ANOTHER LIFE

Sara MacDonald was born in Yorkshire and travelled extensively as a forces child. She attended drama school in London and worked in television and theatre before she married, living abroad for many years before moving to Cornwall with her two sons. *Sea Music* was published by HarperCollins in 2003.

By the same author

Sea Music

SARA MACDONALD

Another Life

HarperCollins*Publishers*

HarperCollins*Publishers*
77–85 Fulham Palace Road,
Hammersmith, London W6 8JB

www.harpercollins.co.uk

A Paperback Original 2004
1

This novel is entirely a work of fiction. The names,
characters and incidents portrayed in it are the work of the
author's imagination. Any resemblance to actual persons, living
or dead, events or localities is entirely coincidental.

A catalogue record for this book
is available from the British Library

ISBN 0 00 717577 9

Typeset in Sabon by Palimpsest Book Production Limited,
Polmont, Stirlingshire
Printed and bound in Great Britain by
Clays Limited, St Ives plc

For
Lizzie Cynddylan

Prologue

Montreal, Quebec 1998

Mark went down to the basement to take one last look at Isabella before he wrapped her up in bubble wrap and placed her in the crate. He had become so used to her being down there that it would seem strange not to have her dominating the room. Despite the ravages of her age and the sea, her presence filled the space. Her eyes in the damaged face watched him with a look that was mysterious and resolute, as if she had seen everything and nothing could surprise her any more.

Her expression seemed to change in the varying light. A face that was made up of such a multiplicity of emotions that Mark thought the carver must have known his model well. This was not a face merely glimpsed or remembered. This face he had created was mobile and frighteningly alive. Her carver had seen and captured the essence of the woman, and even now, a decade later, Mark believed he could glimpse an innocent sensuousness. A consciousness of self that was part of being a beautiful woman and seeing herself reflected in a man's eyes.

The paint had flaked on the left cheek giving her an air of having been abandoned. There was a deep cut in the wood above her right ear, probably made by a propeller. When Mark first saw her in the garden of a house he never meant to revisit, he had been startled, for it seemed to him that he must have been guided there solely in order to rescue her.

Who better than a historian to discover her origins?

His exasperated family admitted that no one else would be foolish enough to ship her from Newfoundland to a basement in Montreal in order to find out who she was and where she had come from.

'You're so fanciful, Dad. I guess you believe she was waiting for *you* to come along, huh?'

Of course, he wouldn't admit to it. Neither could he quite understand how his family were not equally enchanted by her.

'In the right place, I might be,' Veronique said. 'But not in my basement, watching me. Her eyes follow me about. I forget she is in here and at night when I switch the light on she gives me a terrible fright.'

'This is one of the loveliest figureheads I've ever seen. It's worth preserving,' Mark said. 'Pity she belonged to a British schooner, not one of ours . . . Various bodies in England are funding most of the cost, but it's the same over there as it is for us here, they have to fight for every penny they get.'

Mark turned and Inez was standing behind him, hip jutted out to support Daisy who was sleepily sucking her thumb. Inez put her on the ground and they carefully started to wrap the figurehead in layers and layers of bubble wrap, until she resembled a mummy and her face and features were distorted by plastic.

Sitting on the floor, Daisy looked up and pointed. 'Poor lady gone?'

Mark picked the child up. 'Yes. She is going to fly on an aeroplane over the sea and someone a long way away is going to make her better.'

'I like lady,' she said. 'What name?'

'Isabella.' The child's hair smelt of butter. 'The lady used to stand on the front of a ship and swim through the waves and look very beautiful. Her name is Isabella, and we have wrapped her up in a thick coat of bubbles so she won't get hurt on the aeroplane.'

'Poor lady,' Daisy said again as they went up the stairs, and

Mark wondered how he could appease his wife for flying off with his wooden angel.

He was not ready to give her up yet; and he needed to know who he was going to give her up to.

Chapter 1

Through the trees Gabby could see the yellow arm of the mechanical digger in the top field. It was the end of an era. No more cattle or the sweet grassy smell of them bringing the flies into the garden in summer. No sound of cows' teeth munching the new green blades in sharp little stretch and pulling sounds. No wheezy human-sounding bovine coughs making them jump in the dark.

Charlie had occasionally ploughed a portion of the top field for cabbages or kale, and when Josh was small he and his friends had wrinkled their noses at the smell of rotting greens. But cabbages had been infinitely better than executive houses.

'I wouldn't have sold an acre of land if I'd had a choice,' Charlie said miserably, watching the digger throwing up dark earth in all directions like an angry elephant. He was secretly appalled by that great arm tearing at his sacred field. Gabby and Nell could see that, despite his effort to appear businesslike, he felt as sick as they did.

'We'll get used to it,' Nell said quickly. 'We'll make a windbreak to hide the houses. We can fill the gap with trees.'

'Of course we'll get used to it,' Gabby said, wanting to cry. 'Charlie, you had to do it, we know that, it's just . . .'

'*I know*,' Charlie said abruptly, turning away and striding in his muddy boots across the farmyard. He hoisted himself up into the Land Rover and drove noisily down the lane to look at his pheasant chicks, something he always did when he wanted to be alone.

'Oh, Nell,' Gabby said. 'This is far worse for you; you've lived here longer than either of us.'

Nell lifted her shoulders in a pragmatic little shrug.

'I hate seeing any of the land go, Gabby, but we have to survive and it's better than losing the farm or having the financial worries Ted and I had. Charlie is more businesslike than his father. That huge field had its limitations; it slopes, it's exposed to the wind, and it's stony. At least we keep the south end and the views. Those houses are going to lose the sun early and they won't have a view. It's just that we're all sentimentally attached, it's such a beautiful field. Does Josh know work has started?'

'No, not yet, I've avoided mentioning it. You know how Josh likes things to stay exactly the same, he and Charlie argued about it last summer. Josh knows Charlie had no choice, but he refused to see why the paddock by the road couldn't be sold instead. He wouldn't accept that the paddock wouldn't bring in enough money. Also, Nell, he feels guilty about minding so much when he's not prepared to take on the farm himself.'

They walked slowly back towards the house, and as Nell reached her cottage she said, 'You realize Charlie hasn't given up on that one? He thinks Josh will come into the business later when he's a bit older, when he's tired of doing his own thing.'

Gabby hesitated. She was sure Josh would not change his mind. He had chosen his career and she felt, so strongly that it shocked her, that she did not want him to change it.

'He might, Nell, but I doubt it. He loves it here, it's his home, but farming isn't something to do lightly or for sentimental reasons, is it? It gets harder every year. He would have to go to agricultural college, he'd have to be totally committed, and who knows what farming is going to be like for his generation? I mean, few jobs are for life any more.'

Nell laughed. 'You sound like a little old general.'

Gabby made a face. 'Do I? How is that huge picture of yours coming on?'

'It's a nightmare! Come and have a look. It feels like the Forth Bridge. All I've done so far is run some tests.'

They went into Nell's chaotic cottage. Her two old cats lay curled together in the lid of a sewing basket in front of the Aga. Nell led the way, treading over old Sunday papers that littered the floor, into her pristine workroom where Mahler was playing quietly. Gabby never ceased to be amazed at how Nell managed to keep this one room like an operating theatre when the rest of the house grew more like an animal refuge every year.

Both women stood staring at the painting of a stout, bosomy lady clad in pearls and evening dress in an attractive oval frame. The painting looked as if it had been housed in a damp attic for many years, and Nell rather wished it had stayed there.

'It's a lovely frame,' Gabby said. 'The woman is . . .'

'. . . Hideous!' Nell snorted. 'The canvas is in a bad way, as you can see, but it is a quality painting, although I'm unsure if it's as valuable as the Browns believe it to be. I've told them to seek expert opinion; I'm out of date with valuations.'

'I suppose they want you to clean and restore it before they have it valued?'

'I think they hope to send it to Christies.'

Gabby peered more closely at it. It had craquelure or crocodiling almost everywhere and the paint on the dress was flaking badly. In the hands of someone less expert than Nell the picture could end up more restoration than painting.

'Nell, I'm not surprised you're quailing. This is going to take a lot of work. I thought you were going to refuse larger paintings?'

'I was. They caught me at a weak moment. They've dated her around 1892. She's been restored before, twice they think, possibly in the 1930s. It looks as though it's been consolidated with wax-resin and just surface cleaned, but I'd have said it had been cleaned at a later date, possibly in the 1950s.'

Gabby and Nell stared down at the painting. The discoloration of both the varnish and overpaints had affected the image, and excessive restoration in the background meant that no detail could be seen and all sense of the painting was impaired. Gabby was interested in the process of the restoration.

'I could come and help you as soon as I've finished cleaning *The Cobbler's Cats*.'

'I thought you had this figurehead restoration in St Piran coming up?'

'Peter's asked me to go and look at it but I'm not sure I'll get the job, Nell. I haven't got any experience of figureheads. Anyway, I could help you in the evenings.'

'See what happens before you commit yourself to helping me. When are you going to see it?'

'It's arriving in London from Canada and is being driven down to Cornwall next week. Oh, Nell, I'd really love to be given the chance of restoring her.'

'There's absolutely no reason why you shouldn't be offered the job, Gabby. You've got a growing reputation and it reflects the work you're starting to be offered.'

Gabby smiled. 'I've had an excellent teacher.'

Nell patted her arm. 'Coffee?'

'I'd better get to work, Nell, half the morning has gone.' Gabby preferred her coffee without cat hairs in it. 'Let me help you get this doughty woman out of her frame before I go.'

They eased the painting out of its frame and laid it carefully on Nell's table, face up and uncovered to avoid any more paint loss. The portrait was large and had obviously been moved frequently as there were lines of stretcher marks where it had been folded, and the craquelure followed the lines of a stretcher and had caused the most damage.

'I wonder if she was passed from one family member to another in desperation, constantly being removed from her frame, poor old dear,' Gabby said.

'Well, someone loved her enough to commission a huge

six-foot painting of her. Removing the overpaint is going to take the most time.' Nell peered at the woman's bosoms with a magnifying glass. 'I'll remove that varnish with iso-propanol. Can you see? There's a thin layer of discoloured natural resin. I'm going to have to remove most of the more recent restorations. I suspect . . .' Nell moved over to the foreground of the lady's sumptuous dress '. . . that each restorer has altered the tone of the previous overpaint, rather than removing it. I'm pretty sure I'll find layers concealing more damage . . .'

Gabby smiled as she watched Nell. She was already caught in the excitement of restoring. Her face had come suddenly alive as her eyes darted to and fro, assessing the damage with a keen and professional eye. It was this, Nell's passionate interest in her work, that had fired Gabby's imagination and curiosity all those years ago.

Gabby walked across the farmyard back to the house. Despite the distant noise of the digger a feeling of content-ment filled her. She had been afraid when Josh left home that the gap he left would yawn before her, yet slowly but steadily the work had come in to distract her. She had now got to the stage of having to refuse commissions. For the first time in her life she was able to make a financial contribution to the farm, and it felt wonderful.

She walked through the kitchen to her workroom, which was the oldest part of the house with a cobbled floor that had once been Charlie's office. The window looked out on the small, walled garden which dipped downhill to the daffodil fields.

At the start of every daffodil season Gabby would stand transfixed by the green and yellow sloping fields full of emerging buds and the startling vivid blue of the ocean behind them. The scene was reminiscent of the poster of daffodil pickers that had been stuck on the classroom wall at school. It had been that poster that had enticed her to run away and climb on a coach to Cornwall.

She moved away from the window to the small painting

propped up on an easel. She wanted to finish it today. It was the last of her backlog as she had decided not to take on any more commissions until she had seen the figurehead next week.

Ever since Peter Fletcher, the curator from the museum in Truro, had rung her she had felt restless with anticipation. She thought about this lost figurehead making its way from Canada on its last voyage home. She tried not to think how disappointed she would be if she was not offered the job of restoring it.

She picked up a swab of cotton wool on a stick from the jam-jar beside her and started to work, concentrating, engrossed, as her fingers moved deftly, defining detail and discovering small hidden surprises out of layers of dirt. She smiled as she discovered under the old cobbler's hands, not darkness, but a beautiful drawer of nails.

Chapter 2

Gabby set off to see the figurehead at St Piran a week after the digger started to scar the top field. At the top of the hill she got out and climbed onto the gate. She looked down on the farm crouched in the trees, so familiar; and yet, as she gripped the top of the gate all seemed suddenly unfamiliar, as if she was a stranger looking down on a homestead containing the lives of people she knew nothing about.

A small figure came out of the barn and walked across the yard. Charlie? She could not see from here. The odd sensation persisted. The hot, still day pressed down on her, the heat shimmered above the grass and hedgerow. The morning swelled with the sound of bees settling on the honeysuckle in the hedge. Horseflies hovered in petrol-blue clouds over the cowpats in the field beyond the gate.

Still she stood on the gate looking downwards, suspended and held by the day that slowly wound forward to the next minute and the next and the next. In her mind's eye she saw the hands of a clock crawling round the face in slow motion, so imperceptibly towards something that she was afraid they might stop altogether and she would forever be suspended, held here, above her life, waiting.

The sun bounced and glinted off the sea, dazzling her. Her hands on the gate seemed extraordinarily translucent, her body torpid and yet light as if she might blow away like a leaf, hither and thither across the field having no weight at all. She thought suddenly, *I would have no place down there if it wasn't for Josh. If my child had never existed Nell*

11

and Charlie would be a memory only. A memory I reached for in the dark because it reminded me of what I had been running from, that first cold day when I stood here looking down at the pickers bent to the tight green buds of daffodils in a freezing wind.

She stared beyond the gate, away to the horizon, across Charlie and Nell's five hundred acres below her, then she turned abruptly and got back into the car.

As she drove away from the sea she began to think about the figurehead. Peter Fletcher had told her, briefly, that it had come from a trade schooner called the *Lady Isabella*, which had set sail from St Piran and foundered in Canadian waters in 1867 with all hands on board.

The figurehead must have been salvaged years ago, but had only recently been discovered by a Canadian historian who had taken the time and trouble to trace a figurehead, from a foreign vessel, all the way back to the small Cornish port from where it had started its journey.

Gabby had been to the library and got out everything on marine figureheads she could find. Nell had given her a list of maritime museums and suggested she go over and visit Valhalla on Tresco to view the collection of figureheads more closely. She had also dug out old restoration books from her lecturing days which she thought Gabby might find useful.

Gabby pored over the photographs, fascinated by the wealth and beauty of the ships and figureheads inside the books she had borrowed. She had surprised herself with her sudden overriding conviction that this figurehead was a commission she must have. It was the first time she had been approached for the sort of work Nell herself had never undertaken and it astonished her that her opinion was being sought; that she had credibility on the basis of her own work, not Nell's reputation.

Nell was sure that one of the reasons Gabby had been approached was her skill with intricate church panels. Gabby was more patient than Nell had been in her younger days. On wood it was necessary to peel away centuries of wax, stain and varnish, to reveal, after a tiring and lengthy process, if you were lucky, a hidden painting. The moment of discovery, the moment a fleck of colour appeared under your fingers like magic, was incomparable. Gabby never tired of the excitement and anticipation of a discovery. Nell preferred the satisfaction of simply transforming what she was working on to the comparative rarity of finding a concealed painting that had not been ruined.

As Gabby entered the village a small wind gusted from the sea, rocking her car. It carried with it a sudden presentiment that was disturbing. She felt a sharp stab of anxiety that made her breathless. She parked her car near the small museum and walked towards the group of people waiting for her in the porch.

For a moment Gabby hesitated with her hand on the latch of the old Methodist chapel that was now a museum. The group of men waiting for her were in shadow, she could not see their faces.

There was a second when she could have turned and run back to the car, driven away fast, back to the farmhouse lying squat and secure amid small trees all bent one way by the winds like figures frozen in a Russian landscape.

She could have run and never known the possibilities the future could hold. But someone called out and the moment slid away into impossibility. She opened the gate and passed through it, towards the men who stood in shadow and the sound of her name being called.

Chapter 3

It took Gabby a moment to adjust to the darkness of the museum as the vicar of St Piran, John Bradbury, guided her through the door. Her heart sank as she spotted Councillor Rowe. He and Nell had been at war for years and she firmly maintained he was a closet misogynist. He was already puffing himself up like a bantam as she approached.

John Bradbury, with his back to the councillor, gave Gabby a wink of encouragement.

'Gabrielle, come and meet everybody. You know Peter Fletcher from Truro Museum. Tristan Brown is from the *Western Morning News*. Councillor Rowe, I think you've met before. And this is Professor Mark Hannah, from Montreal. Mark has been entirely responsible for the safe return of our beautiful figurehead to St Piran. Mark, this is Gabrielle Ellis, our local restorer.'

Gabrielle looked up into the amused eyes of the Canadian. He held out his hand.

'Great to meet you, Gabriella.' His hand was warm, the fingers long and thin, his grip firm. Suddenly self-conscious, Gabby looked away, smiled at Peter Fletcher, and then they all turned and walked towards a corner of the museum where the figurehead lay on her back on a worktable, swathes of bubble wrap still around and underneath her like an eiderdown.

Gabby stared down at the wooden figure, held her breath. Lady Isabella was so much more beautiful than she had imagined. She moved closer and looked at the high cheekbones, the sightless eyes, the scarred face and neck. The wood was dry with small cracks, the paint flaked, remnants of colour caught in the corner of her eyes like tears.

The face was extraordinary, so meticulously carved that it seemed to have an expression of combined sensuality and haunting sadness. This face, Gabby thought, had been carved with a doomed or careless passion.

The Canadian, watching her, said softly, 'Meet Lady Isabella.'

Gabrielle was unable to keep the thrill out of her voice; 'She is exquisite.'

Mark Hannah laughed. 'She is, isn't she.'

'Where on earth did you find her?' Gabby asked.

'Pure chance. I was in Newfoundland giving a series of lectures at the Marine Institute of Memorial University. I had a couple of days there and I decided to go walking. I suddenly spotted her in a garden in Bonavista Bay, among the usual flotsam brought up from the sea. She was wedged between two trees.

'I knocked on the door and the man who lived there told me she had been given to him as part of a debt owed by his brother-in-law who had once lived in Malpeque Bay, Prince Edward Island. He thought she had been exhibited at some time, maybe at the Green Park Shipbuilding Museum on the west side of Malpeque Bay. I could see a crude attempt to restore her had been made but she was beginning to deteriorate and I asked if he would be willing to sell her to me.'

The boy from the *Western Morning News* was scribbling fast into his notebook.

'After a lot of haggling I bought her for the sum of the whole debt owed to him. I told myself I wanted her because I thought she would make an excellent research project for some of my students, but it was love at first sight. I had to have her.'

Gabby, watching him, thought, He must have told this story many times and yet the excitement of the discovery is still with him.

15

'I wonder how long she was exposed to the elements,' she said, looking at the wood-rot and damage at her base.

'The man told me he had kept her in his old boat shed and had only put her in his garden when he needed his shed.'

Peter Fletcher touched Gabby's arm. 'Thanks to Mark's detective work I was able to trace the original plans for the schooner *Lady Isabella*. They were in the marine archives in Devon. She was a two-masted ship, commissioned by a wealthy master mariner, an ex-naval gentleman called Sir Richard Magor whose family were big in shipbuilding here in Cornwall and Devon, as well as Prince Edward Island.'

Gabby felt a surge of excitement. 'Do you have the name of the man who carved the figurehead?'

Peter grinned at her. 'Oh yes. His name was Tom Welland. He was quite a famous woodcarver in his day. His figures were unmistakable.'

Gabby turned back to the figurehead. She longed to touch that frail face, but knew she must not. The Canadian came to stand beside her.

'Tom Welland went in for detail. Not all figurehead carvers did, many were quite primitive. He became well-known, not just in England but on the continent as well as Canada and America. He was an artist and was able to pick and choose his commissions. He appears to have travelled widely when he was young, probably as crew on the trading vessels, because traces of his work can still be found in Mediterranean ports. Then he just seems to have stopped carving. No one knows what happened to him. John tells me his family lived and worked around St Piran all their lives.'

'They did indeed,' John Bradbury said. 'Most of them are buried here, but not Tom.'

'It's wonderful to have a date. It means we know exactly when she was carved and what materials they would have used,' Gabby said.

'But how did you connect her to Cornwall?' Tristan from the *Western Morning News* asked Mark Hannah.

The Canadian smiled at the boy. 'I knew she must be European, possibly British from a trade schooner. The nearest we have to your schooners or barques are Boston trawlers, and the figureheads differ. I went to the public archives. Prince Edward Island was once a British colony and there had been a thriving shipbuilding business between the island and the West Country in the nineteenth century.

'I couldn't find any sign of a trading ship called *Lady Isabella* registered as being built on the island, but records get destroyed or go missing and when I turned to the register of wrecks it jumped out at me. A schooner, the *Lady Isabella*, lost in a storm in 1867 off Bonavista Bay. Instinct told me this was her. There was no mention of the schooner carrying a figurehead, so I asked an English colleague to check for me in the Lloyds List, London, and there she was, listed and described *with figurehead* alongside the date of her sinking.'

Peter Fletcher took up the story again. 'Thanks to Mark's detective work we looked at the most probable Cornish owners and builders of that period. I went to the Public Record Office to look down the Lloyds Register. Trading vessels had to be registered to get an insurance certificate.

'I found that a schooner called *Lady Isabella*, built in Prince Edward Island in 1863 had been granted an A1 certificate of seaworthiness by Lloyds London in 1864. Then I went to the Guildhall Library, where Mark's colleague had already looked, to double-check the Lloyds List. This also stated that *Lady Isabella* was wrecked off Newfoundland with all hands in 1867. By that time she was owned by a Daniel Vyvyan, but it was common for ships to be sold on when tonnage was profitable.'

'So,' Gabby asked, 'was this Isabella, Sir Richard Magor's wife?'

John Bradbury said, 'We don't know, bit of a mystery there. Peter and I have been going through the old parish records. The Magors were not from the parish of St Piran, they were an old Falmouth seafaring family and many of

17

them were master mariners. Sir Richard lived in Botallick House, now owned by the National Trust in the parish of Mylor. In the Mylor parish register there is no record of him marrying in the 1860s. None at all.'

'What about this Daniel Vyvyan guy, who owned her when she sank?' Tristan asked.

'The Vyvyan family have lived in St Piran for generations. They owned the mausoleum-like house you see on your right as you come into St Piran. It was Perannose Manor and is now a Christian conference centre. Daniel had two wives, a Helena Vyvyan, née Viscaria, and a Charlotte, née Flemming; both are buried with Vyvyan in the family crypt.'

'What about daughters?' Gabby asked.

'Ah, I was coming to that. Helena and Daniel had a daughter Isabella in 1846 . . .'

'What?' Everybody looked at John Bradbury.

He laughed. 'I have more! I was talking to a long-retired vicar of Mylor, a bit of an amateur historian and sleuth. He maintains there *was* an Isabella who was the first wife of Sir Richard Magor. No one knows what happened to her, she is not buried in Mylor or here in St Piran. Legend has it that a page in the parish records registering a marriage in 1864, containing that of Magor and Isabella Vyvyan was torn out, destroyed shortly after that marriage . . .'

'Maybe that's why Richard Magor sold the ship to Isabella's father, if she had fallen out of favour,' Gabby said.

'Quite possibly,' Peter said. 'And of course our research is ongoing. What we do know is that in the years the *Lady Isabella* was built, St Piran had a thriving boat-building business employing many men in the area.'

'This is all very interesting indeed,' Councillor Rowe said, 'but the business of the morning is who is going to restore the figurehead now she is here. The rest we can look forward to hearing later.'

They all stared at him. How on earth could he not be interested in a piece of history that he was hoping to raise money for, Gabby wondered.

'Quite right!' Mark Hannah looked ⟨...⟩ trouble not laughing. 'The business of the ⟨...⟩

They turned back to the figurehead. Mark Ha⟨...⟩ Gabby, 'One of the reasons Tom Welland becam⟨...⟩ known and sought after was that sailors believed his ca⟨...⟩ were blessed because his faces always looked so alive.'

'It's true,' Gabby said. 'Her face is disturbingly alive. It's the eyes, I think.'

'Mark has offered to go on researching the history of the *Lady Isabella* for us in London, when he has time between his lecturing engagements and writing his book, and we're very grateful. Of course, we will go on delving this end too, and hopefully we will discover more about the schooner. We do have a great deal to thank you for, Mark,' Peter said.

'Indeed we do,' John Bradbury agreed, looking pointedly at Councillor Rowe.

Councillor Rowe cleared his throat. 'London is where I think this valuable piece of local history should be restored. We need a London expert. It is only right and proper that we have the best we can afford.'

Gabrielle knew she was being rebuffed and the councillor wanted to ease her out, but she was not going to give him the satisfaction of seeing that she suddenly felt unsure of her credibility; for it was true, she *had* never restored a figurehead. She felt the Canadian's eyes on her, but when she looked up she knew instantly he was rooting for her.

He said in his soft drawl, turning to Rowe, 'I've heard excellent accounts and seen for myself some of Gabrielle's work. Peter took me to the church of Saint Hilary to see the panels and the two painted wood sculptures Gabriella restored. I also drove to Lanreath to see the painted medieval oak rood-screens she worked on. I can see no good reason for this figurehead being lugged to London if it can be restored professionally here. What do you think, Peter?'

'I have no doubt whatsoever that Gabrielle is more than qualified to do the job. I've worked closely with her before and I'm sure she will do it justice. She's been working with ppleby, who is one of the best fine art conservators in the county.'

He turned to the councillor. 'I'm sure you must remember the two major sculptures that Nell and Gabrielle restored about two years ago, Rowe? The seventeenth-century Spanish gilded wood carving of Saint Joseph; and the one of Saint Ann, probably fourteenth-century? It was Gabrielle who found the fragments of original paint.'

Gabby turned away from the men to the wistful wooden face, to the shaved and battered bodice, to the carved fingers with the arms held down close to her body so she could fly through the water.

'I know you will need to do a proper inspection, Gabrielle, but is it possible to give us a quick assessment?' she heard Peter ask behind her.

Gabby got out her magnifying glasses and knelt beside the figurehead, bending close, careful not to touch any of the painted sections. She talked the group of men through the various methods she would use, the tests she would carry out before she started. As she talked and examined the face, the cheekbones looked suddenly warm and smooth, and as Gabby's fingers hovered over her face a strange feeling of familiarity flooded through her as if she was bending to the face of someone she knew well. She wished Nell had come, the detail was breathtaking.

'The work in this . . .' Gabby marvelled as she examined an eyelid, the relaxed and languid lips, '. . . is such a labour of love. She must have seemed so alive and vivid in her once blue dress with the water rushing past her.'

The Canadian's expression was intent, as if he needed to gauge Gabby's feelings and the care she would take with his beloved figurehead.

Peter Fletcher smiled. 'It is the most wonderful find. Gabrielle, would you be willing to take her on?'

Gabby looked up, was about to answer, *Yes, oh yes*, when Rowe said, 'However proficient Mrs Ellis is, a figurehead is quite a different matter to a sculpture or painting. This has been immersed in salt water for many years and has been half-ruined with modern paints. I believe we decided to discuss the restoration carefully before we offered it to anyone . . .'

'That is exactly what we are doing, discussing it,' the vicar said crossly, cutting him off. 'That is why we have two experts in front of us who know what they are talking about . . .'

'There is a question of *cost*,' Rowe said, interrupting in his turn.

Gabby looked at the vicar. 'I can't estimate the time it will take off the top of my head. But of course I would come and do a proper detailed inspection before I sent you a quote.'

Peter was also getting annoyed with Rowe. 'I can tell you now, the cost of the figurehead being restored and insured outside the county is going to be far more than any quote from Gabrielle. You are quite wrong; it is *not* a different skill. A figurehead is like a panel and Gabrielle is expert at wood treatments and polychrome. Which in lay terms, Rowe, are painted surfaces. She also has knowledge of pigments from medieval to contemporary paints. We have an expert on site, so I am unsure what your reservations are.'

Gabby felt like whispering, *I'll do it for nothing, just let me have the chance*, but she knew it wasn't professional and Nell and Charlie would explode.

Rowe opened his mouth to argue and the Canadian said evenly, 'I suggest that having got the figurehead safely home to Cornwall, not without some difficulty, it would be foolish to move her again. She is damaged and had I thought she would *not* be restored locally, I would have left her in London.'

There was an uncomfortable silence. Rowe was an unpopular councillor but he was good at obtaining money from various sources. The Canadian winked at Gabrielle then watched the councillor with veiled amusement.

'I think,' the vicar said, 'we should all repair to the pub and discuss this over lunch.'

'Good idea,' Peter Fletcher said.

'Indeed,' Rowe said. 'I can then go on to talk to the Heritage people. Well, Mrs Ellis, thank you for coming, we will inform you of our decision.'

'I meant,' the vicar said coldly, 'for Gabrielle to accompany us and be part of the discussion.'

Peter took Gabrielle's arm as they walked out of the church. He was a polite bachelor and he deplored Rowe's crassness. 'Let's go and see if we can find a table.'

Gabrielle smiled at him. 'Peter, really, it's fine. I should be getting back anyway.'

They all emerged into the harsh sunlight. Gabby put on her sunglasses with relief.

Peter said, 'I think it's important that you stay, Gabby. We are keen that you do this restoration, that's why we rang you, and I'd like to talk this through with you.'

'I agree,' the Canadian said, falling into step the other side of her. 'It would be good to talk with you, if you have the time. That figurehead has been my baby for quite a while.'

'Settled,' the vicar said. 'Come on, Gabrielle, off we go.'

Peter moved away to talk to him and Gabby was left with the Canadian. She felt suddenly, infuriatingly tongue-tied. From the moment she entered the church she had been aware of his eyes constantly on her face.

He was a tall and lean man, and in the sunlight she saw he was older than she had first thought. His eyes crinkled with amusement as he bent to her.

'Now what the hell could you have possibly done to upset that asshole?'

Startled, Gabby snorted with laughter. 'Not me! Nell, my mother-in-law. She upset his brother, an untrained restorer, who ruined a valuable painting belonging to an old friend of hers and then charged her the earth. Nell wrote an article in the local paper. She didn't name him but everyone knew exactly who she was talking about. It was the end of his career. Councillor Rowe has never forgiven her.'

They sat inside in the cool and Rowe pointedly ordered himself a pasty and orange juice and left. As the door closed behind him everyone relaxed. The young reporter started to quiz Mark on the details of shipping the Lady Isabella back to England while John Bradbury ordered sandwiches.

'How's Nell?' Peter asked Gabby. 'Still working, I hope.'

'Oh yes. Nell will never really give up. She's working on a huge painting at the moment.'

'I met a guy in London who knew your mother-in-law,' Mark said suddenly. 'She's still very highly thought of. I understand she worked for the National Portrait Gallery and then gave it all up to become a farmer's wife.'

'I don't think she's ever really stopped restoring. She just took on work locally instead of from London, when Charlie was old enough to help around the farm.'

'Your husband?'

'Yes.'

'Are you Cornish?'

'No. Charlie is.'

Now, why did she not want to talk about Charlie, as if it might make her less interesting to the Canadian?

'They have the most beautiful farm,' Peter said, 'miles from anywhere and hell to find.'

The Canadian – *Mark*, for heaven's sake, he has a *name* – was still firmly concentrating on her rather than the reporter. Gabby, who hated the focus of attention being on her, turned the conversation back to the figurehead to the relief of the earnest young man.

Back in the church car park they said their goodbyes. The two men thanked her for coming. The young reporter got on his motorbike and roared off. John Bradbury walked home to his vicarage. Peter sent his love to Nell and went to unlock his car and open all the windows.

The Canadian took Gabby's hand and looked down on her in the amused way he had, as if laughter was never far away. She wondered if he found them all very quaint and British and tried to draw her hand away, feeling suddenly

23

cross with him for staring, for making her tongue-tied, when she would think later of all the questions she wanted to ask him. He hung on to her hand, still smiling down at her.

'Please could I have my hand back?' she asked.

'Of course you can,' he said. 'I'm only borrowing it – for now. It's a very nice hand indeed.'

He let it go. 'It's been great meeting you, Gabriella. I'm so happy Lady Isabella is going to be in your hands. She will be, you know.'

'I would really love to restore her,' Gabby said, hot all over. 'Goodbye.'

She climbed into her car and banged the door shut, deeply grateful to her sunglasses that she hoped were hiding her face.

'Goodbye, Gabriella, take care,' Mark said through the window and turned and walked back to Peter, who waved at her as she drove quickly past, eager to get round the corner and back onto the road home.

The sun was beginning to fade and the shadows over the fields lengthen. Cows were making their way down a field to be milked. She wondered how long Charlie could keep his herd and how diminished the farm would be without the sight of them in the yard every morning and evening. Wistfulness for everything to stay *exactly as it was* overtook her so suddenly that tears sprang to her eyes. She made the little car go faster, as if the farm might have disappeared altogether in the time it took her to drive home.

Chapter 4

Nell watched as the girl and the small boy crossed the edge of the daffodil field down towards the coastal path. The morning was still, the wind from the south-west soft and teasing. The sky and sea merged in the distance, blue on blue.

The day was held, breathless and hovering, like the kestrel poised, wings fluttering, over the hedge of the field where the girl walked.

It was one of those days that was too still, the lack of wind unnerving, making the morning seem as if it had drawn in on itself, gathering and collecting in a silence that should be listened to.

Nell stood, shading her eyes, holding the bowl full of corn, staring out towards the small figure of the girl in the distance. There was no hint of cloud, just the endless shimmering ocean meeting the lush green of the fields dotted with buds of emerging daffodils.

She could hear the tractor now, moving along the farm track. As it came into sight above the hedge the girl stopped and lifted the child, and he called out, waved vigorously with his small, fat hands. The driver stopped and jumped out and walked to the field gate that lay between them. The child let go of his mother and ran along the stony edge of yellow daffodils so fast he fell, and the man leapt over the gate and scooped him up, threw him up over his head. Nell could hear the child's laughter blowing over to her like dandelion fluff on the fragile stillness of the day.

Maybe it was going to work, Nell thought, against all the odds. Watching from a distance they looked like a little textbook family; content, happy in their skins. Charlie had a son. He had never doubted for a moment that his firstborn would be a son. That had made everything easier.

The man ruffled the girl's dark hair lightly and they stood talking for a moment before he lifted the child up onto his shoulders, walked away and climbed over the gate and placed the child in front of him on the tractor. The engine started up again and they continued down the lane, towards where Nell stood in the yard holding the bowl of corn for the hens, watching.

Silently the kestrel dived, steep and sharp. Nell could hear the sudden squeal of the baby rabbit as it was caught and pulled out of the hedge. The girl turned, startled, and clapped her hand over her mouth in horror.

'No. No. No,' Nell heard faintly on the wind. Then the girl made little runs up and down, crying and shouting in impotent anger at the kestrel, which lifted its prey swiftly upwards over the hedge and away in low flight.

The girl was left small and alone in the vast rolling greenness of the field. Some nebulous, disturbing feeling caught at Nell as the girl, shading her eyes, watched the kestrel until it was a pinprick in the sky.

Nell had rarely seen any show of emotion in this girl. Placid, cheerful, so careful to fit into country life, to be accommodating, to be loved. Nell realized in that brief moment that her daughter-in-law had been smothering any spontaneous expression of anger, joy or misery. She suddenly perceived Gabby as a sleepwalker in her own life. It was safer to sleep sometimes than to question how or why we came to be in a particular place at a particular time with a particular person. Nell knew this protective passivity only too well.

She turned away from the figure making its way back towards her, a small, clear silhouette against the horizon of sea and sky. She clucked at the hens and scattered the corn in a wide arc as she identified this intangible feeling of

26

unrest. What happened when Gabrielle woke up? No one could sleep for an entire lifetime.

Nell turned Josh's postcard over and looked at the soldier on horseback. How quickly the years had slid away. Hard to think of that little curly-haired boy in uniform. Hard to watch the green field he loved so much with its annual rash of mushrooms, disappearing into piles of earth, forming trenches for foundations that would house another generation on land she knew like the back of her hand.

Who would have thought Josh would become a soldier, not a farmer? Who could have guessed he could permanently leave the farm he loved, the friends he had grown up with? She slipped the postcard into her pocket. She loved Josh with a fierce love and pride and was suddenly shocked at her own duplicity.

She understood exactly why Josh had turned his back on the farm. How could she, of all people, not feel honest and grateful that he had needed more than a lifetime embedded in the harsh Cornish landscape? That he had chosen not to be smothered by the seasons, the weather, disease, and animal husbandry.

She would have been bitterly disappointed if he had grown up incurious about anything outside the parochial world in which he had spent his childhood. There would be no more grandchildren, she had had only one chance to instil in him a need for something outside the farm and county, a craving to learn; for him to soak up like a sponge all that a country childhood had made him, by distance, ignorant of.

She had taught him about paintings, about art, about conserving the past, the environment; all that she herself felt passionate about. Gabby had given him a ferocious love of books and Charlie an abiding pride in the land they owned. This was why Charlie had difficulty in understanding how Josh could turn his back on the physical thrill of working land that had belonged to four generations of his family.

Yet, Josh, the scholarship boy, had come away from

27

university with a first and gone straight to Sandhurst. Nell found it mystifying. It was also humbling. What right had she to try to mould Josh, from a baby, to compromise? Here she was, believing she had widened his horizons when he would have certainly done so without her help. Josh had always seemed to know what he wanted from life. Possibly, it was away from the two women who loved him, in a way, Nell had begun to realize since he had left, that might well have been suffocating.

She and Gabby had each other, their restoration work, and Charlie. Josh must forge his own life. Nell smiled. The lorries had gone, the cows were coming up the lane for milking. Soon Gabby would be home to tell of her day.

She took Josh's postcard out of her pocket and placed it in the centre of the mantelpiece. Thank God for Gabby.

Chapter 5

Extraordinary. Mark did not know who he was expecting. A middle-aged spinster? An earnest academic? A hugger of trees in ethnic sweater and bright sandals? Whoever it was, it certainly was not this small, dark girl hovering on the other side of the museum gate.

She stood peering at them in an enormous pair of sunglasses that hid most of her face. With her hand on the gate she seemed poised for flight and ready to bolt. The kindly priest next to him turned and saw her, called out her name, and it was only then that she lifted the latch and walked towards them.

The little pompous guy was telling Peter that he considered Gabrielle Ellis to be too inexperienced. He was cut off by the priest who moved away to greet the girl. Introductions were made and Mark saw, closer, that Gabrielle Ellis was not a girl, but a small, very pretty woman.

They had unpacked the figurehead on the ground floor in a corner near the window at the back of the museum where there was the most light for Gabrielle to look at her. He watched Gabrielle's face as she caught sight of the Lady Isabella. A little involuntary sigh escaped her. She moved forward to peer at the wooden face he had grown to love, tentatively, as if the impassive face of Lady Isabella was alive and carried secrets from the ocean she would love to know.

Gabrielle Ellis had dark hair to her shoulders and she tended to flip it forward to hide her face. As she listened to everyone her face was concentrated and rapt. She kept glancing back at the figurehead, bending to look at her face and neck, her fingers hovering and framing Isabella's face as if she longed to touch or was offering comfort to a patient.

As she leant forward to examine the many small craquelures and fissures, her hair fell forward to reveal, against her suntanned shoulders, a tiny triangle of startling white neck, as soft and tender as a baby's. Mark had this sudden overpowering urge to place his lips upon that tiny place of whiteness.

He brought himself back abruptly to the conversation. The councillor seemed determined that Gabrielle Ellis was not going to get the job of restoring the figurehead. This project, he thought, has been my overriding passion for too long. If a local restorer can do the job, I'm damned if I'm going to let this sententious little man, with some agenda, ship her back to London.

Mark said his piece and a sticky silence followed. He wondered if Gabrielle was feeling undermined by the attitude of the councillor, but he watched her face and it did not appear so. John Bradbury was beginning to get mad, though, he could see a small tic starting up in his cheek, and Mark grinned to himself.

As they walked over to the pub he made Gabrielle laugh, but she seemed shy and talked little over lunch. She scribbled a quick estimate on a pad and it was obvious that both John and Peter Fletcher wanted to give her the job. Cock Robin disappeared in high dudgeon and he wondered who had the deciding vote; the council, the Heritage people or the museum.

He studied Gabrielle while he ate his sandwich. Without the sunglasses, and out of the dim church, her face was small and elfinlike. She had extraordinary blue eyes with flecks of grey and brown in them. Her hands were small, like a child's, with dimples in the wrists. Dear little hands.

It was her stillness that struck him most. Her movements were slow and tranquil, but somehow detached, as if a piece of her was somewhere else. He knew he was making her self-conscious by looking at her for too long, too intensely, but he found it almost impossible to turn his gaze anywhere else. As soon as he tried to concentrate on the Tristan guy, who was earnestly trying to elicit information for his local rag, his eyes would return to her face as if pulled by a magnet.

They all walked back to the car park to go their separate ways. Peter was driving him back to his Truro hotel. The afternoon was still hot but the colours were changing as the sun got lower in the sky. The sea beyond the languid fields was aquamarine. Loneliness seized him; he did not want to return to his impersonal hotel room, he wanted to watch the sunset on a cliff top with this woman.

He took her hand, held on to it, said goodbye, smiled down at her with the pure exultation of a discovery. She asked, rather severely, for her hand back, got into her quaint little English car, still hidden by those ridiculous sunglasses, and sped off.

He felt, as he held that small hand, such a surge of desire that her hand in his had trembled. He knew, as he felt the heat emanating from her small body and down into her hand like a tangible thing, that she was as acutely aware of him as he was of her.

He turned and walked away to Peter's car. The curator was watching him with an expression Mark found impossible to read, and he thought suddenly, *I am a married man, at least twenty years older than Gabrielle Ellis. I have a wife I love and five grown-up daughters.*

The car turned out into the road and they both reached out to pull the visors against the sun moving down the sky in front of them. They had to stop while a herd of cows idled along the road in front of them, flicking their tails. Huge great beasts with sweet, grass-smelling breath, shoving against each other and mooing noisily as they turned into a muddy farmyard to be milked.

'I'd like to take you out to supper,' Peter said.

'That would be great.'

31

'Can I pick you up about eight?'

'Sure, I'll be ready. I'm not taking up too much of your time?'

'Not at all. I'll bring someone I think you'll enjoy talking to, an archaeologist friend of mine. You have confidence in Gabrielle Ellis to do a good restoration? It must be hard to hand Lady Isabella over.'

'It is hard, but I'm sure you're right in wanting Gabrielle to restore her. How much pull does that councillor fellow have?'

Peter laughed. 'We don't have to take the help of council funding or the conditions the council might impose for that funding, but, as you know, to gather private donations, even with National Heritage help, is difficult and time-consuming. We do have ways of persuading Councillor Rowe to our way of thinking. He is a very vain little man. Give him the limelight, lots of press coverage, photos . . . The Heritage people find him as much of a bore as we do.'

'Good. Does Gabrielle have children? I mean, is she able to work full time on this project?'

Peter glanced at him. 'She and Charlie have one grown-up son. He didn't want to go into the farm, which was a blow for Charlie. He went straight to the army from university instead.'

Mark was amazed. 'A grown-up son? She can only be about thirty, surely?'

'Somewhere in her thirties, I should think. She came down to Cornwall to pick daffodils one school holiday. She and Charlie fell in love and she never went home. I think she had her son at about seventeen or eighteen.'

'My God, that's almost child abduction.'

'Romantic, isn't it,' Peter said dryly, 'because they are still together and as far as I know, very happy. An improvement on marrying first cousins – that used to happen a lot down here.'

Is he warning me off, in an understated British way? Mark wondered. Then suddenly shocked at himself, thought, *He should not have to. If I am a decent human being I close my mind to this woman.*

Later, as he was shaving, Mark met his own eyes in the mirror. He thought of home, of early evening, of how the light slanted mellow across the rooftops at the end of a day as he prepared to leave the campus and return to his rambling house that was always bursting with people. He would stand at the door for a second, listening to Veronique calmly reigning supreme in the huge kitchen in the middle of the chaos of his daughters, grandchildren, their schoolfriends, hangers-on, neighbours.

Veronique blissfully, radiantly content. He had always thought of himself as trying to be an honourable man, certainly not one who had habitually been unfaithful to his wife or gone out of his way to commit adultery. Nor one who had ever pursued a happily married woman, or any married woman for that matter.

He continued to stare at himself with a strange falling-away sensation. His own eyes locked with those of his reflection as if he were two separate people, one trying to stare the other into submission. He caught a quick glimpse of the future in the moment when it was still possible to retreat, and also the moment when he knew he was going to ignore that warning voice as piercing as a house alarm, and reach out deliberately for the self-destruct button.

Chapter 6

Gabby turned left and instead of driving down the lane to the farm she followed the narrow road that led to the coastal path and the next cove. The sun was hanging spectacularly over the sea and the day was cooling. She turned again and bumped along a track until it ended in a gate. She got out, locked the car, climbed over the gate and walked across the field until she came to a small cottage standing on its own, facing the sea.

The door stood wide open and she called Elan's name, even though she knew exactly where he would be. She walked on across the field towards the coastal path until she saw his familiar figure sitting on his collapsible stool, painting with his back to her. He had picked a place relatively sheltered, where the cliff path started to descend down to the cove.

Gabby did not disturb him. She sat some way behind him, cross-legged, watching the sun leach and bleed into the sky, spread out like a crimson stain and then dissolve into the sea until it too was molten. She knew as soon as the sun slipped behind the horizon the last heat of the day would disappear as suddenly as the colours melted, and Elan would pack up his paints and turn for home.

She was unsure why she had suddenly felt the need to see him, but turning towards his cottage had been instinctive. He had been Nell's friend long before Gabby came to Cornwall, and he still was, but she and Elan had the immediate rapport of the outsider and the solitary.

He was Josh's godfather. His name was Alan Premore,

but Josh had always called him *Elan* and the name had stuck. After his parents and Nell, Elan had been the first name Josh had mastered and Alan had, from that moment, signed his paintings *Elan Premore*. This was partly because he unashamedly adored Josh, but also because he had begun to exhibit seriously the year Josh was born.

Gabby loved this spare, reclusive man unconditionally, and accepted, without it ever being mentioned, that he loved her in return. He turned now and saw her as the sun set on one more day. As on many other days he had no idea that she had been sitting silently behind him. He smiled and gathered up his paints, folded the small easel.

'Darling child, how long have you been there?'

'Not long.' She got up and he kissed her forehead and they made their way back to his cottage. He never asked Gabby why she came, for that might have indicated she had to have a reason, and being insular himself he understood the need to be near someone who would not question why you were there, just that you were.

As they walked back to the cottage Gabby told him about her day. Her excitement was catching and Elan had rarely seen her so animated. He was interested in the story of the figurehead and its return to St Piran.

'John Bradbury still vicar?' he asked.

'Yes, he's just the same, so is Peter. So is Councillor Rowe.'

'Dear heavens, Gabby, hasn't he been voted out yet?'

'Nell says every time he's voted off the council, he somehow gets himself voted on again.'

'Mainly, I suspect, because no one else wants to be elected. And this Canadian, what was he like?'

'Oh, fine. He seemed nice. I didn't really have time to talk to him properly.'

Elan propped his things against the hall table. 'Let's have a drink, child, I have a cold, very good bottle of wine all ready in the fridge.'

Gabby laughed. 'But you didn't know I was coming.'

'I always keep a bottle just in case you come. Pour me my tot while I open the bottle.'

Gabby reached up for his heavy tumbler and poured him a hefty whisky with a burst of soda from his archaic silver soda siphon.

'Can you still get bits for this siphon, Elan?'

'Just.' He handed Gabby the glass of wine and they sat at the kitchen table in front of his ancient Rayburn. 'Now, this Canadian historian fellow sounds interesting. Any good for an isolable painter?'

Gabby laughed. 'What a lovely word. Afraid not. I think, well, he's heterosexual, Elan.'

'What a shame, I do like a transatlantic drawl.'

Elan watched Gabby's colour change. This was surprising and he teased her gently. 'What makes you so sure, if you didn't talk to him *properly*?'

'He . . . well, of course, I cannot be sure of anything, but he seemed heterosexual. Elan, could I ring Nell?' Gabby asked, changing the subject. 'She might be wondering where I am.'

'Of course you can.'

Gabby got up and as she phoned Nell, Elan thought how little she had changed over the years. How young she seemed. Yet, he also sensed a buried agitation or tension in her. For the first time he glimpsed what Nell had hinted of; something crouched and waiting in Gabby. Her stillness could be unnerving, but tonight there was an intangible change in her. Her movements seemed quicker and more nervous. Perhaps it was merely the excitement of seeing the figurehead, but Elan thought not. He knew from experience he would have to wait to find out. Gabby was like a bird; startle her and she would be off, a dot on the horizon. She could perversely, casually drop small bombshells, and Elan had learnt that his reaction had to appear insouciant in order to share her rare intimacies.

Watching her chatting on the phone to Nell, he thought back to the first glimpse she had obliquely given him of her past.

'Come on, child,' he once urged. 'Have another glass. I don't drink wine and it will be wasted.'

'No, Elan, no more. I'm hopeless, I can't drink more than one glass, truly. You know that.'

'But you and Shadow are walking, you haven't got to drive. Come on, Gabby, it's such a good wine.'

Gabby had placed her hand over her glass firmly and looking down at the table she'd said, quietly, 'Please, Elan, don't press me. I only ever have one glass, not because it will affect me, but because I am afraid it *won't*. It is in my genes – I have to watch it.'

She had sat opposite him, avoiding his eyes. He was ashamed of his crassness in not just accepting her refusal. He had gone round the table and kissed the top of her head. With his hands on her shoulders he had apologized, promised he would never browbeat her again.

She had stood up, smiling. 'I've got to go. I'm collecting Josh from Cubs.'

At the door Elan had said gently, 'Gabby, I don't believe for a moment you are genetically predisposed to alcohol abuse. It would certainly have manifested itself before now, so banish that thought from your head.'

'OK.'

She was gone, over the fields at a trot away from him. He knew she would immediately regret having given him even the briefest glimpse of her past. He resolved never to be tempted to repeat to Nell anything Gabby said to him. She needed to trust him absolutely. It was not that Gabby was not close to Nell, it was that she was too close. He knew Gabby's childhood was a taboo subject, an uncharted and forbidden landscape.

As Gabby replaced the phone now he pushed the cork back into the bottle of wine for her to take home. He watched her walk, a small, neat enigma, across his field. He stood in the open doorway and lifted his whisky glass to the navy blue sea.

'God bless Gabby and keep her from ever having her heart broken – especially by a sodding Canadian.'

Chapter 7

After supper, when they had cleared away the supper things and Charlie had left for the pub quiz-night, Gabby got out the folder Peter had given her containing the Canadian restorer's report on the figurehead of Isabella, and laid out all the photographs and the better quality JPEG images of areas of damage.

She had been inspected by a Valerie Mischell, of Collections and Conservation, Museum and Heritage Services, Culture Division, City of Toronto, at the home of Mark Hannah, '. . . who discovered the figurehead and generously provided much of the following information which forms part of his research into marine shipping and wrecks of the 19th century.'

Gabby scanned the first page of the report; it would be interesting to know more about Mark Hannah and his work.

'The purpose of the inspection is to provide information for the Victoria & Albert Museum in London . . . describing any obvious work that might be necessary in the opinion of the person carrying out the inspection . . .'

'These are very good photographs of her,' Nell said, coming and peering down at the array of images. 'What an interesting face.'

They both studied the photographs. Isabella lay with a gold headpiece around her hair. Her right hand held a lily, and Nell stared down at the flowing lines of her robe and at her hands. The right hand was beautifully carved, fingers splayed, with a thin gold band on her little finger.

'Mark said she had been cut away from the bow timbers, Nell. She is flatter in the back, and can you see, here . . . her left hand is damaged and has been remodelled.'

'You're lucky to have such a detailed report, Gabby, from someone of obvious experience. It will be of enormous help to you.'

'If I'm given the job, Nell.'

'The figurehead has been painted several times. Many elements have been painted with gold-coloured oil paint. Evidence of an older cream-coloured paint layer under the white coating . . .' Gabby read from the report.

She picked up another photograph. 'Detail of crack along neck. Head secure but some paint loss reveals a thin layer of plaster underneath the paint . . .'

'Look at the detail of the right ear as it disappears into her hair,' Nell said, entranced.

'Oh, Nell, you really need to see the figurehead itself to appreciate the detail. Look at the robe, the wrist, the curve of her arm at the elbow as it disappears into her robe . . . This would be such a wonderful project to work on.'

Nell smiled. Gabby's enthusiasm was infectious and Nell felt a whiff of envy at Gabby's chance of working with something so beautiful.

'The neck and upper body seem the most damaged.'

'That left hand . . . it's a terrible reproduction, totally out of proportion.'

'Mm, I can see that. What else does she say?'

'Image 01-0193 . . . Traces of blue-green paint in upper rear right gap.' Gabby jumped on the last sentence and photograph. 'Great! Nell, she found some original paint!'

'Don't get your hopes up, Gabby, until you've done a detailed inspection of your own.'

'You are going to come and see her, aren't you?'

'I'd certainly like to see her before you start. You just can't wait to get your teeth into this, can you?'

'I haven't got the job yet, Nell!'

'I know Peter, Gabby. He wouldn't let you take this report away unless he wanted you to restore it.'

The phone went and Nell got up. 'It's probably Elan.'

He and Nell phoned each other most nights. But it was not Elan, it was Peter.

'Were your ears burning?' Nell asked.

'Why? Should they have been?'

'Gabby and I were just looking through the report that Mark Hannah brought with him.'

'Good, I can catch Gabby in work mode. How are you, Nell? I hear you've been landed with the Browns' enormous picture.'

Nell had a clear picture of his wolfish, cerebral face crinkling with amusement. 'Glad you find it funny, Peter. I trust you had nothing to do with them coming to me with it?'

'I merely advised them that if anyone could do anything with it, you could.'

'Thank you very much! Well, I hope when I am a bent old crone still working on that masterpiece you will have the grace to feel guilty. I will hand you over to Gabby.'

'You will never be an old crone, Nell. We must have lunch soon?'

'Look forward to it,' Nell said, handing the phone to Gabby. How ridiculous that a certain tone of voice, like a code or secret signal, could still contract her stomach with memory of love.

'Hello Peter,' Gabby said, breathless.

'Gabby, I've come up with an idea that might satisfy all the various bodies responsible for the funding for the museum. I've spoken to John and he thinks it is possibly the answer, if you are agreeable.'

'Right,' Gabby said nervously, wondering what was coming.

'As we explained, funding is always a problem, and unfortunately we have to depend on councillors like Rowe, who are good at drumming-up money for Cornish artefacts.

'We want to get the figurehead into a condition where we can exhibit her in the museum by the end of June, before the influx of visitors. We wondered if you would be willing to work on her in two stages. Initially, make sure she is sound and make all the immediate repairs that are needed to safeguard the whole, plus the superficial ones that affect her appearance.

'When you are happy that she is in a condition to be exhibited in June, having made whatever tests and analysis you consider necessary for further more detailed work later on, would it be possible for you to go on to other work and return to the figurehead at a later date, possibly when the museum is closed at the end of the season? Does this sound feasible to you?'

'Of course, Peter. John says that the museum is kept at a regular temperature so we don't have to worry about humidity. That would be fine. I would like to see her again, properly, out of her wrappings and in position. This inspection report is very helpful. I'll make my own inspection and give you a quote for all the initial work I consider vital before she can be exhibited. After I've been working on her for a while, I'll then submit a more detailed quote for the next stage of her restoration. Would that be OK?'

'Perfect. Thank you for being so accommodating. By then we will hopefully have more funding and voluntary contributions coming in from interested parties. I can now appease Rowe, Penwith Council, the Heritage people, and the Cornish Historical Society. Bless you!'

Gabby laughed. 'Does that mean . . . ?'

'Of course it does, Gabrielle! John and I have always been convinced you are the best person for the job. We just have to tweak terms and make it official. You'll get a letter in a few days.'

'I'm really looking forward to restoring her, Peter, it's very exciting.'

'It is, isn't it? We are all hoping Mark Hannah comes

up with more history for us. Goodnight, Gabrielle, and thanks again.'

'YES!' Gabby said, replacing the phone and punching the air.

'I told you you had nothing to worry about,' Nell said, laughing. 'I'm off to bed.' She nodded at the report. 'I should remove those papers and photographs from the table. Charlie will come home and drip egg sandwich all over them.'

'Oh, God! That wouldn't look very professional.'

She walked to the back door with Nell. 'Look, a new moon.'

They both looked up. It was a clear, cold night and the stars stood out like a child's drawing on black paper.

'Do you remember Josh and his telescope?' Nell asked. 'I wonder what happened to it. It was one of Elan's extravagant presents, wasn't it?'

Gabby felt a sudden wrench for *that time* again, for the simple, innocent pleasures of Josh's childhood. 'Josh used to get crazes on things, do you remember? Absolute passions. Then he would go on to the next thing.'

'Don't remind me. Do you remember the fish?'

'Which all died, because he never took any notice of the man in the aquarium and mixed and matched them because he liked their colour or shape. Months of his pocket money eating each other up before he learnt a hard biology lesson.'

'The fishy mess in the sink when he cleaned them out.'

'Always at Sunday lunchtime!'

'And the stick insects he begged for and then could not bear to touch.'

'And the rabbits.'

'Then the guinea pigs.'

'He stuck to his bantams, he loved those. And the calves.'

'And Hal. That gelding was the love of his life. I still stop in the village and he whinnies and canters over.'

'I know. He's a lovely character.'

'I wonder how he's doing. Josh, I mean. I think he's finding Sandhurst harder, physically, than he expected.'

'People are always saying that it's because the young are not as fit as the last generation, but Josh has always been sporty and fit.'

Nell snorted. 'How many late-rising youths know their way around an assault course? Or readily accept being bellowed at? Or want to trot round Dartmoor in a blizzard with a great pack on their backs? Total masochism if you ask me. Absolutely bonkers.'

Gabby began to laugh. Josh and Nell argued about the army every time he came home, but she knew perfectly well, as Josh did, he could do no wrong in Nell's eyes.

'Goodnight, lovie,' Nell said, making off across the yard, watching her step in the dark.

''Night, Nell.'

Gabby whistled for Shadow who had scooted off into the dark. She looked up at the stars once more before shutting the door. On her way upstairs she paused and pushed Josh's bedroom door open. Funny how a room always retained the faint smell of a person. Odd how strong a sense smell was, taking you faster than thought to a place or a person you loved.

Chapter 8

The noise from the top field was horrendous. They were tipping concrete into the foundations. Nell, who could not bear the thought of this noise continuing for months, phoned the local nursery and ordered twenty trees. If they could plant saplings as soon as possible at least they could screen the building site and maybe it would dull the sound of machinery.

She was planting succulents in the small, walled garden she and Gabby had resurrected from a decade of neglect. They had banned all livestock; no geese, hens or dogs were allowed inside their hallowed plot.

There had been no time to garden when Ted was alive, and Nell thought, not for the first time, how released she felt. Free to be herself, to express herself in ways she had never dreamt of doing when she and Ted were running the farm on a strict budget, when they had had to labour, metaphorically, side by side.

Some mornings, when Nell woke, she also felt guilty about not missing her husband more. She would stretch luxuriously across the whole double bed and lie contemplating her day, waiting for the sun to rise beyond the top field and to creep up the covers towards her face. She felt warm and spoilt and relaxed as she heard the back door of the farmhouse bang, heard Charlie whistling for Shadow and Outside Dog. Then silence would descend and she would lie waiting for the sound of Matt, the herdsman, bringing the cows down the lane and into the yard below.

The smell of them would rise up to her window, the milking machine would start up, a dog over the fields would bark in the first light. All so familiar that any small disturbance in the pattern of a morning would make Nell rise up on her elbow, ears strained for the cause of the minute change in routine. Through it all, like hugging a secret she never got tired of, the knowledge that she did not have to get up and go out into that cold darkness ever again.

She missed the farmhouse not one jot. Most of the contents had belonged to Ted's parents; heavy Victorian furniture to fill the large rooms. When Charlie married Gabby, Nell thought with glee of her escape to the cottage. She had gone out and bought small, light, inexpensive furniture for the tiny rooms and had taken from the farmhouse only the small pieces she was fond of.

Charlie, who missed her in the house with him and had seen no reason for her to move out, had, in a rare and overt show of affection, had the cottage centrally heated for her. This, for Nell, was like being given an invaluable, never to be taken for granted, Christmas and birthday present rolled into one. She could sit restoring for many more hours and it seemed to her that she was warm for the first time in her life.

She stopped planting for a moment and looked over the grass at Gabby, who was lying on her stomach reading a huge library book on marine architecture, seemingly absorbed despite the thunderous noise of the lorries now depositing granite blocks in piles onto the once lush green field.

Sitting back on her heels Nell realized her thoughts had subconsciously formed a circular route back to Gabby. In her life with Ted there had been little female companionship, scarce time for close friendships. Gabby had not been a substitute for the daughter Nell had never had; she and Gabby did not have the intimate and critical relationship mothers and daughters often have. They had a deep, inviolable friendship and an unspoken admiration for each other

45

which had started in that freezing cold spring when they first met.

Nell had watched, protectively, a girl who refused to be beaten by the elements or by the endless taunts of seasoned pickers. Gabby had been humbled by the sheer volume of farm work Nell had been expected to get through each and every day, as well as her restoring, all to keep the farm solvent.

They had rescued each other. Nell had plucked Gabby from the fields to help her in the barn. Help in the barn had freed Nell to restore and to talk to someone. In the days before Charlie qualified and came back to the farm, Nell could go for months without having a proper conversation with anyone.

Ted had been a man of few words. Or, Nell thought now, so long after his death, maybe he only got out of the way of using words to me. Whatever, this second part of my life is *mine*, and I would not change a thing.

Gabby suddenly sat up and pulled small earphones out of her ears. 'I'm sure the earth is shuddering, Nell. I can feel it over the music. This is worse than it's ever been. It's unbearable.'

Charlie appeared suddenly, shutting Shadow firmly on the other side of the gate. He looked hot and fed-up.

'I've been up to the site and complained about the noise. We were given a strict understanding that they would build one house at a time to limit the disturbance. I've got two cows calving and number four is so distressed I've had to bring her in and put her in the barn. I've had two complaints, one from the primary school and one from Tom Eddy. He says two of his sheep have aborted.'

Nell and Gabby stared at him. 'This is serious, Charlie,' Nell said. 'What did the site manager say? We can't afford to fall out with our neighbours.'

'He assured me they've almost finished unloading the granite for the day and he's sorry about the noise, but he's only doing what he's been instructed to do.'

'Stuart something of Roseworthy Developments gave us a hotline number in case of any complaints.' Gabby got to her feet. 'Shall I get it?'

'It's OK, I've got the number in the office. I've told Alan to ring, he's got more patience than I have. I'll end up yelling down the phone. In the end, all they'll say is that they've got to build the houses as fast as possible.'

'I don't suppose they want to alienate people either, if they can help it,' Nell said, conscious that Charlie had chosen to sell the land cheaper and take a percentage of the profit of each house built. And each house built was way out of most local pockets.

'What I came to ask,' Charlie said, changing the subject, 'is can you keep an eye on number four. She's fine at the moment, but she could start to calve any time and I have to drive Darren to the industrial estate to pick up the tractor.'

'Do you want a cup of tea before you go?' Gabby asked, getting up. 'I was just going to make one.'

'No, I'd better get off ... hey, the noise has stopped, perhaps they've packed it in for the day.'

'Oh,' Nell said. 'Isn't silence wonderful?'

'Gab,' Charlie said as she came out of the gate. 'Don't wait until I get back to call David out, will you? If she starts calving, she'll need help. Her calf is going to be breech.'

Gabby linked arms with him and walked him to his car. 'Trust me. I should know what to do by now.'

Charlie grinned. 'I know. I'm just fond of that cow. This will be her last calf and she's done us proud.' He opened the car door. 'See you at supper. I've got my mobile if you need me.'

'Goodbye, hard farmer man.'

'You can mock,' Charlie retorted. 'Who still cries when the fox gets one of their bantams?'

Gabby watched him hurtle down the lane. The building site was deserted, all was quiet again. She stared across the field to the sea, trying to visualize the houses. Horrible, like being invaded. Nothing would ever be quite the same again.

47

The magic and tranquil stillness of the field was gone forever.

Nell, behind her, said, 'I've ordered trees. Probably more than we need, but I think it's important we don't have to look at the wretched houses springing up, even if we can hear them. I'll make a cup of tea. You check that cow of Charlie's, Gab.'

Gabby made her way to the barn. Number four was breathing hard and she was restless, but there was no sign of her being in labour yet. Gabby scratched the cow's head; this cow had been hand-reared and related to humans on a bovine level.

Charlie had never let Josh name the livestock. 'They are not pets, son. Animals get sick and die. Don't name them, don't personalize them, because eventually they will end up on your plate.'

So Josh did not name the orphan calves, he curled up in the straw feeding them by bottle, secretly calling them by numbers. Gabby and Nell would have to proclaim loudly to each other when cooking their own stock, 'Number six got a good price at market, Charlie says. Tom Eddy is going to breed from her.'

Josh, ears pricked, would regard the meat on his plate with suspicion.

'Who is this?'

'Josh!' Charlie would say crossly. 'I've told you not to name the calves. Giving them a number is exactly the same as naming them. Eat. It is probably not our meat anyway.'

'But,' Josh would retort indignantly, 'if you feed them you've got to call them something, you can't call them *nothing* . . .'

'Call them *cow*. Eat.'

'Mum and Nell give the bantams names.'

'Yes, and you know what a fuss they both make when one goes missing or the fox gets into the pen. Bad enough to lose livestock without giving them damn silly names to make it worse . . . Women rushing around the yard squeaking . . . "Oh! Oh! Virginia Woolf has fallen off her perch . . . Dear,

dear . . . Freda is headless . . . Fie, fie, Elton John has been in a fight and lost his pretty little tail feathers . . ."' Charlie had bounded around the kitchen throwing Nell's apron over his head, giving little girly skips and talking in a falsetto.

Josh, by now hysterical with laughter, would decide he must be a man like his father and they would all sit down and happily devour number six. To be a vegetarian on a farm would have been like being evangelical in a strict Roman Catholic household.

'I'll be back in a while,' she said to the cow. 'I'm just going to check my answer-machine.'

Taking tea into her workroom she saw there were three messages. Message number one was from Josh, telling her she should get a mobile as he could never get hold of her. He sounded husky and dispirited. They were never off the parade ground. He was worried he would fail his next fitness test. He was finding out about suitable places for Charlie, Nell and Gabby to stay . . . if he ever passed out. He would ring again on Sunday . . . He was really looking forward to a weekend home.

Message number two was from Peter Fletcher.

'Gabrielle. We considered your quote very reasonable indeed, even our mutual councillor friend. An official letter is in the post.

'My other reason for ringing you is Mark Hannah. Before he goes back to London he's keen to go and see the figureheads at Valhalla on Tresco. Unfortunately, I'm completely tied up with meetings next week. Forgive me if this is an imposition, Gabrielle, but would you be free to fly over on the helicopter with him? We will, of course, pick up the tab. It seems inhospitable to send him on his own when he has done so much for us. I will quite understand if you are too busy. Could you give me a ring on this number . . . ?'

Gabby shakily put her tea down on her desk. Message number three.

'Hi there, Gabriella. Peter gave me your number, do hope you don't mind. He couldn't get an answer so he left a message. Is there any chance of you having the time to accompany me to Tresco to see the figureheads? I would sure love to see them. I'd be grateful if you could let me know as I need to book my train ticket back to London . . .'

The sun was setting below the fields. Shadows lengthened across the stubby lawn outside. Bantams pecked the grubs in noisy little groups like fussy old women at a W.I. meeting. Gabby sat very still, pulling a thread from the hem of her tee-shirt. If she did not pick up the phone and dial his number this instant she would not be able to do it. She opened her diary to see which day she would be least missed from the farm, then, feeling sick, she picked up the phone and dialled Mark Hannah's number.

As she waited for him to answer, the sun slid away, and despite the flushed sky, dusk descended quickly. Damp rose up from the grass and into the open window. In the kitchen behind her, Nell switched on the six o'clock news and lights sprang up suddenly, away on the far peninsula. A fleeting sadness, an ache, a sensation of being beyond the warmth of lighted windows, of being extrinsic within a house she knew and people she loved, descended on Gabby.

In the darkening room there was just her, holding a phone which was ringing out into a hotel room where a man lay on a bed with his hands behind his head, watching, as she did, evening come, with a sudden longing for home; for the smell of cooking and laughter and bottles of wine being opened, of small children being bathed. The safe embodiment of a familiar routine.

He lay still, waiting to see if the phone would ring, and when it did he could not answer it, as if frozen by the knowledge of what answering it might mean. Just as Gabby gave a shaky sigh of relief and made to replace the receiver, Mark Hannah, in one swift movement, turned and grabbed his up from the bedside table, aware as he did so of a premeditated and deliberate crossing from a place of safety, to something quite else.

*   *   *

In the early hours of the morning Charlie and David, the vet, fought to save number four and her calf. The cow managed after a long, painful labour to give birth to a healthy heifer, but collapsed and haemorrhaged immediately afterwards. Gabby knelt by her head, talking to the old cow and stroking her trembling limbs. Nell brought out more hot water and they put a blanket over her to try to minimize the shock of a difficult birth.

She managed to turn and nuzzle her calf to her shaky, stick-like feet and then she gave up the fight and with a tired, sad little sound the breath left her body. The calf bellowed and slid down to the floor again, nuzzling her mother for milk. They watched her suckling, then, still leaning against her mother, the calf fell asleep. Charlie rubbed her gently down with straw, admiring her.

'That's a good calf you've got there,' David said, 'but I'm sorry we lost the mother. Is there a cow you can try her with, rather than hand-rearing?'

'Yes,' Charlie said. 'Just one. She lost a bull calf last week. She's young and skittish, so I don't know if she will accept this one, but I'll certainly try her.'

They moved out of the barn into the cool dark night.

'Come and have a drink, David,' Nell said. 'Gabby, go to bed, you look exhausted.'

'Yes, go on Gab, I won't be long.'

'Goodnight,' David smiled at her before the men turned to follow Nell to her cottage.

Gabby walked across the yard to the house, the image of the dying cow still with her. She knew that it did not matter how long you farmed, you never got used to losing a healthy animal.

She showered quickly, then climbed into bed and lay on her back trying to relax. She switched her small radio on low and listened to the comfortable ragbag of the World Service and tried to drift off. She wanted to be asleep before Charlie tripped exhausted up the stairs, full of Nell's whisky.

Gabby knew the pattern of Charlie's drinking after a long

hard day. If she was still awake she could time Charlie's clumsy movements in the dark. He would wash his hands but would be too tired to shower. He would fall into the bed beside her with a grunt of relief and either reach out for her or fall asleep in a second on his back and start to snore gently.

Gabby preferred the latter. The smell of straw and disinfectant would still cling to him, mingling with the not altogether unpleasant sweat of hard labour. With whisky blurring any moral sensibility he would mumble in her ear, push her nightdress up to her waist, part her knees roughly with his, enter her, come immediately, or, worse, complete this isolating little act with difficulty.

Gabby would lie under him, looking out through the open curtain at the night sky, detaching herself from her inert body being rammed rhythmically under his. As he rolled off her, already asleep, Gabby would feel the bleakness of the spirit confronted by the inevitable fact of its separateness from another human being. She saw in her mind the cockerel pouncing on his bantams or the bull in the field clumsily mounting a heifer.

If Gabby was aware, in the telling and unforgiving dark, that her passivity in allowing her body to be used was colluding with the act itself, she would have had to face, head on, her own facility for smoothing over all cracks to maintain the polished facade of what she believed a marriage to be.

It was easier not to confront. Charlie would not have understood the word violation, and it seemed too strong a word for something that lasted minutes and did not hurt the flesh, only left the soul in a cold, dark place. It was simpler to make some areas of her marriage off limits.

If Gabby had understood that by avoiding communicating to Charlie on any intimate level she denied him the chance of acknowledging any responsibility for the way he sometimes behaved, she would have had to own that she did not have the courage to go there. She was comfortable, on the whole, in the place she occupied, in the marriage she had. Two people who shied carefully away from emotional intimacy. And she was sure Charlie was, too.

Tonight she slept and was only dimly aware of Charlie falling into bed beside her. He patted her bottom. 'G'night,' he mumbled.

''Night,' she mumbled back, and, feeling sudden affection, 'Sorry about number four, Charlie.'

But Charlie was already asleep. In three hours he would have to get up for milking.

Chapter 9

Gabrielle and Mark stood before the figureheads in the peace of an early morning. The helicopter had departed with a roar back to Penzance and the only other people in the Abbey Gardens were the gardeners, unseen and silent. A spade stood upright in the soil, a robin pecked in the new-turned earth. A jacket lay folded on a bench, there was the sound of someone sweeping a path and the smell of damp blooms mixed with spearmint rose from the ground.

They had permission to go into the gardens before they opened to the little ferryboats full of tourists and gardening clubs. They walked silently, along paths that curled round vast tropical plants and beds of succulents of such colour and variety that occasionally they stopped in their tracks, awed by the sheer scale of the planting.

'Each time I come I think of *The Secret Garden*,' Gabby whispered, as if her voice might shatter the illusion of paradise. 'There's always a spade or a fork placed just so, yet I've never seen anyone working.'

Mark smiled. 'Perhaps the gardeners are from some other world. Nothing would surprise me here. What an amazing place! There's something mystical and timeless about being inside a walled garden.'

Rounding a corner they came upon a clearing and there before them lay Valhalla Museum, with the array of figureheads, bright against the lush undergrowth, extraordinary in their garish beauty. Mark drew in his breath, and Gabby, turning to look up at him, thought how open and un-English he was; unafraid to show his excitement.

They both stood silently admiring while the birds swooped and darted fearlessly at their feet, for there was little in these lush gardens to threaten them. They moved closer to examine the carvings. Gabby was especially interested in the faces, because on the St Piran figurehead the face and neck were going to be most difficult to restore.

'Trophies of the sea,' Mark murmured. 'Each figurehead an individual offering of respect and affection, regardless of whether they were carved by a naïve seaman or a carver of distinction.'

Staring into an enigmatic wooden face with eyes that gave nothing away, Gabby thought of the figurehead carvers and of the sailors who had manned the ships and watched as their figureheads rose and plunged out of the waves, carrying them precariously to battle in the duty of a monarch.

How many lives, from the moment of carving to the moment of her ship sinking and being salvaged, did a carved face touch in so many different ways? Gabby could see in her mind's eye a Napoleonic battle or a great storm breaking up a galleon. The sails unfurling at speed, masts falling with a great crack, like trees, and the screams of men jumping away from the sinking ship to drown in the angry waters.

There the ship would lie on the seabed, broken, its hull becoming a sad skeleton over the years as seaweed and barnacles enveloped it. Then, one day, divers would descend; the salvage men, swimming round the wreck in slow-moving sequence with waving arms and excited thumbs-up as they discovered a poignant wooden face, staring blindly upwards, the heart and soul of the dead vessel. They would bring her up from that fathomless dark to see once more the light of day and the lives of men.

Gabby became conscious of Mark staring at her in the amused way he had.

'Come back,' he said softly. 'Where have you been?'

'I was just thinking that each figurehead must have a story, a life of its own, and we'll never know what it was, we can only imagine it.'

'You would be surprised how much we can learn from a ship, Gabriella. Like compiling a profile we can build a history, based on fact. We might never discover all the names and faces of those who built or sailed in the ships, but with a date and a time we can catch a glimpse, find records, form an idea of the way these mariners lived their lives.

'We don't have records of the building of the early ships because the shipwrights were often illiterate so no plans were drawn up. However, models were made and some of these survive and are as beautifully detailed as the real ships.'

They moved around the display of figureheads: a sailor, a king, a damsel, a god.

'Did the figureheads become a way of denoting wealth or origin, or just a way of honouring a monarch or a country?' Gabby asked. 'I know the Vikings had them on their ships until the thirteenth century and then they changed the front of their boats for war or something. We had to draw eleventh-century Viking boats from the Bayeux Tapestry endlessly at school and I'm afraid I was bored rigid.'

Mark laughed. 'I'm probably boring you now, Gabriella. The figureheads became superfluous when the Vikings developed the forecastle on the front of their boats. But before that happened the Viking longships carried serpents and dragons. There were two in the British Museum, as well as on the Bayeux Tapestry, which you must have seen, depicting William of Normandy's invasion fleet of 1066, all decorated with lion and dragon figureheads.'

Gabby said hastily, 'I'm not in the least bit bored. There is a huge difference between being taught by a bored nun with no interest in the subject herself, and going to the British Museum, which I loved. Or standing here in front of figureheads, some of which have been pulled up somewhere out there on the rocks . . .' She gestured towards the sea.

Mark stood looking down at her. Gabby had never met anyone who looked as if they were always about to laugh, as if life itself was one huge joke. It did not fit in, somehow, with her idea of a historian.

He turned back to the figureheads, casually placing a hand under her elbow.

'A figurehead could be many things. Originally it was most likely religious. The head of an animal sacrificed to appease a sea god. Then it would have become symbolic and a means of identification. The Egyptian ships had figures of holy birds or eyes painted on the sides of the bows so the ship could see. The Phoenicians used horse heads symbolizing speed, and the Greek rowing galleys favoured bronze animals, usually a boar's head, their most hunted and frightening animal . . .'

Gabby listened to Mark Hannah's fluid and easy voice. It had a beautiful rhythm and symmetry. His enthusiasm was catching, making it all the more . . . *seductive* shot into her mind, and she jumped away from his hand under her elbow as if this thought could transfer itself up her arm into his hand.

'Can you give me five minutes?' Mark was rummaging in his haversack and brought out a small tape recorder. 'I just want to make some notes, then we can go look for a coffee?'

'Of course.'

Gabby wandered away. She could hear voices now, the day was waking up and the gardens would be open soon. Visitors would begin to stream in and the helicopter would return. The ferry would arrive at St Mary's and the small boats would chug to and fro from the islands, depositing visitors until dusk.

She sat on the grass cross-legged and closed her eyes and held her face up to the sun. She felt an unaccountable surge of happiness. Scilly always felt like another country. Only a few miles of water separated them from the mainland and yet it always felt *abroad*.

Gabby felt that small, familiar tug of longing which surfaced occasionally and which she would quickly squash. A sensation that the world was flowing fluidly on without her.

It was not unhappiness, it was not boredom. She could never catch and hold on to the feeling. It slid slyly away from her, as if momentarily her soul had migrated to a dry desert, a landscape without feature or water, or enough life to sustain her.

Like running through sand, she knew that beyond the horizon there was an oasis, a lighted city twinkling and pulsing with life, but somehow her feet could never retain the momentum to reach that place of light and laughter. The days of her life slid by in an effortless rhythm, each day dissolving into the next with little change or interruption, each day forming a pattern, a whole, indivisible except for the tiniest domestic detail.

Since Josh left home she had started to get up early with Charlie in order to get through her work. Each morning she took Shadow for a walk across the top field and down the coastal path to the small cove. She would watch the sea mist lift to reveal another day, then she would return to the house to cook Charlie's breakfast, already thinking about the painting waiting in her workroom.

After hours working, stiff, she would get up from her chair and stretch, lean out of the window perfectly content, and a sudden yearning for something indefinable would swoop, a burning ache, deep in her bones, for something to break the continuity of the measureless days.

Behind her the faint sound of the soft Canadian drawl had stopped. Her back prickled, the heat of her body felt strange to her. She kept her eyes closed, focusing on the sun blobs behind her eyelids, merging into the soft noises around her and the heady, dizzy smell of flowers.

What she felt in every nerve of her body and what she determinedly allowed herself to think were horribly diverse. It made her want to run away down the narrow paths dripping with flowers like bright jewels. It felt too bright, too nightmarishly large and foreign and unknown. An unmapped landscape, the geography a language she had never learnt and felt stunned to recognize.

She opened her eyes when Mark blocked out the sun. He was standing in front of her, not smiling, his expression unreadable as he gazed down upon her. She looked up into his eyes and they were both still, staring at one another. She glimpsed a sudden hesitancy, a fleeting loneliness or vulnerability.

The strength of emotion that flooded Gabby must have shown in her eyes for Mark smiled suddenly and put out his hand to pull her up from the grass, and somehow, on the narrow paths, where it was necessary to walk close, he forgot to let go of it until they reached the café.

Chapter 10

Charlie crossed the yard to the old hay barn where Alan, his farm manager, worked. Once the land had been sold and Gabby started to bring money into the farm he had decided to hire a farm manager to free him from paperwork.

Up until a few years ago Nell had helped with the accounts, but she had made it plain to Charlie that it was about time he got someone else, *and that does not mean Gabby,* she had said firmly. Charlie did not blame Nell, it took hours of her time and there was always a last-minute panic. All the same, with Josh gone Gabby had more time on her hands, and if Nell had managed to restore as well as balance the books, he could not see why it would be such a big deal for Gabby to take over Nell's work.

However, he had begun to rely on Gabby's small financial input, which made a difference, so he grudgingly hired Alan. It had been an excellent move. Alan had managed to slice a sizable chunk from their feed bills and he was way ahead of Charlie and Nell when it came to what they could and could not put against tax. Charlie had to admit the man earnt every penny he paid him. Alan came from a farming family himself and he had plenty of sound ideas on farm management. Today, however, his face was serious.

'Look at this, Charlie.' He picked a bulb from a bag on his desk and held it in the palm of one hand. He gently scratched the surface with a fingernail and the bulb crumbled.

'Shit.' Charlie picked the bulb up and peered at it. 'Eel worm. Which field?'

'The two-acre field at Mendely.'

'We stored the bulbs from that field on their own, didn't we?'

'Yes, b—'

'Thank God for that.'

'Charlie . . . listen! We stored the bulbs from that field on their own, but, if you remember, the red barn had a hole in the roof, so while it was being fixed we also put the bulbs from the small home field in there.'

'Oh, shit!' Charlie said again angrily. 'We've lost two bloody fields, then, and that barn will be useless until we've disinfected it.'

'It could have been worse, Charlie.' Alan pointed outside his office where layers of bulbs filled the barn. 'Matt and I have checked the bulbs in the other barns and as far as we can see everything is fine. If we had to get eel worm, much better it was one of the smaller fields away from the farm.'

'We'll have to buy in, then, as soon as possible,' Charlie said. 'Have you got time to go through the catalogues for main breeders this afternoon?'

'Yes. About three o'clock, before milking? I've got the meal rep coming at two-thirty.'

Charlie turned for the door. 'Let's make it three-thirty. It will give me and Matt time to plough up the field at Mendely. See you then. I've got my mobile if anything else crops up.'

Charlie came out of the barn in a bad temper and collared Nell who was feeding the bantams.

'Have you seen Matt, Nell?'

'He's taken the repaired tractor to the far field, he asked me to tell you.'

'Oh, for heaven's sake, why couldn't he just wait until he'd seen me this morning?'

'Charlie, he didn't know where you were. What's put you in a foul mood all of a sudden?'

'Eel worm. All the bulbs from Mendely are contaminated, plus we stored the bulbs from the small home field with them, so two whole fields will have to be chucked.'

61

Nell sighed. 'That is bad luck. Did you get that hole mended in the red barn?'

'No!' Charlie snapped. 'I haven't quite got round to that. I can't be bloody everywhere. Look, Nell, can you get Gabby to go and find Matt and tell him to leave what he's doing and meet me at Mendely. I want him to plough up the field so I can spray it immediately. Even if he's got his mobile phone he won't hear it.'

Nell sighed and scattered corn in an arc. 'Gabby isn't here, she left shortly after you this morning. You can't have forgotten, surely? She's gone to Scilly to look at figureheads. I'm sorry, Charlie, but I can't go either. I've got a client collecting a picture in ten minutes.'

'Fine, fine. I'll go myself. Obviously I'm a one-man band around here. Why Gabby has to go swanning off on a weekday is beyond me.'

'Charlie,' Nell said quietly, 'come on, eel worm is serious, but you've caught it early. If it was one of the large fields it would have been far worse. It's happened before and it will happen again. We've been farming long enough for you to know disease is an occupational hazard, with bulbs or livestock.'

She smiled at him. 'Don't do a Ted on me. You know how it used to drive you mad.'

Reluctantly, Charlie grinned back at her.

'Come on, I'll make you a coffee before you go out.'

Charlie followed her into the farmhouse, sobered by the thought of turning into his father. Ted, at the slightest setback, would lugubriously pronounce instant bankruptcy. Indeed, he constantly predicted doom lay in wait for all farmers, but it crouched in particular waiting for him.

'Do I really sound like Dad?' he asked Nell, leaning against the Aga and pulling a hand through his hair irritably.

'Sometimes you do.' Nell took the heavy kettle off the Aga and poured water into two mugs. 'Your language is worse, you get angry rather than depressed, and your bad temper blows over more quickly than your father's black moods.'

Charlie took his mug of coffee from her and asked suddenly, surprising himself as well as Nell, 'Were you happy with Dad, Nell?'

Startled, for this was so unlike Charlie, Nell was momentarily lost for the right words. Eventually she said slowly, 'I don't think I had the time to even think about it. We had a busy life together and I believe I was perfectly content. We both loved the farm and had the same goals . . .'

Nell added, because she knew it was what Charlie wanted to hear, 'Your father and I understood each other very well. We had a whole life together.'

Charlie grinned and drained his mug. 'Good. I'm off. I won't be back for lunch, I'll grab a pasty as I go through the village. See you later. When is Gabby back?'

'Not till this evening.'

'Why does she need all day to look at figureheads?'

'Peter Fletcher couldn't go, and he asked Gabby if she wouldn't mind going with Mark Hannah, the Canadian, to see the figureheads and to show him around Tresco. It would be a waste of money to just go out there and come back on the next helicopter, don't you think? She did tell you, Charlie, you don't listen.'

'Probably not,' he said proudly and went out of the door.

Nell, irritated, thought, he *sounds* just like his father sometimes, too. It was a glorious morning and she hoped Gabby was enjoying every minute of a day's escape.

It was odd. Gabby was such a small, unobtrusive person. Often they would not see each other all day, yet when she was away from the farm Nell felt the lack of her presence in her small workroom, missed glimpses of her flitting around the farm, somehow always registered the weight of her absence.

She thought about her duplicity in answering Charlie's question. Of course she had had time to think about her happiness with Ted. Too much time. Working with your hands freed your mind to fly to places better not visited, but that did not mean she had wasted her life in wanting to change what she could not. The one thing she did envy about Ted back then, and Charlie now, was their ability to accept as truth anything she said with quiet conviction. It was something she had perfected over the years, for in the moment of saying it she too believed the power of her own unambiguity.

She picked up a bowl and went back outside to check the chicken houses and surrounding area for eggs. She found six perfect speckled-brown eggs in the long grass by the hedge. Looking up at the cloudless sky, listening to the roar of the sea in the distance, Nell smiled, thinking again of the small simple pleasures that sustain, that never change and count as happiness.

Chapter 11

'Actually, it's Gabrielle, not Gabriella,' Gabby said, as they sat outside on a wooden bench drinking coffee and eating biscuits.

'I know,' Mark said. 'I know it is. But I like the sound of Gabriella, it rolls off my tongue. Gabrielle, Gabriella – the name reminds me of Pre-Raphaelites floating down rivers in gossamer dresses.'

'Like the Lady of Shallot!'

'Yep. That's it!' They smiled at one another.

'This is heaven,' Mark said. 'Have we time to explore the whole island?'

'Tresco isn't very big and we have the rest of the day.' Gabby was amused.

'Maybe we could gather a picnic together. Is there a shop?'

'There's one shop on the other side of the island. It isn't exactly a supermarket and there is a pub right next door to it if you felt like a drink or somewhere to have lunch.'

'I thought it might be fun to walk, if you're happy to, then we can stop when we feel like it. I'd like to leave time to have a last look at Valhalla before we catch the helicopter back.'

'We'll do that, then.'

They circled the walls of the castle and walked along the tree-lined road past fields, birdwatchers' huts and timeshare cottages to the other end of the island. In the shop they bought filled rolls, crisps, a bottle of wine, chocolate and two apples. Mark stowed them away in his small backpack.

They turned and walked along the coastal path for a while and then stopped at a small white sandy beach. Gabby kicked her sandals off; the sand was already warm under her feet, the sea a shade of violet.

Mark Hannah removed his socks and shoes and rolled his trousers up and they walked along the edge of the sea. He asked her about the other islands: St Agnes, St Martin's, Bryher and St Mary's. Gabby explained that each island was entirely different and unique in its own way.

'Each summer all the islands become full to bursting. Accommodation is at a premium, even the campsite on St Agnes gets overbooked. People book a year in advance and then boat-hop between the islands. There are also trips out to visit the seal colonies, the pre-historic sites and to Samson, which is unpopulated now.'

Mark sighed. 'How I wish I'd booked a week on one of the islands before the hotel in Truro instead of visiting a colleague's family.'

'Maybe you'll have another opportunity?'

'Not this trip. I have to get back to London to see my publisher, but I'm stopping off in Exeter and hiring a car to do a couple of days' research and to visit an old aunt. I wouldn't have minded wasting a week in St Mawes if it had been fun, but the couple I stayed with kept having these God-awful dinner parties and I was trundled out like a decaying trophy.'

Gabby laughed, although she felt sympathetic. 'It's because people down here love having anyone of note to show off to their friends. It's a good thing you weren't visiting at Christmas, you'd have been swallowed whole.'

They stood for a moment watching the sea. In the distance a small boat packed with holidaymakers chugged its way past to the small jetty behind them. The water at their feet was crystal clear and tiny fish darted between their legs.

'Whenever I've come before it's been on *The Scillonian*. It only takes a couple of hours, but it always seems more exciting somehow than the helicopter. You can pretend on a short sea voyage that you are making a journey to a foreign place. You can't do that in a twenty-minute helicopter ride.'

'Do you often come over here?' Mark asked.

'Not really, considering we're so near. We used to come every few years when my son was small. Getting in and out of boats and running wild and exploring are a child's idea of heaven.'

Mark smiled. 'And a grown man's.'

They turned and walked inland through the salt marshes. Gabby's memories were of walking with Josh here while Charlie fished or chatted to the locals. Charlie always met someone he knew, wherever they went. They would talk bulbs and farming, the weather and tourists. Charlie, who grew bored and restless after about two days away from the farm, relaxed here because he knew that in any crisis he could be on the helicopter and home within a few hours. But holidays had often been with Nell as they could never all leave the farm together.

If this was your first trip to the Scilly Islands you would be awed at the vivid colour of the sea and marvel at the row upon row of varying yellow daffodils in spring, sloping downwards from tiny fields rimmed with stone walls. The heat and the silence, even in summer, would press down on you. If you closed your eyes you could almost believe you were on a Greek island.

Gabby thought suddenly of home. The milking would have finished; Nell would be feeding the bantams. Charlie would be doing his rounds, checking up on everyone. And here she was, *someone else*, island-walking on a clear, cloudless blue day with a man she did not know.

Moorhens shot out of the undergrowth and a heron stood on one foot perfectly still. Mark and Gabby walked on in companionable silence.

Mark was considering how his life had changed since he found Lady Isabella. What began as an interest became a quest. *Obsession*, Veronique had said. While he was away, the house would become even more packed with his daughters and their families. Veronique would be standing at the stove cooking dinner. Or, he was a bit hazy about the time difference, she would be sitting at the large Shaker table chatting to one of the girls, keeping half an eye on any grandchildren playing at her feet. She would be utterly content to be surrounded by chaos, for that chaos was her family and her whole life.

Mark could no longer remember when they had last had an evening meal alone together. He could no longer remember what his wife looked like when he first met her at university, but he never forgot how clever she had been and how shockingly eager, almost thankful she had seemed, to submerge that marvellous intellect into babies and domesticity.

Would anyone, passing them on the path as he walked with this small dark woman who was not much older than his eldest daughter, think he was her father? It was the last thing he felt. Away from his family, that ballooned alarmingly each year as if it was a contest, how different, how . . . free he felt. As if he was another man altogether.

They walked until they reached the small harbour, with fishing boats pulled up onto the foreshore. There was a gallery, the pub, and beyond, tucked away in the trees, lay the island hotel.

Mark went off to explore Cromwell's castellated fortresses rising from the water while Gabby sat on the wall, lifting her face to the sun and listening to children playing around the boats. Sound and smell; sun-coloured floaters on her closed lids rose and fell soporifically. The heat warmed her already-brown legs and arms. All life faded to this small second on the wall.

She slowly opened her eyes and got up and walked into the gallery. Most of the artists were local. Gabby was immediately drawn to two of Elan's paintings, a watercolour and a gouache, neither of which she had seen before. She was standing studying them when Mark joined her.

They both stood looking at the two small paintings for

a long time. Elan could capture a mood so exactly that it made your skin prickle. The sheer power and range of his emotions transformed his work. The moral sensibility behind a deft and seemingly simple scene was as real and true as the fierce weather or the muted colours of the start of another day.

Sunrise over Cove, a watercolour, had a haunting quality. *Cottage before a Storm* was full of a strange and intense yearning. Both paintings seemed to capture the artist's longing for another human being to share in the sparse and beautiful landscape he painted.

Gabby felt overwhelmed. She had never suspected the extent of Elan's loneliness. No conversation with him could have revealed so much. It was a shock to learn all over again how little it was possible to know those you love.

Elan went for days without speaking to a soul. It was how he had chosen and needed to live in order to paint, but Gabby saw now the extent of his longing for the companionship he once had with Patrick.

Mark, too, seemed unable to tear his eyes away.

'I'm going to have to have those two little paintings, Gabriella.' He peered at the list of prices. 'So . . . I don't eat for a while. No bad thing.'

'Elan Premore has a cottage near us. He's one of our closest friends. He's a kind and lovely man . . . I never realized how lonely and isolated he must sometimes feel.'

Lonely seemed too tame a word for the passion glimpsed within the paintings. It was raw and bleak. Like waking in the dark and reaching for a person no longer there.

Mark looked down at her. 'Is he a recluse?'

'In a way, I suppose. He lives in a tiny coastguard cottage in the middle of nowhere.'

'Completely on his own?'

'At the moment. He had a long-term partner, a doctor. They'd been together for years, then suddenly one morning Patrick left without a word of explanation. He just vanished. Elan was devastated for a while. I thought he'd got over it, he is always so cheerful, so flippant with me . . .' She swallowed. 'Obviously he hasn't got over it.'

They both turned back to the paintings.

'I don't think he ever will.'

'Yet,' Mark said, 'he is able to turn an emptiness that destroys a man into something lasting. A painting as resonant and as instinctive as a piece of music. A thing we ache to own because we understand he is showing us, more succinctly than we could ever articulate ourselves, a universal human condition.'

Gabby was silent. While the paintings were being wrapped, she said, 'Elan would have enjoyed talking to you.'

'I'd love to meet him one day,' Mark said.

'He's having another exhibition in London soon. I'll find out when it is. He would be glad you bought those paintings . . . you understand them so well.'

'It's possible only to capture a glimpse of what your friend was feeling when he painted those landscapes, those two distinct moods. But that glimpse is more than enough to recognize the spirituality within his work. Each person interprets what they see in subjective ways, but we can all intrinsically relate to those pictures to a greater or lesser degree.'

'Like listening to a piece of classical music we don't quite understand, and yet it makes us cry.'

'Yes, Gabriella.'

Mark reached for her hand and brought it to his lips. A tiny gesture, instinctively done, his eyes smiling again as he smoothly banished any introspective shadow that threatened to cast itself over their day.

They walked slowly back the way they had come towards the Abbey Gardens and the long, white, curving stretch of beach to have their picnic. They found a sheltered place backed by rocks and sat on their sweaters and leant against them. Mark opened the wine with a remarkable penknife that seemed to have a blade for every eventuality.

'Boy Scouts penknife. Obligatory male weapon, never know when it might come in handy.'

Gabby smiled and undid the egg rolls from their clingfilm. She had forgotten how pale and anaemic shop eggs were; they did not look very appetizing. Mark saw her face.

'Sorry, I'm afraid it was egg or processed cheese. I thought eggs might be fractionally better, forgetting that you probably haven't tasted shop eggs for years. I suppose yours are the colour of the sun.'

'Well, yes. Small eggs, though, we keep bantams. These are fine, what does it matter what they taste like . . .' She indicated the duck-egg-blue sea, waved her arm skyward at the cloudless sky.

'Very true,' Mark said softly.

There was hardly a sound except the lapping of small waves. The sun glinted and danced on the surface of the water making it iridescent. Mark handed Gabby a beaker of wine and held his up to her.

'To this beautiful day and to the future.'

His eyes rested on her with an expression that made her stomach lurch. They touched plastic glasses and Gabby, feeling the heat spreading over her entire body, made herself busy stowing away little clumps of clingfilm, then she turned and studied the horizon and the small boats still making their way back and forth to the island.

They munched the rolls in silence, washing them down with sharp white wine. Alarmed, Gabby thought, I mustn't drink too much.

As if reading her thoughts, Mark said, 'An island must be the best place of all to drink at lunchtime. You can't drive. There's no escape, the only thing to do is relax.'

He turned on his back and lay with his head on his sweater, his arms under his head. 'What made you become a picture restorer, Gabriella?'

Gabby sieved grains of sand as smooth as silk through her fingers. 'Watching Nell, my mother-in-law. She used to let me help her with small, simple jobs that didn't need any particular expertise. I began to get so interested that she encouraged me to train properly, get a qualification. But really it was Nell who got me started. I learnt so much from her, she was a wonderful teacher.'

'So I understand. Peter Fletcher has huge respect for her.'

'They go back a long way, I think they trained or worked together in London at some time. It's been much easier for me to work in Cornwall because Nell forged the way. When she started restoring it took her years to build up a business and a reputation. She was helping her husband run the farm, too. I don't know how she did it.'

Gabby slid onto her back. The wine was beginning to make her sleepy. She closed her eyes. One of the reasons Nell had encouraged her to study properly was to banish her longing for another child. It just never happened. Despite months of tests and medical advice and marking the calendar religiously, she had never conceived again. She had enrolled at Falmouth College of Arts to study Fine Arts with a quaking heart, but had loved every minute.

Through Nell she acquired a talent for something she was good at and loved, but would never have thought of doing. Her touch was light and instinctive and when Nell began to slow down she had taken over some of her work and steadily gained a reputation of her own. By the time Josh left for university she had her own clients and a fledgling business.

'I owe Nell so much,' she murmured, her body relaxing into the warm sand.

'You sound close.' Mark turned slightly on his side towards her, away from the sun in his eyes.

'Yes, I guess we are.'

Mark smiled. 'If you've never had to think about it, you are. Does Nell still restore?'

'She just takes on work she enjoys now, and friends' paintings. She used to do all the museum work and the heavy and sometimes monotonous cleaning of huge paintings of local dignitaries in council offices . . .'

'Like Councillor Rowe!'

Gabby laughed. 'Exactly like Councillor Rowe! Now I've

taken over all those and I think she's finding it fun and a huge relief to pick and choose what she wants to do for the first time in her life.'

'So she's a widow?'

'Oh, she's been a widow for twenty-odd years . . .' Gabby stopped as a sudden thought occurred to her. She could not believe she had never thought of it before.

'What is it, Gabriella?' Mark propped his head on his hand and peered at her.

'I've suddenly realized that Nell must have been a widow for almost as long as she was married. It's such a strange concept . . . Nell has always seemed embedded in the farm, yet . . .' Gabby tried to work it out. 'She must have been, heavens, around the age I am now when Ted died.' She stared at Mark, startled.

'Nell could have left the farm when Ted died. She could have gone back to London and resumed her career. She could have had another life altogether, while she was still young enough.'

Supposing Nell had longed to leave and Charlie and I never thought of asking her what she wanted?

Mark was thinking, *How startling this girl's eyes are. They seem to mirror every emotion, leaving her guileless. At times they appear a deep forget-me-not blue, as now. At other times they seem a hazy grey like seeing the sky or sea through mist. There seem to be brown flecks in them somewhere; perhaps they turn that way when she is angry. Is this sleeping girl ever angry? And why do I think she's sleeping?*

Had he spoken aloud? He was unsure.

'I guess,' he said, 'it's not really as simple as that. Can you really go back? The life you had once as a child or a student is long gone. You exchanged it, moved on to the life you have now. Whether your adult life is happy or not it takes courage to return to your roots or a memory of happiness. Most people, perhaps wisely, don't risk it. A place and the people you left behind don't stay frozen in time, waiting for your return. Everything changes, moves on. It can't be

73

recaptured. Isn't returning a way of saying that the whole life you have lived since has not been worth the leaving?'

'Or the living?'

'Or the living.'

He watched her eyes, fixed on his, cloud, change colour alarmingly quickly. For a second he was afraid of what he glimpsed, so stark it looked. He reached out his hand to touch hers and her fingers felt cold. He closed his hand firmly round hers.

'Banish it. Don't let a ghost walk over your grave.'

She smiled and lay back on the sand, closing her eyes, letting his fingers hold on to hers. They both drifted sleepily without talking any more.

A place and the people you left behind don't stay frozen in time, waiting for your return . . .

No. But in your mind they do. In your mind they stay exactly as you left them.

That is why you must take such care with the life you have. It must never be taken for granted. It seemed to Gabby, sometimes, that people did not understand the importance of this. People had rows, screamed at each other, spoilt their lives in cruelty and quick tongues, in passion and in hate. It wasn't worth it. It really wasn't.

She thought of Josh. Josh leaving the life he shared with her for another wider world. She was glad of it, it was how things should be, and yet they would never be so close again. He would grow away from her, the process had already begun. As his world enlarged she would grow smaller. He would bring girls back and the things they had laughed at and done together he would now share with someone else.

And yet . . . she too had moved on to another place; she was not in the same place that he had left her. In those first days of his leaving she had flown to his empty room just to breathe in the smell of him. The pain that cut deep into her ribs, making her breathless with loss, eased, as she too slipped into a separate life without him.

Mark and Gabby both slept facing towards each other. The sun dipping slowly lower over the sea cast a shadow for their faces out of the jutting rock. Their fingers relaxed, but remained touching. Both perfectly at ease, felt, in their sleep, intense happiness.

Gabby woke first and watched Mark's face as he slept. It was a surprise to find how familiar his face seemed. Like a map she already knew her way around. It was a shock to realize that at the end of this day she would never see his face or experience this stab of recognition again.

He suddenly opened his eyes as if her gaze had woken him. They looked at one another in silence. His eyes were serious, she could find no hint of laughter in them. He closed his fingers around hers for a moment and then sat up yawning.

'I suppose it's time we went.' He looked at his watch. 'Just time for one more look at the figureheads?'

'Yes, we've got time.' Gabby gathered the beakers and the empty wine bottle and Mark put them back in his haversack. A small wind got up and Gabby pulled on her sweater. Mark, smiling, reached out to pull the collar of her tee-shirt free at the neck. While his hand was there he could not resist taking a wisp of dark hair from her cheek and tucking it behind her ear.

Gabby experienced such a violent lurch of desire that she wobbled about, her feet sinking into the sand. Mark steadied her, and taking her hand in his they walked back towards the gardens. Standing in front of Valhalla, Mark got out his camera and took some more photos of the figureheads.

'Now, one of you, Gabriella . . . standing right there . . . that's it.'

'OK,' Gabby said. 'Now I'll take one of you, for your book and for your family.'

Around them birds scuttled and squawked in the undergrowth as the sun started to slip into the sea. Gabby bent and took out a piece of roll she had kept. Sparrows hopped around her for a second or two, then suddenly a brave one landed on her hand and grabbed a crumb, then another and another until it seemed as if birds were springing from her fingertips. Gabby threw back her head and laughed silently for the sheer joy of the moment.

Mark snapped her again and again with his camera. He did not know why, but something deep inside him felt as if it was fragmenting, as if he had witnessed and captured a moment he might never have again.

Voices faded, the garden grew full of shadows and the scent of spring flowers more intense as they retraced their steps out of the garden. Above them the helicopter hovered noisily, and landed.

Mark stood beside his hire car jangling his keys. Gabby's car was next to his and she opened the door and all the windows because the windows had misted up in the damp old car. She said awkwardly, 'Goodbye. Have a good journey to London and good luck with your research ... It was a wonderful thing you did, returning the figurehead ...' She petered out.

Mark took her hand. 'Thank you for coming with me today.' He seemed to be laughing and he showed no sign of letting her hand go. It appeared to be a habit of his. He brought her fingers to his lips again, then in a small quick movement drew her towards him and said softly, 'Gabriella, do you really believe that we will never see each other again? That I can say goodbye and just walk away?'

Gabby could not speak. He shook her hand gently so that she looked him in the eyes. 'Do you?'

'You live in Canada. I live in Cornwall. When this trip is over you will go home.'

'Yes. But I have an English publisher and I will be coming over regularly.'

Gabby stared at him, her eyes giving her away. Joy soared and she did not care.

'Have you got a mobile phone?' he asked.

'Not yet, but I am getting one. Josh is always complaining about not getting hold of me.'

Mark let her hand go and dug into his pocket for a piece of paper.

'Right, this is my mobile number. Do you know how to text?'

'I think so.' She laughed nervously, a part of her not believing she was having this conversation.

'When you get your phone, text me your number. I know you won't ring me, because you will have decided by the time you get home that we did not have this conversation. I'm in Devon for one night, then in London for two more before I fly back home.'

He picked up her hand again. 'I will be in hotel rooms, which I hate. It would be great to talk to you.'

Gabby heard the first note of anxiousness in his voice.

'I'll ring you, even if I don't have a mobile phone.'

He bent and held her face between his hands, kissed her mouth quickly, then turned away to his car.

'Au revoir, Gabriella. Drive carefully home.'

He sat behind the wheel until Gabby had finished demisting the windows of her car. She waved, then turned out into the road and was gone.

Mark started his engine. The wind had got up, whipping the sea into white. He did not like the thought of her driving into the wilds of nowhere in the dark, in what looked like an unreliable car. It was a long time since he had had the chance to feel protective about anyone.

He thought about the lights of a farmhouse with people he did not know waiting for her and felt a pang of jealousy. He could not ring her, and there was a chance she would not find the courage to ring him. He knew this. A day can fade so easily, changing shape, becoming an amorphous thing, a trick of the imagination.

Back in his hotel room, he undid the two small paintings and sat on the bed staring at them.

Cottage before a Storm. There, in front of him, the inherent, inescapable dark night of the soul. Spirituality glimpsed. A loneliness so stark it had to be skilfully transformed into colour and paint; the dark shape of pain captured forever in violent colour. Too recognizable for comfort.

Something lost. This small house dwarfed by the fierce landscape and angry sky, rendering all to a speck, as nothing, impotent to change one aspect of the hidden power of the elements or the isolation of the human spirit.

To understand what it is you have lost. To recognize so suddenly an area of your life you have hidden from yourself; an unease, a pointlessness that has been threatening for some time, is unnerving. Mark, his imagination coloured by whisky, almost believed he had been led to this painting, convinced himself this picture had been painted just for him. An omen. Facing the demon within. He determined to write to this Elan Premore, to explain the impact this small painting had on him.

The sunrise was for another day. The sunrise was full of hope. These two pictures were painted before and after some personal crisis. They belonged together, Mark was sure of this.

Chapter 12

Charlie, washing his hands at the sink, turned his wrist to look at his watch.

'Shouldn't Gabby be home by now?' he asked Nell.

'Any moment, I should think.' Nell was getting a casserole out of the Aga and peering at it. 'The last helicopter is about seven or seven-thirty. Is Matt doing the milking?'

'No; Darren. Matt's been out at Mendely with me all day today, he's whacked, I've sent him home to Dora.'

'Oh dear,' Nell said, 'I'm sure to bump into Dora in the village.'

'*He's not as young as he used to be . . .*' Nell and Charlie intoned together. '*I hope your Charlie isn't taking advantage.*' They grinned at each other.

'I'm dreading him retiring,' Charlie said, reaching for a towel. 'The younger lads just don't have the interest or staying power.'

Nell finished stirring the casserole and put it back in the oven. 'You can't blame them, Charlie; low wages, long days in all weathers.'

'I don't,' Charlie said. 'I just can't afford to pay more. You'd think the incentive of a tied cottage would be attractive, but not in the middle of nowhere, it seems. I look after those cottages, too. You should see the state of the accommodation John Tresider offers his workers. His houses have to be seen to be believed. It gives all farmers a bad name.'

'Then it's a disgrace,' Nell said crossly. 'There's no excuse, they got a huge grant last year. His father was as bad. He couldn't keep his workers either. I'm surprised the environmental health people haven't been round to condemn them.'

'It's only a matter of time.'

This was a conversation Nell and Charlie often had in different guises, and both fell into comfortably.

The wind hit the window in a sudden squall.

'I wonder where Gabby's got to. It's getting late and there's a gale coming in. I'm just going out to check on Darren.'

'Charlie?' Nell knew Charlie liked everyone safely in before dusk and as Gabby did not like driving in the dark. She was not often late. 'I do think it's about time Gabby had a new car. She's starting to go further afield now and that old Peugeot is not reliable. She really needs something with a large boot to hold paintings.'

Charlie was irritated because he knew Nell was right.

'Nell, I can't afford to buy a new car at the moment.'

'Look, Charlie, Gabby puts everything she earns into the farm. If she didn't, she could afford a new car for herself. Doesn't that strike you as rather unfair?'

'No, Nell. It's how we survive. We have to pull together like you and Dad did. Gabby only has to ask, you know that, she doesn't go without.'

Nell stared at him. Sometimes it was hard to swallow her frustration or stifle a sharp retort. It did no good. It had alienated Ted and it alienated Charlie. Once entrenched, neither would budge an inch, and she was never sure whether it was obstinacy or misplaced pride.

In her marriage to Ted she had perfected a duplicity which she guiltily maintained over the years of her marriage. Like Gabby, she had pooled her income back into the farm willingly, but she had withheld a small amount each month for her own needs. She had bitterly resented having to ask Ted for things from money she herself had earnt.

When she had first married she had been nineteen and in those days she was unable to open a bank account until she was twenty-one. For her twentieth birthday she had desperately wanted a portable radio. Her parents had sent

80

her a large cheque so that she could choose her own. Ted had cashed the cheque, but when she found the radio she wanted he refused to let her have the money. He told her it was a sheer waste to spend that much on a radio. He bought her a cheap plastic one and the rest went towards a new bailer.

Nell never forgot or forgave him. The meanness froze her heart. Her mother coming to stay and seeing the cheap radio had been quietly livid. Her generous and liberal parents never made the same mistake again. They had, all their lives, schooled Nell for a career and independence. Even as a child Nell had always had a small allowance and it taught her to budget. From the age of sixteen she had never had to ask anyone for anything. The marriage her parents had thoroughly disapproved of had been a shock.

Nell, on the rebound, had married young, full of hope, captured by a good-looking face; seduced by a long hot Cornish summer and Ted's single-minded intent which she had mistaken for devotion.

When she became twenty-one she had persuaded Ted it would be a good idea to have a joint account so that she could write cheques on behalf of the farm. Eventually, as she was doing the farm accounts, he had reluctantly agreed, but had made their joint account a business account, while keeping the personal account in his own name, thus keeping control of all domestic transactions. Even then he had perused each statement for evidence of female waste or frippery, but when he saw none he had relaxed.

What he did not know was that Nell often asked to be paid in cash for her restoring, and this money she placed in her own secret account.

'Good girl,' her friend Olive had said. 'Every woman should have a running-away account.'

From then onwards it was Nell's R.A. account. When Ted died and she saw the amount in his personal bank accounts, she stopped feeling guilty. She just felt sad at a lifetime of endemic meanness. They had had to work so hard all their marriage, then when they could both have slowed down and relaxed, enjoyed what they had, he had let her go on believing they owed the bank money.

He had not even been able to enjoy the money himself, just given himself an early heart attack. She realized she had never really 'done the accounts' for Ted, just faithfully added up the milk quota and feed bills Ted put in front of her.

Later, when sadness turned to anger, she had been glad of Ted's thrift. It had enabled her to help Charlie and Gabby and put a lump away for her beloved Josh.

She said now to Charlie, knowing it would annoy him further but needing to say it, 'How on earth would you know if Gabby goes without? She would never say. You would never even notice.'

'What's got into you, Nell? Gabby often tells me what she's bought. Things for Josh, usually. We have a joint account, for goodness' sake.'

'I know you do, but has Gabby ever bought anything biggish, or personal – clothes, for instance – without asking you first?'

'Of course not. We have to budget, we both need to know what we can afford and what we are spending each month.'

'So you talk it over with Gabby before you buy anything major, like a new tractor, do you?'

Charlie clicked up the latch of the back door. He knew it was pointless trying to talk to Nell when she was having what his father used to call 'a feminist moment'. Or, and this had on one occasion caused Nell to throw one of his grandmother's vases at Ted's head, 'the wrong time of the month'.

'You know perfectly well that Gabby and I have a joint domestic account and I run a farm account with Alan that has absolutely nothing to do with Gabby. It's business.'

'Yes. But you hold the strings for both accounts. If Gabby contributes largely to the domestic account, why can't a new car for Gabby, who is also running a business, come out of the business account she indirectly contributes to? That would be fair, don't you think?'

Charlie stared at her in much the same way Ted used to; as if she had flown from another planet and was talking a foreign language impossible to decipher.

'Nell, I don't understand where you are suddenly coming from. When I can, I will buy Gabby another car, perhaps at the end of the summer. I can't afford one before that. Gabby hasn't mentioned anything about her car. You seem to be the one with the problem.'

He shut the door carefully behind him.

Nell stood in the middle of the kitchen, staring at the closed door. She had been dismissed so often in the years of her marriage, she should be used to it. But the small personal trigger spread like a stain across her heart. Like an interior bleed spreading into something beyond tears. An isolation that might have turned into a wail of anguish, if she had ever let it.

This moment in the flagstoned kitchen, full of the things I touch every day, is the life I led with two strangers. Until Gabby.

Charlie was right, in a way. It was *her* problem, this terror of meanness; because meanness slid slyly into all areas of life. Emotion, time, love and sex. But she knew her attitude to Charlie was coloured by Ted, and this was not fair. How could Charlie possibly understand why she randomly pounced?

People blamed mothers for selfish or thoughtless men. Nell did not. She believed it an entirely genetic thing that might be mitigated by example, but that was all. Despite Ted's rampant chauvinism Nell had always insisted that Charlie helped with certain chores and cleared up after himself. As a child he had complied, but as soon as he married Gabby he appeared to take it for granted that all domestic chores were now her role.

Gabby, young and eager to please, had been complicit in this assumption. Once started, how difficult habit and conditioning were to break. There was nothing offensive, not even self-conscious selfishness on Charlie's part, but his and Gabby's roles were clearly delineated.

Charlie, like Ted, had never bothered to find out how painstaking and scientific restoring could be. How tiring. Hours of matching and patching, testing, waxing – all with someone else's precious property.

It pained Nell to watch Gabby clearing up after her son. Mud under the table where he had not bothered to take his work boots off. Never replacing the lid of the marmalade. The paper would be left scrumpled in a heap as if a cat had had a field day with it. It never occurred to him to carry his plate or mug the short distance to the sink. Small, thoughtless things, not important in themselves, yet indicative of his general attitude to who it was who cleared up after him.

Out of the kitchen window the day was dying, the sky crimson, covered with dark cigar-shaped clouds. In the fields a cow mooed repeatedly for her calf. Nell thought of Elan, standing with his whisky watching the same sky from his cottage. No children, no lover. Just the fading embers of another day with canvases full of the thing that lay unspoken in his heart.

She stood listening for the sound of Gabby's car. Elan had said once, watching a childish, pregnant Gabby, 'The girl wraps herself so close, Nell. She is too contained, too careful to oblige. This Gabby is easy to love, yet I have a sense of someone else, infinitely more complex, carefully hidden, but I don't think we are ever going to be allowed to glimpse *that* little person.'

Out of the growing darkness Nell heard the sound of Gabby's car coming up the lane. She relaxed, smiled, moved quickly flicking lights on, busy creating order and warmth at the end of the day. As she had always done for Gabby, so that she should never come home to darkness and an empty house.

Chapter 13

'I'm going into town, I need some materials for work,' Gabby said to Charlie over breakfast. 'Do you need anything?'

Charlie looked up. 'You could go to Industrial Farmers for me. I ordered a new hay feeder.'

'Will it go into my boot?'

'Just, I think, but it'll go on your back seat if you slant it towards the back window.'

Nell came into the kitchen and Gabby turned to pour her coffee. She said quickly the thing she had been rehearsing in her head and which was now easier because Charlie wanted a favour.

'While I'm in Penzance I thought I might buy myself a mobile phone. It would be useful when I'm out working. It means I can take calls, and I won't lose business.'

Charlie reached for another piece of toast. 'What's the matter with the answer-machine in your workroom? People leave messages if you're out. Mobile phones aren't cheap, you know.'

'You've got one,' Nell said before she could stop herself.

'I have men all over the place, Nell, and I need to know where people are and that they can contact me.'

'Well,' Gabby said, 'the other reason I thought it might be a good idea was if my car broke down. It would be quite nice to know I could ring someone, Charlie.'

'I think you should definitely get one, Gabby,' Nell said, meeting Charlie's eyes and holding them. 'Especially with the age of your car.'

'The good thing is I could put it against my business, Charlie.'

Charlie grinned at her. 'You are sweet, Gab, you haven't earnt enough to pay tax yet.'

'That's because I haven't been working full time. Now I am, the work should come in.'

Before Nell could interfere again, Charlie said, 'It's up to you, Gabby. It seems a waste of money to me, but if you want a phone, go ahead.'

Nell felt like saying, *big of you*, but she bit her lip and made for the door.

'If you are going for supplies, Gabby, I need some more Japanese tissue and beeswax.'

'OK,' Gabby smiled, relieved; horrified at how easy it was to lie.

'I'm off.' Charlie got up from the table. 'I'm going to check the pheasant pens, then straight on to the auction at Tresillian to try and get that bailer. Did you remember to make me a flask of coffee and sandwiches, Gabby?'

'Yes, they're in the old scullery next to your cap.'

'Thanks.' He shrugged his jacket on.

'What are the chances of you getting the bailer?' Nell asked.

'Well, I'd be lucky to. I looked at it yesterday; it's in good condition for its age, so there will be a good bit of bidding. I'm taking Alan with me – to make sure I don't get carried away and spend too much money.' He grinned at them both and disappeared out of the door.

'Good luck,' Gabby called as she carried his plate and mug to the sink.

The buildings and harbour in Penzance were bathed in early yellow light. With the figurehead in mind, Gabby spent a satisfying half-hour gathering materials together. She treated herself to a new ultraviolet light and x-ray equipment. Solvents and adhesives, oil paints and waxes. Japanese tissue and beeswax for Nell. Fine brushes and powder pigments, swabs of cotton wool on slim sticks, some new pots to hold the solvents so that they wouldn't spill, and, finally, resins to make varnishes and some new scalpels.

It was a good thing Charlie could not see the size of the cheque she wrote or know that the estimate she had given for work on the figurehead was on the low side. She happily flicked through the manuals lying on the counter. She loved this, this checking out new chemicals, chatting to the girl who ran the shop, sometimes meeting people she knew and swapping the merits of new brands of cleaning components or varnishes.

It had been all this, Nell's array of little bags and boxes of resins, drawers full of varnishes and paint pigments and unknown substances, that had first fascinated Gabby. In the beginning, before she knew anything about restoring, it had seemed as if Nell worked a form of magic; an alchemist, transforming a painting, bringing out the subtle colours, reverting it to all its former detail.

And it was the detail that was so satisfying. Working out carefully and scientifically testing and patching, watching something damaged coming slowly alive under your fingertips. Even the smell of the potentially dangerous chemicals used to clean canvas or wood excited her with their possibilities.

Gabby knew the importance of wearing gloves and a mask, and sometimes she felt like a surgeon about to perform a tricky operation. She still felt thrilled at an unexpected discovery and the fact that each painting had a history, a story behind it. Each restoration was entirely different and often revealed secrets and questions as the cleaning progressed. Sometimes the point of interest was merely in the people who had once owned a painting, carefully setting it in a time and a place in history.

When she had finished she peered in the windows of the myriad mobile-phone shops and picked one at random. A boy as thin as a pencil in a shiny suit that flapped strangely round his thin ankles swooped, and with a cherubic smile began to explain with enthusiasm the various wonders of each phone.

His boss, an older, stocky man, very dapper in a suit with enormous lapels, brought her coffee, and Gabby suddenly wanted to giggle. The two men looked so incongruous, like the Mafia in a bad American film.

The boy like a pencil set it all up for her, showed her how to text and how to use the answer-machine. Flushing painfully, he put various numbers in her phone book, including his own in case she got stuck, and Gabby suddenly realized he was rather taken with her.

She emerged from the shop, triumphant with mobile phone. This was the first major transaction she had ever made on her own and she felt heady. *Per-lease*, she thought, *I'm pathetic*.

She sat in her car, seeing if she could remember how to text Josh. Her anticipation was out of all proportion. HI JOSH. SEE GOT MOBILE LUV G.

She started to drive home when she remembered Charlie's hay trough. She turned back, loaded it into the back seat and set off again, worrying guiltily about the waste of a working morning, the primary object of which had really been to buy the mobile phone.

As she turned off the main road towards the Lizard, she avoided the question, too, of whether she would have the courage to phone Mark Hannah; but the *possibility* that she could if she wanted to lay there like a shiny washed pebble.

As she drove into the yard Nell came out of the cottage in her walking shoes with Shadow bouncing excitedly beside her.

'The Canadian, Mark Hannah, rang, Gabby. He said he would ring again. He said to tell you he had traced some graves and turned up something quite interesting about Tom Welland.'

Gabby got out of the car and bent to lift her packages out. 'Heavens, he works quickly, or he must have loads of contacts.'

'He probably has research assistants or something,' Nell said, then, looking into Gabby's car, 'I really don't think Charlie should ask you to carry farm stuff. If that had fallen on you, Gabby, it would have been nasty.'

'It was tightly wedged, Nell, I don't think it could fall anywhere. I've got your stuff and some new brown varnish I'm going to try.'

Nell smiled. 'Interesting. I shall look at it later. I'm tired of the monster, I'm going to walk over and see Elan. Did you get yourself a mobile phone?'

'Yes, it took ages, there are hundreds.'

'Well done. See you later.'

Inside, Gabby made herself a coffee and took her phone out. She put Mark Hannah's name in the phone book then turned again to the instructions to text him. RE TOM HOW EXCITING GABBY.

As the message vanished down the line she saw Charlie drive into the yard for an early lunch. She went to her room and put the phone into a drawer. Coming back, she placed bread and cheese and pickle onto the table and put the kettle on the Aga. Charlie was pulling the trough out of the back seat.

She saw the sun was not going to last; dark clouds were gathering over the sea. Even if it rained Gabby knew she must walk this afternoon. She could not stay inside, she felt jittery and wound tight. She would work tonight. She felt as if a part of her had detached itself and was poised, waiting. The other part of her turned to Charlie and said automatically, 'Hi there, how did you get on? Did you manage to get the bailer?'

Chapter 14

Gabby drove over to St Piran the next day. She wanted to run some tests and take photographs of the figurehead before she started the restoration. She had been given an airy space to work in on the first floor of the small museum; the light was good and she had plenty of room.

Lady Isabella lay carefully wedged on her back on a large table as if she was sleeping. Gabby saw now in the better light that the wood section at the central lower front, under a fold of drapery, was rotten and would have to be investigated. This had caused deterioration in both gesso and paint layer. The gesso had become crumbly and the paint was flaking. Most other wood sections appeared sound and the adhesive secure.

Lady Isabella measured approximately sixty inches/152.4cms high. Her core consisted of vertical rectangular pieces of wood, glued and possibly nailed together, although the nails were invisible. The outer wood was carved into the figure shape. The paint layer was mainly cream in colour, probably oil and white lead. There was, as Valerie Mischell had said, evidence of an earlier cream paint and traces of gold and blue.

Gabby had brought Nell with her and she too was captivated. Gabby knew Nell would not give advice unless she asked for it so she outlined the initial treatments she intended to follow before she asked Nell for her opinion.

'There seems to be about four areas of paint loss and missing gesso beneath the neck, with cracks in between . . .

on the upper chest there . . .' Gabby got out her measuring tape
'. . . and here, Nell, see? Those vertical cracks following the
underlying wood edges, they are . . .' Gabby measured them
carefully '. . . six centimetres apart on the lower half and skirt
front. And here, the edges of the restorer's paint are chipped on
the lily she's holding, and here on the dark edges of her hair.'

Nell peered down at the figurehead. 'She doesn't appear
to have a varnish layer.' She borrowed Gabby's magnifying
glasses and moved slowly round the table. 'Rot has set in
there, definitely. You can see the wood is more fragile here.
Damage to the area has caused loss of paint and wood. This
area will have to be carefully prepared, Gabby, before she is
moved again, so as not to cause further loss. It will need to
be consolidated . . .'

'Mischell said the same thing. To start with I'm going
to treat all the flaking edges of paint with conservation
consolidant and then test the stability of the wood and any
poor areas I find. The central lower front section here can be
injected with resin B72. The gesso and paint losses I thought
I'd fill, texture and retouch to match the present colour and
tone down the brightness of her hair. The lily leaf and the
braid on her robe could be toned down with muted tones in
acrylic paint. What do you think?'

'Gabby, have confidence. You don't need me to advise you,
you're spot on. I would do exactly as you've outlined. But I
wouldn't spend too much time on toning the rather garish
paint from the more recent renovations. It's possible there
will be a future repaint as the museum researches the original
colours. Concentrate on conserving and repair. Modify the
colours by all means, but leave evidence when you clean of
natural wear and tear.'

She touched Gabby's arm. 'Before you begin, it really is
important to investigate the structure and run tests, which
you are doing . . .'

Nell suddenly bent and peered again at the flowing robe
under Lady Isabella's damaged left hand. She picked up a
pair of tweezers.

91

'Mischell found traces of original blue-green paint, didn't she?'

'Yes.'

'Don't get your hopes up. Later, to get at the *exact* colours, you must be sure to find the right pigment. You see the dress here? This blue, if you look carefully, differs from that piece in the crack there . . .'

She lifted the tiny piece of blue paint and dropped it into a small polythene pocket Gabby held out for her. 'My only advice is don't hurry, take your time. Never assume there are only one or two differing paints applied, there will probably have been many over the years, with only a vague thought to the original colour or period. Run as many tests as you think necessary, until you are absolutely sure. How much time have you quoted for?'

'I couldn't be absolutely sure how long it would take me, but I told them I would rather overestimate. I said possibly two months.'

'Good. It's taken long enough to reach its resting place, a few weeks here or there in the interests of getting it right should be immaterial. Your quote for the figurehead was rather low, I thought.'

'Well . . . Nell . . . it's good experience.'

Nell bent to Isabella's face. 'Her face is exceptional, wonderfully carved. It seems familiar, somehow; perhaps it reminds me of a painting I've seen. Tom Welland was an extraordinary carver. He went into such detail, and of course his speciality was faces. Like a photographer, he seemed to capture the person behind the face; imbued wood with the tangible essence of a live woman, in the same way an artist does.'

Gabby stared at her. 'Nell! What do you know about Tom Welland?'

Nell laughed. 'I looked him up in one of my father's ancient marine books when Mark Hannah mentioned him the other day on the phone. There was only one short paragraph.'

'So what did it say about him?'

'It just commented on the high quality of his work and how well-known and sought-after he became in France and Spain and Canada, where he spent some years. He was at the height of his career when all record of him disappeared. It was rumoured that he may have upset some sponsor and moved abroad for a while. There is no record of what happened to him.'

'That's what Mark Hannah and Peter found, too.'

'All my old books will be in research libraries. There is a huge growing interest in figureheads and marine wrecks. Mainly because there are so few records and so many figureheads have been allowed to just rot away.'

Nell went downstairs to talk to John Bradbury while Gabby took her samples of paint and placed them into the little self-sealing polythene pockets. Elan, who was joining them for lunch in the pub with John, came up the stairs and sat and sketched the figurehead while Gabby made notes of what she would need initially. Looking up into the blind wooden face of Isabella she longed to make those eyes see, replace colour and life into her face, dress her in her blue and gold.

They walked over to the pub and Gabby was amused at the shorthand Nell, Elan and John had, in the way of people who have known each other for a long time.

'Why is your Canadian researching in Devon,' Elan asked Gabby, 'when the *Isabella* was registered in a Cornish port?'

'Sir Richard Magor, who built and owned the *Lady Isabella*, grew up in Devon. His family had a big ship-building business near Appledore and also in Prince Edward Island.'

'The 1860s,' Nell said, 'when the *Lady Isabella* was being built, was an amazing time for trade around the islands. These ships travelled all round Britain, and Tom Welland's work must have been admired everywhere. It's such a pity there are so relatively few photographs or records left of the carvers of figureheads of that time.'

'I suppose the women on some of the figureheads had to sit for the carvers, like a muse for a painter,' Elan said. 'Lots of room for naughty dalliance.'

'I shall view your evocative paintings in a different light from now on,' John Bradbury said dryly. 'There I have been, humbled and admiring of your spirituality, when it was possibly lust.'

Elan laughed. 'Chance would be a fine thing. You know how rarely I paint people. However, standing in front of that figurehead this morning I thought what a challenge that face would have been to paint. So much there. Such a contradiction of innocence and sensuality. I hope your Canadian discovers who she was and what sort of life she led.'

The conversation turned to what everyone wanted to eat. Gabby wished she had brought her own car as she longed to get to Truro to send her samples off.

'Lunch is on me,' Elan said. 'I've sold quite a few paintings this month and I am very pleased indeed.'

'Did you know Mark Hannah bought two of your paintings on Tresco, Elan? As soon as he saw them he had to have them.'

'No, I didn't. How touching. Hurrah for Canadians.'

'He would like to meet you. Perhaps when you have your London exhibition?'

'Be delighted. What are you going to eat, child?'

'Oh, a sandwich – prawn, I think.'

'Is that all?'

'Gabby wants to be off,' Nell said. 'Elan, if I lend Gabby my car, would you give me a lift home?'

'Of course, but the child must eat her sandwich first.'

Gabby grinned. 'Yes, Daddy. Will you all think I'm rude if I leave straight afterwards? I want to go back via Truro to post off my paint samples.'

John Bradbury winked at her. 'Poor girl, stuck having lunch with the camp and the aged.'

'Speak for yourself!' Elan and Nell chorused together.

*   *   *

94

The wind was getting up by the time Gabby drove out of the car park. Spring squalls could erupt and as quickly subside before the sun set. The sea had turned into a mass of white angry waves and a tanker was heading for shallow water. The fishing fleet were coming in early but the sun was still warm on her hands as she drove in Nell's wonderful high-sided Land Rover. Gabby only noticed the limitations of her own car when she drove Nell's.

As she parked in Truro her mobile phone bleeped. She picked it up and studied it. She had two text messages. The first was from Josh. WELL DONE. U CAN TEXT! WELCUM 2OC. GOT LNG WKEND. WILL RING. LUV JOSH.

Gabby decided to save her rude reply until later. She looked at her second message. WHAT GOOD TIME TO RING. BE NICE TO TALK. TRAIL GONE COLD. MARK.

Gabby posted her samples at the post office then drove home. The farmyard was quiet, she had the place to herself. Shadow, who objected to being left, was ecstatic to see her and pranced round her like a horse. Gabby made tea and sent two replies to the outside world:

DON'T BE RUDE. LOOK FWD WKEND, LUV GX.

Then, to Mark, SIX QTE GOOD TIME. GABBY.

She got Shadow's lead and they both skirted the scarred field and jogged along the coastal path down to the cove. The tide was coming in and Gabby ran along the sea's edge to the rocks at the end of the cove. She loved the power of the rough sea which blew spray in great salty bursts into her eyes. The wind, cold against her face, was as light as air as she ran. She felt a wonderful euphoric freedom that made her imagine she was flying, or poised on the crest of a turning wave with the combined exultation of a seasoned surfer and the equal terror of the pull of the sea.

Small waders rose in flocks in front of her with tiny faraway cries. The waves crashing against the rocks drowned out all sounds except her breath, and the plop of her feet and Shadow's paws on the wet sand as she ran. She stopped by the rocks, panting and laughing, and bent and hugged the dog.

What was happiness? No more than a fleeting moment such as this. Seabirds, dog, vast waves rolling inexorably towards her with the same raw energy that she felt within her. This small single moment separated from any other, entire in itself, held so perfect and timeless that she might lift her head from Shadow's rough fur, turn for home, and this tiny second of happiness would vanish; leaving only a memory like a threnody in the place it had been.

Chapter 15

Josh, on a twenty-four-hour pass, surprised them by turning up suddenly on Friday night for the weekend.

Gabby, Charlie and Nell were astounded at how he had filled out. Gaining muscle made him seem bigger, stockier.

'We do nothing but yomp, with packs on our backs, stumble badly around the parade ground, hurl ourselves round assault courses, hang from ropes in the gym, polish everything in sight . . . and eat.'

'I've never heard you complain about eating!' Charlie said.

Josh laughed. 'I'm not complaining, Charlie. I should be used to piles of food, growing up on a farm, but at Sandhurst we have a cooked breakfast, coffee with buns mid-morning, lunch, afternoon tea, and dinner in the evening. All those carbs just to keep us going.'

'Or alternatively to develop obesity and alcoholism,' Nell said fondly.

'Right, I'm off to start the milking. See you later, Josh. We'll go to the pub after supper, have a few jars.'

Nell went to phone Elan to ask him over to eat with them. Josh went around the kitchen touching things, prowling. He always did this when he had been away, as if to reassure himself all was still the same.

'Is everything OK, Josh?'

He went and leant with his back to the Aga. 'Sure, Gabby, everything's fine.'

But he had hesitated for a split second. Gabby, watching him, said carefully, 'There's something worrying you. It's such a long way to come for a short weekend . . .' She went to hug him, 'But, oh, it's lovely to see you.'

Josh said quickly, looking at the door, 'I just needed to come home; touch base.' He paused. 'It's a tough course. Sometimes it seems as if there is always someone shouting at you. It's all for reasons of discipline, obviously, but after university it feels like going back to school. I just wanted to feel like a grown-up human being for twenty-four hours.'

'If you've made a mistake, you know . . .'

'No, Gabby, it's nothing like that. I haven't made a mistake and I've made some really good mates. It's just . . .' Josh looked at his feet and wiggled them as he always did when he was thoroughly miserable.

'What is it, Josh?'

Josh looked up. 'There was this guy from Ghana in my year. He was a bit useless, but our sergeant definitely had it in for him, seemed to think he was bucking the system, not trying, taking the piss. We went up to the Brecon Beacons last week to train and this guy kept saying he felt unwell. He hated the cold, he just couldn't cope with it, none of the Africans can, so we end up wrapping them in silver foil as their body temperature just plummets.

'Anyway, this particular night there was a clear sky and it was absolutely freezing and Ojai's teeth were rattling so much he could hardly stay upright. Two of us were each side of him holding him upright, keeping him on his feet, or he would have fallen. We came to this river that we were supposed to swim across and Ojai just rolled his eyes in terror. It was obvious he wasn't up to it so we used the radio to get him casevaced back to camp, but this sergeant insisted he went across with the rest of us, said he wasn't having anyone on his course who thought he could pick and choose what he could and couldn't do. He said if any of us wasted any more time we would all be on a charge.

'Me and this other guy roped Ojai to us and told him the river wasn't deep, which was a lie, and that we'd make sure he got to the other side. He was frozen and scared, Gabby;

98

he hated water, he was such a lousy swimmer he was having extra coaching. Anyway, we all descended into this bloody river and we were fine until we got to the middle, where obviously it was deeper and faster.

'Ojai started to panic. Everyone was calling from the other bank, encouraging him on, but he completely lost it and started to flail around. The current was stronger than it looked and the three of us were being pulled downstream and under. We had to cut the rope, because if we hadn't we'd have all drowned. We tried to keep hold of him, but . . . it was impossible.'

Josh stopped, looked away. 'He drowned, Gabby, they found him downstream. There is an inquiry on. All the officers are pissing themselves in case the press get hold of it.'

'Josh, that's terrible. Poor, poor boy. I hope the sergeant loses his job.' She could see Josh was still upset. 'You don't blame yourself, do you?'

'Not really. It's just we lied, we said the river wasn't deep, we said we would make sure he stayed with us and got to the other side, then we had to cut him loose to drown. There was no reason for him to die, he could have been back-coursed or just sent home as unfit. He died horribly frightened a long way from home, for bloody what?'

Gabby bent and got a beer from the fridge, opened it and handed it to him.

'Thanks.' Josh smiled. 'Anyway, I just wanted to get home for a bit. Let's talk of something else.'

Nell came into the room. 'Elan is on his way.'

'Great,' Josh said. 'Gabby, is it all right if I go and have a long hot bath?'

'Josh, you don't have to ask. Go and relax, my radio is still in there . . .'

She went to the door with him. 'I'm glad you came home, it was the right thing to do.'

Elan, Charlie and Josh had gone to the pub, and Nell and Gabby were clearing up the supper things. They had both been invited and had both refused as they knew they were supposed to. Gabby told Nell Josh's sad little story.

'I knew there was something,' Nell said. 'I still cannot fathom the attraction of the army; I never will.'

Gabby smiled and changed the subject.

When Nell had gone back to her cottage, Gabby went into her workroom. She got her mobile phone out. One missed message. It was from Mark.

'Hi there, it's Mark Hannah. Just to say I'm back in London, slight change of plan. I'm following a small lead that may be a wild goose chase, but may give us a clue to Isabella.'

Before she lost her nerve, Gabrielle pressed return call. It rang and rang, and then a breathless Mark came on to the line.

'Hello, it's Gabrielle. I got your message.'

'Hi there, Gabriella, it's great to hear from you!'

'I'm sorry I wasn't here at six. Josh came home unexpectedly for the weekend.'

'That's great. Hey, you don't want to be talking to me . . .'

'It's OK. They've all gone down to the pub.'

'I only rang to tell you . . . Gabriella, hang on while I get a towel, I was in the shower.'

When he came back, Gabrielle said, 'Sorry, sorry, this is why I hate phoning people . . . It's always the wrong time.'

'Gabriella, it's exactly the *right* time. I am stuck in a hotel bedroom trying to decide what to do with myself. Stay in and get bored or go out and eat alone, which I hate.'

'Oh dear.'

'Oh dear, indeed.' Mark laughed. 'I thought you might be interested. One of my researchers found a Welland grave in Yorkshire. There were three generations of carpenters, all in the parish records of the time. A Ben Welland moved to Cornwall where his wife originated from. It is unclear whether he moved from his own county to please her or whether he left Yorkshire to find work in the Cornish boatyards. He had three sons and a daughter who survived beyond childbirth and one of the sons must, I believe, have been our Tom.

'Ben Welland must have gone home to die, or asked to be buried in the same churchyard as his parents, not his wife, which seems a bit strange.'

'So were there were no records of the names of Ben Welland's sons?'

'All the sons who died in infancy were entered and legible, but the bottom of the page was damaged by water marks.'

'So, no grave for Tom in Yorkshire?'

'No grave for Tom, or his wife or children, if he had them. So, Ben was buried in Yorkshire, his wife and children in St Piran, and Tom presumably died abroad, maybe Canada, Australia or New Zealand. There was huge migration at that time, as you know. As the mines failed, hundreds of people left Cornwall and brought back stories of fortunes to be made.'

'Anything about Lady Isabella?'

'Not yet. I am purely following a hunch at the moment.'

'Sounds intriguing . . .'

In the kitchen the phone was ringing. 'Mark, my other phone is ringing. I'd better go.'

'Thank you for ringing me back, Gabriella. Tom was just an excuse to ring you. Hearing your voice has cheered me up.'

His voice was soft and Gabby shivered. 'I'm starting work on Lady Isabella on Monday.'

'Good! Keep me posted about progress. Goodnight.'

The phone in the kitchen had stopped ringing and Gabby dialled 1471. It was Zoë's number, an old girlfriend of Josh's. She dialled.

'Zoë? It's Gabby. Did you ring?'

'Yes. Hi Gabby, I just wondered if Josh made it home. He said he might.'

'Yes, he did, they're in the pub.'

'Oh, great! Are you coming?'

'I might actually. Is it coincidence you are both back home on the same weekend?'

'Well . . . Josh rang and told me he was hoping to come home and I was planning to come this weekend or next . . . OK, Gabby, see you down there.'

Zoë had been in love with Josh for as long as Gabby could remember. It seemed she still jumped at the chance of seeing him and to Josh she was just a mate, no more than that. Gabby hoped Zoë had no residual hope in that direction.

She pulled a comb through her hair and pulled a jacket on, then went out into the yard and started her car up. She stopped at Nell's cottage.

'I've changed my mind. Come on, Nell. Josh might not be home again for ages, let's join them. Zoë is on her way, too.'

Nell hesitated, loath to move from her warm house. Then she said, 'You're right, let's go. Why should the men have all the fun? I must not get old and fuddy-duddy. But we'll go in my car, if you don't mind, Gabby.'

Gabby laughed. 'You, fuddy-duddy? I don't think so!'

Nell thought, *How pretty she looks tonight, how excited and alive. It is true, sons do keep their mothers young.*

Gabby, driving down the rutted track, thought, *How amazing that a voice can enfold you like velvet, go on holding you.*

Later, in bed that night, with Charlie snoring gently beside her, Gabby lay awake listening to the sea. The pub had been warm and full of people she knew. Charlie, Josh and Elan had been so genuinely pleased to see her, Nell and Zoë, that Gabby had felt surprised and touched.

They sat round a large scrubbed table while Elan told his outrageous stories. Gabby had looked round at the flushed and laughing faces of her family, for Elan counted as family; at Zoë and a couple of Josh's local friends, and she felt a surge of contentment in Josh being home. In the evening. *In joining in.* In Charlie's pleasure in the fact that she *had* joined in.

It's odd, she thought, as she turned on her side to sleep. It is as if I am viewing my life suddenly from a tiny, imperceptible shift in perspective.

Chapter 16

They stood in the yard saying goodbye to Josh. Gabby watched him mooching about, inspecting the bantams. He had loved Elton John, a Welsomer who had pranced showing off his glossy petrol feathers of flame and green and chestnut – the current cockerel was not so spectacular. Shadow was following Josh about anxiously, her long nose pressed to his calf.

Josh always put off the moment of leaving. As a small child he had run back two or three times to Gabby before he could get himself through the school gates.

Zoë stood by the car, also watching him. Josh was giving her a lift back to Bristol. He walked back towards them. 'Get in,' he said to Zoë. 'I'm just going inside to make sure I haven't left anything.'

Nell and Gabby smiled at each other and Charlie raised his eyebrows but said nothing. Seeing Josh off always took ages.

'Drive carefully,' Nell said when he came back out.

'Yes, Granny,' Josh said grinning, and Nell clipped him over the ear.

He hugged Nell and Gabby, then he and Charlie did their usual slightly self-conscious hand-slapping and 'Wahoo' at each other before Josh bent and got into his car, which had been a present from Nell.

Gabby leant in at his window. ''Bye, Zoë. Josh, have a good week. Ring me.'

'I will. Good luck with your figurehead.'

They watched the car bounce down the track until it was out of sight, then Charlie went off to get the cows in and Nell and Gabby went inside to tackle the remains of Sunday lunch. Watching Charlie's shoulders, Gabby felt a stab of pity. Every time Josh came home she knew Charlie secretly hoped he would announce he had done the wrong thing. If they had had another son it would have made all the difference.

Neither she nor Nell talked much as they worked. They both hated the aftermath of Josh leaving and the hole he left for an hour or two until their lives slid back into a rhythm without him. Nell would go and nap while pretending to read the Sunday papers. Gabby would walk Shadow until it was dark, following the progress of Josh's car in her mind until it was time to make sure he had got back safely.

'I miss going over the Tamar Bridge,' Josh said. 'It used to feel more like coming home and leaving again.' Like a definite marker as the wide river swirled underneath, full of boats and the small ferries chugging from one side to the other. A marker between home and the rest of the world.

Occasionally he got called a Cornish pasty by an instructor who wanted to annoy him. Josh did not rise. He did not have to prove anything. He was glad he had gone home this weekend, but it made returning worse. It felt like going back to school. He would never admit to his parents that he was afraid of failing the next fitness test, of being back-coursed, of not being up to it.

He practised press-ups in the gym until he was purple in the face and sodden with sweat, but he knew if he could not increase the strength in his arms he would fail the assault course, and he was furious at this physical weakness when he had lifted bales since he was twelve.

'You've forgotten the traffic jams. You've forgotten how long it took to get in and out of Cornwall. It's bad enough as it is,' Zoë said.

'What? Oh ... No, I haven't forgotten. All the same,

Cornwall will be one long dual carriageway lined with housing estates and supermarkets in ten years' time.'

'You sound like my dad.'

Josh laughed. 'So, how's the teaching going, then?'

'OK. I like Bristol. The house I share is in a really nice area. I can walk to school.'

'Got a boyfriend?'

Zoë hesitated, hope flaring for a second. 'Mind your own business,' she said lightly. Then, 'Have you? Got a girlfriend, I mean.'

Josh glanced at her. 'No time at the moment. I'm at a sort of premature middle-aged crisis. I can only think about one thing at a time, which is staying fit and not pulling a muscle or doing my back in, or breaking a leg or a knee going from yomping . . .'

'Yeah, well, you must be a barrel of laughs! Do you have girls on your course?' she asked suddenly.

'Yes.'

'Are they like men, you know butch and lesbosses?'

Josh suddenly felt thoroughly irritated with her. 'For heaven's sake, Zoë! They are no different to any other bloody women. Pretty, plain, fat and thin. Stupid remark.'

Stung, Zoë was silent. It was unlike Josh to snap.

After a moment, he said, 'Sorry.'

He knew why he was annoyed. He knew her too well. She had made the remark in the hope he would agree, thus reassuring her he wasn't interested in anybody on the same course. He just wished she could find a bloke and they could go back to being mates.

Then you shouldn't have bloody well slept with her, should you?

Josh groaned inwardly. He wished he could take that evening back. He had been pretty pissed, and she was so up for it, it had seemed almost insulting to walk. It had felt like incest, like fucking your sister. He was too familiar with the geography of her body; there was nothing to discover, no surprises in limbs he had known from childhood. It had all felt wrong, like the biggest mistake he had ever made. But not for Zoë, it seemed. He didn't have the courage to say, *I don't fancy you. You are a perfectly attractive girl, but there is no chemistry. I have never felt like that about you and I never will.*

They had both been too drunk to use anything and Josh had spent a month in a cold sweat every time he thought about the possible consequences. He had been lucky. It was too near home. His parents were obviously OK, but he hadn't needed to be a brain surgeon to work out Gabby must have been pregnant when his parents married.

Gabby and Charlie were suited. He and Zoë were definitely not. When he picked a girl it was not going to be one he had gone to kindergarten with.

He saw he had really upset her. She was staring out of her side window biting her lip, trying not to let him see she felt like crying. He turned the radio on low in an attempt to lighten the atmosphere.

'How are your parents?'

Zoë blew her nose. 'Bloody awful. They seem worse since Andrew and I left home. Every time we go back they argue and contradict each other and vie for our attention. They are far worse than any of my infants. Andy and I don't know why they don't just separate. Now that we've left home they have absolutely nothing in common.'

Josh grinned. 'Except arguing. Perhaps that's what keeps them going.'

'Andy reckons he was on the way and they had to get married. Awful, really, the way people mess up their . . .' She stopped and flushed red. 'God! Listen to me . . . One drink too many and it can happen to anyone . . .'

Josh took a deep breath. *Get it over with.*

'Zo, what I most regret about that is we are not mates any more.'

Zoë looked startled. 'Of course we are! Whatever makes you think that? We still ring each other. I tell you nearly everything.'

'It *feels* different. As if you want more. I love you, Zoë, but not in that way.'

Zoë was silent, then decided on truth. 'I suppose it *is* different. It's like it never happened, or was so unimportant to you that it wasn't worth mentioning, let alone repeating. If it had been with anyone else I would have felt much worse. At the time, I suppose I thought I've got to lose it sometime and I would rather it was with someone I knew.

'The evening wasn't . . . like calculated, it just sort of happened. It's not like the earth moved for me, Josh. I just wanted you to acknowledge that it *had* happened. It's as if I have to make something of it or file it under humiliation.'

Josh turned the car abruptly into a lay-by and stopped. He didn't look at Zoë for a moment. He felt ashamed and embarrassed. She asked abruptly, 'Do Gabby and Charlie ever argue or interrupt each other? Only, I've never heard them.'

Thrown, Josh looked at her puzzled. 'No, I don't think so. Not in front of me, anyway. Charlie and Nell argue a lot. What an odd question to suddenly ask.'

Zoë smiled. 'You should know my magpie mind by now. I just thought, Gabby is quite young and I wondered if she got caught, like my mum; but your parents always seem happy.'

Josh turned in his seat. 'We are talking about *you*, Zoë. I'm an insensitive bastard. I'm sorry. I guess I was ashamed . . . of myself,' he added hastily and picked up her hand. 'I'm sorry I've hurt you. It just felt wrong, Zo, like . . . incest . . . I know you so well . . .'

'I suppose that was my . . . point. I'm sorry, too, let's forget it.' She bent and kissed his cheek. 'The stupid incident will fade anyway . . . in time.' *Like a bruise*, she thought.

Josh said, because he must, 'Despite what I've just said, never think it wasn't a lovely experience for me. It was. I'm glad you chose me.'

He pulled her to him and hugged her so she could not see his face, and felt her relax against him. He did not like himself, or lying, and the dichotomy of his words did not stand up to scrutiny.

'Tell you what,' he said carefully, letting her go. 'I'll ask you up to the next party and introduce you to some good-looking soldiers.'

'OK,' she replied, matching his tone. 'You're on.'

After he had dropped Zoë off in Bristol and had criss-crossed onto the right motorway, Josh suddenly remembered what she had said.

Do Gabby and Charlie ever argue or interrupt each other? Only, I've never heard them.

Josh tried to think of an instance of his parents having a long conversation, about any issue other than the farm. He couldn't. He tried to remember them arguing or having a heated debate or throwing things or raising their voices at each other, and failed. Nell and Charlie argued all the time, and Gabby and Nell talked to each other in the shorthand of familiar conversations. But he could not make a picture come of Gabby and Charlie engaging together in any fiery exchange, affectionate or otherwise. For some reason this unsettled rather than reassured him.

At the gates to Sandhurst, as he showed his pass to the soldier on the gate, he suddenly spotted a tall girl with blonde hair and sunglasses waiting to drive out the other way. He whistled under his breath and the soldier laughed.

'Out of your league, sir. She is the Commandant's daughter.'

Josh smiled at the girl. *She was a stunner*. He got back into his car and drove up the wide road to his barracks. It was dusk and the huge trees made shadows across the road. He realized with relief that he was actually glad to be back. He had put last week out of his mind. It had been good to go home, but Zoë had reminded him of one of the reasons he had needed to leave Cornwall. In a small village it was just too easy to get trapped in the wrong life.

Chapter 17

The room on top of the museum was warm when Gabby arrived. John Bradbury had been over and switched on a heater and left her a kettle, a jar of coffee, tea and a packet of biscuits. The sun streamed in at the large window over the graveyard and glistened on the sea in the distance; sea that met the sky so seamlessly it was impossible to tell where one ended and the other began.

Lady Isabella still lay on her back, cushioned by foam. Before Gabby began to treat the flaking paint with consolidant she walked round the figurehead, carefully looking for anything she had missed. Then she photographed Isabella from all angles for her record of work in progress.

She had to stand on a stool to take the photos, and as the camera clicked it seemed to Gabby a flicker of expression passed over Isabella's face. Gabby knew it was a trick of the light, the lift of her arm causing a shadow, the sunlight full of dust motes making her blink; but all the same her heart leapt and she experienced a strange and sudden physical reaction as she looked down on that impassive and beautiful face.

Shakily, she moved away and got her magnifying glasses, a plastic pocket and tweezers. *This won't hurt, this will make you see again. I need to discover the colour of your eyes.* With the tweezers she lifted a speck of paint from beneath one eyelid and dropped it into the pocket. The blind eyes stared upwards, unblinking.

Gabby then laid Japanese tissue gently over the damaged

eyes and held it in place with a weak solution of gelatine. The wood under her fingers seemed to grow warmer. Gabby closed her own eyes for a moment. The sun streamed into the room and outside the birds sang among the gravestones. Gabby, with her fingertips pressed to Isabella's bandaged eyelids, felt the silence swell and grow inside the room, as if time had stopped or was holding its breath. As if this single touch of her fingers on the damaged face could, like a surgeon, reactivate a life unfulfilled.

The sensation was so real, so profound, that tears came to Gabby's eyes. She felt overwhelmed by an intense and incomplete emotion she could not place, and the sudden powerful need to know who Isabella had been.

Isabella noticed that the snowdrops were out under the trees and the daffodil buds were unfurling to show cracks of yellow and green. Below the lawn, where she stood beneath the branches of the macrocarpa, lay the creek on a full tide. The branches of the great fir were reflected in the water, rippling and moving, changing shape dizzily as she watched.

Everything in the garden was about to burst forth in a riot of colour. Isabella could feel the excitement tingling in the tips of her fingers. The birds felt this, too, she was sure of it. They swooped and flew low, beginning to gather twigs and moss for their nests. Spring was poised, waiting, it seemed to Isabella, for the sun to breathe warmth upon the tight buds; and like magic the garden would be transformed and radiant.

Isabella looked upwards. The sky was Prussian blue with small floating scraps of cloud. Far away down on the creek curlews called out, small lonely echoes like a madrigal. She closed her eyes, her face upturned to a sun not yet warm, and she experienced a moment of pure exhilaration in being alive, in being there in the garden; in being Isabella.

So acute was this sensation of herself, it felt like pain. It caught in her throat, made her shiver with some primitive instinct that she should not acknowledge this happiness, but recognize the transitory power of joy. Yet, this knowledge of herself was set so perfectly in this fleeting moment of her own life that she did not yet have the wisdom to pay homage to fate. She gathered the folds of her long skirt, lifted the heavy material above her ankles and set off in a run across the grass. Her footsteps made small indentations on the wet lawn and her laughter carried in little pockets of sound across the still garden.

Isabella was fourteen years old, and her body, like the garden, was beginning to stir. She felt acutely alive, but in waiting. Confused and excited as if she was poised on the edge, the very beginning of her adult life. As she ran across the garden she laughed without knowing why. Perhaps it was a last goodbye to childhood or just the sensation of being part of the earth, part of this cycle of nature; hidden, but stirring with new life and about to burst forth upon a waiting world.

Her dark hair flew out behind her, blue-black in the sunlight, blue-black against the whiteness of her pin-tucked blouse. Her black riding habit held high above her ankles, revealed slim black-clad legs and small riding boots.

Her mother, Helena, dressed also in a riding habit, watched her from the window of her bedroom and smiled. Isabella was still free. Free to be anything she chose, God willing. She watched the girl run and duck under the lower branches of the fir, circle the small fountain and head for the path to the lake.

Helena suddenly saw from a distance what she had been avoiding facing. Isabella was no longer an angular child, but fast becoming a rounded young woman. A child may charge around the garden like a highly strung horse, but it would be considered unseemly in a woman.

Helena had tried and failed to get Daniel to educate his daughter as he would have educated his son, if he had had one. Helena was sure that his disappointment in not having an heir was not the reason. Each time she asked, he smiled indulgently.

'What is the point, my love? My daughter is going to be a beauty like her mother. She will marry and have children and have no need of an education.'

'But, Daniel, education is a means of broadening Isabella's mind and will help her converse on a range of subjects. I know you think

111

my music and my education is wasted, but it is not. I may not often play for anyone else, but I play for myself . . .'

And while she was saying these words to her husband, the waste of her own talent would often consume Helena, for she knew her words were as dandelion fluff blowing across the fields. Daniel had closed his mind to her arguments.

Helena knew that in questioning Isabella's narrow education she was also questioning her own life. This yearning she had for something . . . something more than this comfortable, undemanding existence.

She moved away from the window and walked into her sitting room. She stood for a moment looking at her beautiful piano, then she lifted the lid and sat down letting her fingers rest lightly on the keys. Music was an extension of herself, part of the nature of who she was. The only way she had to express herself.

Her father had considered ambition in a woman unseemly and had been afraid her music would prevent her finding a husband. Despite assurances from Helena's professor of music in Rome that she had a rare talent, he had resolutely insisted that to even consider playing at concert level was out of the question. Helena's fingers played a sombre little tune. She could have travelled to Vienna, Paris, London . . . She closed the lid gently. She had been separated from her music professor and sent to study English in London, with the Vyvyans. If her marriage to Daniel Vyvyan had not been exactly arranged, it had been hoped for. Both her father's family and the Vyvyans had known each other for generations.

Daniel had generously bought her the piano as a wedding present. He played himself, jolly little popular tunes, and he had thought it would be nice for them to play together when they had guests. However, Helena's playing, even if she tried to match her playing to his, so outshone his own ability, so impressed and astonished their friends, that Daniel felt inadequate.

Daniel Vyvyan did feel threatened by Helena's intelligence, by her musical talent and her undoubted beauty. He wished her sometimes more . . . ordinary in all aspects of her character. He was twenty years older than his wife and he was intensely jealous of the young men who gathered around her like bees attending their queen. It was not just young men either, he was much envied by his friends.

On occasions, riding over his land, he would kick his horse to a gallop, furious that Helena should have turned out not to be as compliant as he would wish. The point of marrying a much younger woman was that she should be malleable, not have an intellect that made him feel exposed.

Politics and philosophical debate should be kept for the club and had no place in the drawing room. In his view, women should exchange gossip, run the household, and look pretty.

Helena, seeing the time, ran down the wide staircase to the hall. She picked up her own and Isabella's riding crops from the rack by the front door, which stood open to the morning. Benson had brought the horses round and they stood in the spring sunshine, shaking their heads, restless to be away.

Isabella rounded the corner of the house, her face flushed with running. Her eyes lit up when she saw Helena and the horses.

'Mama, I thought you were never coming, it is the most wonderful day to ride.'

'Indeed,' Helena said, smiling at her daughter when she should have scolded her dishevelled appearance.

'Isabella, you will need your jacket, it is not yet warm enough to ride without one. Go quickly and pin back your hair securely or it will catch in the trees and unseat you.'

Once mounted, Helena and Isabella turned their horses away from the house and down the long drive. Isabella glanced back at the huge ungainly house. The many windows of her home always seemed like eyes watching. So many of the rooms lay empty and unused.

'I thought we would ride to the old stables, Isabella, to see how Mr Welland is getting on with your chest of drawers.'

'Could we ride down to the cove, Mama, and then up the cliff path to the village? The horses love the sea.'

'I think it better we return that way. It is near noon and we must not disturb the men's luncheon.'

They rode in companionable silence, skirting around the top acre field on the edge of the wood towards the village, which lay in the

113

valley below them. The mist still lay over the houses and only the spire of the church protruded above it.

A small three-masted schooner with all her sails unfurled to catch the wind was heading out to sea as graceful as a butterfly on the surface of the water. Isabella, watching her, asked, 'Papa says he might buy a small trading ship, Mama.'

'I believe he is seriously thinking about it, Isabella. Trade is so good these days, and he and Sir Richard Magor are talking of sharing the cost.'

The horses shook their heads and snorted, and Helena and Isabella set off down the hill, only loosening the reins and giving them their heads when they reached the flat. Isabella rode ahead and her laughter came to Helena like small birds' cries on the wind. She smiled, wanting to laugh out loud, too, for the sunshine warm on her face, for the changing colour and beauty of the fields, for the sea below them and for the intense pleasure and wonder she had in her daughter who was so much a part of her and Daniel, and yet so uniquely herself. Helena lifted her face to the sky. She had much, much to be grateful for.

Isabella sniffed in the scent of wood shavings and glue as they entered the boatyard, which was housed in the old stables belonging to the Vyvyans. There were three men working on the hull of a boat, sanding and planing planks of wood. It was evidently hot work in the sheltered yard for one of them had removed his shirt. He had his back to them and seemed engrossed in what he was doing. His fair hair flopped forward, striking against the darkness of his skin. His back was long and smooth and brown, and the muscles in his arms moved and swelled as he planed a piece of wood, back and forth, back and forth.

Isabella could not move. She was transfixed by the sight of the half-naked boy. Her heart hammered in her chest. Her mouth felt dry and her body strange and hot as if she had a fever. She could not turn her eyes away.

Ben Welland lifted Helena down from her horse and came round to help Isabella dismount. He followed her eyes and issued a sharp command to his son.

'Thomas – get thy shirt on, we have company.'

114

The boy looked up startled and noticed the women for the first time. He stared straight at Isabella with vivid blue eyes, so deep they were almost purple. With an easy and laconic grace he unhooked his shirt from a piece of wood and pulled it over his head, then with a curt nod turned back to his work.

Ben Welland led Helena and Isabella to the edge of the yard and opened one of the stable doors into a workshop. Isabella hardly listened to the conversation between her mother and the carpenter. She was feeling very odd indeed.

Isabella's chest of drawers lay in a corner covered with a sheet.

'I hope this pleases thee, Ma'am.'

Ben pulled the sheet away and Helena and Isabella gasped. A small, exquisitely carved piece of furniture was revealed. Helena had ordered a chest of drawers for Isabella's room and this far exceeded her expectations.

The wood was plain and light with capacious drawers, polished smooth as an apple; but it was the work on the front of the drawers and all around the edges of the top of the piece that was so skilfully done. Instead of brass handles there were round knobs carved in the shapes of leaves and flowers.

With a cry Isabella moved forward to touch and look closer. There were slender trees and birds nestling among the flowers. Squirrels and tiny dormice, all carved to fit the piece and make it seem as one piece of wood.

'Mr Welland,' Helena exclaimed, 'this is an exquisite piece. I have never seen a piece of furniture like it. I know your work and expected it to be beautiful, but this ... Isabella?'

'It is perfect, Mr Welland. It is ... wonderful. I thank you so much for it. Mama has had my room newly decorated, and this ... I love it! I truly love it.'

Mr Welland was well pleased, but he was a dour Yorkshireman and not given to excess. 'Well, Miss, don't take on. It is my son, Tom, thee has to thank. I carved the piece, but it was Tom who wanted to try the decoration. He said the wood lent itself to shape and there is no doubt he was right.'

'It looks as if he will one day be as good a carpenter as his father,' Helena said diplomatically.

'Aye, and more so. He grows bored sometimes with the plainness of wood. He sees shapes where others do not. I let him have his way with the drawers on the understanding if thee did not approve or thought it too fancy, he must make more plain ones for thee.'

Helena smiled. 'How could we not approve? For a gentleman's room it might be too ornate, for a young girl it is imaginative and skilfully done. Is this his first work of this kind?'

'Aye, it is, Ma'am.'

'May we thank him?'

Mr Welland hesitated and Helena, noticing, said, 'You must be proud of him?'

Ben Welland looked at her with eyes that were possibly as vivid as Tom's once, and were now the colour of a faded sky.

'Aye, Ma'am. I am proud, but I hope to keep the lad with me. Keep him here in the yard. But he is restless for more intricate and complicated carving, for which I know he has the skill. Trading ships are being commissioned faster than we can build them and we could not live by furniture alone, fancy or no. Tom has always been skilled with a piece of wood, even as a bairn.'

Helena smiled again, understanding. 'But, interesting as boat-building is, Tom will need more imaginative work one day and you are afraid of losing him. Our praise of his work might hasten that day.'

'Yes, Ma'am, I believe so. But it is his due and I cannot deny him.'

He turned and they followed him out into the sunlight again. Ben called out to his son and the boy turned and stood awkwardly in front of them. Helena congratulated him on his work and assured him that he would be rewarded above the original price mentioned. She also told him that when people saw Isabella's piece he was sure to gain more commissions.

Isabella, staring from beneath the shadow of her hat, believed Tom Welland to be the most beautiful person she had ever seen. At the mention of her name, Tom's eyes turned to her, and she said, her face reddening, 'Thank you . . . it is lovely.'

She turned away abruptly and walked to her horse. Tom

watched her and when he saw she was going to mount without help he moved forward. He cupped his hands so that she could put her small foot into them and carefully lifted her to the saddle. Ben Welland was busy helping Helena onto her horse.

Isabella gathered the reins in her small, gloved hands. When she looked down the boy was still watching her, his face grave, but she had a distinct suspicion that he might be amused by her. She said suddenly, 'Please do not make another chest of drawers the same as mine for anyone else. I wish mine to be the only one or it will be spoilt, the magic will be gone.'

Her brown eyes met his blue and he held them. The amusement was gone, they held a sudden regard that struck her like lightning. Her bodice felt suddenly too tight, her breasts against the cloth ached. She turned her horse abruptly away before he could answer, brought her whip lightly down on the mare's flank so that the horse leapt out of the boatyard with Helena behind her.

Helena had witnessed Isabella's confusion and she sighed. The boy was uncommonly handsome as, probably, the father had been before him. Helena's thoughts of the morning returned. She was right, Isabella was no longer a child but a young woman with a passionate body difficult to control.

How to tell her, Helena wondered, without putting her off marriage forever, that the men women were often attracted to were not the ones, in general, suitable to marry.

Isabella was now a long way ahead. They had entered the stony cliff path that led down to the cove. Helena did not call out or try to catch up, she wanted to let Isabella compose herself. She would have to talk to her, but not yet, not the second her daughter discovered desire. She must let her have privacy and time to accept her changing body.

Helena remembered her own first thunderbolt of unfulfilled yearning for a friend of her brothers ... Claudio ... that was his name.

Isabella had reached the bottom of the cliff path and turned her horse to wait for Helena to catch up. Helena was not concentrating. She was back in Rome, remembering the beauty of a young body. Why, she had almost forgotten what desire felt like ...

Her mare stumbled on the loose stones and Helena realized she was holding the horse's head too tight and loosened the reins.

Isabella was having trouble holding her horse. It was plunging and dancing, impatient for a gallop by the sea. Helena called out to her, 'Let her go, she will unseat you. I will be right behind you.'

Isabella swung her horse round and started to canter towards the edge of the sea. Helena's horse whinnied in frustration, wanting to be off the stony path onto the sand. Helena spoke to it soothingly.

'Wait, wait, we are nearly at the bottom ... steady now, wait till we are off these stones.'

At last they reached the bottom of the cliff and the beach lay tantalizingly ahead. Isabella was already melting into the distance. Helena's horse leapt forward, snorting with excitement. The stones skidded under its feet, and as it lurched Helena was thrown forward and lost her stirrup. She gathered the reins in and tried to hold the horse, but the mare reared up on her hind legs and plunged ahead again. Helena flew over the horse's head and landed on the sand, but the back of her head connected sharply with the black rocks lying at the foot of the cliff. She died instantly.

Isabella was still galloping to the far side of the cove. She had regained her composure and felt exhilarated by her ride along the edge of the waves. Laughing, she turned her horse round to watch her mother coming towards her.

The riderless horse, stirrup flying and thumping into her side, was pounding her way, and Isabella could just make out a small figure lying crumpled and motionless near the black rocks. She gave an anguished cry that was lost in the sound of the surf and the seagulls screaming above her.

The light was going. The room was suddenly cold. Gabby shivered. She had done enough for one day. She finished filling Isabella's robe, where the wood had rotted at the back of the figurehead where it would have abutted the ship.

She tidied her things and prepared her bottles and jars for the morning. Pink clouds had gathered, coloured by the setting sun. The face of Isabella was caught in golden light from the window and in the rays of the dying sun the face looked as smooth and sad as death.

Chapter 18

It was not until Gabby was on the train to London that she stopped to think about what she was doing. She had told herself that she could not do any more work on the figurehead until the paint samples she had sent up to London had been analysed. This was not quite true, for there were other things she could be doing, such as grouting out all the dead wood from the base of Isabella while she waited.

The sun bounced off the sea as she left Penzance. Nell had wanted to drive her to the station but Gabby had persuaded her it was much too early. Guilt and excitement gnawed at her stomach and she felt odd and jittery as if watching herself from a distance.

It was a long time since she had been on a train on her own. It felt wonderful. *No man's land*. She looked out of the window; to her left the Hayle estuary lay full of waders and the sea beyond the sand dunes was rough, rolling in below the cliffs on a high tide.

As the train rattled inland she thought about a time before the railway was built and how once tin, copper and coal had to be transported by hundreds of mules and horses. There were many depressed little towns left by the mining industry and Cornwall constantly struggled to survive. It was going to take her five hours to reach Paddington, but in Isabella's day London must have seemed as remote as New Zealand.

Gabby's book lay unread on her knee. Whenever her mind came back to the end of her journey her stomach contracted and her tongue stuck to the roof of her dry mouth. Nell had booked Gabby into her old-fashioned club which was conveniently near to Paddington.

She went slowly over her conversation with Mark. She had rung him excitedly when Nell had rushed in to her mid-morning, waving a catalogue.

'Gabby! I knew there was something familiar about the face of your figurehead. Look, I've been rummaging through my files and found this. Don't you think this face is similar? I cleaned and restored her in the sixties while I was at the Portrait Gallery.'

Gabby looked down at the photograph of a dark young woman in a rich ruby dress, looking pensive. It was quite hard to tell; after all, they only had a wooden face and blind eyes with which to compare her. Gabby went to her drawer and got out the photos she had taken of the figurehead and placed one of Isabella's face next to the catalogue. Gabby and Nell peered down and both women shivered in excitement. The shape of both faces was the same. So were the placing of eyes and mouth, the expression in them almost identical.

Gabby looked at the description: *Helena Viscaria. Believed to have been painted on her eighteenth birthday by her cousin, Bernardo Venichy, as a wedding present for her husband, Daniel Vyvyan, whom she married in 1844.*

'Definitely the same family, don't you think?' Nell asked, pleased with herself.

'Yes. Oh yes!' Gabby turned to Nell. 'What on earth made you remember restoring this painting? It was so long ago.'

'Quite extraordinary, the subconscious. The face on the figurehead seemed familiar and it niggled at me. Last night I kept dreaming of a red dress, and in the morning the face of the painting was clear in my mind so I went looking for her, not really believing I would find her in my chaos.'

Gabby laughed. 'Nell, you pretend to be disorganized, but you aren't really. If I moaned about you making me keep records before, I never will again!'

'I think the other reason I remembered was because it was such a beautiful painting and was in really bad repair having been stored in a damp loft or cellar. A young member of the family had found it and of course Venichy was having a spectacular revival in the sixties when the painting was brought to the gallery. I'm not sure, but I believe the gallery eventually bought it from the Vyvyan family, or they have it on permanent loan somewhere.'

'I wonder,' Gabby said, 'if this is what Mark Hannah was chasing. He said he had a lead about the family in Manchester and was going to try to visit the Portrait Gallery before he went home.'

'Possibly,' Nell said. 'It might have been hanging in Manchester at some point. Why don't you ring him? I'll make some coffee.'

So she had, and he too had been excited. 'Gabriella . . . your Nell is a wonder. This is such a bonus. I . . . I know this is a lot to ask, but could you possibly bring that catalogue up to London? It would make my job of finding out about the family much easier. Is that at all possible?'

Startled, Gabby had mumbled, 'Um . . . well . . . could I ring you back on that one?'

Nell had come back into the study, and Gabby replaced the receiver with nervous hands. 'He *was* chasing that painting and it *did* hang in Manchester. Nell, he wants me to rush up to London with the catalogue so that he can take it to the Portrait Gallery with him.'

'Today?' Nell asked, startled.

'Not today, Nell. It's far too late to catch a train today.'

'What if we photocopied it and put it in the post tonight. He would, with luck, get it in the morning.'

They looked at each other doubtfully. 'With *luck* is the word,' Gabby said. 'I told him I'd ring him back. I'll have to think. It would be much better if you went, actually, Nell. You restored the picture.'

'Gabby, I'm not haring up to London for a day. Chelsea Flower Show is my next trip. My dear girl, if you feel like a gallivant to the National Portrait Gallery with your Canadian, you go. It might be quite good for you. I can ring my club and book you in for the night, and you can catch the train home the following day.'

Gabby bit her lip, thinking of Charlie. Nell said quietly, 'Gabby, if you're worried about the expense or what Charlie will say, don't. You're earning your own money. I'll pay for the night at the club. I'd love to, that's what it's for, to be used. If you think it would be fun and you can put up with five hours on a train, go.'

'Nell . . . thanks.'

'Ring him back. I must get to work. I'll see you at lunchtime.'

'Gabriella? Thanks for ringing back. I've delayed my flight a day and managed to get a meeting with a friend of a colleague at the National Portrait Gallery. If it is the same painting I've been trying to trace, it was loaned to the gallery by the Vyvyan family for one of their retrospective exhibitions in 1964.'

'That's right. Nell restored it in the early sixties. Just before that exhibition.'

'She is a star! This is what I love about tracing history, the leads that suddenly appear when you are least expecting them . . . Gabriella, have you had time to think? Any possibility you could come up to London and go to the gallery with me? It would be so good to have you with me.'

Gabby felt almost angry that his voice could wreak such havoc with her stomach, but she said, 'I'll come up on the early train. What time is your appointment with the gallery?'

'Two-thirty. Can you make it for then?'

'On the early train I can.'

'I'll meet you at Paddington. Let me know the time. Then I'll take you out to lunch, before we go . . .'

Gabby wobbled down the speeding train to get a coffee. It was following the sea wall at Teignmouth. In rough weather the waves came up over the sea wall, a great grey tower looming over the trains in a terrifying way before the line was closed.

She could see her reflection in the window and closed her eyes against herself. She could not relax, she felt poised, on the brink of something. She kept visualizing herself getting off the train, walking along the platform to the barrier, looking round for him . . . then, what? Smiling and waving? Shaking hands? Being businesslike?

How had they parted? What exactly had he said? Gabby tried to remember. People often said things they did not mean. Sometimes they pretended they had not said the things they did not mean.

The countryside raced past and still she could not concentrate on her book. The train followed a canal; rows and rows of bright barges were lined along the banks, bicycles and flowers and pushchairs up on their roofs. A family of ducks were settled on the riverbank, the gander's bright green feathers glinted in the sun.

She felt rather as she had when she had smoked a joint with Josh, to see what it was like. Everything stood out, bright and separate. Stark and noticeable. Beautiful and highlighted, as if she was marking her trail to a foreign land and must take note in case she could not find her way back. Her limbs felt stiff with anticipation. She made herself breathe deeply, tried to think of nothing outside her direct vision.

Her mind moved to Isabella. What had excited Mark so much about the figurehead that he felt the need to accompany her thousands of miles?

In her imagination Gabby suddenly saw his wrist. The way the long dark fingers lay curled around the smooth face of a female figurehead on Tresco. The way the hairs on his wrist curled into his shirt cuff. She shivered as she remembered how badly she had wanted to touch that place between cuff and wrist, lay a finger there to feel the heat and pulse of him. *The heat and pulse of him.*

The train swayed and groaned as it gathered speed and she closed her eyes, half-asleep, voices rising and coming to her in small waves.

When they reached Reading, Gabby went to the loo and

brushed her hair, put on her pale lipstick which never stayed on. Sprayed herself with something expensive Nell had given her for Christmas. She looked at herself critically. Her dark skin was tanned and devoid of make-up, which, except for lipstick, she never wore. Her eyes, framed by naturally dark lashes, seemed too intense, too blue and nervous. Like a horse about to bolt.

For heaven's sake. You are just taking him a catalogue. You will have a pleasant lunch, an interesting afternoon, and then . . . She reached up for her overnight bag and pulled it to her. *Then maybe an early drink or supper and he will put you in a taxi for Nell's club, and you will have enjoyed the day with him and be glad you came.*

She got out of her seat as the train slid into Paddington, letting the people in a hurry go in front of her. Then she walked slowly down the platform towards the barrier, holding her ticket. She saw him first because he was tall. He had on cream linen trousers and a crumpled jacket and still looked casually elegant. His eyes were scanning the people pouring towards him, rather anxiously.

Gabby stopped dead in her tracks and watched him. A powerful feeling of familiarity swept through her, so strong and strange was the sensation that she had done all this before. Slowly she moved on towards him and when he caught sight of her his face lit up. Once on the other side of the barrier he hugged her hard.

'It is so, so good to see you. I guess I couldn't really believe you would come.'

Gabby laughed. 'I said I would.'

'Sure you did. But things can go wrong. Something might have prevented you.'

'Well, nothing did,' she said softly.

'Nothing did,' he repeated, taking her hand and bringing it to his lips. He hooked her holdall over his shoulder.

'We'll take a taxi. I found somewhere to eat near the gallery so we don't have a panic about getting there.'

It was an Italian restaurant and looked expensive. Gabby

was glad she had worn a newish pair of white trousers and a navy denim jacket that Josh loved her in.

Mark openly stared at her. 'You look wonderful, Gabriella. Just give me a moment, then I will stop gazing at you and order wine.'

A waiter brought them huge menus and Mark ordered two glasses of white wine, remembering this is what she drank.

'Could I also have some mineral water?' Gabby asked the waiter.

She bent and got Nell's catalogue out, and handed it to Mark with the photos that Nell had given her of the dates and times and process of the actual restoration. He was fascinated.

'I guess I should have, but I never realized the amount of work in restoring paintings. This is a wonderful painting to see, even if it should prove a false lead.' He stared at the face. 'Very beautiful, and yes, so very like our figurehead.'

'What did you find in Devon?' Gabby asked.

'Well, I told you about the Welland graves, didn't I? Well, by chance I was talking to the curator of a gallery in Manchester at a university dinner they had arranged in Exeter for me. He was interested in my research and when I showed him some photos of Lady Isabella he mentioned how Italian she looked. I told him she had been carved in Cornwall by Tom Welland and he suddenly said, before I could tell him any more, "Maybe she is a Vyvyan. They are an old Cornish family who go back to Doomsday."'

Gabby nodded. 'It's a very Cornish name. There are a few in the telephone book, all spelt differently. Some are still landowners.'

'He told me what we already knew, that one of the Vyvyans married an Italian, but he also mentioned her portrait had been painted by Bernardo Venichy before her marriage. She was quite a beauty. It came to the Manchester Gallery in the late sixties when the exhibition moved there from London. But he has no idea where it is now.'

'Perhaps we will discover this afternoon.'

'Hopefully.'

'But the gallery might only know about the painting, not about the family it belonged to.'

'That's very possible. But I have learnt, over the years, that one thing tends to lead to another. You can sometimes gather little scraps of information which don't connect, then suddenly it all begins to make a whole and you are able to piece a life together. With lots of little gaps, of course.'

'You must be very patient.' Gabby smiled at him.

He held her eyes. 'I am very patient when I want something.'

Mark's contact at the gallery was a young woman called Lucinda Cage. Gabby liked her immediately. At first she seemed more interested in Nell's restoration technique than in the painting they were there to discuss.

'I used Nell Appleby as part of my thesis on medieval colours. She was a brilliant detective, you know. I reckon she knew nearly as much as an analyst. I went to a lecture she gave once. She was brilliant; utterly passionate about her work. My tutor used some of her restoration techniques as an example of how to conserve.'

Gabby glowed with pride. Dear, self-effacing Nell, who never blew her own trumpet.

'I'll tell her, she'll be so surprised.'

Lucinda turned to Mark. 'I've been looking up some files and asking colleagues about this painting of Helena Viscaria. As you know, it was found in the early sixties in a bad state. A great deal of the damage had occurred by storing or hanging on a damp outside wall. It was brought to us by a David Tredinnick in 1961 with a view to selling after renovation.

'Nell Appleby undertook the restoration and when it was finished I gather there was some family problem with selling to us. Various members wanted to keep it in the family. After the Venichy retrospective it was loaned to us on a permanent basis. It travelled round the regional galleries for about eighteen months then returned here.'

She looked at Mark and Gabby. 'I'm really sorry to tell you that it was bought by a private Italian art collector and taken back to Italy in 1989. We do not know whether he had any connection with her family or just wanted to acquire the painting.'

'What was his name?' Mark asked.

Lucinda glanced down at her file. 'A Signor Alfredo Manesco.'

'The opera singer?' Mark seemed surprised.

Lucinda shrugged. 'I'm afraid I haven't a clue.'

Mark laughed. 'Of course you haven't. You would have still been in nappies.'

Lucinda blushed. 'Not quite. If you come this way, I'll make a cup of tea.'

Gabby suddenly saw that Lucinda found Mark attractive. Then immediately thought, Well he *is*, so most women will.

For some reason this dampened her spirits.

As they had tea, Lucinda asked Gabby if Nell still worked. 'We could do with her up here. One of our restorers has just gone on maternity leave early because of health problems.'

'Nell still restores, but in her own time. She's sort of semi-retired . . .' Gabby smiled. 'I'm not sure you could lure her out of retirement.'

'I was only joking, really.'

'Gabby is restoring the figurehead of Lady Isabella,' Mark said.

Lucinda stared at her. 'Oh, sorry, I am thick. I never listen to names. I didn't realize you were the same person.'

'No reason why you should,' Gabby said easily.

As they left, Lucinda asked, 'Are you going all the way back to Cornwall tonight?'

'No,' Gabby said. 'Tomorrow.'

'Have you got ten minutes?'

Puzzled, Gabby glanced at Mark. 'Yes, of course.'

Lucinda led the way into the gallery and along some long corridors to a small back room. She pointed to a portrait of a young boy sitting with riding whip and a spaniel, with a river and trees behind him.

'Tell me what you think?'

Gabby went closer. She was appalled. The painting had been brutally cleaned with little concession to its age or original paint. The boy's face had been over-cleaned, so that it seemed to lack expression. The trees behind him, which should have been cleared of yellow varnish, had been left. This really should never have happened. It was a complete mess.

Lucinda was watching her face. 'Thank you, Gabrielle. You do not need to say a thing. Is it irredeemable?'

'Did it come to you like this?' Gabby asked. 'I can't believe anyone here could be responsible. Lucinda, its value has possibly been reduced by this restoration. Surely no one untrained had a go, did they?'

'It came to us from a private collector. He had it cleaned by a restorer who came to him recommended. The collector brought it to us in tears.'

'I'm not surprised,' Gabby said. 'He should not be allowed anywhere near a painting. No, it isn't irredeemable. A good restorer could undo some of the damage, but not all, I'm afraid.'

'Thank you for confirming what we've already been told. Would you mind not mentioning this to anybody? And Gabrielle, may I have your phone number?'

'It's all very cloak and dagger. Perhaps your little councillor's brother struck again!' Mark was trying not to laugh as Gabby scribbled down her number.

The afternoon was dark as they left the gallery and people were pouring to the tube station. Mark managed to hail a taxi. He turned to Gabby inside the cab.

'Would you like to go to your club to shower and freshen up? Or could you bear to come and see this house of my aunt's that I'm going to be renting all next year for my sabbatical. I'm dying to show someone, it's bang on the river and I'm very much in love with it.'

'I'd like to see it.'

'Then, if you don't feel I'm monopolizing you, I could

bring you back to the club and wait around in the bar for you? You needn't hurry, I'll be quite happy. I have hundreds of daughters, I'm used to waiting. Then I can take you to supper.'

'There is a great little French place within walking distance of the club,' Gabby said. 'Nell and I go there sometimes.'

'Perfect. We've got the day sewn up then.'

'I didn't realize you were going to take a sabbatical over here.'

'I've only just stopped dithering and, encouraged by my English publisher, made a definite decision.'

They smiled at one another, and then turned to look at London sliding by.

Chapter 19

The wind battered the long stalks of opening daffodils so that they lay on the banks and borders with their heads bowed like a defeated army. Apart from the relentless rain spattering and running down the panes, the house was deathly silent.

The heart, the very core of the household was gone. Vanished in the moment it took for a horse to rear. Isabella waited and waited for her father to call her to him, for them to comfort each other, but the door to his study remained firmly shut.

She was overcome by shock and sudden shaking fits. Her teeth rattled and her limbs jerked. She could not get warm, and Lisette, Helena's maid, her own eyes red with weeping, put her to bed and lit the bedroom fire.

The doctor came up to her room and gave her a powder, told Lisette what she already knew, that Isabella was in deep shock. Isabella could hear the doctor and Lisette whispering at the door and she cried out, 'Where is Papa? I want to see Papa.'

The doctor came back to her bedside. 'Isabella, sleep now. Your father is grieving too. You will see him later. Now close your eyes and sleep.'

Isabella fell into a nightmarish half-sleep. The same scene played over and over in her head. Mama somersaulting over her horse's neck and lying as Isabella first saw her, motionless on the ground. Her head ... her head ... Isabella squeezed her eyes tight against the recurring image.

Lisette lit a small lamp and brought a bowl of warm water and gently washed Isabella's face and hands, weeping as copiously as Isabella until the two embraced so that they did not have to look

131

upon each other's reddened faces and swollen eyes.

'Papa blames me for Mama's death, does he not, Lisette?'

Lisette, busy with Isabella's pillows, replied, 'Your father is grieving, Isabella. He is in shock, as the doctor told you. He cannot face anyone.'

She could not meet Isabella's eyes and Isabella knew then it was true, her father did blame her, and yet he had not even come to her and asked her what had happened.

Isabella went over and over the sequence of events in the days that followed Helena's death. They left the boatyard. She was in front, Mama behind her. If she had ridden with or behind Helena? If she had dismounted when she reached the bottom of the cliff path? If she had waited? If she had turned sooner on the beach and ridden back towards her mother?

Over and over, back and forth she went, reliving that morning of their ride. Eventually, fearing she would go mad, she left her room to go and find her father. She found him in the library with his agent. It was early in the day but he was already drinking.

He stared at his daughter blankly when she burst in. Before he could speak, Isabella said, clasping her shaking hands in front of her, 'Do you blame me for Mama's death, Papa? Is this why you will not see me or let me tell you what happened?'

Her father poured more whisky into his glass. 'I do blame you, Isabella, for the cause of the accident lies with you. Your mother never rode to the cove on her own. I understand you rode ahead of her, despite being the better rider. The fact is, had you been less impatient and waited for your mother, her horse would not have bolted and she would be alive now.'

Isabella was stung, flushed with misery. 'It was because my horse was exciting Mama's that I rode on ahead. Mama asked me to. I am sorry, Papa, that you think I am to blame . . .'

She bit her lip. She did not want to cry in front of her father.

'You do not think you are to blame, then, child?'

Mr Trovorrow, the agent, standing with his back to the fire, stirred uneasily at this. Isabella did not answer. Young as she was, she was aware that her father must blame someone.

132

Trovorrow cleared his throat. 'Sir, there has been a tragic and shocking accident. No one is to blame, surely? Horses are unpredictable beasts.'

Isabella's father opened his mouth as if he was going to be rude and then thought better of it. Isabella turned and left the room. There was no point in talking to her grieving and angry father when he had been drinking.

She walked through the hall and out of the front door. She walked down the steps to the drive and kept walking. She felt light and disembodied. There seemed no one to turn to. Had she caused her mother's death? Was her father right?

She turned, dwarfed against the vast chestnuts that lined the drive, and looked back. She had always hated this view of the house, neither softened by scarlet creeper nor the shutters Helena told her all Italian houses had, which framed a house softly like eyelids as well as keeping it cool.

So many empty rooms, and now dust covers would soon hide her mother's possessions. Her father had locked the door to Helena's rooms and she could not even go there to smell her mother's scent, touch the silver brushes, sink into the folds of her bed and breathe her in. Helena was lost to her forever and Isabella did not know how she could bear it or where she could turn for release from this unremitting pain.

She turned as she heard a trap coming up the drive and saw two horses pulling a cart. She moved aside to let it pass, but it stopped beside her and Ben Welland got down from the cart. He took his hat off.

'Miss Isabella. The family are sad and sorry to hear about the accident to thy mother.'

He twisted his hat and met her eyes and held them steadily.

'Thy mother was a good and beautiful woman.'

Isabella was overcome, for the carpenter was the first person to openly speak of Helena. She stood in the drive trying not to weep, nodding her head vigorously. The man went to the cart and lifted a piece of the tarpaulin.

'I thought this would bring thee comfort, lass, for it was thy mother's birthday present to thee.'

Under the tarpaulin lay the beautiful chest of drawers. Isabella touched the wood. 'Yes,' she whispered. 'Oh yes. I thank you, Mr Welland.'

Lying in bed that night Isabella could see the dark shape of the chest and smell the faint scent of polish. She could remember her mother's lovely face admiring it. For the first time since her mother's death she felt comforted. She would have this one piece of furniture all her life and it would always remind her of Helena. This was her mother's last birthday present to her, and Isabella thought, I will hand it on to my child and so it will go on, Helena's chest giving pleasure to child after child down the years.

The following day they had a private service for the family and the household in the small chapel in the garden. They buried Helena with all the other Vyvyans in the family crypt. The small chapel was packed with estate workers and their wives, the women openly crying. Helena had seemed to these poor and hard-working people so different from the English aristocracy. She had been warm and young and approachable.

Daniel Vyvyan was of the old school. He was respected, but he had no idea of their daily lives; of their illnesses, tragedies or poverty; of their hopes and dreams. It would not occur to him that they had any, beyond being employed, having a roof over their heads and enough in their pockets on a Friday night for a pint.

It was Helena, and sometimes Isabella, who knew that a sick child had died, or a family were in debt, or a husband too long down the mines had consumption. It was Helena who had taken food or vegetables and persuaded her husband to let the gardeners cultivate a small field for their own use to sell on to other workers.

Daniel Vyvyan sat directly in front of the coffin, his face stiff and grey with loss.

Isabella sat in the same pew, but far from her father as if they were people from a separate family. Lisette, watching that straight little back, knew suddenly that she was the only person who could take care of Isabella now. All thoughts of a life out of service must fade.

Daniel shared a drink with his workers in the courtyard to receive their condolences. Isabella, watching from her window, saw Ben Welland and his family among them. Tom's fair head stood a head taller than the others.

When everyone had gone, Isabella sat on the window seat looking out. A mist hung over the lake and a Cornish mizzle, light but drenching, blew in fine curtains across the drive.

What will happen to me now? I never imagined a life without Mama. I never thought about growing up without her. It feels as if I have lost both parents at once. I don't know what to do. *I don't know what to do.*

Two days after the funeral her father called her to him and told her he had decided to send her to cousins over on the Helford River. They had agreed to educate and finish her with their own three girls and then ... Daniel obviously had no idea what would happen after that.

'Papa, are you punishing me? I hardly know my cousins or my aunt. Why are you sending me away from my home? Am I to lose everything?' Her voice broke.

Her father looked at her for the first time since Helena died.

'Isabella, of course I am not punishing you. Without your mother you will be lonely. Lisette is the only female you talk to. I am going to travel and possibly visit your mother's relations in Italy. I do not want to leave you alone in this house.'

'I could come with you. I could look after you, Papa. Please, please let me come with you. I could see my Italian cousins, my aunts, please ... please, Papa.'

She watched her father's face close.

'Do not make me go away. I would rather stay with Lisette here than go to strangers.'

'I am sorry, child,' he said, closing the subject. 'I am doing the best thing for you, believe me. You will see this later.'

'I only see that you cannot bear to have me near you,' Isabella cried and turned and ran from the room.

This was true, but not for the reason Isabella believed. She was so like her mother in looks and character that Daniel did not want to be reminded daily of something precious he had lost. A beautiful and clever woman he loved, but took for granted. The knowledge

135

of her value, witnessed by the grief at her funeral, bit and gnawed at his innards. He had to escape this.

However, he decided Lisette must go with Isabella to keep her company. He took his daughter's cold little hand in the hall.

'Isabella, I will write. You will be well looked after ...' He hesitated. 'I was not myself ... after the accident. Of course it was not your fault. Forget my words, I did not mean them. In no way are you to blame. Will you forget them?'

'Yes, Papa,' Isabella said dully.

He took her hands in his. 'Now, come, smile at your papa before you leave so that I can remember a happier face on my travels.'

Isabella could not smile. But she reached up to kiss her father then turned with dignity to Lisette waiting by the carriage.

Daniel walked to the door, knowing he was sacrificing his only child. He groaned at his own selfishness and weakness, but he could not stay in this vast, empty, inherited mausoleum alone.

His last image of his daughter was of a small, frightened white face peering out of the window at him, before the carriage turned down the drive and out of sight.

Chapter 20

The taxi dropped them off near the bridge so that they could walk along the river path to the house. Mark pointed; 'It's three-quarters of the way along the path. Can you see, the house with the creeper growing up the front?'

His voice held a proprietorial excitement that made Gabby smile. It was late afternoon and people were beginning to leave offices and shops and go home. Even the river seemed busy with small tugs and cruisers. The path was wet from a high tide and they negotiated the puddles.

'The river floods on a regular basis at certain times of the year,' Mark said. 'All the houses have flood barriers at their front doors to stop the water entering the houses. Sort of quaint, isn't it? People dash out to put them up as the river rises.'

'Do the barriers work?' Gabby wondered. 'How awful to come back to a flooded house. You could be out when the river rises.'

'According to my aunt, if in doubt, put them up anyway.'

Gabby peered into windows. 'What lovely houses. Why did your aunt leave?'

'She's nearly eighty. Most of her friends in London have died. I think she was lonely and the house got too big. She's gone off to live near Exeter with a friend, but she doesn't want to sell her house until she knows whether living with someone else is going to work. So this arrangement is ideal for both of us.'

'She's very wise. How come she is living over here? Did she marry an Englishman?'

'She did, but he died some time ago. They never had children, which was sad. She's a great person. I'm her godson and she has always been very good to me.'

'I expect you've been good to her, too.'

Mark smiled and they stopped for a minute and watched the river. Beyond the houses on the far side the sky was a flushed pink and gold as the sun sank below the buildings.

Mark got the front-door key out of his pocket and they walked up three steep steps to the entrance of a small three-storey house with creeper growing up its walls. The front door was dark green with a brass knocker. As he opened the door, Mark turned to Gabby and said, 'I'm like a kid. I can't believe I'm going to live here for a year. There's no place I'd rather be. Come in and look, Gabriella.'

There was a long hall that led into a sitting room on the right, which had a view across the river and was now full of buttery yellow light. It was partially furnished, but it was obvious that furniture and ornaments had been removed. A fine layer of dust lay on the mantelpiece.

The left room was empty, but had once been a dining room.

'I don't think my aunt ever used it after her husband died,' Mark said. 'There is a kitchen at the back, facing the garden, which is much warmer.'

The stairs went straight up from the hall and a narrow passage continued to the back of the house and into a surprisingly large kitchen, which had a small Rayburn and pine dining-table and chairs. Gabby could tell immediately that this was where Mark's aunt had spent most of her time. It was an L-shape, and Mark went in and opened up old pine shutters which led back into the sitting room. Immediately the room was flooded with light from the dying sun.

'I don't think she ever closed these when she lived here.'

Gabby was silent, drinking in the light and the sound

of the river. Listening to the boats hooting as they went under the bridge, to the distant growl of traffic and a blackbird somewhere, calling on one note. If it is possible, she thought, to fall in love with a house at first sight, I have just done so.

Mark, seeing her face, said, 'I see you understand now why I am so childishly excited.'

'Yes,' Gabby said. 'Oh yes.'

'Come upstairs and then I'll open a bottle of wine and show you the garden.'

They climbed the steep stairs to two bedrooms at the front and one at the back. Both front bedrooms were empty of furniture. The windows, stretching from floor to ceiling, looked down on the fast flowing river and the sounds of people calling to each other at the end of a day.

Mark had obviously been sleeping in the bedroom at the back of the house. There was a clock and books on the bedside table. A shirt hung on the door. A pair of trousers were neatly folded over a chair. The room looked down on the small garden, not much more than a large yard. Next to this room was an old-fashioned bathroom. On the third floor was an attic room.

While Mark went back downstairs Gabby went into the bathroom and brushed her hair, stared at herself in a crackled antique mirror hanging above the basin. Put some moisturizer on her lips. Sprayed a little of Nell's scent on her wrists and behind her ears. She had no idea who taught her to do this small, timeless act. As she met her eyes in the mirror she saw how clear and calm they were. The blackbird was still singing as if its heart would break. Clear into this moment Gabby stared, transfixed, looking into the mirror as if she had never seen herself before.

I'm home, she thought. *I'm home*. She closed her eyes and gripped the edge of the basin, as peace, and something far beyond peace, flooded through her.

She walked slowly down the stairs and back into the kitchen. Mark had opened a bottle of wine and had poured out two glasses. He was leaning against the work surface, looking out into the garden. His face looked more serious in profile when his mouth and eyes were invisible.

He turned as she came into the room. She stood just inside the doorway, suddenly unsure. He did not pick up a glass of wine and hand it to her, he did not move at all, he just stood looking at her. The atmosphere in the room became electric and unbearable. Gabby held her breath. The moment hovered and grew, needing to be broken with a laugh. Needing to be broken.

Gabby swallowed and moved into the room towards him. He moved at the same time and they met somewhere in the middle. He placed his hands on the top of her arms and bent and kissed her forehead and both cheeks then drew back to look down into her face. Gabby could not take her eyes from his bottom lip. She longed to bite it. She reached up and kissed his mouth, once, hard.

His eyes changed colour, his hand came up to touch her face and he bent to her mouth, gently at first, almost a question mark. Gabby, holding on to his arms for balance, opened her mouth to him, pressing against him. He pulled her to him, kissing her urgently now, and there was only the sound of their short sharp breaths in the warm room.

He lifted her suddenly to the edge of the room so that her back was against the work surface, bent to her neck, pressed her so close to him she felt part of his body. She held the back of his head, pushing him to her skin as one of his hands started to undo her shirt. She could feel his hand trembling, then his fingers cold on her breast and his mouth warm on her nipple.

With a small cry she started to shake off her shirt, pulling her arms out of the sleeves. Mark undid her bra and removed it, threw it behind him, stood away for a moment to gaze at her; then he gently took her bottom lip in his teeth and held it there as if he was about to eat her.

Gabby's hands moved to his belt and started to undo the buckle. Still kissing her, Mark helped her, sliding out

140

of his shoes at the same time. He kicked his trousers and boxer shorts out of the way and slid her trousers and underpants down her legs, bending and pulling off her shoes and socks. There was the brief, awkward moment of their own nakedness before he pulled her to him again, kissing and touching her until she could bear it no longer.

He lifted her up onto the work surface and slid into her making her gasp, lowering and holding her onto him. Gabby, gripping his shoulders, cried out as they moved together and came immediately. Then they were both motionless in the dusky kitchen. The sun had disappeared behind the buildings and Gabby was grateful for the coming darkness. One of Mark's hands stroked her hair as she stayed buried in his neck.

She shivered involuntarily and Mark held her away and whispered, 'You're getting cold.'

He carried her upstairs and wrapped her in his towelling robe and placed her under the duvet. Then he made two trips back downstairs to get the wine and their clothes which he folded neatly together on the chair. Finally he got back into bed beside her and held her to him, and they floated between sleep listening to the last of the birds skittering and calling in the dusk.

After a while he switched on the bedside light so that he could see her. He wanted any awkwardness to be dispelled. Gabby half sat up, concentrating on her wine, not looking at him. He turned her face to him and smiled. She met his eyes.

'Just in case you were wondering, Gabriella, that was not a wham, bam, thank you, ma'am.' He was laughing again.

Gabby smiled. 'Sure?'

'Oh, I'm very sure.' He bent forward and rubbed her nose with his.

She looked at him. 'Even if it was . . . I don't regret it . . .' She flicked her hair forward in the small nervous habit she had. 'It was lovely . . . I've never had an orgasm before.'

Startled, he held her hair away from her face. 'What? Never!'

'No. So . . . thank you.'

He pulled her on top of him. 'Obviously we'll have to practise, don't you think, to make sure it wasn't a one-off?'

'Oh, you think so?'

He manoeuvred her robe away. 'I do, Gabriella. Practise makes *absolutely* perfect, as you English say. We must make sure we've got it right.'

'Mark, you're leaving tomorrow.'

'But I'm coming back, Gabriella. I'm coming back.'

She smiled, sleepily. 'So you are.'

'I wanted you to see this house. I wanted to see if you thought you might come here sometimes.'

'It's a long way from Cornwall.'

'But not impossible?'

'No,' Gabby said, 'not impossible. This house almost seems . . . familiar, as if I have been here before. I love it.'

'I'm so glad. Now I'm going to be sensible and make you eggs on toast and put you in a taxi before you turn into a pumpkin.'

Gabby stirred against him. 'I'm not all that hungry.'

Mark groaned. 'Unfair, hussy. I wish you could stay the night, Gabriella, but you can't, can you?'

'Nell might ring the club. I can't really, Mark. I wish I could.'

'Next time?'

'Next time.'

'We'll get up . . . in just a second . . .'

But they didn't.

In the taxi to Nell's club, Gabby watched the wet streets slide by, full of the sounds of police sirens and night-time traffic. In the warm, impersonal room of the club she ached and throbbed. She was acutely aware of her own body, felt sensually absorbed into it, stunned by the way it had reacted so instinctively and physically to Mark. It felt as if

142

she had grown a shiny and voluptuous second skin that was as startling as it was dangerous.

She felt that she could not be responsible for this hedonistic and earthy other person. She did not know her at all. Or, and this sudden thought was more frightening, did she know her only too well? Had she hidden her, buried her deep and tight, so that she might stay forever buried under a life she could only handle if she were stifled?

At six in the morning, Mark rang her.

'Just checking you have no regrets,' he said softly.

'None,' she said. 'Have you?'

'Not one.'

'Mark? Even if it was a moment of madness, don't worry, I will never regret it.'

He laughed. 'I think you know what it was. Time will prove it to you, Gabriella. What time is your train?'

'Ten-thirty.'

'Paddington?'

'Yes.'

'I'll meet you there. I want to see you again before I fly.'

She laughed. 'OK.'

On the train back to Cornwall, Gabby thought, *Nell and Charlie will notice I'm different. My mouth aches. I ache. I've got five hours to turn back into myself. Five hours to metamorphose back into the person I've always been . . .*

At Plymouth, her mobile phone went. She jumped up and went into the corridor. It was Lucinda from the National Portrait Gallery. She asked if Gabby would be interested in restoring the small painting she had showed her, as their restorer would definitely have to take all her maternity leave.

Gabby was startled and unprepared for the suddenness of the offer.

'Um . . . well, I'm tied up for a while doing this figurehead, but yes . . . I guess . . . When were you thinking? I mean, how quickly do you need someone?'

'We need it to be done before the exhibition opens in July. Would it be possible for you to come up, say one or two days a week, while you are still doing the figurehead? Look, I've bounced this on you, do you want to have a think and ring me back?'

'Yes. I'm on the train home, Lucinda. Can I ring you back when I get home?'

'Sorry, I didn't realize. Look, I'll ring you tomorrow morning on the number you gave me. Is that OK?'

'It's fine. I'm sure I can juggle . . . I'd love to do it.'

'It might just lead to other work. Of course, I can't promise. Oh, and by the way, don't worry about accommodation; I've got a spare room so that needn't be an expense. I'll speak to you tomorrow, Gabrielle.'

Gabby flopped back into her seat so excited she had to ring Nell.

Nell, answering straight away, was as thrilled as Gabby.

'We'll talk when you get home, but believe me, it is not something to turn down. Oh, you clever girl!'

'I did nothing, Nell. Not a thing. It's your reputation I'm trading on. I was just there.'

'Being "just there" is sometimes enough.'

'Serendipity?'

Nell laughed. 'Something like that. See you when you get home. If that car of yours won't start, ring me, I'll come and get you.'

Gabby leant back and closed her eyes.

Being there is sometimes enough.

Chapter 21

It was the Commandant's cocktail party. Josh, entering the mess with two fellow cadets, felt the buzz in the room. The passing-out parade was getting close and every cadet officer felt edgy.

The three men scanned the full room automatically for talent.

'Mmm, quite a few yummy mummies here tonight,' David said.

'Commandant's wife really is a stunner.' Guy whistled low under his breath.

'I've heard the daughter is tasty, too. Wonder if she's here.'

Josh said nothing. His eyes were still roaming around the room. He had passed this daughter – whom he now knew was named Marika – frequently on his runs and they had grinned at each other as they sweated past, neither stopping to speak.

A crowd of people in the far corner parted and Josh saw her suddenly, surrounded by instructors. David and Guy grabbed a drink from a passing tray and made an unswerving and obvious beeline for that end of the room. Josh stayed where he was, his heart sinking. What was the point? She was hardly going to be interested in talking to cadet officers when she had the pick of the mess.

He drank two gins in quick succession. Nell was probably right, a career in the army was certainly going to affect his liver. He continued to loiter on the outskirts of the noisy flow of conversation and bursts of laughter. Sunday tomorrow. After church parade he would go for a long ride. If he had not had this passion to fly he would have chosen a cavalry regiment because of the horses. But flying was a little world of its own and he couldn't wait to join it.

It had been great to ride again, though. He had the pick of the horses at Sandhurst, beautiful thoroughbreds. Riding always relaxed him. He had missed Hal when he left home. Nell and Gabby had lent his horse to a girl in the village because Hal had needed regular exercise and they could no longer find the time to ride every day.

At the far end of the room he saw Guy and David had got themselves into the circle of people surrounding Marika. She was tall, as tall as some of the officers, and very blonde, that sexy pale Scandinavian blonde. Marika and her mother, Uli, were Croatian. Everyone knew the Commandant had met and fallen in love with her on his tour in Bosnia. He had eventually brought Uli and her daughter back to England. No one knew what had happened to her first husband, though fantasy and speculation were rife. Jokey rumours abounded of the Commandant having him shot.

Josh looked up and across the room, searching for someone he wanted to have a conversation with. He was being unsociable and he was not circulating, and this was expected of him. He sighed. He was bloody knackered after two sessions in the gym. Josh could not bear to fall below his own standards. He had a horror of failing, of not being quite good enough.

At that moment he caught Marika's eye across the room. She moved her mouth in a half smile and lifted her eyebrows slightly, her eyes signalling *Rescue me*.

Josh made his way across the room to her little entourage, amused.

'Hi,' he said when he reached her. 'I think we've passed each other running, puffing in opposite directions.' He held out his hand. 'I'm Josh.'

The girl laughed and took his hand. 'Yes, but your speed is greater than mine.'

'Oh, so you already know Josh?' David said in a peeved voice.

'Notice you kept that quiet,' Guy said, *sotto voce* out of the side of his mouth, the art of subtlety having passed him by.

'We have not spoken,' Marika said, still staring at Josh. 'I am Marika.'

Josh laughed. 'I know!'

How sweet that she would think anyone in Sandhurst might not know who she was. Waiters moved about with trays of canapés and people drifted and moved, broke up and re-formed, leaving Josh and Marika together.

'Would you have even come to talk to me if I had not made signs across the room?' Marika asked him accusingly.

'It would never have occurred to me that you might need rescuing.'

'I see. So you would not have come to speak with me? You would have ignored me all evening, despite the fact I have passed you every day running? How very rude.'

Josh burst out laughing at her injured tone. 'Marika . . .' How lovely the name sounded, saying it for the first time. 'You are always surrounded by the entire military establishment. I was not going to jostle and hassle for your attention.'

'But do you not realize how frightening this is, to be surrounded?'

Josh looked at her closely and saw that she meant it.

'I hadn't, no.'

Close up, she was amazing. Peachy skin and strange, unfathomable eyes, a sort of greeny-blue. They regarded him steadily and something fleeting passed through Josh, a déjà vu, gone before he could catch it.

'Are you busy when this finishes or could you have supper with me?' Josh asked quickly.

Marika's face lit up. 'I thought you would never ask me. Come, talk to my parents. They are, of course, having a

147

dinner party for the instructors, but I don't think they will mind if I abscond.'

She guided him firmly towards the Commandant and Josh's heart sank. She introduced him to her mother. 'Uli, this is Josh . . .'

'. . . Josh Ellis.' Josh shook her hand. Same eyes. Similar smile.

'Hello, Josh,' she said, her voice very English.

'Sir,' Josh said nervously to the Commandant.

'Would it be all right to go and have supper with Josh? I know you were expecting me home . . .'

Her mother laughed. 'Why, Marika, are you trying to get out of our little dinner party?' She turned to her husband. 'Darling, would you mind? It is her last night?'

The Commandant smiled. 'Of course I don't mind.' He shot a glance at Josh. 'Bring her back at a decent time. You are on church parade tomorrow.'

'Yes, sir.'

Josh guided her out of the room quickly before his friends caught up with him. They ran down the steps clutching hands while Josh pulled his mobile out of his pocket to ring for a taxi. They walked under the trees and along the wide road towards the gate in silence. Happiness soared in Josh. Ever since he had caught a glimpse of Marika at the guard house returning from Cornwall, he had, in a way, been certain this would happen.

Marika turned to him under the shadows of the chestnut trees.

'I have a confession to make.'

'Oh yes? You are married with twins?'

She smiled. 'Don't be silly. I changed my running time to the afternoon in the hope that you would speak to me.'

He pulled her closer. 'Did you now?'

'But you never stopped.'

'Ah, but I take my training very seriously! And I couldn't bear to seem too keen, or to get the brush-off.'

'Would you have ever spoken to me if I had not smiled at you tonight?'

'Oh yes. I saw you at the guardhouse once, but you didn't see me. The cheeky bugger on duty said you were out of my league, but . . .'

Marika kissed his mouth and retreated quickly. 'Every day I see you running. I watch you in church and in the mess and once in town, but you never come over to me. Everybody but you . . .'

Josh wound his arms round her and she leant against him, closed her eyes.

It seems to have taken so long to be here, in this place.

Josh. She had practised his name silently on her tongue. He was dark, enigmatic. A clever face that gave little away . . . a fantastic body . . . So many good-looking officers buzzing round her like bees, except him. *And now, this.*

She sighed, and they continued to the gate where their taxi waited. Inside it Josh picked up her hand.

'I guess,' he said carefully, 'I was afraid of making a move. Also, truthfully, I am preoccupied with passing out, Marika. A lot rides on it. Acceptance in the regiment of your choice . . . and it's bloody physically demanding . . .'

'Oh, I understand. I am in the middle of my finals,' Marika interrupted. 'It is not the right time to get involved, I know this. But I also know that I must have you . . . to . . .'

She searched for words. 'For the future . . . so we don't miss each other. Do you understand?'

Josh grinned. 'I think so. You mean it's not the time to get involved at the moment, but we can sort of make a claim, a declaration of intent, for later?'

Marika laughed. 'Yes, yes. Something like that.'

'So what are we doing tonight? Having supper, forming an understanding . . . then saying goodbye?'

'No. Tonight, I hope, we are sleeping together because we must.'

Startled, Josh laughed nervously. 'My God, Marika, you don't beat about the bush, do you?'

'That is what my stepfather says to my mother. But, you see, we have lived with war and so we must not lose a moment in English reserve. We say what we mean.'

As they paid the taxi, Josh thought of the complications of sleeping with the Commandant's stepdaughter, while knowing it was exactly what he wanted and was going to do. They booked a room in the best hotel and ordered room service as both of them were starving. They pooled their limited resources, giggling. One night here was practically one week's wages. But, as they said later, it was worth every penny to circumnavigate weeks of socially circling each other. It also felt right. No awkwardness, just an immediate feeling of belonging. They lay and talked in the dark impersonal room, and Josh felt happier and more relaxed than he had for months.

'You do not talk to your friends about this, I hope?' Marika said sleepily.

'You are joking?'

'How lovely if we could stay here all night together.'

'We've got a whole lifetime.'

'Yes. How is it we already know each other?'

'Haven't a clue. You're a witch.'

'A white one.'

'Of course.' Josh sat up and looked down at her and felt suddenly overwhelmed. 'You are the most beautiful woman I've ever seen, Marika. How am I going to bear it, knowing that every other male will be lusting after you?'

'First, I am not the most beautiful woman, there are squillions, and secondly, it is the same for me.'

She sat up and held his face. 'It is the same for me. I think you are the sexiest and most lovely man *I* have ever seen. I've noticed the way girls look at you, and you have that air of not being interested which makes you irritatingly irresistible.'

'Do you think it possible we could be biased?'

'I'm not.'

'Well, I'm certainly not.'

'What if we had been terrible in bed together? You know, one of those fumbling farces?'

Josh did know, only too well. He laughed and got out of bed. 'It wasn't going to happen. It is something you instinctively know. It's chemical.'

'Like an experiment?' Marika sat up and jiggled the bed up and down happily.

'Marika, get dressed! We must watch the time. I don't want to do extra orderly officer, even for you.'

Marika made for the shower. 'Do we just brazenly walk out of this hotel together? How do we leave with dignity?'

'I'll order a taxi while you shower. Then we walk down to reception with utter aplomb and say that we have just had an urgent phone call and must leave immediately, and I'll pay the bill while you go outside for the taxi. Of course, they know perfectly well, we have no luggage, but we leave insouciantly with panache.'

Marika nodded gravely. 'We leave with insouciant panache. Got it.'

Josh threw her dress at her. 'GO! Shower quickly!'

In the taxi, Marika suddenly looked vulnerable. 'I leave at midday tomorrow, back to Durham. I won't see you at church tomorrow, Josh. Uli's driving me to London because the Sunday trains are crap from here.'

'I've got your mobile,' Josh said. 'I'll ring you while you're on the train. I'll try and ring you every day, even if it is a quick one. OK?'

'Don't lose my number. We can text, too, and I could leave messages, couldn't I?'

'Of course you can. After my passing out and your finals, we'll take off. Goa, perhaps – somewhere right away, just the two of us.'

'Don't forget me, Josh.'

'No chance of that. I've been head-over-heels in love with you for weeks. Love at first sight.'

'Well, I loved you before I even spoke to you.'

'Clever girl!'

They hugged each other until the taxi turned into the married quarters. Marika slipped out and ran to the front door, turned and blew a kiss and was gone.

Josh could not sleep. He could still smell and feel her in the dark. Would he be able to focus tomorrow? Thank God it was Sunday. Only church parade and curry lunch in the mess. Then a long ride . . . He thought of home. Charlie, Gabby, Nell. They seemed so far away, like a different life.

As he began to fall asleep, he saw clearly, in one of those moments when it is difficult to know whether it is fantasy or truth, a glimpse of his own future. He saw himself in an unknown landscape. There was a woman beside him who had a small child by the hand. Her stomach was swollen and distended with another. The dream was erotic and visceral; that woman, those babies, his. The dream or fantasy felt so real and sensual that Josh was desperate to hold on to it in the dark, but it slid away into oblivion leaving a strange hollow place where it had been.

Chapter 22

Mark stopped for a moment before he opened his front door. His plane had been delayed and he had rung Veronique to tell her he would make his own way home. Usually one of his daughters came to the airport to meet him, as Veronique did not like driving at night. As he sat in the taxi he marvelled at the way in which a journey home could seem like a small act of loneliness.

This feeling was immediately enhanced as he put the key into the lock and pushed open the front door. The noise of conversation, of voices raised in rowdy debate, hit him. A wall of sound, not deafening but eager and involved.

He leant against the inside of the door, outside the pool of light, looking down the hall into a kitchen full of daughters, sons-in-law and children. A small girl sat at the large table among the remnants of a meal, drawing; a bunch of imported pink roses dropped petals on the tablecloth.

The conversation was political, good-natured and heated. It did not pause or slow, indeed no one had yet noticed him standing in the dark hall watching them. It occurred to Mark that he might be a ghost returning to see how life went on without him, and the answer was that it went on very well.

The feeling of dislocation he had had in the taxi returned, as if he had opened a stranger's front door and found himself in the wrong house and the wrong life. He felt a dramatic urge to turn and wrench the door open again and run out into the velvety night.

The small girl at the table, Mercy, her tongue wedged on

her top lip in concentration, raised her head at that moment from her drawing and saw him. She beamed and jumped off her chair, crying, 'Grampie! Grampie!'

She ran down the dark hall and Mark caught her, whirled her up in his arms.

'Hi there, tadpole!'

His youngest daughter, Nereh, peered round the kitchen door.

'Dad! You're back.'

Mark moved into the room and Veronique came across the kitchen to kiss him. She smelt of garlic and herbs and her lips tasted of red wine. He turned to three of his daughters, five of his grandchildren, two of his sons-in-law. Everyone talked at once.

'Chéri! We waited for you. Only the children have eaten.'

'What was the flight like?'

'Did you deliver your figurehead?'

'Have you been to the back of beyond?'

'How was London?'

'Grampie, Grampie . . . look, look, I've lost a tooth.'

'Well, I've lost two teeth . . .'

'Grampie, look, I've drawn a sailing boat with a head in front, eyes, everything . . .'

Helena, Nereh, Inez, Elle. Jean-Pierre and Mike. Mercy, Naimah, Daisy, Violette, and the baby, Flynn, Nereh's youngest. Tiny Flynn, who would be ruined in this household of women, eventually perpetuating in all his female grandchildren the historic and unfair role of the longed for male child.

Mark was drowning in a sea of voices, suffocating under happy faces and the sheer volume of noise. He took the wine Inez handed him over the children's heads. He felt deathly tired.

'Have I time to shower?' He smiled, ruffling heads, cheerful; jolly, even.

'Go!' Veronique called, smiling affectionately, turning from the stove to him.

But she does not see me. When did Veronique last really look at me or try to read what is in my face? Mark willed her to meet his eyes, register his tiredness, but she was already bent to the girls, to her grandchildren.

'Vite! Vite! Clear the table. Elle, fetch a new cloth. Inez; mats, candles. Jean-Pierre, will you see to the wine?'

Nereh, the baby crooked in her arms, saw her father was white with tiredness. She moved to the door. 'Dad, shall I run you a bath?'

They moved out of the kitchen and Nereh shut the noise firmly in. They stood in the dark hall.

'You're knackered, Dad, you just want to go to bed, don't you?'

Mark leant towards her and placed his index finger into the baby's tiny hand. For a moment, in the light of a passing car, Nereh saw a profound and sudden sadness in her father's face, then he turned for the stairs.

'I think a shower will jolt me awake. I might fall asleep in a bath, but thank you, honey. Put the hall light on, you might trip with the baby.'

'Dad?' Nereh called after him. 'I'll make sure we all leave straight after supper. I did suggest to Maman it would be better to leave a family meal until the weekend, but . . . you know Maman.'

Mark stopped at the top of the stairs. 'I do.'

He smiled down at the daughter most like him, at her sweet, open face, dark eyes and tight curls that made her look touchingly young. She grinned back, and then disappeared into the lighted kitchen.

What is the matter with me? Mark wondered under the shower. *Middle-aged angst? These are my children. This is my family.*

Dressed once more in clean shirt and linen trousers, he felt more human, less humourless. He took his mobile phone out of his briefcase and switched it on. It bleeped. A small envelope appeared: HOPE YOU HAD SAFE JOURNEY HOME, it said. Mark smiled and gently deleted the message.

In bed, later that night, his hand lightly over Veronique's hip, he thought, *I am jetlagged, that is all. All will be well in the morning.*

He woke early. Sunshine was slanted in little leaf patterns across the beige carpet. Veronique was still asleep. He slid out of bed and went downstairs in bare feet. He pushed his feet into somebody's moccasins, plugged coffee in among the chaos of the kitchen, opened the screen and outer door and padded out into the yard.

This was the garden he and Veronique had planned together and had filled with plants and tubs and trees over the years. Balls and toys lay on the lawn, wet from the dew. He saw a small rose was trampled and carefully pulled away the broken branch.

Out under the trees the grass was cold and wet around his ankles. A dove called somewhere. A summer sound. A sound of childhood. Long days running wild, when everything lay ahead, stretching out to a future both terrifying and exciting.

Everywhere he turned in this garden there was evidence of his children's children. Swings, play-pit, seesaw. Grass scuffed and trampled by small feet, netball nets.

He closed his eyes for a moment and tried to visualize an immaculate English lawn, a wooden bench, table and garden chairs. Flowerbeds full of subtle and delicious colours. No sound except the birds singing as he worked in his own peaceful, silent garden, empty of children and the trappings of childhood. Sometimes, *just sometimes,* empty of his children and his children's children.

Mark tried thinking of a time when there was only Veronique in this house. Only he and Veronique eating a meal, having a conversation; and he could not remember that far back.

He thought of a three-storey house by a river, the noise of traffic a gentle growl. A house devoid of possessions. Empty rooms with sunlight sliding across the polished floor from long windows. He imagined the pieces he would buy to furnish the rooms of that house, that was waiting for him to the sound of water.

No small footsteps dotting and carrying up the stairs. No toys and piercing cries. No chatter. Peace. Just him in another life.

Chapter 23

Isabella stared at herself in the mirror. The dress she wore was beautiful. Sewn into the bodice and gown were hundreds of small pearls. It fitted perfectly to her small waist. Against the darkness of her skin, which her aunt had always disliked, Isabella knew it looked well. She was like a portrait of a grown-up woman she did not recognize.

She stared into her own eyes as if they belonged to another. During the last few weeks she had lost weight, and her eyes seemed too big for her face and had shadows beneath them.

Isabella thought of Helena, of how she should be beside her this day. But she would not be here in this room if her mama were alive. She would not be in this house. She would be in her own house about to marry a man she loved. She closed her eyes quickly against her reflection. This was no time to remember Mama.

She moved to the window and looked out across the garden to the bay. The sea was like glass, too little wind for the white and tan sails of the small boats idling there. She looked across to the far side of Helford Passage. Verdant green fields and woods rose up from the water. She remembered the day she had arrived here, and that, despite her sadness, she had seen how beautiful it was.

From the open windows of the drawing room below her she could hear laughter and chatter. Soon she would have to walk down the aisle in her wedding dress and everyone would turn to stare at her. Isabella felt unsure she could bear it.

She heard her father's voice and she tried to swallow the bitterness that rose up in her. She tried not to think of this as a second betrayal. For a moment she wondered what would happen if she changed her mind, if she refused to go down the stairs, get into the carriage, walk into the church. If she refused to marry a man nearly as old as her father.

Her heart jumped for a moment in hope. Then she thought of the consequences of having to stay here and they were more unbearable. There was also Sir Richard Magor to consider. He might be old – Isabella suspected he neared fifty – but he had always been kind to her.

There was a knock, and then the door flew open and Sophie burst in. Isabella's small cousin stopped in the doorway and gasped.

'Isabella, you look just like a princess. Why are you alone? Where is Lisette?'

'I was thirsty so she went down to the kitchen to find me a drink.'

Sophie shut the door and came into the room. 'Mama is coming presently to help Lisette with your veil.'

Isabella sat carefully on her dressing-table stool so that she did not crush her dress. Sophie was watching her intently in unaccustomed silence. Then she leant towards Isabella and said urgently, 'Isabella, you do not have to do this. You look so sad in your wedding dress. I wanted to talk to you before Mama comes. I am sure she would learn to understand if you have changed your mind. So would your father ... if you told them you are so unhappy ...'

She trailed off. The words hung in the air and even Sophie did not believe them. Isabella smiled for the first time that day. Sophie was the only person she would truly miss. This youngest, plainest daughter; the clever one; the only one who did not resent her in any way.

'You know I cannot remain here, Sophie. Your parents have been good to have me for so long. I am grown up and not their responsibility.'

Her father, confronted once more with the problem of what to do with Isabella, had made it plain that he intended to re-marry, to a woman called Charlotte Flemming, the daughter of a friend.

Sophie turned away, paced the room anxiously.

159

'It is my mama who has driven you to this. You cannot help it if you are prettier than my sisters and far less stupid. It is as if she thinks you attract all the attention on purpose ...' She came and knelt in front of Isabella, her small, sweet face earnest. 'I cannot bear you to throw your life away. You have been pretending you are happy to marry that old man all these months. I am so angry with your papa, Isabella. I am sorry to speak of him like this but he is grown into a very selfish man indeed.'

Her voice was so portentous in a girl of fifteen that Isabella laughed.

'I think Papa is a man who is afraid of growing old and being alone in that huge house.'

Isabella got up from the stool and pulled Sophie to her feet, shook her hands so that she listened to her.

'Sophie, in a moment your mother will be here. I made a promise to marry Richard Magor. I am not going to change it. I cannot remain here and I cannot return home ... Help me to be strong ...' Isabella's voice wobbled. 'I need your friendship today, Sophie, more than I ever have. There are things I cannot change and I must make the best of them. I will especially need you when I return from Italy to my new home.'

Sophie's eyes filled with tears. 'Isabella, he is so old, how will you bear ...?'

Isabella interrupted her cousin swiftly. 'He is kind to me, Sophie, and I believe he will go on being kind. I am going to live in a beautiful house by the sea. It is not so bad, and we can see each other often, can we not?'

'Of course! I will come whenever you need me, Isabella.' She hovered at the door. 'Isabella, at night when I cannot sleep, I have such strange and lonely thoughts. What is the purpose of being a woman, apart from having babies? No one takes us seriously. I wish I had been born a man.'

Before Isabella could reply to this outburst, Sophie heard her mother downstairs and with a small moan disappeared quickly down the corridor to her room.

Lisette came in carrying a tray of tea for Isabella. 'The kitchen is in turmoil. Your aunt is displeased with the flowers and Cook is having an argument with Tilly. For pity's sake, Miss Isabella, you should have had this tea before we dressed you. Do not spill it down your dress. Wait, wait, I will cover you.'

Lisette threw a sheet over Isabella and she took her tea gratefully, for her throat felt parched.

Lisette watched her anxiously. 'Now, let me throw your veil out upon the bed ...'

Isabella waited. She knew Lisette well. She wanted to talk to her of intimate things but was having difficulty finding the right words.

'I will be in the new house waiting for you when you return from Florence, Miss Isabella. Botallick House is a beautiful house, is it not? I believe you will be happy there.'

'Yes. I am so near the sea I can walk to the beach from the garden. Did you know that, Lisette? There is a hidden path down to a small private cove. It was once used by smugglers.'

'Indeed, Miss?'

'Yes, it is true.'

'I believe you will feel much ... freer at Botallick, Miss Isabella, to be yourself. Why, you will be your own mistress!'

'I think it will be very peaceful there. I believe I will grow to love that house.'

Lisette said gently, 'I believe, too, Miss, that you will grow fond of Sir Richard, for he seems a kind man.'

Isabella's eyes suddenly filled with tears. She bit her lip hard, but could not answer. Lisette made herself busy straightening her veil, then she said in a little rush, 'Miss Isabella, at first ... relations in marriage are not ... easy. It grows easier with time. Your mother is not here, so I ... I will tell you little ways of being more ... comfortable. Do you understand me?'

Isabella nodded. She understood only too well. 'Thank you, Lisette.'

It was a thing she tried not to think about. She had looked at women of her acquaintance who were married to old or ugly men and they appeared perfectly content, so it could not be too dreadful. Perhaps these women kept their eyes firmly shut.

Isabella's aunt appeared at the door, positively joyful at the prospect of her niece's departure, and today her voice held no edge. There had never been open hostility from her, she was much too well-mannered, but it had been implicit and had grown worse as Isabella got older. .

Her aunt bustled round her. 'You look very well, Isabella. Very well indeed. Your father will be proud of you.'

'Thank you, Aunt.'

Isabella hesitated, then, risking rebuff, she said, for it was true, 'Aunt, I know it must have been difficult to have yet another girl in your household for so long and I thank you for taking me in.'

Her aunt's face grew red with surprise and something else Isabella might only guess at, for her aunt and her father were very alike in their transparency.

'Isabella, you are my brother's only child, what else would I do but welcome you into our house? Now, come along, it is time to leave for the church, your father waits downstairs.'

She touched Isabella's arm briefly. 'I wish you happiness, Isabella.'

Lisette adjusted her veil. Isabella wanted her to hide her face but Lisette would not let her do so until they had descended the stairs.

'You will break your neck, Miss Isabella.'

Daniel Vyvyan stood in the hall looking upwards. She watched his face closely. She wanted to see the pain in it, although she knew that it was wrong to have these thoughts on her wedding day. She was quite aware of how like her mama she looked today and she wanted her father to remember this day, always. To remember Helena. To remember that Isabella was her daughter, a part of the life they once all shared and he was renouncing for the second time. She wanted him to remember her, exactly as she was at this moment, untouched, before he gave her away to an old man.

Oh, the pain was there, making his face suddenly grey and old, but it gave Isabella no pleasure, only sadness. She reached him and Lisette pulled the veil over her head, hiding her face, and they walked together, father and daughter, out of the front door, down the wide stone stairs to the waiting carriage. Her father had not said one word.

At the church her cousins waited in their creamy primrose

dresses to walk behind her. Her father took her arm to walk her up the aisle.

'How did you grow so suddenly beautiful?' he whispered. 'My God, you are like Helena. It breaks my heart.'

It was as if he was seeing Isabella for the very first time as a grown woman.

The dark chill of the church was a shock after the warm day and Isabella shivered. All eyes turned to watch her. Isabella wanted to run. She wanted to run, screaming her mama's name, along the sea's edge. She wanted to be free of this. She wanted to be free.

Her father, feeling her tremble, squeezed her arm. They stopped in front of the vicar and her father vanished suddenly from her side as he had always done, and she was alone next to Sir Richard.

Her eyes, hidden behind the veil, did not have to express anything as she looked into his face. He took her hand gently between his own, smoothed it as if he wanted to smooth away the ache in her heart. Tears sprang to Isabella's eyes, rose up in her throat. She looked away, to the crucifix, to the vicar, and concentrated hard on his opening words. The tiny pearls on her wedding gown glistened and moved in the candlelight like thousands of tears.

Chapter 24

On Monday morning Gabby returned to the upstairs room of the museum and continued to fix the loose paint on Isabella, concentrating on the main damage around the neck and chest region. The gesso or ground layer beneath the paint was brittle and thick as it was chalk or gypsum based. She decided to use a weak solution of gelatine so that it would penetrate through all the layers. She had kept an eye on the temperature in the room and the humidity was stable so there was little danger of fungal activity.

Gabby had brought the small CD-player Nell had given her last Christmas and she put Beethoven on low. The day was heavy and overcast, the sun, trapped behind cloud and sea mist, pressed down making her head ache.

She had been tense all weekend. She had walked and gardened and fidgeted, guilt and astonishment at herself making her jumpy. Now, in the silence, away from the farm and Nell and Charlie, Gabby felt her limbs begin to loosen as she concentrated. A form of peace flowed through her and into her fingers, making them sure and steady.

She stopped working for a moment and went to switch her mobile on. *Just in case.* Her stomach lurched as the memory of Mark's hands reaching for her played, as it had all weekend, through her head. She had thought Charlie must notice the difference in her and had fought to seem normal as she discussed with him whether or not she should take work in London.

'It doesn't make sense, by the time you've paid your train

fare and accommodation, you'll be no better off, Gabby. Just exhausted,' Charlie had said.

'My accommodation is free, for this job anyway, and I'll get paid far more than I get down here.'

Nell had said quietly, trying not to interfere and failing, as she poured Charlie a beer, 'I would discount money, keep it out of the equation. You've been offered a job by a prestigious gallery, Gabby. Are you excited by the work? Is it interesting? Do you believe you can do a good job? Might it lead to more work? If the answer is yes to all these things, what do you have to lose? The only consideration you have is the figurehead. It must be in a condition to be exhibited at the end of June. That is your first responsibility. I would have thought you could manage both.'

'Yes, I could. I'm sure I could. The NPG already know I am committed to work on her for another two weeks.'

'I am not against you taking the job, Gabby,' Charlie had said. 'But you know what the summer is like. I'm out all daylight hours and I rely on you being here for whatever crops up. If you're away, all your jobs fall on Nell . . .'

'Charlie, for heaven's sake, we're talking about three weeks at the most. This is Gabby's future. You can't have it all ways. You are permanently trying to devise ways of bringing more money into the farm and restoring is how Gabby and I contribute.'

There was no answer to this and Charlie had been silent. Eventually, draining his beer, he got to his feet.

'Well, it's your decision, Gab. It's money, I guess, and as you say, it is probably a one-off. I suppose we can manage without you.' He had grinned at her.

'I'll be finished long before harvest,' Gabby had smiled back, feeling treacherous.

'OK. Go for it! I'm going to the office to catch up on paperwork. I'll shut the hens in for you.'

'Thanks, Charlie.'

'This girl from the gallery is ringing you again tomorrow?' Nell had asked.

Gabby had suddenly felt exhausted. 'Yes.'

'Go to bed, Gabby. I'll stick these in the dishwasher.'

'Sure?'

'Positive.' Nell had paused, carrying plates to the sink. 'I really don't think Charlie was trying to be obstructive, Gabby. He's just so used to having you around. Men are odd, you know, they rely on women far more than they'd ever admit.'

Gabby had stared at Nell, surprised. 'I didn't think he was being at all obstructive, Nell. I thought he was being very reasonable. He was only pointing out that if I swan off it makes more work for you, which is true. But it's doubtful this is going to happen too often, and apart from the figurehead I do usually work from home.'

Nell had thought later, Does Gabby ever think about what she actually does for Charlie? Things that he could very well organize for himself, or a housekeeper or extra cleaner could do. Roles, she thought, form such a comfortable habit that we stop questioning them and they become hard to break, like a comfort zone.

In the museum the phone bleeped. Text message. Gabby ignored it and went on working. After an interval that she judged businesslike, she went over to the phone. It was Josh, not Mark. Anxiously she scanned the message:

MET FANTASTIC GIRL LUV JOSH.

Gabby smiled. Must be fantastic to text your mother during the day. So Josh was, at last, smitten. She went back to Isabella and looked down on the face that gave nothing away. *What do you know about love, Lady Isabella?* Then, out of nowhere, the thought came; *Were you married off to an old squire and the young men could only paint or carve your likeness?*

Gabby gazed down on her, feeling sure she was right. She started to prepare a fine chalk-based filler, texturing it to match the chest and neck damage. She found herself murmuring to Isabella as she worked, almost believing Isabella was listening.

In the silent room, with Beethoven playing softly, the figurehead seemed tangibly real. Flesh and blood, like a second person in the room. A patient lying flat, while the doctor bent working over her, stitching her deftly together, healing her wounds, mending the ravages of the past.

When Gabby left the museum at the end of the day the heat haze which had never lifted had swallowed the sea, locking the village into the landscape, muffling and distorting the disembodied voices coming eerily above the throb of the engines of the returning fishing fleet. The evening seemed diluted, like a child's watery painting, the colours running into each other, blurring all edges.

Gabby drove slowly, unwilling to return home. She stopped to do some food shopping and as she climbed back into the car, the phone rang.

'Hello?' she said breathlessly.

'Gabriella! Tell me if it's a bad time.'

'No . . . It's fine, really.'

'I just wanted to say "Hi", and to hear your voice.'

Gabby closed her eyes, said inanely, 'You got home safely?'

'Sure. I got in last night. How are you doing?'

'I'm driving home after a day with your Lady Isabella.'

'How's it going?'

'Very well, but it's looking doubtful whether we'll discover any more original paint. I'm just waiting for the last of the tests I sent to be analysed.'

'Looks as though Valerie Mischell was right, then?'

''Fraid so. Mark, you know the girl, Lucinda Cage, at the National Portrait Gallery? She rang and asked me if I would try to undo some of the damage to that painting she showed us, before their exhibition in July.'

'Hey, that's wonderful. Congratulations! I hope you jumped at it?'

'Yes,' Gabby said smiling, 'I did.'

'When are you going?'

'When I've completed restoring the first phase of Isabella. In about two weeks.'

Silence at the end of the phone and then Mark said, 'I'm still going to be over here. Oh, what bad timing, Gabriella.'

'Yes . . .' Gabby said. She had been hoping, perhaps . . .

'Is there any chance of you getting more work with them?'

'Well, maybe, if I'm lucky. And if they're happy with my work.'

'If I could get back earlier I would, but . . .'

'I know.'

'I have to go . . . I miss you,' he said softly.

'Me, too.'

'We'll speak soon. Take care, Gabriella.'

'Mark, thank you for ringing me.'

'The pleasure's mine!' She could see him vividly, head slightly on one side, his eyes laughing.

The sea fret began to lift to reveal a pearl grey sea like a millpond. Her headache had miraculously flown. She realized that in accepting Lucinda's offer in London and waiting all day for that one telephone call she had made a definite declaration of intent. A deliberately placed foot forward.

Chapter 25

Charlie always enjoyed ordering in new strains of daffodils. Their very names conjured up exotic images. He walked the fields where the daffodils had remained unpicked so they could die back into their roots. After three years all daffodil fields had to be alternated or disease would get into the bulbs. He had spent the morning with Alan, ordering in from the catalogues, and now he wanted to inspect the fields that had lain fallow.

Two fields away towards the coast he could just see Jason ploughing, oblivious to all but his music playing full blast on his earphones. He'll be deaf before he's thirty, Charlie thought, watching the furrows the boy was ploughing critically.

The morning was unusually still, what his father used to call a 'given day'. He paused, whistling to Shadow and Outside Dog to wait. Leaning on the gate he gazed into the shimmering horizon. From this gate he could look across his land in every direction. It was the highest point between the sea and the farm.

There was no sound except the birds and the distant tractor. He squinted upwards at a bird of prey above the hedge of the next field. It hovered, waiting to swoop, deadly as an arrow . . . there it went sure and true to its prey, too small for Charlie to see.

He thought suddenly of Josh. What a difference it would make if he could have gazed across this land knowing he was going to hand it over to his son. He still hoped, he could not help himself. Something deep inside him refused to believe he would be the last Ellis to farm this land. There was a remote chance that if Josh had a son . . . but Josh would not be able to turn his back forever, Charlie was convinced of that.

It was odd. When Josh was small, and all the time he was growing up, it had never occurred to Charlie that Josh would not want to farm. University, yes; Josh was a bright lad. Gap year, travelling a bit, that he could have understood; it was a rite of passage for the young. But the army! Charlie turned away from the gate abruptly and continued walking the edge of the daffodil field. The shock when Josh told him. He had laughed at first; had been about to say, *Good one, Josh.* Then he had seen Josh's face, miserable and anxious.

'Why the army, for God's sake?'

'Dad, it's something I've been thinking of for a long time. It was just hard to tell you.'

'The army is a bit different from being a cadet at school, Josh. I know you enjoyed all that, it's a part of growing up.'

'More than enjoyed, Dad, I loved it.'

'So is this the result of the recruitment officer bending your ear?'

'He didn't have to. There are so many opportunities in the army . . . Dad, I want to fly. I want to fly helicopters.'

'There are the same opportunities outside the army. You are deliberately going to waste a good degree.'

'Rubbish, Dad, it's because I've got a good degree that the chances of promotion are higher. Everything is computerized and highly technical now. It's not Dad's Army.'

'I can't see why you have to join up. If you don't want to farm you could just as easily be a civilian pilot.'

'I'm joining up because I like the whole ethos: the challenge, the fitness, the competition, the camaraderie, the whole life, Dad. Moving on, new postings; it's what I want to do with my life. I'm sorry.'

Charlie had stared at him, then said bitterly, 'Can you so

easily turn your back on all this? The Ellises have farmed here for generations.'

Josh had stared back, unflinching. 'I know. And each year it gets harder to make a living. It's not a job, Dad, it's a way of life. It's like a yoke round your neck. I love this farm, it's my home, but I don't want it. I'm sorry, I'm really sorry, I knew you would take it badly.'

Josh had turned away, upset at Charlie's white face.

'How the hell do you expect me to take it?' Charlie had bellowed. It felt like a precious gift had been thrown back in his face, somehow devaluing it. It was like being slapped by the most important person in your life. Charlie was reeling. He had gone off for the whole day, in turns furious with Josh and then deeply hurt.

Farming was all he knew and had ever wanted and he could not understand how Josh could give up this inheritance. He had thought the day Josh told him, and he thought it now, *If only I had two sons, or even a daughter*.

His deeply buried secret resentment surfaced. He blamed Gabby. It wasn't much to ask, after all he had . . . Here he stopped, guiltily admitting unfairness, but if someone could get pregnant by mistake, surely they could get pregnant one more time. Surely one more pregnancy wasn't too much to ask?

Secretly he also blamed Gabby for Josh's choice of career. Nell and Gabby had mollycoddled him, encouraged him to travel, to enjoy things outside the farm; put ideas into his head.

Nell had said to Charlie, 'It's not personal, Charlie. Josh is not sticking two fingers up at our way of life, just choosing another life.'

'How can I take it, but personally? How the hell do you expect me to feel?'

'I mean that Josh choosing the army isn't a slight. It's not done to hurt you, although it must have done and that has made him thoroughly miserable. It was hard for him to come and tell you, Charlie, probably the hardest thing he has ever had to do.'

Charlie was not listening. He went to the pub that night and drank morosely until closing time, whereupon the publican drove him home.

The field still carried the strong scent of daffodils. He used to walk here with Ted as a small boy, and the smell could take him straight back to total recall of his father's face and his old tweed jacket and cords, pipe in his mouth, flat cap on his head.

He made his way slowly to his Land Rover parked on the far side of the field. How could Gabby bear to be in London in summer? Odd she did not seem to mind the days spent inside working in a city. At home she could never bear to be inside for long, and the doors and windows would stay open from dawn to dusk.

He had never imagined she would have a real career, just dabble at her picture restoring. She was such a hermit and had from the day he married her hated being away from the farm for long. Then, suddenly, when Josh left she seemed to grow more confident of her skills or perhaps it was the figurehead that had been the start of the change.

Gabby had been going up and down to London three days a week now for three months, and she did not seem to be getting tired of it. With her work in Cornwall she was, for the first time, making real money. Charlie admitted this helped to compensate for the fact he had to make his own breakfast when she was away; fend for himself; do all those irritating little jobs he'd never had to do before; or Nell had done for him and seemed to think he could manage for himself now.

He opened the back of the Land Rover and the dogs leapt in. There had been a little write-up in the local papers about the figurehead.

'You must be proud of Gabby. Isn't she doing well?' people said to him in the village.

'Got to pull your own weight now, boy,' the old boys joked in the pub. Gabby had been the only wife who took his lunch to the fields in the old days when they were first married. Lunch and tea at harvest. He smiled. Gabby had always been good like that.

These days she came back from London all excited and hyperactive. She rushed around trying to make up for her absences, cooked meals to save Nell the trouble and put them in the freezer. Ran about cleaning the house as if she could not stop still; and she was definitely losing weight. She and Nell talked endlessly about paintings. It seemed to Charlie that restoring was becoming a bit of an obsession.

People also said, 'You must miss her?' He did, but he missed the slow-moving, hesitant, dreamlike Gabby; that was the person he missed. He was used to that person. He was not sure about the new confident Gabby, it made him uneasy.

For the first time ever Gabby was not going to be home for the weekend. It was Elan's preview on Friday evening and she was staying up in London to support him.

He stopped in the lane and looked at his calves. They were coming on beautifully. Charlie began to whistle contentedly. Darts match tonight and he was playing cricket on Sunday. It had been a good summer so far; he was even paying off the bank. Not a bad life. Not bad at all. He wouldn't change it. One day when Josh was his age he would regret his decision. Charlie had no doubt of that.

Chapter 26

Josh, coming down the stairs of the Hershon Gallery where Elan was exhibiting, caught sight of the back of a woman who seemed familiar to him. She was half turned away from him as she stood inspecting one of Elan's paintings. She was wearing a stunning, very expensive-looking little black number and strappy little shoes. Her dark hair was shiny and cut to just under her chin. David, beside him, was staring at her, too. Her arms were tanned and something about her was exotic, relaxed, sexy.

At that moment she turned smiling to the tall, dark man beside her, and Josh saw with a sick shock that it was Gabby. Rooted, he could not tear his eyes away from her. He felt a strange falling away, a glimpse of a person he did not know, a snapshot of someone other than his mother. He wanted to turn and run out of the gallery, but he could not move.

'Do you know her?' David asked, seeing Josh's expression.

'Yes, I know her,' Josh said under his breath.

'Well, come on, introduce me. Wow! I want to be her toy boy.'

Josh was so angry he wanted to slam his fist into David's jaw. He was going to leave now, quickly, before Gabby saw him; but at that moment his mother turned his way. A strange thought flashed through Josh's mind as Gabby saw him. For one second, he wondered, *Is it really her? Is it her double?* Gabby had had her hair cut and she never wore clothes like that. *Is her face going to fall with shock at the sight of me?*

Gabby gave a start, her eyes widened in shocked surprise,

then she gave a small instinctive squeak of pleasure and rushed towards him holding her arms out. She was hugging him, smiling at David, turning to introduce the man she was with.

'Josh, this is Mark Hannah. He brought the figurehead I've been working on back from Canada. Do you remember? I told you about it.'

Josh breathed out suddenly. *God, I'm stupid.*

'This is my son, Josh,' Gabby said proudly. 'Darling, what are you doing here? I thought you couldn't come tonight?'

Josh grinned and relaxed. 'You've had your hair cut! I didn't recognize you!' *It was all right. It was bloody all right. For a second he had thought ... but it was only Gabby in work mode. How extraordinary to see it for the first time. As if she was someone quite else.*

'This is David Matthews,' he said. 'We're on the same course. I thought I wouldn't be able to make it, but our last-minute rehearsal was changed to Sunday, so change of plan.'

Gabby shook David's hand. 'We've been here quite a while, we were just leaving. Elan's done some wonderful work.'

'Is he here? I was hoping to catch him. I bet he's done a bunk as usual?'

'I think he might have. He didn't think you were coming. I tried to persuade him to have supper with us but he was sloping away somewhere.'

'Trolloping off, was he?' Josh grinned, turned to David. 'Elan hates his own previews. I'll just go and see if I can find him, he might have got waylaid.'

'We were just off to eat round the corner, in that little Italian place. Can you join us when you're done here?' the man called Mark asked. He had an American accent.

'I can't, I'm afraid,' David said. 'I'm meeting my sister and some friends at Marble Arch – it's her birthday – but you stay, Josh, we'll meet up later.'

Josh said quickly, 'No, let's stick to our plans. Why

don't we have a quick drink with you, Gabby, when we've finished here?'

Suddenly and unaccountably Josh did not want to eat with his mother and a stranger, and the tension was there in the back of his neck again.

'Fine,' Gabby smiled at them. 'See you both later. Elan's done terribly well; lots of red dots already.'

Later, much later, Josh, David, David's sister and a group of her friends, erupted from a club and drunkenly got a taxi to David's sister's flat to crash. When Josh woke sober and with a dry mouth early the next morning, he lay thinking about that strange meeting with Gabby and the Canadian.

The man had been charming, neither too friendly nor too interested. He was much older than Gabby, older than Charlie, too. Josh had watched him with Gabby. He had no reason to think they were anything but two people who worked together. But something niggled at him. Why wasn't Gabby going home tomorrow? It was the weekend. Why, apropos of absolutely nothing, did the man, Mark, carefully introduce the topic of his family as if he was afraid of what Josh might be thinking? And, if he had thought Josh might be suspicious, did it make it true?

Josh felt a strange, sharp pain at the memory of his mother looking young and . . . really great. So great that David had gone on about it.

Your mother was your mother and she had no right to look . . . attractive to people of your own age.

He was used to having a young mother. He had been proud of it at school, but his eyes had been sharply opened by the fact that Gabby had a life he knew nothing about away from the farm, away from Nell and Charlie; away from him. *An entirely separate life.*

He knew it was incredibly childish, when he'd left home, had his own life. What did he want? Would he like Gabby to be patiently waiting in familiar surroundings, doing what she had always done, keeping to a routine he knew like the back

176

of his hand? The gentle rhythm of his childhood remaining the same each time he went back home, to be sure somehow that Gabby's life revolved around his?

The answer was yes, yes he did, and Josh was appalled at himself.

Chapter 27

There were times when Isabella felt like a spoilt child with too many toys. She had more clothes than places to go. She had two horses. She had a gardener who had been told to humour her every whim, which did not endear her to him, for she knew nothing about flowers although she was trying to learn.

Some days she thought she would turn into her own grandmama before she reached twenty years. Time passed slowly like a meandering, infinite summer. Isabella felt suspended, like a dragonfly hovering in one place over the river. There was nothing to complain of save that her life seemed to have little purpose.

Botallick House, Richard's family home, lay above the mouth of a small creek near Falmouth. The windows at the front of the house faced down to the small quay and natural harbour, where sailing boats and small trading schooners were moored. When Isabella was in the garden she could hear the boats swinging about on their anchor chains, moving and turning on the tide, their rigging clinking and whistling in the wind. It was a comfortable, lazy sound, somehow reassuring for she found sailing folk to be jolly and friendly.

Richard kept his own small sailing boat down there and occasionally Isabella would go out with him if the weather was calm. But she was not a natural sailor; she mistrusted the sea having grown up on the north coast and seen what a calm sea could so quickly turn into.

Her husband, however, was in his element. He respected the sea but appeared to have no fear of the sudden unexpected savageness of tide and wind despite his adventures as a naval captain, which he was fond of recounting to Isabella at length, usually at meal-times.

Unlike her father, who rarely conversed at any length with her mama, Richard would talk animatedly of his plans to Isabella.

'My love,' he would burst into the room, disturbing her day-dreams, her book-reading or gardening. 'My love, what did you think of Sir Penrose? I saw that you talked to him at length last night. Women are so good at defining character. Is he trustworthy? Does he have a steady heart, do you think, for the business of investing in trading vessels? Is he a fair and honest man?'

Isabella would consider slowly and seriously for she knew that her husband had already made up his mind and hoped only that she would verify his own opinion. She also suspected that if she had talked too long with any one gentleman at dinner, Richard needed to know what she thought of him. She had learnt to be measured in any approbation and careful over any reservations she might have. Generally, though, she gave her honest opinion, especially if she thought her generous husband was being exploited or that his assessment of character was awry.

Isabella did not believe there was any schooner or brigantine that Richard did not know and revere. He was interested in all manner of shipping and in business he was very astute, this she had learnt before her marriage from her father. Daniel Vyvyan had been so impressed by Richard's success with trading schooners that he had taken up a partnership in one.

Her husband owned four two-masted schooners of his own which traded around the British Isles, South Wales, the Scottish coast and Ireland. He traded in all manner of diverse goods: coal, tea, slate, furniture, farm implements, drink and foodstuffs.

Richard was Devonshire-born, but as well as inheriting Botallick House he still owned a small family summer house in St Piran where many of his ships were built or refitted. His larger vessels, the three-masted schooners, were jointly owned by three or four families who held shares in the ships. Indeed, Richard had taken out shares in Isabella's name and taken the time to explain exactly what this meant.

This year he was having a ship built in Prince Edward Island in

Canada, for the wood and labour were cheaper. He planned to take emigrants out to the colonies in this new schooner and to bring lumber and exports back in the empty vessels.

The trading ships disgorged such a strange assortment of cargo upon the beaches and harbours. Lisette and Isabella set off sometimes to Falmouth to watch the vessels unload. It was a veritable treasure-trove, a meeting place of diverse utilities and personal items. Candles, salt, bags of nails, soap, a piano, a toy horse, a puncheon of rum.

Smuggling was rife everywhere, but Isabella could not blame these men, for the mines had been closing for years as the tin had dried up. She had heard that the farmers were resorting to violence at the wilful export of foodstuffs needed here at home after poor harvests. Drink, of course, was the most smuggled item. The coastguard had recently found ninety kegs of rum as well as tobacco and wine in a cave just below Botallick House.

All these little things diverted Isabella's days. They also helped her to view an outside world she had never been a part of, only viewed from a distance, only glimpsed from a vantage point of a large house.

Richard appeared before her one day.

'Tomorrow,' he announced excitedly, 'I have a surprise for you. Leave the morning free, my love. We will ride together into Falmouth.'

'Tell me!' Isabella begged. 'I cannot wait until tomorrow. Please?'

'Indeed I will not,' he placed his hand on the back of her neck. He was very pleased with himself, 'for then it will not be a surprise.'

Isabella moved slightly away, for his hand was heavy. He squeezed her arm. She could not move away again or she would hurt his feelings. The shadow was back; she did not like his touch and tried hard to hide it, not to shiver. His hands were large and in private, in their bed, she felt as if he was going to swallow her. She closed her eyes, banishing the image of a pig bending to the trough. He was so eager and excited and clumsy and she was repelled.

Lisette, without a word exchanged between them, had helped Isabella with this difficulty. She left porter by his bedside so that he often fell asleep before he could turn for her. Lisette also

180

explained to Sir Richard that Isabella had always slept badly and must have a room of her own where she could toss and turn without disturbing him.

Of course this did not stop Richard visiting her, but Lisette, who always seemed to know, would leave her a small glass of milk and brandy. Isabella took it like medicine and it enabled her to float away from her body, to detach herself from what he was doing.

Afterwards, when Richard slept or had gone back to his own room, Isabella would cry silently for a thing that was taken from her, a thing she could hardly bear to give. Then she would be angry with herself. This was her husband. It was his right.

That night, during his expected visit, before the promise of tomorrow, Isabella tried hard to hide her revulsion and the act was blessedly quick. As he slept beside her Isabella tried to think of what his secret could be. She was more than a little intrigued.

Chapter 28

Gabby watched Mark. He was moving the small desk they had just bought on the Portobello Road, a little to the left, then a fraction back to the right, so that it was exactly in the middle of the small alcove of the sitting room. She smiled at his concentration, his total absorption in the smallness of the task, in the exactness of its position.

She sat curled up on the sofa with the Sunday papers. It was early evening and the birds were singing their nightly hymns outside. She was soporific from the wine at lunchtime and quietly exultant to be there, to have had one whole weekend with Mark before he flew to Paris to see one of his daughters.

Through narrowed lids she watched his languid movements. He was wearing a coffee-coloured short-sleeved shirt and his cream linen trousers. He wore clothes as if they were a second skin; effortlessly. His arms, dark against the shirt, were muscular from chopping logs in cold Canadian winters. They gave Gabby a frisson, made her want to leap off the sofa and bite gently into the flesh of his forearm just to hold his skin between her teeth.

Mark, feeling the intensity of her gaze, turned and met her sleepy half-closed eyes and was stopped by her feline languor. They stared at each other, both in awe of this endless craving they had for one another.

Then Mark was across the room, bending and pulling Gabby to her feet. He lifted her up the stairs and threw her gently on the bed. Laughing, they pulled at each other's clothes and threw them over their heads onto the floor.

It was like having a fever, Gabby thought, as she bent to his mouth; a wonderful, terrible, insatiable, burning fever that consumed and seared the flesh. *You. You. Only you.*

They slept lightly as the summer day faded, their bodies curled around each other, perfectly still, as if they had both stopped breathing. They were holding these moments of a stolen life with care as they always did when they were together.

Behind their eyelids as they lay in the rumpled bed, their other lives played in the background like a slow-moving film. Gabby dreamt of a purple evening sea, engine sounds carrying over the water as the small fishing fleet made for the harbour.

She could almost smell, in this London house, the cows ambling back down the lane to their field after milking, flicking their tails against the flies. She tried not to think of Nell and Charlie moving about the yard or kitchen, for her heart would jump guiltily with sharp sadness.

She was cheating. She was no longer the person they thought she was, she had become someone quite else, a woman grown clever at secrecy and evasion. Nothing seemed to touch her when she was with Mark. Guilt came on the train home or when she was alone.

As the summer slipped by, Gabby had got bolder, less hesitant and less guilty about spending time with Mark. She travelled up to London on the early train on Monday, going straight to the National Portrait Gallery or wherever she was working that week.

Sometimes she could work from home, in the house by the river, and she restored in a corner of what had been the dining room, watching the river outside and listening to music.

Mark had a desk in the bedroom above which also looked down on the water. On the days when he was writing and not lecturing they worked companionably in the house together, both disciplined but very aware of the other in the silence or with soft music playing.

They would stop for lunch and walk by the river, hardly

daring to breathe or articulate their happiness in case some God was listening. But there were also long days when they left the house early and got back late, battling back tired through the rush of the city. Sometimes they met in a wine bar to wind down, eat supper and make their way home together.

And although it was all new, this life they shared until Thursday, it sometimes felt to both of them as if they had done it forever.

On Thursday Gabby caught the train home, used the time to do her paperwork. Back at the farm she had a late lunch with Nell, took a long walk with Shadow to ease her back into the familiar routine. She would tackle the chaos of the house, answer any messages left for her. Ring Mark.

On Friday and Saturday she delivered or collected paintings, restored in her workroom, washed and ironed Charlie's clothes and did any jobs he had asked her to do on the farm. On Sunday Nell made her lie in and cooked Sunday lunch and she went to bed early for the train back to London on Monday morning.

Mark, on his own in London, wrote, went to an exhibition, lunched, had supper with colleagues, missed Gabby.

The previous Thursday Gabby had felt unwell and had rung Nell to say she thought she was coming down with flu and would stay up in London. She had sounded dreadful and Nell, worried, had said, 'You're doing too much. I'm trying to get you help in the house.'

Gabby had slept for two whole days. By Saturday she had felt wonderful. She and Mark had had a leisurely weekend with time to wander about together slowly with no particular aim. Just having fun. Gabby was reluctant for it ever to end. She had stopped spinning through her two lives and relaxed. Mark always managed to surprise her with plans for their days together, taking her as a tourist around a London he knew better than she.

They walked hand in hand the wide London parks that separated the city, and breathed in the space and the trees;

sat on benches and talked and talked of other cities they might visit together one day. They peered through the railings of private gardens, wandered along wide roads and looked down into expensive basement kitchens where lives so different to Gabby's were lived.

Once they had stopped fascinated to watch a little Asian boy on a kitchen stool playing the violin, and the sound of the music issuing from below the pavement in the dusk was somehow surreal.

They went to the theatre and Mark had introduced Gabby to opera, carefully chosen because she was unsure. She had loved being enveloped for an evening, loved the splendour of it and never got sick of emerging into the West End at night, with all the lights that defied the shadows, the endless excitement and bustle of a city that did not sleep.

Lucinda and Gabby were often given tickets for exhibitions and spent their lunch hour in the galleries Gabby used to read about in Cornwall with longing. She saved the catalogues to show Nell, feeling constantly tired but vitally alive, loving every moment of this city life.

Mark's thoughts also returned home on Sunday evenings. He saw a faded cream clapboard house, its possessions spilling out into the yard full of children's toys and rugs and old garden chairs. The house would be bursting with friends drinking beer in small groups in the leftover day. His daughters would be traipsing in and out bathing small children, who would reappear in their clean pyjamas smelling of baby powder.

The smell of cooking would pervade the house as his daughters and Veronique filled the table with too much food. The sacrosanct Sunday meal, all the family together, children scrambling into seats or being placed into baby chairs; the noisy sound of a close-knit family, chatting, laughing, arguing, doing what it did week in and week out with little variation, because they all enjoyed being together and took such pleasure in the sheer weight of their numbers.

Mark ached for the loss of a need to be there with them,

part of it all still. It frightened him, this strange disconnection with his family; flesh of his flesh. They were the wife and children he had worked his butt off for; *they were the meaning of his life*. Always had been. Five successful, bright daughters; happy, as far as he could tell, with their lives.

They are the meaning of my life. Not any more. The sentence formed itself, chilling him with its certainty. Was he other than himself, then? Was this a passing fantasy, this life he might have led with this woman in this London house? If he had been younger, single and available?

Was he subconsciously angry with his family for existing, for being in the way of . . . ? He smiled cynically at himself and opened his eyes. *Don't go there. Don't start all that crap*.

On the wall opposite he had placed Elan's two paintings. They were the first thing he saw in the morning and last thing at night. Apt. *Before and after*.

His eyes wandered round the bedroom. He had found the small nursing chair in a junk shop and had had it re-covered in yellow brocade. There was a small built-in wardrobe and a neat chest of drawers with brass handles he had bid for in a sale. On it Gabby had placed a vase of sweet peas which he could smell in little waves from the bed.

The floor was polished and had two cream rugs either side of the bed. No clutter, minimal furniture. The house could breathe and so could he.

He turned over carefully so that he did not wake Gabby and propped up on one elbow to watch her sleep. He could never get used to the smallness of her: her dimpled hands, like a child's; the slimness of her wrists which he could encircle twice with his fingers; her newly cut hair, a shiny dark bob that framed but did not hide her face, heightened her cheekbones. He felt choked with love. If only it was just sex. But it was not. It was not.

Gabby's shoulder was cold and he pulled the covers up over her. He got out of bed and padded to the bathroom for his robe and went downstairs. He went to the fridge, pulled out a bottle of wine and opened it, held the glasses up to the dusky light from the window to make sure they were clean. Polished them quickly with a cloth, watching himself performing these pedantic little domestic tasks with surprise.

Why? To preserve an illusion of perfection that did not exist? He did not know why he was suddenly giving weight to unimportant things, behaving in this slow and precise way; as if each simple task he undertook was somehow giving validity to normal everyday life here, making it real and tangible and *true*.

See, here are my hands doing the things people do every day, all the time, making a careful symmetry, finding a certain place in the house I share with Gabriella, for these are the small objects that unite us.

In the tiny garden a tortoiseshell cat sat watching him hold a perfectly clean glass up to the dying light. He filled the glasses and went back up the stairs. Gabby was awake and lying on her back in the almost dark. Mark placed a wine glass on her bedside table and she sat up, reached out to him, and placed her mouth into the palm of his hand. His long fingers almost covered her face.

He felt her tears and did not move, closed his own eyes against the ending of this. When she let his hand go he moved away, lit one small bedroom lamp and got back into the bed beside her. Gabby smiled and lifted her glass to him, wanting to banish the Sunday-evening blues, where church bells rang and children telephoned their parents. Where families gathered for scrambled eggs and bad television. *Where people were where they belonged.*

'Skol!' she said, wrinkling her nose at Mark.

'Bottoms up, old fruit!' he replied, and their eyes met in an understanding. They snuggled down together in the bed.

'Tell me the story of how you came to live in Cornwall,' Mark said.

'It's a boring story, honestly.'

'I'll be the judge of that, madam.'

Gabby giggled. 'Went for a holiday, never really left. That's it.'

Mark peered down at her. 'Well, if you are going to be obtuse, tell me about your childhood.'

'Nothing to tell. Nothing.' Her voice had changed. She moved abruptly and picked up her wine. The room was suddenly silent, full of distance.

'I'm sorry, Gabby . . .'

'It's OK. I never talk about my childhood, Mark. Never.'

The face she turned to him was devoid of expression. It was not a face he had seen before.

He touched her cheek. 'I'm sorry,' he said again.

Gabby did not answer. She moved closer to him, tight into him as if she wanted him to absorb her. Mark stroked her hair rhythmically and she ran her fingers down his body suddenly, surprising him; bent down to him, making him groan.

'*Fuck me*,' she whispered. '*Now.*'

What the hell demons am I slaying? Mark wondered.

They slept, woke, got up to eat, went back to bed with their books. Josh rang Gabby on her mobile. She got out of bed and walked onto the landing, and stood in the dark talking to him. Officially she was staying with Lucinda.

Gabby shivered with guilt as Josh relayed his week . . . Sunday evening, cleaning kit time . . . passing out was getting near . . . the sergeant-major was an absolute bastard. He was marching in his sleep and dreaming he mucked up at Chaos Corner . . .

'What's Chaos Corner?'

'It's a corner of the parade ground notoriously difficult to manoeuvre. It's where we all have to turn, but it's so tight everyone usually ends up colliding with the guys in front.'

'Well, if everyone always mucks up, it's nothing to have nightmares about. You'll all go down like little spillikins!'

Josh laughed. 'Gee, Gabby, I feel a whole lot better now.'

'How is your love life? Will we meet her?'

'Hope so, but she's in Durham and it's exam time, so my

188

love life consists of e-mails and texting. I can't wait to take off on holiday . . .'

When he rang off Gabby ran a bath and she and Mark both got into it, giggling and squirming and threatening to flood the bathroom. Then they returned to bed.

'I don't think I have ever spent so much time in bed.' Mark was laughing, relieved Gabby was happy again.

'Bed is an island. Some days I think about going back to bed all day. Bliss! Utter bliss!' Gabby wriggled down under the covers, picked up her book, but did not read.

'Your favourite place?' Mark asked lightly, bending and kissing her nose.

'I spent ninety per cent of my childhood in bed,' Gabby said suddenly, with a small shrug. 'I used to lock myself in my bedroom so my bed became home.'

'A safe haven?' Mark asked gently.

'A safe haven, until I got to Cornwall. Josh was the reason I never left.'

Slowly, hesitantly at first, Gabby started to talk to Mark of her long-buried childhood with Clara. Not everything, never everything, but it was a beginning.

Chapter 29

It was the spring of her A-level year when Gabrielle decided she would go daffodil picking. She knew nothing about it, but one of the supply teachers had come from the Scilly Isles and had put up a wonderful poster in the art room. Green fields full of yellow daffodils with a backdrop of aquamarine sea. It looked idyllic. Gabby imagined herself in skimpy shorts and tee-shirts getting a tan against that exotic horizon. Bending and picking vivid yellow flowers in tiny green fields with groups of cheerful pickers.

She had one overriding need – escape – and she had planned it for weeks. She was on study leave so she was able to catch a coach to Cornwall before the school officially broke up for Easter. The daffodil season was short and she wanted to earn as much money as she could.

In the dark she had unlocked her bedroom door, stepped over the various sleeping bodies, left a note for her comatose mother and crept out for the early coach to Penzance.

She never reached the Scilly Isles. By the time she reached Penzance the weather was appalling, the ferry had been cancelled and she could not afford the crossing anyway. She had seen from the coach various large signs on the roadside saying, 'Daffodil Pickers Wanted'.

With desperate courage, pretending she was much older, she booked herself into one of the numerous bed and breakfast places in Penzance, and the next day, after asking her landlady the way, she took a bus to the farm. The farmer refused to take her on. He wanted experienced pickers who worked quickly and he could tell at a glance she was a city girl.

That night, huddled in her room surreptitiously eating fish and chips, Gabby saw in the local paper that held her chips that other farms were advertising. Her landlady told her there was a shortage of pickers due to the government clamping down on immigrant labour. There were swooping inspections now for foreign workers without papers.

The next morning Gabby hitched a lift to the farm. She had looked at a map in Smith's and decided to go as far off the beaten track as she could. It was a bleak, dismal morning and the wind bit into her face, stinging and vicious, making her gasp. The sun had not shone once since her arrival and the entire world seemed to be encased in cold grey cloud.

By the time she reached the farm down an endless rutted lane, her rucksack felt like lead. She was cold and wet and already unsure what on earth she was doing. Two dogs barked wildly in a farmyard that seemed deserted, but away on the other side of the farm buildings, in a large, sloping field sheltered by hedges, she could see two covered wagons and figures bent in the rain to the yellow-green rows of daffodil buds.

A woman came out of the farmhouse to see why the dogs were barking. She was wiping her hands on a cloth and smiled across at Gabby shivering on the other side of the gate.

'Are you a picker?' she called.

Gabby nodded earnestly.

'Come into the yard, the dogs won't hurt you.' The woman shouted at the dogs and Gabby pushed the gate open and walked in.

'You'll need to see my husband,' the woman said. 'At the moment everyone is up with the wagons.'

She stared at Gabby and smiled. 'You do look cold and miserable, come in for a minute and I'll make you coffee.'

The kitchen was warm and fuggy and smelt strongly of

turps, as did the woman herself. She went to wash her hands at the sink.

'Tea or coffee?' she asked.

'Coffee, please,' Gabby said, leaning against the warm Aga. The woman reached in front of her and lifted a huge kettle off the hob and poured hot water on instant coffee. Gabby was to remember the smell of that coffee and of turpentine and dog as the moment her life began to change.

'If you don't mind me saying,' the woman said, 'you don't look like a daffodil picker. Have you done it before?'

'Well, no,' Gabby said. 'But I'm a hard worker and I can learn fast.'

The woman smiled at her doubtfully. 'It really is back-breaking work. Where do you come from?'

'Oh,' Gabby said quickly, 'I'm staying with friends in Penzance for Easter and I wanted to earn a bit of money, before I go to uni . . .'

Gabby's heart raced at this outright lie. She was unnerved by the way the woman was looking at her. She disliked lying and the woman was kind. She gulped down the hot coffee gratefully, in silence.

When she had finished the woman said gently, 'I can hear the tractor. It's probably better if you wait outside and then you will seem more like a seasoned picker. Good luck . . .'

'Looking for work?' the farmer asked, walking towards her. He was an unsmiling man in his forties.

Gabby nodded.

'Don't suppose you've picked before?' He was looking her up and down.

'No,' Gabby said, for there was no point lying.

'I'll take you on trial for a week.' His lips twitched in an imitation of a smile. 'Most don't last that long.'

He bent and uncoupled his trailer of picked and bunched daffodils and hitched another empty trailer to the tractor. He motioned her to get into the trailer and then he went into the house.

Gabby stood miserably in the trailer as an icy wind blew

192

at her from the sea. She was cold and hungry and the day had not even started. The farmer and his wife came out of the house together and the woman handed Gabby a small bag.

'It's a piece of cake, I should eat it now. Once you start picking there is virtually no stopping until the end of the day.'

The farmer started-up the tractor and they lurched up the lane towards the yellow daffodil fields. He pulled in behind other wagons that were filling up with the tight green buds and Gabby climbed self-consciously out of the trailer.

'Now,' the man said, 'I'll start you off with a seasoned picker and they'll show you how it's done. There's a knack and a speed to it, some people get the rhythm of it and some don't. The ones that don't, don't last. It's too tiring and you won't earn enough. A good picker can earn thirty to sixty pounds a day. I pay five pence a bunch. There are no stops other than a half-hour lunch break. A wagon will pick you up at the end of the day and take you to the end of the lane at five p.m. for the bus. We start at seven-thirty in the morning. Come this way.'

He hesitated and looked down at Gabby. 'Some of the women are rough and you'll get some stick, so it won't do to be too sensitive. Just close your ears and pick.'

He called over to a boy and he stopped picking. 'Go over there to Jason. Off you go.'

'Right,' Jason said, 'what's your name?'

'Gabrielle.'

'Too posh, I'll call you Gabby. Now, you mustn't pick too short or too long. The stems must be of uniform length. Ten stems a bunch. Here are your rubber bands. Pick and bunch like this . . .'

He bent and his fingers moved deftly, picking the stems swiftly at the same place and bunching them expertly with a leaf before going on to the next. He made it look easy.

'Either put your bunches on the ground as you go and collect them later or move them along with you and put them in the basket at the end of a row.'

Gabby bent and picked quickly. Ten stems a bunch. Two heads of the daffodils broke and as she tried to bunch them the sticky sap from the stems stuck to her fingers and they fell in a heap at her feet. Jason smiled, not unkindly.

'I should get some gloves, the sap can irritate. Don't try to go too fast. Pace yourself the first day and don't expect to earn much. Fast-pickers – some can pick with two hands – get the best rows, I'm afraid. OK, let's get on. You work those four rows . . . I'll be over there.'

Gabrielle looked quickly across the field at the other pickers then bent her head and bent and picked, bent and picked. She was so slow the boy Jason was way in front of her. She picked for hours without establishing any rhythm. Her hands stung with the sap and she had great trouble picking stems of even length. Bunching them up was even worse.

She was so thirsty her tongue stuck to the roof of her mouth. How on earth was it possible to go a whole day without food or drink? It was slave labour, that's what it was, she thought miserably. Then she noticed the pickers had water bottles in their pockets and would throw their heads back at intervals to drink.

Jason walked back along the row and offered her a drink from his bottle.

'People don't drink more 'an they need for obvious reasons. It's over there if you need it.' He pointed to a corner of the field which held a small blue mobile loo. 'It's time lost.' He looked down at her little heap of daffodils.

'You are not doing bad. Keep at it.'

The day stretched into eternity, punctured by the wind and the murmur of odd snatches of conversation or ribald teasing. Gabby could not feel her feet or her hands; her back felt it was going to break in half and she wanted to howl her misery into the wind. And this was only the first day.

Then, as if by some silent, magical signal the pickers stopped as one and began to leave the field, carrying their last bunches of daffodils to the wagons. Each bunch was counted by one of four men. The farmer's wife who had given Gabby coffee sat at the wheel of one wagon, ready to drive them to the road. Embarrassed, Gabby clutched her miserable bundles and queued like the rest.

'No good. No good. OK. No good. OK, OK, OK. No good . . .' the man at the trailer chanted when Gabby placed her bunches before him. Twenty bunches OK, five substandards. Ten pounds ten. Seven-thirty tomorrow.'

Four pounds fifty! For a whole day's work! Gabby shook with tiredness.

'You'll do better tomorrow,' Jason said, appearing suddenly by her side.

'No she won't!' a woman behind her cackled with scorn. 'You can smell 'em a mile off. *One-dayers*. She won't be back, will you dearie? Look, she's nearly in tears! She'll run back to daddy as fast as her legs will carry her . . .'

'Shut your mouth!' Jason said abruptly, and swung Gabby up into the trailer taking them to the bus.

'Ooooh!' There was a chorus of laughter. 'Jason's in love, Jason's in love!'

Gabby could feel her face burning. She just wanted a hole to open up so she could disappear into it.

Jason said quickly, his own face red, 'Don't let them get to you, or they won't stop. Ignore them.'

Holding on to the edge of the trailer Gabby shook with exhaustion.

The bus was waiting at the top of the lane. The farmer's wife smiled at her.

'Well done,' she said kindly.

Gabby fell in the door of the bed and breakfast with only one thought: bed. She was even too tired to be hungry any more. Olive, the landlady, came out of the kitchen when she heard her.

'Look at the state of you, my bird!' she exclaimed. 'Get in my warm kitchen and I'll make you a brew.'

She sat Gabby down and put a mug of steaming tea laced

with sugar before her, and then she turned to the stove and began to fry eggs and bacon and sausage. As soon as Gabby smelt the food she realized she was starving.

'Get that down you!' the landlady ordered.

'But,' Gabby started to say, 'I can't . . .'

'Hush your noise and eat. I don't want paying for a bit of eggs and bacon, for heaven's sake. I know what picking daffs is like, believe you me . . .'

She paused and watched Gabby eat. The girl was small with a thin childlike body encased in mud-splattered jeans. She said quietly, 'I've just got one thing to ask you. Do your parents know where you are? Sorry, my bird, but I don't believe you're nineteen. I've had daughters myself. I think you're still at school. Am I right?'

Gabby nodded. This adventure was not turning out to be fun. The thought of another long day picking was a nightmare. Gabby wished she had thought of anything but daffodil picking. When she had finished eating the woman brought the phone over to the table.

'Ring your parents. Whatever you think, they'll be worried sick.'

Gabby felt dismay. Her hands on the white cloth were stained and they stung. She stared at them. *She couldn't, wouldn't go home.*

For a moment Gabby did not move, then she pulled the phone towards her.

OK, if it makes Olive feel better.

She dialled. It rang for a long time. Relieved, she was about to put it down when a man answered. There was laughter and music in the background.

'Wait a minute,' the man said when Gabby asked for Clara.

Gabby could feel Olive watching her. Pride and shame pricked her eyes, made her suddenly hot and flushed in the close room.

Please, God, don't let her be . . .

'Gabby? Where the hell are you?' The voice was thick and slurred.

'Did you get my note?'

'What note? What did it say?'

'It said I was going to Penzance. I left it in the kitchen.'

'Penzance? What the hell are you playing at?' Clara's voice was rising. She had obviously not sobered up enough to even realize Gabby had gone.

'I was just ringing in case you were worried . . . to tell you I'm in Penzance,' Gabby said in a slow false voice for Olive's benefit. She could hear people calling her mother. She could hear the music getting louder, hear the raucous laughter. She could picture the scene exactly. She had lived it a thousand times. This was the end of lunchtime drinking. The evening for Clara had not even begun. Gabby waited. Clara laughed, called out to someone and put the phone down on Gabby. Gabby hesitated then carefully replaced the phone in its cradle. She would rather be in this shabby kitchen – safe – than in her room which she had to lock each night.

'It's OK,' she said, refusing to meet the woman's eyes. 'It's cool.'

The woman got up, touched Gabrielle's shoulder gently and began to clear their plates away.

'Go and have a bath, the water's hot. It will warm you up. If you want to come back down and watch the telly, feel free, dear, I'm on my own tonight.'

In bed, in the dark, Gabby thought, *The first day is always the worst . . . It may be warmer tomorrow. I'll get used to it. Or I'll look for something else. I'm not going home. I'm never going back. Nobody will ever do that to me again. Nobody is going to touch me with their drunken, filthy fingers ever, ever again. I'd rather be in the daffodil fields.*

She thought of her friend Amanda, the only person who had suspected something.

'You can't give up your exams, Gabby, this is going to affect the rest of your life. What's happened? What's made it worse at home? You've only got one year to go, then you are free of your mum and you can go to uni.'

Gabby had been silent. A year was too long. It was not something she was going to talk about to anyone.

She moved down in the bed and tried to sleep. Her back ached and the sap had brought a rash out on her hands making them itch.

Downstairs in her faded kitchen, Olive Trelaw hesitated over the telephone and then pressed redial. Was she meddling or just being protective of that small, thin, sad-eyed little thing? A woman answered. There was a lot of noise in the background and Olive wondered if it was a pub. Clara's voice was slurred and when Olive said, 'I am sure you must be worried about your daughter,' the woman became offensive. Olive put the phone down.

An almost forgotten, bitter anger rose up in her. She had had a daughter she loved and that daughter had been snatched away in a random single act of violence. How could this drunken woman take her child for granted? How could she not care? How dare she get drunk and abandon a vulnerable teenager to this dangerous, uncertain world? If children could not be protected by their parents, who could they trust?

She would never forget the look in the girl's eyes earlier as she had replaced the phone. She had wanted to gather her up and tell her to stay here with her; she would look after her. But she couldn't. Just because she'd lost her own child it didn't give her the right to interfere in lives she knew nothing about. All she could do was keep an eye. That was all she was entitled to do. The girl reminded her of a deer – startle her and she would be off and over the horizon.

Gabby woke at six, bleary-eyed. She dressed quickly and crept downstairs. On the hall table she found a little worker's bag containing a flask and sandwiches with her name on it.

Gabby stared at it, tears of gratitude welling up in her eyes. As she ran for the bus station a small, warm place opened up inside her. It had been so long since anyone had done an intuitive and kind thing for her.

'Olive Trelaw was my first friend in Cornwall,' Gabby murmured into Mark's shoulder. 'She eventually contacted social services and became my guardian. I went to a sixth-form college in Penzance after Easter, when the daffodils were finished.'

'You went on daffodil picking? Brave little thing you must have been.'

'Not really. Nell took me into the barn to help her sort out the bunches; much easier.

'Nell was my second friend. Eventually, Olive became Josh's godmother and Nell became my mother-in-law. I never, ever went home.'

'And Charlie?' Mark asked softly. 'Where does Charlie come in?'

'He came back to the farm that Easter from agricultural college, that's how I met Charlie.'

'Fate, then? A third friend.'

Gabby was very still. Did a twenty-two-year-old boy suddenly pushing and rushing you into the hay barn on the way back from the pub count as a friend? But he had married her. He'd done that without any hesitation. That had been an honourable thing to do.

Gabby shivered violently with that familiar sense of betrayal. She had thought Charlie must be safe. Kind, like Nell. She had thought Charlie liked her, really liked her. He had said nice things, picked her out to talk to when he arrived home. She had almost glowed in the dark from the attention.

Then, all of a sudden, without any words at all, there she was on her back in the scratchy hay while he pulled at her knickers. He wouldn't listen. She couldn't make him stop or hear her small, frantic cries.

He hurt her, and in the end she lay quite still. At home she had known who the enemy was and fought hard. It was a

199

lesson too late to realize that an enemy comes in many guises. He had driven her home, back to Olive's, without one word. Olive gave her hot sweet tea and held her as she wept, put her to bed and then they talked and talked and decided to put it behind them, *because of Nell*.

Gabby had gone back to college, but not for long. Olive, white with fury, had then marched over to see Nell. Charlie was sorry. He had been very drunk and was truly mortified and ashamed. He had tried to make it right.

These things she did not say to Mark, but he watched the memory of them play across her face, caught her sadness.

He said, softly, 'I love you, Gabby.'

Gabby swallowed, raised her head to him. He had never spoken of love before. She said abruptly, holding his hand against her face, 'Olive died of stomach cancer when Josh was sixteen. An awful death, Mark. She deserved a better life. She gathered in waifs and strays and I loved her dearly. You should have seen the church at her funeral. It was packed, people had to stand out in the street . . . Oh, God, why am I telling you this? I never cry.' She sat up crossly.

Mark said quietly into the dark, 'Everyone cries, Gabby, if they are human.'

He was aware that what Gabby did not tell him was as important as the small pieces of her life he was allowed to glimpse.

Gabby turned her face to him. 'I am so afraid that you will go on a trip to see your family and they will reclaim you. You will never come back. It will be as if you have never been and I don't know how I will bear it.'

Mark, laughing softly, reached for her. 'I just told you I love you, Gabriella Ellis. Perhaps you didn't hear me?'

Gabby put her fingers over his mouth. 'I heard you,' she said fiercely. 'I was afraid of acknowledging your words in case a jealous God was looking down.'

'Oh, I see. Thank you for telling me.'

Gabby giggled. 'I love you more than I have ever loved anyone, Mark Hannah.'

Mark was silent and then he said lightly, for although he did not believe in jealous gods he did not want to test fate too far, 'Apart from Josh and Charlie and Nell, of course!'

'You know what I mean.'

'Yes,' Mark said, 'I know exactly what you mean, my darling, and I am afraid this cannot end happily ever after for all of us.'

'No.'

They stared at the image of their faces in the dark.

'I don't think I can sleep.'

'Let's go down and make coffee and walk out into a sleeping London and watch the sun rise and talk of happy things.'

Outside the window it was growing fractionally lighter. Gabby looked down at her fingers entwined with his. It hurt, this love. It was frightening, the power of it.

It was not just her life or Mark's life, but the heartbreaking, ripple effect of treachery on other lives happily going on as they had always done.

Mark brought her fingers to his mouth. 'We won't look too far ahead, Gabriella, or we will drown. Get dressed and I will walk you through a medieval London and tell you what shipping was like on the river in far-off days. It will be good practice for my lecture next month.'

Gabby bounced out of bed. 'My God, kick me out of bed in the middle of the night for a history lesson, why don't you?'

She was wiggling into her jeans, her small breasts bouncing, and Mark, watching her, said, 'On the other hand we could just go back to bed and . . .'

'Absolutely not! History lesson it is, I'm out of bed now. And stop looking at me like that!' She turned her back.

'What a shame.' Mark started to hum softly as he dressed. Outside, a new day was just beginning.

Chapter 30

Isabella could hear the rain before she opened her eyes; gentle, steady rain that brought a delicious smell of wet earth through the open window. She got carefully out of bed so that she did not wake her sleeping husband. He was snoring gently, curled in a large lump under the covers.

She was surprised when she went downstairs half an hour later to see that Richard was dressed, shaved and had had the horses brought round to the front door. His excitement was catching and they ate a quick breakfast together, both anxious to be on their way to Falmouth.

By the time they emerged from the house the rain had almost stopped and the sun was trying to break through the clouds. As they rode under the dripping trees Isabella turned to look at the garden, vividly lush and green after three weeks' drought. She sighed with pleasure for the long ride ahead and the beautiful morning opening up before them.

They rode in comfortable silence, but Richard seemed preoccupied and at intervals took out his pocket watch to check the time.

'Are we late for something?' Isabella asked, eventually.

'I think not.' He smiled at her secretively. 'I want to reach the other side of Flushing and be up on the headland within the half-hour.'

'Why is that?'

'Wait and see, my dear. Wait and see.'

Isabella pouted, pretended to be put out, for it gave Richard such pleasure to surprise her.

'Well, I think it is too bad to keep me in the dark.'

Her husband laughed. 'It is only for a little while longer, my dear.'

As they left the shelter of the trees and gained the top of the cliffs within sight of the harbour, Isabella was surprised at the roughness of the choppy green sea below her.

She looked out to sea and gasped at the sudden sight of two small brigantines and three schooners out in the Carrick Roads, headed for the harbour in full sail. Listing into the wind, huge white sails taut, they were flying across the sea like a flock of magnificent swans, their hulls seeming hardly to touch the water.

'Look!' she cried. 'Look, Richard. Where have they all come from? Why are they here? The bay is full of them. They are so beautiful!'

Richard was laughing. 'Indeed they are!' He turned to her. 'Come, we will have a gallop down the valley. I want to be at the harbour well before they arrive.'

'But Richard, they are moving much faster than we are.'

'Aye, they are, but they must reduce sail any minute now or they will sail straight past the harbour mouth. They will have to tack and mind they do not run into each other. That takes time. Come, let us ride.'

As Isabella turned her horse away from the sea and rode after her husband down the valley, she saw that there were streams of people on the coast road; in wagons, on foot or on horseback, all making their way steadily towards the harbour. So many vessels at once was an unusual sight even for Falmouth, for the larger ships usually made for Appledore or Bideford and the trade goods were then transported by train further east.

Once they reached the Falmouth road she and Richard were slowed by the volume of people hurrying excitedly along the promenade towards the harbour.

'Follow me closely,' Richard called to Isabella. 'I know a way round.'

'What is happening, Richard? Why are so many ships and people coming here today?'

Before Richard could answer, Isabella saw her father waving. His wife, Charlotte, was clutching his arm as if her life depended upon it.

'Papa is here, too!' she cried, surprised.

'Indeed he is. For you see, Isabella, every schooner in the bay belongs to our syndicate. These people here, so dressed up today, are all shareholders in those trading ships. Do you know how far some of those brave little schooners and brigantines have sailed? All the way from Newfoundland. Is that not something? I have organized this, so that your father and the other shareholders may see their investment and realize fully the true potential of sea trade, for it has always been the way forward.'

For a moment, Isabella felt disappointment. What was a syndicate to do with her? Was this her surprise?

All eyes were turned seaward to watch the first two schooners negotiate the harbour. Their sails were carefully furled and the first ship to come alongside had only a small foresail up. There was much yelling and encouragement from the bystanders, much prodding with oars and rushing about with buoys by the crew so that the schooner did not scrape her sides as she came alongside.

'Come!' Richard took Isabella's hand purposefully and people parted for them as they walked along to the end of the quay. Her father was smiling as he turned with Charlotte and followed them.

When they reached the schooner, Isabella looked down at the men busy on the deck and quayside making her fast. She was a pretty little ship, made of light, polished wood with a long sprit. She seemed neither too heavy nor too light and swayed steadily on the swell. Richard guided Isabella forward and with a flourish pointed down. There, in bold gold lettering, lay the name of the ship: *Lady Isabella*.

Isabella stared at it and then up at her husband's smiling red face. She was so moved, the tears sprang to her eyes. It was such a gesture of love.

'Oh!' she said. 'Oh ... what a lovely surprise ...'

She reached up quickly to kiss Richard's cheek. 'Thank you. Thank you. She is such a beautiful little ship.'

Richard looked down upon his wife. 'Indeed, how could she be otherwise? She carries the name of my wife. She must go to St

Piran to be fitted and finished off, but I think now is a good time to christen her, my love, in front of all these good people.'

A bottle of champagne was brought and tied with ribbon to the bowsprit. Richard instructed Isabella to throw the bottle at the side of the ship and name her.

'You must cry loudly, "I name this schooner *Lady Isabella*"!'

But Isabella felt suddenly overcome and her voice was soft as she aimed the champagne bottle at the side of the ship.

There was a cheer from the crowd and the men raised their hats and someone called, 'Three cheers for Sir Richard and Lady Magor! Three cheers for our trading vessels!'

Richard was still smiling down at Isabella, then he said quietly, 'This schooner is not just named after you, my dear. Your name is on the title deeds with mine. You own her, too. All the other boats are part of our syndicate, but not the *Lady Isabella*, she is yours and mine. And when I die she will be all yours, as will all the other ships I own.'

Isabella saw the startled look on her father's face. She was overwhelmed, for she understood the generosity behind Richard's words. She took his arm, hugged it to her with her eyes closed in gratitude. When she opened them she looked at her father. Her husband had made a declaration not only of his love but of her importance in his life. In that small ship he had given her an equal share. She was not a commodity to be handed on. She was Lady Isabella.

Her eyes were piercing as she stared at her father, for she was thinking too of Helena. Isabella remembered clearly her mother having to justify all expenditure to her father, despite bringing considerable money into his estate on her marriage.

He could not hold her gaze and looked away. Charlotte, Isabella knew, would fare no better financially than Helena.

Isabella turned, suddenly becoming aware of what was happening around her. The schooners, two berthed on the quay, three anchored offshore for some were flat bottomed, were disgorging their wares. Crates were being rowed ashore or carried from the quay and laid out along the shore for the crowds. The beach was as full of noise and barter as a weekday market.

That was what the crowds were hurrying into Falmouth for. Isabella would have loved to have gone among them to look at all the differing materials and foodstuffs being sold below her, but she knew there were too many people there today. The crowd, eager for a bargain, would end up in fights and drunken arguments.

At that moment, though, everyone seemed to have a sense of wonder and excitement in the strange and foreign goods emerging out of the small dinghies.

She looked up and saw a tall figure making his way along the quay. There was something vaguely familiar about him as she watched him approach. His walk was unhurried, almost leisurely. He walked the way a tall confident man walked, with a total sense of his own being.

Richard was suddenly beside her.

'Now,' he whispered, 'for the second part of my secret. Though I must admit this is perhaps more for my pleasure than yours, my dear wife.'

He turned to the man who had reached them and held out his hand. The man's face was tanned and his hair was bleached almost white by the sun.

'I am glad to meet you again, Mr Welland. This is my wife, Lady Magor ...'

Tom looked down on Isabella and there was shock in his face. For a moment he could not speak. Isabella stared back; she also was speechless. The moment hung, threatened to grow into something more, and Isabella hastily put out her hand and said, 'Tom Welland. It is a long time since we last met.'

Tom took her hand and held it. 'It is, my Lady. I am sorry, I had not expected it to be you.'

Isabella turned to her husband. 'Tom and his father used to work for Papa. He made my carved chest of drawers, the one I have in my room.'

'Indeed! Did he now? It is a pretty piece. I had not realized you knew my wife's family. Isabella, you will approve, then, for I have commissioned Mr Welland to carve the figurehead for the *Lady Isabella*. I want him to carve your face upon it. He has sailed

206

back with her from Prince Edward Island and he comes highly recommended by my brother.'

Tom was watching her intently, and under his gaze Isabella dropped her own.

She said, 'Did you and your father emigrate, then?'

'No, my Lady.' Tom appeared amused. 'My father is still at the boatyard at St Piran. I had an offer to work with the boat-builders in Prince Edward Island and I took it. We called in at Newfoundland for salt fish before we set sail for England.'

'Mr Welland has gained a reputation with his figureheads, Isabella. Now you have seen my wife again, do you feel confident you can carve a good likeness? It must be quite as beautiful as my wife.'

'That will not be difficult, Sir,' Tom said quietly.

Isabella's stomach gave a sickening leap. She suddenly wanted to be home. Under the thick riding coat, she burned. Tom was no longer the boy of her imagination and memory, but a grown man and in no way servile.

He was so intrinsically part of the day her mother died that Isabella could not look at him and not remember Helena lying so still against the rocks.

'So, let us make a date for you to sketch my wife. Is this how you start?'

Tom smiled. 'I have already chosen the timber from our cargo, and the wood is to be delivered to your shipwright, as you asked. I would like to come over next week if Lady Magor has the time. I begin with a sketch, but for the best result I carve from the real face, which I am afraid needs some of your time, my Lady.'

Isabella met his eyes, and believed they were so pale she could see herself reflected in them. They held amusement, as if he was still seeing the fourteen-year-old girl of his memory seated upon a nervy pony, not a grown-up Lady Isabella, eighteen-and-a-half, now the wife of Sir Richard Magor, ex-naval captain, aged fifty-two.

'My wife has time,' Richard said proprietorially. 'Let us make it Tuesday afternoon, say three o'clock or thereabouts. Is that as good a day as any, my dear?'

'I believe that day is clear, as far as I can recall,' Isabella said stiffly, mortified that Richard had highlighted the aimlessness of her days.

Tom Welland gave a small bow. 'Then I will see you on Tuesday afternoon, my Lady.' He hesitated. 'I am glad to make your acquaintance again.'

'And I you, Mr Welland. Please remember me to your father.' Her voice sounded odd and high but Richard did not appear to notice.

They watched him walk away through the crowd of people. Richard said, 'According to my brother, Tom Welland is a master at carving. He has come home to honour his commissions. He is becoming rather famous and we are lucky to get him. News travels fast in the world of shipping. I believe he is sought-after in the Mediterranean ports where they appreciate art of this kind even more than we do.

'Now, my dear, let us find your father and take some refreshment before we ride home. You look tired and must rest before our big dinner-party tomorrow evening.'

Isabella's mind was reeling. She would have liked to have galloped home then, on her own, but she could not. She could still feel the firm grip of Tom Welland's hand. She could still feel his eyes upon her, resting upon her, holding her own. She could still feel that swoop of familiarity as he touched her, as if they had been bound together in memory of that day so long ago when her childhood ended.

It was not just that Helena lost her life that dreadful day. It was also that she, Isabella, experienced her first and only overpowering rush of desire. So strong she had been careless of her mother. So strong that today, years later, her legs felt as if they might give way and tumble her onto the wooden-planked quay which held a small schooner that her husband had named after her in love.

At dinner that night, Richard said, concentrating on breaking his bread roll with undue interest, 'I had not realized that you were well acquainted with Tom Welland or that he once worked for your father.'

Isabella knew the tone of her husband's voice and replied carefully, 'I am not well acquainted with him. He carved my chest of drawers. A gift from Mama, that is all.'

Silence. Richard pushed his meat around his plate for a while, drank his wine. Isabella waited.

'It is just,' her husband said, still not looking at her, 'I somehow gained the impression you knew each other rather better than as acquaintances.'

Isabella felt suddenly weary and sad. This constant questioning of her was suffocating. She put down her knife and fork, gave up trying to swallow food she did not want. She said quietly,

'Perhaps my papa never told you that the morning Mama took me to the boatyard where Tom Welland and his father worked, was the morning she was killed. We had been to look at the chest of drawers Tom and his father had made for us. Mama's horse threw her as we made our way back home along the beach. A few days later Tom's father delivered my chest. He was so kind to me, for I was distraught. Papa blamed me for the accident ...' She looked her husband in the eye. 'If you saw any understanding between Tom Welland and me, Richard, it was because he too was remembering that last time he saw me, the terrible day Mama died. Everyone loved my mama.'

Richard closed his eyes. 'My love, I am so sorry, I had not realized ...'

Isabella scraped her chair back. 'Please excuse me, Richard, I am very tired.'

As she passed him she stopped. 'Thank you so much for naming your ship after me, it was a lovely surprise.'

She bent and kissed his forehead and was gone. Richard sat there, feeling ashamed. He had no heart for the cheese and waved it away. He must stop this confounded jealousy. He had a young wife, of course men were going to register it and be surprised, as the carver obviously had been. Time he got used to it instead of behaving like an adolescent.

He got up from the table and took his wine into the study. He remembered suddenly what an old friend had said on hearing of his marriage to Isabella.

'Many men will envy you your young wife, Richard, but I do not. When is a man to relax if not in his fifties? With a young wife you will notice every younger man in the neighbourhood. You will notice your increasing girth and your decreasing stamina and whether your wife be guilty or not of a roving eye, you will eventually accuse her of all manner of things, conjured by your feverish imagination and growing jealousy.'

Damn it, he thought, as he went to his table and viewed the huge map of the trade routes. I wish I had command of my feelings for my wife as I do over my ships and my business.

He lit a cigar and sat by the fire. He would not disturb Isabella tonight. She looked pale and tired after the excitements of the day. He would ask Lisette to take her breakfast in bed. He would go out early and pick one of his roses for her tray. She would understand that his tongue was only unguarded because he loved her so dearly.

Chapter 31

An icy wind blew across the parade ground, although the sun shone down on the anxious cadets standing motionless in rows. The excitement in the air was palpable. Josh felt sick. He had been chosen to carry the sword of honour. His hands in his white gloves felt slippery with nerves. *Please God, don't let me foul up.* He thought of his parents and Nell somewhere out there in the crowd and his anxiousness grew.

Charlie, Gabby and Nell sat leaning forward, peering at the ranks of sparkling soldiers all looking identical; most a sort of standard, medium size, a few short, a few tall. Charlie was looking through his binoculars.

'Can't make him out. Impossible,' he said. 'He could be anywhere.'

'Josh told us last night he was carrying a sword, in the front somewhere,' Nell said, clutching her hat as a gust of wind tried to whisk it off her head.

'But they are all wearing swords,' Charlie said.

'Maybe he carries one later on. I think he said he's got to hand it to some VIP so it can be presented to the best cadet.'

No wonder Josh had been nervous for weeks. Gabby sent out little calming mantras his way. She was glad now she'd decided against a hat. She'd found a tiny dark blue veil attached to a thin band, no more than a large slide which she had pinned to her hair. After many forays down Oxford Street she had also found a beautifully cut white suit, reduced because it was a small size and had not sold. Gabby was feeling wonderfully sophisticated in it.

Nell looked stunning in lavender, and even Charlie had been persuaded into buying a new suit, not gracefully, but when he had arrived that morning he was very glad he had. People were smart, very smart.

A small fleet of staff cars swished up the beautiful avenue of trees, little flags flapping importantly on the bonnets. The Commandant of Sandhurst emerged with various VIPs who got out of the other cars. A discreet murmur of anticipation ran through the crowd. The parade was about to begin.

For a second there was an absolute, tense silence. The waiting soldiers stood rigid, appeared to be holding their breath. Suddenly a loud, barked order cracked out into the silence and was echoed through the parade ground.

The soldiers jumped to attention and the guest of honour marched out with the Commandant to inspect the cadets. He walked slowly up and down the rows, stopping every now and then to talk to one of them. It seemed to take quite a long time.

'I wonder what he says to the cadets,' Gabby whispered.

'What's a nice boy like you doing in a place like this?' Nell whispered back.

Gabby giggled.

'Ssh!' Charlie said. 'Behave yourselves! I wonder if some unfortunate cadet is ever picked out for having something wrong with his uniform.'

'Too awful to contemplate,' Nell said. 'Oh how Elan would have loved this.'

'He would,' Gabby said. 'Such bad luck having an American exhibition at the same time.'

'Well, I expect he will enjoy the money,' Charlie said dryly.

The Commandant and the VIP were being escorted back to their seats, and there were more barked orders flung out into the wind. The ranks presented arms and were still again like clockwork soldiers. The band flared up and the men turned as one and began marching and turning, marching and turning in perfect unison. In and out of each other in tricky little sequences like a dance. No one appeared to put a foot wrong. The sight was quite spectacular and Nell and Gabby felt choked with pride.

Charlie, too, felt pride, and something else; respect for Josh. As if he had for the first time recognized his son as an adult, quite independent of him and the farm. No longer a boy. Making his own choices, sure of what he wanted from his life.

Charlie could not imagine what that felt like, to have to make a choice, because his life had been mapped out for him. It had never occurred to him to question his destiny. Perhaps, because it *was* right for him, he had never considered anything else. But Charlie also knew that he had never had the intellectual curiosity to look beyond what was offered, as Josh had.

Watching his son in the serried blue ranks before him, executing complicated manoeuvres, Charlie was struck by the discipline needed to be that perfect. He had always loved his son, thanked God he had a boy, but suddenly he was able to view Josh's life as separate from his own. Accept his decision.

Nell and Gabby were watching Chaos Corner nervously, worried for Josh, but they had no idea which group of cadets he was in so they watched them all bunch up together for a minute's irregularity in the spaces between them, then they were quickly back in formation again. Unlike Josh's stories, which he had relayed to them with relish, there was no catastrophe with rows of soldiers falling like dominoes.

Nell and Charlie were taking photographs and Gabby picked up the binoculars. She was suddenly sure that the cadet standing at the front of one squadron was Josh. She steadied them as the band finished and the soldiers halted and shuffled themselves into exact formation, equidistant to each other. It was Josh, she was sure of it. A soldier was marching up to him and giving him a sword lying across a military cushion.

213

'Charlie, look, it's Josh.' She handed him the glasses. 'Have a look.'

Charlie peered through them. 'Yes, I think so, but I'm not absolutely sure.' He handed them on to Nell.

The speeches began and prizes were handed out. Then came the sword of honour for the most outstanding cadet at Sandhurst. Josh marched forward on his own to hand the sword to the Duke, who then presented it to a cadet who had marched up to receive it.

Charlie said, picking up the binoculars again, 'Poor little sods, both their faces are as white as sheets. I can see Josh clearly now he is nearer.'

Both Josh and the star cadet marched back to their ranks. Everybody clapped, the band started up again and the parade was over. The cadets marched away and up the steps of the college, and disappeared inside the large entrance doors followed by a beautiful white horse, which shimmied up the steps and through the door after them like a horse in a fairytale.

'Phew!' Charlie said, impressed. 'That was quite something.'

'Wonderful!' Nell exclaimed. 'I wouldn't have missed it for the world, despite being totally baffled by why so many young men opt to be clones.'

'Honestly, Nell, you get more left wing the older you get, I don't know where it comes from,' Charlie said.

'From myself and from observing life cynically, which I am allowed to do at my age.' She linked arms with him. 'I'm teasing, I am inordinately proud of my grandson.'

They made their way slowly across the parade ground towards the college buildings. There was a little arrow on the map on their invitation cards where Josh would meet them for drinks. Nell and Gabby made for the ladies', and when they emerged Josh had found Charlie.

'Josh, that was spectacular and very impressive,' Nell said.

Josh hugged her. 'Nell, you look ravishing. And you, Gabby, I love your outfit.' He kissed the top of her head.

214

'It was wonderful,' Gabby said. 'We are all bursting with pride.'

A waiter appeared at their elbow with a tray of drinks and they stood looking around them. They were in a huge and beautiful room filled with the noise of hundreds of parents, grandparents and friends.

All very, very smart. A different world, Charlie thought, fingering his collar. *He will grow away from us. We will not be sophisticated enough for him soon.*

'All right, Charlie?'

Charlie took another gin from a passing tray and handed it to Josh. He held his glass up. 'To you, son! As Nell said, very impressive. Well done.'

Josh was touched. 'Thanks, Charlie.'

They looked at each other for a moment, then Josh grinned. 'I can't believe it's all over. I've passed out. Phew!'

He hugged Gabby suddenly. 'I've got my blue beret! Now I've just got to pass the flying course.'

'You're brilliant and we're not a bit biased,' she said.

As they entered the huge dining room, Gabby and Charlie felt suddenly daunted by the size and splendour, by the gleaming glass, the silver, the formality and the flowers.

Nell paused. It reminded her suddenly of a small piece of her childhood in India. *An immense table, each place decorated and laden with silver, bowls of frangipani petals filling the room with their pungent smell. Overhead, slow-moving fans lifting the edges of the tablecloth and her hair as she stood holding the hand of her Ayah, pausing for a minute on her way to bed.*

Josh sat between Charlie and Gabby. Nell was opposite and immediately into conversation with the man on her right. Gabby smiled at the man next to her. He smiled back nervously and leant towards her.

'If I use the wrong fork, lass, nudge me.'

Gabby laughed and relaxed. 'The same goes for me.'

There were natural gaps in the polite conversation and Gabby was glad for she wanted to watch and listen and store

215

this day of Josh's away, to take it out and examine it in the moments before she slept.

Josh would have girlfriends, he would marry; he would have a life she imagined but did not know and would never be familiar with. The closest person to him would be another woman. Their time together had gone and sadness rose suddenly in her like a lament for the child that had gone, for the simplicity of her life when he was small, the purity of pleasure in her child, the absoluteness of that love.

Even while she was living that time she could never take it for granted. She hugged herself close, neither looking forward nor back. Just living the days, drifting, allowing nothing to disturb the equilibrium of her time with her son.

Nothing must threaten the security of Josh's childhood. He must never doubt his parents' love. Unlike her, he must have a perfect childhood to look back on, to last him for the rest of his life.

She had never argued with Charlie as Nell had argued with Ted. The only time she would react was over something that affected Josh. She had been lucky, for Charlie had adored Josh from the moment of his birth so it had not been difficult.

Josh was saying something to her and she turned to him. He was working hard to put her and Charlie at ease, to ensure they were both happy and relaxed. How grown-up he was suddenly, how grown-up and excited about the life stretching before him.

'There's someone I want you to meet. She's come down from Durham especially to watch me pass out, and for the ball tonight . . .' His voice was anxious. 'The Commandant of Sandhurst is her stepfather . . .'

'This is the someone special?'

'Yes.'

'What are you two whispering about?' Charlie asked, turning back to them.

People were beginning to rise from the table and leave and

Josh got up, too. 'We'll go outside. I was just saying there is someone I'd like you to meet.'

They walked outside into the grounds. The wind had dropped and people were standing in little groups, or sitting on the grass. Some of Josh's friends came over with their parents and Josh introduced them, but he was distracted and kept looking over his shoulder.

Suddenly Gabby saw a tall blonde girl making her way across the grass towards them. She was exceptionally beautiful. Charlie's mouth fell open as Josh called out to her.

She was nervous, Gabby could see that, not overly confident in the way beautiful girls often were. Josh sprang towards her, his face lighting up.

'Marika!' He took her arm. 'Come and meet my family. This is my grandmother, Nell, and these two are Gabby and Charlie, my parents.'

Marika, startled, started to laugh. 'You call your family by their Christian names?'

Nell shook her hand. 'It is lovely to meet you, Marika. He always has. He was born precocious.'

Marika held out her hand to Gabby with a quick assessing look. 'I am so happy to meet you.' Her accent was too English to be English. 'You have all had a happy day, yes?'

'Wonderful,' Nell said.

Charlie was still speechless. He shook Marika's hand without a word.

'I think your fun is only just beginning,' Nell said, indicating a fun fair that was being set up on the other side of the parade ground.

Josh laughed. 'Nell, you are very welcome to stay.'

'Don't be so ridiculous! You would have a fit if I took you up on it. We'll be on the sleeper home before your ball even gets going.'

Charlie was still frantically trying to think of something to say that would not sound like an old man in a raincoat. His brain was not helped by the wine at lunch.

They sat in the sun with cups of tea, feeling reluctant

for the day to end. Josh could hardly take his eyes off Marika and she would turn from a conversation to touch his arm, leave her hand there. They were very conscious of each other but seemed comfortable, too, in the way some relationships were.

The way it is sometimes, Gabby thought, *a form of shorthand, circumnavigating courtship. I know you; I have always known you.*

Mark slid through Gabby's mind although he had been kept at bay all day because he belonged to another life, to a different woman called Gabriella.

That was a lie. Her other life moved like a second skin under her old. It was there always, like a hidden breath, even on a family day such as this. Part of her, moving with her, like her shadow.

Gabby got up quickly and crossed the grass to the room this male institution had made into the ladies'. She stood looking at herself. Her short hair was still a shock she had not entirely got used to. *She had always been so careful to guard Josh from hurt. She was not being careful now.*

Marika came in and they eyed each other carefully through the mirror, both acknowledging they needed to like the other.

'Hello.'

'Hello.' They smiled at their images through glass.

'I need to pee. Will you wait?' Marika asked suddenly and disappeared without waiting for a reply.

This girl could be the first to break Josh's heart. Gabby pulled out a pale lipstick. *Where are you, Mark, at the moment I colour my lips?*

Marika came out and over the basin she stared at Gabby quite openly, then suddenly conscious of being rude, she said quickly, 'Sorry! I had not expected you to be so young. It is a surprise.'

There was no answer to this and Gabby laughed and said, 'What are you taking at Durham?'

'History of Art. You are a picture restorer, aren't you?'

'I am. What do you hope to do with your degree?'

'I'm not quite sure yet. I may do something quite different for a while. Whatever I do needs to be something I can practise anywhere. I am Croatian.'

'You plan to go back?' Gabby asked, surprised.

'Not to live. But I want to go back to work for a while. My home does not exist any more. England is now my home. My mother and stepfather are here . . .'

She hesitated as if she wanted to say more, then smiled and held the door open for Gabby and they went back into the late afternoon.

Gabby asked her, 'How long have you known Josh?'

Marika was gazing towards Josh who was standing laughing with Charlie.

'Always,' she said under her breath, then quickly, 'A few weeks only. He has been down here and I have been in Durham. So . . . many e-mails and phone calls . . .'

She turned and faced Gabby. 'Because of the life I have led, time is a thing I do not trust. It can whisk away all familiar things if you let it. Love must be seized and held tight in the time that you find it, and never taken for granted in case it disappears.'

She dropped her eyes. Gabby was an Englishwoman who could not possibly understand where she was coming from.

'I am sorry. I must seem very . . . odd,' she said quietly.

Gabby put out her hand. 'No, not odd at all, Marika, just mature and very honest. Because of the life you've led, you've discovered what it takes most of us a lifetime to understand, and then usually too late . . .' Gabby's voice wobbled, 'You are right. When you find something good . . . each moment should be treasured for what it is.'

The girl took Gabby's hand for a moment, both somehow understanding the need they would have for each other, one day, in the future.

Josh drove them back to the hotel to collect their bags and then to the station for Paddington and the night train to Cornwall. He was off sailing with friends, then taking Marika to Goa. When he got back he would go straight off to Middle Wallop to learn to fly, but he would be home for Christmas. He kissed Gabby.

'It was such a lovely day,' she said. 'I like Marika, she *is* special, so take care of her.'

Josh's face lit up. 'She *is* amazing, isn't she?'

Josh and Charlie hugged awkwardly and then he enfolded Nell.

'I'm so glad you came, Granny.'

Nell laughed. 'I wouldn't have missed it for the world, lovie. Take care of yourself.'

On the train, Nell and Charlie walked down to the buffet for a nightcap.

Nell asked, 'Do you understand Josh's decision any better after today?'

Charlie thought about it. 'I respect it, I suppose. I can understand the allure and I got a glimpse of the sort of life he's going to be leading. It doesn't stop me wishing he would come in with me and farm . . .' He sighed. 'It just seems a pity, having had a son young . . . Josh and I could have had so many years doing things together . . .'

He trailed off and Nell said, 'It is hard, Charlie, very hard. I think you have handled it very well, and today meant a lot to Josh, you realized that?'

Charlie grinned, 'Yes, of course I did. What would you like to drink? I think I'll have a whisky.'

In the night in her small bunk on the rolling train, Gabby went over the day. Underneath her in the bottom bunk, Charlie was snoring gently; he always did when he had been drinking.

Had they been close today? Gabby tried to remember if they had turned once, at any time, and *touched one another* in excitement or pride. Did they think to themselves, This is *our* son passing out over there, *we* conceived him and despite everything *we are together after twenty-two years*?

Gabby grieved for a moment in the dark for how it might

have been between them. No noticeable difference to anyone else, but to share the intimacy of the moment with the father of your child. How wonderful that must feel. *How wonderful*. The difference, so slight, was not Charlie's fault or hers. It was just how their lives were. Too late to question or change it now.

The train hooted in the dark, reminding her of her room as a child and the loneliness of an often empty house at night. She would lie in that bed by the window thinking of all the people in the lighted trains out there, while the house creaked and moved alarmingly without a grown-up to hear or guard her.

Now, here she was on a night train, while other people in their houses listened sleepily to the speeding of her train through the velvety night, and she still felt alone. She formed Mark's name on her lips and thought of the house by the river, her safe house, as the train sped through the darkness taking her home.

Chapter 32

The timber is beautiful. I have taken great pains to ensure its quality, for it must withstand exposure and the battering of the sea. The wood is oak and perfect for my purpose, being free of knots for a good two feet. I lay the wood out and arrange the planks carefully so that the end grain will not be in a critical carving place such as the face, neck and hands. The grain of the wood should also run in the same direction for carving her drapery. Her costume must flow as if it is one with the water.

I tried my brothers' patience sorely. I had the wood yard in turmoil as I searched for the perfect timber that I had seen on board. I knew exactly what I wanted and I searched until I found it.

I had the oak cut into six-foot lengths. The plank sizes vary and the thickness in them differs, so I will have to plane the surfaces. I will have to bolt the wood together from many pieces for the body of the figurehead, for it will have to weather all manner of extremes as well as salt water.

I am glad to be back in England, yet it is strange, for all seems to be exactly as I left it. The St Piran boatyard thrives, thanks to my father. He now has many men in the yard, as well as my two brothers. Although he seems always short of skilled carpenters, for they are much in demand at this time and many skilled workers have emigrated to seek a better life in the colonies.

It occurs to me for the first time that my father's ambition might well have been stunted by my mother's need to remain in one place. I watch my father's face sometimes when I am talking of my travels and I believe I see wistfulness there, for what might have been.

I owe my father a great deal. He let me watch him carve as a small boy and allowed me to experiment as an apprentice. I long for him to be his own man as I intend to be, for he sees none of the profit of the shipyard, only takes a wage.

When I was offered the chance of working in the boatyard in Prince Edward Island, and then taking passage to sail the schooners home to England to be fitted, my father did not hesitate or ask to keep me. He advised me to take the opportunity to better myself.

I started my new life by carving and embellishing the prows of small schooners, and when this proved successful I tried my hand at a small figurehead for a Cornish brigantine which then sailed home to Falmouth.

Sir Richard Magor saw this figurehead in Flushing and sent word, via his brother in Prince Edward Island, that he would like me to return home to carve a figurehead for one of his own schooners. The offer was such that I could not refuse and I felt the need to see my family after nearly a three-year absence.

This is my most important commission to date. Sir Richard is an influential man who owns many small trading ships. He is also a naval man, knowledgeable about ships and the sea.

My father tells me that Sir Richard is seeking to build bigger boats with detachable bunks in order to take emigrants. He plans to replace the bunks with timber and sundry goods for import on the return journey to England. His schooners, brigs and barques will sail home via Mediterranean ports where he can unload and take on foreign cargo. He is undoubtedly a shrewd businessman.

I could be afraid that I might fail to do justice to Lady Isabella, fail to capture the likeness of her, but I am not. I fear only the excitement in beginning such a project may affect my hands at first. However, such is the quality of the wood, such is the beauty of the face I am to carve from it, that I am anxious to begin.

Once I start carving I will be lost to all but the work of my hands holding my tools, and to that face. A face that is haunting and sad at the same time. A face impossible to forget, for the eyes pierce my heart with the memory of a child collecting her birthday present, sitting proud on the back of a small grey mare.

The years between that day and this have taken the laughter from Isabella's face and masked her eyes, and yet, as I looked into her face once more, I saw that the spark still lay somewhere, hidden, but not dead.

It was a shock to see the child of my memory a married woman, for she is a girl still. She cannot be more than eighteen and looks that age despite her smart clothes. From awkwardness she has grown into a beauty, yet she seems somehow subdued.

The woman I gazed at from the end of the quay was indeed a beauty, but she no longer had that sense of joy, of living in a world where everything is before her. She has lost it, that restless excitement I glimpsed in her as a child. I wonder if it had started to fade even before that tragic day ended.

Chapter 33

Mark had complicated-looking maps, notebooks and ancient sailing manuals all over the floor. Gabby stood in the doorway watching him. He had his half-moon glasses on which amused her, and he was concentrating so hard he had not heard her come in.

'What are you doing?' Gabby asked, kneeling beside him.

'One second, sweetheart . . .' He reached out to touch her without taking his eyes off some equation he was making in a notebook. Then he threw his pencil down.

'Navigational skills are definitely not my strong point.'

Delighted to see her he took her face in his hands and gently kissed her mouth, his eyes laughing behind his professor-like glasses as he examined her features. This was what Gabby loved most about him, his even temper, his capacity for happiness. She stared back, her heart contracting with love.

Mark removed his hands from her face. 'Dear little face. If I look at it any longer I shall get sidetracked. I'm trying to work out the timings of the old trade routes before the railways connected the West Country with the rest of England. This is for my lecture at Greenwich for combined London schools next week. I was trying to calculate how long a so-called commuter route to Newfoundland and back would take . . .

'See, here on this map . . . this is where the packet ships carrying the mail used to sail. So did the small trading ships of the nineteenth century, with variations, of course, as they discovered new ports of call, new places for trade . . .'

Gabby smiled. Mark was off. She knew he would be brilliant with schoolchildren; his enthusiasm could enchant a slug.

'You see, I've been wondering about the *Lady Isabella*. We know she sailed the long trade routes but she was a smallish schooner, which is interesting. I would have thought she would have been better suited for trade around Britain, France, Spain, all round the Med. So I think she must have been built for speed. She was really quite sophisticated for that time if you study the plans.

'I've been doing a bit of sleuthing. This Sir Richard Magor owned quite a few vessels. In those days owners formed a sort of syndicate, the profits and costs would be shared by many investors. This guy was forward-looking and later he co-owned quite large vessels for the long hauls which would have been far more cost effective in terms of carrying imports and exports.'

Mark turned to Gabby. 'Although I couldn't find evidence of the *Lady Isabella* being built in Prince Edward Island, I'm pretty sure she was. They built fast, light little schooners, and despite the shipwright's plans for her construction found in the archives in Devon, I don't think she was built in St Piran.'

'Peter sounded so sure. Why would she have been registered at St Piran if she had been built elsewhere? And why would the plans for the *Lady Isabella* have been found in Devon? I think the museum would far rather believe she *was* built in St Piran.'

'What I believe might have happened is that she was basically built in Prince Edward Island, sailed home and was refitted in St Piran. This was not uncommon for those who had business interests out there.'

Mark got up off the floor. 'Let's have a drink. I need one.' He grinned at her. 'One always imagines on a sabbatical that there will be plenty of time to pursue various little anomalies. I daren't start researching any more on the *Lady Isabella* until I've finished my book. I've had my publisher on the phone and I bullshitted. I'm nowhere near completing.'

'Oh dear.'

'Oh dear indeed!' Mark opened the fridge and took out a bottle. 'I keep getting sidelined. One little bit of research leads to another and another and I get sidetracked.'

'Apparently, the figurehead is drawing in visitors to the museum; it's their best year yet. John says Lady Isabella stands in her corner looking down and enchanting everyone. It would be great to have funds to do the second phase one day, Mark.'

'When I last spoke to Peter, he was delighted with all you'd done. He said you'd worked wonders with her face.' Mark said wistfully.

Gabby smiled. 'I guess it must be frustrating not to be able to pursue a project you started. I know the museum want to bring a booklet out detailing the *Lady Isabella*'s history eventually, but John told me they were well aware researching is very time-consuming. And just think, when you've finished your book and stopped giving lectures to every deserving case who asks you, you'll have all the time in the world to pursue your little peccadilloes.'

Gabby placed two wine glasses in front of him and he kissed her nose.

'I don't feel it's solely *my* project, Gabriella. That's the wonderful thing about a find like Isabella, the whole community gets involved. Both Peter and John have got retired volunteers who have the time and patience to painstakingly sift through records. Little clues will turn up all the time.'

'I was thinking, Mark, apart from the fact that the figurehead was named Lady Isabella, and so she was most likely married to Sir Richard Magor, mustn't there be parish records or a population census which could prove Isabella was in a certain place at a certain date, and so must have been his wife?'

'Oh, definitely. Yes, there will be. I've two young researchers from Exeter University who are going through parish records for me in Bideford and Appledore, where there were two big and vibrant boatyards at that time. They might have gone to live in Devon for all we know. This Sir Richard rather interests me.'

He poured out the wine and lifted the bottle. 'This should be rather good, try it.'

Gabby laughed. 'Honestly, I wouldn't know, Mark. I hardly drank before I met you. All the wine you buy tastes great to me.'

'Gee,' Mark said. 'I've driven you to drink, Gabriella.'

'What I want to know is,' Gabby said, ignoring him, 'is this lecture of yours going to include the *Lady Isabella*, then?'

'Sort of. I guess I'd like the life of mariners on the high seas to come alive for the kids, not just turn into a boring old history lesson by a dull old prof. I thought I would use a ship like the *Lady Isabella* so the kids could relate to the real-life example of one ship and her crew. I'd give the crew names and take them through one voyage to, say . . . Newfoundland, to illustrate the hardships and the deprivation as well as the adventure of such long voyages. A few gory details of how apprentices, young boys of fourteen and sometimes younger, were bullied and horribly mistreated. Bring in pirates on the high seas, terrifying waves as high as mountains, a few wreckers, and the startling discovery of new lands . . .

'Not only have I got to keep their interest in a relatively short burst, I want them to enjoy and understand how rich history is and how much the minutiae of their lives inform us of how people lived then . . .'

Mark paused, out of breath, and grinned at Gabby. 'I'm not used to this younger age group. What do you think, Gabriella?'

'Mark, you'll captivate them. You couldn't be boring if you tried. You never talk down, that's the great thing about you. You always assume everyone knows as much as you do, and it brings us all up to your level. Honestly, it sounds wonderful. I know Josh loved anything like that. Oh, by the way, Lucinda asked me if there was any chance of her sitting in on the lecture. Something to do with an exhibition of warships they are putting on next summer. She knows you are lecturing to children and on a later period, but thinks it would be helpful. But, actually, I think she fancies you,' Gabby said suddenly.

Mark laughed. 'Come here, you.' He enfolded her, still laughing.

'What's so funny?'

'You. You make me so happy.'

'Do I?' Gabby peered up at him.

'You do. Especially when you're jealous and I'm an aged historian.'

'Of course I'm jealous! I've seen the way women look at you. I don't like it at all,' Gabby said seriously.

Mark was trying to stop laughing.

Gabby stared at him. 'You are always so content with life, Mark. It makes me feel . . . peaceful. Even when you are serious I know it's not for long.'

Mark poured more wine. 'I have much to be content about, Gabriella. I am doing work I love. I have you. You remind me how to be young. We have this house we share. We have love. What more could I possibly want?'

He raised his glass to her. Gabby thought, *We have love. But not forever and ever. We haven't got this forever and ever.*

As if he could read her face, Mark said gently, 'Sometimes we can spoil the moment by wanting more. This is our moment, my beloved Gabriella, and we mustn't waste a second in looking forward or back. Just live it.'

'Yes,' Gabby said, 'I know. It's a gift, this living the moment. How did you learn it so well?'

She walked towards him, leant against him, wrapped her arms tight around his waist. 'Teach me,' she whispered. 'Teach me the art of it so that nothing can get through the cracks.'

Mark held her and was silent. Then he said, 'I cannot teach

it. It has somehow to be learnt. I cannot always do it myself. It is like happiness, never a permanent state, not for anyone. If I lose it, which I do, I go back to my beginnings. I look at what I had and who I was a long time ago.'

Gabby leant back to see his face. He tucked her hair behind her ears, distractedly, and then he said, with difficulty, 'I was born and lived in Bonavista Bay, Newfoundland, until I was four, with a mother I hardly remember. Apparently we lived in abject poverty. I never knew who my father was. My mother died suddenly and I was about to be shipped off to a children's home when two anthropologists arrived in Newfoundland for fieldwork. They adopted me. The chance of that happening to a "Newfie", a derogatory term used by Canadians, was zero.

'From that day onwards it was up. Perhaps that's why I always feel I was born the day they found me. I was adored. I was educated. I had the most wonderful parents it was possible for a child to have . . .'

He smiled wryly. 'The Newfie in me, however, is always there, hoping to trip the happy me with memories of those first years I don't want to remember, for reasons I can't recall. Those are the nasty little fissures ready to trip you into their cracks if you let them. That's when you have to conjure joy from a tiny thing, remind yourself of how far you've come, how very lucky you are.'

Gabby moved away, disturbed, trying to assimilate his words with the so different childhood she had imagined for him.

'That's why you understand me.' Gabby saw it suddenly. 'I don't know who my father was either. I don't think I'll ever do it, Mark, this accepting, this not looking back or never looking too far forward.'

'Gabby, you will. I am much older than you. It has taken me a lifetime to get to this point. If I hadn't met you I might never have realized I had reached a point of acceptance long ago.'

'A facility for happiness?'

Mark smiled. 'If you like. Which might mean many things. Accepting that you might never know who you are or where you came from. Approving of the person you've become or maybe having the courage to change, to be true to yourself for the first time.'

They stared at each other. Reading her eyes, Mark said softly, 'Don't ask which is true of me, my darling, for I cannot give you a simple answer, or one I know to be entirely truthful. I have that yet to discover. I only know that each moment with you is more happiness than I deserve and I won't test the Gods for more . . .'

He kissed her nose; grinned. 'Have we done philosophizing? Shall we head out for a meal?'

Gabby smiled. 'I love you, Mark Hannah.'

'Thank God for that, Missy Ellis.'

As they walked in the dusk down the river path on a summer evening, fingers lightly touching, Gabby thought, *How can I not look forward? How could I go back to a time without this man when I am so changed by this love every single day?*

When I think of a life without him a great chasm opens up before me in a terrifying way. I could never leap it. I would just fall into darkness.

The emptiness of a life without Mark rendered in Gabby such a sense of panic that her heart raced and her mouth went dry. She would shake her head violently and whisper in the dark somewhere, *no, no, no,* like a mantra. God, she prayed, I'll settle for less, for little, just let me have him somewhere in my life. *Just somewhere.*

This was new to her, this all-encompassing love which filtered into every aspect of her life. Underneath her fingers, his. Long, slender, pianist's hands. Here, on the river path, their bodies moved together, as close as it was possible to walk. The river was silver and racing. Soon, as the sun got lower, it would turn a cloudy pink.

Men and women walked hand in hand; talking, laughing. Two little boys in peaked caps – twins, perhaps – ran past carrying sticks, chasing each other. Here they were, like anyone else, one more couple wandering towards the pub or a restaurant where they could sit and look out over the river on an evening in the middle of summer.

Mark hooked his fingers round hers for a better grip and started to hum. Gabby smiled, shook her head as if to free herself from thoughts which would affect the moment she had now. What was it Marika had said? Cherish the moment, for time would snatch it away if you let it. Gabby was not going to let that happen. She had this moment on a river path with the man she loved.

Chapter 34

At last Isabella was in bed and alone. She asked Lisette to leave the curtains open so she could see the sky. She asked her to please make sure she was not disturbed. Lisette brought her herb tea on a tray. It tasted unpleasant, but it always eased her head.

It seemed so long ago since this morning when she woke that she felt as if she was in another day.

'You are hot, Miss Isabella, you should not have been out riding so long in the rain. I hope you are not coming down with a fever.'

Lisette fussed and tucked and fiddled and folded until Isabella thought she would scream. At last she said goodnight and left the room. Isabella knew that she would go straight downstairs to Sir Richard and complain that he had kept her out too long, that she was overtired and now must be left to sleep. Isabella smiled. Richard was a little afraid of her Lisette.

She watched the clouds scud across a navy sky studded with stars, and little by little she let her mind go over the moment she turned and saw Tom Welland again. When she had suddenly recognized who it was her heart beat so loudly she thought Richard must hear it. She remembered that earlier time in the boatyard with the smell of sawdust and a boy with his shirt off, bent to his work.

Mama had been watching her and she had ridden ahead of her out of the boatyard so that she might not read her face. She needed to keep to herself, to hide this strange excitement. Then, suddenly, like a punishment, Mama was snatched from her. Isabella could never look upon her beautiful face or talk to her again. She was gone in the moment it took her to reach the sea.

On the quay, standing next to her husband, the same feeling flooded through Isabella with such force as she looked at Tom Welland once more that she thought her knees would give way, that she would fall onto the wooden boards of the quay in front of all those people.

Isabella had felt sick to her heart, angry with herself, that until the day she died, Tom Welland would be inextricably linked to the memory of Mama's death and her neglect of her. Yet, clear to her, clearer even than the memory of her voice, was the treacherous way she had reacted at the sight of him. Faint, like a schoolgirl. Breathless when he looked upon her.

Isabella sits in the shade of an apple tree, watching me. Lisette has sent the gardener's boy out with a garden chair and a rug although the day is warm. Isabella looks stiff and self-conscious and cannot relax. There is tightness in her shoulders and mouth and still I have not picked up my pencil to sketch her.

Finally, in exasperation, I ask, 'Are you comfortable, Miss ... Lady Isabella?'

'Quite comfortable, thank you,' she says coolly, though it is obvious that she is not.

I pick up my drawing pad and do a quick little drawing which I show to her.

'Who on earth is that?' Isabella cries crossly.

'Why, it is yourself, your ladyship.'

She looks up sharply. 'Please do not call me that! That drawing looks like a cross old spinster lady.'

'Indeed?' I peer at it. 'So it does. I only draw what I see. So what shall we do about this? Shall Sir Richard have the only cross figurehead in the world? It may, of course, start a fashion. Captains of the fleet may compete to have their wives carved upon the prows of their ships in order to see their scowling little faces plunged through the waves ...'

Isabella giggles. 'I think it is the chair. I would rather sit upon the ground. I cannot relax in the chair.'

I take the rug and place it under the tree, and Isabella sits leaning against the apple tree. I sigh; at last a face I can draw.

'Will you close your eyes for a moment and talk to me of something that gives you pleasure?'

Isabella closes her eyes. She is silent for a while then she says softly, 'I like the early morning and the sound of the sea which breaks into my sleep. It is wonderfully soothing, the rush and slap of the waves ... I like the moment before I open my eyes when there are infinite possibilities before me ... I like my new rose garden and the scent of the roses that floats over to me as I lie reading ...'

The voice stops and I see she is watching my fingers moving across the page as I sketch her likeness. Her eyes are dark and fathomless and my fingers holding the pencil grow slippery under her gaze. Even with her eyes closed, those intense eyes seem to scorch my skin. Hot, I shake my head to free my hair from my eyes, breathe slow to steady my hand upon the page.

There are bees in the apple blossom above where Isabella sits and the orchard is full of their gentle noise. My fingers move fast and true over the page and I catch that faint, secret smile upon her lips. Now her features are relaxed I can capture the beauty of her cheekbones. Her hands in her lap are upturned as in sleep. Small, white hands.

I ask her to open her eyes and when she does they are somewhere far away. Although she does not know it, those eyes which look so directly at me sear me with their sense of innocence and loss.

Over the white page my fingers fly as if possessed, for I must capture these first moments of her face unguarded; capture this heavy-lidded, sleepy expression that makes my hand tremble. I must carve a face from wood that will last long, long after we both are dead.

Chapter 35

For the first time on the train back to Cornwall Gabby felt a sense of dread. The sky was a cold, closed battleship-grey. A November sky. The train half-emptied at Reading and a sort of titanic hush descended on the remaining passengers in the carriage, all the way back to Penzance.

Gabby drank relentless cups of bitter coffee that made her feel squeamish, and the heavy emptiness in her stomach refused to budge. She would have two, maybe three months without Mark, who had flown home to see his family ahead of Christmas. His foster mother was still alive and being cared for by his half-sister. He had friends and colleagues he wanted to catch up with. He had a house that needed attention. He had a wife and five daughters.

There lay the rub. There lay the chill of the human spirit. Gabby, watching the bare wintry trees and small Lowry figures muffled up and bent into the wind on a sea wall landscaped by a vicious cold sea, hurt. Was stilled and dumb with misery. She sat huddled into her seat, bent towards the window, bent away from contact with other passengers.

She had travelled up and down on this train through a spring and a summer. Up and down, using the journey to settle back into the life waiting at the end of it. On that first trip to London the hawthorn blossom had been out, great mouthfuls of it flaming along the track. Gabby had watched people cycling along canal paths, running with dogs across fields, all getting in the mood for a summer that was hovering, just around the corner.

That first glimpse of London, breath held for she was meeting Mark again, was stamped indelibly on her memory. Magnolia buds like upheld mouths were beginning to open in small town gardens. Cherry trees were already out on the pavements. Delicatessens and coffee houses had wiped down chairs and tables placed outside in the spring sunshine. People had cautiously left their coats at home and sat at the tables pretending they were in Paris.

Great trays of plants and flowers had flowed across the pavements next to antique and newspaper shops, bicycle and betting shops. The sun, Gabby thought, changes everything. She longed to travel back in time, to have that spring and summer all over again.

She had trailed down the wide roads observing the routine and ordinary lives lived in a city, watching mothers wheeling children and walking dogs to the shops, and she had thought suddenly, as she gazed into the windows of houses where all these millions of lives were being lived out, *Why, I could live here. I could melt into another person. I could metamorphose into someone who has a town life. As long as I could see from my window a green tree, have great pots of colour in a yard; as long as I could walk in a park. How is this? I never believed I could live anywhere but by the sea.*

I could have been one of these women who wheeled her child along these pavements. I could have been a city girl who jumped off and on tubes without blinking an eye. I would have taken my child to galleries and museums. To the V&A. To the Tate and to the river to watch the boats.

As the train travelled along the coast a watery sun appeared, glazed behind hazy cloud. The moon was already out over the sea. The tide was high and Gabby felt she could almost stretch out to reach the water from her carriage. It was as if the train was travelling through it.

As evening came into the near-empty train, Vs of birds flew south. Seagulls followed a fishing boat like a swarm of butterflies.

At Teignmouth the sky above the sea wall as the sun set

looked like some tinged and misty Jerusalem. Love for this familiar landscape welled up in Gabby like a small wave. I am schizophrenic, split into two, she thought, as puffs of smoke rose from houses and a moorhen scooted across the calm surface of the water. Gabby felt choked with the certainty of belonging, but to whom? To what?

It was as if the merging of day and night mirrored her confusion and identity. The silent transference from golden dusk to darkness, of lights snapping on in houses. Of the last rays of the sun staining the sky like a mirage then fading in the blink of an eye behind a fall of land, only to appear again ahead of the train. It was like following a flame into darkness.

Then the light was truly gone and the day had died. The train travelled over the Tamar in blackness with street-lights and the lights of ships below them. Over the bridge it slid into Cornwall. Home at the end of the world.

As the long-empty train pulled in to Bodmin, Gabby was in the end carriage beyond the platform and lights, beyond the opening and banging of train doors. She was in a little pool of darkness, in the middle of nowhere. This was just a long journey home and yet Gabby felt suspended. She had left herself behind somewhere and was travelling forward in limbo. Fear rose. If she had lost herself, who was she now? What might she become?

As the train got closer and closer to Penzance she felt as if all her nerve-endings were on the surface of her skin. Throughout the whole journey she had felt acutely aware of insignificant things. Small observations barely noteworthy were heightened and seemed important; like a dream sequence singled out to seem profound. Yet, as in a dream, there was this abiding sense of loss that made the familiar strange, a known landscape foreign. There had been a surreal quality to this train journey that deeply disturbed her with its uncertainty and sense of threat.

Gabby stared at the perfect half-moon as they drew into Penzance. Thought of the relentless tug of time and tide, of the ephemeral fleetingness of human lives. She thought of that same moon shining down on Mark's house, a house which contained his wife and daughters. Loneliness, like a shocking icy wave, swamped her.

Nell was waiting on the platform. She had Shadow on a lead. The dog barked with joy as she spied Gabby and strained at the lead and Nell let her go. She raced towards Gabby with little yelps of pleasure.

Gabby dropped her bags and bent to her thick fur, buried her head into the dog's neck, hugged her fiercely, fought the relentless urge to burst into tears and howl on the deserted windy platform.

By the time Nell reached her, she was able, just, to leap up, willing herself jolly.

'Hi Nell!' she said, hugging her.

'Hello lovie . . .'

She held Gabby away and examined her face. 'Gabby, how thin you are. It's a damn good thing you have a long break for Christmas. You are getting to look like a pale city girl.'

As Gabby climbed into Nell's truck she vowed to leave the city girl behind her, to practise happiness. Shadow, in the back, draped her long pointed nose and head over Gabby's shoulder like a fox fur, breathing doggy breath down Gabby's neck.

Gabby sighed, closed her eyes, leant back into the seat and caught the whiff of Nell's familiar scent. She would think no further than this moment. This small intimate homecoming in the darkness with Nell and her dog.

Chapter 36

Mark stood in a glade surrounded by Norwegian spruce, holding the small mittened hands of two of his grandchildren. Elle and Naimah were marching indecisively through rows of firs looking for the one perfect Christmas tree among thousands. Apparently their Christmas depended on the exact height and width, the exact space and shape and form of branches, of a tree he would have to strap to the roof of his truck.

Daisy and Violette, holding his hands, were cold. Mark was cold. He swallowed the desire to bellow down into the small green forest, *Oh, for God's sake, girls, what does it matter? Just pick a tree and let's go home.*

Instead, he hitched a child under each arm and walked towards his daughters. Daisy took off a mitt and placed a freezing little starfish hand to his cheek and left it there as if to warm it. When she removed it the place where it had lain burnt like a small brand. *Traitor.*

'Look,' he called, keeping the impatience out of his voice. 'Here is a great little tree and just the right size.'

The two girls moved quickly back towards him. 'Mmm, that's one of the ones I liked too . . .' Naimah said.

'Yeah, it is quite a pretty tree . . .' Elle agreed.

'Come on you two, make up your minds and go tell the man, these kids are cold and hungry.'

'OK, Dad.' They flashed him smiles that took him back to their childhood and disappeared to find a man to dig out the shallow-rooted fir grown just for Christmas. Veronique

insisted on a tree with roots every year, which was commend-
able, but every year another tree died in one or other of his
daughters' gardens.

At that moment Veronique would be cooking and bottling,
icing and storing, shopping and hiding so frenetically, that by
Christmas day, the whole point of all this yearly palaver, she
would be exhausted yet triumphant. Nothing had changed in
this Christmas ritual since his first daughter, Inez, was born.

It was as if the entire happiness of their Christmas
depended on these small, everlasting rituals, not the fact that
they were all together sharing a Christian festival. *Something
at odds with my wife's Catholicism*, Mark thought. *You
would think that religion would predominate on this feast
day, but it does not.* Going to Mass interfered with the
perfection of the turkey.

Love makes us cruel to those we have stopped loving.

Standing holding these babies, flesh of his flesh, Mark felt
as detached and dislocated as if he had suddenly awoken and
realized he was someone else. This year he could conjure no
interest, no joy in this regular, vast family Christmas in which
he was about to be swallowed.

He set the children on their feet and indicated to his
daughters, who had now found a man with a spade, that
he was going inside the café to buy these cold children a hot
chocolate. Ten minutes later they joined him, took charge of
their infants, found small plastic beakers with non-spill lids
in which to pour their drinks.

He caught Elle sliding a quick, knowing look at Naimah.
She said, 'Dad, would you mind if we had lunch here? I know
it's a bit grim, but we're here and everywhere else is going to
be so crowded . . .'

'Do they serve beer?' he asked hopefully.

'Sure they do,' Naimah said. 'I'll go get a menu.'

They ordered scrambled eggs for the children and they ate
cardboard sandwiches, but the beer hit the spot and Mark
cheered fractionally and joked, 'Are you sure your mother
isn't back home cooking a four-course lunch for us?'

241

Again his daughters exchanged glances.

'Come on, spit it out!' he demanded fondly. 'Less of those loaded glances I know so well. What are you hatching?'

'Oh, Dad!'

Mark had always been able to read his daughters and it annoyed them greatly. It was what he loved most about them, their openness, and for this he had Veronique to thank.

They avoided his eyes for a minute or two, popping mouthfuls of egg into small open mouths like mother birds. Then it came.

'Dad, while you've been away we've been wondering about what we could do . . . how we could . . .' Naimah eyed Mark miserably.

Elle said quickly, 'We thought of ringing you for advice, but we all decided you deserved this sabbatical in peace, away from us all . . .'

'You have been such a brilliant dad . . .'

Mark was worried now. 'What's happened? For heaven's sake . . .'

'Dad, Dad, nothing has happened, it's just . . .'

'We don't want to hurt Maman, she's so great . . .'

'She's a wonderful mom . . .'

'We love her to bits . . . You too, Dad . . .'

Mark banged his beer glass down. 'If you two don't come to the point I am going to get off this chair and knock your heads together!'

Silence. Then they dropped the bombshell.

'Maman's got to let us go, Dad. Let us have our own lives. It's affecting our marriages . . .'

'We're grown up now. Sunday meals and weekday suppers are lovely every now and then, but not every Sunday, not every week . . .'

'We'll always be in and out of the house, it's our home and we love you guys, but Maman has got so she expects us all to be there when she wants . . . I know she picks up the children and feeds them and has a meal ready for us, and it's sweet of her . . .'

'. . . But we need to get back to our husbands, our chores, our studying, our lives, Dad. The men are getting pissed off.'

Mark had no idea they felt like this. *How selfish of me. How blind and insensitive*. He closed his eyes, jerked out of his shocking, convenient, complacency. He had always thought, *If I ever leave, Veronique has the kids*.

'I had absolutely no idea you all felt like this. You should have spoken to me sooner . . .'

'Dad, please don't look so shocked . . . it's no big deal . . .' *Oh, it is. It is.*

'We've been racking our brains over how to say something without hurting Maman.' Naimah touched his arm anxiously and Mark picked up her hand.

'How can we do it, Dad?'

'She's going to be hurt, initially, there's no way round that. I think you'll have to withdraw slowly. Hopefully, when she sees you're all still around, that nothing threatens her relationship with all of you . . .'

'Inez has been trying to get her to think about going back to college, to do a course or something. We found her grades and dissertation in the attic the other day. She was very clever, you know, Dad. We were surprised at some of the papers we found.'

Mark smiled. 'Oh, she was exceptionally clever; bright and witty, too. The sort of girl who could have done anything she set her mind on . . .' he paused, '. . . but a girl with no ambition.'

He heard the wistfulness in his voice and was surprised.

'Except to have a family,' Elle said quietly. Both girls were looking at him as if he had now surprised them.

'Did you mind, Dad?'

'I was surprised,' he said carefully, 'because I just assumed with a first-class degree she would want to work, or teach – use her subject, for a few years, anyway. We were very young, as you know. We got married straight after university, and we were absolutely broke . . .'

243

'We all thought that you hadn't wanted Maman to work . . .'

'Especially when we found all her old university stuff. We assumed that you preferred her at home. You know, because she had been beautiful and clever and men of your generation liked their wives to stay home . . .'

Mark laughed again, but it was a hard little laugh, too ironic to be kind. He stared back at his daughters. 'You thought perhaps I felt threatened by a clever wife? That I encouraged her to stay at home?'

Oh, how wrong they were! He had married Veronique because he had thought she was as passionate about history as he was. At twenty-three, he had had romantic visions of them nesting in a little flat talking endlessly of their fulfilled days. Eventually, one day, a couple of kids, but basically an academic, a professional life together.

'I had taken it for granted she would want to go on to do a PhD,' he told them, 'and to have a working life.'

'So,' Naimah said slowly, 'it was Maman who never wanted to work . . .'

They were both having trouble absorbing this. Had it been a well-worn mantra started by Veronique, as an excuse to daughters who all worked and had families, because that was the norm now?

Both his grandchildren had fallen asleep with small flushed faces, leaning against their mothers. Mark said, getting back to the subject, 'Let's get Christmas over and I'll think of the best way of initiating the subject before the New Year.'

'You won't hurt her, Dad?'

'Of course I won't. I can prepare the ground, but you must realize it has to come from you lot, not from me. Imagine how your mother would feel if she knew we were talking like this behind her back.'

'Dad, she is young enough to do something, have her own life still, isn't she?'

'You girls are her life,' Mark said quietly. 'You have to remember Maman is still very French in her attitude to family. Remember your French grandmother? She was formidable, pure Mafioso in her attitude to family first.'

He grinned at their solemn faces. 'Don't let's get this out of proportion. I think the more casually this is handled, the better. Withdraw slowly but firmly. Of course she needs to realize you have your own lives. I'm pretty annoyed with myself for not realizing something I should have seen clearly, then all this agonizing for you could have been avoided.'

'Come on, Dad, you've been away a lot and you've always been so busy.'

'Someone has to bring in the bacon, we know that.'

Ah! An ancient, buried resentment surfaced. All those years ago Veronique was determined to have a house and garden for her babies. Not a rented flat. She had worked until they had enough for a deposit and then she had got pregnant without discussing it with him. Mark had had to give up his lowly paid research post. He had been straight into a mortgage and a job to process it.

He got up. 'Come on, let's get these kids home.'

He did not regret his daughters. He adored every one of them, even if it had been a longer academic climb. He lifted a sleeping child's dead weight and carried her out to the truck with the Christmas tree neatly attached to the roof. Snow was falling again. Mark buried his nose for a second into the warmth of the child, into that dusky, powdery baby smell.

Out of the blue, like the piercing point of a knife under his ribs, *I want Gabriella to have my child.*

Chapter 37

Within a few days Isabella had grown to love the smell of wood, the sharp gluey smell as the chips fell to the ground around Tom Welland's feet as he chiselled into the solid piece of wood that would one day be her face.

Isabella had not expected to feel so excited to be back in St Piran, but she was. She was touched at how the villagers remembered her and Mama and she was relieved to find it was the happy memories she associated with the place she grew up, not that tragic last memory.

Richard's family had had a summer home there for decades. Rumour had it that it had been his grandfather's love nest. Neglected for years, Richard had now had the house renovated and Isabella called it the Summer House. She and Lisette were installed there until Tom Welland had completed the figurehead.

Lady Isabella was being fitted out down on the wooden quay. Sheltered harbours were few on the north coast and the smaller ships, if blown by a vicious onshore wind, could beach themselves up on the cove if they needed shelter.

Richard, despite a childhood in Devon, wanted the local people to have pride in *Lady Isabella*. St Piran was his wife's birthplace, and if trade went well the community would also prosper in her success.

He had less altruistic reasons, too. He must maximize the success of the trade routes he had established over the years. He must constantly evolve his business interests, note where the new trade lay, and take risks.

Trade was good, but he and others like him, small local shipping dynasties, knew they had maybe ten years more and then steam and iron vessels would overtake the wooden schooners and brigs. They would be overwhelmed by progress.

His beautiful wooden ships would be in decline, but, God willing, by then he would have a son, and he would have to move with the times as his family had always done. But for the present he was the happiest and most fulfilled he had ever been. He knew where every one of his ships registered around Cornwall and Devon lay, and the reputation of every master. After a season or so, when tonnage was good, Richard would sell on one or two of his boats, for the right price.

While Isabella was taken up with sitting for the figurehead, Richard decided to travel to Devon and then on to London. It was a good time to do business without feeling he was neglecting Isabella.

In case she should be lonely or bored he arranged for Sophie, her cousin, to stay for a few days.

'Will you visit your father and his wife, Isabella?' Richard asked her before he left. 'Do you not think it is time to make your peace? It is somewhat awkward when your father and I do business together for you are very distant with him. Could you try to like his wife a little, for my sake?'

Isabella looked at him with an expression he was coming to know well.

'Richard, I am perfectly cordial to my father. I have no opinion of his wife whatsoever. I neither like nor dislike her. My father knows I am here with Lisette. It is my father and his wife's place to invite me, for I am the visitor here.'

Richard sighed. Isabella could be childishly wilful. It really was not that poor woman's fault that she had taken Helena's place. Charlotte seemed constantly to be in Helena's shadow, no one seemed able to even remember her name.

'I will be gone for three weeks, Isabella, for I must go on to London from Exeter.'

Isabella smiled. 'Richard, I believe it is all just an excuse for you to travel on the railroad, which I know you love!'

But she was overjoyed to have the time on her own.

'It is a new and revolutionary invention that excites me, I admit, every time I travel. The time it saves to reach London has transformed our lives down here. By the time our children are born the railroad will have reached Truro. There will hardly be any part of the world that does not have a railway, you wait and see.'

Sophie had arrived in St Piran with her drawing book, happy to escape her French tutor and her mother who was determinedly grooming her for her season in London. While Isabella sat for Tom, Sophie sat upon the cliffs and sketched.

Isabella had been sitting for a long time. Her feet had gone to sleep. Tom stood up and stretched, looked at Isabella.

'What do you think about while I carve?' he asked. 'Your face changes in small ways all the time. It is like the shadow of rippling leaves across your face.'

Isabella stood up too. She turned away for a moment to hide the colour which had suddenly come to her face. She had been watching his hands as they chiselled and his concentration on the block of wood. She had been watching his hair as it fell across his face, lines of fairness that the sun had bleached. His bent back was powerful, the muscles under his shirt moved tightly.

Had she been thinking? No, she had not. Sleepy with having to stay so still, she had just let the sensation of Tom waver over her in the warm afternoon. Absorbing him into her in the flickering of light and shadow across her face.

Isabella walked over to look at her likeness emerging from the smooth, honeyed wood. The huge block of wood was held by a chain at an angle. It was strange, a little eerie. Her face was half-formed, a metamorphosis, the wood inanimate without life. A frozen half-face. Isabella shivered. It was like someone had died while giving her birth and here she was unformed and lifeless, caught in unbeing for eternity; a grotesque half-life.

Tom said quickly, 'If I were a painter you would not be allowed to look before I finished you. The wood looks strange now, but I have to break when my fingers ache, for the face must be right, it leads all the rest of the carving.'

He smiled down at her. 'I start by carving the shape of the head and face and then I go on to the body and return to capture the detail of the face later.'

Isabella turned away. 'Lisette brought me orange juice. Would you like some?'

'If you have some to spare. What about your cousin?'

'Lisette has gone with Sophie to the cliff path above the cove. Sophie wants to paint the sea and Lisette is afraid she will fall over the edge of the cliff and insisted on going too. We are all very much afraid of Sophie's mama.'

She handed Tom a glass of orange and they smiled. They stood together looking across the cove, squinting against the sun bouncing off the sea. They could not see her, but *Lady Isabella* was laid upon wooden staging on the quay while her carpenters, Tom's father among them, climbed aboard her like ants, working hard to finish for her maiden voyage fully fitted.

From where they stood the sounds of hammering and voices and the occasional swearing carried up the cliff in disembodied echoes. Tom flexed his fingers and turned away from the sea.

'So, you have not told me what you think about as you sit so patiently, Lady Isabella?'

Isabella's smile was enigmatic. She could say it was lovely to have her bed to herself, or how free she felt in the boatyard with Tom, away from Richard, away from Lisette. She could say that she understood now the ache of belonging, that a sense of the place you were born always remained.

For so many years she had put her childhood and her mama out of her mind. And suddenly, as Tom carved her likeness, the happy memories were creeping back. She could see Helena laughing again, not dead.

She said to Tom, 'I think of many things. Sometimes I visit the rooms of my father's house once more and try to remember how each room was furnished, but only my mama's room remains truly clear to me.'

'You miss your home?'

'No, not the house itself, it was too big. Papa used to say he could spend three weeks just trying to find Mama. I loved my own room and Lisette's little room off the nursery. I loved Mama's drawing room, it was full of lovely Italian furniture and glass. I liked the room off the kitchen where Lisette and the maids used to sew. It always smelt of newly baked bread. What I miss most are the gardens where I used to play – they were beautiful. I loved the lake and the stables . . .'

Tom, watching her, laughed softly.

'Why do you laugh? You asked me a question and when I answer, you laugh at me.' Isabella was mortified.

Tom hastily became serious. 'I am sorry, Miss . . . Lady Isabella. It is just the way you reel off the rooms of your house, the ones you can remember! It is difficult to even imagine so much space. Many cottages only have two rooms for a whole family. I was not laughing at you. It is the . . . difference that struck me, for where you might have envied more simplicity, my parents with three sons and a daughter would have envied you your excess of rooms.'

Isabella was embarrassed. 'I am sorry . . .'

'There is nothing for you to be sorry for, my Lady. My father, my two brothers and I are all in work, and we were able to buy old Mrs Trevean's place two years back. I believe my mother to be the happiest woman alive.'

'You mean the little thatched cottage? The last cottage after the chapel near the coastal path that leads into the village?'

'I do.'

'Lisette used to walk me past there, her mother was friendly with Mrs Trevean. She had a goat in her front garden who ate her roses, did she not?'

Tom laughed. 'She did. When I was little I got chased by that goat, I was mighty scared of it. Now, will you sit for me a little longer?'

Isabella sat.

Tom said, 'I need you to be very still for one more hour while I finish the shape of your face. After that it will be much easier and we can talk if you feel like it.'

He went to Isabella and lifted her chin gently with his finger, then measured with his finger and thumb the width of her head. His hands were surprisingly square and small and strong. More than half an hour passed and he was bent to his wood in total concentration, glancing up every now and then. Little beads of sweat formed on his forehead and top lip. His tongue was caught between his teeth.

In the long afternoon as Tom carved her features from wood, Isabella was finally able to lay Helena to rest, to remember small precious moments and to banish that last image of her mother for another, far truer memory.

Her mother had once given an impromptu concert when her piano had still been in the downstairs drawing room. The French windows had been thrown open to a hot summer day such as this one. Their house guests had sat enraptured, inside the room and outside on the terrace, listening to Helena play for more than an hour, play as if she could not bear to stop.

When she did, a mistle thrush in a tree went on singing like an encore as the sun sank beneath the sea. There had been an awed, breathless silence as still as the dying day. Helena's audience were reluctant to let the evening slip from them by moving or clapping. Isabella, sitting on the steps, had been so proud. She had felt like the thrush puffing up his chest for the glory of being alive.

Isabella looked on the face before her. Tom Welland looked exhausted, as if all his energy was spent. His eyes were a faded yet startling blue, exactly like a rash of forget-me-nots against a green lawn.

'Extraordinary,' she murmured.

Tom smiled, removed his hand, focusing once more on the flesh and blood Isabella.

'What?'

Isabella blushed. 'Oh ... your eyes. Exactly like forget-me-nots. Sophie will be interested,' she added hastily.

'Why will Miss Tredinnick be interested?' Tom did not move away. Dared not laugh at her again.

'Because she paints,' Isabella said inconsequently.

'Ah,' Tom said. 'I do not know the colour of your cousin's eyes but yours are like tiger's eyes, the stone as well as the beast. They are not English eyes. They make you ... different, Lady Isabella.'

He blinked as a bead of sweat fell in his eye. Isabella took out her handkerchief and pressed it above his eye, then the other. Dabbed his forehead gently, soaking up the moisture on his face.

When she reached his mouth her hand trembled as she pressed the flimsy cloth to the beads of moisture on his top lip.

Tom did not move. When she met his eyes he held them. Then, gently, he took the handkerchief from her.

'Thank you. I am very hot. I will ask my mother to wash this for you.'

His voice sounded a little strange. 'Come, I will walk you home or I will have Lisette to deal with.'

He walked away to his wood and covered it, tied the cover over her likeness with rope although it was under cover of a rough roof. Isabella thought, How could I have touched him like that? What will he think of me?'

She walked over to him, her eyes on the ground.

'I do not want you to look at the figurehead again until I am quite finished.'

Isabella looked up. He had her handkerchief to his mouth and was breathing deeply.

'Lavender?' he asked.

'Yes.' Her voice caught in her throat at the way he was looking at her.

He put the handkerchief in his pocket and they walked together out of the empty boatyard. As they walked up the hill, Tom said, 'Would the day after tomorrow be all right for you? I have to help my father all tomorrow.'

'Yes. In the afternoon?'

'Yes. Would you like to leave it until later when it is cooler?'

Isabella smiled. 'You are the one who must choose the time, for I am not the one who grows hot with working. I just sit.'

'But,' Tom said softly, 'I cannot create your likeness without you.'

They saw Lisette coming down the road towards them. When she reached them she said immediately, 'You have been out in the sun far too long, Miss Isabella ...'

'I have been in the shade, Lisette. It is Tom who has been in the sun.'

Tom was grinning at Lisette and she glared at him in mock anger.

'Do not go giving me your best smile, young man. I have better things to do than worrying about where my lady is. You should have seen she was home long before now. We have a ten-minute walk now before supper ...'

'Lisette, it will do me good. I have been sitting all afternoon ...'

'Well, I have not!' Lisette said crossly.

'I would offer to carry you on my back, Lisette,' Tom said, 'as for some strange reason I am to blame for you having to use the two good feet God gave you, but my arms might break and I would not be able to carve, so ...'

Lisette swatted him. 'You cheeky young beggar! Just because you have, by all accounts, been living with the gentry in those foreign parts, don't you go giving yourself airs here ...' But she was laughing.

'The day after tomorrow, my Lady, at three o'clock?' Tom turned to go back down the hill.

'Yes, I will be there,' Isabella called, watching him walk briskly away.

'He is a worker, I will say that,' Lisette said as he disappeared. 'He will be down to the quay now to help his father and brothers pack up for the day.'

'Oh, I thought he would go home for his meal and rest now. He seemed so tired with the heat and the carving, which is difficult work, Lisette.'

Lisette gave Isabella an amused look. 'Ben Welland and his boys will have been up working the boats since first light, Miss Isabella. Ordinary people do not have the luxury of thinking about whether they are tired or not. You work till the work is finished for the day. That is all you know.'

Isabella was silent, then she said in a small voice, 'Is this how it is for you, Lisette, looking after me?'

She felt ashamed. She had never ever considered Lisette's private life.

Lisette was silent as if she was considering the question, then she said, 'No, Miss. Your mama, and now you, are my life. I do not wish another.'

Isabella stopped on the road. 'But you have never married or

253

had children. Is this because Mama died? Would you have left us to marry, Lisette, if Mama had not died?'

'Goodness, Miss, how do I know what might have happened? You are quite enough for anyone, and how do you know anyone ever asked me to marry them?'

'Well, did they?'

'Once, Miss.'

'When? Why did you not accept, Lisette?'

Lisette said quietly, 'It was the wrong time. Your mama was killed the day after I was asked. Everything changed then. Everything.'

'Oh, Lisette! I am so sorry. I never even stopped to think about you. You must talk to me about ... things. You must help me not to be so selfish and self-centred.'

Lisette laughed. 'You are neither, Miss. You were born to one way of life, I to another.'

'Without you, I would have jumped into the sea after Mama died, truly, Lisette.'

'I believe you might have done, but I was never going to leave you. Look, Miss, there is your cousin waving from the garden. Now there is a handful if ever there was one. A mind of her own and where she gets her notions from is anybody's guess. I hear Mrs Tredinnick is at a loss to know what to do with her ...'

Isabella laughed and waved back. There in the Summer House, with no grandeur or pretence, few servants and no husband, it was possible to feel free and to say and do whatever filled your heart and mind.

Chapter 38

Elan was walking over Waterloo Bridge to meet his agent at the Savoy when way ahead of him he saw a familiar figure. Something in the walk, the angle of the back of the head. Elan began to walk more quickly, conscious of the increased speed of his heart, of the old familiar pain lurking for moments such as this.

By the time he had crossed the bridge and was turning into the Strand, full of lunchtime crowds, it was impossible to make any individual out in the bobbing heads in front of him. He walked into the Savoy, wondering if he would ever stop seeing Patrick; in the street, at a party, in a gallery, in his sleep . . . Patrick, the kindest of men, who had made such a puzzling, unkind, treacherous disappearance.

His agent lowered his newspaper and jumped to his feet to greet Elan. He had said on the phone he wanted to talk about Elan's next exhibition. The fact they were in the Savoy meant, Elan knew, that George either wanted the impossible or something unexpected had cropped up which was worth an expensive lunch.

It turned out to be both. A gallery in New York wanted some of Elan's paintings for an exhibition of British painters in February of next year. Could Elan conjure enough paintings for them to choose twenty when the New York gallery owner came over in January?

Elan was horrified. It was December 15th now.

'How many unsold paintings from my last exhibition?' he asked George.

'Four. The large seascape, a smaller gouache, *Storm Window*, and one small one, *Rocks off Bryher*. How many can you re-call locally?'

Elan tried to think while George ordered him a drink. Two at Penlee. About four in St Ives. At least six or seven sitting in Falmouth and National Trust galleries. He had no idea what he had hanging in Truro and Penzance. Not all of those paintings were necessarily ones he would choose to send to New York, but he must have enough for the gallery owner to pick and choose. It was possible . . . just . . . if he did not go away for Christmas.

He sipped his gin and let George stew for a minute or two, then he said, 'Well, if I recalled most of my work . . . I guess I would need to paint at least five or six more canvases. I might be ready, just.'

George let out a huge sigh of relief. 'Great! Elan, if you get well known in New York it is going to be a whole different ball game. I thought I would bring Natasha Farini, the gallery owner, down to Cornwall. Great PR for her to visit your house and studio, see some of those wild places you paint . . .'

'George!' Elan reined him in. 'You must remember that in the event this woman likes any of my paintings, I am not, nor will ever be, one of those painters who can churn out stuff at a rate of knots. I mean that. I would rather stop painting and turn to the bottle.'

'Of course, of course. I of all people understand the quality of your work, Elan, you know that, after all I am your agent. But this really is a prestigious exhibition, vastly different from Chicago, though you did pretty well there . . . New York will do wonders for your profile. Now, let's see if our table is ready.'

It was only when they had been sitting in the dining room for some minutes perusing a vast menu each, and George had chosen a bottle of very expensive champagne, that Elan looked up and around the room.

At the other end of the dining room, sideways on, profile

to Elan, with a woman Elan recognized as his sister, sat Patrick. Recognizable for shape of head and long limbs. Unrecognizable in the sickly pallor of his once beautiful face and the painful thinness of his wasting body.

Instantly all was clear to Elan, and the agony of this understanding made him almost cry out, double-up in pain. *Oh, Patrick! You fool, you bloody, bloody fool. How could you have done that to me and to yourself?*

He was gripping the sides of the table and George, staring at him, said in alarm, 'What is it, Elan? Are you ill?'

He turned in his chair, following Elan's eyes, then swung back to face Elan, shocked.

'God! It's Patrick.' He stared at Elan. 'He hasn't seen you. Do you want to leave, old thing?'

Elan had already made a decision.

'No, George,' he said quietly. 'I am not leaving until Patrick has finished his meal. I do not know if I can eat, but I can certainly drink.'

With trembling hands, Elan looked down at the menu again and ordered.

When the champagne arrived, George asked, as he watched Elan's pale face, 'What are we going to drink to, my friend?'

Elan smiled faintly and lifted his glass. 'To understanding. To resolution.'

And George, the tough agent, said suddenly, 'Love, old thing. I think we will drink to brave, unselfish, unconditional love.'

Their eyes met. Elan lifted his glass, but choked, could not speak. He was already, in his imagination, on the other side of the room, bending to the chair which held his lifetime love and saying, 'Did you really think you could hide this from me? We share this. We share it. Do you understand?'

Chapter 39

Gabby was standing at her bedroom window watching the rain gust sideways in great billowing misty sheets. She could not feel less Christmassy or more miserable. The house and everything in it felt damp. The only really warm places were the kitchen and Nell's cottage. If it was not for Charlie she would have been tempted to let poor Outside Dog in from the barn. He looked just like Gabby felt.

There was so much to do and she had no inclination to do it. It was as if all her energy, the vitality needed over the summer to pursue the volume of work and a secret life, had suddenly evaporated leaving her shaky, burnt out and reluctant to leave her bed.

Josh would be home in a few days. The house must be cleaned and decorated. While she had been in London, Nell had arranged for Alan's daughter to come in and clean, but the girl was erratic and prone to sudden ailments and now Gabby had returned Charlie said she was useless.

Gabby pulled on two sweaters and went downstairs. The remains of Charlie's breakfast were on the table and the kitchen floor was full of muddy boot and paw marks. There was a note from Charlie propped up on the marmalade jar.

'*Could you find my dark blue work jeans and thick overalls? I can't find them anywhere. Also, Alan has a cold and is not coming in so could you get the milk quota up on your computer for me. See you at lunch. Sandwiches will do as it is the shoot supper tonight, did you remember? C.*'

Gabby slumped on a chair. *I don't want to be here. I can't do this any more.* Suddenly it seemed too much effort to make herself a pot of coffee. *What's the matter with me? I'm going to ruin Christmas for everyone. Josh loves Christmas, everything must be just as it's always been. I am so tired. I want to go to back to bed and sleep forever.*

She got up and took the kettle off the Aga and made a strong pot of coffee and some toast, willing herself into the day. *I'll make a list, then I'll go through the list and tick off everything I get done today and then I'll feel better.* She switched the radio on and the warm kitchen, a place in which she had spent so many hours, began to soothe her as the storm raged outside. First on the list: washing.

Gabby went out into the old scullery to the washing machine and dryer and saw a vast heap of dirty washing on the wet floor. When she opened a cupboard to find the soap powder a smaller pile of clothes fell out: shirts, still buttoned up and arms carelessly half inside-out, Y-fronts, socks and the dark blue jeans. She stared at them. Had the girl pushed them in there, or Charlie? Shoved them in a cupboard to wait for her, Gabby, to do. *Part of her job as a good wife. Part of her job description.*

Blind rage seized Gabby. The shirts had done it. Not only had they been left for her to wash, but left for her to unbutton first and pull the sleeves the right way. *How dare he?* She kicked at the pile, screamed;

'Bastard! Weeks of it. How dare you? How dare you leave it smelling and rotting for me to do? These are *your* clothes. *Yours.* All you have to do is push them in a machine, fill a container with powder and switch on. But oh, no, not you, Charlie. You've got to make a point. I should be here to look after you, *you*, Charlie, the head of the household . . . Well, I brought in money this year . . . I can't do everything . . . I can't . . . I can't. I can't . . . I'm so tired of it . . .'

Gabby turned, sobbing and choking, past caring, beside herself, and saw Nell standing startled and white-faced by the back door. But she could not stop now, she stood there shaking and heaving, looking at Nell like a small overwrought child.

Nell, who had quickly taken in the floor full of washing, moved over to her and held her, wordlessly, until the shaking and sobbing subsided. The sight of Gabby kicking at the pile of washing, screaming like a banshee, had shocked Nell to the core. She felt utter dismay. It was as if the great dark wave she had been waiting for all these years was suddenly looming over her. All her secret fears rose with it. There was going to be one almighty undertow to Gabby rebelling at last.

Nell understood. It could have been her standing there a decade ago amid Ted's debris left for her to clear, swamped by a familiar sudden rush of despair. *Nothing was going to change. Ever.*

And it had done her no good. Ted was as tone-deaf to her distress as she feared Charlie would be if he ever witnessed Gabby's age-old cry of lament first-hand. For it had merely illustrated to Ted, and, she feared, Charlie too, imbued with genetic smugness, the mental instability of a certain type of women who thought they were too clever by half.

Men like Ted and Charlie, who made it clear they did not like their wives to work or have interests outside their own familiar world, would never recognize in a million years that what they really feared was the perceived threat to themselves. The woman you married young must remain the same, must not move on, in case they moved away from the most important job in the world. *Them.*

Nell held Gabby, finding to her horror that she had never entirely let go of her own overpowering anger of a life dedicated to an implacable man. *To the loss of love.*

She led Gabby back into the warm kitchen, sat her down and made her more coffee. She went back into the scullery and piled a load of washing into the machine, and came back and poured the coffee into two mugs. Gabby was still sitting in the same position. Nell stopped herself issuing forth clichés. *You are just tired; Christmas does this to people;*

it's the weather. She sat beside Gabby and pushed the mug towards her.

'Drink your coffee, lovie,' she said gently.

Gabby gave a little shiver as if she was waking up and looked at Nell. 'Nell . . . I'm so sorry, I . . .'

'Gabby, you don't have to apologize or explain to me.'

'No.' Gabby smiled bleakly. 'I feel as if I am ploughing through treacle. I'm so disorganized this year. There's one week to go and I haven't even done any Christmas shopping or made out menus or cleaned the house properly or stocked up . . . Josh will be here on Saturday.'

'Gabby, the world is not going to come to an end if the house does not sparkle. We can do that together, and Gabby, Josh is grown-up now, you do not have to re-create every single little ritual of childhood, lug sacks of food home because that is what we always have on the table. Josh is in love and will not notice or mind if there are not glass bowls full of crystallized fruit or nuts, or if he doesn't get a sackful of presents. Gabby, you've worked harder this year than you ever have. It has been a protracted and concentrated summer in which you wanted to prove yourself in London. You have commuted back and forth for months. Of course you feel like this, it would be odd if you didn't . . .'

I had a love affair all summer. Betrayed you, Nell; betrayed your love and your trust.

'. . . Please, just go easy on yourself for once. We live on a farm, for heaven's sake. I've organized the duck, the turkey and the ham. This year there is only Elan for Christmas day, just family. We have enough food for a siege for Josh's usual Boxing-Day crowd as well as our own droppers-in. There is nothing to get exercised about. Relax. The only thing that will worry Josh is if he comes home and you are tense and stressed . . . for no reason . . .'

Except I miss Mark Hannah so much I feel physically ill . . . bereft . . .

'I know, Nell. I know I've lost my sense of proportion.' Gabby got up and went to look out of the window.

'If this clears, why don't you walk over to Elan's with Shadow? Get some Cornish air back into your lungs?' *I can do jolly, jolly well*, Nell thought. 'Then, maybe go and hit the shops with a positive list for presents and by tonight you can relax . . .'

She paused, then said quietly, 'Charlie is not going to change now, Gab, it's too late. You've always done everything for him, he expects it.'

'I know.' Gabby turned from the window and smiled at her. 'Bless you, Nell.'

As she left the room, Gabby stopped at the door.

'This Christmas thing I have with filling the table to overflowing, it's childhood stuff, the terror of suddenly going back to an empty table, an empty house. All the little rituals I've always done here are like a superstition. As long as I religiously maintain them, all will be well.' *All will be well.*

'But all of a sudden it seems like such a lot of work. Not Charlie's fault, Nell. *Mine*. Sorry.'

For a second, Gabby's small face under the new short hair was as desolate as the day outside. Then she was gone.

'Oh, God,' Nell sighed. She had glimpsed something disturbing she did not wish to recognize.

Chapter 40

I can see Lady Isabella and Miss Tredinnick sitting up on the cliffs above the boatyard. I know it is them because of their large white hats. Miss Tredinnick, as always, has her sketchbook.

I pause for only a moment as I measure a length of wood, but my eyes are drawn upwards to those still figures. That one figure above me on the cliffs.

It is a hot day with barely a cooling sea wind and I have tied a kerchief round my head to stop the sweat falling into my eyes and blinding me as I work.

I long to be up in the old boatyard with my figurehead. I wish I could just carve all day, every day, in the peace and isolation that I need. I am concerned that I will lose the moment, that moment when her face will become alive, almost flesh and blood to me, when Isabella's expression will emerge, when I will have captured those intense eyes. My fingers work fast as if guided by another and I wait, poised for the moment, there, there, when the essence of Isabella lies before me, captured in the wood under my hand.

The thrill makes me weak and sick just thinking about it.

The figurehead is the last thing I look at night and the first thing I stare at each morning. When I came back from Prince Edward Island my mother's cottage was overflowing with my brothers and their children and so I made a room for myself up in the sail loft above the old boatyard.

I am mighty pleased with my home. It is warm and I can see the sea from the broken window and look up at the sky as I lie beneath the skylight, newly mended. My brothers and their wives swept and cleaned the loft, moved old sails and boxes away into one corner and placed a mattress under the skylight with one of my mother's patchwork quilts over the top. The sound of the ocean in the dark soothes my aching body to sleep. Below me, the figurehead stands. I have left the detail of the face until last. I want to concentrate on the angle of neck and shoulder, where it meets the bodice of her dress. Then I must catch exactly the flow of her robe, the angle of her arms and hands, for when she is out on the spar, plunging into the waves. I consider before I sleep what decoration I will place in her hair. Should she hold a flower in one hand?

I think it is an odd place for the two women to sit, for the noise of anvils and hammers and sawing and general disturbance of men working must reach them and disturb their peace. I bend again to my piece of wood, take a lead pencil from beside me and mark a line.

Perhaps they sit up there so Miss Tredinnick can sketch the harbour. She showed me her sketches, shyly, as one artist to another, and I was greatly surprised at the detail in her work. She seemed fascinated by the building of the schooners and wanted to know the workings of the rigging and the design of the boat.

I was amused and praised her work, told her she would have to become a travelling artist to foreign ports of call, commissioned by master mariners to paint their vessels under full sail. I assured her a lot of money was to be had for a good painting from a grateful owner.

Her eyes had widened.

'I hope to travel. It would be ideal if I could earn my own living. It is a good idea ... Of course, I must grow more proficient,' she had added hastily.

Isabella, seeing my expression, had smiled. 'Miss Tredinnick is unique, Tom. She believes that with education and opportunity, women can succeed as well as any man.'

'And you, Lady Isabella, what do you believe?'

Isabella met my eyes. 'I believe my cousin is right regarding most things, but she is braver than I am and younger. I am also sure that she will be famous for her views one day.'

'I hope also to be famous for my paintings, Isabella!' her cousin had laughed. 'If you knew my mama, Tom, you would understand how vital it is for me to make my own way in the world.'

She is an unusual young woman and I am impressed by her. The plainness of her face matters not for she has character and she is devoted to Isabella. When I glance upward again they are gone. Pleasant as she is, when Sophie Tredinnick goes home I will have longer to carve and more time with Isabella.

Sophie had been trying to capture the *Lady Isabella*. She was anchored up on pit props on the quay. Men swarmed beneath her and on the decks, adjusting her rigging, banging nails, hammering, uncoiling rope. The faint smell of tar and sawdust wafted up to the top of the cliff.

Isabella, sitting beside Sophie, looked downwards. Her eyes focused on the man like a pirate she knew to be Tom Welland. Stripped to the waist he was the only carpenter wearing a kerchief over his head. Occasionally he stretched and looked upwards, but mostly he was bent to the deck sawing wood. His back was dark, almost as dark as her furniture. He would not be able to see her staring from down there.

The two women needed shade. It was too hot to sit in the sun. Isabella fidgeted and Sophie threw down her pencil.

'It is no good,' she declared. 'It is too difficult and I am too hot.'

'I imagine it is difficult,' Isabella said. 'Sophie, why do you want to draw the ship in the process of being finished? It will be much easier once she is in the water, besides, you can see no detail from up here.'

They walked slowly back to the house and Sophie said, 'I was trying to capture it for a record in progress for your husband, Isabella, but I do not have the skill yet.'

Isabella took her arm. 'How sweet you are. I believe you are rather taken by Richard?'

To her surprise, Sophie blushed and said quickly, 'I merely find him interesting, Isabella. I have always loved boats and sailing and he has sailed to so many fascinating places, has he not?'

'Indeed he has,' Isabella said. 'I have heard many of his interesting adventures ... more than once.'

Sophie turned to face Isabella. 'Do you not have a burning desire to visit places you know nothing about, Isabella? Do you not long to see the places on maps, to see what they are really like? So different from England ...' She pointed to the cliffs and sea, '... India, China, America, Japan. Isabella, our lives are so small and contained. We know nothing. We do not even know what it is like to live in a large city in our own land.

'Culture!' she said bitterly. 'When we visit London or Bath, is it the history that interests Mama? No, it is only the parties to promote the sale of daughters to the highest bidders.'

Isabella wished she was having a different conversation, for this one triggered her own longing for more. They had left the noise of the boatyard behind, and she viewed the shimmering violet sea once more before they turned and moved inland across the fields towards the house.

'Dearest Sophie, it does you no good railing against being a woman of a certain class, but perhaps it will help you to achieve whatever it is you want. I do understand what you are saying for I know your mama ...' Isabella took her arm. 'The trouble is that you have grown too clever.'

They reached the gate of the small house.

'I love this summer house,' Isabella said. 'Do you not think it is just the right size?'

'Yes,' agreed Sophie. 'It is a happy little doll's house.'

Both women walked in through the open front door. They took their hats off and regarded their reflections in the large gilt looking-glass in the hall.

'I have caught the sun. Mama will have the vapours,' Sophie said. 'I miss you, Isabella. At home I have no one to talk to. There is no one to try my ideas out on.'

She bent to the looking-glass to tidy her hair and Isabella, watching their reflections, suddenly saw an older, grown-up, short-haired Sophie haloed with a man behind her whose mouth was tight with disappointment. When she turned round startled it was only Richard standing there, smiling jovially at them both.

'I am home early, my dears. Just for the one night. I can accompany Sophie home to Falmouth tomorrow. Now, come and have luncheon and tell me all your news. How is the figurehead progressing?'

There was nothing tight about his lips, he was as cheerful a man as ever, and as Isabella went to greet him the image faded but left a faint aftermath behind, like an omen.

Richard had decided to accompany Isabella to the old boathouse to inquire how long it would take Tom to complete the figurehead. He wanted only to see it once it was completed.

'How are you progressing, Tom? I understand that some days you are needed by your father in the boatyard?'

'I am, Sir. There is much to do on the schooner if we are to finish on time and we are a carpenter short. My father knows the quality of my work and is loath to employ another.'

'So I understand. I have offered to send a man over from Falmouth. I know his work and your father and I have agreed that I will cover the cost of him. I do not want *Lady Isabella* to sail late or without her figurehead, Tom.'

Tom had been relieved. 'Working on her every day will speed her completion, but I am still at the stage where I need Lady Isabella. I can do much from my drawings, but I cannot do the face. Maybe two weeks more? Then the figurehead will be fitted to the schooner.'

Richard had nodded. 'If I plan on the *Lady Isabella* being ready to sail one month from now, is that time enough?'

'What does my father say, Sir?'

'He believes with an extra hand he can complete the refit in three weeks. That leaves one week to fit the figurehead.'

'I believe I can do it,' Tom said. 'It is just that sometimes my work cannot be hurried, Sir.'

Richard laughed. 'There speaks an artist, Tom. I understand, but I am a businessman and I am afraid you must give me a date.'

Tom smiled. 'Four weeks it is, Sir.'

Isabella had been sitting on her chair in the shade, listening. Richard had gone over to her.

'Isabella, can I leave you here in St Piran for a little longer? I cannot stay, I am afraid, I have to return to Falmouth and then back to London to register my schooners and visit the house. Will it be too dull without Sophie?'

Isabella's heart had leapt. 'No, Richard. Of course, I will miss Sophie, but you know I love it here. I have my books and the garden and Lisette. I can walk, I will be quite happy.'

She lowered her voice, wanting to please him, 'When Papa returns from France, I will even steel myself to go and visit him, if it would please you, Richard.'

'It would please me very much.' Richard sighed. 'All is settled, then. Tom, you are happy?'

'I am, Sir.'

'Right. I will leave you with my wife and I will go to speak to your father. I will see you in an hour, my dear.'

When he had gone it seemed quiet in the yard. Tom stood very still, staring across at Isabella. Then he walked over to her.

'Will you stand, Lady Isabella? I want to see how your skirt falls.'

Isabella stood and he watched the way the folds of her skirt gathered and dropped from waist to ankle. How tiny her waist was.

I long to place my hand there.

Touch me. Touch me. Tom was so close Isabella could feel his breath.

Tom bent to the dusty yard to see where her skirt skimmed her ankles.

Small narrow feet. He straightened up, stood back and viewed the whole.

'Turn slightly to the sea,' he said.

Isabella turned. Tom went back to the figurehead and looked back at her, then came back and with his finger turned her chin slightly upwards, left his finger there on the warmth of her skin as if to remember the difference between wood and flesh.

Isabella met his eyes.

'Isabella,' he whispered, 'stay just like that.'

Tom had moved a tiny damp piece of hair from her hot cheek and placed it carefully behind her ear. Her ears were like small shells.

I want to place my lips to an ear. I want ...

Isabella had seen what was in his eyes and they both shivered, and then he had stepped quickly back and had gone to pick up his tools.

The sun was sliding behind the old glass houses and the scent of flowers and damp earth came in from the open windows. A robin was singing on a branch just outside one window and another answered from across the garden. Isabella was filled with a sudden sense of her childhood.

Richard laid large maps across the floor of his study and they all knelt on the floor and peered at it.

'Now, you wanted me to show you maps, so here they are. For her maiden voyage, fully fitted, *Lady Isabella* will sail from here, St Piran. She will do a short hop to Bideford, here, where she will pick up my good friend Captain Trelawney. He will skipper her to Ireland and from there she will cross the channel to St Malo. She will coast the Mediterranean ports, picking up cargo, mostly fruit, and then she will return to Falmouth. Once I have Captain Trelawney's report on the ship's ability, and if there are no problems, this, my dears, is the route she will follow ...'

Richard folded the map and pulled out another and flattened out the creases with his large hands. 'Now then; North America ... This is Prince Edward Island, where *Lady Isabella* was built. Here in Malpeque Bay ...'

Isabella and Sophie peered at the names: Malpeque Bay ... Cascumpec Bay ... West Cape ... North Cape ... Greenwich ... Hunter River ... Charlotte Town.

'Can you show me the sea she sailed, Richard? How long did it take for her to sail back to England?'

Richard got out some charts. 'It is hard for you to conceive of the distance, my love. It took twenty-four days for her to get to Plymouth, but she took it easy. I did not want anything to go wrong before you had seen her ... Now, fully fitted, why, she will do it in twenty-one days, on the home trip.'

Sophie asked, 'Why is it not the same distance both ways?'

Richard laughed. 'Because of the Westerlies, my dear, which are a battle for all shipping.'

'All this is sea with no land at all? What do all these arrows mean? I do not see how it is possible to learn navigation,' Isabella sighed. 'You are right, Richard, I cannot get a sense of the distance.'

Sophie pointed down at the chart which could convey nothing of the adventure of sail to her. 'And I cannot get a sense of how men can stay at sea for so long in rough weather, with no land anywhere, and not die of terror. I love the sea, I am a good sailor, but, when I look at these charts, well … It is like … like a launching into nowhere … a frightening endlessness. I wonder if I could ever be a passenger on a long voyage.'

Richard sat on his heels, amused. 'Sophie, my dear, I do not believe you have sailed beyond the Helford! That, my dear, is only dinghy sailing …'

He folded the charts up. 'I must try and think of a way of conveying the wonder and possibilities of sea voyages to you both. The trouble with your schoolgirl globes is they cannot show you distance, only the geography of one country to the next … Perhaps when we get home I will make a large wall map for you …

'However,' he looked at his watch, 'I think it is time to change for dinner.'

Isabella was staring down at one of the maps. 'The island of Newfoundland. I do remember learning about that. It is a wild and inhospitable place, a whaling place with no civilization.'

'It has one of the richest fishing fields on the planet, my dear. Inhospitable it may be, but its indigenous population were massacred in the last century, leaving the Irish and the English …'

'It became a colony,' Sophie cried, triumphant, 'with a British Governor. I remember …'

Richard laughed heartily. He loved the company of women.

'Very good,' he said. 'Now will you change quickly or we will be in trouble with Lisette, whom I am afraid of, and also with Cook.'

Sophie and Isabella got to their feet. Sophie said, smiling, 'You must not patronize me, Richard. I am more than conscious of the gaps in my education. I am trying to address it.'

Richard looked at her, but did not laugh this time.

'My dear, just be yourself. You are too quick ever to be dull.'

Isabella was filled with tenderness for her husband. He was a kind and a good man. She saw Sophie was touched. For, however a woman pretended it did not matter, it was easier to have a pretty face. Sophie was struggling to find her way in the world and Isabella could not bear the thought of her being hurt.

That night when Richard turned to her, she tried to remember his kindness, tried to banish the image of a man with sun-baked skin, a kerchief over his head; tried not to see his naked back and the way she felt as she watched his long fingers carving her likeness.

But Richard, either with the wine or tiredness, slept before he could make love to her. Isabella, in the dark, her back to her husband, shivered. Her body felt liquid and ached. She pulled her knees up to her chin, curled for sleep, one hand across her heart, the other carelessly over a breast.

Chapter 41

Gabrielle ran through the rain to her car with Shadow at her heels. The dog leapt onto the rug in the back seat with a sigh. She drove down the lane and made for the next cove. If the rain stopped she could walk over the headland to Elan's cottage. She parked in the empty car park and watched the violent sea run at the rocks, hit them with a sound like thunder and spray upwards towards the sky.

Further out, rounding the cove, a small fleet of fishing boats were battling home along the coast to Newlyn. She could see the skipper at the wheel and the crews in their heavy sou'westers trying to stow away the nets.

She watched them anxiously. A small green boat seemed to be in trouble; she could see men leaning over the stern looking into the water. None of the boats battling against the sea seemed to be making the progress they should towards the headland and comparative shelter.

Gabby sat up, mopped the misting windscreen. Something was wrong out there. Should she do something? She reached out for her mobile telephone and at that moment the maroon went off for the lifeboat. Gabby jumped, her blood running cold as she heard the sound of the rescue helicopter above the clouds.

She got out of the car still clutching her phone. The rain had stopped but the wind nearly blew her off her feet. She hung on to the car, peering out to sea. Two of the fishing boats had made the far headland and disappeared, but the other one manoeuvred dangerously round to go back to the stricken little boat. Gabby could hear clearly the roar of protesting boat engines as they battled not to get blown onshore. Hugging the cliff she edged forward, ignoring Shadow's indignant barking.

The air-sea rescue helicopter had descended from the cloud and hovered over the green boat. The crew waved at it and pointed down into the water, and Gabby saw with horror a small yellow figure rising in the water behind the boat. He appeared caught in something, then a huge wave rolled in and they were lost to sight as they sank into a trough.

When the boat came back into view two fishermen were leaning dangerously over the stern towards him. The helicopter was now winching a crewman down a rope into the water, but the wind kept blowing him away from the desperate yellow blob fighting in the huge swollen belly of the sea.

The helicopter hovered like an angry wasp as the crewman tried to get a line round the fisherman. The second fishing boat rocked dangerously, men leaning out, waving encouragement to the man in the water.

Suddenly, riding, plunging, ploughing through the waves, the lifeboat came into sight and the second fishing boat began to manoeuvre out of the way. Knowing there was nothing she could do to help now, she turned and headed for the harbour beyond the headland.

The crewman was now in the water with the lifeboat as near as it could get. Gabby realized she was praying. 'Please God . . . please God . . . please God . . .'

Now, on the wind she could just hear the faint shouts of men over the storm, and that meant they were all being blown onshore towards the rocks.

Villagers' cars were beginning to fill the car park as well as the people hurrying to the cove on foot. A shout went up, 'I think he's got a line. Thank God.'

But the helicopter could not lift the two men out of the water. Gabby could see the winch man peering down from the bottom of the helicopter. A man beside her said, 'They can't lift the weight of the fisherman in full wet-weather gear and the crewman . . . Or the fisherman's caught in some tackle.'

All at once the yellow figure was pulled free and was being drawn upwards out of the water. He hung suspended, swinging perilously in the wind, then slowly he was reeled upwards to waiting arms leaning down to gather him in to safety.

'The crewman's still in the water. God help him . . .'

People had brought binoculars but Gabby could see nothing now except the lifeboat frantically turning so the towering waves did not catch her broadside on.

'He's going to be blown ashore onto the rocks unless they get him . . .'

Gabby saw the tiny figure rise up on the crest of a wave like a rag doll. An echo of fear rippled through the watchers, like a lament. Gabby's teeth chattered and she was shaking from head to foot.

They saw a line thrown from the lifeboat before a vast wave crashed over it, hiding them all, and rushed like an express train towards the rocks in the small cove where they stood. The small crowd, including Gabby, turned and ran for safety, before it crashed over the rocks and sprayed up in a volcanic explosion over the car park and the nearest cars.

Oh my God, Gabby thought. The airman would be on the rocks. It was then they heard the whirring blades of more helicopters. Elan was suddenly beside her.

'I recognized your anorak. Culdrose must have been scrambled.'

They clutched each other, peering out at the empty sea, but there was the lifeboat still riding safe in a trough and the man with binoculars called, 'They've shot another line out . . . He's got it . . . There are two men in the water . . . One of the lifeboat men has jumped in . . . They are pulling them both in . . .'

Two helicopters still hovered overhead. After that last huge wave the sea seemed momentarily calmer and then the cry went up . . . 'They've got them . . . They've got them! They're safe!'

'Thank God. Thank God,' Elan said. 'You look dreadful, Gabby. Come on, off to my place; brandy, that's what we need. You're shaking like a leaf, darling, I'll drive your car.'

'You walked in this?' Gabby asked through chattering teeth. They got quickly into the car with the sulking dog.

'I saw the fishing boat send up a flare from the cottage and I rang the coastguard. They had already had various radio messages that a fishing boat seemed in trouble. It seems a young lad got pulled overboard and was caught in the nets and they couldn't pull him back on board. That first helicopter happened to be exercising in the area. Just as well.'

Elan drove up the hill to his gate and parked. They climbed over the stile with a more cheerful dog and ran with her into the warm cottage, slamming the door against the weather. Elan threw more logs onto his fire and then cried, 'Brandy! I hope all those rescuers are having stiff ones. I'm wondering, Gabby, if that fisherman could have survived in the water so long. I do hope so.'

At that moment Patrick called from upstairs, 'What happened? Is everyone safe?'

Elan called, 'Yes, all safely out of the water . . .'

He turned quickly to Gabby and mouthed, 'Patrick home. Very ill, don't look shocked.'

Startled, Gabby turned as Patrick began slowly to descend the stairs. He smiled down at Gabby.

'Hello small one.'

'Hello tall one.'

Gabby went to hug him. 'Oh what a wonderful Christmas present, to have you back,' she said, terrified of holding him too tight for there was so little of him left.

'So good to be back, my sweet.'

He sat abruptly at the kitchen table, small beads of sweat collecting on his upper lip. Elan was fussing, finding clean glasses.

Gabby said, 'Excuse me a minute, I must go to the loo.'

She leapt upstairs to the bathroom and sat on the upturned loo taking deep shaky breaths. Patrick was dying. He was even the colour of death. And yet . . . yet there was something peaceful, even radiant about him. Elan, too. The sadness was missing. As if they had both reached a point of acceptance or understanding; two of them in the place they wanted to be, together.

What a strange unnerving day this was turning out to be. She looked out of the bathroom window at the trees bent to snapping point and the sea beyond full of angry white waves; at the rain, continuous now, lashing the panes. Yet, she could see blue sky in the distance, the storm was blowing itself out.

I wonder what you are doing at this moment. I miss you. How I miss you. I want to tell you about this. Want to hear your voice . . . need you.

She splashed cold water onto her face and went back downstairs, calling as she entered the kitchen, 'Hey, you guys, I am now a drinker!'

Elan's eyebrows lifted. 'Since when?'

'Since London.' She sat at the table.

'Who has corrupted you, small person?' Patrick asked, laughing. 'I mean, what are we talking here, alcoholism or two glasses of wine?'

Elan handed her a brandy and Gabby sipped and made a face. The two men grinned at one another.

'Pathetic!'

'A drinker? *Not!*'

They ate bread and cheese and then went and sat by the fire and Elan put on his old Noel Coward records. He and Patrick sang along, imitating Coward beautifully and camply, making Gabby giggle. She drew her feet up into one of their old squishy chairs and fell asleep.

When she woke, Patrick lay fast asleep opposite her on the sofa. The cottage was silent, the wind had dropped and it was dark outside. Elan sat by the window, painting, with

Shadow at his feet. Firelight played over the walls. Gabby did not want to wake up or to move away from that room. She felt secure and held. There was peace here and faith and a strange happiness.

Both the men in the room had reached a place of safety. A steady calm that would last through the painful moments to come. It would live on in the house when one or both were gone, as things profound and worthwhile always did, giving inanimate things an aura of good, soaking the walls of the house with the past.

She felt ashamed of her outburst of the morning. Self-pity *was* shameful. She had stood and watched a helicopter and lifeboat crew risk their lives in terrible seas to save an unknown fisherman. She had sat by firelight listening to two people revisit their youth, gently singing, one to the other, ironic little Noel Coward lyrics, their eyes meeting in a form of joy. One was dying. The other was going to be left alone. Yet, look at what they had in the firelight together as the wind beat outside against the granite walls of a small cottage perched on the coast. Look what they had decided to make of tragedy.

What had Mark said? *Never ask for too much. Don't lose the moment in wishing for more.*

Her mobile bleeped suddenly in her pocket and she took it out and quickly pressed the button so she did not wake Patrick. A text message.

GABRIELLA. GABRIELLA. GABRIELLA. I CANNOT LIVE WITHOUT YOU.

Gabby closed her eyes, trembled, felt inexpressible joy. Then a sharp sudden fear of the destruction to come. *What of the life she had here? The life now in this room with people who love her, with people she has spent more than half her lifetime with.*

She sat up and leant towards the fire to text Mark back. I LUV YOU LUV YOU AND IT HURTS. She pressed send.

Elan, cold, stretched and came back to the fire. Patrick woke up slowly, came from a long way away.

'Hello, dear people, I have had such a lovely dream.'

'Tell us.'

'I was a small ship, a sloop perhaps, with huge square-rigged white sails. I flew like a bird over aquamarine seas as still and clear as glass. I could see all the fish and coral and bright seaweed below me, a whole glittering world. Dolphins leapt at each side of me like a guard of honour. There was nothing in sight, just me with my sails unfurled, flying on and on . . . I felt this overwhelming and encompassing happiness . . .'

His voice wobbled. 'I did not want the dream to end; I did not want to wake up.'

He closed his eyes again, lay very still.

Elan mouthed 'Morphine' to Gabby.

She got up. 'I'll make you both tea, then I must go,' she whispered.

'I rang Nell, just so she knew where you were, darling.'

'Thank you, Elan.' Elan looked up. Gabby was not talking about a telephone call.

'For what?' he asked gently.

Gabby hesitated, then smiled. 'For being you. For always being you.'

She went to put the kettle on.

At her car, Elan, taking his torch back, said, 'Drive carefully. Love to Nell and Charlie.' He met her eyes. 'Be careful, very careful, with your life, beloved Gabby.'

Driving off into the dark with the road strewn with branches and the eerie stillness after the wind, Gabby thought how long it felt since that morning, *as if I have covered a great distance*. In the face of tragedy your perception suddenly changed, you swung round and viewed things from a different angle and in that one small movement everything shifted slightly, changed its place and importance; became small and simple and clear.

There was this new, frightening clarity. A place suddenly reached. *I love this man and my life feels hopeless without him*. Life mattered. Life was tenuous and frightening and lonely and could be snatched away any second of any day.

In the dark the car felt like some small capsule skimming through space. There were no other cars on this branch-strewn road. She was glad of Shadow's doggy presence in the back for everything seemed oddly unfamiliar.

She turned down the lane and negotiated the ruts and puddles. *Gabriella, Gabriella, Gabriella. I cannot live without you.*

Wasn't that what the morning with the washing had been about? *Not, I can't do the washing any more. Simply, I cannot live without you. I do not want to do this any more.*

Gabby got out of the car and let Shadow out. She stood for a moment in the dark. The kitchen lights were on but no one seemed to be in and Nell's cottage was in darkness. It was only then Gabby remembered with a start: she should be at the shoot supper with Charlie and Nell.

She looked at her watch, fed Shadow, had a quick bath, changed and headed out again. Her face in the mirror looked just the same.

This Christmas she must do all she had ever done. Behave and be as she always was. *She could do it,* for she had had the first glimpse of a future she might have.

Chapter 42

Nell, Charlie, Gabby and Josh cooked and transported Christmas lunch over to Elan's cottage. They carried the kitchen table into the sitting room and Patrick, whose bed was now downstairs, lay by the fire, pale but peaceful. He had a morphine drip he could administer himself at the press of a finger. The nurse had gone to her sister's for two days.

Josh and Elan had decorated the cottage with candles and holly and single glass baubles which reflected the light. All looked beautiful. All was well. Patrick felt surrounded by love.

Josh surprised Gabby with his mature and gentle support of Elan. He made lists of things Elan and Patrick might need. He shopped and went to the pharmacy because Elan was afraid of leaving the house, petrified that Patrick might die without him. But Patrick was determined he would have this last Christmas on earth.

After the meal, Elan played his out-of-tune piano and Charlie and Josh sang rousing sentimental Cornish hymns and even more rousing local songs and carols, while Patrick smiled and slept his drugged sleep, his fingers moving jerkily over the covers.

In the late afternoon Charlie left to do the milking, awkward, sad, but glad to be away. Nell and Gabby cleared up and packed the things away while Elan and Josh watched *The Great Escape* for the umpteenth time on television, sitting one each side of Patrick.

When Nell and Gabby were ready to go, Josh refused to

leave Elan. He wanted to stay and help him with Patrick. It was the only time Elan was near to tears. Patrick woke as they left, stared at them.

'Goodbye, darlings – thank you – so lovely – the day – so happy.' And slept again.

In the early hours of Boxing Day, Elan rang for Father O'Callaghan, who battled out in the dark to administer the last rites to Patrick. At two-thirty he died, slipped away, Josh told Gabby later, holding their hands.

Josh felt devastated; for Patrick's shortened life, for his dying, ravaged, at fifty. For Elan who would be alone again. Patrick had brought Josh into the world and he had watched Patrick leave it.

Elan was dignified and busy, calm and tearless, but a shroud of loss clung to him like an invisible cloak. Patrick's funeral was without delay, on the thirtieth of December at the tiny Catholic church. Only Patrick's sister, Nell, Gabby and Josh went on to the crematorium with Elan. It seemed hardly possible that Patrick could be alive for Christmas and was dead and buried before the New Year. Elan left that evening for Gatwick and a flight to India.

'I have to,' he said. 'I can't be here for New Year.'

No one felt like celebrating and Gabby thought Josh should get away too. He was restless and sad.

'Is it too late for you to spend New Year with Marika?' she asked, knowing he would not be up to seeing his usual noisy crowd of friends. 'I think it might do you good. You've been marvellous, Josh. I've felt so proud of you.'

Josh smiled. 'Will Charlie mind if I take off before New Year? Will Nell?'

'You know they won't. Charlie might go for a pint at the pub. Nell and I will stay here. I just think it will be so flat for you. It is a New Year, Josh, and I think you should celebrate it. Enough of sadness.'

'I've had plenty of invitations in the village, but what I would really like to do is spend it with Marika.'

'Go and ring her then.'

Within an hour Josh was packed and beside his car.

'Drive carefully, please. There will be idiots on the roads,' Nell begged.

'Will you be home again before you go back to work?' Charlie asked.

'I'm not sure, Charlie. I'll ring.'

Josh hugged Gabby. 'Love you lots,' Gabby said.

'You too, Mum. I'll ring to say I got there . . .' He grinned. 'Thanks.'

'What for?'

'For not minding me leaving early, not spending any of New Year with you.'

'If anyone understands how you're feeling I would have thought Marika would?'

'Oh, yes, Marika will.'

The three of them watched Josh's car bumping along the lane and out of sight.

'Not a jolly Christmas for him, was it? Poor Josh,' Charlie said.

'That's life, Charlie,' Nell said. 'Josh is grown up now and boy didn't he prove he was this Christmas. I might even revise some of my prejudices about the services!'

Gabby smiled, pulled on a coat and whistled for Shadow.

'I'm just going for a walk,' she said, feeling for her mobile in her pocket. She negotiated the wet, loose stones on the cliff path carefully, and she thought about Patrick and the moving little funeral and Elan winging his way alone to India.

Beyond the cove, on the stretch of beach this side of the headland, there was a single line of banked clouds and in front of them three huge, coloured kites danced against a violet winter sky. Gabby watched them for a long time. It had been a strange, sudden end of a life; end of a year. So much had happened. All their familiar routines had altered, had subtly changed course, like breaking a spell of continuity.

A time in her life was ending. Christmases for the child that was Josh had gone. At the thought of a future Christmas with just Nell and Charlie, Gabby felt a terrible monotonous heaviness. *I've moved on. I can't go back now.* Then she thought, *Maybe we all have.*

One of the kites billowed out, then down and into the sea. Gabby's mobile rang as she had been sure it would. Her heart soared. She felt as light as those kites silhouetted against a vivid blue sky.

Chapter 43

'I could look for a job near you,' Marika said, 'but I've heard you blue-beret boys live in a little bubble and talk aeroplanes to the point of catatonic boredom, and the trouble is you don't know where you are going to be posted, do you?'

Josh turned and wound a piece of her hair round his finger. They were in bed in a luxurious flat in Kensington belonging to a friend of Marika's. The owners were away, skiing, and Marika was house-sitting.

'I haven't got my posting through yet. It might be Germany, but . . .' His voice was cagey. 'I think you must concentrate on getting a job you really want, Marika, otherwise you're going to be left in a place where you don't know anyone a long way from home.'

Josh pulled her over on top of him. He was not going to tell her he had applied for the Air Assault Brigade. There had been rumours flying around before Christmas and Josh wanted to get in on any possible action.

'It is difficult to know where to aim for, Josh. My step-father too will be posted this year. So both you and my home are constantly moving.'

Josh laughed. 'Poor little orphan!'

Marika rolled off him. 'Do not be cruel. I am going to make coffee.'

'I had other ideas,' Josh said.

'I am sure you had, but I do not have sex with men who are about to cast me off as a loyal camp follower!'

Josh sat up. 'The truth is, I could be posted anywhere and

I want to know you're safe and near your family if I do get posted abroad.'

Marika went and sat on the edge of the bed. 'Do you know something you're not telling me, Josh? You seem so sure you are going abroad.'

'Well, if you call Germany abroad, yes. I already told you that.'

'I was not meaning Germany,' Marika said, watching his face closely.

Josh thought there was not much he was ever going to be able to conceal from this woman, but he was not about to worry Marika about something that might not happen.

He smiled and kissed the end of her nose. 'Stop interrogating me. I will always, always make my way to wherever you are, so please go for the job you really want.'

He moved her gently out of his way and leapt out of bed. 'Am I going to get that coffee before next Christmas, Doris, or not?'

'DORIS!' Marika squeaked. 'What sort of name is that . . . Boris? Doris?'

'It is the name for little old ladies who . . . ow.' Marika jumped on him and he fell back onto the bed.

'Happy New Year!' Josh said sleepily later.

'Happy New Year, soldier boy.'

It was quite some time before either of them surfaced for coffee.

Before everyone arrived for their New Year's Eve party, Mark went down to the cellar to check the pressure on the central-heating boiler. Veronique had said the bathroom radiator was not working. He looked at the gauge without interest. It was fine. He supposed the boiler needed a service. He went back upstairs.

Veronique looked wonderful; luscious in a red dress. Her dark hair had gone almost white in places and it suited her, those wings and streaks of white. She had a new red lipstick, darker than usual, and there was something defiant about her.

'You look lovely,' Mark said. 'I like the new dress.'

Veronique looked up from the table she was finishing laying. 'Thank you.' She smiled. 'Could you get the wine glasses, Mark, the hired ones in the box by the door?'

Mark began to take them out, held them up to the light in habit to make sure they were all clean and placed them on the table. They were having a buffet supper as there were too many people to sit down at the table. The kitchen seemed empty without the girls. He ironically longed for the noise and the chaos of children underfoot and for the chatter and gossip of his daughters.

The kitchen was too quiet. He should be filling the silence with his own minutiae, but he had lost the knack somehow; lost the thoughtless art of small talk with his wife. The house seemed huge, their proximity to each other overwhelming. He wondered, suddenly, *Did we ever chat inconsequently to one another? There were always babies, I can't remember a time before we were caught up in feeding bottles, bath time, sterilizing, school runs, homework . . .*

By the time the last child left home I had left too, although you did not know it.

'All the girls are coming?' he asked Veronique.

'Of course! They always do,' Veronique answered, but her voice was tight. Words had been said between Christmas and New Year. Veronique had listened to her daughters in a dignified silence, then made light of it. Shrugged, in her very French way; 'Pouf! Why did you not say before? That is OK. You tell me when you would like to come for meals. I will wait to know if I am to pick up the children from school. Yes?'

His daughters, surprised, had rushed in quickly, for in order to work they did need their mother's help with school pick-ups. Veronique knew this and was making a fair point. His daughters could see that, too.

'Maman,' Inez had said. 'You know how grateful we all

are. We do need you, you know we do, and we do love coming to have meals. All we are saying is, perhaps not every week or every Sunday. We think it is too much for you, too.'

Veronique had shrugged again and thrown out her arms; 'Fine. OK.'

Then she had gone out of the room leaving her daughters feeling wretched.

Veronique had announced the following day that this New Year would be different. If her daughters wanted to come to the party, fine, they could come as guests. They must not feel they had to come hours before, to help.

Mark said now to his wife, 'Veronique, I think the girls love to be involved in getting ready for the New Year party. They didn't mean to hurt you, you know. They only meant that on working days they find it difficult to spend so much time here. That's understandable, isn't it?'

Veronique looked up at him. 'I am not hurt. Of course I understand.'

She was lying, and Mark, putting the last glass on the table, said, 'Then why shut them out of coming to help for New Year? It has always been a big family thing we all do together.'

Veronique did not answer. In punishing her daughters for wounding her she had only succeeded in punishing herself. It had been a great shock, for her whole life was caught up in theirs and without them she felt panic. This was what the defiant red dress and lipstick was about. *See, don't worry, girls, I am my own person with plenty of friends . . . plenty to do.*

Mark went round the table and placed his hands on her shoulders, made her look at him. He said gently, 'Veronique, you are the most wonderful mother. Your children and grandchildren adore you, they always will, but you are also a very clever woman with many talents. Maybe it's time for you just to think of yourself for once. Not bury yourself in the girls. Think of what you might like to do with your life now they are grown up. The amount of time you expend on your family . . . why . . .' he laughed, shook her a little, trying to get her to smile '. . . you could be running a vast business empire!'

Veronique did smile, but not before he caught the panic in her eyes at the thought of having to do something else with her life, leave her womb-like home.

'Let's make this a really happy evening. No atmosphere, no coolness, just the beginning of a new year with family and friends,' Mark said automatically, and heard his treacherous self saying it.

Veronique moved away. 'Yes! We always have a happy New Year party, don't we? There is the bell, will you get it?'

She added, suddenly, 'You need the girls filling the house, too, don't you, Mark?'

Something in the way she said it made him turn quickly, but she was taking a dish out of the oven and he could not see her face.

He threw the front door open and a cold blast of air filled the hall. The couple stamped the snow off their boots. Behind them the branches of the tree in the front yard were bent with great wedges of snow which slid and dropped with a heavy plop. Mark closed the door and greeted the woman in the way he always did; 'How is the most beautiful doctor's wife in Quebec, then . . . ?'

An hour later he sprinted up to his study and grabbed his mobile, checked his watch, and dialled Gabriella's mobile.

'I'm on the beach,' she said, 'watching some beautiful coloured kites sail against a vivid sky . . .'

Outside the snow began to fall again and the window-ledge, which he had not cleared of earlier snow, built up in little frozen peaks. The noise of laughter and voices floated up the stairs to him. *Across the world she stands on a beach against a winter sea.* The pain caught him off-guard, contracting his throat, spreading across his chest.

'Happy New Year, Gabriella,' he said, forcing himself to breathe. 'I cannot say it on the stroke of the hour.'

'I know. I know. Happy New Year, Mark.'

'Our year, Gabriella, this will be our year.'

Nell had not stayed up for New Year and Charlie was not yet back from the pub. Gabby went out into the night and looked up at the stars. As the hour struck she lifted her glass of wine to a moon she could not see. *Happy New Year for all those I love. Good things for Josh and keep him safe. For Nell and Charlie. For Elan. For Mark and me.*

The house seemed very empty. She made a hot-water bottle and went upstairs to bed. She paused outside Josh's room, peered inside, smiled and then closed the door. She climbed into a freezing bed and curled into a ball.

Our year, Gabriella. Our year.

The house seemed full of ghosts, empty of its heart. People no longer filled its rooms but loitered on the edge like strangers passing on the stairs. The beloved kitchen was the only room still beating with a last little pulse of its own.

Gabby listened to the house creaking as if it ached. It needed small footsteps climbing up and down the stairs, clinging to the old heavy banister rail. It needed its windows thrown open to the sun and wind to dispel the smell of damp and dust from the corners. There was a room with a piano that was no longer played. A dining room with heavy furniture, no longer used. Nooks and crannies, stairways, hall, landings and cupboards, cobbled and flagged floors, old faded Persian carpets full of generations of dog hairs. Still the same place, always the same, but changed because they were no longer loved and polished, swept and lived in, and Gabby knew the heart of a house died when it was no longer cared for. It slowly faded like the lives it had lost.

She sat up to listen to its rhythm, the sound of the creaks as the house cooled down. She could hardly hear them, realized she had grown away from its steady heartbeat. The song she heard now was the flow of a river and distant traffic as it drove over the bridge, the edge-of-a-city sounds, far away from the beat of the sea.

For the first time she realized the enormity of what Charlie had lost. No Josh and his wife filling this house with their children. Josh was the only chance he had had of the next generation living in his family home. No hide and seek and children's bikes littering the yard. No retirement to a little warm cottage like Nell.

Gabby rocked with the sudden clarity of both their lives in the soft darkness of a house she had loved and cared for so long. *You have a choice. You could make a decision, now, before you see him again. You could do the right thing. You could be content again. It would not be that hard. Charlie and Nell do not deserve this. They gave you a whole life, a refuge, a place ... You've fought to have the perfect family, why do this to Josh now ... why blow a whole good life away?*

Gabby was part of the dark. An owl hooted somewhere and a dog barked in the distance. She thought of that house by the railway line and the room she had spent so, so many hours in. She remembered the feeling of never feeling safe. Of having to watch out for herself from the moment she could reason. Of knowing where dangers lay and that the most danger lay in the fact she was a little girl, cute and dark and pretty. They came, her mother's boyfriends, and rattled the locked door. But of course there were other places to catch you, you could not stay in your room forever. But she was clever, she bit and scratched and clawed and yelled. Not all had evil intent, but how was she to know in the pawing and lifting and touching what might have been kindness and what intent. Her biggest dangers came when she was wearing school uniform.

Clara, the drinker, chose her friends in the club from the bottom of a gin glass. She was a sought-after croupier, it was her one talent, and she was in her element working at night. She had all day to sleep off excess. The drinker became the heavy drinker, then the alcoholic. The more her looks faded, the more she loathed her blossoming daughter . . . *but to hate me that much, to not want to believe or protect me . . .*

Gabby leapt out of bed and went to the window, shivering with cold. *I am not going to remember. I am not.* Olive had said, 'I wonder why she did not give you up for adoption or place you in care? She *must* have wanted you, Gabby. Perhaps she just lost her way, grew evil through drink.'

Perhaps. And the irony was, Gabby ran. She ran all the way to this house and Nell and overdosed on her kindness. Mistook lust for affection. Mistook respectability for safety because Charlie was Nell's son. Blurred by the wine Charlie had bought her, startled by his sudden lunge, she did not scratch and claw, she just *gave up*. She had fought for so long and run so far, and for a second, like a child, she thought she might seem ungrateful for all the attention Charlie and Nell had given her. She was too weary and disillusioned to run any longer. *She just gave up.*

It had taken about four minutes. Four minutes that dictated her future; and Charlie's. The reason she was here now. The reason Josh was. The reason she was a picture restorer; the reason she had met Mark. The reason she was here now, remembering. All this in four minutes. Terrifying in its simplicity. *One small, unthinking moment in time changes the map of our lives forever; dictates the future.*

I gave up, gave in, and lived a contented, sleep-walking, safe, safe life.

Was it living, this life without passion or growth or danger? Or was it living a whole life lost in other people? A life you thought you wanted.

Our year, Gabriella. Our year.

Chapter 44

Tom put his tools down and looked down at his afternoon's work. The head, apart from details of the face and the front piece, was almost finished. He stared at the alignment of the arms from the shoulder, looked down at his sketches then across to where Isabella was standing. He went to her and rearranged her right hand. She needed to hold a flower of some kind in her hand.

He peered at the front of the figurehead. He was happy with the folds of the dress and the skirt to ground level, but he was going to have to be careful when he bolted the back section to the front. The bolts must lie just behind the sash, which would be painted gold, and the hand holding the flower would be in front of the sash, which meant the angle of that right hand . . . he pencilled a line down the figurehead.

Isabella watched him, marvelling at his concentration. She had stood for a long time and was tired but she would not say anything, for she could see he was exhausted and after all he was working, she had only to stand.

Tom walked towards her. 'Are you tired? I can do no more today. I will make a mistake if I go on.' He smiled. 'You can sit down now.'

Isabella sat and bent to the basket Lisette had brought and handed him an orange. He took it with a smile.

'I will walk you home,' Tom said.

'Really, there is no need, Tom. I can walk up the hill on my own.'

Lisette's mother was ill and she had asked Tom to see Isabella safe to the house so that she could stay on with her mother in her cottage.

'I had thought of walking you home by the cliff path, then across the fields so that we can catch the breeze above the headland, if you are not too tired?'

Isabella's spirit soared. She had no wish to go back to the house.

'I am not tired,' she said, 'and it is a much nicer walk than along the road.'

Tom covered the figurehead and shut the gates of the boatyard. They walked up the road and then turned off for the coastal path. He took the basket for the climb uphill. At the top of the cliff the next cove glittered below them. The sea was enticing, a deep navy. They walked on the soft dry grass, full of clover and little yellow and blue cliff flowers, for half a mile or so and then started to descend to the next cove. The fields above the cove led back to the Summer House.

Tom took Isabella's arm down the path full of loose stones, but even so she kept losing her footing. She tried to keep the image out of her head, she even hummed a little out-of-breath tune to deflect herself, but as she neared the bottom of the path and the loose stones rolled and bounced to the dry white sand the image flashed again, as clear as in her dreams. The reality she never actually saw: Mama flying over her horse's neck and her head connecting with the jagged rock lying ... there ... there, in that same place.

Isabella could remember turning at the sea's edge and seeing the crumpled figure lying motionless like a broken doll. She could remember the terrifying gallop back across the sand towards that still figure as she hung on to the reins and saddle, screaming, 'Mama, Mama, Mama. No! No! No!'

They had reached the bottom of the track and were onto the sand, and Isabella was shaking. Tom, startled, looked down at her ashen face.

'What is it, Isabella?'

She pointed to the dark slash of rock. 'Mama ... died there.'

'Oh!' How could he have forgotten that was the place?

'Of course ... Isabella ... I'm sorry. Come ...'

He took her hand and made her run towards the sea away from

the rock and the image of Helena's blood soaking into the sand. They reached the sea out of breath.

'I am sorry,' Tom said. 'I did not think, Isabella . . . I had forgotten it was here.'

'It is all right. I am all right now, Tom. It is just I never came back here . . . It is the first time . . .'

Her hand in his was burning.

Tom touched her cheek with the backs of his fingers.

'You are so hot! Isabella, do not get heatstroke or I will be blamed for keeping you in the sun too long. I am not conscious of time when I am carving. You must call out when you are tired . . .'

'I am fine, Tom. It is just uncommonly warm for June and we have had no wind for days.'

Tom looked down at her. 'Go into the sea. Take off your shoes and go in. The water is cold and will cool you.'

Isabella blushed painfully. 'I cannot. No, I cannot.'

Tom realized suddenly that she would have to take off her stockings. He sat in the sand and took his boots off, rolled his trousers up to the knee.

'I am going to walk into the sea. Take your stockings off, I will not see. Then come into the water.'

Without waiting for an answer he moved away, walked into the small waves leaving Isabella standing awkwardly not knowing what to do. She longed to take her thick stockings off, release her feet from the prim lace-up ankle boots, to feel the sand between her toes again as she had as a child.

The sight of Tom moving about in the shallow water was more than she could bear. Quickly she lifted her skirts and rolled her stockings down, pulled her boots off and placed each stocking carefully into a boot. Then, released, she ran into the sea, holding her skirts free of the small, slapping, cooling waves.

Tom turned to see Isabella's laughing face. Her hair was coming loose and she was so extraordinarily beautiful he forgot to breathe.

'Oh,' she cried. 'This is good! I have not been in the water for so long . . .' She stopped as she saw his face. Tom stood there staring at her, transfixed. For the first time in her life, Isabella felt the exhilarating power of her own beauty. It was exciting and blindingly powerful. She lifted her skirts a little higher and turned from him and began to run through the shallows, splashing and laughing, not caring if the salt ruined her dress, not caring how wet she became, only wanting to hang on to this feeling of freedom.

The cold sea against her ankles was intoxicating and she ran and ran, wishing for the first time she was just a girl from the village who could do this every day if she felt like it. She skirted out of the sea but kept running on the wet sand along the edge of the waves.

Tom had come out of the water and picked up the basket and their shoes, and was walking in the shallows towards her. Isabella could see when she turned that he was laughing at her. She waited for him to catch up and they stood smiling at each other, then he said in that particular voice that made her stomach turn over, for it seemed to be saying something quite different, 'I must get you home, Lady Isabella.'

'Indeed?'

'Indeed, indeed!'

Isabella giggled. They moved onto the dry sand and Tom handed her the basket with her shoes and stockings. He took his shirt off and bent to dry her feet. He carefully brushed away the wet, clinging grains of sand from her toes, and when he had dried both feet as well as he could, he placed them on his rough blue shirt and stared at them a moment. He could still see the faint marks of her ankle boots on her skin.

He touches me. He touches my feet. His fingers brush the glistening, scratching grains of sand. Those fingers which carve my likeness now touch my skin.

Tom got up abruptly and walked towards the far rocks where he turned his back to put his own boots on. Isabella stood on his shirt and quickly pulled her stockings back on, then sat on the sand to do up her boots.

When she was done she lifted Tom's shirt and shook it free of sand, but there on the front was the clear imprint of her feet. She lifted the shirt to her face and breathed it in, breathed in the smell of Tom.

Tom turned and saw Isabella's face bent into his shirt. Desire shot through him like buckshot. He turned quickly away to the sea before she looked up. The water was bright with sparks, the sun was sinking lower at the end of the day, and Tom fought with himself, confronted the enormity of his feelings. No fantasy, this, no flight of his imagination. This thing between them was a factor he could no longer control.

Isabella reached him and held out his shirt.

'Thank you,' she said to his brown naked back.

Tom turned to take the shirt. Isabella stared at the fair hairs running over his chest. Everything about this man was beautiful. Before she could stop herself she had reached out and touched the warmth of his skin, startling herself as much as him. They stared at one another, fascinated and afraid. Tom battled with himself, breathing hard. Isabella was willing him; touch me, touch me. Oh God, touch me.

Tom broke eye contact, quickly took his shirt and pulled it over his head, bent to take the basket, and they walked in complete silence across the sand and up the path to regain the fields. Tom helped her over the stiles without meeting her eyes. He could find no words to say that would sound right, although he rehearsed them in his head. He felt her embarrassment and wanted to break the silence, but he could not trust himself to say what he should.

They came out on the road, just below the small house.

'Will Lisette be home?' he asked finally before he left her at the gate.

'I do not think so.' Isabella took the basket. 'Thank you for walking me home. I hope that you will not have missed your meal.'

'Will I see you tomorrow? It will not be long now before I finish. I will try not to keep you too long.'

Isabella nodded. 'I will be there if you need me. Goodnight, Tom.'

Her voice was small and tight and miserable. She looked as wretched as he felt.

'Goodnight, Isabella,' he said.

Isabella looked at him then, caught something in his voice, then she turned and went inside the house and shut the door.

*   *   *

That night I toss and turn. Sleep evades me. I am angry with myself. I burn and the bedcover suffocates me. I kick it off. Isabella's face keeps passing before my eyes. She had gazed at me like a small flower opening. She reached out and touched me and I turned away. I wounded her for I did not have the wit to play light of it, to pass it off as play, to talk of other things, to distract her as I should have done.

Isabella is without guile. Her feelings play across her face openly. She is like a child who has been too long restricted by adults who would like to keep her safe in the nursery, and I feel a sudden, unjustified anger towards Sir Richard.

I see her face pressed into the blue of my shirt. Her hair is dark against it. I see her small childlike hands and those narrow, confined little feet trapped in boots ...

I throw the cover off, leap out of bed and climb down the ladder and out into the still night. Not a breath, only the infinite distant roar of the ocean. I begin to walk and find myself climbing the hill towards the house where Isabella will be lying asleep.

I know Lisette will not be there tonight, my mother told me Morwenna Penrose is dying. Isabella is in the care of the cook and one housemaid.

The house is in darkness and I have no idea why I have come or what I will do. Neither do I know which room Isabella sleeps in. Isabella has told me she can hear and see the sea from her window. So she must sleep at the front of the house. I stand looking up at the windows. The middle window must be a landing so it must be one of the rooms to the right or left of the front door.

The left room has light cotton curtains and I decide this must be where Isabella sleeps, and I stand in the dark looking upwards.

Isabella could not sleep. How could she, a married woman, have touched him, again?

I did not mean to, she kept whispering over and over, *it just happened. I reached out like a sleepwalker and now I have to endure the torment of having embarrassed Tom and myself. Oh, if only I could have the afternoon back and begin again ...*

Isabella threw herself on her back in agony as she remembered.

She had thought … What had she thought? That he … She thought back to how he had looked at her in the water … It was unmistakable, that look.

Admiring you does not mean he will … will … What had she wanted him to do? She closed her eyes … She did not know. She was not thinking, just feeling …

She thumped the pillow. She would never sleep now, and she would look pale and drawn tomorrow and would wake ugly and he would not be able to carve her likeness … She jumped out of bed and walked round the little room. Thank God Lisette was not there … *How selfish I am, I have not thought about poor Lisette and her mother once.*

Isabella went to the window. There was a half-moon and clouds were racing past it. Then, under the tree by the gate, she made out a figure. She drew back a little, her heart thumping, gazing downwards, and the figure moved forward towards the window and stood on the lawn looking up. It was Tom Welland.

Startled, she opened her window and whispered down,

'What are you doing here? Is it Lisette? Is she all right?'

Tom shook his head. 'She is still with Morwenna. I have something I must say to you, Isabella. Will you come down for a moment?'

Isabella stood gazing down at him, then shut the window and pulled a wrap round her and tiptoed down the stairs. At the bottom she put on a pair of slippers and opened the front door, undid the bolt slowly, holding her breath. Then she turned the heavy key and she was standing outside, facing Tom.

He smiled. She was all in white like a snowflake.

'What is it?' she whispered, avoiding his eyes.

'Isabella … this afternoon … I am sorry … Please look at me.'

Isabella reluctantly met his eyes.

'Isabella,' he whispered. 'You did not mistake my feelings. They have been there ever since I met you again.'

They stood in the dark, facing each other in silence, and the night rustled around them moving inexorably towards daylight. Then they both moved together and Tom was pulling her to him, bending his mouth to hers, holding her face to his, kissing her again and again, and Isabella leant against him feeling his body move against hers; young, firm, exciting and unknown.

Then he drew back, pressed her head into his shoulder for a moment.

'Isabella,' he whispered. 'Go and sleep now. I will see you tomorrow.'

'Tomorrow.'

She was gone through the door. He heard the bolt and the key. Isabella raced upstairs to the window and he held a hand up to her and melted into darkness.

The sea sounded louder in the dark, but Isabella could hear her heart thumping in the silent room. After a while the birds started, slowly at first, then the whole world was full of the sound. Something stirred in Isabella. She felt the sudden smallness of herself in the world. It was a chilling, isolating sensation and, shivering, she moved down under the bedcovers.

She could not know that she and Tom had taken a step that was irrevocable. That one day she would pay a terrible price. She could not know of the hurt she would cause, or the lives she and Tom would damage, but she had a second's fleeting intimation in the dawn of a new day.

Chapter 45

Nell was thinking of going on a spring cruise to celebrate finishing the monster picture. She had taken so long its owners seemed to have forgotten about it. She missed Elan and knew there was a chance he might not come back, or at least not live there permanently.

She was cleaning his cottage to combat the January blues. She did not want him to come back to the cottage just as he had left it, with all the paraphernalia of a dying man still in the house. It had rained solidly for days and she had watched Gabby itching to get back to London to work. Nell didn't blame her. She had never grown sanguine about Cornish winters either.

Lucinda seemed to be finding Gabby plenty of work with the gallery and with private collectors. She had stopped taking on local work, apart from small paintings for loyal clients. It was a shame, Nell thought, that Gabby couldn't strike a balance, somehow. She knew the money Gabby earned in London had been a godsend for both Gabby and Charlie, but she looked thin, tired and permanently preoccupied.

Nell looked down at the pile of things Patrick had needed that must go back to social services. She thought of Gabby's exhausted outburst before Christmas. It had been startling and disturbing.

Gabby was changing, Nell realized. She was suddenly seeing what Nell had tried to warn her about from the start of her marriage. Charlie's casual selfishness. It had taken far longer for Gabby to build up a healthy resentment to her marriage than it had taken Nell with Ted.

She threw open the kitchen window, which stuck. She saw the ledge was rotting and took in the air of neglect, the smell of damp that granite cottages so quickly assumed when unlived in.

Come home, Elan, I miss you.

Oh, how she missed his sometimes bitchy humour and the knowledge he was here in his cottage painting, always glad to see her. They went back such a long way and there was a shorthand old friends used which could never be replicated. A moving through life together, watching a familiar face grow older and yet seem exactly the same as ever.

Life moved on. Patrick, the dedicated and tireless GP, was dead. Elan was floating, looking for a place to land, and that might mean anywhere and everywhere. Gabby, the biddable and pliant housewife, had moved on, too; Nell was unsure where she was roosting or how this commuting back and forth was going to work out in the long-term.

She was amazed that Gabby could settle happily in one room in London, especially in spring and summer. Gabby had always come alive when the weather changed. She lived outside, revelled in the sun and colour of the sea, had never ceased to be enchanted.

Nell knew this Lucinda existed because she had spoken to her on the phone. Gabby insisted her room was lovely and the two of them had obviously become friends. It was surprising, for she would not have said Gabby was ambitious, but she obviously was.

The figurehead seemed to have given her confidence and kudos. In all the years she had been on the farm Nell had never known Gabby make a close friend of her own age. Of course, young mothers came in for tea with their children when Josh was small, but Gabby never had a *mate*, never telephoned or gossiped.

When Nell had pressed the young and self-contained Gabby, she had said, 'Nell, I have you and Josh, the farm and Charlie. I don't need anything or anyone else.'

Nell, standing in Elan's tiny sitting room, realized with horror she was yearning for the days when Gabby needed her; when the work of the farm threw them together, day in and day out.

Dear God, I'm lonely, Nell thought. *Which means I haven't moved on and I damn well should have.*

Gabby drove over to St Piran to look at Lady Isabella. Peter had rung and told her that donations to the museum had been surprisingly good. They had started a 'Friends of St Piran Museum Fund' and many locals had contributed. It had been a good summer opening. Lady Isabella could draw in the crowds.

Gabby walked over to the vicarage for the key. John was taking an adult confirmation class and mouthed, 'Come back after you've checked Isabella, we'll open a bottle.'

Gabby grinned at his expression; it was obviously going to be a long afternoon.

Isabella stood in her corner, as majestic and beguiling as ever. She had not deteriorated any further in the even temperature of the museum. Gabby checked her base where the rot had begun to set in and which she had treated. It was stable and had not spread, but would definitely have to be treated again at some point.

Isabella's right hand possibly once held a flower and both hands must have been beautifully carved.

'Your arm, I think, is a priority, Isabella, and an insult to your original carver. I will come and fix that soon, I promise.'

She stood looking at the beautiful face in the faded light of the museum. Isabella gazed steadily back. The more Gabby stared at her face, the more warmth and feeling seemed to enter the wood and give Isabella's face fleeting expression, like the shadows from the branches of a tree playing across a window.

Gabby shivered but could not move away. The wooden

eyes were dark, dark brown, and held her, mesmerizing her with their intent. It was as if Isabella was trying to tell Gabby something. The hairs moved on Gabby's arms. The figurehead seemed suddenly large in this confined space and the winter light was dying. Gabby felt too spooked to move away, then, out of nowhere, she had a clear image of a grave; overgrown, hidden and covered in lichen. Then it was gone and Isabella was just a figurehead once more, standing in a dusty little corner of a museum, quite still and inanimate.

Gabby shivered again and went out of the door, locked it, and then found herself walking not down to the gate but through the narrow paths of the old, overgrown graveyard. The rain had stopped and the earth smelt damp and lifeless, but in spring it was a beautiful place full of colour and life and wildflowers.

She was drawn to a far corner of the graveyard where the headstones were ancient and ornate. Two faced the sea. They were hidden with dead grass and brambles. Gabby bent and pulled at the nearest until she could read the name inscribed on it. The words on the grave were worn and disappearing:

Morley Penro e 1802–1840
A mariner n th arm of t   sea he loved.
Hu band of Mo wen a Penrose
Fat er of Lisette

Then, added at a later date:

M rwe na Penrose 1810–1866
Beloved Mot er of Lisette

The names meant nothing to Gabrielle. She pulled the dead winter grass from the second grave. The brambles were huge and tore her gloves as she moved them up and behind the grave to read the inscription. She crouched in the wet grass peering down at the grave. She could feel her heart racing with excitement but she did not know why.

Lisette Penrose 1827–1890
Faithful servant and friend
To Thomas from 1867–1890
And to Isabella, his mother, before him

Isabella . . . his mother! No surname for Thomas or Isabella.

Gabby straightened up. She was trembling with cold and something she was struggling to remember. She felt strange and light-headed.

She made her way slowly to the vicarage. John Bradbury opened the door and exclaimed over her ashen face, wet, muddy jeans and scratched hands. As he took her waterproof jacket, Gabby saw her face in his old spotted mirror in the hall. Her face was wild. For a second she thought she saw a reflection of another dark young woman behind her, then it was gone and she was left staring at herself and at the vicar's startled expression behind her.

She turned to John Bradbury. 'I've found Isabella's name on a grave.'

Chapter 46

It was late April and Elan was crossing Paddington Station to pick up the 'Cornish Riviera' train to Penzance, when he spotted a small familiar figure in the flood of people flowing off the incoming train. She was wearing jeans with a snazzy little suede jacket he had not seen before. A pale mauve scarf was knotted fashionably at her neck and she looked for all the world like a seasoned city girl. She was scanning the barrier ahead and Elan was just about to wave and call out, 'Cooee, darling – what a surprise!' when he saw her face light up. She was laughing with pleasure, throwing back her head in sudden joy.

Elan turned and looked to his right through the crowds. A tall figure stood watching Gabby hurrying towards him. It was the Canadian Elan had briefly met at his exhibition before he had made his escape.

As Gabby reached him, Mark Hannah held out his arms and Gabby walked straight into them, and they stood there to one side of the barrier just holding each other. *What a risk they are taking standing there for all to see near the platform for trains to Cornwall. What a risk.*

Elan watched with a sinking heart. Still they stood there holding each other and rocking slowly amid the crowds, and Elan saw it was a homecoming, a coming to rest, a serious thing. Not an affair, a fling, a light-hearted tryst.

At last they broke away, gazed at each other for a second in a way that made Elan ache to remember. *It's you. You.*

Then they turned and disappeared into the crowd. Elan's

train was being announced and he moved stiffly with a sigh. He suddenly felt very old. What a kaleidoscope life was; jiggle a little and all the colours shifted and changed position.

He thought of Josh. Grown-up or not, Josh would never accept what he would see as Gabby's betrayal, if she ever left Charlie. He adored his godson, but Josh had never had a thing go wrong in his life, just three adults – four, if he counted himself – who thought he was the bee's knees. He would not handle this sort of shock well; of this Elan was sure. If Gabby chose to go off with this Canadian she would lose Josh . . . but maybe it would not come to that.

He could not picture Gabby away from the farm. More than half her life had been spent there. Against all the odds, Gabby and Charlie had stayed together. As he boarded his train he thought of Nell and of the wonderful four days they had had together when she had flown out to join him in Venice.

Then Gabby's joyful face came back to him, a lighting up of something deep inside her, a radiance he had never seen before. A different Gabrielle. *Such happiness*. It would be short-lived, as she would learn, for it would have been gained at the expense of other lives.

Elan climbed into his first-class carriage with a sigh. No, he was certainly not going to say anything to Nell.

Chapter 47

Mark and Gabby were sitting in a restaurant by the river which was gilded in spring sunshine. Ducks flippantly turned tail and swans floated elegantly past in the quick current, like dignified judges. On the other side of the river under the trees a man and a child threw bread into the silvery water for them.

'I've just had a letter from John Bradbury. He's met an old lady in a nursing home who remembers the last family of Vyvyans living in the village when she was a child. He says she is a fount of knowledge about her childhood in St Piran, but keeps wandering on to other subjects just as it all gets interesting!'

Mark laughed. 'I've been there. It takes endless patience, oceans of tea, and then just as you're leaving the dear old thing will drop into the conversation the one thing you've been angling for all the time. We ought to have a national grid to tap into the memory and recollections of the old sitting out their lives. Whole pieces of history and perspective lost because none of us have time to listen . . . Oh, Gabriella, I'm on my soapbox again. Has that nice priest recovered yet from the sight of you at Christmas with your hair on end, burbling about graves?'

Gabby laughed. 'I think so. Apparently I kept saying Isabella had led me there and he kept saying I was overtired and I must remember that the museum had been a church, and churches can be atmospheric in the dark and lead people to think they have had supernatural experiences.'

'You would have thought a man of the cloth would be the first person to acknowledge the supernatural!'

'In the morning I wasn't so sure I hadn't dreamt or imagined the whole weird experience. I'm glad John drove me over to the house that had once been Perannose Manor. It is now a huge Christian conference centre. I wanted to look at the inscriptions above the Vyvyan crypt.

'There she was: *Helena, née Viscaria, Beloved wife of Daniel and mother to Isabella.* Then Daniel Vyvyan at a much later date and then his second wife, Charlotte. It suddenly all seemed so real to me. Isabella must only have been a child when Helena died. I felt, looking at that huge family crypt and finding those graves in the Methodist graveyard, that Isabella meant me to make a connection . . . I know that sounds . . . strange.'

Mark leant towards her. 'No, not strange at all to me.'

Gabby sipped her ice-cold wine. 'It would be wonderful to find Isabella's grave and know when and how old she was when she died.'

'I'm rather jealous that I don't have the time to go on digging around myself. I couldn't justify any more time, even as a research project. University budgets don't extend to international flights to the UK for students! But you know it's great that the village is getting involved. You'd be amazed what people come up with. My best researchers back home are retired. They have the time and the patience to look and listen.'

'I know the museum is repaying you for the cost of transporting Isabella from Montreal, but it must have cost you a bomb to get her from Newfoundland. And you made a gift of her to Cornwall. You are amazingly generous, Mark Hannah, and I love you for it, but you are no businessman.'

Mark smiled. 'So my wife tells me.'

He poured Gabby more wine and picked up her hand.

'We may both be barking, Gabriella, but I believe you were meant to find those graves in the same way that I discovered the figurehead. I had no intention of going to Bonavista Bay

308

the day I found her. In fact, the trip to Newfoundland and the Memorial University weren't even strictly necessary, more a sudden odd need to visit my birthplace . . .'

He stopped for a minute, looked away and twiddled his wine glass.

'As you get older the past seems suddenly more relevant. Perhaps that's the reason I've always loved history; there is so much to learn that connects in surprising ways. Research often throws up such unexpected and exciting things that link human beings through the ages.

'The garden where I first saw the figurehead belonged to the house I'd once lived in as a child. I stood at the gate and I couldn't take my eyes off her . . . I don't know whether something about her reminded me of my mother, for I have no conscious memory of her or the house. I only knew I had to own that powerful wooden face.'

Gabby shivered. 'Did you think that you were there to take her home, to *her* birthplace?'

'No. Not at that moment. I just simply had to have her.' Mark grinned. 'It was not a practical decision if you live in a suburban house with a large family and an already crowded yard . . . I guess what spooked me most was why I had been drawn so powerfully back after so many years to the house where I was born. Perhaps a sudden subconscious need to check my origins or to see if there really had been a house where I began my life. If I had been a week earlier I wouldn't have even known the figurehead existed because she had been kept in a shed, so the motivation that drew me there seemed of great importance . . .'

He closed Gabby's fingers round his own. 'And, in the light of meeting you, my darling, it makes me tempted to believe nothing is really chance . . .'

Gabby said slowly, turning his hand in hers, 'You brought Isabella thousands of miles back home, and even if the real Isabella has no grave in St Piran, the figurehead marks her birthplace.'

'The real one is haunting us, too, Gabriella. I believe the

answer lies with her carver, Tom Welland. You only have to look at Isabella's face to know how the carver felt about her. It's all there, the sensuous abandon and intimacy. It is unlikely there could have been a happy ending.'

The river outside was rising and a waiter came to take their order. For a moment a small shadow obliterated the weak heat of the spring sunshine. Mark and Gabby stared at each other. The joy of being back together made them both reluctant to break the spell and talk about practical things. For the moment it was possible to have each other and it was easier not to face the future. Soon, very soon, they would have to address it, but it was only when they were apart it became unbearable. Now, together again, the weeks slipped by and it seemed possible to put off hurting other people for a little longer.

Gabby said now, 'Mark, when I've finished this picture at the Tate, I'll have to go home. Charlie is driving Nell mad with eclipse fever. She says the whole of Cornwall is going potty with avarice and Charlie is the leading contender.'

Mark smiled. 'I like the sound of your Nell. If you believe the papers the whole world is headed west!'

'I doubt it, if people are going to have to pay a thousand pounds for a few days in a cottage!'

Mark whistled through his teeth. 'Ouch! Smugglers and wreckers, ever?

'Do you realize, Gabriella Ellis, we have known each other for more than a year?'

Gabby sighed. 'I can hardly remember a time before you, Mark Hannah!'

Mark slid a small, beautifully wrapped box across the table.

'What is this?' Gabby turned it in her hands.

'I waited until I saw something I thought you would like.'

Gabby unwrapped the box and took out a thin silver chain with a tiny pearl encased in a silver acorn. Mark watched her face. She held it up and the silvery sunshine caught it. She swallowed; met his eyes. She had never owned anything so beautiful.

'I love it. I simply love it, Mark . . .'

She leant forward and took his face in her hands, and kissed him lingeringly on the mouth. She did not care who was watching.

'Thank you *so* much, it is utterly beautiful.'

Other people sitting out by the river gave a little cheer and started clapping.

When they were home Mark fastened it for her as they stood in front of the mirror in the hall. Between her white shirt and dark skin it lay like a perfect little tear.

Gabby watched Mark sleep. He could relax like a cat, fall instantly asleep, and breathe so shallowly he seemed not to breathe at all. His limbs seemed, to her biased eyes, languid and infinitely desirable, even in sleep.

His long legs protruded out of the bottom of the duvet or lay curled against hers. She loved those moments of waking and watching him, unaware, sleeping. Tenderness and wonder that it was possible to enjoy and love a human being in the way she loved Mark amazed her.

He was such a beautiful man, must always have been so. Did his wife still see him this way? Would it ever be possible for Mark to seem ordinary and everyday to Veronique? Could she still see him with those first eyes now, many years and many children later?

Gabby leant forward and placed her lips against Mark's arm. His mind and body excited her, and how lucky was that.

Mark stirred at the feel of her mouth on his skin, and without seeming to wake turned to scoop her to him and they lay length by length, bodies touching as the flicker that was always there slowly ignited and tenderly they explored one another all over again.

Gabby could not have imagined there were so many ways of loving; she had only ever known the fumble and the mostly silent act in the dark. Nothing had prepared her for the sheer power of passion or the sweet melancholy of intimacy which could make you feel so alone when separated from the one you loved.

Gabby also found it frightening growing so close to someone, for other things began to loosen and unravel like a grubby bandage she had worn too long. Lying close, limbs wrapped round limbs, she had suddenly found herself forming words and sentences she had never wished to disclose, and it was only her terror of bringing ghosts into their lives that stopped her. That, and a feeling that if she once started the thunderous Niagara of emotion that surrounded her childhood with Clara, she might never be able to stop.

Mark sensed her need, but knew he must wait. He hoped as the months and years went by Gabriella would, in fits and starts, open up to him.

For Gabby the healing had already begun, diminishing the power of memory. The pinching of budding breasts, the laughter at the hands reaching up under her little pleated uniform skirt, fingers ready to grab before she understood what it was they wanted to take.

Desire, the love of a man's body, the excitement and tenderness it produced in her, was a revelation to Gabby. She could never have believed that sex and love could come together in one mind-blowing fundamental act and this simple wonderful fact made her understand how badly she had been affected. How perverse her view of sex and love.

Love was not passive and should not be confused with contentment. Never getting angry, avoiding all confrontation. Willing yourself happy, never ever daring to think you were not, would not do.

Gabby knew the time was coming when she would have to let go of her ghosts. She was too happy for them to intrude now and she and Mark had the rest of their lives to talk, she was surer of that than anything.

Chapter 48

In the two months before the summer eclipse Charlie and Alan drove up to the three large fields on the west side of the farm. They were cleared and ready with an extra standing tap which had been linked to the mains from the old piggery. Charlie had had another one put in the lane, beside one of the farm cottages. The mobile toilets had been ordered as well as litter-bins for all four corners of the fields.

Alan disapproved. 'You're taking a risk, Charlie. You've seen the papers, there are too many locals prepared to rip visitors off. I really believe a lot of people will stay away. Some of the prices being asked for cottages and camping spaces are abhorrent. Word has got out that Cornwall is in for a killing and if people don't come in the numbers expected, if you've misjudged the cost of hiring all this, it's going to leave you with a red face.'

'Of course they'll come, Alan, it's a once in a lifetime experience. Every one of the cottages are booked, have been since Christmas.'

'Yes, because Nell took the bookings and asked a perfectly reasonable price; above the norm, but not excessive.'

'Don't you understand, Alan? The farm is in an absolutely perfect position for the eclipse. People will come in their thousands and I want to be ready and organized, not to have to chase people from my land.'

'Charlie, I warn you, you are putting the land at risk. Very few people can afford to pay what you're asking, especially the kids. Last-minute travellers will pitch anywhere, whether you like it or not. You are advertising your fields widely. This land will already have been spread all over the Internet as available. Charge a reasonable price and you will at least fill one or two fields with people who you won't have a problem with . . .'

'Alan, how often does a chance like this come along? I could clear the remainder of my overdraft . . . We've had a pretty good financial year, this is the icing.'

Alan stared at him. 'You're the boss, Charlie, but I disapprove of what you are doing.'

'You're my accountant as well as my farm manager. What problem can you have with me hiring out my fields to those who want to see something they will never experience again in their lifetime?'

'You could say it was their right to see a natural phenomenon without getting ripped-off. You know the problems, Charlie, as well as I do. You are going to have horrendous litter and noise and drugs, and that equals trouble. Hawkers will descend with vans, selling environmentally hazardous food, and worst of all, what about the travellers who will not leave at the end of the weekend . . .'

God, what an old woman he is, Charlie thought.

Charlie had had numerous rows with Nell over this. In fact she was as angry as he'd seen her for some time. She had called him greedy and irresponsible and now Alan was going all tight-lipped on him.

They got into the Land Rover and headed back to the farm in silence. Nell came out of the back door and called, 'Charlie, Josh has been on the phone, he wants you to ring him back.'

'What did he say? Is he in trouble?'

'No, he's being posted. Ring his mobile, Charlie.'

Charlie was concerned. Josh never rang him during the day. He dialled Josh's number as he walked across the yard.

'Hi, Charlie.'

'Hello, son, what's up?'

'Just to tell you I've suddenly been posted. Gabby isn't going to like it, so I thought I'd better tell you first.'

'Where?'

'Well, you know I told you I was with Joint Helicopter Command? It's an attack and observer squadron. We are just off to the Gulf. It's more or less a training exercise really. We'll be based on an aircraft carrier monitoring the no-fly zones.'

'A bit dodgy out there, isn't it?'

'It's safe enough, Charlie. I'm not flying jets!'

'Do you have time to come home before you leave?'

'I doubt I'll have time, there's a lot to do. I'm replacing someone who suddenly got ill, so they jumped me into his place.'

'When do you leave?'

'Saturday morning. Four days' time.'

'How do you feel about being "jumped", Josh?'

'I'm excited, Charlie, it's great to be picked. It's what I joined up for. I don't want to sit around on my arse!'

Charlie felt uneasy. 'Isn't it a bit early to send you on that sort of mission?'

'If they didn't think I could do the job, they wouldn't be sending me.'

'True.'

'Gabby's still in London, isn't she?'

'Yes. She's due home on Friday, why?'

'Well, I thought if I couldn't get home I might get up to London to see her before I leave.'

'Nell will know exactly where she's working this week, I don't, but you've got her mobile, haven't you?'

'Yep. Charlie, I have to go. I'll ring again, soon. OK?'

'OK, son.'

He looked at Nell's face and saw Josh had already told her.

'Nell, it is no good you and Gabby getting all female and jumpy every time Josh is posted to a trouble spot.'

'Have I said a word?'

'No, your face says it.'

'Actually, I have every faith in my grandson to take care of himself. After all, he's not going to war.'

Charlie didn't answer. He was sure Josh would be all right, but those damn helicopters occasionally had a habit of falling from the sky.

The following day Josh drove to London with another pilot who was also bound for the Gulf and wanted to say goodbye to his parents. They parked in Chelsea Barracks, and when Josh had finished finding some equipment he needed he set off to meet Gabby, who was working on a private commission in a little gallery near the Portland where Elan exhibited.

He found her alone and she showed him into a back room where she was cleaning an early oil of a young girl on a horse. Josh peered at it.

'I'm always amazed that women managed to stay on, riding side-saddle. I can't see how they didn't fly over the horse's head.'

'Someone once told me that they had a pummel to hold on to which made up for not being able to grip the horse, but I'm not convinced either. Imagine hunting, side-saddle!'

'Great painting. He could certainly paint horses, makes me long to ride again. Have you just uncovered all that detail, Gabby, with the reins and the girl's fingers?'

'Yes. It's fascinating, I don't think this painting has ever been cleaned and I'm uncovering little treasures everywhere. It's a lovely painting to work on. Anyway, let's go for lunch. I've just got to lock up as Arabella's also at lunch.'

Josh looked around the small trendy gallery with the latest mod lighting and mooched round studying the paintings on the walls while Gabby got her jacket and fixed the alarm.

Josh grinned. 'You're getting to know an awful lot of girls called Lucinda or Arabella . . .'

'Mmm, and Catriona and Minty.'

They walked along the street and Gabby hugged Josh's arm.

'This is so nice, me taking you out to lunch.'

Josh looked down at her. Gabby looked very pretty in linen trousers and a light jacket. Different, somehow. 'You're getting really established up here, aren't you?'

'I am getting quite a lot of work, thanks to Lucinda who refers people to me. But, you know, restoring comes in fits and starts so I'm not complacent . . . I thought we'd eat here in this little Italian place, it's the only one I've tried and it's pretty good, I think.'

When they were sitting down, Josh said, 'It's quite weird having lunch with you in London. I always picture you at home, even though I know you work up here quite a lot.' He looked at her closely. 'I'd never have thought you could live in a city away from the sea, Gabby. When I was small it was a major deal getting you to Truro!'

Gabby laughed. 'I surprise myself sometimes, but I've made good friends and work contacts here and I enjoy London, mostly, and . . .'

'. . . You know you can always go back home to Charlie and the sea.'

Oh Josh. 'Yes,' Gabby said. 'Now concentrate for a moment, darling, what are you going to have? Choose anything.'

They both stared at their menus. *We are skirting the Gulf. I don't want him to go. I want to pretend we are just having lunch because he happens to be in London.*

Their drinks arrived and they ordered their meal. Josh noticed Gabby had white wine. *Gabby drinks now,* he thought fondly.

Josh sipped his cold beer and said, 'I'm out there for such a short time, Gabby. No more than a training exercise really. Pilots have to gain experience in the climate they might have to work in. When I've gone you mustn't go reading the papers and believing everything you read if there is a lurid article on Iraq. Servicemen are in and out of the Gulf all the time . . .'

He watched her. 'I'll probably spend a lot of time sitting around with the Navy guys getting drunk.'

'No change there, then?' Gabby said lightly, smiling. 'Josh, don't look so worried. This shooting off to places I'd rather you didn't go is something I'm going to have to get used to, isn't it?'

Josh laughed. 'That's what Marika said.'

'Will you have time to see her before you go?'

'We're going to drop in to see her on the way back. She's home at the moment. Gabby, I've written names of the various officers to contact in case of any emergency. I might have occasional access to a computer and I will e-mail you, but you might not be able to e-mail me back.'

'You'll have cabins, will you? Are there barracks or a mess or anything in Kuwait?'

'I'm not sure what the form is yet. I haven't really been briefed properly. I won't be swinging in a hammock from the masts, Gab!'

Gabby felt suddenly anxious. 'Those photos of helicopters you e-mailed me, they seem so huge and complicated. You haven't been flying for five minutes. Why can't they send someone more experienced?'

'Gabby, how would I gain experience if I didn't fly? This is part of my training. Stop worrying, these new helicopters are amazing machines.'

Their food came and Josh said, 'Wow, I'm going to enjoy this! Not sure what the food will be like out there . . .'

'Josh,' Gabby said abruptly, 'what about jabs, what about malaria tablets?'

'It's OK, we all had to have the injections as a regiment, in case we got suddenly posted, and I started my malaria tablets as soon as I knew I was going out there.'

'We could rush and get you stuff you'll need from Boots. We could do it after lunch . . . Josh, you should take soap and sun stuff and Imodium and mosquito repellent, talc, you know, and foot things . . .'

'Gabby, stop! Eat. You haven't touched your food. If

there's time, thanks. But don't worry, Marika is also getting stuff for me, it's giving her something to do . . .'

'Please take care, Josh, *please*.'

'Of course I will. You know me!'

As they walked back towards the gallery, Josh said, 'Gabby, would you mind if I shot off now? It's just Marika . . . I won't have much time with her.' He hugged her. 'I promise I'll take a crate full of medicine out with me . . . half of Boots!'

Gabby held Josh tight. 'Love you lots . . .'

'Love you, too. Thanks for lunch. It was great seeing where you work. I can sort of imagine it now while I'm away . . .'

'I'm going home on Friday. Will you be able to ring before you fly out?'

'Of course! I've had my orders from Nell. I'll talk to you all on Friday, Gab. Take care.'

''Bye, darling.'

Josh turned and started to walk away, and as he did so Gabby was seized by a terrible, irrational fear. She started to run after him, stifled, '*Josh, wait!*'

She stood watching his figure until it disappeared into the crowd, her heart beating absurdly in the crowd of a city afternoon. She went back to the gallery which Arabella had opened and told her she was going to finish for the day.

On the way to the tube she started to ring Mark and then remembered he was giving a lecture. She thought of Nell, hesitated, but did not ring her. She made her way to the National Portrait Gallery and Lucinda gave her coffee and made her laugh.

That night Gabby said to Mark, 'It's so illogical and childishly superstitious, this need to be in Cornwall when Josh leaves, as if Josh is going to be any safer whether I am here or at home . . .'

'Go home, my sweet. Superstition does not come into it. It's perfectly understandable.'

Mark turned to Gabby. Mahler was playing, beautiful but

achingly sad. A mistake, he thought, and got up to turn it down.

'No,' Gabby said, 'leave it, I love it. It is my favourite piece.'

'But sad, my darling, very, very sad.'

In bed, in the dark, they made love to the echo of the music and afterwards Mark said, 'We don't talk about the future, Gabriella. Are we afraid of it?'

'Yes.' Gabby held Mark's face to hers in the dark. 'It's frightening. I love you so much I dare not talk . . . in case you've changed your mind . . . in case it spoils this life we're living . . .'

Mark laughed quietly. 'Change *my* mind. Oh my darling Gabriella, that is not going to happen. But it is easier for me, my ties are across an ocean, yours are five hours away . . .'

'But they are there, Mark, in exactly the same way.'

'Yes. It's just gathering the courage to hurt . . .'

Mark sat up and pulled a pillow behind his head. He felt his age suddenly. Old and wise and . . . resigned? He was not sure whether resigned was the word, but he was aware that he could lose Gabriella any moment. There was a pull for her of a life unfinished. His children were older and leading their own lives, totally independent of him.

That was not quite true. It was what he thought when he imagined himself leaving Veronique permanently for this life he had with Gabriella. He had known since Christmas that he wanted to share his life with this woman, but if she went back to her own life he would not go back to his.

'Have you . . . changed . . . ? Do you feel different, Mark?'

Mark smiled in the dark. 'Oh, no, Mrs Ellis, I haven't changed. I am just as irresponsibly besotted as I was that first time in your funny little museum.'

'You stared horribly and embarrassingly.'

'I couldn't help it.'

'Of course you could!'

'I could not. I was expecting a very earnest, rather large Cornish lady in socks and sandals with fierce iron-grey hair

320

pulled up into a bun, or with an ethnically long plait down her back . . .'

Gabby giggled. 'Why? Is that what Canadian restorers are like?'

'I've only met fierce ones who gave me nightmares.'

'You do talk a lot of codswallop, as Nell would say.'

She kissed his wrists, which she found incredibly sensuous.

'But you are very good at diversion tactics . . . I will go back, tomorrow. It's not just Josh; Nell and Charlie have had another huge row about the eclipse and she sounds very depressed. It's unlike Nell.'

Gabby paused in the dark then said it.

'I can't live without you, Mark. I love the people in my other life, but I love you more. For the first time I feel I am living the life I want, not dictated by circumstances, but by me.'

Mark did not move in the dark. *The life that I want. The life that is me.* Rilke?

Then he said quietly, 'To do what we intend to do takes an amount of selfishness and a certain fixed ruthlessness. It is not going to slide into place with anyone's blessing, my darling.'

'I know.' Gabby wrapped her arms around him. 'I know.'

Mark, sliding down into the bed, his mouth on her hair, thought, *I don't think you do, wonderful little person. I really don't think you do.*

Chapter 49

The figurehead is raised by a chain to a horizontal position at exactly the angle I will fix it to the *Lady Isabella*. Today I am concentrating on the scrolls. The figurehead has been raised so that I can get an idea of the end result, the feel of her when she is fitted against the hull of the ship, for I must follow the angle of the bow carefully to about seventy degrees. Later I will return to the face.

Before I start to carve a figurehead I spend much time assessing the shape of the ship's bow, its length and the rake of her bowsprit, for this dictates the size of a figurehead. The trail boards, the scrolls pattern that runs each side of a figurehead should fit perfectly, so that the finished figure fits exactly under the bowsprit. I know however much I calculate I will need to modify the figurehead once she is in place. I have to make sure of the depth and breadth of her so that she will not be in the way of the heavy martingale backstay and bobstay chains that lead to the dolphin striker that lies on the bowsprit.

Isabella has come early, before the heat of the morning builds to an unbearable closeness, for the days are as humid and windless as the tropics.

Lisette's mother died during the night and Lisette is sad and preoccupied. Isabella has insisted she can look after herself, to release Lisette for family duties.

I pause in my work to wipe sweat from my eyes and look across at Isabella.

'Tom,' she asks. 'How do you get the figurehead down to the ship without damaging it?'

'We use a cart which is set on the old tramlines left from the mine to get her down to the quay, then she will be winched up to the vessel where we will bolt her to the ship. I will use old sails to wrap her on the downward journey, but she is bound to be marked or chipped a little. I have to expect this and put it right when she is in position.'

I wriggle my shoulders to release the cramp in my neck and move towards her.

'Normally, I would carve in the boatyard down near the harbour where I can turn and judge the shape of the vessel while I am carving the figurehead, but I work better up here where I am not interrupted and it is quieter.'

I look up at the figurehead. 'My father came up this morning to make sure she fits into the cart. Time is short and he wants nothing to hold us up.'

Isabella gets up and wanders round the carving, looking at the way I have carved deep ruts into the wood for the drapery, incorporating it so the line is fluid behind the scrolls, so that once the figurehead is in the water she will seem to rise up from the waves as part of the ship.

'It is beautiful, Tom. I do not understand how you can create movement and life from a piece of wood, but you do.'

Isabella is wearing a white blouse of some thin material and a skirt that is of a dark shiny material, held to the waist by a belt, the clasp of which is shaped like a butterfly. The sun has given her skin radiance and lifted her hair so that small pieces glint like shiny copper. She looks very beautiful and foreign and it is hard to tear my eyes away to continue my work.

She turns and moves away under the old sail loft to the window. Out at sea there is a schooner in full sail, passing the cove swiftly. Noises from the shipbuilding yard below rise upwards; strident, hot, busy.

I see she is uncertain of the thing that lies between us, but I am also uncertain. My father this morning eyed me in that way he has as he measured the figurehead.

'Do you need Lady Isabella up here so often, Tom?'

'I have still to go back to the face and I need her for the fall of the drapery.'

'Aye, I see that, but for the moment you are doing the tail-boards, son.'

'I am, but I need to finish the face before Lady Isabella returns to Falmouth. We have such a short time to complete.'

'Aye,' my father says again, then struggling with himself, 'Do your work, son, and let Lady Isabella depart with Magor. She is too much in this yard and tongues will wag. She is no' but a girl, it's up to you to do what's proper, protect her reputation. Offend Sir Richard and we will all be out of work, lad.'

I did not answer him.

Isabella turns. We are close and I place a finger on her bottom lip.

'I must go back to work, Isabella.'

She nods, but we do not move. She is so near to me I can feel the warmth from her body. I bend swiftly to her mouth, kiss her, my mouth just touching hers. Our lips part a little then we stay quite still like two birds.

There is such sweetness in this long chaste kiss that I see tears behind her closed eyelids. At length I draw away, whisper again, 'I must carve. Should you go home?'

Isabella shakes her head. 'No. I may walk a little or read. Go, carve, I will not disturb you.'

We smile at each other.

'I carve better with you here,' I say softly, going back to the figurehead.

Isabella turned again to the sea. The schooner had almost disappeared into the horizon. She looked out at the empty sea and wondered about that time before she was born when the cove had been full of sailing ships. All those men and boys taking a voyage into the unknown, never sure if they would reach their destination.

She turned and looked about her, saw the ladder up into the old sail loft and climbed it to see what lay up there. She was surprised to find a bedroom of sorts, neat and swept, a mattress upon the floor with a clean patchwork cover, a small chair and table holding a carafe of water.

Tom sleeps here! Isabella climbed into the room. What a view! Across the small harbour and beyond was a last white sail in the distance, and red and green fishing smacks and red lobster buoys bobbing beyond the harbour mouth. She sat on the mattress. Above her the sky, blue as his eyes, with small wisps of white clouds flying past. Why, it is the perfect bedroom! Isabella lay back, enchanted.

I concentrate on the scroll head I am working on. Have I got the angle right? Carved exact to the shape of the bow to meet the start of the trail boards? I can feel the familiar tension already, the anxiety of getting measurements wrong or even out by a fraction.

When I finish the scroll I am exhausted for I have been carving since early morning. I tidy my tools and look around but Isabella is nowhere to be seen. I pull my shirt off, visit the closet in the corner of the yard and then wash under the pump. I look to the sun to gauge the time; it must be near five of the clock.

I climb up the ladder to fetch a clean shirt and I am startled to find Isabella asleep on my bed, her knees drawn up like a child's. As I stare down at her I feel tenderness, not lust. I lie on the bed, careful not to touch her, and fall instantly asleep.

When Isabella woke she could not think where she was and felt a moment's panic, then turning she saw Tom asleep next to her. The sun was low, she should go, but she lay where she was watching him sleep. He had not put on his clean shirt and she knew his skin would be warm to touch. How smooth it was, that skin, how firm and brown and young. The image of Richard's white body floated into her mind. The way, when he lay with her, she could feel the flabbiness of his stomach against her own. She shuddered and sat up and Tom woke.

He stared at her and moved towards her, still half-asleep. Isabella's heart leapt as he pulled her to him, bent to her mouth, her face, her neck, put his hand over her breast. Isabella held his head to her and Tom began to undo the buttons on her blouse quickly and deftly, until he could place his hand inside her blouse and feel the warmth of her skin. Isabella gasped as he bent and took her nipple in his mouth and began to undo her belt. He could not find the catch on the waistband of her skirt and he pushed it up to her knees.

He was excited by the feel of her stockings but she pulled away, undid her skirt and wriggled out of it, then undid her stockings. She was left in her bodice and petticoats and Tom was transfixed as she took the pins out of her hair and let it fall in a small provocative gesture around her shoulders. He reached out to touch it, long, thick and shiny between his fingers.

He unbuckled his belt and pulled his trousers off. Isabella looked away, the colour rising in her face, then Tom pulled her on top of him and she bent to kiss him, her hair cascading around his face until he was buried in it. They rolled on the mattress, kissing and biting until their mouths felt bruised, and then Tom was inside her and Isabella cried out.

'Ssh,' Tom whispered, and gently covered her mouth with his own. Isabella came so violently her body shuddered for moments afterwards.

'Mine,' Tom thought, holding her. 'Mine.'

Isabella floated, felt the smoothness of Tom's skin under her hand, experienced a sense of euphoria. They lay like cats facing each other, rapt.

This idyll was broken by the sound of Lisette's voice.

'Tom? Tom Welland, I'm looking for Lady Isabella.'

I dive for my trousers but Isabella is paralysed. I put my finger to my lips and go to the hatch.

'What is it, Lisette?' I ask, faking a yawn.

'What time did Isabella leave here?' Lisette demands. 'Did you walk her home?'

'I did not,' I say, 'for it was still light and she was taking a walk, I think to her father's gardens.'

'It is too bad,' Lisette says crossly. 'Why can she not stay put instead of gallivanting around the countryside? As if I have not enough to do.'

'Then why do you not leave her to her day instead of shepherding her every move like a sheepdog, Lisette? No wonder she escapes. She is not a child and you have disturbed my rest,' I add, pretending at petulance.

'I am sorry for that, Tom, but I have been to the house to find her and I am now to my mother's cottage for the preacher. Isabella is in my charge and I have no idea where she is ...'

'Lisette, go to the preacher. I will go to try and find Lady Isabella for you and tell her ... what shall I tell her?'

'That I will be back to the house by nine and Cook has a cold supper ready and she should stay in the house ...'

I try not to laugh. 'Now, Lisette, does she need help to eat this cold supper, should I stay and spoon-feed her ...'

Lisette tuts crossly at me. 'I would be grateful if you could find her before dark, Tom Welland. Sir Richard expects me to ...'

'Then I will find her, Lisette,' I say kindly, for I am sorry for her troubles. 'Even if it means I miss my own supper.'

But Lisette has already turned and is hurrying across the yard to the road.

Isabella has been lying quite still, her eyes large with fear, but now she begins to laugh with relief.

'I must dress, Tom ...'

I watch her, fascinated by the complications of women's clothes. She starts to pin her hair back up. Her eyes are shining and her dark skin is flushed.

I would know immediately.

'You are very beautiful, Lady Isabella,' I tell her softly. The shadows of the dying day are caught across her face and I am suddenly alert to the danger of her getting home unseen.

'Wait! I will go and make sure the road is empty. Most people should be having their tea.'

I go down the ladder and across the yard to the gate. The road and coastal path are deserted. I go back and call her.

'Come, Isabella, quickly.'

Isabella comes down the ladder looking suddenly small and afraid. I touch her arm.

'Go and take the coast path and walk until you come to the stile which leads down to your house. I will take the road and join you there as if I have been searching for you.'

Isabella moves swiftly up the hill and bears right to the cliff path. I follow, but along the road until I reach the path. I turn onto it and see Isabella coming towards me.

'Why, Lady Isabella,' I say loudly, although the road is deserted. 'What a surprise! I am sent by Lisette to find you and escort you home before dusk. Where have you been?'

Isabella is out of breath. She laughs, but I can see she is nervous and will be glad to be indoors. I walk with her to the front door.

'Isabella, I will come and find you when I need you again for the face. We must be careful. You should not come to the yard too often. Lisette is like a guard dog where you are concerned.'

Isabella is silent. I see she is unsure whether I am distancing myself. I lift her small hand and hold it to my cheek. 'I could not think less of you, Isabella, ever. It is not that I do not want you near me, only that I do not want to put you in danger. You see that?'

'Of course.' Her small mouth trembles. 'I must go inside, Tom.'

'Yes.' But I cannot let go of her hand. 'We will try and meet elsewhere ... down in the cove. We will find a way ...'

Isabella looks me in the eye and reads clearly all that I feel. She smiles.

'Goodnight, Tom.' Her hand slips from mine and she is gone through the door.

Bats swoop down at my head in the dusk as I walk back down the hill to my mother's cottage for my meal. I would avoid going home but I am extremely hungry. My family are already at the table and all look up as I walk in.

'Your tea is near spoilt,' my mother says crossly.

I decide on a half-truth. 'Lisette arrived in a state. She could not find Lady Isabella and the preacher was due at her mother's cottage, so I said I would go and find her.'

'And did thee?' my father asks.

'Yes, she was on her way home.'

'Not with you, then?' one of my brothers laughs crudely.

'Obviously not,' I say shortly.

'We'll have none of that,' my mother snaps. 'You may all have known Lady Isabella since she were a child, but she is a respectable married lady now and don't you forget it.'

I eat my meal in silence. Since my years in Prince Edward Island I have grown away from my brothers. In the house I shared with the architect's family I was treated almost as an equal. I learnt to converse, to listen, and to read. I learnt there is more to life than putting a meal on a table. I learnt that the world is vast and there is much to discover away from the land of your birth. I learnt that I want more of a life than the one my parents and brothers lead here in the village.

God gave me a gift. Through my fingers, through my love of wood lies the way forward to a better life.

I walk back to my room through the hot summer evening. It still feels close and I watch the glow-worms by the side of the road and feel a strange, sick longing for a woman not of my own kind, who belongs to someone else.

In the sail loft the covers are still rucked up and disordered. I catch the smell of Isabella on them. I lie exactly where she lay and fall into an exhausted sleep.

At dawn, when the sun was edging up, hazy in sea mist, blood red over the sea, glittering on the water as it burnt off and flamed into a new day, Tom finished carving the haunting and sensuous face of Lady Isabella Magor; as he remembered her, lying under him, arched and abandoned in that first act of love. The date was June 15th 1865.

Chapter 50

A thin blue airmail letter arrived from Josh at an RAF air base in Kuwait. He sounded excited. He was about to leave for his 'floating airfield', somewhere he could not specify. He was flying a Lynx Mark 7 and extolled its virtues in the enthusiastic way pilots talk about their aircraft.

The aircraft carrier had left British waters before Josh had been picked to take over from a sick colleague, and he told Gabby he was looking forward to joining the rest of his squadron.

> There is quite a lot of frustration here in Kuwait among the pilots flying the RAF Tornados over the no-fly zones in Iraq. The living quarters are quite basic, with overcrowding and not enough washing facilities or air-conditioning. Added to this, there is a lot of rumbling about the high temperatures affecting the jets, which are designed for cold war air-defence. The Yanks flying side by side with us have far superior equipment, so you can imagine the envy of British pilots!
>
> Gabby . . . This is just a quick bluey while I'm on dry land . . . got to go . . . Hope all is well at home . . . Give my love to everyone . . . Love you lots, Josh.

Gabby smiled and tucked it in her pocket. It was seven days old. Josh would be on the aircraft carrier by now. She looked up at a clear sky. How far away he seemed.

How different Cornwall seemed, too, Gabby thought.

People were beginning to descend on the coast in the run-up to the eclipse and the roads were full of foreign cars and television vans. The landscape seemed to have been hijacked and plundered. Even the beach no longer belonged to her and Shadow. There were figures doing strange dances to the rising sun and sitting in yoga positions and chanting and drawing strange circles in the sand.

'I even found someone in my garden,' Elan said indignantly, 'and when I asked him why he was there, he said "The cliff top belongs to everyone, man."'

'I suspect you told him exactly who it did belong to?' Nell said, trying not to laugh. 'The television companies are camped out on Marazion beach. It is quite festive down there, actually.'

Nell, who had thought the smallest cottage beyond the barn too shabby to rent out, had been offered a ridiculous amount by a Dutch television station.

'I showed them round first,' she told Gabby and Charlie, 'and they jumped at it, though where they are all going to sleep is a mystery.'

'I wouldn't worry,' Charlie said. 'I expect they have an expense account for twice the amount you are asking.'

The days were hot and sticky, the air full of anticipation and something elemental too. There was an unnatural lack of wind to lift the heat haze which hung over the fields. Everyone longed for a breeze to come off the sea, cool and sharp.

Nell reluctantly set off for Truro one morning with a painting. She was going to lunch with Peter, but could have done without a morning in a town. Charlie left early for the auctioneers in St Austell with some cattle, and Gabby set off along the coastal path to the village with Shadow to buy stamps, airmail letters and bread.

She met Susan Dale riding Hal through the village and the horse tried to bury his nose in her pocket. Gabby laughed, stroking his whiskery old face. The two women talked of Susan's children and Josh for a few minutes and moved on.

Gabby felt restless. She thought of Mark. Now she was here she ached to be back with him in London. Should she walk over to Elan? She decided against it, she would go home and write to Josh.

As she came up the path which skirted the top field, now full of almost finished houses, she spotted a black car moving fast down the lane towards the farmhouse. Something about its speed alarmed her and she broke into a run as she entered the yard.

Three men got out of the black car and stood outside the front door which was never used. Two were in naval uniform. One was a padre wearing a black cassock. Gabby called out to them and they turned towards her, their faces serious. For a moment she thought they must have come to the wrong house and were looking for someone else, then something grim in their faces alerted her and she stood quite still as they moved towards her.

'Mrs Ellis?'

Gabby nodded. *Please God. Please God. Please God. Josh!*

'Could we go inside, Mrs Ellis?'

'Please . . . tell me . . .'

'Let's go inside.'

Gabby turned like a sleepwalker and they followed her round into the yard and through the back door into the kitchen. She saw one of them had a roll of paper in his hand and was preparing to read a statement from it.

'Is my son . . . ?'

'No,' the padre said quickly. 'Your son is not dead, Mrs Ellis.'

They kept asking her to sit down. Gabby sat on a chair and the naval officer said, 'I'm Lieutenant Commander Paul Drew. This is the naval family officer, Don Watts, and our padre, Commander Paul Mitchell. We are here on behalf of the army as your son was operating from a Royal Navy aircraft carrier in a multi-service operation.'

He nervously unrolled his piece of paper and stood in

front of Gabby and formally read out in a monotone:

'I regret to inform you that at fifteen hundred hours yesterday, your son, Joshua Ellis, along with his co-pilot and two passengers, was reported missing in hostile territory. All the British soldiers involved were participating in a training exercise with an Air Assault Brigade.

'It is believed that Captain Ellis was forced to land his Lynx helicopter through bad weather or hostile fire. Search and rescue were immediately mounted. We regret that at the present time we do not know the whereabouts of your son, his co-pilot, or the other two British soldiers, and they are now listed as missing.'

Gabby felt the strange displaced feeling of sudden shock. The naval officer lowered his piece of paper and looked at Gabby anxiously. The family officer hovered at her side. She realized they were waiting for her to break down.

'Let me make some tea,' the family officer said.

'Are you saying that the helicopter was forced to land somewhere in Iraq?'

'I'm afraid so, Mrs Ellis. More information is coming in all the time. There had been a sandstorm earlier in the day and that alone could have brought the Lynx down.'

Gabby stared at him. 'But the helicopter didn't crash?'

'No, it had a forced landing.' But the Lt Commander did not meet her eyes.

'How do you know this?'

'The Lynx was traced. Radio contact was maintained after it was damaged and forced to land.'

'I don't understand. If you had radio contact, why don't you know where the men are? Why wouldn't they stay with the helicopter so they could be rescued?'

The Lt Commander sat down opposite her at the kitchen table. Gabby saw he was anxious and very young. Perhaps it was the first time he had had to do this sort of thing.

'Mrs Ellis, we are constrained by the nature of this operation as to what we are allowed to divulge. The political situation is extremely tricky . . . The helicopter, once on the ground, would have had to be made inoperable in case it fell into Iraqi hands . . .'

'You say missing . . .' Gabby's chest was so tight she could hardly breathe. 'You mean captured, don't you? You mean captured . . .' She heard the kettle boiling behind her, held on to the edge of the table.

'No. Not necessarily. The four men would have had to split up in order to evade capture. Unfortunately they will also be unable to use their radios because if we can pick up their signals so can the Iraqis. But you must remember, Mrs Ellis, all those men have been trained for this sort of eventuality.'

'My son had only been out there about two weeks.'

'I assure you, if he had been picked for this operation he would have been training for months.'

'But not in desert conditions.'

They all looked at her. 'He would definitely have trained in desert conditions, Mrs Ellis.'

Gabby felt sick. There was so much about Josh's life she did not have a clue about, obviously could not be told. There she had been, thinking he was safely flying a few hundred miles up the road in Wiltshire, and he had been somewhere quite else, thousands of miles away in Kuwait, training for this. *Every week they had talked. Every single week.* But she should know, for God's sake she should know, with a mobile phone you could be anywhere.

She got up to find clean mugs and pointed out the tea, got the milk out of the fridge. Everything had gone into slow motion and she was watching herself calmly doing these things. She forced herself to ask, 'If they are captured, what will happen to them? Will you know? Will they be paraded in the streets like those two poor RAF officers in the Gulf war . . . ?' She could not bear it. Josh beaten-up, humiliated . . . maybe alone and frightened.

'We are not at war with Iraq. We are maintaining a UN-sanctioned no-fly zone for the protection of Northern Iraq, the Marsh Arabs, the Kurds, and countries such as

Turkey and Saudi. Unfortunately this means constantly being under Iraqi fire, but I do not believe Iraq wants a diplomatic incident at the moment.

'Mrs Ellis, there are a lot of people out looking for your son and the other officers. This includes the American helicopter pilots. God willing, we will find them before they are captured.'

'You . . . really believe this?'

The young officer paused. 'I do, Mrs Ellis. There is a concentrated effort being mounted to find and air-lift them out . . .' He swallowed and met Gabby's eyes. 'We must remain optimistic that all four men will come out . . . safely.'

To his credit he did not flinch from the truth, but Gabby was suddenly very cold. He had just stopped himself saying, *alive*.

'However, the situation is extremely grave. We have a Foreign Office minister flying out to Kuwait tonight. I promise you everything that can be done is being done.'

A cup of tea was placed into her hand. *In a moment*, Gabby thought, *I will wake up*.

'May I say that you are taking this remarkably well, Mrs Ellis.'

He sounded so relieved. Gabby smiled. What a horrible job the poor man had.

'Your husband? Can we ring him for you?'

Charlie! 'He's in St Austell. I'll ring his mobile.'

Charlie picked up straight away. 'Gabby, this isn't a good time.'

'Charlie, please come home. I have some naval officers with me. It's Josh . . . Josh's helicopter has come down over Iraq . . . he's missing . . . Charlie, he is missing . . . maybe captured.'

Gabby was suddenly shaking as the words began to sink in.

'Jesus,' Charlie said. 'I'm on my way now.'

The Lt Commander said to Gabby gently, 'I need to reach one more family in Plymouth in case the news breaks at six p.m. Apart from alerting the families we are trying to keep this low profile for obvious reasons relating to safety. So any information you are given is restricted, Mrs Ellis, to immediate family. I have to make you aware of this. I am so sorry to leave you. Would you like the padre to stay?'

Gabby shook her head. 'No, I'm fine, thank you.'

'The family officer will stay with you for as long as you need him and certainly until your husband gets here. This is a contact number to ring for information. Give them about twenty minutes for new information to come in.'

'Thank you.'

The Lt Commander smiled at Gabby. 'Take care, Mrs Ellis, I will speak to you tonight.'

He disappeared with the padre and Gabby heard the helicopter overhead and the black car speed down the lane towards it.

'How are you getting home?' she asked the family officer.

'I left my car at the bottom of the lane.'

Nell! Gabby thought suddenly. Oh my God, Nell must know. She grabbed the phone and dialled Nell's mobile, but Nell had switched it off. How long would it take Charlie to get home? She walked around the room willing Nell and Charlie to be there with her.

Josh. At this moment in some frightening, unimaginable landscape, while I got dressed, ate my breakfast, walked and laughed . . .

The family officer – Don . . . John . . . ? She did not like to ask – was saying something to her, but Gabby could somehow make no sense of it. She could see his mouth moving as she walked round the kitchen tidying and wiping and placing things in cupboards, but his words did not seem to reach her brain. She felt as if she was in a bubble.

After a while he gently took her by the shoulders and guided her to a chair, put another mug of hot sweet tea in her hand and went on talking and talking, words that flowed over her as she watched his mouth intently.

* * *

336

Nell was in Truro Museum with Peter.

'We should lunch more often, Nell, you always cheer me up.'

Nell smiled. 'Do I?'

'You always did.' He stirred the teapot and found cups. Nell felt sudden tenderness. Peter must be one of the last people on earth who loathed teabags and mugs.

He started to pour the tea and Nell was watching his long, pianist's hands when she heard this piercing cry deep inside her, eerie and childlike. She jumped, her heart jerking, and leapt out of her chair.

'What on earth . . . ?' Peter looked at her in alarm. 'Nell, you're as white as a sheet. Are you ill?'

Nell could not answer. She was gripped by terror. She stared at him and then grabbed her bag. 'I must get home. Sorry, I have to go.'

She turned and literally ran down the corridor with Peter behind her, calling, 'Nell, what . . . ?'

Nell was in her car and starting up the engine. She zapped the window down and looked out at him. 'Something has happened. Don't know what.'

'Nell, for heaven's sake, wait, we'll ring Gabrielle . . .'

'No time, must get back.'

She was gone, her silver Honda joining the flow of traffic. Peter stared after her, disturbed, then went back inside to ring Gabrielle but found the line engaged.

Nell, who rarely drove fast, raced down the dual carriageway willing herself home. Her body was tense and hunched and what she felt was icy cold fear without knowing why, for that terrible cry had been one of terror.

'*Gran!*' Josh had screamed. Not Nell, *Gran*.

She looked at the radio and turned it on. There was a woman rabbiting on about pensions and Nell was leaning forward to switch it off again when the programme was interrupted by a newsflash. Nell steeled herself. Prayed she was wrong.

'*We are getting uncorroborated reports of a British*

helicopter being shot down over Iraq. The helicopter is thought to be part of a joint operation between . . . part of multi-service . . . It is thought that as well as the two army pilots there were two British soldiers aboard. The Foreign Office refuses to confirm or deny that two of the soldiers were part of an SAS team . . .'

'Oh, my darling boy,' Nell whispered.

Charlie had never found the route home so endless. *Josh will be OK,* he kept repeating to himself. *He can look after himself. Was he alone? Unlikely. They must be trained for this sort of situation. They know what to do. Yes. They can handle themselves. Know how to play it cool. He'll be all right. Of course he will. Of course he will.*

Gabby rang the number on the piece of paper. It was engaged. It was engaged every time she tried. She tried to keep the panic out of her voice when the phone suddenly rang in the silent kitchen.

'Mrs Ellis? This is James MacDonald-Brown. I was Josh's Commandant at Sandhurst. We met briefly when Josh passed out. I've just heard. I am so sorry. I know you must be worried and if there is anything at all I can do to help . . .'

'Please,' Gabby cried, 'I've been given this military number and I can't get through to get any more information . . .'

'Mrs Ellis . . . Gabrielle, isn't it? Give me the number. I'll ring you straight back.'

Gabby replaced the phone and watched it. If she took her eyes off it, it would not ring again. The family officer viewed her in silence from across the table. There was nothing left for him to say. All he could do was just be there.

In a few moments James MacDonald-Brown rang back.

'Gabrielle? Have you got a pen? This is the new number you need to ring. You will be contacted shortly. An officer will be assigned to you to answer any queries and to give you all information as it comes in.

'This is my telephone number, please ring me if I can help

in any way. Gabrielle, I have every faith in Josh, he is a very mature and competent officer. They are all trained for this eventuality, dwell on that. But of course, my thoughts are with you.'

'Thank you. How is Marika? Does she know?'

'Not yet. Her mother is frantically trying to contact her in case the story breaks on the six o'clock news.'

'Please give her my love.'

'Thank you, I will. Goodbye.'

Outside there was the sound of the Land Rover sliding across the yard. Gabby threw open the back door and ran out.

'Charlie, Charlie, Charlie . . .'

Charlie grabbed her. 'Gab. It'll be all right. Really. Come on, Gabs.' He led her back inside and took Don Watts' hand as he introduced himself.

'Thank you for staying with Gabby, it was kind.'

'Not at all. I'm sure there are questions you want to ask and then I'll go. You will want to be on your own. I'll ring later and come and see you tomorrow. This is my phone number. Please contact me at any time, it's what I'm here for . . . I am so sorry.'

'Thank you.'

Nell turned into the lane as Don Watts climbed into his car. She stopped and wound down her window.

'Are you something to do with Josh? I'm his grand-mother.'

Don walked over to her car. 'Yes. I'm the naval family officer . . .'

'Is my grandson . . . ?' Nell's voice quavered.

'No,' Don said hastily, 'he's not dead. I'm afraid his helicopter came down in hostile territory . . . Captain Ellis, his co-pilot, and two other British soldiers are missing. We have every hope they will be picked up by our forces soon. I am so sorry.'

'Thank you.'

Nell drove on up the lane and into the yard. Gabby and

Charlie heard her coming and went quickly out to meet her. Gabby was shocked at how grey Nell was.

They all held each other, standing there in the doorway like drowning men, then Charlie went to the cupboard.

'Would you like a drink?' he asked Nell.

'Yes,' she said. 'A strong brandy.'

'Gab?'

She shook her head.

It was five forty-five and they switched on the news with dread. The phone went suddenly and it was a soft-voiced officer on the other end, rather breathless.

'Mrs Ellis? My name is Simon Cottrell. I am your contact. I am afraid the story is about to break now on the six o'clock news. We were unable to keep it from the public domain. Be prepared.'

It was all so unreal. Gabby felt numb. Charlie, looking at her from the other side of the kitchen, thought how small she looked, as if she was shrinking.

'This line is open for you and your family. You can contact me night or day for any reason or no reason. Often it just helps to talk. I will ring you as the situation develops. You will not hear anything on the news before I have spoken to you. Please ring me if you have any concerns. We are all thinking about your son and the other soldiers. Please remember they have been prepared for this sort of situation. They will not be panicking or putting themselves at risk or danger.'

'Thank you. Thank you so much.'

As Gabby replaced the receiver the six o'clock news started. Before the announcer had even spoken there was footage of an aircraft carrier sailing through tropical waters, the camera zooming in on the helicopters tied to its deck. Then there was footage of the RAF's Ali Al Salem air base in Kuwait where helicopters filled the sky.

There are unconfirmed reports of a British Lynx helicopter being shot down over Iraq today. The pilot, co-pilot, and two British soldiers are missing, feared captured.

'It is believed the incident happened while it was taking part in a multi-operational exercise between the three services. Lynx helicopters are regularly used by the British army for sorties over Iraq. These particular helicopters are flown from the aircraft carrier . . . serving in the Gulf.'

The announcer handed over to a colleague with a huge map and enlarged photographs of helicopters.

'The Lynx helicopter is used by the British army to counter the threat posed by enemy armoured formations. It can be armed with eight TOW missiles and is currently the mainstay of the British armed helicopter fleet . . . In addition to its role as an anti-tank helicopter the Lynx can be used for fire support, operating machine guns, troop lifts, casualty evacuation . . .'

'What was Josh into out there, for God's sake?' Charlie said, white-faced.

The announcer faced the camera. 'It is believed that a Gazelle helicopter was flying with the Lynx but why it did not land to lift the stricken crew out is not known. Neither the Foreign Office or the Ministry of Defence were forthcoming, and in the light of the current political situation and the safety of the missing soldiers there is little information about the details of the incident or what the helicopters were doing in that area.

'The safety and whereabouts of the servicemen are unknown. Their names have not been released by the military. The situation is considered grave and a Foreign Office minister is preparing to fly out to Kuwait tonight.

'This incident highlights the dangers of all pilots monitoring the UN-sanctioned no-fly zone over Iraq. Any capture of British or American servicemen could trigger a highly volatile and unpredictable situation. We will be giving you news as it comes in, meanwhile . . .'

Before the announcer had finished speaking the phone began to ring. It was Elan, breathless.

'Gabby? I've just caught the news. It's not Josh, is it? He's only been there five minutes . . . Oh, child . . .'

Then Peter; 'Nell, my dear Nell ... I'm so sorry. My thoughts, please, to Gabrielle and Charlie.'

Marika asked for Gabby. Her voice was shaky and Gabby could hear she was in a bad way and talked to her calmly. 'Marika, Marika, listen to your stepfather. Josh is going to be all right. He is going to come out of this. OK? Now we'll talk again, soon ...'

Friends and neighbours in the village, anxious and unbelieving: 'It's not Josh? Please say it's not Josh?'

Nell and Charlie fielded most of the calls.

'I only want to speak to Simon,' Gabby said.

She sat bolt upright on the old kitchen chair with her knees drawn up, watching the turned-down television, willing it to newsflash.

At nine o'clock they turned the sound up. Again, the same footage. No more.

At ten the phone suddenly rang. It was Simon to warn them the names of the missing servicemen had been released.

Then, suddenly, startlingly, there it was on screen.

'The four missing British soldiers in the helicopter believed to have been shot down over Iraq are: Captain Josh Ellis AAC, the pilot. Captain Duncan Rivers AAC, co-pilot. Major Andrew O'Conner, 16 Air Assault Brigade, and Sergeant David Mackenzie, Air Assault Brigade.'

Charlie poured a tiny drop of brandy into a glass and forced Gabby to drink it.

'So much for restricted information,' he said.

'I imagine with journalists out in Kuwait and probably on the aircraft carrier it is almost impossible to keep it from the public arena,' Nell said.

Gabby was so pale and cold, Charlie did something he had not done for years. He wrapped his arms around her and pulled her onto his knee, holding her tight.

Nell took an old sweater from the kitchen door and they pulled it over Gabby's head. Her eyes were still glued to the screen.

At eleven o'clock a Special Branch officer arrived wanting

a description of Josh; a recent photo, any distinguishing features, birthmarks. Colour of eyes, what kind of eyebrows, colour of skin. Fair? Dark? Build? Height? Weight?

Gabby gave them the latest photograph they had. One of Josh and Marika at the dinner the night after he had received his wings. Josh in dress uniform. Marika in a dramatic dress of aquamarine blue. Both laughing.

Blessed and beautiful people, Nell thought, *full of life stretching seamlessly ahead . . .*

The policeman stared at it without comment.

'I'll return this to you if I can, but I have to forward it to my London colleagues.' He was thinking, *Thank God this is not my son.*

Charlie, Gabby and Nell did not ask him why he wanted all this information; they knew. It was the moment they all acknowledged the stark reality they might have to face; the possible identification of Josh's body.

Gabby handed the photo over with difficulty. It was her only copy of this particular snapshot. 'I would like it back, please, it's the only one I have.'

The policeman nodded. He said, as Nell and Charlie answered the constant ringing of the phone, for it was the only practical help he could give, 'It might be an idea to put a special line in for you and then it can be kept clear for important calls and your contact with the army. It will also mean the press cannot get hold of you. I am afraid they could begin descending at any time. I'll leave a car at the bottom of the lane. If there are any problems, contact me on this number.'

He paused. 'Everything that can be done is being done. We hope for the safe return of all those officers as quickly as possible.'

Before they went to bed, Simon rang and gave Gabby his home and mobile numbers. 'If you need to talk in the night, it doesn't matter, ring me. If I hear anything at all during the night, I'll ring you. Try to get some sleep.'

'Thank you.' Gabby was touched. 'Thank you.'

Do they pick special people, she wondered, with soft voices that soothe, with an ability to imbue comfort by just an inflection?

Nell made up a bed in the spare room. Charlie walked down to the village with Shadow to warn the publican, the post office and friends and neighbours to close ranks when the press arrived. Not to direct them to the farm. He knew it was pointless, they would be found, but it was something positive to do and he was touched as well as mortally afraid by the reaction and warmth of people he had known most of his life.

Josh was one of their own; born, baptized, schooled and grown up among them, and one of their own was in danger. Walking back up the lane, Charlie stopped for a moment to speak to Darren, the young policeman sitting at the bottom of the lane in a police car.

'Thanks, Darren. I'm sorry, it's going to be a long night for you.'

'Not as long as Josh's, Charlie,' Darren said quietly. 'I'd be here even if I wasn't getting paid. Josh and I go back to primary school and Cubs, remember?'

Charlie nodded, not trusting himself to speak. He walked on up the lane and stopped in the yard and looked upwards. Milky Way, Great Bear. Infinity.

Don't let him die in some terrible way, God, so far from home. God, I beg you, if You exist . . . this is my son . . .

When he went in, Nell told him Gabby was in the bath with the telephone next to her. Nell was in her dressing gown. Charlie poured himself an enormous whisky and sat at the table. Nell put her cup of tea down and went behind him, placed her arms around him and kissed the top of his head.

'Charlie, Josh is going to come out of this alive. He is. Keep saying this. Believe it.'

Charlie nodded, held on to Nell's hands. 'Let's go to bed.'

Gabby was curled up in bed with her Walkman, listening

to the news all over again. Charlie knew she would lie listening to the World Service all night. He fell heavily into bed beside her.

'Wake me if you hear anything. If anything happens, Gab.'

'Of course, Charlie.'

'Josh is going to be OK. He is going to come out of this.'

'Yes,' Gabby said, dully. 'Yes.'

They sabotage the helicopter and split up quickly. Shock makes Josh slow at first. At least the Gazelle was unharmed. Josh and Duncan split up, each pairing with the two special-forces soldiers. In a situation like this there is no one else Josh would prefer to be with. Andrew has done time in Bosnia and Northern Ireland. Both men's thoughts are with the soldiers they had been sent to airlift out. Now they are in the same danger.

The first night is the worst as the temperature plummets. Andrew uses his beacon every hour to try to alert their position for rescue and then they move on quickly. They have calculated the risks, as both men know the longer they are on the ground the greater their chance of capture. Josh thinks how different this feels to his escape and evasion exercises on Dartmoor. The adrenaline rush, the fear, changes everything.

They come to a river and work their way along it cautiously. Both men pore over the map with a torch, pulling their jackets over their heads and the map so that no glimmer of light escapes into the cool desert night. They calculate they are two hours from where they were headed in the Lynx to pick up the four Hereford boys doing surveillance. They decide to head in the same direction; risky, but easier for rescue.

As dawn comes they find a deserted village. Not a house remains standing. The surrounding area is strewn with shells and burnt-out tanks. The atmosphere is pungent and stilled by death. The two men crawl into a derelict house and lie at

345

the outer edges of the walls to be in shadow and try to sleep. As the sun rises Josh falls into strange and hallucinatory dreams.

He and Andrew wake to the same noise at the same time and peer up into the muzzle of Kalashnikovs held by two young and nervous Arabs. They are poked roughly and told to get up. Outside the derelict building stand twenty more men, hard-eyed and threatening, who yell into their radios.

They are quickly stripped of their radios and equipment, watches and Andrew's wedding ring, and bundled back towards the river. The Arabs seem unsure and argumentative and both Josh and Andrew realize they are not regular militia despite their camouflage combats and equipment. In the distance both men can hear the faint clatter of helicopters. Without warning Josh is suddenly knocked to the ground and made to kneel while his hands are tied behind his back. He feels a knife pressed into the back of his neck, is aware of Andrew also on the ground.

This is what fear is. Josh prays. Let it be clean. Don't maim me. Kill me outright. Make it clean and quick.

He thinks of Marika, of Gabby and Nell and Charlie. Of home. This is what it feels like, the moment before you die. A sudden strange calm.

Chapter 51

Josh's room was still and dark as if holding itself in. Gabby switched on the bedside lamp that he had made at school. The bulb was low and cast a small pool of yellow light into the room. Silver riding cups and coloured rosettes lay in a thin layer of dust on his chest of drawers. His small possessions lay around the room, waiting to be picked up and replaced affectionately when he returned.

A cricket bat, metalwork and pottery objects, driftwood, a surfboard, school photos on the walls. Lucian Freud, Elan, his own A-level paintings. A photo of a once-loved ginger tomcat stuck into the side of his mirror, curling at the edges.

Gabby examined his bookshelf. VS Naipaul, John Keegan, Garcia Marquez, and E Annie Proulx. Max Hastings sat next to Wilbur Smith and Bernard Cornwell. TS Eliot and Rupert Brooke sat next to Hornby and Amis. There was a technical shelf of modern warfare and art books. *Keeping Bantams*; *Keeping Goldfish*; *Keeping Guinea Pigs*.

Outside the window the night was still and thick with silence. Gabby lay on Josh's bed, under the old dusky-pink eiderdown that was once Nell's. The BBC World Service was on low and Gabby was alert to every news bulletin. She willed Josh to *feel* her sitting there awake and know he was not alone. The silence pressed down, crushing her into the room so full of his life.

Horror crept towards her. Josh could be hunted, frightened, or lying beaten-up in some hellhole, terrified, wondering if he would ever make it home. Her ears picked up Iraq and she turned the small radio up. A journalist was telling a colleague what might happen if any British officers were captured on Iraqi soil.

He described the kind of humiliation and torture meted out to captured pilots during the Gulf war and listed the various atrocities of Saddam's Special Guard. He then went on to list in detail the particular dangers any captured servicemen could be facing or enduring.

Gabby snapped the radio off angrily. *Didn't they realize families would be listening?* The sheer crass sensationalism and irresponsibility infuriated her. She got off the bed and went over to Josh's small chest of drawers, which had once been hers. She stroked the soft wood, curled her hands around the carved handles. She let her fingers wander over the worn indentations as she had done as a child. She opened the drawers and began to tidy each one. She matched socks, folded shirts and placed them in neat little rows one on top of the other. Then she moved to his sweaters, making a little pile of those that looked as if they needed washing. She would wash them in the morning, then she would clean his room out and polish the chest and chair and bedside table so that all was ready for when he returned.

She touched his riding rosettes, trying to smooth them straight. Josh on his first pony in tiny riding jacket, hat, whip, small legs akimbo on the plump little mare. Over the jumps they had gone, that fat little pony and the small eager child, and Charlie had tried not to look as if he was bursting with pride as the small crowd smiled and clapped.

She looked down at the yellowing cricket sweater she was going to wash, remembering long summer evenings taking him to cricket practice at school or on the village green. She used to sit with the other mothers drinking tea from a flask, occasionally Pimms. School plays, sports days, detention.

Josh. A whole childhood and growing-up with Josh that she had never taken for granted, painfully aware, even while she was living them, the days were precious and finite. She had wanted to be there for all the big and important events in his life because she knew what it felt like not to have anyone care enough to chart the course of your childhood.

There had been no danger of Josh's landmarks slipping by, for as well as Gabby there had always been Charlie, Nell and Elan, as well as the older farm-workers all rooting for him.

Josh had always seemed to sail through life. *The good die young,* suddenly shot into Gabby's brain and she shook it away with a small moan and got back into Josh's bed and turned the lamp off. Her eyelids were heavy and dry with tiredness.

She thought of Clara. *Clara is Josh's grandmother.* Was she still alive? Would she read and connect Josh to Gabby? Would she even remember the name Ellis?

Of course not. Why was she even thinking about it? Clara would either be in a home or dead by now. Gabby had hardened her heart long ago. It had been impossible to explain, even to Nell, who had insisted Clara had a right to know when Josh was born. Clara had never acknowledged Nell's card. Gabby knew she wouldn't and it was the last time Nell had ever interfered.

It had been the hardest lesson of her childhood to finally understand that a drunk had to really want to stop drinking. And if she couldn't, she found others like her, until suddenly one day you could not remember anything nice about her, only the smell of gin and a house full of drunks and a life you didn't understand which had become dangerous. You had no chance of looking out for the mother you loved, despite everything, because you were too busy looking out for yourself.

Clara had had one sister, Bella. Bella was nice and fat and jolly. Gabby had liked her more than anyone and she would often get a bus to the other side of Bristol after school. Then, Bella left England for a new life with a new man in America. She had offered to take Gabby with her, but Clara would have none of it, and Gabby had never understood why.

Bella had said before she left, 'I'll write, kiddo, as soon as

I have an address. Now, you are to write and tell me if things get worse. I'll come back and get you.'

'Won't Chuck mind?'

'No, he won't. He says your mum's got a screw loose . . .'

Bella had said she hated leaving her but she had gone all the same.

'Don't believe all your mother says, kiddo. She knows exactly who your father was. All I know is that she met him on holiday in Plymouth and got her heart broken. She was always an odd little girl . . .'

She bent to Gabby. 'I told you our mother died when we were tots. I was older and I coped better than Clara. Dad was an odd one, too . . .'

She stopped abruptly. 'You're fourteen and bright. Get out as soon as you can, kiddo . . . Please don't cry. I am only a plane ride away, I'm not forsaking you.'

But she had. No word came, although Gabby had waited and waited. No letter with an address ever came. Clara had said, 'You silly little honey-bun. Did you really think Auntie Bell loved you more than I do?'

Gabby, lying in the dark, heard Elton John start up his crowing. Soon Charlie would get up for milking. Gabby had a sudden sense and shape of herself and her life as she lay where Josh had slept. She heard Reverend Mother's voice: *We pay for our sins.*

In crisis we regress, Gabby thought. What we scorned in childhood we confront in terror at the first hint of tragedy. *My mother.* She could have so easily been that child again, believing that if you loved someone as hard as you could they would eventually love you back. She could have turned in the dark and whispered some of these thoughts to Mark, but she must shut her mind to Mark.

I dare not, must not, let him into my thoughts or this house. She bargained with her God. Pleaded. She was sure of only one thing. If anything happened to Josh she did not want to go on living.

Chapter 52

The next morning, Darren deposited flowers, plants, bread, casseroles and eggs up by the back door of the farmhouse, all messages of hope and support from the village. He also delivered an array of the national newspapers. The stricken helicopter crew had made all the headlines and it was a weird, sick feeling for Nell, Gabby and Charlie.

Simon had rung first thing that morning, and assured Gabby that there was an alert and concentrated search going on to find the crew of the helicopter. There had been no intelligence regarding the capture of any British soldiers.

'Let's hope today brings us good news, Mrs Ellis.'

Charlie came in from milking. 'I can't lie in bed. I'm better doing what I always do.'

They spread the papers out over the kitchen table and read them all with a sense of terrible unreality.

HELICOPTER CREW SHOT DOWN ON RESCUE MISSION IN IRAQ

HELICOPTER CREW MISSING FEARED CAPTURED

Charlie read slowly, trying to understand what Josh had got himself into.

'The danger of this "forgotten war" being waged daily in

the skies over Iraq was dangerously highlighted by yester-
day's downed helicopter containing a crew of four British
servicemen taking part in "Operation Thunderbird", a multi-
service operation.'

Nell was skimming because she could hardly bear to read. It seemed a military spokesman had refused to discuss rumours that a covert operation involving an SAS undercover unit was involved, and that the Lynx had been on its way to pick them up.

She glanced at Gabby, then down at the page. Gabby was reading intently.

'The fear is that if any of these pilots are captured by Saddam's forces we will have to face the spectre of them being paraded and beaten through the streets of Baghdad. The Foreign Office were quick to make clear that British pilots fly over Iraq with UN sanction and any capture of British servicemen will be viewed as an act of aggression . . .'

'Lovie . . .' she said gently, 'it also says that the capture of any service personnel under the auspices of the UN will have grave political repercussions . . . I am sure, Gabby, the Iraqis won't risk an international incident.'

But Gabby's eyes were still riveted to the acres of news-print. *'As part of a covert operation these soldiers would receive little mercy from Saddam's men.'*

There it was in black and white, not someone else's son, but theirs. Gabby turned the newspaper so Charlie could read it.

'The British soldiers will be out there, isolated and hiding in the heat of the day and moving at night when the temperatures plummet. They will all have been trained for such an eventuality as being shot down over hostile territory, and could be making for some arranged point for rescue. But unlike SAS officers they will not have had extensive survival training. Each day that passes diminishes their chance of rescue and increases their chance of capture . . .'

'Enough!' Charlie jumped to his feet and gathered the papers up and placed them in a pile on the table. Nell went to make more coffee. Charlie touched Gabby's shoulder.

'What are you going to do today? Will you be all right if I go out? I can't sit by the phone, Gab, I'll go mad.'

Gabby, in a daze, looked up at him. 'I'm OK. I'm going to wash some of Josh's sweaters. I have to stay by the phone, Charlie, I have to, but you go out, it's pointless two of us waiting. Don't turn your phone off, and keep within range for the mobile, please.'

'Of course I will. I'm going to go up to the barley field and then I'll be in the office. It will take me minutes to get back home. OK?'

Nell walked out into the yard with him. 'Keep faith, Charlie. I won't leave Gabby. Try and keep occupied.'

Charlie looked down at her. 'It's so bloody real when you see it in print, Nell.'

'I know,' Nell said, 'I know, lovie.'

She turned and saw Elan and John Bradbury walking down the lane.

'Could you do with some company, some moral support, or are we imposing? If we are, we'll disappear, you know us well enough . . .'

Nell burst into tears. The whole situation suddenly seemed insupportable and she had never been so glad to see anyone in her life.

The day was hot and they opened the French windows to hear the phone and sat in the little walled garden. Gabby saw how hard Nell had been working in there while she had been in London and was guilty that she had not noticed before. She kept looking at the phone, moving it slightly in case she had not replaced it properly. The radio was next to them so that they could listen to the hourly bulletins.

Josh's sweaters were soaking in the old scullery, but Gabby had forgotten them, and Nell, when she went back inside, rinsed them and hung them on the dryer. At lunchtime Gabby rang Simon, desperate for news, but there was none.

The day crawled, the heat pressed down, and Nell and Elan made jugs and jugs of iced tea. Charlie came in at lunchtime.

Alan had been right; he kept finding people trespassing on his land and was infuriated. The only positive aspect was the press were busy with eclipse stories and seemed to have left them alone so far.

Nell had cobbled salad and ham together and everybody tried to eat something, except for Gabby. She went inside and read the papers all over again. Folded them obsessively into the right creases.

By six o'clock there would be some news, they were all sure of it. But there was none. Then Simon rang to warn her there was a rumour, but it was only a rumour, that two British soldiers had been picked up and were on their way back to Kuwait.

John Bradbury left at four. He was going to say an Anglican Mass for the missing soldiers in the village church and afterwards the bell-ringers wanted to peal.

Dusk came. Charlie and Outside Dog had seen the cows back to the fields and the birds sat up in the small cherry tree singing their evening hymns. The bells rang out suddenly into the still evening and Gabby, Nell and Charlie stood and listened to them in the garden at the farm, and for the first time Charlie turned his face to the fields and wept.

How did you bear it if something terrible happened to your son? How did you bear it? Knowing each morning you woke that your only son died so far from you.

Gabby turned to the sea. Small, becalmed white sails dotted the horizon. Over the fields came the poignant and dramatic sound of those bells, filling the air, making people stop in their tracks, chilled at the ancient sound of warning. Gabby thought of the bell-ringers eagerly giving up their time, ringing out with all the heart they could muster because it was the only way of showing the Ellises up at the farm that they were not alone; there was always hope. Gabby was touched and humbled by the solidarity and kindness of it.

Standing in the garden she had a sense again of the reason she had wanted to stay here all those years ago. Something she had perhaps taken for granted. The comfort of being part

354

of a place, part of the land and a community that dug in close to its own when anything threatened a part of them. Gabby supposed this was how people got through; when tragedy struck they had to turn to each other. The sea had taken so many, how could the people here not understand what Gabby, Charlie and Nell were going through? Whole generations of fishing families had been lost in one night.

Elan put supper together from the array of dishes that had arrived on the doorstep. Gabby was talking to Simon on the phone and Charlie was sitting at the kitchen table, watching something on the television which he was obviously not taking in. Elan heard Outside Dog barking and saw a man climbing the fence in the corner of the top field. He whipped outside and intercepted him before he got into the yard.

'You are trespassing.'

'Are you Charlie Ellis?'

'I am not. Will you please leave before I call the police.'

The man got out a card. 'Look, I'm not a weirdo. I work for the *News of* . . . I just want to offer my condolences and to ask how it feels . . . to have your son as a hostage . . .'

'I suggest you leave now before I clobber you one. I don't know how you lot sleep at night . . .'

'Now, come on, I'm . . .'

'I don't care who the hell you are . . .'

'All I want is five minutes . . .'

He stopped as Charlie came out of the kitchen. Charlie was much bigger than Elan and Shadow was with him making a low threatening warning in her throat. Charlie unleashed Outside Dog and then went on walking towards the man with the two dogs each side of him eager and growling nastily.

The man started to back away. Charlie said softly, 'If you are not out of here in one minute I swear I will set both these dogs on you.'

The man turned and started to move away quickly. Charlie

rang the police car at the bottom of the lane. Darren was off-duty but the copper inside was waiting for the unlucky reporter when he arrived.

'Well done,' Elan said to Charlie.

'You spotted him. Right, you two dogs can stay out here, on guard.'

They went back into the house and said nothing to Nell and Gabby and the second day crawled to an end.

From somewhere behind them comes a screamed order. They are lifted roughly to their feet, blindfolded and made to walk. The men holding them argue incessantly as they jerk and pull Josh and Andrew along.

They reach a village – they can hear chickens and children – then suddenly they are thrown inside a small hut. Their blindfolds are taken off but their hands left tied behind them. The bare room is about six foot by twelve with a grille in the door.

Both men know straight away these are only ordinary Iraqis who have little idea what to do with them, but it will not be long before the arrival of the militia who will know exactly how to extract information.

This is when I find out how brave I am, Josh thinks. He turns to look at Andrew but his throat is so dry he cannot form words.

'Let's hope the other two made it,' Andrew mutters. 'You OK, Josh?'

Josh nods solemnly. 'Never been better, Andrew.'

They grin at each other wryly.

The door is opened and they are pulled outside. A small group of villagers come and stare at them with hostile faces. All men. One spits at their feet.

'American! Pah!'

'British,' Andrew says. 'We are British.'

They are quickly surrounded and pushed and poked with sticks, from one Arab to another like a rough playground game organized by the school bully. They begin to chant

356

and the chant gains momentum. Josh feels sick. They are revving each other up and as the punches grow harder and harder both men know that if they fall they have had it.

Josh, giddy, wills himself not to stumble. Charlie used to frighten him silly with his warning about pigs: 'If you fall in a pigpen they will savage and eat you.'

There is the sound of a Land Rover and an Arab festooned with armoury and headdress leaps out and shouts at the men. The punching and shouting stops immediately and the group grows ominously quiet.

The Arab looks at them both and then indicates they are both to be taken back to the derelict building. Ten minutes later two dirty mattresses are thrown through the door. Then a chair. Their hands are untied. The man comes and sits on the chair back-to-front and both Josh and Andrew have a mad desire to laugh. He has obviously seen too many old Westerns. He has a bottle of water and two glasses. He politely pours water and hands the glasses to Josh and Andrew who drink greedily. This is Mr Nice Guy.

'Who are you?' he asks in English.

'British helicopter pilots.'

'Why you here?'

'Our helicopter was damaged by Iraqi fire; we had to make an emergency landing.'

'What you doing in helicopter?'

'Maintaining the no-fly zone.'

'I say what you do?'

'Just observers. We are observers.'

'I think spies?'

'No, we are both army pilots, not spies.'

The sweat trickles down Josh's face and into his eyes.

'You?' the man says. 'Why you afraid if only pilot?'

'I'm not afraid, I'm hot. It is very hot in here.'

Andrew says quickly, 'We are pilots with a damaged helicopter, that is all we are. Look at how we are dressed.'

The man stands up. 'We will see,' he says and leaves abruptly.

357

Josh crawls onto the filthy mattress and closes his eyes. Andrew follows slowly.

'What are you thinking?' Josh asks without opening his eyes.

'I am thinking, Josh, we must take any chance to escape. There was something odd about that guy. Something not quite right.'

Night comes and they are left alone. They have been given water and inedible dry biscuits. They hear the guard outside coughing and spitting, and he keeps them awake twiddling the knobs of his radio. There is a constant coming and going of vehicles and an air of tension.

Both mattresses are full of lice and they lie, itching and scratching, unable and unwilling to sleep.

Their guard stops twiddling his radio or cleaning his gun and peers through the grille every now and then to see if they have mysteriously disappeared.

Josh and Andrew realize he has tuned into the BBC World Service, probably by mistake. As they crane to listen they are horrified to realize that their guard must be listening to the eager imagination of a journalist describing with relish the various gruesome torture and treatment Saddam and his henchmen might inflict on any captured servicemen. He also speculates on the feelings of the missing servicemen if they have been captured, and what could be happening to them right now.

'Fucking idiot,' Andrew mutters.

'Arsehole,' Josh agrees. 'Let's hope the guy outside doesn't understand a word of English.'

Both men vow to find the journalist if they make it back home.

There is a flurry of activity outside and the door is thrown open. They are ordered outside and into the Land Rover. They are surrounded by nervous Iraqis waving their guns about and shouting. Something seems to have unnerved them.

Is this it? Josh thinks. Are they going to be driven to Baghdad to be interrogated? Or killed somewhere where no one will ever find their bodies?

Gabby and Nell were watching the midday news and suddenly clutched each other in excitement.

'*There is an unconfirmed report that two of the British soldiers from the stricken helicopter shot down over Iraq have been rescued. We will bring you news of the situation as it comes in.*'

The phone rang and Gabby reached for it, her heart pumping. It was Simon. She felt giddy and breathless.

'Gabrielle? Are you watching the news?'

'Yes.'

'We have an unconfirmed report that two British soldiers have just been airlifted out of Iraq by an American helicopter crew and are on their way to the American air base in Turkey. Until they reach the safety of the base we cannot announce or confirm their names. Stay by the phone and I will ring you as soon as I know.'

'Thank you. Thank you.'

The officer's voice was cautious. 'Gabrielle, it might not be Josh.'

'I know. I know it might not, but it's hopeful isn't it . . . ? If they've found two the others could be picked up any time . . . couldn't they?'

'Yes, they could. I will ring you as soon as I hear anything.'

Gabby turned to Nell. 'Good news! Two soldiers from the helicopter have been airlifted out and are on their way back to the American air base in Turkey.'

They looked at each other, suddenly sure that it was going to be all right. Nell said quietly, 'When will we know whether it is Josh?'

'Soon. Simon is going to ring straight back.'

'You stay by the phone. I'll go and find Charlie.'

'Nell, we don't know yet if it is Josh.'

'I know, but he will want to be kept abreast.'

Alone in the kitchen, Gabby thought, *There are four mothers or wives feeling like I do. If it is Josh, it is not one of their sons.* She knelt and stroked Shadow's ears. The dog placed her paw on Gabby's knee and licked her cheek, a thing she never did for Shadow was fairly haughty with humans. Gabby smiled, bent to hug the dog ... *Who says dogs don't understand?*

The phone blared out into the room making her jump. She stood up and grabbed it from the cradle.

'I'm so sorry,' Simon said. 'I am afraid neither of the soldiers was Josh. Gabrielle ... are you still there?'

Hope had risen so high and was now so cruelly dashed. The officer on the end of the phone could hear the small desperate sound Gabby was making and felt powerless.

'Gabrielle, I am so, so sorry. But it is good news, the rescued soldiers will be able to tell us much about the situation and it really does bode well for the safety of the others.'

'Sorry,' Gabby managed.

'Don't apologize, it's why I'm here. I wish I could give you better news. I cannot imagine what it feels like ...'

His voice was concerned, upset. 'Are you all right now? Is anyone with you?'

'Yes, I'm fine, really.'

'I'll see what else I can find out and ring you during the day. Ring me with any worries or if you hear anything you want to confirm or discount. Remember the media are not always correct.'

Elan came in, breathless. He had been down to the village for the papers and goodies he knew Gabby might eat.

'I've just met Nell ... ?'

'Two of the crew have been picked up, but not Josh, Elan.'

'Oh, darling ...'

Elan dared not touch Gabby. She held her hands up to ward him off, knowing she would dissolve and she must not yet.

'It won't be long now, Gabby, I am sure of it . . . Look, I've bought straw bugs and fruit so I can make you a fruit salad.' He pulled them out of the bag. 'They will slip down your throat, you won't even notice . . .'

Gabby smiled, 'I'm so glad you're here, Elan.'

Elan kissed the top of her head. 'These days will pass and seem a distant dream, darling. They will.'

He began to unpack the rest of his bag.

'It is rather a treat to be close enough, just, to walk to the village. Now I'm old I miss that . . . I'm so forgetful. Gabby, so many people have sent their best wishes. I met John, too, he is coming up later. Prayers are being said in all the village churches and in Truro cathedral.'

'Josh would be amazed.'

'He would indeed.'

Elan went on talking and Gabby was grateful. She could not listen for long, could not concentrate even on the papers. She opened them up. It was so odd to see Josh's name in print. It was all so speculative. Why were there always so many experts?

Gabby folded the paper away. 'I'm just going to my workroom, Elan. I want to see what is on the Internet.'

'Is that wise?' Elan turned from the sink where he was washing fruit.

'It gives me something to do. If the phone goes I'll answer it in there.'

As Gabby switched on her computer her incoming e-mails came up. Lucinda. Various people she had worked for. The curator of the National Portrait Gallery. *Mark*.

Gabby looked at that familiar e-mail address and trembled. She opened all the others and their messages touched her. She wanted to open Mark's e-mail so badly it hurt. She imagined what it would be like for her if he was going through something bad and he shut her out. Yet to touch that button would be a betrayal to Charlie and to Josh.

She e-mailed Lucinda, knowing she would pass her message on. By the time she had been on the Internet and printed stuff off for Charlie and Nell to see, there was a reply from Lucinda.

Dearest Gabby,

So relieved to have your e-mail. WE have been so worried about you. Just know WE are thinking about you night and day, do not feel alone. Two soldiers are out and it will be Josh soon. Hang on to that. Know too that we are both here any time. I wish I could find the words to let you know how much we both care and we are thinking of you every moment.

With love,
Lucinda xx

Gabrielle sniffed and replied: '*Thank you. Your e-mail means a lot.*'

The phone was silent, all day it was silent, and when she could bear it no longer and rang Simon, he said gently, 'I was just going to ring you to see if you were all right. You have not rung all day.'

'I was trying not to bother you.'

'Then don't. Ring as much as you like, OK?'

'OK. Simon, there is no news, is there?'

'I am afraid it is very silent. We have heard nothing.'

'Is that bad?'

'No. It can be for a number of security reasons. Believe me, there will be a lot of activity going on behind the scenes. We have to be patient.'

'Yes.'

'Goodnight.'

'Goodnight, Simon, thank you.'

Another day ended with Josh missing. Gabby, held in like a spring, was unsure how much more she could bear.

Chapter 53

The sun was trapped behind cloud so that the heat still pressed down, unrelieved. Gabby would not walk beyond the garden in case she missed the phone. She moved round and round the house, in and out, and Charlie and Nell watched as she began to fragment.

When the newspapers arrived the missing helicopter crew were no longer headline news, and for all of them this was somehow worse than the screaming headlines. Gabby could not bear it, for the world was moving on and there were still missing soldiers out there and they were going to be forgotten. She raked through the papers for some significant mention and could find none.

She rang Simon.

'It is odd,' he said. 'We think there's been a news blackout. Hang in there, Gabrielle, obviously there is something major going on behind the scenes and as soon as I find out anything I'll ring you.'

Elan had had to go home for the day to fetch paintings he needed framing and take them into Penzance. Charlie could not decide what to do, how far from the house it was safe to go. He could feel the situation coming to a head and instinctively knew it could go either way. There would not be a press blackout unless the situation was dire.

In the end he got in the Land Rover and went round his fields, checking the water and the litter-bins and how many people he had on his land. Nell, like Gabby, had not slept for days and felt exhausted. She made an attempt at cleaning a painting which she had brought into the farmhouse kitchen to be near Gabby, but her heart was not in it.

Gabby was relentlessly cleaning Josh's room, even taking down the curtains, but her interest and concentration kept wandering and she left things half done. Nell followed in her wake, gathering and putting back.

They were both in the old scullery when the phone went. Gabby ran and snatched it up. *This has got to be news.* But it was a woman who had somehow got through and wondered if Gabby could restore an old painting of her grandmother's.

Something snapped in Gabby. She screamed down the phone: 'Get off the line! Get off this line this minute. You are blocking my calls, do you hear me? You are blocking my calls.'

Nell took the phone and apologized, and explained to the mortified woman. Gabby had rushed from the room out into the garden. She was shaking from head to foot and was so weak from lack of sleep and food that she had to crouch on the grass. It was as if she no longer had a spine to keep herself upright and she felt strange and light-headed as though she might blow away.

Nell came and walked her back inside, made her lie down, placed the phone beside her and went and made tea. When she returned, Gabby had fallen into an exhausted sleep. Nell sat in the chair opposite her, leant back and closed her own eyes.

She concentrated hard on an imagined place Josh might be and tried to will the missing soldiers safe; *feel* an outcome, as she sometimes could. But all Nell could see and feel was a blurred fuzziness and she knew that the fate of those boys must hang in the balance.

Charlie came in at lunchtime and they sat and watched the one o'clock news. There was a small feature on Baghdad, on the ordinary people in the street who suffered most from the stringent UN sanctions and who wanted peace. Then there was a mention of the ongoing negotiations to find out the whereabouts of the two remaining British soldiers: the pilot, Captain Josh Ellis, and the senior officer with him, Major Andrew O'Conner. The fact that the Iraqi regime had not come forward with names of any British servicemen gave hope that they might have managed to evade capture.

Charlie felt better. 'You hear that, Gab? That's really good news, something to hold on to.'

Josh's colonel and Marika rang in the afternoon and Gabby was glad to talk to them. They talked on Gabby's mobile so that the main telephone line was free. Marika had rung every day and Josh's colonel was upbeat, but if he knew anything he was not telling Gabby.

Gabby was sitting in the garden with the radio, pulling weeds half-heartedly out of the border when there was a newsflash: *'It is believed one of the two remaining British officers from the downed helicopter has been rescued and airlifted to safety . . .'*

The phone rang out and Gabby grabbed it.

'Simon?'

'One British soldier has been picked up . . .'

'Do you . . . ?'

Simon said quickly, 'Gabby, we don't know who it is yet.'

'Please, ring me as soon as you know.'

'Of course.'

Nell was standing in the doorway.

'They've found one soldier.' Gabby's voice wobbled.

Nell was suddenly tearful. 'Please, please God, let it be Josh.'

Gabby had resumed pacing. *Please . . . please . . . please . . .*

The phone rang again and Gabby reached out for it, and Nell's hand, too.

'I'm sorry, Gabby. It's not the pilot, not Josh, but the senior officer. I am so sorry.'

Gabby burst into tears. 'I'm not sure how much more I can bear.'

Simon let his breath out. 'It is so very hard.'

Silence. Both were reluctant to put the phone down.

'Gabrielle, you are doing so well. It's a terrible waiting game, I know. I will ring when I've heard more details. Try and hang in there. OK?'

'OK.'

White-faced, both women stared at each other. *It meant Josh was somewhere out there alone.*

Charlie came in and they told him. The cows were brought in for milking, their sweet milky smell filling the yard. Charlie poured himself and Nell a whisky. They switched the early evening news on.

Suddenly there was an interruption and a newsflash and fuzzy pictures on the screen, of the American air base in Turkey. Darkness and distant shots of American soldiers and trucks standing in groups by an airfield. Then the announcer said excitedly, *'We have news of the possible rescue of the last missing officer, the pilot of the stricken helicopter . . .'*

Gabby was already dialling, 'Simon . . . Simon . . . on the news . . . now . . . It says the last British officer might have been rescued?'

'Gabrielle, I've heard nothing. I'm sorry, I think it might just be a rumour. I don't think it's true. Stay on the line, I'm going to check . . .'

Charlie was going into Ceefax. 'Tell him it's up here in black and white, Gabby.'

Simon came back on the line. 'Gabrielle, please don't get your hopes up, I can't verify this. I will get back to you, I promise, but I can't confirm.'

Gabby and Nell and Charlie stayed glued to the television all evening. Gabby could feel her heart swelling with hope. There was no more coverage and by mid-evening they were all beginning to think the BBC had made a mistake when there was a sudden and frenzied switch to the American air base. The pictures were still in darkness but there were now Land Rovers with Red Cross on the sides and heavily armed troops everywhere. There was a feverish air of tension and activity.

Oh God! Oh God! Josh. Josh. Is he hurt? Wounded?

The announcer said, '*The tension is palpable here at the Incirlik American air base in Turkey. There has been a complete news blackout for the last twenty-four hours but journalists based here believe there has been a huge British and American covert operation to find and airlift all the missing soldiers to safety. The dangers involved do not need to be illustrated. It is probable that the Special Forces unit that the Lynx helicopter had been deployed to airlift out of Northern Iraq when it came under hostile fire has been crucial in finding three of the missing helicopter crew and airlifting them back to the American base here in Turkey . . .*'

The announcer suddenly stopped and cried, '*News is coming in now . . . We believe the last missing British soldier has been found and picked up . . . We think the last British soldier is out . . .*'

Gabby was watching and dialling Simon at the same time.

'Tell me exactly what you are seeing and hearing!' he said excitedly. 'You are getting the news by satellite faster than we can access it.'

Gabby repeated every word to him as it was coming over on the television.

'What can you see now?'

'Nothing. The picture is fuzzy and dark . . . just Land Rover lights and soldiers rushing about or huddled in groups . . . Everybody is waiting. Please, Simon . . . you must be able to verify this. Is Josh safe? Has he been picked up?'

'I can't confirm it. Sorry, Gabrielle.'

'But they wouldn't say it and film it if it wasn't true.'

'I will ring you back.'

Gabby replaced the receiver. 'Simon won't confirm it,' she said to Nell and Charlie.

'It's happening! . . . Look, we've seen the military waiting, Gabby,' Charlie said.

'I believe they've picked Josh up, I really do, Gabs,' Nell said.

Marika rang. 'I'm sure it's true, Gabby . . . it's got to be.'

'Yes,' Gabby said, but dared not hope yet again.

They had the radio and the television on at the same time. In the sitting room ITV ran; in the kitchen the BBC. None of them dared take their eyes off the screen in case they missed something. Elan came panting in with a bottle of good whisky which he and Charlie made inroads into. Ten o'clock came, and still Simon had not confirmed any rescue.

There is a lot of argument going on as to who is going to travel in the Land Rover with the captured British. Mr Nice Guy is definitely in charge.

Andrew leans towards Josh. 'Don't look at me. Listen. If I or anyone yells at you to do something unexpected, do it. Don't question it. Just go, go, go. OK, Josh? Now stay on the ball.'

The Land Rover speeds jerkily out of the village and into darkness. Mr Nice Guy sits in the front, gun across his knees. Two of his fierce-looking henchmen stand watching out of the back, equally armed to the teeth.

Tiredness is making Josh feel as if he is somewhere a long way away from this surreal journey through barren desert. Mr Nice Guy suddenly shouts an order to the driver and he slows down. The nervous tension of the four Iraqis in the vehicle alerts Josh. He glances at Andrew and sees he is watching Mr Nice Guy intently. The latter speaks rapidly into a handset and then turns and yells at the two Iraqis behind them. All at once both Josh and Andrew see lights behind them and the Land Rover speeds up again. Mr Nice Guy turns and looks at Andrew.

'British, when Land Rover slows again I give word. You jump and then follow me quick, very quick.'

Andrew nods, glances at Josh. Josh can feel his heart thumping, all tiredness suddenly gone. Both men move to the edge of their seat, place the weight on the balls of their feet. Mr Nice Guy speaks quietly into his radio and then touches the driver's arm. The vehicle does a sudden circle facing the way it has come and Mr Nice Guy yells, 'Now!'

The two guards at the back jump out of the way. Josh and Andrew leap out. Mr Nice Guy is already running and they follow, pounding after him into the darkness. There is the sound of gunfire behind them and more vehicles converging. Josh and Andrew keep running but it is hard-going on sand. They slowly become aware of other shadowy figures moving with them in the dark. Josh is glad now he kept his running up, but he sees Andrew is beginning to lose pace and watches horrified as he stumbles and falls. Josh rushes to help him up, but two shadowy Arab figures appear. One pulls Josh away and on and the other bends to Andrew. Josh hears shouting and gunfire and he tries to turn back, but the figure beside him yanks him firmly onward and suddenly there is a vehicle ahead and he is thrown into it, and the man leaps in after him as it shoots away. They scream through a village and on and on through darkness as Josh crouches, miserable, worrying about Andrew.

His rescuer is shouting into his radio and the vehicle suddenly stops, turns back and drives towards an abandoned village where it parks inside a derelict building. Suddenly Josh hears the sound of a helicopter and his hopes soar. He sits up. It has landed somewhere near. He looks at the Arab eagerly and points to the sky.

'British?'

'American.' The man shrugs his shoulders and shakes his head, points out into the darkness. 'No good. Saddam soldiers. Too late, helicopter.'

Suddenly the helicopter is airborne again, its lights disappearing into the darkness. Josh has never felt so alone in his life.

'Who are you?' he asks the frightening-looking man beside him.

'No like Saddam.' He makes a realistic cut-throat motion. 'He kill family.'

He is driven further into a village consisting only of men, and given an Arab costume to wear and water with dry biscuits.

Josh tries not to think of home, tries not to feel abandoned. The Arab lies on the straw near some chickens and promptly falls asleep. Josh sits there, determined to stay awake and alert, but tiredness overcomes him.

He is woken abruptly and yanked upright. A hand is clamped over his mouth from behind. The Arab is awake and pulling out a knife. The man holding Josh says something quietly in Arabic to the Arab and he nods. There is shouting outside and the sound of a vehicle arriving and men jumping out. Footsteps come towards them. The Arab rises silently in one movement, knife in hand, and flattens himself against the wall. The footsteps start to go away and then stop, turn, and start to come back. Josh can feel his heart thundering, sees a uniform briefly as a man comes into the building lighting a cigarette, then the Arab's knife flashes and the intruder is eased to the ground in absolute silence. Josh shakes with shock and the man holding him says, 'OK, boss, we are going to have to move fucking fast now.'

He lets Josh go. Josh turns to look at a dark man dressed as an Arab.

'No time for introductions . . .'

He says something to the Arab, who is peering out into the darkness. All the men are round the vehicle at the other end of the village.

'Right. Out and behind this building, quickly.'

They move quickly and silently round the broken wall and begin to run, still in darkness. Josh runs as he has never run, keeping pace with the two men. After twenty minutes he wonders how long he can keep this pace up.

'Five minutes, boss,' the man beside him says. 'Keep going. They are going to find that dead man any minute.'

He talks quickly into a handset and two more men appear out of the blackness and move with them. They can hear vehicles behind them now, but something else, too, the clatter of a helicopter overhead. And then there it is, a great big dirty American Black Hawk dropping from the sky a hundred yards ahead of them.

Hope flares. Josh, almost sobbing with relief, makes his tired legs fly. Ignoring the pain in his side, his eyes are on the opening door. He can see faces and uniforms . . . just ahead, so near . . . please . . . so nearly there.

Suddenly before them on the screen, in a darkness they could not see through, there was a huge helicopter landing and a rush of activity. The Land Rover with the Red Cross on it sped towards the helicopter.

An excited journalist shouted, 'We think this is it! The army pilot is out! We believe the last British soldier is safely out!'

But on the screen there was nothing to see except the blur of vehicles. Gabby rang Simon who answered on the first ring.

'We're watching, too, Gabrielle . . .'

'He's out! They're all out. The young helicopter pilot is out and safe!' the announcer yells. *'This has been an incredible combined British and American rescue mission . . .'*

'Simon!'

'I can't confirm, Gabrielle. I can't confirm. We don't have satellite.'

The trucks were turning and whizzing away now, back along the road to the base, flags flying.

'They are all out. Josh must be out,' Charlie yelled. 'The trucks are leaving. They would not dare to announce it if they were not absolutely sure.'

'Yes!' Nell agreed. 'Gabby, they are safe. Josh is safe.'

Gabby nodded. She thought so, too, but she could not quite believe it until the voice she had come to rely on confirmed it. She hovered by the phone and they switched channels repeatedly to see the same thing over and over again to convince themselves.

Josh was safe.

The phone went. Simon was laughing with relief. 'Gabrielle!

I can confirm Josh is out. All British servicemen are now out. Josh is out and safe!'

'Oh!' Gabby sank to her knees, relief literally making them give way.

'Expect a call from your son very soon.'

'He's really all right?'

'Yes, but very shaken. I am so happy and relieved for you all. This is such a good result.'

'Simon, thank you so much. Thank you for everything!'

'My pleasure. Sleep well.'

Gabby, Nell and Charlie stood with Elan and held each other without speaking. Then, Nell, suddenly overcome, needed to be alone and went back to her cottage. Charlie and Elan went back to the whisky bottle. Gabby sat by the phone.

When it rang she snatched it up. 'Josh!'

There was silence then a faint sound that tore her heart. *'Mum.'*

'Josh . . . Josh . . .'

She could hear him fighting for control.

'It's all right,' she said, 'it's all right, Josh.'

'I didn't think I was going to make it home.'

'Oh, Josh.'

'I . . . all so quick . . . I . . .'

'You don't have to talk, darling. You're safe, that's all that matters.'

Charlie came in and Gabby handed him the phone.

'Hi, son. How are you? God, you gave us a fright . . .'

'I'm OK, Dad. I can't talk long because other people need the phone . . .'

'You take care, Josh. It's so good to hear you, boy. We'll talk soon. Get some rest. Here's your mother again.'

'Mum, I'll try to ring you tomorrow when I'm back in Kuwait. Some really brave guys got me out and they need to phone their families too.'

'All right, darling.' Gabby was reluctant to let him go. 'Josh, are you really OK?'

'I'm fine, Gabby.'

'What will happen now, darling?'

'De-brief. Have a shower! Then go to thank the Yanks. We are invited to their mess. Then bed. I'm too tired to talk to Nell, will you give her my love?'

'Of course I will. Sleep well. Oh Josh . . .'

'I'm OK, Mum, don't worry.'

'Love you, Josh.'

'Love you too, Mum.'

Gabby went into the kitchen. Charlie smiled at her and Elan got up and kissed the top of her head. 'Go to bed, child, and get some rest.'

Charlie was so relieved his son was safe that he was on a high, and certainly wouldn't sleep. Gabby saw that he and Elan were going to get pretty drunk.

She walked across the yard to see Nell. Nell had been crying. They sat with the cats in Nell's sitting room and both nursed a brandy.

'Nell, Josh has never called me Mum before. His voice was so small, as if he was a child again for a second. It seared me. How could we have borne it if something had happened to him?'

'It doesn't bear thinking about. Josh has had the most frightening experience, Gabby, and it will undoubtedly affect him for a while. Will they send Josh and the others home?'

'I think he would hate to be sent home, Nell. His colonel said they would probably have a short leave to see their families. It will probably be up to them.'

'But surely he won't be flying over Iraq again?'

'Nell, I don't know. Knowing Josh, he will want to go on flying.'

Nell sighed. Gabby saw suddenly that Nell was beginning to grow old. Somehow she had aged so gently over the years it had not seemed noticeable. Now it was becoming so. Gabby got up and gently kissed her forehead.

'Nell, stop worrying. Get some sleep. Thank you.'

'For what?' Nell snorted.

'Always being there.' Gabby smiled.

'Gabs?'

'Yes?'

'You did awfully well, small person, as Elan would say.'

Gabby smiled and went out into the dark. She looked up at the stars. At this moment she could light a candle to thank God. Shadow slunk from the darkness.

'Where have you been, girl?' Gabby asked. 'I know, you've had no walks, have you? Tomorrow we'll go down to the cove, I promise.'

She said goodnight to Elan and Charlie who were eating bread and cheese and making no sense, and after a hot bath she got into Josh's bed where she would not be disturbed, and she dreamt strange dreams of loss.

Mark was torn. He should fly home. The girls had rung and told him Veronique had a breast lump and was going into hospital for a biopsy. He should be there. Of course he should, in case the news was bad.

Yet to leave England now would feel like abandoning Gabriella. It made no sense for there was nothing he could do here. She was with her family. He could neither comfort nor sustain her. He understood her silence, how could he not? All the same, he had been glad to have Lucinda's phone call.

He would decide that evening. He had no lectures for a month as he was concentrating on finishing his book. He was still behind and having difficulty focusing on what he needed to do. A deadline seemed unimportant in the light of the tragedy looming for Gabriella and her family.

Mark had some research to do and decided he would go to the Guildhall Library before meeting his publisher for lunch. For the past three days he had paused in front of every television shop, blindly watching the news unfold. The newspapers didn't help his dreadful sense of unease, either.

Both his and Gabriella's lives were starting to unravel, as if fate had been waiting, watching for an opportunity to shit on them from a high place. If Veronique had cancer . . . If, God forbid, Josh died . . . it would be the end of their brief life together. Neither love nor happiness could be snatched at any cost. Mark knew that neither he nor Gabriella would or could turn their backs on the innocent.

He also knew that Gabriella would never be the same again if anything happened to Josh; and he would be helpless, thousands of miles away, unable to love, cherish or coax her back from the brink.

Mark walked over the bridge and stopped and watched the muddy water flow beneath him. *I am going to lose Gabriella. I might already have lost her.* For even if Josh came home safely, and please God that he did, Gabriella would have re-learnt the powerful pull of family. As *he* would, if the woman who had borne him five daughters and who he had shared a long married life with was threatened by cancer.

I suppose, Mark thought, life is dictating our future. We are losing each other, for I could never turn my back on a smitten Veronique. She has been such a huge part of my life.

I shall have to fly home. I will book this evening.

He looked up at the sky. All this fever about the eclipse. Everybody moving ritually and instinctively towards the ocean. How small we are in the scheme of things, he thought, and how often we need to be reminded.

Chapter 54

We meet down in the cove at the end of each day. Sir Richard is due back in St Piran any day now. Our days together have an unreality about them, like this heatwave that goes on and on like a dream; yet they seem truer to Isabella and I than real life. We lie naked with wonder and ease with each other. We talk and sleep and love on our deserted and lonely beach and look no further than the end of each day.

Daniel Vyvyan has not yet returned from the south of France, and Isabella takes me to the cool of her father's garden. We trespass and she shows me the hidden places where she used to play as a child.

Lisette is grieving for her mother and is much less of a guard dog. Morwenna is to be buried in the Methodist chapel. The village stops work for the funeral to pay their respects. Lisette's father had been a French fisherman who saw Morwenna and never returned home. Both he and Morwenna were loved and respected.

Only those working on the *Lady Isabella* return to work that afternoon, in order to finish the small outstanding jobs before Sir Richard's return. The village love a wake and it will go on long after the sun sets.

I go down to the quay with my father and we make the final adjustments to the figurehead. My calculations were accurate and I am mighty relieved. The figurehead looks, as she should, part of the ship. She is now ready to start her voyage through the oceans.

It had not been easy getting her down the hill. It had taken eight of us, four each side of the cart to steady her, for she was heavy and unwieldy.

My father and I stand side by side, viewing her. It is the first time my father has had the chance to look at the figurehead properly.

'It is skilfully carved,' he says. 'The best carving thou hast ever done.'

But something in his expression as he stares at Isabella's face disturbs me, as if I have somehow given him a glimpse of our secret.

'Sir Richard should be well-pleased, son. Thou hast done a good job.'

I stare at the face I am beginning to know better than my own.

'I would not have finished her, Pa, if you had not freed me to work on her full-time. You have done well to finish the schooner in three months.'

My father nods. 'I could not have worked the men so hard if it had been for anyone but Sir Richard, who is generous with his bonus.'

Yesterday I took Isabella down to the quay to show her the inside of *Lady Isabella*. Newly fitted, pristine, ropes curled and ready. Foredeck, aft deck, cabins and hold, gleaming and waxed, swabbed and polished. Isabella explored every little nook and cranny of the ship, fascinated by the order of everything and the smell of new wood and glue which filled her nostrils.

I leave my father now and go back to the top boatyard to tidy and pack my tools away. My next commission is in Falmouth, then St Malo. I walk up the cliff and make for the cove where I am meeting Isabella. The heat of the day has driven her into the water and she stands up to her ankles, trying to keep cool. She has on a large straw hat and a thin white dress which suits her dark skin. As I approach she runs towards me laughing and I catch hold of her and whirl her round.

We move into the lee of the cliff where there is shade, and lie on a rug. Isabella takes off her dress to keep cool and lies in her petticoats. I take off my shoes, shirt and trousers and we lie holding each other, skin touching skin, talking.

Then we are both silent, and I say, because I cannot believe it, 'The day after tomorrow you will be gone from here, Isabella.'

Isabella closes her eyes and leans against my hand.

'I feel as if I have been here forever.'

I take a strand of her hair and hold it to the light.

'I have been working so long on your likeness, now I am going to lose you both ... My wooden angel and my real one.'

Isabella's small face closes. She does not want to hear these words.

'Tom, are we never to see each other again? You told me you were coming to Falmouth, to ...'

'I am. And no doubt I will see you with your husband ... but never like this ...' I push her gently backwards onto the rug and kiss her. 'It will never be like this again. It will seem like a dream ... and one day I will see that you are mortified at the memory of me and you will look through me ... turn away ...'

'Never!' Isabella cries vehemently, kissing my mouth. 'Do you hear me? Never ...'

I touch her warm dark skin. 'Never?' I smile, wanting to hear it again.

I roll with her back onto the rug. Our lovemaking has the urgency of a leave-taking. This is our last time in the cove, where the cliffs rise high above to hide us and the seabirds mew and wheel overhead, resting in the thermals. The sea is violet, reflecting the sky. From high above on the cliff-top path, Isabella and I would look as small and insignificant as the stones on the shore or the driftwood. Cliff, sea, sky and cove will remain much as it is, but nothing will remain of these moments of our life here.

Shielding Isabella's nakedness, I want to tell her all that I feel for her has gone into my carving of the figurehead. I will do other carvings, some beautiful, some clever, I know this, but there will never be another moment when my heart and hands come together to make a whole and almost perfect piece. I know this.

I know that if the small schooner makes old age she might lie on the bed of some creek and her figurehead be taken to adorn a public house or sold to a naval establishment. If the ship is ever wrecked in a wild sea or on some far shore, a part of me will sink to the ocean bed and be lost forever. A part of Isabella and I lost in the deep.

I would like to express what I feel to Isabella but I do not have the flow of words, only these fleeting thoughts, only these hands to carve feelings men cannot speak of.

378

When I look up I see she is crying without sound.

'I love you, Tom. I love you. I believe I loved you from the first moment I saw you with Mama.'

I am wretched in my turn for I can do nothing about our situation. I try to make her smile. 'Why, you were "no' but a child", as my father would say.'

I wrap my jacket about her shoulders, draw a finger across her wet cheek.

'Isabella,' I say gently. 'Come, we must start walking. It is late.'

Isabella gets to her feet but she is watching my face for the something I cannot give her: hope. Desperately I take her hand.

'Love is something we dare not think about, Isabella. We have different lives. I have nothing to offer you, even ... Come ...'

We walk up the steep incline silently, hand in hand. At the top Isabella takes her shoes off to remove the stones and leaves them off. She always likes to walk with the wildflowers under her feet.

'Tomorrow,' I say eventually, 'your husband will see the figurehead for the first time, and in position. How does it feel, Isabella, to see your likeness set up there on the prow?'

'Strange,' Isabella says after a while. 'Proud, and not a little guilty for although Richard called the schooner after me, the figurehead up on the front of the ship will always remind me of you.'

'Then you will not forget me?' My voice gives me away.

Isabella turns to me. 'You know the answer, Tom, for I have already declared myself. I do not know how I am going to bear my life. It is so empty and you have been my friend. I can talk to you about anything.'

Her words strike me with sudden dread, for I realize the truth of them. With Isabella I have been myself. We have talked and loved and been together so much that the emptiness she speaks of opens up before me like a gaping mineshaft. I put my hand over my heart and I can hardly speak for this sudden knowledge in me.

'When you doubt my feelings, Isabella, look at the drawing I gave you of your face. Look into the face of my figurehead. All that I feel for you is there, and here ...' I place the flat of my hand across my heart.

Isabella smiles and places her hand over mine. It is enough. We turn and walk on, careful now not to touch on the path. At the fork to the village I leave her.

'Lisette will be home before you. Do you have an excuse ready?'

'Yes.'

'I will see you tomorrow, Isabella. When you are sad, remember these were our days, yours and mine.'

'How lucky we were to have them, Tom. How very lucky.'

'Indeed, my Lady. Indeed.'

I cannot let her go. 'Isabella ... when you feel alone, I am somewhere thinking of you. You know ... what I feel ... Run home, Isabella, run home ...' I say fiercely and turn abruptly away.

Isabella runs from me down the path and I can hear her little intakes of breath as she cries. A curlew above me calls out sharply. The weather is going to break. The seabirds are coming inland. There will be a storm.

Isabella reached the gate of the house and stopped dead. There were two horses outside and Richard's groom was leading them round to the old stables. Richard was back early, he was not expected until the morning.

Isabella replaced her shoes and moved swiftly round the side of the house, up the servants' stairs and into her room. She took her sandy clothes off and washed carefully, and changed into a dark dress with a high neck to hide where the sun had caught her skin. She tied her hair back tightly into a knot, but there was nothing she could do about the brightness of her eyes or the sense of well-being that gave her a radiance that would not last, unless she guarded it carefully.

She went slowly downstairs. Richard turned as she came into the room and he was stopped by her beauty.

'My dear Isabella ...' He rushed over. 'You look wonderful. The heat must suit you ...'

He kissed her cheek. 'Have you missed me?'

'Of course,' Isabella smiled, her heart sinking at the look in his eye. Covetous, as if he was reclaiming a prize, which of course he was.

'Have you ridden all the way from Falmouth?'

'No,' Richard turned for his whisky, 'from Truro. It is a special day tomorrow, is it not? Is Tom Welland pleased with his work?'

'I believe he is.'

'I asked for the figurehead to be covered. I will not look until the morning when we are together. Are you excited, my love?'

'I am. It is not every day that I have a ship named after me, or my likeness carved.'

She went and kissed Richard's cheek. 'I thank you for it, Richard.'

Richard took her hand and kissed it fervently. 'There is nothing I would not do for you, or for our children, once they come.'

'Come,' Isabella said gently, 'let us go into the dining room or Cook will give in her notice.'

As Lisette helped Isabella to get ready for bed she exclaimed over the amount of sand in the room.

'Lisette, you know I cannot resist going into the water. I am sorry.'

Lisette stopped turning down the bed and sighed. 'I believe it is time you grew up, Isabella. You cannot recapture your childhood or the times here you had with your mama. Life is not all that we wish it to be. You lead a comfortable life. Sir Richard is a good man who loves and respects you. What more could you want?'

Isabella said in a small voice, 'I do not love him, Lisette ... I ...'

Lisette stared at her. 'I know you do not love him, but he asks so little of you. Love grows, if you let it, Isabella. If you tried harder ...'

'I do try.'

Isabella climbed into bed and leant against the pillows. A small tear of self-pity trickled down her cheek. Lisette relented and sat on the bed.

'Miss Isabella, I know that you find the ... married relationship difficult. I try to help ... It gets easier, especially once you have children. The demands get less and it is just something you get used to.'

'It will not get easier for me, Lisette. I will never get used to it, I know this.'

Lisette smiled. 'You cannot know, Miss Isabella. Children change everything.'

381

Lisette was fighting with herself, for she did pity Isabella with her beautiful body, for Sir Richard might be kind, but she doubted he was skilful in bed, being a bachelor so long. She said astutely, 'It is of no use you comparing a young man with an older man. We all do this when young ...'

'Even you, Lisette?' Despite herself, Isabella was laughing.

'Even me.'

'What would I do without you, Lisette?'

'Sleep, now.'

At the door, Lisette turned. Isabella was lying, eyes closed, dark against the white pillow, a suspicion of a smile on her lips. Isabella's looks seemed somehow to have changed this summer, but Lisette could not fathom in what way this change had taken place.

A small shadow eased its way into her mind and she hastily dismissed it. As she shut the door, she thought, I am afraid sharing a bed with Sir Richard is something my mistress is going to have to learn, for it is a duty like any other.

Chapter 55

Ben rose early to go down to the quay and make sure that all was ready, that nothing had been forgotten. He knew Sir Richard would inspect it with an acute and critical eye and anything missed he would surely notice.

He looked up at the sky. It was a deep, bruised purple, colouring the sea, and the morning was strangely muted, as if poised, waiting. Even the birds, sensing the change in the weather, seemed to be lulled into silence.

'The weather is going to break,' Tom said.

'Aye. Let us hope it keeps off till this afternoon.'

Something in the brooding morning made Ben uneasy. The bakery was lighting the ovens up early, for Sir Richard wanted all the men to celebrate with a pasty and beer, and the smell of warm bread hovered over the quay, filling the still air.

Isabella too had woken early and threw the window wide onto the airless day. She chose her dress carefully and picked out the brooch that Richard had brought her from London. This was his day and Isabella wanted it all to go well.

Richard was already having breakfast when she went downstairs and Isabella took fruit and tea. Then they left the house with Lisette and Cook holding umbrellas, and the kitchen girl, the groom and the gardener all following behind them as they made their way down to the harbour.

There was a little trail of people walking down the hill and they greeted Sir Richard and Isabella with a cheerful air of excitement at this small holiday. The quay when they arrived was festive, with chairs and tables laid out around the harbour and a small brass band all ready to start playing.

Isabella laughed. 'Why, it is as if someone famous or royal is about to arrive to launch my ship!'

Richard smiled and looked down at her. 'My dear Isabella, to me you are both famous and royal, and I would have no other to launch your namesake properly now the refit is completed but you.'

His eyes were so full of devotion that Isabella had to look away, for she could not return his look with the same feeling. She turned away and met Tom's eyes, for he was standing with his father ready to greet Sir Richard. He held her eyes for a moment before looking away.

Richard had not yet looked up at the schooner and the covered figurehead. He was almost afraid to have her uncovered. He had had a vision of her in his head for so long that he was afraid of disappointment and his inability to hide it. He saw the bottle on the small table, tied with ribbon and attached to the ship for Isabella to throw, and he felt the sudden stillness in the small crowd as they waited for the figurehead to be unveiled.

He nodded at father and son and they turned and signalled to the two young boys holding the ropes of the cover. They let the ropes go and the figurehead was revealed.

A sudden wind got up and swung the ship round on its moorings. The face of Isabella veered round to the quay and Richard and the villagers gasped, for the beauty of the carving far exceeded anything imagined. It was a work of art, and yet . . .

Richard stepped forward and peered across the small stretch of water at the likeness of his wife. It was not . . . somehow . . . an expression he had ever seen on her face. He searched in his mind for a memory that eluded him, then the wind turned her slightly profile and it was his Isabella exactly, and he turned relieved and beamed at Tom and went to shake his hand.

'Well done, lad! I couldn't have asked for more. Well done, I say.'

The carpenters lined up on the quay clapped and the crowd joined in. All except Ben and Lisette, who were standing a little apart. Neither could take their eyes off the wooden face of Lady Isabella.

384

Lisette's hands flew to her mouth. She saw so clearly what the sensuous curl of Isabella's mouth and the lazy heaviness of her eyes meant, and she could not believe that no one else could interpret that expression. Yet they did not seem to.

Then she saw Ben Welland's face. It was tight-lipped and shocked. Their eyes met briefly in recognition of impending disaster.

The band started to play softly, and Ben, collecting himself, handed Isabella the bottle of champagne. Two men pulled at the ropes to swing the *Lady Isabella* closer to the quay, and Richard touching Isabella's shoulder urged her to swing the bottle hard in order that it broke.

Isabella swung it as hard as she could, crying out, 'I name this ship *Lady Isabella*. May God go with her!'

At that moment there was a huge clap of thunder, and lightning streaked across the sky. People gasped and scattered, the bandsmen leaving their metal instruments. Richard hurried Isabella into the lee of the cliff by the bakery, followed by everybody exposed in the open on the quay.

There was another huge clap which rumbled and roared across the black sky and they waited for the lightning. No rain, just the violent breaking-up of the heat-wave, the dry cracking of the sky. For ten minutes the storm flashed and then was gone. The air was clearer, but the sky, though no longer so violent, was a strange clouded and threatening mauve.

'Right!' Richard called out, holding Isabella's arm. 'Let the band play and refreshment be brought out, in thanks and celebration of a fine and finished vessel. I thank you all for your good work.'

There was mumbled applause and a few claps and the bandsmen resumed their places, but the older, superstitious villagers crossed themselves. It was a bad omen this sudden storm, no two ways about it. They looked towards the ship with the beautiful figurehead silhouetted against the brooding sky. So much work in her. So much labour ... But a bad beginning ...

Yet when everyone was full of beer and pasties the good humour that comes with a day off work returned and the storm faded into proportion. Those sailing in the schooner that afternoon with Sir

Richard got themselves ready, for there was extra money in the short sail and a story in *The Cornishman*. Richard, who had not yet sailed in the *Lady Isabella*, wanted to take her out to gauge the feel and pace of her before he handed her over to her skipper.

Tom, watching Isabella from a distance, saw how Sir Richard must touch his wife all the time. He gritted his teeth. He could not bear the thought of her husband pawing her, could not bear to think of him ... It was wrong, an old man and a young woman ... She should not have to bear it ...

He threw his beer back angrily and did not notice his father following his eyes, reading him all too clearly. Ben wanted to believe that weariness had made him fanciful. Now he knew for sure that what he saw was the truth. The beer tasted sour in his mouth and he put his glass down. There was no way he could swallow a pasty. He was not a particularly superstitious man, but he knew disaster when it faced him and he prayed it might be diverted.

'Let's get on board and be ready. Call the crew,' he said abruptly to Tom.

'I will leave you, my love. I want to inspect the ship before we sail. Lisette, will you see Lady Isabella keeps dry if the weather breaks? If there is another thunderstorm she must not go out, lightning is dangerous ...'

'Do not worry, Sir, I will see Lady Isabella home safely.'

'I will see you in Truro tomorrow, Isabella. We will fetch up in Newlyn or Penzance tonight. It is too precarious to sail back here in the dark.'

'Take care, Richard, for she is a new ship and you are not used to her.'

Richard laughed heartily. 'I have been sailing in ships new and old all my life, my dear, I do not think much can happen between here and Penzance ...'

Isabella knew it was tricky sailing out of the cove, and a while later she stood with Lisette and the villagers and watched the schooner turn gently on small reefed sails until they were free of the harbour and outlying rocks.

There was a scurry of activity as they turned and tacked, ready to head for the open sea. Isabella could see one man at the spanker-sheet and guy, and two boys at the maintopsail; the rest of the crew were on the mainbrace.

She remembered Tom telling her how every man had a place and a job on board, and smiled. She heard Richard shout, 'Helm's a lee.'

And there was an answering shout: 'Helm's a lee.' And then the head sheets were loosened.

'Well the fore-topsail yard!'

'Topgallant yard's well!'

'Royal yard too much!'

'Haul in to windward!'

'Well that!'

'Well all!'

The jib sheet was hauled down and a tackle attached in case the wind got up. The villagers standing on the quay caught the excitement and cheered.

'Haul taut to windward!'

And she was gone out of earshot, a dream of a boat, sails up and furled. Out to sea she raced on the late afternoon tide where the wind was fresh. White sails and varnished wood against a vivid sky sinking into blood-red as the sun lowered. The figurehead before her proudly plunged through the waves. There was a gasp of admiration from the men watching and they turned and smiled and nodded at Isabella. They watched the schooner until she was a speck on the horizon, then turned for their homes. Isabella and Lisette turned also, in silence, and walked back up the hill.

Isabella glanced at the boatyard as they passed. She and Tom would never have time together again. Tomorrow it would be a social round in Truro which would try her deeply, and then they returned home to Botallick House.

She closed her eyes and smelt honeysuckle from the hedge and the faint smell of roses. Nothing could ever take these summer days from her; nothing. This long, hot and wonderful summer, Isabella thought, will have to sustain me for a whole lifetime. I will never regret it, ever.

Chapter 56

On the day before the eclipse the weather broke. Unrelenting rain beat down, turning the fields and the lane to mud and the tents to soggy masses of canvas. The skies remained heavy and grey as the forecast had predicted. General disappointment, as well as being continually wet, subdued the visitors.

On the morning itself, however, people rallied. Even if they missed the actual eclipse they were going to enjoy themselves and there was always hope the weather would blow itself out in time. Charlie directed his campers to various different beaches and coastlines, for then at least some of them might glimpse the actual event they'd travelled so far for.

Most of the village trailed under the grey sky along the coastal path which ran parallel to the Ellis's land and down to the cove. The beach near Elan, locally known as Cow Beach, was also popular as it was more accessible than the cove where Shadow and Gabby walked and swam.

There were various parties going on in the village, but neither Charlie, Gabby nor Nell felt up to joining in. They were still shaken, and although they had all spoken to Josh on the phone once he was back in Kuwait, such was their level of terror over the four days he was missing that it was no longer easy to relax back into a normal routine.

The amount of people who had flooded the village and countryside, the unaccustomed noise and air of expectancy, disturbed Gabby. It felt as if she had entered a nightmare, and when she'd woken up her world had changed and the isolation she depended on had disappeared and been replaced by a strange circus. All she wanted was to have her quiet and steady world back, to see and touch Josh so that she knew he really was all right; safe and himself.

She walked with Nell and Charlie down to the cove although the cloud did not look as if it would clear. Elan was going to watch it from his cottage on the hill.

'It is a pity,' Nell said, 'when it has been so hot and clear.'

As they descended the cliff path they saw a mass of small boats in the bay that had sailed and motored round from the harbour. There were bright-coloured sails everywhere and the small day ferries were full of visitors who wanted to watch the eclipse from the water.

It all looked so festive and celebratory that Gabby stopped and stared around her at the cheerful excited little groups waiting by the ocean.

Why could she not feel happy and jubilant? Why wouldn't this tension leave her? She had spoken to Josh that morning. He was going about his normal duties after only forty-eight hours. But today he had a day off and he and some friends were driving off to some beach to drink beer and swim.

England and the eclipse seemed so far away, he told Gabby. Like another world. He was looking forward to some leave. It felt bizarre to Gabby. Days before his life had hung in the balance and twenty-four hours later he was going on as if nothing had happened.

'Well, that's the army isn't it?' Nell had said crossly.

Gabby moved away across the sand to stand on her own. She needed space between herself and other people. As the eerie darkness approached and the sun was eclipsed, the sea birds fell silent and the water lay in front of her like molten glass. People gazed upward through glasses, the small boats were still and silhouetted into black and white, captured like an aged photograph.

It all felt surreal; the silence of the birds; the darkness. Gabby felt caught and trapped in an unmapped landscape.

She felt an unnatural lament begin low and deep inside her. It burrowed up from somewhere unknown and seemed to encapsulate not only the anguish of Josh's capture but all the moments of isolation and fear and unknown dread that had lingered like some shapeless and malignant shadow on the pathways of her life.

Josh was safe. But the fear, the terrible presentiment of disaster remained lingering and clutching at her entrails, nebulous and unformed. The reality of his release and safety could not touch her yet. Overwrought, she remained in a state of inner terror.

She tried to subdue this chilling sound inside her, moved further towards the rocks. The cloud cover had hidden the sight of the eclipse from the watchers gazing skywards in the cove, and a small sigh of disappointment filtered like a rippled echo along the shoreline.

When the wounded sound escaped from Gabby it came as harsh as a seagull's cry. She terrified Charlie and Nell who jumped and turned towards her in horror as Gabby crumpled onto the sand. Gabby was aware of nothing, no one; she was that primitive howl of despair, enveloped inside it to the exclusion of all else.

Nell moved quickly over the wet sand and bent and held Gabby to her, but the painful racking sound only increased. Charlie stood ashen, embarrassed, watching Gabby lose complete control. He was appalled and frightened for Gabby and for the effect that rhythmic sobbing started to have on his own self-control.

He could feel the tears begin to choke him; for Gabby's distress, for his own, and for the crisis they had just been through together. For the son they had so nearly lost. He walked across the sand and put his arms around Gabby, and Nell, surprised, moved away.

'Enough,' Charlie said softly. 'Enough, Gab. It's all over now. Gabby . . . it's over.'

Nell saw how choked he was, fighting with his own emotions, and she turned and left them in a little crumpled heap on the wet sand. She laboured up the cliff path feeling very old.

A little group of neighbours caught her up and she was touched to see how concerned they were, carefully circling Charlie and Gabby.

'Poor little thing.'

'Dear of her.'

'Your Charlie will see she's right.'

'Thank the Lord it ended well, Nell.'

'Very best to that grandson of yours when you next talk, Nell.'

'Shaken up, I'll bet he is, poor soul.'

And so Nell reached the top of the cliff path, glad to be reminded of the kindness of strangers as she headed for the blessed stillness of her cottage.

Gabby turned close into Charlie like a child and let him hold her. She could feel the hammering of his heart and his own sniffing. At this moment he was the only person in the world who knew exactly how she felt, who could share this with her, and she clutched him until she was calm. When they both looked round the cove it was completely empty of people and of boats. They were completely alone.

Charlie kissed her forehead. 'Better?'

Gabby nodded and looked at him, and it seemed to her she had not looked at him for a long, long time. She could not read his eyes, they were dark and careful; wary, maybe. She kissed him gently on the mouth and Charlie kissed her back, and they went on kissing and suddenly they were on their backs in the sand, desperately pulling at each other's clothes, unaware of anything but the need for the other. It was fast and passionate, both of them active and involved in a way they had never been in the whole of their married life.

When it was over they looked at each other rather shocked, and laughed, embarrassed, adjusting their clothes, brushing the wet clinging sand from their limbs. Then they climbed up the path together in silence, feeling strange.

Gabby could feel Charlie looking at her sideways, but

he said nothing. She moved closer to him as they walked, puzzled about her own feelings, and Charlie jumped as she brushed against him, moved imperceptibly away, yet Gabby felt it.

She thought suddenly, blindingly, *it is like two strangers having sex*. Afterwards they are awkward and have nothing to say to each other, and the man wonders, *What demands is this woman going to make on me now?*

She stopped on the path and turned to look at him, and Charlie stopped too and could not meet her eyes. She wanted to laugh gently and say, *Don't worry, Charlie, I am not going to cling and demand and change the order of our undemanding marriage. You are safe.*

But what she actually said was, 'Shall we ring Elan, cook that goose, open a good bottle of wine and then the four of us can have our own little eclipse party, to toast Josh?'

Charlie grinned, relief lighting his face. 'Good idea. We'll knock on Nell's door as we pass.'

Gabby turned the Aga up high and went to have a bath. From the bedroom she looked over the waterlogged fields. The clouds had lifted and the evening looked like a vast watercolour painting. She did not know how long she stood there. She did not consciously think at all, just let what she had learnt today settle and filter through her into a form of understanding.

There were some things that did not translate immediately; they needed to lie still in some inner place until she could fathom the full implications. Gabby knew she hurt because of this new abrupt understanding of Charlie, and yet in a strange way the pain was welcome because it put everything else into context.

It pared away this mellow sadness. For a moment, maybe that was all it had been, a moment, she had felt down there in the cove that there was something left for her and Charlie. On the path home she had looked into his eyes and realized it was not true. It had all been illusory, the rawness of heightened emotion. It felt, in the second Charlie could not meet her eyes, like a slap in the face.

Gabby pulled on clean jeans and a shirt and went down into the kitchen and placed the goose into the oven. Charlie was nowhere to be seen. She peeled potatoes and washed vegetables then she laid the table with all the best silver, glass and linen. She went into the garden and picked bright nasturtiums for the table. She placed candles alongside them. She leant against the sink and viewed the kitchen, full of warm cooking smells. The round table looked as good as a Sunday-supplement photograph. The room was reflected in the window. Outside the sun set, and she could see Charlie and Matt talking behind the cows.

Under her feet, the huge slate flagstones of the old farmhouse. Gabby swallowed. This perfect scene was the one she always used to strive for. Perfect marriage. Perfect home. Welcoming and secure for Josh. *Without love it was as unreal and as fleeting as this afternoon.*

A mirage, too easily created by superficial things without any real substance or painful hard work. Flowers on a bright tablecloth, glass and silver. A lamp shining into dark corners where the dust collects.

A deception. A revelation.

It hurts. Because I made this whole flimsy fantasy my life's work.

She watched Nell walking from her cottage in a new dress, saw her stop and talk to Matt and Charlie and then move across the yard towards the back door. Gabby's heart ached, for Nell would see this as the celebration it was meant to be and not the goodbye Gabby knew it really was.

She left the room and climbed the stairs with her mobile phone. In her room she dialled Mark's mobile number, not knowing if he would be there or whether he would have flown back to Canada.

She trembled as it rang. The longing to hear his voice was overpowering. At last he answered and she could not speak.

'Gabriella? Is that you, my love?'

The strength, the warmth behind his voice made her collapse on the bed.

'Yes,' she whispered.

'Oh, how good to hear you!'

'And you. Oh! And you.'

'I am so, so glad Josh is safe. Are you all right, sweetheart?'

'Just. Mark, I need to see you.'

'I'm here.'

'I'm very muddled.'

'I'm not surprised!' There was laughter in his voice and Gabby smiled.

'I thought of coming . . . maybe tomorrow . . .'

Nell called up the stairs.

'Mark . . . I have to go.'

'Just e-mail or ring with train times and I'll meet you, my Gabriella . . .'

'Goodnight,' she whispered.

'Goodnight . . . I love you so very much.'

Just hearing Mark's voice again took Gabby back to a point of safety.

Charlie would never know how willing she had been as she lay on the cold wet sand, how willing, as they engaged each other physically and emotionally for the first time, to try anew, to make solid and tangible the fleeting act that had been the only real and true moment in the whole of their detached and undemanding marriage.

In that second of complete clarity, as Gabby felt Charlie withdraw from her in embarrassment, she had understood that it was not that Charlie did not want to give emotionally. It was simply that he did not love her.

She ran down the stairs. Tonight would not be a charade, for every person in the room was a part of her. She wanted to remember and be remembered for the evening of the eclipse, when Josh was safe, drinking beer in some Middle Eastern resort, and she and Nell, Charlie and Elan were last all together in the life she and Charlie had grown out of.

Chapter 57

Back at Botallick House, Isabella saw the summer was turning, the colours in her garden fading and overblown, sliding into autumn.

Isabella, on returning from St Piran, promptly caught influenza. It was a relief she could not admit to, for although feeling unwell and running a fever, her illness kept Richard from her bed.

As she lay feverish she missed Tom so acutely that she spent hours with her eyes closed tight against the room she was in, talking to him in her head. Tossing and turning, she longed for the feel of him beside her, the length of their bodies lying on the sand side by side.

'I am cut in half,' she whispered. 'I am cut in half without you, Tom.'

Although Tom was working in Falmouth, Isabella had been too unwell to catch a glimpse of him or to go anywhere.

Lisette watched the weight fall from Isabella with a sinking heart. Isabella seemed to have fallen into some dreamlike state, had withdrawn from her life with Richard and was making, like a child, Lisette saw, her own entirely make-believe world.

When Isabella was on her feet again and once more downstairs she sometimes wandered listlessly around the garden, dead-heading the roses, but for most of the day she sat just outside the French windows, wrapped up against the October wind, staring into space.

Richard was so concerned he wanted to call the doctor back.

'My wife seems depressed,' he said to Lisette. 'Why should this be? Is it due to her influenza?'

Lisette, knowing the cause was Tom Welland, said carefully,

'I do not think she needs the doctor, Sir Richard, but something to occupy her. Maybe Miss Sophie could come to keep her company for a while?'

Richard thought this an excellent idea, but Isabella immediately vetoed it.

'Thank you, Richard, it is a kind thought, but I do not care for company at present, even Sophie's. Later, perhaps. Really, I get better day by day.'

Isabella tried to make a supreme effort at cheerfulness but Lisette would find her weeping in her room. One day, carrying the rags that Isabella would need soon upstairs, Lisette found her at her small desk writing letters with some concentration, and sighed with relief.

'Good, Miss Isabella, I am glad you are writing letters. Maybe you can walk into the village later to post them? The air will do you good and if you feel frail I will accompany you. I have placed new rags in your drawer.'

Isabella seemed hardly to hear. She nodded and continued writing and Lisette left the room quietly.

'Dear Tom, life feels unendurable ...'

'Dear Tom, this is a note to say I hope ...'

'Tom. Tom. Tom. I miss you. I cannot endure this life I have.'

'Tom, without you I am nothing.'

All the notes were screwed into a ball and Isabella burnt them in her grate. She paced the room and suddenly stopped. What had Lisette said? She walked slowly to her drawer and opened it. The rags lay there, accumulating. Isabella stood looking down at them. She tried to think, then went to her desk and looked in her diary, turning back to the last month. Her last monthly bleeding had been due the day before Richard arrived back in St Piran. This month she was three days late. Lisette always remembered the correct dates. Had she noticed the amount of rags in the drawer?

Isabella put her hand over her mouth as her predicament dawned on her. She had not shared a bed with Richard for months. She went and sat on the bed, sick with shock. She sat there for a long time. It was the first time in her life that she had been really frightened.

She got up again and removed some of the rags from her drawer and placed them under articles of clothing in a separate drawer. She left the room and went down the wide staircase and out of the open front door. She walked across the lawn, past the British flag which flapped like washing in the wind, and stood looking out towards Falmouth docks.

She curved her arms round her stomach and closed her eyes, and it seemed to her that she felt a faint answering beat, and despite her fear her heart swelled with the thought of Tom's child lying within her. Part of him; part of her.

I am glad of the cooler weather, but my heart is not in the figurehead of the pirate I am carving. Isabella moves everywhere with me and the heaviness of my heart will not lift as the days go by. I have seen Sir Richard in the harbourmaster's office and down on the quay but I dare not inquire after Isabella. Then, one month after I have been working in Falmouth, I overhear Sir Richard talking with Mr Vyvyan as they stand on the quay near the schooner I am measuring up for my figurehead. Both men have already greeted me and asked after my father.

It is a habit of Sir Richard's to shout, even when talking to a man next to him, and I hear clearly most of the conversation.

'Is my daughter quite recovered now?' Mr Vyvyan asks.

'From the influenza, yes. But her spirits seem very low. I suggested that your niece, Sophie Tredinnick, come to stay. I thought it might cheer her, but Isabella did not feel up to it.'

Mr Vyvyan says, 'Richard, you must not allow Isabella's low spirits to take hold. Her mother used to suffer in the same way from time to time ...'

'Indeed? And what cheered Helena? What brought her back to herself?'

'Isabella. A child made the difference. After Isabella was born, I do not believe Helena ever suffered the same low spirits.'

I hear Sir Richard laugh. 'My God, Daniel, I believe you have given me the answer. Of course! Isabella needs children and a purpose.'

I feel rage, then such sudden despair that I have to hang on to the bowsprit. I know that if Isabella had her way, Sir Richard would never touch her. I swing down from the ship without my measurements and stride past the two men.

In the late afternoon I walk into the village of Mylor. I have no idea what I am going to do, only that I have an overwhelming need to see Isabella. I walk up the creek road from the village and stand facing the gates of the house. I decide I will search out Lisette and ask how her mistress is. I do not care what Lisette thinks. I head off to the right of the gates towards the small wood that runs behind the back of the house. I skirt the wood, then suddenly hear a horse and see Sir Richard, back from Falmouth, emerging from the trees and riding towards the house. I turn away back to the gate. I can think of no good reason to give for being here.

Lisette was in the kitchen ironing one of Isabella's dresses. Something was niggling at her but Lisette could not identify it. As she ironed she thought, *I am going to have to take her dresses in soon . . .* It was then that her unease manifested itself.

Lisette replaced the iron on the stove and went quickly upstairs. She knocked on the door and went in. The room was empty and Lisette went to the top drawer and looked down at the rags. Some had been removed and Lisette felt sudden relief. She went into the bathroom but could find no soiled linen in Isabella's covered bucket.

Lisette felt the frightened beat of her heart. Isabella had been left in her care and she had neglected her duty because of her ill and dying mother. Perhaps Isabella's illness could have changed the pattern of her monthly.

Then she remembered the look in Ben Welland's eyes that had mirrored her own suspicion. She went slowly and heavily back down the stairs to her ironing.

Tom turned back to the gates. Had he continued a few more yards he would have met Isabella, who was walking along the ha-ha towards him.

Chapter 58

Lisette went quickly into Isabella's bedroom. That morning she had woken knowing she must ask Isabella the question she already knew the answer to. She had been hoping for two weeks to see a sign and she dared not leave the situation any longer.

Isabella was still in bed, lying up on her pillows staring out through the window to the sea beyond the garden. Lisette placed Isabella's breakfast tray on her knees and stood at the foot of the bed.

'Miss Isabella, are you with child?'

Isabella started, shocked, for she was not expecting this. She looked at Lisette and her colour rose. Lisette held her eyes steadily and waited.

Isabella said quietly, 'I believe so, Lisette.'

'Have you told Sir Richard?' Lisette needed to discount the possibility of this being a celebration not a tragedy.

'No. Lisette . . .'

Do not make me ask, Miss Isabella, Lisette thought. *Have the courage to tell me.*

Isabella said, 'Lisette, the baby cannot be Sir Richard's. It . . . is not.' She looked down at her tray, fiddling with the lace edging.

Lisette said, 'Can you be sure, Isabella? He did visit you in St Piran.'

'Yes . . . Believe me, I am sure.'

'Then there is only one thing to be done. You must take Sir Richard to your bed as soon as possible.'

'I cannot do that, Lisette.'

Isabella seemed very calm and Lisette wondered if the seriousness of her predicament had dawned on her yet. She felt suddenly angry with her mistress. They stared at one another, neither looking away.

'It is the only thing you can do,' Lisette said finally.

'It would be dishonest.'

'Dishonest!' Lisette almost spat the word out and Isabella flushed.

'What do you have in mind, Miss Isabella? I hope that you are not thinking of going to Sir Richard and telling him the truth?'

'Not yet, Lisette.'

Lisette was now frightened. She went towards the bed.

'Isabella! For pity's sake! You will be ruined and I will be in the poorhouse ...'

Isabella placed the tray aside and patted the bed.

'Lisette! Come, sit down. Listen to me. I have been thinking. It is all I have been doing these past weeks ...'

Reluctantly, Lisette perched on the edge of the bed. She closed her eyes for a moment to still her heart. She did not realize she was wringing her hands and Isabella took one and smoothed it, knowing she should have talked to Lisette long before now.

'Lisette, I need to see Tom.'

'How is that going to help? Miss Isabella, it is not Tom who is going to grow large. It is not Tom whose reputation and marriage are going to be ruined ...'

'Lisette, please listen. When I realized ... I was so afraid, I thought as you do, that I would have to deceive Richard. But I cannot do it. I can neither take Richard to my bed nor pretend he is the father. Lisette, I love Tom, I love him. He has the right to know and I believe he will help me ...'

Lisette snatched her hand away. 'Love? Pah!' She jumped to her feet. 'What were you thinking of to be so careless? Passion passes, Miss Isabella. You won't be the first lady to take a lover, nor the last to have another man's child. It is what you do next that counts. You can ruin your life or you can be sensible. You have deceived your husband. You have lain with another man. Worse, you have lain with a boy half Sir Richard's age and one who works for him. You will never be forgiven. Never. Believe me, Miss Isabella, for I swear to you, if Sir Richard ever finds out

400

you carry another man's child ... God help you, for I will not be able to.'

Isabella had gone pale. She had never seen Lisette afraid. She said slowly, 'I cannot believe, Lisette, that Tom would abandon me or Sir Richard would ever do me harm ...'

'Then you are a fool!' Lisette interrupted. 'What can Tom the carver do to protect you? What can he offer you?'

Isabella leant forward. 'I have Mama's money in trust for me. I thought if I tried to explain to Richard that I am being unfair to him ... that I do love him, but ... not as a husband ... I thought if I bought a little house of my own he might let me go ...'

Even to Isabella those words sounded so unlikely and childish that she stopped.

'Lisette, you are right. I do not quite know what I can say, yet ...' She touched Lisette's arm. 'Oh, Lisette, I want my freedom from this marriage ...'

Lisette shook her head in despair. 'You think that Sir Richard will nod his head kindly, that he will understand your rejection of him?'

'Of course not, Lisette ... I mean only that I want ...'

'You want to hurt and destroy a man's life and you want him to understand!' Lisette walked to the door. 'At this moment I wish your mama was alive, and I a servant only, not a nursemaid.'

She started to go out, then turned. 'I ask one thing of you, Miss Isabella. If I can find Tom, will you do nothing, say nothing to Sir Richard until after you have seen him?'

'I will, Lisette. Say nothing of my condition to Tom. Say only that I need to speak to him. I will meet him on the coastal path near the stile by the wood at three o'clock.'

Isabella was mortified at the tone Lisette had just used. It was as if she was already losing Lisette's respect.

Lisette said, more gently, 'Miss Isabella, you have kept Sir Richard out of your bed for many months now. Absence and illness are no longer the case. I doubt even Sir Richard will indulge you for much longer.'

Then she left the room.

Isabella got up and went to the window and stared out. She

shivered. She could never lie with Richard again. She would rather die.

I watch Isabella coming towards me along the path. She seems smaller and thinner, yet she looks more beautiful than ever. I can feel my body tense with the excitement of seeing her again.

Her smile lights up her face as she sees me and her pace quickens. Oh, that face! I know every feature, it is a familiar map I wander round at night before I sleep.

Isabella reaches me breathless and we stand staring at each other, so glad to look upon the other's face. I hold out my hands and she takes them. She is wearing a dress I have seen before in a shiny blue which catches the light.

I pull her towards me to kiss her mouth and I feel her shaking. Her breasts are tight against the shiny blue of her dress and I can see the swell of her belly. I know every curve of her body, the cut and flow of her dresses, where they are gathered, how they fit and fall around her. I know exactly.

Isabella meets my eyes and the colour floods her cheeks, and it is then that I realize what her new radiance means and why she suddenly needed to see me.

As she waits for me to speak, her eyes hold mine, burn into me. She is waiting to see if I will reject her.

I reach out and touch her rounded belly, then, overcome, I bend to my knees pressing my head against her stomach. Isabella is carrying my child.

She holds my head hard to her and I can feel her weeping. I lay my coat on the damp grass for her and pull her gently down. I am lost for the right words to say, for this discovery is so startling and unexpected.

Before I can say anything, Isabella whispers, 'I have only been with you, Tom. Richard has not shared my bed since . . . you. This child is not my husband's.'

'Isabella, do you really think I would doubt or question you?'

She smiles faintly. 'No.'

'Only Lisette knows of your condition?'

'Yes. But Tom, my body is changing. Richard might not notice but other people will soon. You did.'

'But I know your body as if it were my own ...' I kiss her mouth, feel the familiar ache of wanting her.

'Isabella, I do not know what is in your mind. I have so little to offer you. I am no longer a poor man but against the life you have known I will seem poor, but I love you and everything that I have is yours to share ...'

'You would share a life with me, Tom?'

'I would. But, Isabella, I could love you no less if you stayed with Sir Richard. I would understand.'

'And pass off your child as his?'

I nod, unable to meet her eyes.

'Lisette has already suggested that is what I must do.'

'Perhaps it is,' I say miserably.

There is silence, then Isabella says in a voice that is unsteady, 'Tom, I do not love my husband in the way he would like, and despite his kindness my life is empty. I carry your child and even when I am afraid, it has been like some wonderful secret that has given me strength and made me calm ...'

She takes my hand and holds it to her face.

'Without you my life feels worthless. I would rather be with you than anything on this earth ...'

'Say it once more,' I whisper. 'Only then will I believe it.'

'I love you, Tom. You know that I do! Last summer, when we were together in St Piran, I was the happiest I have ever been in my life.'

I pluck lengths of grass and twist them into a small ring and place it on her finger. 'Isabella, your husband might never divorce you, this might be the only ring I can ever give you.'

'So be it, Tom. In our hearts we will be married.'

'Your reputation will be ruined, Isabella. If you regret your decision you will never be accepted back into society.'

'I know this.'

'You understand that we shall have to move a long way away?'

'Yes.'

'You have always lived in Cornwall.'

'I have always wanted to travel, Tom.'

I tremble, suddenly able to glimpse a life together. 'Is it possible

403

you could sail with me to Prince Edward Island? Start a new life with me there?'

'Yes!' Isabella says. 'Truly I could, Tom. Is it a good place to bring up a child?'

'It is a wonderful place and I am assured of work. I was always going to go back ...' I stop. 'Isabella, I need to think carefully about how we do this, for there is a need to move fast ...'

I get to my feet and help Isabella to hers. Already her movements are slower and I have a sudden fear of being unable to protect her.

'Isabella, you must leave Botallick House without saying anything to Sir Richard.'

'It seems so cruel.'

'What we are doing is cruel. There is no way out of that. Isabella, even good people do revengeful things when they are angry. I want you safe. I need to be safe to protect you ... How quickly could you be ready to leave?'

I see her face is suddenly anxious. 'Isabella, maybe you need more time to think on this?'

'No, Tom, I do not. I was thinking only of Lisette. I do not want to leave her, but I do not know whether she will come with me. Where will we go?'

'I think, London or Southampton. A city will hide us and we can obtain a passage there for New England ... I will get word to you, Isabella, but our safety depends on your silence. Promise me?'

'I promise.'

'Come, it is getting cold.'

Isabella is pale as if suddenly realizing all the wider implications for the first time. She will leave everything behind her. So will I.

I walk a little way back down the coastal path with her. We are silent, our spirits subdued for the troubles ahead. I cannot tell her that I am afraid for us both. I do not doubt our paths lie together but exactly how it is to be executed, at this moment I have no idea.

Chapter 59

Returning to London after Josh's rescue was like finding an oasis. Gabby did not need to explain or talk to Mark, he just let her slide through those first days, sleeping and reading, walking with him and listening to music. When she felt like talking, he was there.

She moved about the London house touching things, glad they were in the same place they had always been, like a cat re-establishing territory after an absence.

Lucinda was proving a good friend. Gabby needed to work but found she could only manage short bursts of concentration and Lucinda, noticing, put her in touch with a couple of clients who had smaller paintings to restore.

It was not just the fright with Josh that had knocked Gabby off course. It was Charlie, her life and Mark. Life suddenly seemed tenuous, in the moment of moving on but not yet reaching anywhere lasting.

She and Mark spent a lot of time walking through parks, where the trees were beginning to shed their leaves, and along the river. Sometimes they walked in silence as they thought about the reality of what they were both about to do. Sometimes they gently rehearsed the things they might say. Both felt joy at the thought of being together and equal dread at the distress and anger and recriminations involved.

Mark had actually booked a flight to return home for Veronique's hospital appointment, but had cancelled it when Gabby rang from Cornwall. He told Gabby about Veronique and she immediately felt guilty.

'Mark! You should have told me. I would have understood.'

'There is no way I could have flown home at that point, Gabriella.'

'But her need might have been greater than mine.'

'It might have been,' Mark agreed, 'and that would have been on my conscience. But it wasn't. Her tests were negative.'

'But,' Gabby said, 'your wife won't see it like that, Mark. She will only see that you didn't travel back to support her when you knew it was possible the outcome could have been quite different.'

'You're right, and that's why I must fly back in the next week or so and talk to Veronique and the girls. My daughters will give me the third degree and I want to be honest.'

They were standing near a huge plane tree. Mark smiled as he put his hand out to touch the vast trunk.

'I bet this guy has heard it all before, the machinations of human beings and what they do for love. I bet he's glad he's a tree.'

Gabby stared at him, suddenly remembering how much more he used to laugh.

'Mark, I have never asked you to leave your family. I can go on as we are . . . or if . . .'

'Hey . . . hey, Gabriella . . . stop right there . . .' Mark pulled her to him leaning against the tree. 'That must have come out all wrong. A sort of feeble joke that sounded cynical. I'm sorry. I'm as much a coward as the next man. I admit I'm dreading having to confront my family. But I can't go back to my old life, I don't want to. I love you, possibly more than you will ever know, Gabriella Ellis . . .'

He placed his hands either side of her face. 'I love you so much it hurts. I moved here to be in an empty house and when it is empty of you the heart goes out of it.'

Gabby reached up to kiss his mouth, hesitated and then said, 'Mark, when Josh was captured I felt the only person who knew exactly what it felt like was Charlie. In a way I was closer to him than I've ever been. Josh was safe, back in Kuwait, but one day I completely lost it . . . just lost control. Charlie comforted me and then we were suddenly making love. Everything was sort of heightened. I thought, for one minute, maybe, maybe we can start again, change and be closer . . .'

Gabby stopped and Mark was very still, watching her, wondering what more was coming.

Gabby laughed shortly but there were tears in her eyes. She moved slightly away from him. 'But you know what, Mark? It wasn't that at all, *it was the end*. Charlie was embarrassed at how we had behaved. He didn't want to be any closer than we already were. He wanted life to go on just as it had before. No emotional demands.'

She met Mark's eyes. 'I'm telling you this because I'll never know if I could really have started again. I do not love Charlie in the way I love you. I never have, and maybe I believed for a second the two of us could reach a place of closer fondness, if not love, because of all that had happened and because we were so lucky Josh wasn't killed.

'What hurt was I would have *tried*, despite loving you. Charlie could not even try, not for even a second. Because you see, Mark, he doesn't love me in the least and he was sweating like hell in case I had suddenly got the wrong impression. So . . . life *is* ironic.'

They started to walk slowly towards the gate. Gabby was cold and Mark tucked her hand in his pocket. They were about to have an early supper and then the university were putting on *Carmen*.

Mark said, 'I knew there was a strong possibility that I would lose you and I would have understood. I knew if Veronique had cancer I couldn't leave her. On my own here I became like Eeyore, convinced fate was going to keep us apart, prevent us from ever having a life together. Let's guard what we have, Gabriella. We are so damn lucky to have a reprieve.'

Gabby stopped walking and turned to him again.

'In Cornwall you seemed so far away. I had this stupid superstition that if I opened your e-mails or rang you Josh would be killed as punishment. When I heard your voice on the phone it was as if I had woken from a nightmare and there you were . . . So wonderful. *There you were!*'

They walked through the underpass and hailed a taxi.

'Will you go back to Cornwall when I fly home?' Mark asked in the taxi. 'Do you know any more about Josh's leave?'

'No. Mark, I can't say anything to Josh yet, it is too soon after his fright. I just couldn't . . .'

'Gabriella, you couldn't possibly do it now. You'll have to judge it carefully, as I will. I mentioned you going back only because I know you're worrying about Nell.'

'I am.' Gabby sighed. 'When I've finished the painting I'm working on I think I will go back while you're away and spend some time with her.'

'Do you believe you'll lose Nell?'

'I think she'll feel betrayed. I think I'll lose her for a while.'

Her happiness was dissipating and Mark said softly, 'Shall we put our other lives away just for this evening, my love? Our time together is precious.'

'Yes,' Gabby said. 'Yes it is. You're right. Just a moment a word, and it's gone . . . Why are you smiling?'

'I see you also have a bit of Eeyore in you.'

Gabby giggled, leant against him in the taxi and watched the swarms of people heading home in the rush hour.

Nell noticed how quiet Charlie was after Gabby decided to go back to London. It seemed so sudden, her departure, although Nell could understand Gabby's need to get back to normal, and she had been disappointed that Josh could still not get home on leave.

Nell had spoken to Josh and he sounded his old self, just rather fed-up as the army were prevaricating about any leave for pilots at the moment. He wanted to come home for a while as much as they all needed to see him. Josh and his colleagues had been told if they wanted immediate leave they must pay for the flight home. Nell had been outraged.

'Don't tell Gabby, Nell, she'll do her nut and write e-mails or something to the BBC and I will get court-martialled!'

'Don't be so sure I won't dash a few letters off myself, my lad.'

'Granny, Granny, please . . .'

Nell smiled to herself, marvelling at the ability of the young to bounce back. She picked up her basket and went to search for eggs. She shooed two broody hens out of the nesting box.

'Come on, girls, it's too late in the year. Go on out or I'll put you in the pot!'

Charlie crossed the yard and heard her. He held up a handful of small brown eggs.

'One of them is laying in the barn again.'

'I thought so!' Nell exclaimed. 'I saw Maisie coming out of there yesterday.'

Charlie placed them in her basket.

'Have you had breakfast?' Nell asked.

'Not yet.'

'Would you like a cooked breakfast with one of these eggs?'

Charlie laughed. 'Good heavens, Nell! Are you really offering to clog my arteries?'

'I just thought you were looking a bit thin.'

'I'd love a cooked breakfast. I'm going to plough up the east field later on. I was wondering . . . I haven't put it to Alan yet . . . about going into soft fruit. Strawberries. Pick your own. What do you think?'

Nell put the egg basket down on the kitchen table and turned the Aga up. She had a distinct sense that Charlie was making conversation in order to deflect anything Nell might have to ask. Am I that transparent? she wondered.

'It's a lot of work. It can be financially rewarding, but so much depends on the weather.'

'Doesn't everything?' Charlie switched the kettle on.

As Nell fried his bacon the telephone went. It was Josh. Charlie grinned happily. 'That's great, son, really great. When? OK . . . No, she's in London . . . I'm sure she won't mind. Give her a ring . . . Oh, right. OK. Nell or I will ring her. Do you want her to meet you off the plane? All right, son. See you soon.'

'He's coming home?' Nell asked excitedly.

'Yes, he's flying back on Friday. He wants to bring Marika with him. He can't ring Gabby because she's on a mobile. Will you give her a ring, Nell?'

'Of course.'

'Why are you looking like that?'

'Well, I just wondered if Gabby might have liked to see Josh on his own.'

Charlie stared at her. 'Honestly! I wonder how Josh cut the apron strings at all!'

'Wouldn't you have quite liked to see him on your own?'

'I'm just happy he's coming home, Nell.'

As if I'm not! Nell would have quite liked to bang the frying pan over Charlie's head. Although of course he was right.

She put his breakfast in front of him and made herself a coffee.

'Everything is all right with you and Gabby, Charlie?'

He looked up. 'Why shouldn't it be?'

'I don't know. She was very upset and frail and she suddenly took off.'

'I expect she was asked to clean a picture or something. Best thing. Pointless her sitting here brooding, waiting for Josh to come home.'

Something in his voice. Nell said evenly, 'You both got the most terrible fright, you know, Charlie. You might not think it, but that sort of trauma leaves an aftermath, in you as well as Gabby.'

'Rubbish! I'm fine.'

Then, abruptly, Charlie put his knife and fork down.

'You know what gets me about women? You must make

410

melodrama out of everything. Analyse every damn emotion until it becomes a major incident. My God, how did people get on in two wars for God's sake? It really bugs me, Nell.'

He went back to his breakfast and Nell, startled, watched him for a moment. There was a small muscle going in his cheek, a sure sign he was disturbed about something. Nell could have said, *In the war people came back with shell shock, with huge emotional trauma which affected them and the people close to them for the rest of their lives.* But she didn't.

I am growing old, she thought. I can't be bothered any longer to engage. When did this ennui start to creep up on me? This feeling of lethargy and pointlessness. A feeling of change and impermanence when there is none. The need to sleep longer, to drink a little more in the evenings.

The pleasure in a new day had vanished. These mornings, when the sun slid in through the window and crept across the bed along with the same familiar noises, Nell thought, What have I got to get up for?

I am not yet old, but I have outgrown myself. A strange feeling.

Charlie said, in a different voice, a sort of apology for his outburst, 'I thought I might go up to the Caradons', speak to Sarah. They've been doing pick and grow for years.'

'Good idea,' Nell said. 'I must get on. I'll ring Gabby from the cottage. Have a good day.'

'You, too. I might have a quick sandwich in the pub as I'm that way, save me coming all the way home.'

Nell walked back across the yard. It would be quite wonderful to see Josh again. For the first time she felt glad he had got away from the farm, from Cornwall. Too invidiously small a canvas. Perhaps she should have gone when Ted died, back to a different life. However, she knew she could not have borne to miss out on Josh or Gabby.

As she dialled Gabby's mobile number a little worm of a thought burrowed upwards. Did Charlie dislike women?

Chapter 60

Richard took his whisky outside and went and stood under the flagpole where he had the best view of the bay. He caught a glimpse of blue on the path and peered into the sun, shading his eyes with his hand. His spirits rose. It was Isabella and he watched her moving towards him.

Her beauty never ceased to thrill him. Daniel was right. Isabella needed children, it was what women were born for, it was their role in life; whatever they pretended, a woman without a child was to be pitied.

As Isabella reached the turn in the path where it became steep, she paused, and like him turned to look out at the bay and the busy trail of small boats making for home. The wind caught her hair and blew it around her face, caught at her dress and blew it tight to her body and the thin material clung to breast and limbs.

Richard stared down at his wife. Since her influenza she had grown thin. It was noticeable in her arms and face. But her body was ... thicker, the material tighter around her breasts and waist. She turned to continue up the path and Richard clearly saw the small protuberance of her stomach as Isabella placed one hand on her side, as if to balance herself as she climbed.

For a second his heart leapt with joy as he fought to remember how long it was since he had shared a bed with his wife. Too long. At least four months. Something cold clutched at him. He might have been a bachelor for a long time but he had sisters, and he knew Isabella was not that far gone. *If it was mine she would have spoken to me.*

She had disappeared around the bend in the path and would

412

reappear any moment in front of him. He wanted to turn and run for the house but he could not move. He could feel the blood draining from his face and for the first time in his life he felt he might pass out unconscious. He clutched the flagpole, his eyes still fixed to the point Isabella would emerge from the path.

As Isabella came from the trees she saw her husband ashen and clutching the pole and ran towards him with a cry; 'Richard, Richard, what is it? Are you ill?'

He could not answer and Isabella, believing he must have had a heart attack, cried out to the house, 'Come quickly. Please come quickly, Sir Richard is ill!'

She went to him. 'Richard, Richard, lean on me. Can you walk? We must get you inside. Oh dear! Richard, can you speak? There, that's it, lean on me . . .'

Richard's steward, Trathan, and the groom came running from the side of the house, alerted by Isabella's cries. They helped Richard slowly back to the house, but he would not let Isabella's hand go and she ran awkwardly beside him as they got him inside and into the drawing room and laid him on the chaise longue.

'Ride for the doctor,' she told the groom, 'as fast as you can.'

'No!' Richard had got his voice back. 'No, it is just a turn, give me brandy. I will recover in a moment.'

The groom hesitated. Isabella said, 'Richard, you must see the doctor in case it is your heart. Go, at once.' She waved the groom out of the room.

She felt Richard's brow; it was clammy. She turned to the steward, 'Could you please find Sir Richard a brandy and call one of the maids to bring me water with lavender?'

When it came Richard leant back and closed his eyes and let Isabella gently bathe his face, the inside of his wrists and between his fingers. Helena had taught Isabella this reviving trick with lavender. Isabella was so gentle and loving that for moments Richard pretended that all was normal. This was his beloved wife tenderly caring for him. This sweet girl would never betray him. Then he saw again the clear shape of her body silhouetted against the dying sun and a light was snuffed out like the sudden movement of two fingers extinguishing a candle.

413

The doctor ushered him up to bed and examined him. His heart rate and blood pressure were up, otherwise he could find nothing wrong with Sir Richard, except perhaps overwork or too much excitement. The doctor viewed the much younger wife from beneath half-moon glasses and ordered, 'No undue exercise or excitement for a week or so.'

He was more perplexed by the undue quietness of his patient, normally so loud and bluff. If it was anyone but Sir Richard the doctor would have diagnosed a malaise of the spirit, a depression. He said to Isabella, in case he had missed something, 'If there are any other symptoms you must call me straight away.'

After he had gone, Richard turned to Isabella.

'Will you stay with me for company? I do not wish to be alone tonight?'

'Of course, Richard,' Isabella said. 'Could you take some soup?'

He shook his head. 'Just ask Trathan to bring me brandy.'

Isabella went downstairs. She had never seen Richard like this. Lisette was waiting for her.

'Is it his heart?'

'The doctor thinks not, but I shall stay with him tonight just to be sure.'

When Isabella was ready for bed she went back to Richard. He smelt of lavender water and brandy and seemed asleep. She climbed into bed beside him and lay on her back, knowing she would not sleep.

Richard was very still beside her. He did not turn or move, his breathing was shallow, but she felt sure he did not sleep. She lay, acutely aware of him and frightened in a way she did not comprehend. His unnatural stillness was disturbing.

Such misery emanated from Richard that Isabella got up quietly and drew back the heavy curtains so that she might see his face. She looked down upon him. His eyes were shut against her but he silently wept for a precious thing lost.

Isabella felt weightless. All was now clear. She felt as if she had struck a child or shot a decent man in the back. What she had done was break a man's heart.

With the edges of her nightdress she dabbed at the steady yet

414

incessant flow of her husband's tears, terrible to see for she had never seen a grown man weep. Isabella's betrayal rose up in her in an anguish that would become part of her. She wept with her husband, bent her cheek to his, sobbing uncontrollably.

Richard brought his arms up and enfolded her, and she lay with her head turned from him, buried in his shoulder, weeping until she could weep no more. Richard thought, *I will have this one last night holding the woman I have loved beyond anything sensible. I will have it, not to remember, but to seal the end of my happiness, when I was a reasonable man and would not hurt another human being. To remind myself of that.*

As a new day edged up over the water beyond their window in a thin straight line of gold, both Isabella and Richard fell into a strange, awkward and unreal sleep. They held each other closer than they had ever done in their short marriage. Held each other in denial of a thing that could not be undone.

Chapter 61

Marika and Josh drove down to Cornwall in her mother's car. Josh had never been so pleased to see anyone in his life. They were going to spend three days at the farm and then go off on their own to Florence, where neither had been before.

As soon as Josh arrived at the farm he felt peculiar, as if he had made a mistake in coming home and should have taken off with Marika straight away.

Gabby and Nell were so overjoyed to see him that he felt impelled to react in a way they expected and not in the way he felt. It was easier with Charlie, who was much more casual and did not make him the centre of attention.

Josh knew he was being unfair, but something in him had to keep Gabby and Nell at a distance. Gabby more than Nell, because Nell was less nervous of saying or doing the wrong thing.

Gabby and Nell had moved his childhood bed out of his room and replaced it with a double bed from one of the spare rooms, and Josh was touched. He and Marika walked miles with Shadow. She was enchanted with Cornwall and was happy to go off on her own when he disappeared on the tractor or to the pub with Charlie, and just as happy to be with Nell or Gabby.

One afternoon Marika and Gabby set off together for a walk along the cliffs. Marika was struck by Gabby's fierce love of this landscape. It was like seeing her for the first time in her own element and Marika warmed to her because being in Cornwall reminded her suddenly of home; her own suffocated ache for the village she grew up in and the mountains that bordered the coastline and were reflected stark and clear in the sea. It was easier not to be homesick – to mingle and forget and be swallowed whole – in a cosmopolitan university city.

Marika sensed Gabby's puzzlement at Josh, who appeared to be avoiding her, and as they walked Marika wondered how she could explain to Gabby what she thought Josh might be feeling. She had been careful not to question him on anything until he felt ready to unload.

When men were in danger or about to die they often called out for their mothers; Marika knew this, she had heard it. When they survived they viewed this as a weakness and had a need to close off, shut out the child in them. It was understandable.

Josh's life was not taken, but he had glimpsed his own mortality, and now knew that even belonging to a military force you believed in did not protect you.

Marika had seen it in soldiers of her own country. Her male cousin had been beaten, stripped and humiliated by a group of Serbs from his own village, in front of his peers. She hesitated to speak because she knew Gabby might see her as a threat to her close relationship with Josh. As they walked, she tentatively started to tell Gabby about her cousin, and how long it took him to put the violent act behind him.

'His mother was the one person he could never talk to about it. I do not mean Josh's experience was the same, only that I think most people want to forget bad things and sometimes pretend they never happened.'

Gabby looked at Marika. She wondered if she had been able to put her childhood, and a life she once lived, so firmly behind her.

Marika met Gabby's eyes and knew what she was thinking. She was silent and then she said, 'No, it is not possible for me to pretend. It is always there inside me, buried, but there . . . so hard to talk about . . . because then it is real again, not like a terrible dream . . . You have to acknowledge it then; *This really happened*. Silence keeps it at bay. Silence protects the present.

'It is all Josh is doing, Gabby. I think he is afraid that if you are alone you will ask him about it and he will be back in that particular nightmare; vulnerable, and not in control.'

Gabby said, hurt, 'I would never question him about anything. Josh must know that.'

'Well, maybe he does, but you are his mother and you are the closest person to him, and I guess that makes him vulnerable because you know him better than anyone.'

They had reached the bottom of the cliff path and crossed the cove for the narrow path up to the next cove and Elan's cottage.

'I suppose,' Gabby said slowly, 'there is an overriding need, if you are a mother, to know your children are safe, mentally and physically . . . and it is this tendency to automatically protect, as you would a child, that threatens the grown adult you love.'

Marika stopped and turned to her; 'Yes! Gabby this is exactly right, you have hit the nail on the nose!'

'Head!' Gabby smiled, delighted.

'What?'

'Hit the nail on the head!'

'Oh!' Marika laughed too.

They perched on a boulder before the climb uphill and looked down at the sea swirling in on the rocks just below them. The waves were quite dramatic and Marika shivered.

'I am in awe of the sea. I do not understand how Josh or anyone can dare go into those cruel waves and surf. My brother and sister shared a boat, they loved the water; but I am like my mother, I like my feet on the land.'

'Tell me about your mother,' Gabby said.

'She is very happy with my stepfather. They have a little boy. She has grown to love England, although of course it was very difficult for her at first.'

'I imagine it must have been.'

Marika was staring straight ahead at the sea and her body was tense.

'She had this need to protect me, Gabby, all the time, even when we were safe in England and nothing more terrible could happen. It was like being buried in her pain. I felt I was wrapped in a shroud because I was the only one she had of another life; I was all she had left of a whole family. The responsibility was . . . terrible.

'I hurt her. I asked if I could be sent away to an English boarding school like other army children my age. I wanted to get away because while I was with her that other life we had lived stood between us and the future. I was not able to get on and pretend I was an English girl of fifteen who had not lost her father and elder brother and sister . . . but she dare not let go of me . . .'

Marika turned away from the sea and looked down at her hands. Gabby sat very still.

'At first, my mother lived her new English life as if it was the only one she had ever known. She threw herself into being an English army wife, frantically volunteering for everything, maybe because she was so grateful to be alive.

'Then she got pregnant with my little brother and . . .' Marika swallowed '. . . she slowly began to fragment. It was very frightening to watch her disintegrating a little more each day . . . She had always been so brave and strong . . .'

Marika's hands trembled and Gabby reached out to take one.

'Marika . . .'

'It is all right.' Marika's fingers curled round Gabby's. 'It is just I have never spoken of it, even to Josh. Now my mother is so together you could not believe she was once so broken . . . She was lucky. She had my stepfather. Army men are not known for their sensitivity, but he is special. He did not call in doctors or therapists, he took my mother away to Italy for a month and he listened to all the things she had never told him, even though he had been there and seen much, and could understand as others could not. He listened and he listened and he let my mother grieve openly for all that she had lost . . . Helped her to see that having another child in another life did not negate or betray the children she had lost. He is a wise and clever man.'

Marika's hand tightened on Gabby's and her voice wobbled. 'You see, my father was shot in our cellar in front of her, at the beginning of the war, while my sister and I were at school. They told her that if she closed her eyes they would shoot to wound him, bit by bit, so she kept her eyes open.'

'Marika!'

'I was the only member of my family not to be hurt. Everyone else but me; my father, my brother and my sister. I carry the guilt of it.'

Gabby took her hands, would have loved to hug her fiercely to her.

'Marika, you must not feel guilty for being alive . . .' *My God!* What right had she to be sad? She had lost no one.

'I know this of course, with my head but not my heart. I am alive and I was given, with my mother, another chance of happiness. I cannot change the past, Gabby, but I must try and enjoy each day that I have . . .'

'You make me very humble and ashamed.'

'Why?' Marika looked at Gabby, startled.

'You look cold, let's start walking uphill.'

They climbed the steep path and reached the top puffing. Gabby thought, Marika is totally innocent in the way children are, unafraid to be honest, to say simply what she means and how things are. It's the courage that comes with having suffered, which strips away cant and shallowness.

'You are a very open and honest person, Marika. I have spent most of my life carefully closed so that no crack of my past escapes. I've never been able to talk about my childhood to anyone, not even to the people I love . . .'

'It is easier talking to strangers, they do not judge.'

Gabby smiled. 'I suppose you're right. When I was very young I made up a make-believe family I talked about at school. My make-believe mother was based on my Aunt

Bella . . . Then she went off to America and got married and I never saw her again . . . My real mother grew to loathe me as I grew up. She was unmarried and would never tell me who my father was. If I've ever been over-involved with Josh, Marika, it's because I had a mother who never put her foot across a school gate and was rarely there when I got home from school . . . rarely there at all.'

Gabby paused. 'My recurring nightmare is that I am a child again. I'm very ashamed of what I still sometimes feel . . . when I hear a story like yours.'

'But, Gabby, I have the most wonderful childhood to look back on, to keep here . . .' She thumped her chest. 'I cannot imagine what I would be like if I had had only one parent, and one who did not care what happened to me every moment of my growing up as my parents did. As you do with Josh. Without love in my childhood I do not think I would ever feel safe. You have managed it, Gabby, Josh says he had a wonderful childhood . . .'

'Did he say that?'

'Yes.' Marika turned to Gabby. 'And you have made a happy life for yourself, despite everything.'

Marika watched an expression pass across Gabby's face. One she did not understand.

'Is your mother dead?' she asked.

'I don't know. I should think so, she was an alcoholic.'

'When did you last see her?'

'When I was seventeen.'

'So . . .'

'I ran away.'

'For a particular reason?'

'For the reason my mother had a predilection for boy-friends who liked schoolgirls and she never, ever believed me.'

Marika watched Gabby's face closing.

'Marika, look to the left, you'll see the roof of Elan's cottage. It used to be the coastguard cottage. He's got a curved granite terrace with a telescope set up over the

421

coast. Josh used to spend hours there . . . I'm hoping we can persuade him to come back with us for a meal . . .'

Marika put her hand on Gabby's arm and bent her tall, slim body down to kiss Gabby's cheek in a small quick movement. They stayed close for a second, then Gabby smiled and they walked towards Elan's front door which was suddenly thrown open and Elan cried, 'Two beautiful women beating a path to my door . . . How wonderful!'

He pointed to his watch. 'And . . . it is ten to twelve and the sun is over the yard arm, I can open something special . . .'

Gabby grinned at him and turned to Marika. 'One thing you will have to learn, wherever Elan is, here or in London, the sun is always over the yard arm . . .'

'But,' Marika looked bewildered, 'what is this arm yard thing?'

As the three days of Josh's visit came to an end, Gabby still had not seen or had a conversation with him on her own. Nell had watched Gabby wounded and puzzled, then quietly resigned, and felt distressed. When Josh came over to the cottage on his own one day she asked gently, 'How are you doing, darling?'

He made a face. 'I'm OK, Nell . . .'

'Do you feel all right about going straight back to the ship, flying over Iraq again, Josh?'

'Nell, flying is what I do. I'd feel mortified to be grounded even for a short time. It's like falling off a horse . . . I have to get back in there. Don't worry, it was just bad luck, it won't happen again.'

Nell picked up something in his voice.

'All the same, it would be unnatural not to be nervous.'

He grinned and swallowed his drink in one gulp.

'That's why I need to take off with Marika somewhere neutral. Do you think I've hurt Gabby by not spending my whole leave here? I just need space, Nell.'

'I can understand that and Gabby would, too. Have you

got time to go for a walk with her before you leave, on her own, and explain it to her?'

Josh turned Nell's glass round in his fingers, staring down at it.

'Sure, Nell,' he said at last. 'It's just . . . I really needed to have Marika with me.'

'Of course. If Gabby and I love you a little too much, a little too eagerly, don't hold it against us, darling.' Nell smiled and refilled Josh's glass.

He glanced at her quickly, didn't know what to say, looked miserable for a moment and Nell said quickly, 'Josh, your emotions are going to be all over the place; expect them to be for quite a while. Go easy on yourself. I don't want any of this stiff-upper-lip crap.'

Josh burst out laughing and Nell said, changing the subject quickly, 'I think you have hit the jackpot with Marika.'

Josh's face lit up. 'I have, haven't I? I'll go and find Gabby. Will you go over and keep Marika company? Dad's conversation is sometimes a bit limited.'

They walked across the yard together. 'Don't you dare give us any more frights, Josh Ellis.' Nell linked arms with him.

'I'll try very hard not to, Granny.'

In late afternoon, before Josh left, the sun came out from behind thin cloud-cover and flared through the turning leaves, making them a mellow gold. The sea was iridescent, forming differing thick lines of blue and green, aquamarine and grey. Nearer, in the cove where Josh and Gabby walked, the white waves were gold tipped by the setting sun.

The cove was deserted and they hung their clothes on the jagged rock at the foot of the cliff path.

'Right,' Josh yelled. 'You've got to run, Gabby, it is no good doing this slowly . . . One, two, three . . . Run . . .'

Gabby ran and yelled, 'I must be mad! It's the end of September . . . Oh my God . . . Josh, it's freezing . . .'

Josh was ahead of her and dived straight into the waves,

coming up like a seal, throwing his hair out of his eyes. He looked frozen. Gabby dived next then swam madly because she couldn't feel her limbs, automatically keeping an eye on Josh. He waited for her to call, 'Josh, don't go too far out, mind the current.' And she did.

He smiled to himself. Something began to shift back into place. It was so good to be home. He loved this place, it was a part of him. Gabby and Charlie and Nell were always exactly the same, waiting for him each time he returned.

He sighed and swam towards his mother. 'Isn't it wonderful? Look at that sun going down. It's not that cold, Gabby, once you get used to it.'

'No,' Gabby agreed, 'but it's bracing! I'm going out to do press-ups! Don't get pneumonia, Josh!'

Gabby ran up the beach and wrapped her towel round her, moved into the last rays of the sun and jumped up and down, trying to get her teeth to stop chattering. She watched Josh swim in and then stand facing out to sea, jumping the waves and surfing in on them.

She had stood here hundreds of times in so many summers, watching Josh do exactly what he was doing now. Barbecues lugged down the path with lots of excited little boys. Lying on rugs in the dying of the day reading the very trying Mister Men; Noddy; Rupert Bear; CS Lewis; *Just So Stories*; *Stig of the Dump*; *A Tale of Two Cities*. Even when Josh could read he loved to be read to. Later they would read avidly side by side for long stretches of the summer. Josh, growing up and needing her less. And it was all right.

He turned and started to wade in, breaking into a run up the beach. The last rays caught his limbs, water shone off his dark skin. Josh. Young and fit and alive. Josh, grown up and gone, madly in love with a Croatian girl. It was all as it should be.

Gabby smiled and held out his towel as she had always done. They both grinned at each other. Everything's fine.

Chapter 62

When Isabella woke, Richard had gone. She returned to her own room where Lisette was filling her bath.

One look at Isabella's face told Lisette everything. They did not speak but went on doing the things they did every morning in silence.

As she dressed, Isabella kept seeing Richard's distraught face. She realized in a blinding moment of truth that, had she not been carrying Tom's child, she might never have been able to leave Richard. It was Tom she loved, but to deliberately injure another human being in the way she had done … She had never understood, or had chosen not to, the depth of her husband's feelings for her.

An unnatural silence hung over the house. The housemaids did not chatter but went about their work in silence. Trathan, who had looked after Sir Richard since his naval days, had the same sense of dread as Lisette.

Sir Richard had risen early, asked for his horse to be brought round, refused Trathan's concerned offer to ride with him and had taken off in the direction of Falmouth. Trathan could have saved him the journey, for Lisette had sent him last night with a message for Tom Welland. Trathan was the only person Lisette could trust to keep silent.

Lisette had written to warn Tom that she suspected Sir Richard knew of his relationship with Isabella. She felt angry. What good could come of a man Sir Richard's age marrying an unworldly girl young enough to be his daughter? And as for Mr Vyvyan, he had sacrificed his daughter for weak and selfish reasons.

'Oh, Madame!' she whispered to Helena, as she carried Isabella's laundry down the back stairs. 'How I wish you were still alive. You would never have allowed this ill-advised marriage.'

Lisette returned upstairs to Isabella in the breakfast room. It was a beautiful day and the French windows were thrown open to the morning. Isabella was drinking tea but had eaten nothing.

Lisette placed an egg and thin slices of bread and butter in front of her.

'My Lady, you have an unborn child to think of now, not just yourself. Eat.'

Isabella looked up quickly. It was the first time Lisette had ever used her title. 'Miss' was now inappropriate as an affectionate reminder of childhood. My Lady, too, seemed an unwise title, for Richard would disown her.

Lisette sat heavily on a seat by the window.

'Sir Richard has ridden off towards Falmouth. I sent word to Tom Welland last night as I guessed Sir Richard knew the situation. Tom must warn Ben of the possible consequences for St Piran, Isabella.'

She got up with a little cry and left the table, went out into the warm autumn day and walked towards the woods. Lisette, fearful of what she might do, called out and ran after her.

'Isabella, stop. Wait a moment ... Please, Isabella.'

Isabella turned. When Lisette reached her she took Isabella's hands, firmly.

'Listen to me. You must keep your head and wait. You are carrying a child. That life is sacred. It did not ask to be born, but it is a life created and your responsibility.'

Isabella held on to Lisette's hands.

'It was created with love, Lisette.'

'Then,' Lisette said gently, 'it is all the more reason for you to take care of yourself. Come, will you rest for a while in the morning room? I will bring my sewing and sit with you and maybe you can sleep a little.'

Isabella nodded for she felt inordinately weary. Once she was settled under a rug in the morning room and Lisette had collected her sewing she asked, sleepily, 'How are you so wise and steady, Lisette?'

Lisette smiled. 'I am far from wise, but if I am steady I learnt it from my father. He was a Frenchman who sailed over to Cornwall and never went home. He was a Catholic who married a chapel-going Cornish woman. He and my mother differed much in religion and temperament and they argued a great deal.

'My father called it debate. He was a fisherman by choice, for he was an educated man. He taught all his children to think things through, before acting. It does not solve everything, Isabella, but it gives an advantage.

'My father was drowned when I was eighteen and your mama took me on as her personal maid. Everything else I learnt from her. Both my father and your mama taught me to keep very still until you know in which direction to move. This, you must do, Isabella.'

Lisette had been Helena's maid but their ages had been only two years apart, and she had become Helena's confidante in her first lonely years in England in the huge, cold house. It was like a circle, a curse, Lisette thought now, my beautiful ladies yearning for more or something different, when they had so much.

When Trathan leaves me, I borrow a horse and set off to ride the narrow lanes to St Piran. What I most feared has happened, and how this should be I know not. It will not have come from Isabella, this I do know.

My father is emerging from the kitchen to the pump with a jug for water and he is startled to see me as I bound through the gate, breathless. He looks upon my face and knows I bring trouble with me. We make our way to the upper boatyard again and we both sit at a make-shift table.

I tell my father of my meeting with Isabella yesterday. My father sucks his tea and is very still. Then he says, in the slow way he has, 'I remember the day thy figurehead was unveiled, and I have been half-expecting trouble, but it is a shock just the same, Thomas.'

He gives me a piercing look of disappointment which grieves me far worse than harsh words.

'Anger will serve no purpose, Tom. Thou hast put the girl out of her own society and made her beyond ours. If Sir Richard knows, St Piran will lose all future building contracts with his syndicate. He will not be made a fool of. Men will be out of work and women and children will go hungry. No one will accept Lady Isabella here. They will blame her, and thee. Did thou have no thought for the consequences?'

He stares at me sadly, for I have always been his favourite son, the nearest to him in character.

'What hast thou done? More, I think, than thou will ever know, Thomas.'

'Pa, I have money saved. I can now command considerable sums for my figureheads. We have talked, Isabella and I; she is willing to sail with me to New England to begin a new life.'

'Will thou take her as a wife or as a woman no longer respectable?'

I am suddenly angry. 'In whose eyes, Father, will she be no longer respectable? In yours? I have no use for society if it judges her. She was sold off to an old man . . .'

'Thomas, I am not thy judge. God will be that. Doest thou think that by putting an ocean between thee and English society thou will be free of it? It awaits thee with a different face in the colonies.'

'I love her, Father. I love this woman. She is having my child, your grandchild. I would marry her tomorrow.'

'Dost thou think Sir Richard will quietly divorce his prize possession for a working man and let thee sail off with her?'

'She carries my child . . .'

'I am sorry, now,' my father interrupts with unaccustomed bitterness, 'that I sent thee to Prince Edward Island with my blessing, for this is the result of mixing too freely with the gentry. Thou hast got above thysen, Thomas. Aye, thou hast money now, saved and well-earnt, but it is as nothing to Sir Richard's money or Mr Vyvyan's. Lady Isabella is used to being pampered and waited on. Mr Vyvyan is the squire of this parish. We have worked for him for most of my lifetime. The Welland name will now be blacklisted from all shipbuilding and carpentry, because of thee, Thomas. God knows what thy mother will say.'

'I cannot believe Mr Vyvyan will ruin you or the village for a thing I have done, Father. You know they have always done well out of us. We build faster and more competently than any firm round here

428

and our prices are more than fair. It would not make sense ...'

'Sense has nothing to do with it, son. Betrayal, everything. Sir Richard trusted thee with his wife.'

I hesitate. 'Pa, I cannot leave Isabella alone with this. I came only to warn you, not to run away from him. If I have to face him I will. I am not a coward.'

'Thomas, thou hast made a fool of an old man without an heir. Thou hast fornicated with his wife and she is having thy child. He will not be able to hold his head up for he has been cuckolded under his nose. He will believe the world laughs at him. That damn figurehead will be a bitter travesty for evermore. Keep away from him. Keep away until thou knows how the land lies.'

I drink my tea and begin to eat my pasty for I feel suddenly weak and light-headed with shock.

'I must sleep, Pa. I have ridden all night and I cannot think.'

'Aye, sleep. I will say nothing and thou must do the same, Thomas. Thou will need sleep, for Sir Richard will come to find thee, of that I am sure. I must go to my work now.'

I get to my feet. 'Father, if I could undo this, I would. I cannot regret Isabella, ever, but I regret the situation I have put you ... and her in. She thought I might abandon her.'

'Some might have. What is done is done, son. Go to thy loft and sleep.'

As Ben turned to go down the hill to the quay he had one hope left. A frail hope, but he clutched at it.

Chapter 63

Gabby's car had given up from lack of use, so Nell drove Gabby to the station to catch the train back to London. She rushed off to buy Gabby magazines and papers, mineral water and chocolate. Ever the farmer's wife, she imagined Gabby would starve to death between Penzance and London.

Gabby laughed. 'Nell! I'm not on a train to Outer Mongolia!'

Nell snorted. 'I know British Rail, or Great Western, whatever they call themselves. They either put on an empty buffet car or run out of everything before you reach Plymouth.'

Gabby hugged her and boarded the train. 'Take care, Nell . . . I enjoyed our few days, pretending we were tourists.'

'So did I, lovie. Don't work too hard.'

'I won't. I'll ring you . . .'

The train started to move slowly forward and Gabby leant out, said quickly, 'I love you Nell!' Then her head disappeared.

Nell was startled. She watched the long train snake out of the station and run along the track parallel to the sea, a little shimmer of heat haze hovering above the carriages. She and Gabby had never gone in for endearments or declarations of love. They had never needed to. She went slowly to her Land Rover where Shadow sat in the back panting sadly. She adored Gabby and hated it when she went.

Nell drove away from the station and out onto the dual carriageway. She intended to shop while she was there. She

430

deliberately put away the sliver of unease, for she and Gabby had had such a happy week, getting back to normal after Josh and Marika had left.

Gabby felt sick. To her right the waves were grey and large, full of seaweed. A winter sea. The train stopped at signals and Gabby glanced left out of the opposite windows and glimpsed Nell's Land Rover on the dual carriageway, with the shape of Shadow in the back.

She had the sudden eerie sensation of catching sight of a life she once shared from the disembodiment of a train. Seeing people blow along a sea wall walking dogs, heads bent against the wind, and knowing it could be her walking there and a stranger glimpsing her from a train window with a sense of recognition.

When Josh left, Gabby and Nell had decided they would have 'outings'. Every day they would drive somewhere different. The Tate at St Ives. Barbara Hepworth and the myriad of small galleries and shops in the small coastal villages which were possible now that the hordes had left and schools were back.

They had sat by the sea and eaten leisurely lunches in Mousehole and Trelissik Garden. They had bought bulbs and plants for the front garden and taken long walks on different coasts. One day they had driven to the Lost Gardens of Heligan to see how the excavation of the Victorian Garden was progressing.

'Isn't it odd,' Nell had asked, 'how we just stopped going to places when Josh left home?'

'I suppose we got busier, Nell. Took on more work and forgot to play.'

'Elan used to call it Cornwallitis. This tendency we all have down here to get locked in and enervated by the weather and being so far from everything . . .'

'Like agoraphobia; the distance just seems too great.'

'Exactly.'

Gabby had picked up on Nell's depression, so un-Nell-like that she made her promise to have a check-up to make sure it did not have a physical origin.

431

Gabby knew there was no way she could avoid hurting Nell and it made her feel desperate. The thought of losing her altogether . . . Gabby could not believe in a life without Nell somewhere in it.

There were notes all over the house from Mark and he had had a telephone line installed with an answer-phone. '*I needed to know I could talk to you any time and mobile phones are extortionate.*'

Gabby had collected flowers on the way home and she filled vases with them and roamed round the house feeling flat and lonely. Mark had booked an open ticket back because he couldn't gauge how much time he would need.

She had one answer-message on the new phone. '*I guess you'll be home about five, sweetheart. Glad you've been having a good time with Nell. I'm not sure how long this is going to take. Inez has moved to New York, so I shall probably take an internal flight to see her. I want to talk to the kids first. My lot are great at Chinese whispers . . . I'll ring you tonight . . . Oh, I nearly forgot, Gabriella. I've left something out for you on my desk. Directly under the photo of Lady Isabella pinned on the board. I think you'll find it interesting.*'

Gabby went and switched on the kettle, then walked over to Mark's desk. He had photocopied two passages and made various notes for her. It was difficult to read as the original couldn't have been clear after so many years and different hands had scrawled in the margins.

With the first entry, Mark had written on a separate piece of paper beside it: '*John Bradbury checked this in the Parish records for me. Thomas Richard Magor was born on April 15th 1867 in the Parish of St Piran, but baptized in the parish of Mylor, near Falmouth, where presumably he grew up. But look at these photocopies, Gabriella. I found the entries for these two vessels at the Public Record Office in Kew. I then checked the Certificates of British Registry, plus Lloyds List information and merchant shipping movements at Guildhall*

Library. I was looking for something quite else!'

Gabby looked down at a register with a list of ship's details arranged alphabetically. The year was 1883.

No.	Ships.	Masters.	Tons.	BUILD	Where	When
43	MORWENNA	A J ROWE	350		FALMOUTH	1880.

Owners.	Port belonging to.	Destined	Voyage.
R & T Magor	London.	Falmouth.	Newfoundland

So the owners were Richard Magor, Isabella's husband, and Thomas, their son. Gabby turned to the second document. The *Morwenna* was holed off Scilly when her load of wood shifted in a storm in 1884. Four of the crew died and the rest were rescued by lifeboat. They were Master S Budd, First Mate; L Wyatt, Second Mate; and Thomas Magor.

Richard's son, now aged seventeen.

Gabby picked up the last document Mark had copied.

No.	Ships.	Master.	Tons.	Build.
15.	Isabella.	T. Welland.	445.	Falmouth.

When.	Owners.	Destination.
1896.	T. Welland.	P.E.I.

Gabby leant back. Goosebumps broke out all over her arms. Another ship named *Isabella*. Another Tom Welland. She looked up at the photo of the figurehead, stared at the sad and haunting face. Oh, Isabella, you and your Tom Welland must have had a child! Oh, God! What happened to you both? Your son was baptized with Richard's name but he changed it later. Gabby brought her hands to her mouth.

I want to know. I want to know what dreadful thing happened to you, Isabella. Because it did, didn't it? What made your son change his name suddenly? Gabby thought back quickly. Richard Magor must have been dead by then. Was it only then that Isabella's son found out who his real father was? Oh, such a tiny glimpse of a story contained in that dry ledger.

She got up and paced the room. Oh, if only Mark was here. *I want to talk to him about this.* I long to know what really happened to Isabella and we're never going to know, are we?

Gabby stared and stared at the face on the pin-board above her. Reached up and touched it with her finger. It was as if the air in the room shifted and deflected and took her to the sick moment of Isabella's disgrace. This familiar face she had so lovingly restored. This face pulled up from the sea would haunt her forever, unless she knew.

She remembered the day in the cemetery and shivered. *You want me to know, Isabella. You want me to know.*

Mark had written: *This perhaps explains why we could find so little reference to poor Isabella in the close-knit villages of Mylor and St Piran. I am so glad we found her and restored her to her rightful place, Gabriella.*

Gabby looked out of the window and sighed. So, Isabella's son Thomas changed his name and called another ship after his mother.

Chapter 64

Richard did not return home that night or the next. There was no word from him or Tom. Isabella felt ill and weak with anxiety. She felt sure that Richard would have gone to St Piran to find Tom or to tell her father of her disgrace.

She felt powerless over her own fate. She had wanted to tell Richard what she felt the night he wept. How deeply she felt for the kind and generous person he was. But she did not love him like a wife and these were words she could not say.

On the third day the winds turned the bay choppy and squalls of rain hit the windows so that Isabella was trapped indoors. She was standing at the window when she saw Trathan ride in through the woods and take his horse to the stables. She knew he would have been sent with a message from Richard and she went downstairs to wait in the drawing room with a quailing heart.

It was not Mr Trathan who came to find her, but Lisette. She looked pale.

'My Lady, I am to pack you a case. You are to go home to your father.'

Isabella stared at Lisette and said coldly, 'Lisette, I am not a child or a horse or an unwanted thing to be sent back to my father.'

Lisette compressed her lips. 'Even so. I do not think you are in a position to argue. Trathan is to accompany you to St Piran where your father's housekeeper will meet you.'

Isabella was suddenly, unaccountably angry. 'I will not be dismissed like a servant, Lisette. I will wait until my husband returns. He must have the courage to dismiss me himself.'

She went to her desk. 'I will write a note for my father and one

435

for Sir Richard. Would you ask Mr Trathan to make sure they are both delivered?'

When the clouds cleared Isabella pulled a cloak around her and walked across the garden. She felt this bitter anger that must have been lying inside her for some time. She was considered mature enough to marry an older man, yet she was treated like a child when all went wrong, bundled back to her childhood home.

Out in the air her head began to clear and she considered the choices she might have. She did not yet know if Richard would divorce her. She did not know how much of Helena's money was settled on her when she married Richard. She knew only one thing. She must have a safe place to live until her baby was born.

She trusted Tom but she did not know what pressure he was going to be put under. She knew she must have something to bargain with.

She cupped her arms round her stomach. Perhaps this new wisdom came with the life she was carrying. As she stood looking out over the bay, she felt a little flutter, a movement as slight as a breath. She knew it was too soon for the baby to move, it was no more than a tic in her cheek or the touch of a light finger on her skin, but the full impact of carrying another life hit her with all its force. Whatever she did, wherever she went, she would be responsible for this life.

There was something admirable about Ben Welland, Richard thought. He managed to be courteous without being servile, but he was nervous.

'Where is your son, Tom? Has he scuttled off somewhere safe?'

'No, Sir Richard, he will not hide from thee.'

'Then he is a fool. Does he not know I can break him, make sure he never works again?'

'Aye, Sir.' Then Ben said softly, 'He has wronged thee.'

Something in the way Ben Welland said, 'Aye, Sir' infuriated Richard. He caught the inflection and the meaning. *You may stop my son working here, but Thomas can work anywhere in the world.*

He banged his fist down on his desk. 'Does he also realize that

I can stop all work in the shipyard tomorrow? I could make every damn one of you redundant.'

'He knows, Sir.'

'And what have you to say to him about taking your livelihood away, Mr Welland?'

Ben looked him in the eye. 'I think it right that my son should suffer, but not innocent people who work hard and have never done thee wrong, Sir. They know thee as a fair man and a good employer and they will not understand why thou art judging us all by what my son has done.'

'You are telling me that no one knows of my wife's disgrace except you and Tom?'

'I give thee my word. Even my wife does not know.'

Richard looked at him in silence. Ben's word was good enough.

'Keep it that way, Ben. I mean that. Where is your son?'

'He waits outside.'

'Get him in here, then.'

Ben stood there for a moment longer then said gruffly, 'I hope thou doest not blame me for this . . . tragedy, Sir. I was that shocked, mysen. Thomas has wronged thee and I am sad and sorry for it. I am not good with words, Sir, I know they don't mend anything, but thou hast always been more than fair by me . . . and I apologize for my son. It is all I can do.'

Despite himself, Richard was moved.

'Ben,' he said more gently, 'my quarrel is not with you.'

I walk up and down in the road outside the Summer House, waiting for my father. I would be on the first vessel out of here, taking Isabella with me, if it were not for my father, who emerges to say Sir Richard is waiting for me. He starts to accompany me back to the house.

'I am not a child that you have to hold my hand, Pa.'

But my father is insistent.

When I walk into the room, Sir Richard's face changes colour. He trembles and he swallows a rage that seems to consume him. He grips the edge of the desk in an effort to control himself. When he speaks his voice is not steady.

'How dare you take advantage of my wife? How dare you abuse my trust so wickedly?'

'I have known Isabella since she was a child. I grew to love her. I had no intention of abuse ...'

'What do I care for your intentions? You knew my wife as a child, yet you are happy to ruin her reputation. What do you say to that?'

'My intentions towards Lady Isabella are honourable, Sir Richard. I wish to take responsibility for the predicament she is in. I would marry her and take her to New England to a new life ...'

Sir Richard leaps to his feet. 'Never! Do you hear me? I will never divorce my wife. Who the hell do you think you are? You will never marry her.'

I stare at him. 'Then it is not me, Sir, who is ruining her, but you.'

Sir Richard becomes red with rage, and saliva hangs in the corner of his mouth. My father moves forward, afraid that he might have a heart attack.

'You think I would divorce my wife so that she can marry you, you ... imbecile?'

'She carries my child.'

Sir Richard moves towards me from behind the desk with surprising agility for a man of his age.

'Aye, and that child will be born a bastard and my wife will live out her disgrace here. Do you hear me ...?'

'Does Lady Isabella have no say in her own life, Sir Richard?'

'She,' Richard spits, 'has forfeited all rights. Her future, as yours, lies in my hands, and like the idiot you are, you do not seem to comprehend this.'

I turn for the door. With my hand on the latch I look back.

'I have always thought of you as a fair and just man, Sir Richard. I have wronged you and I cannot put that right except to seek respectability for Lady Isabella. Your anger is justified. I cannot undo what has happened, nor would I, for I love Isabella and would spend my life with her ...'

I pause. I suddenly see Isabella's beautiful young face. I see that this revengeful, vain old man would like to ruin her to satisfy his own vanity, with no thought to her youth, to her life, which is her own. He had no right to take and hold a young woman like a bird in a cage. I shake with fear for her and my voice is unsteady.

'Isabella is not yet nineteen, she has hardly begun her life. You would blight her life for evermore because she and I have done you injury? I do not call that love. If that is your kind of love then I prefer the love of my sort ... Punish me, prevent me from working in Cornwall. Do not punish Isabella ...'

'Thomas, wilt thou keep thy mouth shut ...'

My father's intervention brings Sir Richard's attention to him.

'It should be of great concern that your son cannot keep his mouth shut when it would be better for all of you that he did.'

I have had enough. 'Aye, Sir, it is easy to threaten my father and the village with loss of work, but how does that save your own reputation?'

Sir Richard smiles and returns behind his desk. 'There is only one way to save my reputation and your livelihoods.'

My father and I stare at him.

'You tell me this affair between my wife and your son is not yet common knowledge?' Richard asks my father.

'Aye, I do, Sir.'

'Then this is what your son will do, Ben ...'

I believe he had not decided until that moment. I could see this by his sudden satisfied smile.

'You indeed will sail for New England, but on your own, Welland. I will not divorce Isabella. She remains as my wife and the child she carries will be mine and I will bring it up as mine. If you do not agree I will withdraw all contracts. No ships will be built in St Piran and I will ensure that Mr Vyvyan does not employ anyone from this village, man or woman.

'Put out of your mind, for good, Welland, any union with my wife. If you leave for New England with her I will make sure no work awaits you there. You accept these terms or suffer the consequences. Have I made myself clear?'

'You would tie Isabella to you for the rest of her life, even though she does not love you? You would give her no chance to speak for herself?'

'It matters not whether she loves me. It matters a great deal that you do not have her and that my standing is not compromised. I will not have sniggers behind my back. Well, do you agree to these terms?'

My father turns to look at me and for the first time I see the fear in his eyes. Because of me my family, a whole community, risk losing all and everything they have worked for.

I turn back to Sir Richard. 'I cannot agree to anything until I have seen Isabella,' then, I add quickly for my father and Sir Richard's benefit, 'one last time, before I leave.'

Sir Richard considers, then smiles, very pleased with himself.

'Very well. On my return to Falmouth you may see her one last time. But, naturally, not alone.'

Chapter 65

In the bath Gabby thought about the face of Lady Isabella. No one could have carved a face like that unless they had been sexually involved. It wasn't possible. She walked around the house in her nightdress opening the windows. The sky was dramatic with strange-shaped clouds of charcoal and pink collecting in great masses behind the buildings on the opposite side of the river. There was not a breath of wind. The last of the day hung heavy and the little house seemed airless. There was going to be a storm.

Gabby did not want to go to bed in case she missed the phone from upstairs, so she curled up on the sofa, put some music on and picked up her book. Two minutes later she got up and went into the kitchen to make some tea. She refused to look at her watch again. She was so afraid the evening would slip by without Mark phoning.

If it was possible for him to phone, he would. Gabby knew this . . . it was just her imagination, and the distance, and his huge family. If she had considered for even a second that she could stay with Charlie, was it not possible that Mark might feel the same about Veronique? He had five daughters he adored, and grandchildren, and a whole full rich life over there.

She remembered what Nell had said once when discussing some mutual friend in the village who was having an affair.

'When the time comes, men so rarely leave their wives, and women never seem to learn this.'

Elan told her once about a friend who planned to leave his

441

wife. He broke it to his wife and daughter, packed a bag and made for the door, but his daughter, aged five, ran and held on to his ankle and would not let go. He walked down the hall dragging one foot, with the little girl hanging on like a ball and chain, being pulled along the carpet behind him, her small face grim and tight with misery. The man knew then it was hopeless, he could not prise those small fingers off his leg, open the front door and walk away.

Gabby's very anxiousness seemed to her a betrayal. She knew it was the reassurance of hearing his voice that she needed because she had made an ending of sorts. The nearest to a leave-taking with love she could manage.

In the distance a low growl of thunder started and Gabby got up and shut the downstairs windows before she went to bed. She listened to Mark's message one more time and smiled. Suddenly, all doubts flew. She remembered their last week together, how close they were and how sure of each other.

She took her mobile phone to bed but left the bedroom door wide so that she could hear the downstairs phone too, and fell asleep almost immediately in the hot room. The thunder rumbled on through the night but came to nothing.

Some time in the early hours she was woken by the sound of her mobile phone beeping and flashing beside her, and half-asleep she lifted it to her ear.

'Mark! I'm so glad you rang, I've been worrying about you.'

There was silence and then a strange man's voice said, 'I am afraid this is not Mark. Am I speaking to Gabriella Ellis?'

'Yes,' she said warily. She looked at the clock; it was two-thirty in the morning.

'My name is David Horsanavitch, I am Mark Hannah's American publisher.'

Gabby tried to gather her wits, wake up properly.

'I am sorry, there is no easy way to tell you this. Mark was killed on an internal flight to Montreal yesterday afternoon. The plane came down in bad weather. There were no survivors.'

What is this man saying? Is it some cruel joke? How does he have her number?

'Are you still there?'

'Yes. It can't be true because I've got a message from Mark. He left a message on my answer-phone yesterday.'

'I am sorry, Gabriella. I am afraid there is no doubt Mark died in the crash.'

She wanted to scream, *Don't call me that, only Mark calls me that.*

I'm dreaming. In a moment I will wake up.

'Oh God!' the voice said. 'I've just realized it must be the middle of the night with you?'

'Yes.'

'I must have woken you with this. I'm sorry, I'm real sorry, shock is making me dumb. I should have thought . . . I'm not on the ball. I saw Mark two days ago and he was real happy with life and the new book . . . It's a terrible shock. He gave me your mobile telephone number a few months ago and asked me if I would let you know if anything ever happened to him.'

No, no, no, no. It's not true. It's not true. God. Please don't let it be true. Please, God . . .

'Gabriella?'

'Yes.'

'I am so sorry. It is an atrocious waste of a life. He had a lovely family.'

Outside there was a burst of sudden rain and the heat eased, the room cooled.

'Thank you for ringing me. Good—'

'Are you all right?'

Gabby could not answer. Breathing seemed difficult, too fast, and too painful.

'I apologize . . . I've been unnecessarily abrupt. It is just that I've known Mark's family for years, one of his daughters used to work for me. I was sad he was going to break his long marriage up for . . .'

'Me,' Gabby whispered. 'For me.'

'There is certainly no doubt he loved you. I'm so sorry to be the one to break it to you. Goodbye, Gabriella.'

'Goodbye.'

Gabby did not know how long she lay in the same position. She heard seagulls and for a moment thought she was back at the farm and had been asleep.

Her mind would not clear. She felt drugged, as if the sudden shocking awakening had released some drug in her brain which rendered her immobile. She did not trust her legs to get her to the bathroom and eventually she wobbled, holding on to the door jambs like an old lady. She splashed cold water on her face, did her teeth because her mouth was so dry, then slid downstairs on her bottom for water from the fridge.

She went slowly upstairs with the bottle, holding on to the banisters, and crawled back into bed. The day outside was closing in, a grey blanket over the river. The rain was steady against the window, forming a rhythm which she listened to with intense concentration to stop her thoughts. *No, no, no, no. Please, no.*

If she could fall asleep to wake to another day all would be well. She would not have had that conversation. She could wipe it out . . . that man . . . his words. The sweat ran down Gabby's body, soaking her nightdress and the bed. She kicked the hot duvet off and tossed and turned, sipped the water. She turned the radio on and tried to listen but her mind slid away and the words kept coming back. She looked at the clock. It was only eight o'clock.

She went under the shower, hanging on to the sides as waves of dizziness seized her. She pulled on aged, faded pyjamas that Mark used to tease her about and looked in the medicine cabinet. There were some old sleeping pills left in a bottle she had brought from Cornwall and she took two and collapsed back into bed.

All through the day she slept and woke and dreamt, tunnelling up through a drugged, false slumber to the same words like a terrible refrain. Her mobile phone went once or twice on her bedside table and she knew it would be Lucinda wondering why she wasn't at the gallery. At four she made tea for her parched throat and got into a bath. She went downstairs and sat in the chair facing the river. The house was an island, closed-in with the sound of water.

Dusk came, the lonely no-man's land between night and day. Gabby stood in the kitchen looking out. A leaf fell like a tawny hand, landing softly in the yard. Lights sprang on, faces appeared at windows, fingers tugged curtains in small quick movements and then the lights were gone, the windows blind, hiding the lives inside.

Gabby opened the kitchen door and went out. The leaf lay face down all on its own. She looked upwards, but could see no tree from which it could have floated down. She bent and picked it up. The colours were extraordinary, with such depth and shades of copper and crimson, as if still attached to a live source and breathing.

She shivered in the damp air and splayed her fingers over the leaf. Her hand fit snugly within it. She turned her wrist and it seemed to her the thin trace of veins resembled her own. A human hand pressed to an ethereal one, like lovers when a train starts to move out of a station. Inside the train, a hand, fingers spread against the glass. On the platform outside, the lover places a hand over hers. Cold glass divides them. Hands together; yours; mine. Us.

It suddenly seemed to Gabby that the leaf was important. She carried it inside, hurried almost, and sat in the dark room facing the river, still holding it. A barge hooted as it approached the bridge. People laughed as they walked along the river path to the pub.

She sat in the silent house as sounds outside faded and became small distant echoes. The house was drawing itself in, waiting, like her, for the sound of footsteps and a key in the lock.

On she sat, her hand upon the leaf, as night gathered. The river settled for night, flowing darkly, silent now, towards the bridge. Every now and then a half-moon appeared from behind clouds that moved as fast and elemental as the water.

It was like a stupor, a trance. Frozen, Gabby stared transfixed at the black water gleaming beyond the path. Felt a terrible cold penetrate her limbs. She felt stopped, like time, to that one moment. *Mark is dead.*

Eventually, the cold seemed to wake her. With a jerk she came to. Shivering, she stumbled out of the chair, carried the leaf upstairs and placed it on her bedside table. Staring at the bed, she lay carefully in exactly the same position Mark always lay, curled towards her, one arm thrown out and over her. She wanted to be Mark, turn into Mark, and vaporize into the same infinity.

She lay motionless for a long time wondering how many pills she had in her drawer, then Josh's face sprang before her and she sat up abruptly. Afraid of what she might do she reached for her mobile phone and dialled Elan's London number. She had no idea if he was still in London.

It rang for a long time and then Elan came on the line, his voice thick with sleep.

'Hello? Hello?'

Relief. Gabby closed her eyes, could not speak.

'Who is this?' Elan asked crossly.

'Elan,' Gabby whispered, 'Elan.'

Elan was instantly awake. 'Gabby? Gabby, what is it? Where are you?'

Gabby began to dissolve. 'Please come. Please come, Elan.'

'Gabby, are you in London?'

'Yes.'

'What's happened? Is it Josh?'

'No, it isn't Josh. It's Mark. He's dead. He's dead.'

'Oh, Gabby!'

Gabby heard him erupt out of bed and move heavily across the room.

'I've got a pen, give me your address . . . OK, I've got it. I know exactly where you are. Don't move. I'm on my way, child.'

It was night again. A whole day had gone. Elan ran Gabby a bath. She was cried out, exhausted. He brought her up a tray of scrambled eggs and tea with sugar in it, as if she was convalescing. She sat up in bed pushing it around the plate, pushing tiny pieces into her mouth and trying to swallow.

'I can't go home,' she said. 'Elan, I can't go home.'

Elan got her to swallow one of the tranquillizers he'd brought with him, left over from his days with Patrick. 'We'll talk in the morning. Don't think about anything for now, Gabby, just sleep.'

'Please don't go, Elan. I am so afraid of myself.'

'I have no intention of going anywhere.'

He took his shoes off and lay beside her on top of the bed.

'I love you, Elan.' Gabby's voice was slurred as the pill took effect.

'I love you too, child.'

Darkness came and Elan lay with his hands behind his head, wide awake. He thought of the farm and Nell and Charlie and what lay ahead, and of the stark fact that by keeping Gabby's secret he might have betrayed his friendship with Nell. He cursed the gods, because this tragedy was going to rend the family apart. It was going to catch everyone in its slipstream, not least his godson, who certainly wouldn't understand his mother's fall from grace.

Nell and Charlie? Nell would be bitterly hurt, she had been so close to Gabby. It was why Gabby never bothered to form friendships of her own age, she had not needed anyone else.

Charlie? Bugger it, Charlie's pride was going to take one hell of a battering. Charlie was Charlie, and, as with Ted and Nell, Elan had absolutely no idea how deeply Charlie cared for Gabby.

The long day ended as it had begun, to the sound of rain and a grey claustrophobic mist that still clung to the swollen river, shutting them in, enclosing them tightly in Gabby's grief. One whole day had passed without Mark.

Chapter 66

Isabella was astonished when Lisette burst in and announced before breakfast that her father's wife, Charlotte, had ridden over from Falmouth with her groom and was waiting below to see her.

'Will you show her into the morning room and make sure she is served tea and breakfast, Lisette. I will be downstairs in a few minutes.'

Ten minutes later Isabella went downstairs and saw immediately how nervous Charlotte was.

'Isabella, forgive this intrusion so early in the day.'

She went towards Isabella and took her hands. Her voice held no hint of censure or coldness and Isabella was surprised at this and the smile she was given. The two women went back to the fire for the morning was chill. Isabella could not think of a thing to say and watched the older woman anxiously, sure she must have come with a message from her father.

Charlotte was shocked at Isabella's colour. Her eyes were huge and her healthy, rounded body had grown thin.

'Isabella, I am sorry that we have not been friends or even acquaintances and I hope to remedy that. Your father does not know I have come but when I heard of your predicament I was anxious to see how you were. I thought you might need a friend . . .'

She looked away and into the fire. 'My younger sister found herself in a similar predicament and I . . . let her down because of pressure from my father.'

She met Isabella's eyes. 'I know that it is a very lonely place to be.'

Isabella found her voice. 'I imagine my father would not like you to be here?'

'He is shocked, Isabella, very shocked. He has been very quiet since Richard's visit, but he has not said one angry word against you ...'

Charlotte smiled. 'Blood is thicker than water, my dear, and he does not like the way Richard is reacting. He sees no dignity in it and is hurt by condemnation of you coming from the lips of someone who professed to love you so much.'

'I have hurt and wronged Richard, Charlotte.'

'You have, Isabella, and of course it is natural that Richard is angry as well as hurt, but you are your father's daughter and, whatever you think, he loves you and does not like to hear you spoken of badly. This is what I came to say. I have realized in the last few days how much he wishes you had both been reconciled; how much he partly blames himself for what has happened to you.'

Isabella's eyes filled with tears for she suddenly realized how much she had missed her father all these years and how she had conjured hate from hurt. She looked at Charlotte, who was quite different from the imagined figure she had made her into all this time.

'Was it Richard who asked my father to take me back to St Piran, away from here, Charlotte?'

'Yes. But your father did not react in the way Richard expected, or I, for that matter. He refused to condemn you in the way Richard hoped, or to make St Piran pay for what he considers a domestic matter. He will not deprive his own community of work. He is angry that Richard, an outsider in the village, would even contemplate revenge in those terms and on people who have never harmed him but only served him well and faithfully. He will not have his name used. Your family have lived in St Piran for generations and he refuses to penalize ordinary people he knows well.'

Charlotte got up from her chair.

'Isabella, I do not know what you are going to do, or what is in your mind. I just want you to know you are welcome to your own home, not as childish punishment, but because it is your home.'

'My father ...?'

'Your father, my dear, did not ride with me this morning, because he hoped that I would do what I had suggested we do together, and come to you. He is a proud man and a man no longer young … he is distressed, not angry, at the way things have turned out for you. He wants you to know his home is open to you.'

Isabella, too, got up. 'Charlotte, forgive me for judging you. Coming here was brave and I thank you for it, for it means more than you will ever know.'

Isabella walked to the door with Charlotte and they waited for her horse to be brought round.

'Charlotte, will you tell my father that I am waiting to talk to my husband when he returns. I am uncertain, as yet, what I will do, but I believe I must have a place of my own and I would be grateful if he could look into Mama's legacy to me so that money may be released for this end.'

'I will. Goodbye, Isabella, may God guide you.'

Isabella watched the two horses walk away down the drive until they were lost in the trees. She clasped her hands together. Her father did not condemn her. He would not put his name to any revenge Richard might have in mind!

I ask my brother Harry to sail me round from St Piran to Mylor. I know Trathan is riding with Sir Richard to Truro before he goes back to Mylor and I want to reach Isabella before he gets home. The wind is strong but it serves my purpose and we fly along the coast in a heavy autumn sea.

When we reach Mylor harbour I write a note to Isabella and send a boy with it up to the house. Twenty minutes later I make my way quickly up to the woods behind the house and lean against a gate, praying Isabella will come swiftly.

Within ten minutes I see her hurrying along the ha-ha towards the wood and I go to meet her. We turn into the shelter of trees and hold each other for a moment, my hand pressing her head to my chest. I can feel the frightened beating of her heart as she leans against me. A feeling of impotence fills me. I cannot protect both her and my family.

Isabella tells me breathlessly what happened after I left her, and of Richard's distress.

'I had to see your husband for my father's sake,' I tell her. 'I saw only anger. Anger and a need for revenge. Isabella, he is never going to let you go. He has threatened to put the whole village as well as the shipyard out of work unless I sail on my own for New England. Worse, he says he has the power to prevent me working in Prince Edward Island if I do not renounce you. Isabella, I can work anywhere but I cannot think of a way of safeguarding the livelihood of so many people.'

'I cannot believe he would carry out his threats, Tom. He is angry and wants to hurt ... Would he tie me to him forever when he knows I carry your child? I do not think so, for I know he does not wish ever to see me again and tried to banish me to my father before he came home.'

'Believe me, Isabella. He is determined we will never be together and he will hurt people to this end. By keeping you and bringing up my child as his, he saves face and revenges us. He is a proud man and I believe at this moment his pride is paramount to all else.'

Isabella leans against a tree. She looks suddenly weak and sick.

'Isabella, are you ill?'

'No, it is just the baby ...' Her face is young and miserable as she looks up at me.

'So, Tom, you must go away from here and I must live out my days with a man I do not love because of his threats to innocent people?'

I smile. 'Isabella, how can you doubt me? I will not leave without you. I will not leave you to his anger and threats. I do not want my child brought up as Sir Richard's, it makes me sick. I lied to him and to my father ...'

'Tom, my father's wife visited me. She wanted me to know that my father is shocked but will not condemn me, and that he will have no part in Richard's wish for revenge on any of his tenants or workers in the village and shipyard.'

I look down at her surprised. 'He said that?' I close my eyes in relief. I hope my father knows this and I pray he will forgive me, not see my escape with Isabella as a betrayal. I pray also that Daniel Vyvyan's influence will prevail.

I take Isabella's shoulders with a sense of urgency, although I do not want to frighten her.

'Isabella, can you be ready tonight?'

Isabella's eyes widen but she nods. 'Yes. Yes, but where will we go, Tom?'

'The quickest way out of here is by boat. There is one in the harbour. I sailed with Harry from St Piran this morning. If we sail first to Truro and then continue to Plymouth we can see what ships lie there. Isabella, are you sure you can do this? Are you sure you can leave this life behind?'

'Do you doubt me now, Tom?' She smiles.

'No.' I take her cold hand. 'It is not going to be easy or comfortable for you at first. And we must travel by dark out of Cornwall, Isabella. Can you wear something plain and warm and bring only what you need . . . ?'

I fold her hand between mine. 'I will buy you the things you leave behind later, I promise. I do not want you to go without . . .'

Isabella smiles once more. 'Do I come to the harbour tonight, Tom?'

'No, I will meet you here. It is too dark for you to walk the coastal path alone. I will be here at nine o'clock for the tide will be right.'

We stare at one another, wishing the deed was done, that we were safely out of Cornwall.

Chapter 67

Elan drove Gabby back to his cottage two days later. She was in no state to go home and in no state to be left in London. He phoned Nell before they left.

'Thank goodness you rang. Elan, we can't get hold of Gabby. Normally she phones me every two or three days. I wouldn't have been worried, but the Lucinda girl from the gallery rang, she hasn't been in to work . . .'

'It's OK, Nell, she's with me.'

'What on earth's happened? Is she all right?'

'Yes, Nell, she is all right in the sense you mean. I can't explain over the phone. I will come and see you tomorrow.'

'Are you bringing her home?'

Elan hesitated. 'Nell, she is going to stay with me for a few days. Is it possible for you not to say anything to Charlie until we've talked?'

Oh God, Gabby wants to leave Charlie.

'All right, Elan, I'll see you tomorrow. Drive carefully.'

'I will, Nell. Take care.'

Charlie was out and Nell sat down heavily on a chair in her kitchen. *Oh, why have I not seen this coming? Gabby taking on more and more London work . . . The last time I put her on the train . . . I love you Nell, she had said. Gabby had been leaving.*

Nell picked up her newspaper from the table and distractedly started to thumb through it, while she thought about what to say to Charlie. Just as she was closing the paper her eyes fell on the obituary page:

Professor Mark Hannah was one of the passengers killed on a Canadian Airline internal flight to Montreal on Tuesday. Currently on sabbatical in London, he was responsible for returning a ship's figurehead to the small Cornish port of St Piran. He was a popular writer of marine history and well-known on the lecture circuit for his innovative and slightly eccentric slant on history. He aimed to make the past accessible and alive and he succeeded. His passion was figureheads from the small trade schooners of the nineteenth century. He was completing a book on this underrated art form when he died. He leaves a wife and five daughters.

There was a fuzzy and much younger photo of a very beautiful man.

Nell closed the paper and folded it slowly and neatly into fours, stepped over her cats and went outside. Charlie was sitting in his Land Rover chatting to Sarah Caradon, who was facing the opposite way in her truck. They were obviously talking fruit and flirting. When Charlie saw Nell, he called, 'I'm going to the pub to pick Sarah's brains, see you later.'

He didn't ask about Gabby and Nell went back inside and put on her favourite Mahler, and continued restoring a small painting for John Bradbury. It was only when she could no longer see the painting that she realized she was crying.

The wind rattled the cottage windows of Elan's house and wuthered round the walls dramatically. Elan had piled wood on the burner so that it stayed on all night and Gabby lay in the dark or wandered round the cottage, making tea and getting as near to the stove as she could.

She found it impossible to accept Mark was dead and swallowed Elan's tranquillizers as if her life depended on it. It prevented her from thinking. It prevented her doing anything coherent or practical and in the end, small dose or not, Elan flushed them down the loo.

Gabby walked miles along the coast in all weathers, but

Elan knew he could not play guard dog. He said quietly, 'If you ever feel like doing something silly, think of Josh, darling, and how he would feel, apart from the rest of us.'

'I do,' Gabby said. 'I do.'

When Elan went over to see Nell she had already guessed. 'It wasn't difficult. You don't have to be a brain surgeon. I saw the obituary.'

Elan was shocked at how defeated Nell looked. She was furious with Charlie because he was so busy with setting up his fruit for next year that he had failed to notice that Gabby had not rung for some time. He was also spending too much time in the pub with the giggly Sarah.

Elan and Nell told him together.

'The fucking little bitch! The deceitful, fucking bitch. She can bloody-well stay out of my sight. Who else knows about this?'

'Apart from me and Nell, no one. John Bradbury might suspect. He came round because he had seen her at the museum and was worried about her.'

'She wasn't working?' Nell asked.

'No. Just sitting in front of the figurehead.'

Charlie jumped in. 'That was the start of this, that bloody, fucking figurehead! I'm glad that . . .'

'Don't say it!' Nell snapped. 'Don't you dare say you are glad another human being is dead.'

Elan got up and went to the door and Nell walked with him. Out of earshot she said, 'I packed Gabby some things, Elan. Changes of clothes, soap, and stuff she might need. They are just inside my front door.'

Elan hugged her. 'Oh, what a mess, darling.'

'Isn't it?' She tried to smile. 'Sorry you've got landed with it.'

'Both you and Gabby were wonderful when Patrick died. It's a sad thing if you can't be there for the people you love. I am not taking sides, Nell. I am simply being there.'

'How long have you known about Gabby and the Canadian, Elan?'

'For a while, Nell. I thought it would blow over,' Elan lied, for he thought no such thing. The first time he spotted Gabby and Mark together at his exhibition, he saw that the Canadian had a magnetic personality, was very much his own man. Elan had liked him and the way he had looked and listened to Gabby as if she was someone very special, which she was. Then, seeing them at Paddington . . .

'I don't suppose she is in any state to think about what she is going to do?'

'No,' Elan said. 'Putting one foot in front of the other is all she can manage. Oh, Nell, this is so difficult for you . . .'

Nell put her hands up to stop him and her pain was naked.

'I don't know how to react, Elan. At the moment I don't even know how to feel . . . Please go before I let myself down . . .'

'Oh, Nell.'

'Go!'

'I'll ring you. I'll ring you, darling Nell.'

As he drove back home Elan thought how glad he was that Josh was still out of England.

Nell felt as if a whole lifetime was about to unravel, pivoting Charlie and Josh out of their safe and sure positions in the family, and there was absolutely nothing she could do about it.

As she scattered corn for the bantams she felt cross with herself, for believing that Charlie could get away with not addressing the inevitable needs and changes in the sad and lonely seventeen-year-old Gabby and the woman who evolved and became so much her own person, with a surprising talent for restoration.

That young Gabby had surprised them all. She had embraced the farm, Nell and Charlie with a single-minded intensity. She had adapted to pregnancy, a speedy marriage and the isolation of this small farming community as if she had been born to it.

She had been so rewarding to teach, so eager to learn. So proficient it had been extraordinary. Something in Gabby's goodness had always made Nell anxious. She had anticipated Charlie's needs, worked by his side, waited on him. Nell had watched his surprise grow. He had done the right thing without pressure and it was working out.

When Josh was born he had been ecstatic. Those had been the happiest years, Nell thought, the very happiest. Later, she had wanted to yell and shake Charlie awake. She had tried to warn him, urge him not to take Gabby for granted; dear God, she had tried.

Charlie had worked hard in those early days to keep the farm out of debt. There was little time or money for even small extravagances, but it was more that Charlie, like Ted, believed that putting bread on the table should be enough. Their hard work provided safety and security. Their women should *know* that the farm and a home was their exchange of love and duty.

Gabby had never given Charlie any reason to believe she did not understand this or appreciate it. *But it does not mean it's enough to sustain a woman from seventeen to seventy.*

If Gabby kept her eyes closed she was back in the sitting room. She could hear and smell the river through the window. She could feel the polished floorboards beneath her feet and listen to the music playing softly as the candles flickered over the walls. With her eyes tightly closed she could feel Mark's touch, feel the warmth of his body as he guided her slowly round the small room that always smelt of flowers, in a dance that was not a dance, just an excuse to be close.

They were both silent, concentrating on their bodies moving in perfect unison, bare feet never faltering on the smooth wood floor. With their eyes closed, they clung to those moments. Those moments that might slide away into an unknown future if they did not hold them, breath held, like a breakable thing.

Round and round the small room they moved to the faint slap of water, light as air, the rhythm of their bodies conjuring a melancholy so sweet and sad it was like joy, for they knew the fragility of that time in their lives as they danced to the sound of the river.

They knew they might have to move back to their other lives, but this, this perfect moment would live on, stored against the second when they heard the same piece of music, played at another time, in another place; and they would fly back sickly and with sorrow to the river, the faint scent of hyacinths and the feel of one another in the dark silent room.

Gabby was feverishly going over every moment she had had with Mark. She was desperate for the feel of his body holding her, his long arm thrown over her hips. For the feel of his breath on the back of her neck as they lay like spoons in sleep.

Nothing was real. Nothing touched her but this loss. This life she had while he was dead was her living, breathing nightmare. His laugh, his enthusiasm, the small habits of every day, the sheer vitality of him existing, of being alive, had been her reality.

She wanted to walk back into that life with Mark. Make time go backwards so that it would never erase the sound of his voice, his face. Mark Hannah. That piece of him that was part of her, that piece of her that died with him. She was smothered and blinded by the suddenness of his absence, rendered incapable by having to go on.

One morning Nell saw her from a distance as she walked Shadow. The dog whined and Nell hastily put her on the lead. She saw the flesh had fallen from Gabby, saw by the way she paced the small beach near Elan's cottage, that she was hunched and haunted by sorrow.

Would Charlie ever understand his own part in this? Gabby had been loved by a man who was, according to Elan, going to leave a long marriage, five daughters and numerous grandchildren for her. *That was some love, some regard.* The same woman Charlie had so casually and carelessly disregarded for so long.

Nell realized that she had been afraid of unleashing something in Charlie; the blind and immovable intransigence of Ted. An inability to imagine any emotion which is not felt by oneself.

Catching sight of Gabby grief-stricken and rudderless was like going back twenty years. Like revisiting an old wound that never entirely healed.

Peter had let her love him for so long. At university they had gone about together for the whole of those years before he suddenly said out of the blue, 'Nell, I think I'm gay.'

They had slept together. They had been inseparable and he had said so casually she had gasped at the pain of it, 'I think I'm gay. I've just fallen in love for the first time.'

So rapt had he been in this love, in this realization, he had been unthinkingly cruel. He had made casual something that had been fundamental to her. He had not even looked into her face.

Her parents had packed her off to an aunt in Cornwall and she had roamed, like Gabby, walking in all weathers, bent huddled with her wound, so gaping, so lonely she thought she might break in two. For she had lost her lover and her best friend in one bitter, burning, astounding sentence.

I'm in love for the very first time.

My God, where did that leave her? It left her with nothing sweet to look back on. She had met Ted and he couldn't have been more different and, at the time, it seemed refreshingly normal and honest.

Nell realized as she trudged home across the fields that she could not feel angry or deceived or hurt by Gabby. *I could not love her more if she was my own daughter and that is how it is.*

I have to look at my own cowardice too. I could not face what I knew to be true. What I knew in my heart was happening. That Gabby had moved on to another place and left Charlie and me behind. Perhaps, perhaps, if I am truthful, I believed in some subconscious way she deserved the blossoming that I saw when she returned each time from London. The coming alive that flared outwards and warmed us all. We all stood in the reflected rays of her happiness and chose not to question it.

The following afternoon, after ringing Elan, she walked over to his cottage with Shadow, and a bag containing the dog's lead and bowl, some dog food and a comb. Gabby needed an anchor, a small reminder of reality, and who better than her dog. Shadow seemed to sense that Gabby was at Elan's long before they reached the cottage. Elan had said he would be out and Gabby was not inside the house, but Shadow, crying softly, held her nose up towards Elan's summerhouse.

Nell shut her in Elan's kitchen, walked across the garden in the late afternoon sun and peered through the half-open door. Gabby was lying curled up with her back to the door on the hard horsehair bed. She was rocking and keening in a low eerie monotone. On her small cassette player Barber was playing *Adagio for Strings*. Back and forth, back and forth Gabby rocked, while outside the sun slid behind the headland and birds skittered and called in the undergrowth.

The day lost its warmth suddenly like a shadow descending, and with it a damp earthy smell rose and filled the summerhouse. Gabby seemed unaware of Nell in the doorway. She was somewhere a long way away, although she must hear the birds and feel the damp for she shivered again as she stared blankly out of the window. Her breath came in little pants. The movement seemed painful as if something was caught under her ribs.

Nell saw that Gabby was groping round like a sleepwalker with no idea how to get through the next, unreal, lonely minute. She turned away without speaking. This was a private grief that had to run. She could not help or get near Gabby. Not at the moment. But Shadow might.

She went back to the cottage and let the dog out and she

bounded with her ears up towards the summerhouse, making little moans of pleasure, and Nell turned and walked home before it got dark.

Chapter 68

In the dark they ran and fear caught and snapped at their heels. Tom kept a tight hold of her hand and Isabella could feel the tension in him. They stopped to get their breath before they descended the coast path down to the harbour.

They walked along to the quay. Tom pulled Isabella closer and peered into the darkness. He could not see the boat, but he guided her onto the small beach where someone whistled softly.

They hurried over the pebbles to the sound. Someone coughed a little way behind Isabella and she jumped and gave a small cry.

'Ssh!' Tom whispered, amused. 'It is only a cow in the field beyond.'

Tom's brother, Harry, waited for them by his small fishing boat.

'Come, let us be off,' he said, 'or we will miss the tide and be here till morning.'

Tom lifted Isabella into the boat and told her to sit as the boat swayed. Both men pushed the boat afloat and jumped quickly in and Tom showed Isabella down into the cabin.

'You will be safer in here for we must get the sails up, Isabella, to catch every bit of wind. If you feel unwell, come up on deck immediately, but it is very calm tonight. Look, I have made a bed for you . . . rest.'

He smiled and was gone. Isabella looked out of the hatch; it was a dark and cloudy night and she could not see the stars. It felt strange to be here on the sea in a small boat at night when her household thought she was safe in her room.

She thought of Lisette going upstairs in the morning and finding her note. She knew how afraid and distressed she would be and she wished it could have been otherwise. She had written to Charlotte asking that she take Lisette into her household for Isabella knew that Richard would not keep her and Lisette would not want to stay.

She lay on the bunk that Tom had made and felt warm and suddenly safe. No footsteps or voices could reach them here. It was but a short sail to Truro and Isabella felt her eyes grow heavy with weariness. The motion of the boat was soothing and she knew in a moment she would sleep ...

When Isabella woke it was to the morning sky. Someone had covered her in warm rugs and they were still sailing. She struggled up on her elbow, still half-asleep, and the sky was blocked by Tom coming down to the cabin. He perched on the opposite bunk and smiled down upon her.

'You are like a little cat. I believe you could sleep anywhere.'

His eyes were lazy and loving and she smiled and closed hers against them, felt the colour and the rush of love.

Tom bent and kissed her on the lips. 'How beautiful you are, even when you sleep.'

'How is it that we are still sailing, Tom?' she asked.

'The wind grew perfect in the night. We are headed for Plymouth. It will save us time. Luck is with us, Isabella, my love.'

She looked upon his face. She had a wonderful sense of adventure as if her world had slid suddenly into place.

Isabella went on deck and Harry handed her cold tea which she sipped and did not like. Both men ate a pasty which they wanted to share with her. The sight of them made her queasy and she turned to look at Plymouth appearing pink-washed ahead like a rosy Jerusalem.

They sailed into the harbour on the tide. Harry jumped out as they came to, tied the small boat up to the wooden quay and went to look for the harbourmaster. Tom and Isabella sat watching the comings and goings. Tom seemed uncomfortable.

'I will find a room to rent, Isabella, so that you can wash ... You must tell me what you need ... I know this is not what you are used to and I swear that as soon as we are settled I will make sure you are looked after ...'

'Tom,' she took his hand. 'It is true that a room to wash would be welcome, but please do not worry about me. I hope I am not so spoilt that I cannot adapt to a little hardship. I am with you and that is all that matters.'

Tom held her fingers to his lips and she thought how lucky she was to be loved by him. They saw Harry returning from the harbourmaster's office and he had found somewhere for Isabella to wash and change.

While Isabella was in the guest house, Tom and Harry went to see what ships were there in Plymouth and whether it was possible to obtain a passage across the channel where they could relax a little without looking over their shoulders.

When Tom returned for Isabella they walked along the colourful streets. There were wares of all sorts, and near the docks there were jugglers and an organ grinder with a poor monkey who was tethered and woebegone. There was much noise and cheerfulness about these streets full of sailors.

It was warm but Isabella kept her hood up for Tom could not relax, he was afraid someone in the crowd might glimpse and recognize her. It was a strange and liberating experience for Isabella to cover her head for she could walk anywhere and no one stared at her.

Here she walked in a busy seaport, her hand in Tom's, in the middle of a crowd so varied and dazzling it took her breath away. And she was part of that crowd. She did not have to worry about the colour of her hat or propriety. She could just be. She could just be part of all this and absorb it into her – the noise, the colour and bustle – as she did the sunlight.

'You are very quiet. What are you thinking about, Isabella?' Tom asked her.

'I am thinking how lucky I am to be here with you on a hot autumn day. How good it feels to be invisible.'

Tom smiled. He said, 'You cannot see that people turn after you have passed. Even hidden in a cloak you walk like a beautiful woman. No amount of wrapping will make you ordinary, Isabella, and it is this that worries me. It is impossible for you ever to be invisible.'

'Tom?' she asked, suddenly overcome by nausea. 'Please could

464

we find somewhere to sit so that I might have some bread and tea?'

Tom looked at her alarmed and quickly found a café. He sat her on a bench outside and ordered tea and bread to be brought out to them, as she could not bear the smell of cooking. Harry joined them. He told them there were passages to be had for Calais that night and St Malo the next morning.

Tom made up his mind. 'It is tempting to take a passage out of here tonight, Isabella, but I think it safer we take a train to London.'

That night Tom and Isabella lay side by side on the narrow bed, husband and wife. Mr and Mrs Jarrard. Isabella did not like this deceit. It made her feel instantly unrespectable. But in the dark, her flesh against Tom's once more, all was forgotten in their joy of one another, heightened by the tension in them, for neither of them could quite relax.

Isabella woke in the night and felt unaccountably afraid in the narrow bed, in the clean but ugly room. She missed Lisette like an ache in her side. When she woke again Tom had gone but he had left a note for her.

It was another clear blue day, but the freedom and happiness of yesterday had deserted her and she could not banish the nebulous anxiety which lay heavy on her heart. She longed for Tom to return. She wanted to be away from there on their journey to a new life.

She turned to walk back to the guest house and a man walked past her. He doffed his cap and wished her good morning and she nodded but did not speak. When he had passed her she thought that there was something vaguely familiar about him. She started to make her way back to the house, her heart hammering at her wild imagination. Tom was still not back and she knew now something was wrong.

She went upstairs and began to pack her things into her small valise, to be ready to leave quickly. She folded the bed back neatly and went downstairs to wait in the shabby little downstairs room where the window faced the sea. She took more tea and tried to calm herself. Where was Tom? What could have happened? What would she do if no one returned for her?

Just as she decided she must go out again to look for him, she saw Tom's figure making his way towards the house with another man who was too small to be Harry.

She rushed out of the door and lifted her skirt and began to run to him. She saw suddenly who the other man was and stopped. It was Ben Welland. Tom's face was pale. As he reached her he took her hands without smiling.

'Isabella, my father is come. Your husband has closed the shipyard in St Piran. Every man is laid off and denied work in any other shipyard . . .'

Isabella turned to Ben. 'My father could not prevent him?'

Ben doffed his cap and replaced it carefully on his head. 'No, Miss Isabella, thy father could not prevent it, although he tried. Villagers are still employed in the big house but it is not enough to keep any family alive for long. Miss Isabella, I am come to ask thee and Tom to return before thee both become public knowledge . . . I do not just ask for mysen, there are near three hundred workers laid off and winter is coming. Doest thou and Tom know what thou art doing to gain happiness for thysen? Hast either of thee stopped to think of what trouble and misery thou wilt leave behind?'

Isabella felt dizzy with shock and Tom led her back into the empty little front room.

'How can it make any difference now?' she asked Ben dully. 'Sir Richard will not take me back as his wife. The damage is done. People know.'

But as she said the words she saw that if Richard could not prevent it being common knowledge he could prevent her being with Tom. He could taste revenge.

Ben said quietly, 'Only I know the real reason he has shut the yard. He has made it common knowledge that there is a business rift between him and thy father. There is rumour in the village but not outside it as yet. Sir Richard gave me his word that if I could find thee and if thou return with me he will reopen the shipyard.'

'But Tom is to stay away?'

'Aye, lass.' Ben looked down on her face and Isabella saw pity there. She felt as if a light was going out and all hope of another life fading.

466

'I will leave thee to talk. I cannot force thee; I can only hope that thou both will do what is right and proper.'

When Ben had gone they returned to their room. They could not speak or look upon the other's face, but they held each other tight, rocking, rocking together in a terrible defeat.

They lay upon the bed, still without speaking, for there was nothing to say. There was no place to go. And Isabella believed they loved each other all the more for knowing they could not turn their backs on their own community.

Tom said, with his face in her hair, 'We will have this night together, Isabella. One last night.'

Tom went out to reassure Ben and then they had the dark to hide in, and they lay and talked and talked as close as two people could be, and Isabella's heart broke for Tom's banishment from his home, his family and his work, because of her.

I am almost relieved for the dark, for Isabella's face is so young and wretched and when I think of what she has to return to I have to draw back for the anger will spoil this night if I do not take care. How weak a man Sir Richard is to harm those who have done him no harm, to punish those he cannot control. How vicious to demand love where it is not given.

'It is perverse,' Isabella cries. 'I would not want anyone near me who did not love me, who loved another. I cannot believe Richard does not feel the same. His aim is to prevent us being together, Tom ...'

'Isabella, listen. We will let your husband think it is over between us. I will go and find work and earn as much as I can for our future together. When I am on the other side of the world your husband will relax and your life will be easier. When we are sure that all danger has passed to others and Sir Richard believes all links between us are severed, I will send for you. You will just disappear, with no connection to me. Then your husband will not have an excuse to punish the whole village.'

'Tom, I have some money left in trust to me by my mama. I am not yet twenty-one but I shall ask my father if I might have it early in order to buy a small house somewhere for myself and my baby ...'

467

'It is a good plan,' I say gently. 'I would like that, knowing you were somewhere safe with our child.'

But I believe it unlikely that Sir Richard will allow Isabella her freedom.

'When our child is old enough for a journey by sea, you will join me, with Lisette.'

Isabella sits up holding on to me. 'Tom, Tom, I must know that you mean this. I am sorry to doubt you, but I must know that you are not just saying this to give me comfort.'

'Isabella,' I take those small hands in mine, 'you are the woman I love and you always will be. You carry my child and I believe we will be together one day. I am sure of this.'

'Then I can wait for you to send for me, Tom.'

And then I love her gently because of the child, and Isabella weeps, 'Tom, when I am not with you I feel a terrible loneliness.'

'Soon,' I say, 'you will have my baby, a part of us both, and you will never be lonely again. I will find a place where we can live together and I will build a small house for us, by the sea. We are young and we have our lives before us. We can be strong, even apart we can be strong, can we not, my love?'

'Yes!' Isabella says. 'We will be strong and we will never break trust with one another or have doubts . . .'

'Never. We know our hearts and we understand one another.'

And the night passes and dawn comes swiftly and we rise early to meet my father. Now we must part and it must be quickly done.

I hold Isabella one last time and whisper, 'Do not let your husband hurt you or make you ashamed. Pretend to forget me. We are as one, Isabella, and neither distance nor words can part us. We will live together one day soon and we will die old together. Isabella, I love you with all my heart. Remember it when you are sad.'

I take my poor father's hand and he closes both about mine. I look into his eyes and see loss there, too. I turn quickly and walk down to the harbour. I do not look back but I know they both stand watching me. I dare not look back.

Isabella could remember little of the long, weary journey home with Ben Welland. It felt as if a mist had come down and she was enveloped within it. Ben too looked dispirited and they had few words to say to one another.

Ben, beside her, twisted his cap nervously between his fingers.

'Ben?' Isabella asked suddenly. 'You are afraid that even my return may not reopen the shipyard?'

'I am, my Lady. Every job is dependent on another, lass. Close one thing down and it affects a whole community. In one week the effect has not bitten home, but it will. Sir Richard means business. This is what he is showing thee.'

Isabella turned to him. 'I understand this, Ben. I will do my best, I promise.'

'I know thou will, lass. God go with thee.'

He got out of the trap and Trathan turned and urged the horses back up the hill to the Summer House where Richard waited for her.

'I bought the carver and his family off far more easily than I might have imagined. I suppose I should not have been surprised. For a sum, Welland was only too anxious to sail quickly away from his responsibilities.'

Isabella looked on Richard's face and saw a quite different man to the one she had held as they wept together a week ago.

Eventually, because she did not speak, Richard looked up at her.

'What have you to say?'

'Richard, I am sorry I have hurt you . . .'

'Hurt! You are an adulterer.'

'I have given you the right to say that. I have wronged you. But no one else is responsible. No one in this village has ever done you harm or been disloyal to you. Please do not make innocent people suffer for a wrong I have done you.'

Richard stared at her. 'I believe people in this community have aided you in your affair with the carver. Why should I reopen the shipyard? Why should I give work to people who have deceived me? I can never be sure of their loyalty or that they will not aid and abet you again.'

'The village knows nothing. You know that they do not, Richard, for I understand the reason you have given for stopping all work in the yard is a disagreement with my father. Do you think anyone in the village would aid me at the risk of their livelihood? Only Ben knows the truth. What can they aid me with? You tell me that you have paid Tom off, that he was anxious to be away.'

Richard stood up and looked at Isabella with such loathing in his eyes that she quailed.

'Do not get clever with me, Isabella, or you will be sorry.'

'Richard, you have every right to hate me, therefore it is better that I go from this house and out of your sight ...'

'What you will do is return with me to Botallick House, Isabella. Nothing more will be said of this incident. In public we remain man and wife. The child you carry is mine and a cause for celebration ...' Richard spat this out.

Isabella was shocked. 'You would keep me and my child, hating us both, just to save face, Richard?'

'I will not be made a fool of by one of the lower orders.'

'Then I am a sort of prisoner?'

'If you like. You are my wife. I am your husband.'

'And if I refuse to stay with you?'

'St Piran will remain closed down. You will put St Piran out of work.' Richard smiled. 'The outcome of this shoddy little episode, Isabella, was never in doubt. You should have expected this. Whatever your carver whispered to you, I assure you he could not get away from you fast enough. If you play the slut, Isabella, you get treated as one.'

Isabella sat suddenly on the chair. She deserved these words, but she would never have believed Richard could utter them to her and in such a way. She had never even heard him raise his voice before. Is this what she had done to him? She longed to run from the room and his insidious and poisonous words.

'So?' Richard said, turning his gaze away, for the sight of Isabella frail and with child threatened to undo him. 'Do we understand each other? I am saving your reputation as well as mine.'

'I have no choice but to agree, Richard.'

She did not say, If you had asked me the night you held me and wept. If you had stayed so that we might have talked as friends, my answer might have been so different.

470

But he had threatened and lied and bullied and that could not be undone either.

She said, without hope, 'I will act as your wife. I will do all that you ask, but I must have a place I can go. I must have a place of my own to live in peace until my baby comes.'

Isabella was not acting now. 'I ask this because I have done you a great wrong. Our marriage is not as it was and I cannot live all year with your hate. I cannot socialize at present, I am unwell, and you can explain my absence by my condition. I cannot pretend that nothing has happened and go on as before, whatever you threaten, I cannot do this . . .'

'Isabella, you are in no position to ask for any favours.'

Richard watched her, then he asked before he could stop himself, 'Would you have preferred banishment, Isabella?'

Isabella looked him in the eyes. 'Yes, Richard, I care little for what people think. It would have been more honest than the life you suggest.

'I would like to live here in the Summer House. I grew up in St Piran. Although we have been estranged I am near my father. You need have no fear of Tom Welland because he is gone and that part of my life is over. This is the nearest to going home I can get . . .' Isabella's voice broke.

Richard thought, If she stays here it will kill all gossip about my reasons for closing the yard . . . and I can close the rift with Vyvyan which will ultimately harm my business.

'Very well. I have no particular love of this place, for obvious reasons. For the period of your confinement I am willing to let you stay here. After that, you return as my wife.'

Isabella got up. 'Thank you, Richard. I would like to go and rest if I may.' She walked slowly to the door, closing it softly behind her.

As she left the room, Richard felt vanquished rather than victorious.

How terrible was a love that refused to die.

Chapter 69

Charlie was fuelled for the first few days by a sense of shock, fury and astonishment. Gabby! Of all the people to go off and have an affair! Charlie had trouble accepting or believing it. Anger catapulted him out of bed in the morning and lured him to the whisky bottle in the evening. His workers learnt to keep out of his way.

There was talk in the village and once when Charlie walked into the pub there was a sudden embarrassed silence and he knew they had been talking about him, for it was followed by hearty offers of a drink and cries of, 'Good to see you, boy.'

After that, Charlie took to drinking alone in his kitchen, growing more morose and maudlin. OK, so she had changed since she started work in London; she'd bought different, smarter clothes, had her hair cut. But she had seemed happy enough to come home . . . and all the time she was planning to leave him. *The bitch*.

He thought of all the times his mates in the pub had joked, 'Your Gabby off to London, then? You'd better watch it, you'll lose 'er, boy.'

And if he'd thought about it at all, it had been, '*What, Gabby!*' Gabby was Gabby, always had been. Part of the furniture. As familiar and comfortable as an old shoe. He shook Nell's voice out of his head.

He went over the terrible week when Josh was captured. Remembered how Gabby had turned to him and his heart had wrenched at her smallness, at her fear and her grief. He had thought, with a jerk of fear, that if anything happened to Josh it would be the end of Gabby. He had felt . . . protective, near to love, nearer to it than he had ever felt.

Then the strange week of the eclipse and the . . . thing that had happened on the beach together. They had both seemed like other people. Not themselves. It had felt as if he was watching himself trying to stop the terrible racking sobbing that seemed to be more, somehow, than fear for Josh, but something extreme that had been waiting inside her to erupt at a certain trigger. He hadn't thought about it straight afterwards, only in the weeks after she had gone back to London. Sometimes he would take the memory out, unsure if it had really happened, that raw, rough sex on the beach. It had been like doing it with someone else; Gabby had never been that keen on sex.

The bit that was painful then, and stabbed at him now, were the moments afterwards. *Something in her had wanted or needed something he did not want to give.* He didn't want anything to change. He was as embarrassed by that sudden passionate coupling in the open as if he had shagged a stranger. He had no idea why he felt that instinctive need to draw away and distance her, to turn abruptly from something he saw in her eyes that scared him to death with its emotional pull. Charlie watched that small lightness of spirit die in her eyes almost before it began. He knew, in the small hours of the morning when truth rushed in whether you wanted it or not, he had rejected an opening, an offer, a chance to move on.

Something in him hated to get too close. Couldn't bear it . . . Couldn't do it. Women sucked you dry with their words and their analysing.

He had thought that the marriage he and Gabby had worked. She wasn't the emotional sort. She didn't lose her temper or throw things. She didn't argue like Nell and she did her share in the house and round the farm. She was just beginning to bring in good money too. She had everything. Why had she done this? Coldly, planning to leave him, Nell and Cornwall? All for what? Some old lecherous American. Josh would be devastated. It would be like a bolt out of the blue for him too.

At this his self-righteous fury would start up all over again. He felt duped, tricked, a mug.

Nell came into the kitchen and said severely one evening, 'Charlie, this drinking binge has got to stop. You can't drink spirits like you're doing and get up at dawn. You've got to get a grip. I know it's a shock, but have some pride. It's not fair on any of the workers. You'll lose their respect.'

'She had everything, Nell. Why did she throw it away?'

'Because, Charlie, someone fell in love with her and she with them.'

'Blah!' said Charlie. 'Love!' He tried to click his fingers and failed. 'I give you that for love.'

'I know you do, perhaps that was the problem.'

'What do you mean?'

'Charlie, have you ever been in love, really loved any woman? Think about it.'

'I had a wife, didn't I? Much good it's done me.'

'She was a wonderful little wife. You just forgot to notice. Come on, let's get you to bed. I mean it. I'll leave too, if you don't stop drinking.'

'Bloody ol' sinking ship,' Charlie said blearily, staggering to his feet.

Having got him upstairs to bed, with difficulty, and taken his shoes off, Nell said suddenly, 'Charlie, did you ever love Gabby?'

'I married her, didn't I?'

'It's not what I asked.'

Charlie closed his eyes to stop the room going round. Then he said quietly, 'I don't know. She's my wife and Josh's mother. We were all right.' He tried to grin at Nell. 'I'm like my father. I don't go in for grand passion.'

Nell sat on the bed. 'Charlie, you never wavered when Gabby got pregnant, not one minute's hesitation, so you must have felt *something*. You seemed fond of one another, especially when Josh was small, and you were a wonderful father. And yes, I think your marriage did work. But to think of you going through life without ever truly loving a woman makes me sad. Maybe, although it can't possibly seem like that now, it will turn out to be the right thing for both of you.'

'Like fuck it is,' Charlie said. 'I wish her in . . .'

'Goodnight Charlie,' Nell said. 'This drinking is doing you no good at all. You and Gabby are going to have to talk before Josh gets home.'

She heard Charlie snoring before she reached the bottom of the stairs.

When Gabby reached the back door she suddenly, bizarrely wondered whether she should knock. Then she took a deep breath and the heavy latch clicked under her fingers.

Charlie was leaning against the Aga reading the paper. He did not look up.

'Charlie?' Gabby said, standing awkwardly.

Charlie folded his paper and looked at her, avoiding her eyes. He had not expected her to look so . . . bloody awful.

'Pleased with yourself, are you?'

'Of course I'm not.'

He skimmed the paper across the room and it landed on the table.

'You've broken up this family. For what? For bloody what?'

Gabby did not answer.

'I suppose you are going to come out with all the trite, fucking rubbish about not being able to help yourself, and that it just happened.'

He was working himself up into righteous anger and Gabby knew it had to run its course.

'Well? Are you just going to stand there saying bugger all?'

'What can I say except I'm sorry if I've hurt you, Charlie?'

'What do you mean, *if* you've hurt me? My bloody wife

shacks up with a bloody American for months and then says "*sorry if I've hurt you*".'

Charlie mimicked a silly girlie voice and this triggered something in Gabby.

'I'm unsure how exactly I was meant to know you cared a fig whose bed I was in.'

'What the hell is that supposed to mean?'

'It means, Charlie, I've never known how you felt about me.'

'Balls! Any second you are going to say it was my fault.'

'No, I'm not.' Gabby turned and switched the kettle on. Her mouth was dry. 'I'm not going to make any excuses, there are none. I fell in love with someone. Of course I felt guilty, of course I didn't want to hurt you or Nell or Josh. What I'm saying is I honestly don't think it is your heart that is wounded but your pride. Charlie, be honest with yourself and with me. I believe you were fond of me, but you have never loved me, been *in love* with me. You did the honourable thing. If it had not been for Josh we would never have got married. You know this and I know it.'

'We've been together for twenty-four years, for God's sake.'

'Yes, we have.'

'So what are you saying, Gabby? That for all those years you've been unhappy?'

'Of course I'm not. You know I'm not. I've never been unhappy with you. I've had a good and happy life with . . .'

'So why chuck it away?'

Gabby closed her eyes and swallowed the loss of it all. She said quietly, 'I met someone who loved me, who was interested in me and my work . . .' Her voice trembled, 'Who thought I was clever and fun and beautiful and I realized what it felt like, to be really loved.'

She opened her eyes and looked at Charlie. 'Fondness is enough, I think, until you know the difference.'

Charlie met her eyes and Gabby held them. 'That day, after Josh was rescued, I . . . thought . . . for a minute it might be OK for us. There might be a way forward. We got close to love, I think, when he was threatened. But it's hard, Charlie, and you couldn't make the leap . . . and I understood, truly . . . that the moment had passed for us.'

Gabby was looking at him and the tears were trickling down her cheeks. Charlie felt the tears suddenly behind his eyes, in the back of his throat, and was appalled. He had let the moment pass and *he knew it*, had known it at the time, but had been unable to summon the emotional wherewithal to cope with what it meant.

He dropped his eyes, dug deep for resentment. 'You have no right to break up this family. We were all right. You've broken up this family for bloody nothing. What do you think Josh is going to feel? You know he's due home in a week or ten days?'

Gabby turned and poured water over a teabag. 'Yes, I know he is.'

Elan had had an e-mail. She knew there would be an e-mail on her computer too.

'Do you want a coffee?'

'No.' Charlie dived for the fridge. 'I'll have a beer.'

'Josh is going to be upset. But he is an adult with his own life now, Charlie.'

'Adult or not, who would like to find out their mother has been living a double life, shacked up with another man?'

Gabby hugged the mug of tea between her hands. She looked at him. Dark, slightly heavy, good looks. Hair that needed a cut and flopped over one eye. At that moment, sulky mouth and eyes full of resentment.

'Forget Josh, just for a moment. What about you?'

'What do you mean?'

'How exactly do you feel?'

'What a fucking stupid question.'.

'Is it? In what ways do you miss me?'

'You're my bloody wife.'

Gabby waited and Charlie banged his beer down. 'I'm not

going to stand here and play silly buggers with you.'

'You can't answer me, Charlie.'

Charlie suddenly with violence threw the beer bottle across the room where it shattered in a corner. Gabby jumped.

'OK. OK. You want the truth, do you? How fucking dare you decide to break up our marriage when I married you, married you because you were pregnant. You had nothing. You were nothing and I gave you everything. You were a pathetic little runaway. You've had a home and a family and financial security. I've been bloody good to you . . . so has Nell . . .'

He stopped. Gabby's face seemed to shrink. Her eyes were huge as she listened to him in shock. Nell had come in the scullery door and was taking her boots off when Charlie's beer bottle hit the corner of the kitchen wall. She stood frozen, unable to believe Charlie's words.

Gabby gripped the edge of the work surface. *So this is how he feels. This is how he has always felt. Here it is out in the open at last.*

'Yes, I was grateful to Nell for taking me in, I loved her from the very first moment. I was happy here, but I would have been grateful to anyone or for anything in the beginning.

'My mother used to bring drunken men back from the pub or the club. They used to come to my room, so I slept in the bathroom with the door locked, but one broke the door down . . . I was fifteen. My mother did not believe me. Then I came daffodil picking and Nell looked after me, and then you came home and you were Nell and Ted's son so I trusted you, thought you must be safe. But you did exactly the same as the man did to me in the bathroom, so I knew it must be *me*, I was a bad person who asked for it.

'You said you were drunk and you were sorry and you married me, and I was grateful all over again. I tried to be everything a wife should be and I used to pretend you loved me and we were fine and it was fine, all the time, except in bed. You take. You don't love. You take without a word.

478

Never a word. I have lived with you for twenty-four years and you have never spoken a word of love. It has always felt like rape, not by a stranger, but by someone I know well.

'You are angry because I was going to leave you for someone who loved me beyond anything. He's gone, but I will never ever regret knowing what love is. Real, painful, truthful love and respect for what I am. *What I am*.

'I'm glad you said what you said, Charlie, because we both know the truth of it now. I'm sad for you, sad, because you don't know what love is and that is a tragedy . . . I may have come from nothing, but I have loved you and Josh and Nell as much as I ever can . . .'

Gabby moved slowly out of the room and pulled herself up the stairs. She lay carefully on Josh's bed. She felt as if she might break in half. She would go as soon as she got her strength back.

Charlie was horrified at his words, that had come spouting and pouring venomously out into the light of day. Why did he say what he had never consciously thought? What had he just done?

He jumped as Nell came slowly into the room. She was white and shocked and looked at him as if he was a stranger. Charlie knew she must have heard. He moved for the door without speaking.

Nell said, 'Remember as you go about your work, the words that you have just used to the mother of your son. You think Gabby broke up this marriage. Take a long look at yourself, Charlie. You wonder what Josh will think about Gabby leaving. I wonder what Josh would think if he could have heard what you have just said. I thank God he didn't. Gabby owes us nothing. We owe her everything. She has given everything of herself she had to give. She has given me more happiness and friendship than I had a right to. Every single day of the last twenty-four years I have given thanks that she walked down the lane of *our* farm. I have never told her, but I'm going to tell her now.'

Nell made for the stairs. 'I don't think the puzzle is that

Gabby is leaving you after twenty-odd years, but how she stayed so long. Charlie, have you ever taken responsibility for the wicked and dishonourable thing you did? Did you think by marrying Gabby it absolved you from any acceptance or memory of it?'

Charlie was silent. He walked to the door, crossed the yard and hoisted himself into his Land Rover, then rattled down the lane towards the pheasant pens. Words could never be unsaid. You could never backtrack and press erase. He saw her face again. Those shocked eyes. He swallowed hard and wiped at his eyes with his hand. Fuck. Fuck. Fuck.

Nell sat heavily on Josh's bed. Gabby was still breathing very hard, harsh little breaths. Nell did not say a word. She picked up Gabby's hand and placed it firmly between her own and held it there. Gabby's eyes were focused somewhere bleak and cold and unimaginable. A place that a Canadian had been able to banish altogether. Nell was afraid suddenly for this beloved girl who determinedly and bravely put it all behind her. Who tried so hard to be the perfect wife and mother. Charlie had just tried to wipe it all away in a second.

Nell cried softly, hardly knowing she did so, and Gabby looked up, came back from the place she'd been and touched Nell's face.

'Nell, don't cry. Oh, don't cry. I'm all right. Really, I'm all right.'

Chapter 70

Elan said one morning, 'Gabby, darling, I think we must start to be a little practical. It's been worrying me. You still have things in Mark's London house. I think we ought to go and get them. It's possible you have no legal right to be there. Did he own the house?'

'He rented it from an English aunt but she died at the beginning of the year and left it to him. Elan, I was going to go back there for a while. I know you must have had enough of me . . .'

'Put that thought out of your head, Gabby. I just think if Mark's family turned up . . .'

'They won't, Elan. They didn't know about the London house. Mark wanted peace and a place to work, uninterrupted.'

'All the same, I do think you should be aware that when his affairs are wound up, the house will come into it. I expect he has an English solicitor who will be involved in the disposal of it.'

Gabby stared at him, aghast. *Soon I will not even have the space we occupied. Mark has a wife and family and solicitors and wills and paperwork to be dealt with, and a funeral I knew nothing about and a place to rest I will never see.*

'I'm sorry, child. I know I'm being horribly realistic.'

Gabby thought of Mark's message on the answer-phone, their personal things, his desk, hers. The sheets were still on the bed. His clothes still lay in the drawers and wardrobe.

481

She was not ready to dismantle that life they shared. *She was not ready.*

'I will go up. I will remove my personal things. But not yet, Elan.'

'I'll drive you up when you feel ready,' Elan said, unwilling to let the business with the house go. *Bad enough your husband dying suddenly without finding out he had an English mistress.*

'Gabs, forgive me nagging, but . . . I think you should go and see Nell and Charlie. You owe it to them, don't you think?'

He watched Gabby grow even paler. 'I've been. I saw Charlie. It was awful, Elan.'

'Child, I'm sorry. What about Nell?'

'Nell is . . . Nell. Not a word of condemnation, but, oh, she is so sad . . .'

Gabby looked out at the cold winter sea. 'It's bloody, hurting people when you can't make it all right. Elan, both Mark and I were not leaving our families easily or without regret, we were leaving because we loved each other so much we could not live without each other . . .'

'I know, child. I know.'

Elan watched the tears collect and roll silently down her cheeks. She was so broken and he could do nothing but watch and be practical. Throughout her married life he had looked on while she had waited on Charlie, spoilt Josh, and worried and cared for Nell. All her life she had been the biddable, self-effacing wife, fitting in with everyone else, trying not to take up too much space in their world. A world she had been allowed to enter with such evident relief.

'Have you thought at all about what you might do, Gabby?' he asked gently.

'Only that I will go back to London. Lucinda wrote to me. There is work if I want it.'

'That's good. You know you can use my London flat for as long as you like. Now I wouldn't offer that to everyone!'

Gabby gave him a watery smile and got up from the table. She knew she must be depressing to live with.

'Thanks, Elan. I'm going to walk into St Piran. John has something to show me.'

'Is it to do with your figurehead?'

'I think so. He wouldn't tell me over the phone.'

'You can take my car, darling.'

'Thanks, Elan, but Shadow and I will walk, won't we, girl?'

Gabby bent and pulled the dog's long ears and looked into her intelligent face.

'Come on, I'm not going to leave you. We'll walk together. A good long walk.'

Elan smiled. Clever Nell.

John led the way into his study where stacks of books, papers and bound documents made the going treacherous.

'I will start from the beginning, Gabrielle. There has been an ongoing dispute between the Church Commission and the county council for months about an area of land just beyond the bottom of the vicarage garden. You can see it from this window, an almost perfect semicircle. The Church Commission insist the land was bought with the house and has been consecrated at some point. The council are equally insistent it is common ground and want to build on that field and the one behind it.

'We . . . the church, that is, have earmarked it for a further graveyard and are fighting them. This has meant going through all the old deeds relating to the house . . .' he swept his arms over his study floor, '. . . which my solicitor held, because, Gabrielle, I bought the vicarage from the Church in 1991 when my parents died and left me a little money . . .

'My dear girl, some of these documents make fascinating reading. It is all here because one family, the Magors, Gabrielle, *the Magors*, kept it for generations as a holiday home and handed it down. It has been neglected and modernized, bits pulled down, rooms put up . . . But that isn't all . . . Come over to my desk. Look what I unexpectedly found . . .'

John was hardly pausing for breath and his excitement was catching.

'Isabella Magor bought this house from her husband Richard Magor in 1867! I looked up the census for that year and *Isabella was in this house!*'

Gabby stared at John. 'You're joking?'

'No, I'm not! She left it to her son, Thomas Magor. Look at the brackets, Gabrielle.'

There it was: *(Thomas Magor, later known as Thomas Welland for the purpose of this document.)*

Gabby looked down at the document in astonishment. She heard Mark's voice. *There is a little trail and sometimes, if you are lucky, it all comes together, all the threads begin to tie up to give us a glimpse of a life.*

As if he knew what she was thinking, John Bradbury said, 'Wouldn't Mark have loved this clue sitting here under our very noses?'

'Oh, he would have been so thrilled. Look, John, in Isabella's day it was called the Summer House.'

Isabella's Summer House. Was this where she ran? Was this her refuge?

'Is there more, John?'

'Not yet. But it should all be here, somewhere, who the house was handed down to. The records are not in order, though, so it is a time-consuming job. I'm hoping we can find out when she died and when the deeds were made over to her son. Then we might find where she is buried. All the documents relating to the house seem to have been kept. Peter is helping me to go through them and I wondered if you might be interested in helping me too, Gabrielle? It is sad Mark is not here, my dear girl . . .'

Gabby swallowed and said quickly, 'John, this is so strange . . . Of course I'll help. I'd love to.' Here was something to do, something to hold on to, part of the life they shared.

'Come with me, there is something else I want to show you.'

John led the way outside and round the house towards the stables.

'It was turned into a vicarage just after the war. Thomas Magor's descendants must have sold it to the church. There are many additions. Once it was a square little Cornish teapot house. This small wing was for servants I suppose. I turned it into a little cottage flat and I rent it for sixpence to clergy and those too poor to afford a holiday. I wondered, if it is not an imposition, whether you would like to stay while you help me go through all the deeds?'

Gabby stared at the little stone-walled house with Virginia creeper climbing over the sides and up the roof. It faced south into a cobbled courtyard and Gabby suddenly felt strange, as if she had seen the house somewhere before.

'Would you like to see inside?' John asked, and his voice seemed to come from a long way away.

'I'd love to.'

Inside, John had modernized it beautifully. A small ground-floor flat with a wood-burning stove, light curtains and polished floors. There were pictures on the walls and ornaments dotted around. It did not look like a rented place, but a home someone had just walked out of. She could feel the age of the place, the stillness, as if the air had stopped moving and the house waited in a silence that seemed to wrap itself around her.

'I'd love to stay here. I'd love to.' She was unable to hide her excitement. 'It's a beautiful little cottage, John.'

'Well, I thought, why shouldn't the poor have lovely things around? So far no one has trashed this place, just loved being in it for a while.'

Shadow had refused to go into the house and stood at the door, growling under her breath.

'Don't be silly, Shadow,' Gabby said. 'John, would Shadow be able to come with me, or is that too much to ask?'

John stroked the dog. 'Ordinarily I don't allow dogs. But

I know Shadow is impeccably behaved, aren't you, girl? So yes, Gabby. Come whenever you like. If you need a lift with your things – I know you haven't a car – just ring me.'

'John, you're being very kind, thank you.' Gabby smiled wryly. 'You'll be helping Elan out. I know I've been gloomy company.'

'My dear girl . . . we are your friends. How about letting us be just that while you heal?'

Gabby was touched. 'Thank you.'

'Forgive me, it is too soon to say this, I know. But do you think there is any chance of salvaging your marriage? I've known you both for such a long time. Sometimes long relationships need a wake-up call.'

'No, John, I'm afraid not. I fell in love with someone else.'

Gabby left the vicarage and crossed the road and walked straight up the cliff path. She stopped for a minute and looked to her left down at St Piran's quay and the ruins of the old shipyards which now housed speedboats, yachts under repair and a small chandlery and car park. Some little shops dotted the quay, selling touristy beach ware and fishing nets. All shut now the season had ended.

She turned to walk back to Elan along the coastal path. In winter the coves and harbour on this coast were particularly dangerous; huge waves crashed over the quay and the road leading to it. Visitors were warned not to walk along the quay at high tide and Gabby knew it had been the scene of a few suicides.

She looked down at a rough sea rolling in on huge waves and crashing against the rocks with a sound like thunder. It made her feel small and insignificant.

I can wallow or I can go forward.

Mark is dead. He is dead and the life she had envisaged had vanished. She would never get over his death, but she could live the working life she would have led with him. Leaving *this*, Cornwall, her friends, for a life in London made her quail, but she knew it had to be done. For Charlie and for herself.

Both Lucinda and Elan had offered her a base from which to start. Gabby trembled as she looked out on a familiar landscape that had been the greater part of her life. Suddenly, she could not think beyond the terror of the bleak reality of London alone without Mark. A whole long life without him.

Her brief spark of optimism faded. She walked fast, her face up to the wind, salt and gusty, grabbing her breath as she hurried.

Elan smiled at her excitement about Isabella and was relieved. Good, John had given Gabby something else to think about. He looked down at her gaunt little face. Thought how bleak and lonely the future must look to her.

'Take small steps and don't look too far ahead, darling. Nell and I will always be here,' he said gently. 'Stay at the vicarage for a while. Do your research. It connects you to Mark, doesn't it? Little clues to something he started.'

Gabby went to hug him and he felt the thinness of her small bones.

'You always know the right thing to say, Elan.'

The following day, Gabby and Shadow drove with Elan and the minimum of possessions and moved into the Summer House. A tiny place of her own. To be still for a while, to heal. A place where Isabella once lived.

Chapter 71

The sparrows woke Isabella each morning. They came to catch the small flies under the eaves. She lay and watched them as they noisily bobbed about the window. They were so busy and cheerful they made her smile.

She had chosen the little room Lisette used as a sewing room to have her baby. She had noticed how private and warm it was, for the pale winter sun entered the windows which looked out on the courtyard and the unused stables beyond.

Isabella had had a cough for weeks. It was partly to do with the weather, for as soon as they moved here the mists descended. The damp penetrated all and the vicious winds chapped her face and froze her hands. She had forgotten how Godforsaken and bitter a winter could be.

Isabella's contentment lay in the knowledge that winter would not last. Spring would come and with it, God willing, her baby. The mists would lift and the months pass to the day when Tom would send for her and their child and they would sail for their new life together. She would be warm again and the damp would cease to penetrate her bones.

Daniel Vyvyan began to visit her, with Charlotte at first and then he occasionally rode over on his own when he had business with Ben Welland. It was hard for them both to begin with. Isabella had hung on to bitterness and hurt for so long, and Daniel had had so little to do with Isabella as an adult that he hardly knew what to say to her. But each time it grew easier.

Isabella saw how old he was getting. His thin shoulders protruded from his jacket and she felt the stab of tenderness she used sometimes to feel as a child. He sent food from the house and fruit. He made sure she always had logs for the fire and worried about her constant cough. Isabella began to learn there were many ways of loving for those who found words difficult.

Every evening she wrote letters to Tom in her old journal. She knew one day in spring the packet boat would bring news from him and she could send this record of her days in return.

Richard came infrequently and only for form's sake, for people would find it strange if he never visited his wife. He combined it with business in St Piran. They were polite and distant with one another. The anger seemed to have gone from him, leaving a space that was neither cold nor warm but contained nothing.

She had stolen his cheerful, innocent bluffness and there was nothing to replace it. The pain and regret she felt was real. She had to live with the knowledge that she had destroyed the happiness of another human being for the sake of her own.

He had told his friends and family that Isabella was having a difficult time and had been consigned to bed rest. Of course there was gossip. Why would Isabella leave the comforts of her home in Mylor and the softer south coast of Falmouth for St Piran? The word, Lisette told her, was that Richard was humouring her because her spirits were low and she wanted to be near her father.

How odd that it turned out to be true.

Her little household consisted of Lisette, a cook and two maids and a gardener who came three times a week. This is what Isabella could afford and each week she and Lisette checked the books to ensure they lived within their means.

This new way of living gave Isabella much satisfaction and helped her to make decisions. Although she was poor by her father's and Richard's standards, she did not feel poor. Lisette told her that by the standards of the village she was very well-to-do.

At first the people of St Piran were wary of her and the trouble she might bring with her. Lisette explained that you could never stop rumours in a village. What the gentry did not know, servants always would.

The villagers who had waved at Isabella all summer often now turned so that they need not pass her. These were Isabella's lowest moments on her arrival at the Summer House. Lisette said she must be patient and that when they saw that her father visited her they would stop being anxious about what Richard might do. Tom seemed so far away from her some days, that despite her dear Lisette Isabella felt a loneliness that was overpowering.

One evening Cook sent Lisette to tell her that Ben Welland was at the kitchen door. Isabella's heart leapt thinking that it might be a word from Tom. But Ben Welland had come to ask her help. His daughter Ada's baby was very sick and he wondered if she had her mother's gift with the herbs. He remembered that Helena used lavender and herbs to make compresses; he had once seen a child's fever banished this way.

'Have you sent for the doctor?' Isabella asked as they hurried down the hill.

Ben did not answer and Isabella realized all of a sudden that they could not afford one.

As soon as she bent over the baby and heard her cough she knew the poor child had the croup. Instantly, she knew what to do, for she had seen and heard this cough many times on her rounds with Helena.

She turned to Ada. 'Put kettles on the stove, I need a good head of steam.'

Ben turned immediately and went downstairs. Isabella went to the window in the airless room.

'This window must be opened, Ada, during the day, both top and bottom casement, so fresh air can circulate into the room.'

'No,' Ada cried. 'It is too cold, my baby will die.'

Lisette picked up the baby who was fighting for breath and said sharply, 'Ada, do as Lady Isabella tells you. There is no air in this room. Your child cannot breathe. How many of you sleep in here?'

Ada said, 'My husband, the two lads, the baby and me.'

Isabella looked at the walls. They were not running with water, but crystal beads stood out, a sure sign of damp. Five people in one tiny, fetid room.

'Who owns this cottage?' she asked.

Ada's husband looked at his feet.

'My father?'

'Yes, M'lady.'

'And when was Mr Rowe, his agent, last round?'

Again they did not answer.

They took the baby down into the kitchen and had her cot brought downstairs. Lisette laid her across her knee near the steam and Isabella applied compresses to the tiny forehead and bathed her thin limbs with lavender water. Then they sat, listening to the terrible croaking sounds that racked her small body until slowly they became easier as the steam worked on her lungs. Finally the rasping noise grew fainter and then ceased altogether as the baby slept.

They laid her in her cot, as near to the constant steam of the kettle as possible. Ada's pinched, tired face relaxed into something near a smile.

'Keep her warm and down here with the steam tonight,' Isabella told her. 'Then in the morning your baby should see the doctor.'

They left the house and Ben walked up the hill with them. Lisette said, 'They will not get the doctor, will they, Ben?'

Ben shook his head. 'Mines are closing. They have no money for the doctor, but I will see what I can do.'

'Mr Welland,' Isabella said carefully, for she knew he was proud. 'Will you go for the doctor in the morning and ask for the bill to be sent to the Summer House. Please do this. I am not a doctor and the baby needs medicine.'

Ben Welland turned to look at her and then said slowly, 'Aye. I thank thee, M'lady. I would not accept for mysen but I will for the child.'

'Good.' Isabella smiled. 'Goodnight, Mr Welland.'

'Goodnight, Miss Isabella. God go with thee.' His faded blue eyes met hers. 'Thou art so like thy mother.' And he was gone back down the hill.

The village began to come to her when they were sick or needed help. Sometimes Isabella could help them and sometimes she could do nothing but soothe them with her herbs.

Her father had been mortified about the state of his cottages.

He rode down to see Ada's house and arranged for the work to be done himself.

People no longer avoided Isabella and she felt warmer for their smiles and their greetings. She was now in her eighth month and Lisette would no longer allow her to walk into the village or let people come to the door. Isabella grew weary quickly and rested each afternoon in her room. Lisette would sit by the fire with her and sew, and Isabella would sleep a little for the movement of her child kept her awake at night.

When she was by herself, watching the firelight play across the walls, in the melancholy time when it was neither afternoon nor quite evening, she would sob with this loneliness and fear that she might always be alone. She felt she had lost her husband, who had once loved her, and she had lost Tom whom she loved beyond everything.

She would look around the room to where her carved chest of drawers stood in an archway that had once been a door. The light played over the small animals Tom had carved and she took comfort from seeing it there, knowing Tom's fingers carved every piece.

Resting on the chest was a small mirror with drawers and the sketch Tom had made of Isabella for the figurehead. Above, on the wall, hung her favourite painting of Helena in a red dress. Her father had brought it over one day and she knew how precious it was to him. She had wrapped her arms around him for a moment in gratitude and he bent quickly and kissed the top of her head.

'You grow so like her, daughter. So very like her.'

One day Ben Welland knocked on the outside door of the courtyard. Isabella struggled to get out of her chair and Lisette said sharply, 'Miss Isabella, stay exactly where you are.'

Ben came in carrying a wooden crib and placed it before her. It was made of light wood and was on rockers. The edging all round was carved with small acorns and the wood was so polished she could almost see her face in it. Inside there were layers of tiny crocheted covers in white, and a tiny lace pillow.

Isabella stared at it, reached out to touch it. She could not speak. The tears rolled down her cheeks and she could not even thank him.

He stood awkwardly and said, smiling, 'My carving is not up to my son's, M'lady. The crib and the covers are from the village, from us all, to thank thee.'

Isabella found her voice. 'Thank you, Mr Welland, it is beautiful. I love it. Thank you so very much ... it is very kind of you. I am so touched.'

She turned to Lisette, for she wanted to talk to Mr Welland alone.

'Lisette, would you ask Cook to make tea for Mr Welland?'

Lisette went reluctantly, and before Isabella could speak Ben Welland went to the crib and from under the covers took out three letters and handed them to Isabella. She clapped her hands to her mouth in surprise. She had waited so long she felt almost faint.

'The packet boat is in from Southampton. Tom's brother brought them to me. He disembarked at Falmouth last night and came over this morning.'

Isabella clutched the letters to her, longing to be alone to read them.

'Did you have word too? Is Tom well, Ben?'

'Tom is well. He asks about thee. He worries about thee and thy condition.'

'Can I give you letters for Tom, Mr Welland? Will they go back on the packet?'

'I will give them to my younger son, Jacob, Miss Isabella. He is going back to join Tom in Prince Edward Island. Have you letters ready?'

'Yes.' Isabella struggled up and went to the top drawer of her chest. She took out all her letters, dated and in envelopes. She sat to finish the last one with a flourish, to tell Tom of his father's kindness with the crib and that she held his letters to her heart to read when she was alone. She placed them in a bag with Tom's name on and gave them to Ben.

'God willing they reach Tom,' she whispered, and Ben repeated, 'God willing, Miss Isabella.'

Isabella looked again at the crib. 'Mr Welland, it is easy to see that Tom learnt his craft from you. You build ships because that is your training. I have no doubt in a different life you too would have carved the most beautiful figureheads.'

Ben Welland's face crinkled and he gave a wheeze which Isabella believed to be a laugh. He bent suddenly and pointed with his finger at the carving at the foot of the crib. Isabella looked down and for a moment she could not see what he was pointing out. Then she made out, between two little acorns, the letters I and T.

Isabella and Tom.

Ben looked her straight in the eye. 'Look on't when thou art sad, lass.'

And he was gone, leaving her in the firelight with Tom's letters.

Chapter 72

When Gabby got to John's little cottage flat she found he had laid a fire for her and put all the basics in the fridge and cupboards, placed flowers on the table with a note propped up against them:

'*My Dear Gabby, Welcome! I am so sorry I have to be out tonight, I would have loved to have given you supper. God bless and sleep well.*'

Gabby was touched and moved around unpacking and placing the few things she had brought with her around the room. It was easier putting distance between her and the farm. She lit the fire, switched the lamps on, drew the curtains against the nights which were drawing in, filled the space, poured wine, and tried not to think. *All these things Mark and I did when we got home, that precious little wind-down at the end of a long London day.*

Shadow padded about, unable to sit still, and Gabby wondered if she had been away too often and too long and Shadow needed to be at the farm with Nell.

She sat by the fire and pulled out one of the three files John had left on the table. She started with the documents, which were sparse, from 1868 onwards, but John was right; at some point they had been muddled and randomly filed. Gabby laid them all on the floor so she could make some order and started to make little piles relating to the varying dates of the documents.

John had established that Isabella had left Summer House to her son Thomas. It seemed when Thomas had changed his name suddenly to Welland in 1884 the solicitors had continued to call him Magor, with Welland in brackets, presumably for legal reasons.

Summer House had stayed in the Magor family until after the Second World War, but Gabby was unsure who Thomas's grandchildren, his direct descendants, were in the numerous names that cropped up. A huge extended Cornish family, cousins perhaps, who used the house as a holiday home?

None of the family seemed to have lived in it permanently and it had been rented out to various tenants since 1914. There were letters from these tenants complaining of the repair of the house and replies from the solicitor or agent filed with them.

What was apparent was that many of the male Magors seemed to have emigrated or gone to work in Prince Edward Island long after it ceased to be a British colony. Presumably they still had business interests there for many stayed and became Canadian citizens, as the letters showed, but they had kept Summer House in the family.

Gabby tidied the papers away and went to the next file. There seemed nothing of interest, sheaves of plans for various improvements to the house. Letters from the War Office to the Church Commission . . . Then, suddenly, there was a deed of will. Gabby's heart gave a jerk. Richard Magor had left Isabella's son, Thomas Magor (Welland), Botallick House, Mylor, in the parish of Falmouth, with the proviso that his second wife Sophie Magor live in it for her lifetime. There were no children of this marriage it seemed.

Presumably after Richard's death this second wife Sophie remarried and moved to London, for there was a document relating to the change of her name, objects she was taking with her to London, and a draft signed by her relinquishing all claims to live in Botallick House.

There were no documents to say who Thomas married, for all the documents in the files related directly or indirectly, through the solicitors, to matters to do with the Summer House and various other properties.

Gabby was turning the dry, faded pages of title deeds, plans for additions to the house, maps and surveys relating to old mine workings, when she came across further deeds of the Summer House. Thomas Magor (Welland) left the Summer House jointly to a David Thomas Welland and a Charles Richard Magor (Welland). His two sons? They both owned the house jointly in 1902. So Isabella's son died young, at about . . . thirty-five?

Gabby kept turning the documents. In 1903, Charles Magor, one of the sons, paid a considerable sum to his brother David and took over Botallick House. David became the sole owner of Summer House. There was still no mention of Thomas's wife, their mother, and Gabby wondered if she might have died young too.

In 1939, Summer House had been requisitioned due to its proximity to the harbour and its long view over the bay and beyond. After the Second World War it stood empty and then was sold off to the Church and renamed The Vicarage. Summer House no longer existed.

Just as Gabby was putting the file away a flimsy piece of paper fell out and Gabby saw part of a letter clipped to a deed.

. . . grateful if you could ascertain his whereabouts for us. My husband is now unwell, so if you could kindly forward this letter to him in the hope it will reach him when he returns from sea. The last we heard he was with a whaling ship in Newfoundland, but it is possible he has moved on. There is some urgency in this due to my husband's age and infirmity. As you know there has been a rift for some years between Sir Richard and his son which has upset my husband greatly, and he wishes to heal this rift between them before he dies.

I have heard rumour that Thomas changed his name by deed poll from Magor to Welland. I pray that

*this is not true, Mr Bray, for it will injure Sir Richard
grievously . . .*

That was all. Clipped to it was a terse note in another hand.
'*Return to British solicitors Bray and Houseman. Magor's
whereabouts unknown.*' And then, '*(Keep with deeds of
Summer House.)*'

Mark was right. Research was sifting and sifting, slowly
and painstakingly, for long and boring hours sometimes,
because it was so easy to miss something. Presumably, Sir
Richard Magor and his adopted son *were* reunited, for
Richard left him Botallick House. Odd, very odd, too,
that Richard allowed Isabella's son to be called Thomas. And
had one of Richard Magor's grandchildren taken back the
name Magor in order to inherit Botallick House?

What on earth had happened to Isabella? If she had died in
childbirth there would be a grave here in St Piran or Mylor, or
in a Catholic churchyard in Penzance or Truro, and all those
places had been checked.

Gabby and Mark had discussed Isabella and Tom's possible fate regularly. Mark was sure Isabella disappeared
abroad with Tom. Gabby believed no woman would abandon her child to a man she was leaving. It was just not
possible.

Both Peter and John Bradbury thought it unlikely that
Isabella would have had the courage to flout the strict
conventions of the time and leave with a man not of her
own class. But in naval circles, Mark told her, wives of sailors
in the nineteenth century often had children obviously not
sired by their husbands, who were away for months and
years at a time. These children were often taken on by their
husbands for form's sake. Maybe Sir Richard was keeping to
some naval tradition.

Gabby put another log on the fire. She wished Mark
were there, he had been so expert at correlating evidence,
seeing what was meaningful and speculating on possible
outcomes. He had always thought he had plenty of time

to come back to Lady Isabella when he had finished his book.

She got up, stretched, and opened the door to let Shadow out before she went to bed. The night was clear, the sky cloudless and filled with stars, and she stood in the damp air listening to the sea in the distance. When she first came to Cornwall she would stand in the dark, awed by the silence, the vastness of the landscape and the rhythm of moon and tide. The faint roar of the ocean filled the space she stood in. She had felt immediately part of it all, in her element, as if she was standing on the edge of the world, insignificant and yet making this sudden and astounding connection deep into the earth. To the young Gabby the mystery of being alive and alone in the universe was exciting and overwhelming.

The hairs rose up on the back of her neck as she looked upwards at the scattered stars in the cloudless night. She could be Isabella. *Isabella, Gabriella*. It did not matter, for this landscape would endure long after they had both ceased to be remembered. Isabella must have stood there too in the house or garden, looking up at a sky with her own thoughts of mortality.

Where was the spirit of Mark in this infinity?

She had once attempted to explain to him the profoundness of the discovery of herself as part of the universe, something she had never felt in a city. How, in a sudden moment on that doorstep of the farm, with her feet firmly on the earth, aged seventeen, she had looked up dizzily to the star-filled blackness and felt herself spring into existence. Such a strange and powerful feeling.

She had watched Mark's eyes crinkle with interest.

'The human spirit is unique and the sense of oneself within the universe necessarily solitary. We live in a fast-moving urban world where we have forgotten to be still and listen to the beat and rhythm of the planet we inhabit. Some people never experience your moment on the doorstep, Gabriella. That sudden amazing feeling of accord and harmonized coexistence with nature . . .'

He had pulled her to him, smiling. 'The endless cycle, the absoluteness, the mystery of human life is what makes it so exciting ... Don't ever lose that feeling, my beloved Gabriella.'

Gabby called Shadow and went inside. Mark. It was like losing a limb. You felt the movement of it, as if it was still attached to you. All the time. Every minute.

Shadow came reluctantly back inside and Gabby locked the door, made toast and Marmite and climbed into bed. She lay with the firelight flickering over the walls for a long time, unable to sleep.

As a child she had once seen a Cretan house left exactly as it had once been. Bed, chair, spinning wheel, jug, basin, pottery oven; all in its particular place, an exact space between each object. Everything you needed in one room. Perfect.

This was how she felt here. The beams of John's car shone across the walls as he came home, then silence. Gabby listened to this heavy silence as the fire died and the room creaked and settled around her.

She turned on her side, bringing her knees up to her chin, taking herself back to the London house. She followed Mark's lean frame around the rooms, watched his familiar habit of raking his fingers through his wiry hair, greying at the temples with single white hairs sprinkled through the rest of his head. The way he folded himself into a chair with unaware grace. Heard that slow throaty laugh and the way his slanting dark eyes crinkled in the corners with amusement nearly all the time.

Mark. A life together ended abruptly almost before it had even begun. A life so vividly real she could almost remember each day. Yet the twenty-odd years at the farm had faded into one long shimmery heat haze of a life, passed safely sleepwalking to the moment Mark stood on the other side of a church gate.

A log shifted in the dying fire and Shadow stirred, and it seemed to Gabby the room shifted too, as if her grief had found an echo. Was this where Isabella stayed while the figurehead was carved? Did Isabella and Tom Welland walk these cliffs? Had Richard Magor banished Isabella here to this Summer House in disgrace, to have a child he later took as his own?

She would never know. She would never know what really happened.

Isabella slept with Tom's letters under her pillow. She knew them all by heart and she touched them in the dark and whispered his words to herself.

My Dearest Isabella,

This, my first letter, is begun off the coast of Spain where we are becalmed. I am afraid I am not good with words. My hands are more used to carving than writing. I fear the voyage to Prince Edward Island is going to be long and troublesome. The Esmeralda is a barque of similar size to Lady Isabella but she is not so seaworthy, nor so comfortable or well-built. I am told the Captain is too ready to take to the bottle at the hint of bad weather. I am praying for wind to hasten this voyage to its end, for then I can start to prepare for our life together.

It is three days since I set sail from Falmouth and five days since I last saw your beautiful face and spoke to you. Isabella, I feel I have deserted you and this causes me sleepless nights. It is then, in the dark, that I think I should have waited, whatever the cost, and that I should have spirited you away, up north, away from Cornwall, and when our child was born we could have sailed for our new life. But in the morning I know we could not have found happiness at the expense of so many.

Our parting and separation are cruel, and in the long nights imagination conjures so much doubt. When I am on dawn watch and the sun appears over the horizon and the dolphins jump beside the ship, you seem so

*far away and I am heading away from you. I ask you,
Isabella, never to doubt my love and fervent intention
to return for you and the child.*

   *I trust Lisette is caring for you well, as I cannot view
my life without you and all I do is for that one end.*

   *One comfort is that my brother, Harry, sails with me
as Second Mate and will return with this letter and
more as I write. Isabella, my thoughts are never far
from you. Feel this in your heart as the days pass.*

   Tom.

I cannot view my life without you and all I do is for that one end.

Isabella took courage from Tom's words for she had become
unwell as her time approached. The doctor had consigned her
to bed and sought a second opinion. Knowing little of Isabella's
circumstances he requested a meeting with Sir Richard to ask his
permission to send for a gynaecological specialist from Plymouth.

'It would have been preferable for Lady Isabella to have stayed
here near Falmouth where it is easier for her to be visited by her
doctors. The access to the main highway is a distinct advantage.
But I'm afraid it is too late to move her now.'

'I'm afraid my wife was insistent,' Richard said. 'You know what
women are like once they have an idea in their heads.'

'I do,' the doctor said. 'I have never been keen on the north coast
myself. And it is certainly not the ideal place in winter for a difficult
confinement. Sir Richard, I am concerned about Lady Isabella. She
is frail. As you know she has suffered from a persistent cough which
tires her and prevents sleep. It is not going to be an easy birth.'

'What do you want me to do?' Richard asked rather irritably.
'I cannot have the child for her.'

'Do I have your permission to ask a second opinion and to take
their advice over any medical practice they suggest?'

'My wife is not in danger?'

'Sir Richard, childbirth always carries danger.'

Richard stared at the doctor. 'I do not want to lose the child ...
or my wife, of course. If it is a boy, he will be my heir.'

'Then I have your permission to seek further advice?'

'You do.'

'Sir Richard, one further thing. Is Lady Isabella prone to low spirits?' The doctor, seeing Sir Richard's face, added hastily, 'Or is it her condition?'

'Her condition,' Richard said briskly and walked the doctor to the door.

As he departed, the doctor wondered if the rumour his wife repeated to him last night might not be true. There was certainly no doubt Sir Richard seemed more interested in an heir than his wife. Odd. Could a man fool himself and others that a child conceived outside marriage was his own? But then, Sir Richard was a man no longer young and perhaps he thought this was his last chance of a son.

Isabella was sure the baby would come early. It moved constantly, restless and turning, disturbing her sleep. Her back ached with the weight she was carrying. Instinctively she knew something was wrong.

What if something happened to her? *Please God, do not let me or my child die. I want to see Tom again. I must be here to take care of my child. There is no one else but me.*

Lisette had taken to sleeping in the chair beside Isabella and had told the midwife to be ready at any time. Lisette trusted the midwife far more than any fancy doctor.

In the few months she had been in St Piran, Isabella had quietly helped many people, and now that she was unwell prayers were said in the chapel and small gifts arrived at the door.

Ben Welland had sent word to Tom by the packet ship, knowing it would only reach him after the birth of his child. He had watched the light and hope begin to fade in Isabella and he saw that Tom must return for her or she would decline here. His message had been to the point. *'Thou should return home, Thomas. I believe the time for trouble is gone. The moment for it has passed. Isabella's spirits are low. She has great need of thee by her side.'*

His wife feared greatly for the lass. She was not built for childbirth, even Ben could see that. He had watched many women die in childbirth and he had seen the loss of spirit which came after the birth. A strange thing it was; a falling away of the body and soul.

Ben was not at all sure that the moment for trouble had passed. But he knew that Mr Vyvyan was trying to withdraw from his business dealings with Sir Richard and he had made it clear that he would protect his tenants and the community.

It was rumoured that Sir Richard was in disagreement with many of his business partners and with his family, and Ben had realized that, without support, Sir Richard's threats were empty. They did not need him, for there was business enough in St Piran without him.

With luck and a fair wind, for the packet ships were fast, Tom could be home in six or seven weeks.

Tom's child made a dramatic entrance into the world. There was no gentle warning but Isabella was seized by a violent pain in her back, and she screamed out and terrified the sleeping Lisette, who leapt from her chair and rushed to Isabella, who was lying whimpering and hot to the touch.

Lisette hastily pulled the bell-pull to alert the household and then went to light the lamp. She took a cloth and immersed it in cool water from the basin and went to bathe her mistress's forehead.

'Now, my bird. Listen to Lisette. Do not hold your breath. Breathe easy and as gentle as you can. Relax your fingers. There! That is better. All is well. All is well. Now, we must time the pain carefully. Do not fight the pain, Isabella. Go with it and it will hurt less.'

Isabella's eyes were huge and terrified. 'Will that terrible pain come again, Lisette?'

'I am afraid so, my lamb. It is your baby telling you it is time to be in the world.'

'But you told me the pains would begin gently at first and then ...'

'I did,' Lisette smiled. 'Do you not think you must have a son, to herald his arrival so painfully?'

Isabella tried to smile.

'Lie still and calm. Good. Now, your body will tell you when the next pain is coming. When the pain is too bad to bear I will give you something, but I cannot give it to you too soon. The calmer you are, Isabella, the easier the birth.'

There was a knock on the door and the two maidservants entered carrying water and lavender.

'Cook has run for the midwife,' one whispered to Lisette, glancing at the bed in awe.

Lisette took the jug of water. 'Good. Now you both know what to do? We will need continual hot water.'

'Yes, yes, we know.'

Lisette returned to Isabella's side. She did not like the colour of her face. Her eyes were closed and Lisette saw the dark rings under them. Isabella opened them suddenly and said quietly, 'Lisette, I am afraid my body is not strong enough to bear this pain.'

'With God's help you will bear it as other women do.'

'Am I a coward, Lisette?'

'You are young and afraid and in low spirits. Some women sail through their confinements. You are not one of them. Isabella, it is but a few hours' pain and then you will have your child in your arms, just as your mother held you. Think of that . . .'

Lisette leant down to stroke Isabella's forehead. 'How beautiful this child will be. Yours and Tom's.'

'Mine and Tom's.'

Isabella and Tom.

Another pain was coming. Isabella could feel it like a vast wave and this time she clutched Lisette's hand, tried not to scream out at the strength of it which seemed to raise her half from the bed.

Gabby was woken by violent stomach cramps and nausea. She just got to the bathroom in time. She sipped water and was sick again and again. A thin layer of sweat lay over her skin. She went back to bed, taking a bowl with her. Every time the pain came she was left vomiting. She could not ever remember being so ill and was tempted to use the bell-pull that John had showed her for when his guests were unwell. But she did not want to wake him so she promised herself after every bout . . . *If I get another pain I'll pull the bell* . . . until the early hours, when she fell into a hot and troubled sleep.

She half woke to the feeling of people whispering and moving round her bed. Shadow was growling under her breath. Her nightdress was drenched and Gabby felt cold, icily cold, but when she opened her eyes and sat up and blearily looked round the room there was no one there. She did not think she had the strength to let Shadow out and fell back on the pillows, closing her eyes again.

The room was full of a sense of urgency, and a faint memory of a man lifting her in a room and holding her to the light of a window to look at her face. She fell into a feverish sleep. She dreamt of candlelight and Mark . . .

I ask you never to doubt my love and fervent intention to return for you and our child . . . I cannot view my life without you, and all I do is for that aim.

Gabby smiled. Mark. Mark. Her hands curled round to protect her aching stomach.

With each wave of pain Isabella's eyes were fixed on Mama looking down at her in her red dress. She pretended Mama was real; flesh and blood and here. She heard again her soft English voice with that Italian inflection. This gave her strength even though her body trembled with fatigue.

There were so many women round her bed. The Catholic priest waited outside. Isabella had called him in case this child, who was taking so long to come into the world, needed baptizing.

Lisette was worried. She wondered how much longer Isabella's body could take this assault. It was now twelve hours of relentless labour.

The doctor arrived and examined Isabella. He looked grave. The baby had turned late. It would be a breech birth and every woman in the room knew what that meant. They did not tell Isabella, but prepared quickly.

The doctor gave her laudanum and the midwife asked her to lie quite still. She must not push.

Anna, Tom's mother, whispered in Isabella's ear, 'Tom is on his way home to you, Isabella … Be brave … soon the pain will be over.'

The doctor cut Isabella carefully and Isabella began to float away. *She smiled. I ask you never to doubt my love and fervent intention to return for you and our child.*

It was going to be all right. Isabella suddenly knew this. Her child was going to be born and to live and have children of his own. Isabella and Tom. Their children. Their children's children. Mama smiled down at her.

'Now, my darling child, now!'

Isabella lifted her head and Lisette supported her on one side and Anna on the other.

'Now, Miss Isabella. Now! Push! One more push!'

With all her strength Isabella pushed and her son slid out into the world, tired but intact.

When Gabby woke it was late and Shadow was sitting by the door. Gabby got out of bed unsteadily and let her out. She felt drained and weak. She made tea and had a bath, then, leaving the stable door open to the morning for Shadow, she went back to bed.

The night came back to her. The feeling of people round the bed, Shadow growling . . . She stared at the mirror above the small table in the alcove and it caught the light and reflected back. She had such memory of a face somehow familiar, as if it reflected her own. Of footsteps slowly walking away down flights of stairs. Of listening to those footsteps until they faded away.

Gabby shivered. She knew she still had a temperature, she must have been hallucinating, but when she closed her eyes she could still feel the sensation of people in the room; as if they were trying to relay some message of hope to her, of continuity.

Shadow refused to come back into the cottage but lay just outside the door in autumn sunlight, watching Gabby anxiously.

507

Gabby sat upright very slowly, propped up by the head-board. She saw clearly and suddenly the face of the figure-head. She placed both hands on her stomach with the same awe and shock as Isabella had once done.

I am pregnant. I am having Mark's child.

'It's a boy!'

The midwife took the silent baby quickly away and turned him upside down and smacked him. There was no sound. The doctor quickly took him and pushed his finger into his mouth and removed mucus, then he turned the baby again and methodically tapped his back hard.

Everyone held their breath. Isabella was too exhausted to be aware that her baby was not breathing. Then there was a small coughing sound, a rasping wail, then a cry, and everybody smiled. The crying baby was bathed and swaddled and handed to Isabella.

She looked down and marvelled. 'How tiny he is.'

The doctor smiled. 'He is early and he is small, Lady Isabella, but God willing he will thrive. Now, I will leave these good women to attend you and then you must rest. You have had a difficult time of it. I will return in the morning.'

'Lisette?'

'I'm here, my bird.'

'Is the priest still outside?'

'He is.'

'Would you ask him to come in?'

Isabella turned to the young priest as he came in. 'Will you please baptize my son, Father? He is small and I want to be sure he is in a state of grace.'

With her finger Isabella stroked the tiny downy head of her infant son and love flowed through her. She felt such joy for his life that she smiled and looked up at the women around her and sought out the eyes of Anna, Ben's wife.

'I will name my son "Thomas Benjamin".'

The priest took the tiny infant from Isabella and baptized him.

'In the name of the Father and the Son and the Holy Ghost, I name this child Thomas Benjamin ...'

Chapter 73

Richard was exultant when he heard that Isabella had had a son. He had intended to be in St Piran for the birth in order to look the expectant father and he made his presence in the household felt as soon as possible.

Lisette made him wait as Isabella was feeding the baby, and this for some reason irritated Richard.

'How is she? The doctor said she had a difficult time.'

'She had a long labour, Sir Richard, and she is still very weak.'

'And the child?'

'He is small, but alive and well.'

'Good. Good.'

Lisette felt anxious. What was going to happen now? Dear Lord, this man was never going to let Isabella or the child alone. He would cart them back to Botallick like the possessions they were. These months of pretending that things might be different were sliding away. Lisette had changed her opinion of Sir Richard. There was something single-minded and relentless about him. He would survive at any cost, but Isabella would not.

When Richard was allowed into the bedroom, Isabella was lying with her eyes closed and the baby in the crook of her arm. He stared down at them both and his heart stirred. Isabella looked pale and drained but more beautiful than he had ever seen her, as if the hard labour of childbirth had made her into a woman. The childish face of the girl he loved had gone. This face was that of a tired woman informed by pain, grateful that she had survived.

Richard felt awkward and large standing in the privacy of her bedroom, and when Isabella opened her eyes he saw immediately that she resented his presence. He moved nearer the bed and looked down at the tiny piece of humanity with its creased little face and downy hair.

'Isabella?' Richard asked. 'How are you?'

'I am well, thank you, Richard.'

'May I see your son?'

Isabella moved the baby slightly and pulled the shawl away from the child's face. Richard peered down. He had never seen anything so small. Tentatively he put out his little finger to a hand the size of his bent thumb. The tiny fingers flexed and closed around his. Richard was enchanted.

'How small he is. How perfect,' he murmured.

Isabella looked up at him surprised. She had yet to understand he had spent nine months convincing others of his impending fatherhood and in so doing had almost convinced himself. He did not look down and see Tom's child but his own, and in a flash Isabella realized this and her emotions were mixed.

She felt a stab of fear for her future, and pity for a man who had married a younger woman in order to procreate. She had wronged her husband and she felt sadness for what might have been between them if she had been a little older, if she had minded less about the physical side of her marriage. If she had never set eyes on Tom Welland again.

If only she could have loved Richard. That moment, as he looked down for the first time on her child, could have been a gift she gave him in return for his devotion. The softening of his face as he reached out to touch his son. These small precious moments that made a union of marriage. If she had loved him. If the child had been his.

They were both still as they looked upon the baby, and in the stillness, Richard, whose nature was to love absolutely when he loved, felt sudden, total and unconditional love for the child in Isabella's arms.

'Have you everything you need, Isabella?' he asked gently. 'What can I bring you until you are both well enough to move back to Botallick? You look pale, should I employ a professional nurse for you? You need to get your strength back. The doctor wanted to send for a London quack and here you are having managed very well on your own!'

Isabella smiled faintly, but her heart sank at mention of her leaving the Summer House.

'Richard, you are kind, but I have all I need, thank you.'

'Then I will leave you to rest . . .'

Richard felt suddenly at a loss. He had married her too young. He saw that now. He had frightened her with his demands. This business with the carver had just been childhood fantasy. He should have let her play it out instead of handling it badly. He should have stayed silent, turned a blind eye. Isabella would never have pursued it if he had left well alone. God! How he wished he could go back and have that time again.

'I will leave you. I go to talk to Ben Welland. I shall be staying at The Western Arms, but before I return to Falmouth I will come and see you, for I must register the child in Truro. Goodbye, my dear.'

Register the child? Richard disappeared and Isabella was left with a dry mouth and shaking hands as she pulled the baby closer. She had baptized the child, Thomas Benjamin. Welland names. This truce could not last and Isabella wished it to. It was so much easier without harsh words and she felt so exhausted she wondered if she would ever be herself again.

Chapter 74

Gabby stood in the hall of the London house. She had had to push the front door open against the mountain of circulars and mail that had accumulated since the day she had left. She bent and picked it all up and placed it in a pile on the kitchen table.

Already the house smelt empty and neglected. Devoid of the particular smell of people living there. She stood looking out over the Thames. Small pink clouds floated past buildings. Leaves covered the footpath and the surface of the river. From the kitchen she saw gardens that lay neglected and sodden now that summer had faded. Just a child's bike or a ball left on a patch of grubby grass.

She walked slowly in and out of the rooms, went upstairs. Everything was exactly as she had left it. Mark's dressing gown still hung on the bathroom door. The unmade bed still contained the same sheets Mark had lain on. Gabby bent to smell the pillowcase and sheets to see if any of Mark remained. It did not.

She stayed for a moment with her cheek to the place Mark had lain then she got up and stripped the beds, gathered up the towels from the bathroom that smelt, and placed them all in the washing machine.

She unlocked the back door and went out into the dank little garden. All the flowering pots they had planted were withered and dead. A steady light rain began to fall. Josh was on his way home, cheerful, thinking everything was normal. She felt sick at the thought of what she must tell him.

She went back inside leaving the door open, and pulled the fridge door wide and piled all the stuff inside in a bin liner. She switched the kettle on, made tea, added dried milk from the cupboard, then she sat at the table and tried to think logically.

Did she cancel all the services? Phone, gas, electricity? On whose authority would she do these things? Her name was not on any of the bills. She did not know the name of Mark's English solicitor. She felt as if her lifeblood was going to be depleted once this house was dismantled. Once it was empty of their things, who was to say she and Mark had existed together here at all?

Mark was back home with his family. Canada, his last resting place. Gabby got up and went into the sitting room and looked down at the answer-machine. Five messages and the first would still be Mark's. She pressed 'Play' and skipped back after she'd heard the others to listen to him. She closed her eyes. The sound of his voice remained.

'Honey, you will just about be home now . . . You will just about be home now . . .'

She could almost, with her eyes tight shut, pretend Mark was in the room.

The other calls were from Lucinda and from a university, expressing shock and sympathy. She zapped them.

'I'll ring you tonight . . . something that might interest you . . .'

Gabby shivered and went back into the kitchen. Had Mark told Veronique he was leaving her before he was killed? Gabby prayed fervently he had not. To lose your husband twice . . . how would that leave the rest of your life? It would colour and taint all her happy memories. All they had had together.

Gabby began to sift through Mark's mail, making a small pile of his letters and throwing the junk mail into the bin liner. There was a small, thin envelope with her name on it in his writing. Gabby opened it with unsteady fingers. It was a Peter Nero tape of 'The first time I ever saw your face'. Mark had been looking for this version for her for a long time. Gabby shut her eyes, holding the tape close to her, and wondered if she would ever bear to be able to play it.

Opening her eyes again, she saw another letter addressed to her: Mrs G Ellis. On the envelope was the name of a solicitor: *'Daniels, Jacob and Lean, Cumberland Place'*. Gabby turned it in her hands. At least she had somewhere to forward Mark's mail. Here it was then, the polite reminder that she had no right to be there.

Grief had kept all practical decisions at a peculiar distance. Blind instinct had told her that she was pregnant and Elan's doctor had confirmed it. It was early days but it changed everything. She had never intended to take advantage of Elan or Lucinda's offer of accommodation. She had to find somewhere affordable and on her own. Somewhere large enough to restore from home. She must earn as much as she could before the baby came and her ability to work long hours was limited.

Practically, she could not afford to live in London and she felt dismay at the thought of being alone in a London that did not contain Mark or the tiniest garden. Should she go somewhere quite new? Find somewhere in Cornwall, away from the farm but near friends; Nell, people she knew, and clients she had built up?

It was hard to think. It was hard to make any decisions. She had only made two big decisions in her whole life . . .

Gabriella, are you going to open that letter or not?

Gabby smiled and opened the envelope.

Dr Hannah instructed us in April 1999 to act on his behalf, in respect of the property 14, Riverside, Chiswick . . .

Dr Hannah left a will with us with instructions that we contact you in the event of his death. He has left 14, Riverside, with all contents and in its entirety, solely to you, Mrs Ellis. We have been in contact with Dr Hannah's solicitors in Canada and they confirm that

this was Dr Hannah's legal and binding instruction in a
more recent will they held.

On the death of his aunt, Mrs Clarissa Shreeve, Dr
Hannah became the sole owner of the property. There
was no mortgage outstanding . . .

We were very sorry to hear about Dr Hannah's
untimely death and we offer you our deepest sympathy.

I would be grateful if you could contact me at your
convenience . . .

Gabby stared and stared at the piece of paper then burst into
tears. Mark had even thought of taking care of her after his
death. It was such confirmation of his conviction they would
have a life together, be together in old age.

Oh, God, Mark, you have given me a home, for me and
our child.

Gabby clutched the letter to her. All things seemed suddenly possible. She looked around and touched the door-
frames of the house. *Mark would always be there in the*
house and it could stay just as it was. She could catch his
shadow in the turn of the stair; hear an echo of his voice as
she stood in this kitchen. Sleep in the bed they shared.

Gabby went upstairs. She had a shower and remade the
bed with clean sheets. She rang Lucinda and arranged to
meet her for lunch. Then she took the coloured basket Mark
bought her in Camden market and she walked out by the
fast-flowing river to the shops.

Marika met Josh at the airport. He looked brown and well.
They hugged and hugged.

'I've booked us into a little hotel for the night.'

Josh grinned. 'Good.' He stared at her. He was home and
everything was right with his world.

That evening he phoned Gabby's mobile but it was
switched off. He left a message. Perhaps she was in Cornwall.
He rang the farm and no one answered. He tried Nell. She
was not there.

Josh had caught an earlier flight than planned. He had thought he would surprise everybody and he felt mildly deflated that everyone was out. He rang Elan's London number and Elan did answer.

'Thank God someone's home, it's like the *Marie Celeste*.'

'Josh! Dear boy, how lovely, you're back in Blighty!'

'I am, but my whole family seems to have evacuated somewhere. I can't get hold of anyone, really weird.'

'Gabby's here in London,' Elan said guardedly.

'Oh, good, I'll try her mobile again later. Charlie and Nell aren't answering either.'

'How are you, Josh? Glad to be home, I'll bet?'

'Very glad.' Why was Elan being so hearty? 'After my leave I'm off to Germany. How's the painting going?'

'Bit of a dip at the moment. I haven't been painting for a few weeks. Where are you?'

'In a hotel with Marika.'

'How lovely for you! When are you heading home, Josh?'

'Not sure, probably within the next few days, but I need some time with Marika.'

'Of course you do.'

'Have you time to meet up while I'm in London, Elan?'

'Of course, old thing. Ring your mother first. Gabby would hate to have missed you. Then just give me a ring and I'll take you all out to supper.'

'Great. Elan, are you OK?'

'I'm fine, dear boy. I'll talk to you soon. Have fun.'

Josh switched the phone off.

'What is it?' Marika asked.

'I don't know. Just a feeling.'

Josh lay down beside Marika and they held each other. She said softly, 'You are tired and all your family are out. It is an anticlimax. When you return from a journey you think everyone will be in the place you have imagined them to be all the time you were away, and when they are not, you suddenly realize that the world has gone on without you. That the people you love are not in exactly the same

516

position waiting for you to return. It is very sad, this feeling. Very lonely. Almost as if you have died and they can get along fine without you.'

'Yes,' Josh said, breathing in the smell of her hair. 'That's exactly it. It doesn't matter how old you are, the need to touch base, to reassure that all is the same as it ever was, remains.'

He turned over on his back in the dark room listening to the noise of traffic outside, and people inside walking down the carpeted corridors sliding cards into hotel locks. Gabby had sent him airmail letters, shorter than usual, and he had had no sense of her days or where she was. There were no amusing little anecdotes about things around the farm or people he knew. Nell had written her witty little missives regularly and Charlie never wrote letters to anyone. Marika had written every day.

He propped himself on an elbow and looked down at her.

'I had forgotten what a wise little witch you are. Will you marry me?'

'No. I want a proper romantic proposal with you on bended knee in some romantic setting.'

'Oh, you're so girlie!'

'I know.' Marika sighed happily. 'Go to sleep.'

Chapter 75

Isabella was feeling stronger and sat in a chair by the glass doors to the courtyard which Lisette had thrown open to let the spring air inside the room.

Lisette was concerned. Isabella was eating little, but she was feeding her baby and must take nourishment. The baby was small and always hungry and Lisette doubted Isabella was going to have enough milk.

Anna came daily to help with the baby. She looked down at her grandson in wonder and love. Thomas was not yet beautiful but he was to Anna. Both she and Ben knew this was a child they would not be able to hold for long or watch grow up.

Lisette watched Isabella. She fed and crooned to her baby but neither read nor sewed, and showed little desire to leave her room but sat staring, staring at the sea, waiting.

The spark in her was gone. She had no spirit. She seemed seized by a listlessness and lethargy that seemed to Lisette more than physical. Anna, too, had noticed.

'I have seen it before in women, Lisette, after a difficult birth. The pain is too much for the body. The mind takes leave for a while.'

'Then we must call the doctor.'

Anna was cautious. 'I do not trust doctors in the pay of gentlemen such as Sir Richard. Have a care that we do not play into his hands. Let us look after her for a while longer ourselves.'

Lisette stared at Anna. 'You mean that to Sir Richard the child is more important than Lady Isabella?'

'I do. I have seen a woman dragged off to Bodmin Asylum when it suited her husband.'

Lisette smiled. 'Anna, I cannot see Sir Richard committing his wife to the asylum. He has a kind, if bitterly proud heart.'

Anna compressed her lips. 'Lady Isabella has baptized her son Thomas Benjamin. Is that an act of a woman who plans to return with her baby to her husband? Sir Richard's gentleness with Isabella is only to this end.'

Lisette was silent. She had been too near to see the truth. If you lived a lie it became so easy to believe it and Lisette did not know which she was more afraid of, Isabella going back to Sir Richard with her spirit gone, or her escaping with Tom to unknown hardship in her fragile condition.

Anna, returning down the hill to the village, prayed Tom came soon. Anna knew the nature of gentlemen. Sir Richard would have his wife home, and the baby, too. His concern for Isabella was only concern for himself and an heir. If Isabella had loved her husband Anna would have been prepared to lose her grandson to the big house, but when she looked at the scrap of a thing, a child only, wedded to that old man, it seemed to her perverted. What Mr Vyvyan had been thinking of, the Lord only knew.

Isabella looked down on Thomas. He made small gurgling noises and stretched his tiny arms, opened his eyes and squinted up at her, not focusing as yet. His eyes were little slits of tiger eyes, not blue like Tom's, but like her eyes, like Mama's.

'Mama, this is Thomas Benjamin. Is he not beautiful?'

'He is indeed, my darling. He will need much love and care.'

'Yes. Do you like his name?'

Silence.

'Mama, I asked Father O'Callaghan to baptize my child Thomas Benjamin.'

'But, Isabella, what surname will he carry, this grandson of mine? Did you make your decision in that single moment and have since forgotten?'

Isabella did not know.

'I was afraid the baby might die without absolution. I chose the names instinctively. I wanted him to carry his father's name.'

'And your husband?'

'He does not know I have baptized and named my baby, Mama.'

Thomas. This was Thomas. Isabella held him up against her cheek, soft and dependent on her as he made his little snuffling noises. Would Tom return? Why did she doubt it? As if it really had been only a dream and was now fading.

Richard seemed always there and panic made her revert to a childlike state of powerlessness. When she thought of returning to Falmouth with him, a great and terrible languor of mind and spirit seized her at the memory of those endless days of a suspended life.

Yet, when she saw Richard bend with awe to this child, touch him with such gentleness and joy, she thought her heart might break for the look on his face, for the generosity of spirit which could make him forget her betrayal and welcome both her and her child back into his life as his own. The pain she felt was confusing and rendered her incapable of coherent thought.

The baby had settled into the crook of her neck like a dormouse. She smiled. Thomas. This is my son, Thomas. For the first time there was a little answering movement deep within her as if he was still attached to her umbilical cord. The connection was made and she gently moved him back into her arms and looked down into his face, whispered with sudden joy, 'My beloved little Thomas. Your papa will soon be here.'

When Richard appeared at her door the child was at her breast. He did not leave but stood watching her from the doorway, blocking the light. Lisette was nowhere to be seen and Isabella felt exposed. A slow flicker of anger started inside her. She met his eyes and saw he was aroused by the sight of her feeding her child.

She lowered her eyes. 'Please leave, Richard, you are disturbing us.'

He did not move from the doorway.

'Will you please leave and return later,' she said coldly.

'I came only to say I have registered the child, it is a legal requirement. Also you have visitors eager to view the boy. We will come back in fifteen minutes.'

Richard's eyes were fixed on her breast and the child's small suckling movements. Isabella felt she was being violated and reached for the bell to call Lisette, but Richard turned as she did so and left the room.

When Lisette returned with tea she saw two spots of colour on Isabella's cheeks and an expression she was relieved to recognize: fury.

'What is it, Isabella? What has happened?'

Isabella took the sleeping child from her breast and handed him to Lisette. She covered herself but was unable to articulate her outrage and embarrassment at her intimacy with her child, her privacy suddenly taken from her. A shock, too, that Richard could be a voyeur in such a blatant and insulting way.

'I understand we have visitors?' she said quietly.

'Yes. Sophie and her mama wait outside.'

Isabella smiled faintly. It would be good to see Sophie again, but she wondered why she was no longer *persona non grata* with Sophie's mama.

'Do I invite them in to see you and the child?'

'Yes, of course, Lisette.'

As she said this, Isabella realized she should have asked them to wait in the drawing room and joined them there with the child. But she had not the energy to entertain and her bedroom would have to suffice.

Sophie rushed in first to hug Isabella, but gave a little cry when she saw her.

'Oh, Isabella, how pale and thin you are, you poor darling. Was it quite dreadful? I shall never have children ...'

Isabella laughed. 'It was not too dreadful. Of course you will have children. It is so good to see you, Sophie.'

She turned to Mrs Tredinnick and rose to her feet.

'Please, Isabella, do not get up, we do not mean to disturb you. We are here to visit your father and his wife and could not pass by without seeing you and your child.'

Lisette was still holding the baby and Richard, who had entered the room last, made it very crowded even with the glass doors open. He moved towards Lisette and took the child from her, turning the baby's small face to the two women proprietorially.

'Meet my son,' he boomed. 'Meet Richard Charles Magor. I have this day registered him. Is he not a sturdy child for one born early?'

Mrs Tredinnick did not see Isabella's face grow ashen or Lisette's startled look, for she was admiring the child. But Sophie did. Something was wrong.

She said quietly, 'Mama, the room is small and we are crowding Isabella. Shall we go outside?'

'Of course. Forgive us for dropping in unannounced, Isabella. Your child is beautiful. I congratulate you both. Thank you for inviting us to be the first people to see your son, Richard. Goodbye, Isabella, we shall see you next at Botallick House, no doubt.'

Richard handed the baby back to Lisette and went outside with Mrs Tredinnick.

Sophie knelt to Isabella. 'Dear, what is it? I saw your face. Did Richard name your son without consulting you?'

Isabella forced herself to speak. 'Do not concern yourself, Sophie. It is just that I am still weak . . .'

'May I come again when you are stronger, Isabella?'

'Of course you may.'

At the door, Sophie turned. 'Isabella, if you have need of a friend, you will send word to me?'

'I promise . . .' Isabella's voice cracked a little and Sophie rushed back to hug her. It was all Isabella could do not to weep.

'Men can be so thoughtless, darling Isabella . . . even Richard . . .'

Mrs Tredinnick gave a loud call; 'Sophie, come at once . . .'

'Lisette, take care of my friend . . . please.'

'I will, Miss Sophie . . . now go quickly or you will be in trouble.'

'Goodbye. Goodbye . . .'

Lisette turned and placed the sleeping child in his crib then poured tea and made Isabella hold the cup, held her fingers round them and whispered, 'Do you remember, my bird, what your mama used to say to you when you were frightened or upset?'

'All will be well,' Isabella whispered. 'All manner of things will be well . . . All will be well. All manner of things will be well . . .'

Isabella was weeping and Lisette took the cup from her and held her. She thought Isabella would never stop, but this weeping for a thing lost needed to be done. Lisette helped her to bed and bathed her swollen face and cooled her hands. In the corner the baby snuffled and the day faded and became chill, and Lisette went to close the doors. Isabella was very still in the dark. She said quietly, 'Lisette, please would you see if Sir Richard is still here. If he is would you please say that I wish to see him?'

'Miss Isabella, could it not wait till the morning?'

'No, Lisette, for tomorrow is a new day and I wish to start it right.'

When Richard came back into the room it was dark save for one small lamp. He could not see Isabella's face.

'You wish to see me, Isabella? I go soon to dine with ...'

'This will not take long. Would you please tell me what registering a baby means?'

'It is a legal document recording time of birth, name, parents, place, and religion.'

'And what did you write on the document, Richard?'

Something in the calmness of Isabella's voice unnerved Richard. He coughed.

'I should have consulted with you over names, Isabella. I got a little carried away. I apologize.'

'Did you write your own name down as the father?'

Silence, then, 'I did.'

'You did not think to talk to me before you did this? You did not consider I had a right to know you were registering my son?'

'I did not wish to trouble you with legal talk, Isabella.'

'Indeed?'

'Isabella, I am afraid I must take my leave, I will be late ...' He heard the rustle of her dress as Isabella sat up.

'On the night my son was born the priest baptized my child. You know that I am a Catholic and believe in absolution. He was baptized with names I chose for him, and they are not the names you put on your legal document, Richard.'

'I did not know he had been baptized in the Catholic faith or given any names.'

'You did not ask and yet I am the mother of this child.'

Richard was beginning to feel alarmed at the cold voice in the darkness. It went on, very composed, very calm.

'When I saw how you looked at the child with such feeling, I was touched. I wronged you and I have always deeply regretted hurting you. I felt confused for I saw how much you wanted a son and I remembered only your kindness, and for a moment, a moment only, it seemed like small reparation to go forward as if he was your own child.

'If you had asked me if this was possible in the moments you first saw him. If you had been as you once were, I do not think I could have hurt you more. If you had treated me as a woman and not as a child or a possession, if you had not paraded names I knew nothing of in front of the Tredinnicks. If you had not stood in my doorway staring at me, leaving me in no doubt of how things would stand if I returned to Botallick House, all might have been different. But you did all those things without thought, Richard, because you were so sure you had control and I had no power or choice to make in my own or my child's future. But you are wrong. My son was baptized with names I chose. His mother is Isabella, née Vyvyan. His father is Thomas Welland of the parish of St Piran. This is who we are to him. And this is who we will remain, no matter what you try to do to us. I will never return to Botallick House with you. Never.'

Isabella took a deep breath. 'I would like to buy this house from you, in order that I may stay with people who have been kind and good to me. If you will not permit this, I will go to live elsewhere. I would be grateful if you would consider this.'

'With what names did you baptize your son?' Richard would not let it go.

'His name is Thomas Benjamin.'

'Ha! And with those names you considered returning to me? I think not, Isabella.'

'I do not care any more what you think, Richard. Names can be changed but I see now that your love is not generous but possessive and will not change. It always has been. Now, I am tired and you will be late for your dinner.'

Richard hesitated then turned to leave. This was an Isabella he did not know and he needed to gather his wits. For she was right, he did not believe his wife had any choice but to return with him to Botallick House.

As he mounted his horse, he suddenly relaxed. For there was one thing that Isabella had overlooked.

Chapter 76

Gabby and Josh sat opposite each other in a small Italian restaurant. Gabby was cleaning a painting in a private house nearby, and it was conveniently near Paddington for Josh to put Marika on the train home for the night before he met Gabby.

Josh had wanted Marika to come and for Elan to join them so that they could all have supper together, but both had insisted, for different reasons, that he met Gabby on his own.

'Josh, your mother has not seen you for months. We are going on holiday together, let her have you to herself for one evening.'

'Dear boy, do come along afterwards, we can do a little foray into late-night drinking. Why don't you stay the night?'

Josh could not get rid of an insidious feeling that something was wrong, and when he saw Gabby he got a shock.

'You look awful, Gabby. Are you ill?'

'Thank you, darling. I love you, too!'

'Sorry.' He hugged her and felt only the angle of her bones.

'You're skeletal. God, you can't be eating.'

'Of course I am.'

Gabby made a great play of ordering drinks and opening up the huge menu for him. He saw that her hands were trembling and she laid the menu down on the table. When the waiter had left their wine she said brightly, 'Oh, Josh, it's so good to see you. You look wonderful.'

She seemed nervous and distracted and her words some-how struck Josh as false or automatic. Was Gabby ill? Had she got cancer or something and was going to tell him now? Perhaps this was why Elan would not eat with them?

'What is it, Gabby? Something's wrong. I've known it since I got back.'

To Josh's horror a tear slid down her cheek and she hastily stemmed it with her finger. She looked down at the tablecloth and up again, and then said quickly, meeting his eyes for the first time, 'I'm sorry, Josh, the timing's bloody . . . I'm no longer living at home. Charlie and I have split up.'

Josh couldn't take this in for a moment. He had been expecting her to say something quite different, that she was dying or something, and his relief was tempered with incredulity.

'What? What on earth do you mean?'

Gabby was watching him anxiously.

'Has Charlie got fed up with you working in London and given you an ultimatum or something?'

'No, Josh, nothing like that. I . . . fell in love with someone else. Charlie has done nothing wrong at all.'

Josh could feel the blood leaving his face. He did not want to hear this. He really didn't need this.

'You mean that Canadian figurehead man?'

'Yes.'

'You are leaving Charlie for him, for God's sake?'

'He was killed in a plane accident three weeks ago, Josh.'

Josh stared at his mother. 'Did Charlie know you were having an affair?'

'No, not until after Mark was killed.'

'Poor Charlie.' Josh drained his wine glass and poured himself another.

'Elan knows, doesn't he?'

'Yes. And Nell of course.'

'You've just fucked up your life, haven't you?'

Gabby did not reply. Josh twiddled his wine glass. The waiter brought bread to their table and asked if they were ready to order. They were not.

'Why?' he asked when the waiter had gone.

'Why did I fall in love with someone else?'

'Yeah, Gabby, why did you need to have an affair?'

Gabby had never heard Josh so aggressive. She disliked it.

'I did not *need* to have an affair, Josh. I simply fell in love with another human being.'

'And he was married and had children so there was never going to be any future in it, was there? Just stupid to risk your marriage . . .'

'It was not a light-hearted fling. Mark flew home to tell his wife. I was going to tell Charlie. We were going to make a life together, Josh.'

Josh scraped his chair back. 'And what the hell are you going to do now, Gabby, now you've fucked up the life you had? Are you hoping Charlie will have you back?'

'No, I'm not, Josh. I'm going to live and work in London. I'm sorry to jump this on you, I know it's a shock when you've just come home, but you had to know. I'm sorry.'

Josh thought he might cry. He looked away, swallowed, threw his napkin onto the table, and said suddenly, 'Maybe Charlie will forgive you. Maybe you can go back, eventually.'

To crawl. To feel eternally grateful. I don't think so. Not again, even if I wasn't pregnant.

'Life is not quite that simple. It never is. We all change, move on, cannot go back to being the people we once were, you know.'

Josh stood up. 'I can't eat anything. It would stick in my gullet. I can't believe you could cheat on Charlie. He would have trusted you implicitly, he's that sort . . .' Josh looked down on someone he no longer knew. 'Well, I hope you're happy. You've buggered up my life and Nell's as well as Charlie's. I've spent months longing to come home, and now . . . this.'

He turned and walked out of the restaurant. Gabby sat, stricken. The Italian waiter came instantly and gently poured Gabby more wine from the bottle.

'Madame, may I recommend the soup, it is light and nourishing?'

Gabby nodded, dared not speak at his kindness. She felt sick and light-headed and guilty. She knew Josh would have gone straight to Elan and was glad. Poor Josh.

'Did you know?'

'For the last few months, yes, I did, Josh.'

'So why didn't you warn Charlie?'

'Because one does not meddle in the lives of one's friends.'

'So, no loyalty, then?'

'To whom, Josh?'

'To Charlie, of course. Gabby was the one having the fling. You should have given Charlie the chance to put a stop to it.'

'Gabby is also my friend and it was more than a casual fling, Josh.'

'So that makes it all right, then?'

'It makes it more understandable. Will you please sit down and I'll get you a drink.'

'You can't answer me, Elan, can you? You knew Gabby was in the wrong, yet . . .'

Elan held his hands up and Josh realized he had never seen Elan angry before.

'Stop shouting, Josh, or leave. Now, would you like a drink?'

'Whisky, please,' Josh said sullenly.

Elan poured two whiskies and went back into the sitting room. Josh was prowling. Elan said quietly, 'Now we can have a conversation, Josh, but what I cannot put up with is you bellowing at me like a petulant sergeant-major.'

Josh threw himself down in a chair and Elan said, 'I realize it must be a great shock, coming out of the blue at you . . .'

'You can say that again!'

'All I can say is I have never seen your mother so happy or fulfilled as she was last year.'

'Meaning she wasn't happy before? That's crap, Elan. Gabby has always been a happy person and she loves the farm and Cornwall.'

'She did and always will, but she was forging a little life of her own and that makes people change . . .'

'But not necessarily jump into bed with the first person that asks them?'

'And how the hell do you know that is what happened? Can you not conceive that even mothers have a life, fall in love, and enjoy the company of people they are not married to? Have interests and pursuits that bind them together? In long marriages people take each other for granted, Josh, and stop seeing anything new . . .'

'She's been married to my father for twenty-four years! Why throw that all away . . . I just can't get my head round it.'

'In my limited experience it is always one half of a couple that makes a marriage last. Your mother has been an exceptional wife and mother for all those years. She and Nell are the most generous and giving souls I know. Are you going to judge your mother because she happened to fall in love with someone who loved her deeply in return? So deeply, Josh, he was leaving his family . . .'

'And you applaud that, do you, Elan?'

'I don't believe I have the right to judge anyone.'

'Are you saying we took Gabby for granted?'

'Yes, I am. She's always been there for you and for Charlie. She did not start to work or use her own talents properly until you left home. You, Charlie and the farm always came first. Was Gabby expected to go on leading your lives, just being there, forgoing any life she might have of her own until the day she died? I will tell you this, Josh, Charlie certainly wasn't interested in Gabby's restoring. As far as he was concerned her life was the farm, full stop.'

Elan was as surprised at his anger as Josh.

'Whatever you say, I know my parents were happy. They never argued or rowed when I was a child. I had the most wonderful childhood.'

'Yes, you did. You were and always will be loved and cherished by both Charlie and Gabby. But it is our mothers who care mostly for us in our early years. It is from women we receive both our sense of ourselves and unconditional love. Don't judge, Josh; give Gabby some understanding and love in return for all she has given you.'

Josh got to his feet. 'I don't think I'll stay after all, if you don't mind. I'll join Marika. Thanks for the drink.'

He made for the door and turned. 'I'm actually going to save my love and understanding for Charlie, Elan. Good-night.'

Elan itched to say, *Oh, my dear boy, if you only knew how implacable and self-righteous you sound.* But he didn't, he said instead, 'Take care, Josh. I'm always here.'

Josh could not wait to get to Marika. She met him from the train.

'You sounded awful on the phone. We are in luck, both my parents are away. I was going to wash my hair and slut about in terrible pyjamas and you have spoilt it.'

Josh did not smile and Marika said anxiously, 'You look shocked. What has happened? I thought you were having supper with your mother and staying with Elan?'

'I need a drink before I even begin to tell you.'

'You smell as if you have already had more than one.'

'Well, I need a few more.'

'It cannot be that bad.'

'Believe me, it is.'

It felt odd driving into Sandhurst again, Josh thought, so much had happened and the time spent there seemed suddenly innocent and uncomplicated.

Once in the house Marika poured him a drink and they sat at the huge kitchen table.

'Would you like scrambled egg or something?'

'Maybe later. Marika, my parents have split up. My mother has been having an affair all the time she has been in London.'

'Gabby!'

'Yes.'

'She told you this tonight?'

'Yes.'

'Well, is she living with him now, at the moment?'

'I guess she must have been, but he was killed three weeks ago in an air crash.'

Marika clapped her hand to her mouth. 'Oh, how dreadful. Poor Gabby!'

Josh stared at her. 'Poor Gabby! What about my poor father?'

'Josh, of course, he will be upset, but Gabby has lost . . . everything.'

'How come every bloody person is concerned with Gabby and this man and not what she has done to Charlie?'

'Have you spoken to your father?'

'No.'

'So how do you know what she has done to him? Suppose he is not heartbroken? Supposing they had grown away from each other? You have been away . . .'

This was not the reaction Josh had expected. 'I thought you, at least, might understand at this precise moment how I am feeling on hearing that my parents, who have never had an argument in their lives, have suddenly and inexplicably split up.'

Marika came round the table and twined her arms round his neck.

'I am sorry, I did not mean to sound callous. Of course it must be a shock. But you know, it may heal itself. If they had a strong marriage up to now . . .'

'This man was going to leave his wife and children. Gabby was leaving Charlie and they were planning a life together . . . I just can't believe it. She and Nell were like that . . .' He snapped his fingers.

Marika went to the toaster. 'I am going to make you comfort food; toast and Marmite.'

Despite himself, Josh smiled. Marika said carefully, 'Then it was not just an affair, Josh. Gabby must have loved him very deeply to be prepared to leave her life in Cornwall, to risk losing you. I saw how she felt about the place . . . She seemed so much part of the farm when I was there.'

'So how does that make it better?'

'It doesn't. It makes it sadder. Gabby has lost someone she loves. Imagine how we would feel if we lost one another.'

'I'm more concerned with how Charlie is feeling. He is the innocent party in all this.'

It was Marika's turn to stare. 'How can you not care that your mother must be going through hell on earth at this moment? She must be lonely and frightened and utterly bereft. I hope you were not beastly to her?'

Josh's mouth twitched at Marika's English. 'I guess I was *beastly*, but I thought Elan was pretty beastly to me. I've never realized he is much fonder of Gabby and Nell than he is of my father.'

Marika buttered toast. 'You need to sleep on this, Josh. In the morning you might regret your first reaction to your mother and then you can ring her, let her know that of course you love her, but need time to . . . be there for her.'

She placed the toast in front of him. Afterwards she was to think of the fleeting random choice of a sentence she had formed in a certain way and of Josh's reply which might have been different, but was not.

'No way am I ringing her! At this moment I don't love her and I see no reason why I should be there for her, Marika. She has ruined my leave, spoilt everything good in my life, and I can't forgive her.'

Marika was suddenly very still.

'*Ruined your leave?*' Her voice was very quiet. 'Ah, I see, this is about *you* and *your* feelings. I had not realized.'

'Am I not supposed to have any?'

'Sure you are. But you seem to have no compassion or

understanding or insight or sadness for your mother's situation. I am sorry, but I cannot get *my* head round *that*, Josh. I cannot bear my mother to be unhappy. To lose someone you love is the worst thing in the world. You are her son and you are judging her while knowing *nothing*.'

'You sound like Elan.'

'Good. You make me afraid, Josh.'

'Why?'

'Because that cold hardness and lack of compassion is what my mother and I fled from. You have had a wonderfully privileged life and I think you are spoilt. I think you have always had everything your way, everybody has gone out of their way to make life happy for you. And when they stop, maybe because they want a little happiness too, you kick and scream because you cannot bear it. You are not thinking of Charlie or Gabby, only of what is spoilt for *you* . . .'

'Have you finished?'

'Yes. Where are you going?'

'To find a hotel.'

'It is too late. I will make you up a bed in one of the spare rooms. You have had too much to drink to go anywhere and you are not thinking straight. I will show you upstairs.'

'I am actually as sober as a fucking judge. Just mystified as to why everyone around me thinks I ought to congratulate my mother for breaking up her marriage to my father.'

'No one is saying that. It would just be nice if you thought about what your mother must be going through for one second. Considered someone else's feelings above your own. Felt *something* for anyone other than yourself. *Loved*, with all the meaning of that word, Josh.'

'I love *you*.'

'As long as I abide by your set of values, presumably? As long as I never fall from grace? Here is your room.'

'Marika, I need to sleep in the same bed as you tonight. Don't punish me for a fucking awful day.'

Marika relented. 'OK. In there. I am going back downstairs to finish the toast.'

Later, when they were both side by side, not touching in the dark, Josh said, 'I've made you sad.'

'Yes.'

'Why do you feel so strongly about my mother?'

Silence, then Marika sat up. 'Because of Uli. My father was shot in front of her, Josh. She was made to watch. She was not allowed to go to him as he died. My elder sister was raped. She committed suicide on the day my stepfather was bringing us to England. We do not know what happened to my brother. Life is so fragile, Josh. It can be taken in a moment. You know this. The thought of you making a person you love unhappy for even a second . . . this breaks my heart.'

Josh reached for her, horrified. 'I didn't know . . . You never told me . . . Come here . . . Oh, Marika, I'm so sorry . . . I wish you'd told me, before . . .'

'I told you now for a reason, Josh.'

'I realize that and I do understand why, Marika. In comparison my little drama is as nothing.'

'Then you will ring Gabby tomorrow?'

Josh swallowed. 'I can't, Marika, I'm sorry. I can't be a hypocrite.'

'What if Gabby died suddenly while you were mad at her? How could you bear it?'

'It's not going to happen, Marika. Everything for you is coloured by your past, it has to be. If I've overreacted, so have you. Let's go to sleep.'

Marika's voice was small with disbelief. 'I tell you something that hurts me to speak of and it has made no difference to you at all. If you cannot find it in your heart to forgive Gabby, I do not want you, Josh, for you are someone else, someone I don't know or understand.'

'Don't be silly. We're both tired. Let's just go to sleep.'

And he did, almost straight away, and Marika lay beside him weeping soundlessly for the happy, witty and carefree man she had fallen in love with when all was going smoothly and his stride into the future with her had seemed graceful and effortless.

It was not enough.

They had had their first row and their last. Marika lay in the dark and worried about Gabby, alone somewhere in London in an empty house, with no comfort but Josh's cruel words echoing in the dark. She brought up her knees in a familiar anguish. If she knew where Gabby lived she would get a taxi, go there herself, so Gabby would know she was not alone. Sometimes it is the people you never think of who are thinking of you in the dark.

In the morning she would walk away.

Chapter 77

Isabella had not seen Richard since the day of Mrs Tredinnick's visit, but she had had a letter from his solicitor containing the deeds of the Summer House. It seemed Richard wanted no payment for the house and Isabella was puzzled. Perhaps he considered she owed him nothing, since her father had given him a considerable sum of Helena's money on her marriage. But why had he so suddenly and completely appeared to relinquish any rights to her and the child? It was not in character and she asked Lisette what she thought.

Lisette, too, felt uneasy. 'The only reason I can think of, Miss Isabella, is that Sir Richard hopes to turn you by kindness.'

Ownership of the Summer House made all the difference to Isabella. She no longer doubted that Tom would come or send word to her, and she now had peace and a place of her own in which to wait.

She began to wake early in the mornings. She threw the windows open and stretched in sunlight like a cat that scented the coming of spring. She felt almost herself once more, as if she had slept too long or had had some fever but was now recovered.

It was the time of the spring tides and the sea retreated towards the horizon leaving acres of pale sand. When it returned, sliding slyly back in a floodtide the colour of aquamarine, it formed a waveless lake as still as the one in her father's garden.

The villagers left small baskets of presents in celebration of Thomas's birth. Isabella felt suddenly weightless, for she had discovered that the fear of something was far more deadly than facing it.

Thomas already had a downy growth of blond hair as soft as

feathers. With his striking dark tiger eyes he was beginning to grow beautiful. He had in a short time made slaves of Isabella, Lisette and Anna, who could not bear to hear him cry for more than a second and competed to rush to his crib at the slightest pretence.

Isabella did not want to miss a moment of him. She carried him round the garden, pointing out the emerging bulbs, shading his eyes from the sun and describing the vivid colours of the dying day to him. She rocked him in Lisette's old rocker chair and they sleepily listened to the birds. She and Lisette bathed him by the fire, watching his tiny legs kick like a little frog in the water.

In the afternoons she rested and Lisette took Thomas down to Anna until Ben finished work. Ben pretended gruff indifference to the child he called, 'A little Pasha, that's what thou art, with thy strange dark eyes that seem to know a thing or two.'

Daniel Vyvyan arrived with Charlotte one morning and surprised Isabella in the garden as she rocked Thomas to sleep. Since the child Daniel had been a regular visitor to the Summer House. He, too, was enamoured of his grandchild. Isabella could not help wondering if her child had been a girl whether she would have commanded the same attention. Daniel had always longed for a boy.

Each time Daniel caught sight of Isabella he was struck to the heart; how as the years passed she grew more and more like Helena.

While he could not approve of her conduct, he ached for her vulnerability. She had put herself outside her own society now, but could not quite enter the carver's. Over the last months he had seen something obsessive in Richard which was not healthy. It lacked dignity and had definitely affected his business judgements, for which Richard used to be renowned. Suddenly handing over the deeds of the Summer House, making it a gift, was not in character with the man of the last few months.

Daniel had heard a rumour and it had upset him greatly.

That day as he looked down upon the child something shifted within him, an instinctive protective emotion for his own blood. When the child opened his eyes and appeared to gaze at Daniel, he was swept by love and regret. If only he had cared more for his daughter instead of abandoning her to an older man so that she was Richard's responsibility, not his own ... What had he been thinking of? Why, she still looked almost a child ... He had stolen her childhood. How could he ever undo this damage?

He took his leave of Isabella and his grandson, reflecting sadly on the fact that his grandson carried the shipwright's name, not his. He said to Charlotte as they took the coastal path home, 'I would take back the years if I could, Charlotte.'

'You cannot take them back, my dear, but you can protect Isabella and her small son's future, can you not?'

Daniel took her arm, thought about this. 'I can,' he said, brightening. 'Indeed I can ...'

He looked down upon his wife. 'Charlotte, I know I have not been an easy man to live with ... I resolve to be a better and a kinder man.'

Charlotte smiled. 'All this ... reflection, my dear, comes from looking down on small Thomas?'

'Perhaps.' He smiled back. 'Or perhaps I grow an old and sentimental man.'

He stopped walking. 'Am I wrong, Charlotte, to no longer wish to condemn my daughter for wronging a decent man? For no longer caring much that she has caused rumour and gossip and will bring up a boy who will not be quite a gentleman?'

'I believe these things are secondary to your anxiety for your daughter's future?'

'Well said, my dear, it is exactly that. I want to believe Richard is behaving well in this gift of the house but, Charlotte, something is wrong. He is too much the gentleman of late. We speak only of business, but he is much preoccupied ... It may be that my anxiety is misplaced and he hopes by leaving Isabella alone she will return ... but ...'

'You wish her to return to Botallick House, to her husband?'

'If you had asked me that a short time ago, I would have said, of course. But I have never seen my daughter so content or at peace.'

Charlotte smiled and said softly, 'And you, my dear Daniel, have the disconcerting ability to shock and surprise. From a lifetime of rectitude and propriety, you have managed today to see only

539

what makes your daughter happy; to suspend judgement and convention, and that is a considerable feat and I believe Helena would applaud you for it.'

'I have had help,' Daniel said, equally softly, 'from a very patient and loving wife.'

'You know it is freedom as well as her son that gives Isabella her peace?'

'I do,' Daniel said and thought: a freedom I denied her by bundling her off to my cold and socially obsessed sister, instead of letting her stay in her own home with Helena's things around her. Then with my hastily engineered marriage to Magor, attractive only to Isabella because she could leave her aunt's restrictive and shallow household. A man only three years my junior, who put her on a pedestal and worshipped her unhealthily to the amusement of his peers.

Charlotte was right, he could not undo those years, but he could make sure his daughter and grandson had a future in this changing world.

There was one thing he was sure of. If Tom Welland was anything like his father he would be one of life's gentlemen. A man with a steady and a loyal heart.

Chapter 78

Gabby returned with dread to the farm to pack up her things for London. Nell was there, but Charlie had purposely gone out for the day. Gabby was beginning to feel like a gipsy. She had clothes at Elan's, a few things left at John's, possessions in the London house and the remainder of her life there at the farm.

Elan was going to transport her things to London in the back of his capacious Jeep, bought to carry large paintings and canvases.

Nell helped her fold and pack and chuck unwanted clothes into a bin liner for the charity shop with a sense of strange disbelief. When Gabby's things were amassed they seemed so little for twenty-odd years of a life there.

Gabby came with nothing and leaves with so little, Nell thought. We have never been a present-giving family. There are no precious or sentimental vases or knick-knacks. Two little watercolours I gave her once and some tiny pieces of jewellery which she rarely had occasion to wear. The only thing I have ever seen Gabby constantly wear is that tiny pearl pendant, which I thought at first she must have bought for herself, but now . . .

Charlie had bought her bantams or chicken-houses, practical things because that was what she had always said she wanted . . .

'Will I lose you, Nell?' Gabby asked all of a sudden, thinking, *Will I fade as if I have never been, as the house and land settle without me?*

'Of course you won't lose me, Gabby.'

'Is it possible you might come up to see me in London?'

'In a while, Gab, when things have settled. If I'm invited.'

'Was Josh still very upset when he came down at the weekend?'

'I'm afraid he was. It seems he had a disagreement with Elan. They have never had words and I think it was a bit of a shock. He was pretty miserable . . .'

'What, Nell? I saw you hesitate.'

'He also had a pretty serious difference of opinion with Marika.'

'But why? Not about me, surely?'

'Marika told him he was acting like a selfish, spoilt brat, apparently.'

'Oh, Nell, this is the fallout. I didn't want this.'

Nell sat on the edge of the bed. 'Gabby, Josh and I had long, protracted and repetitious conversations all last weekend. He does listen to me because I am his grandmother and I am possibly the one person he cannot be rude to. Charlie, like Ted, has something intransigent about him; black is black, white is white. End of story. I have never seen any sign of it in Josh, who has a wonderful imagination, but I am afraid I did last weekend. I came up against a solid and impenetrable brick wall.'

Gabby looked at Nell. 'You mean Josh shows no sign of ever forgiving me?'

'It's very early days, Gab, but it is going to be a while.'

'Do you think, Nell, I could find Marika's address and write and ask her if she will be there for him. I can't bear the thought of him being alone and unhappy.'

Nell was silent, then she said tiredly, 'No, I don't think you should contact Marika. Josh is a grown man now; he has been through enough to make mature and adult decisions. He . . .' Nell found this hard to say about her beloved grandson, '. . . can, it seems, bear for you to be alone and unhappy. He cannot find it in him to stop for a moment, even to be kind or express regret. Marika is right, Gabby.

Josh must grow up and learn compassion and understanding even when he does not like a situation. That is what loving someone means. If he can't he's not going to be a very nice human being.

'Marika is a very wise and astute girl. If she loves him she will leave all doors open. It is up to Josh. I've made it clear that the love we all have for *him* is unconditional, but it does not mean I approve of his attitude.'

'Was he a comfort to Charlie?'

'Of course Charlie loved seeing him. They got very drunk in the pub. But Charlie would not allow Josh to say anything critical about you. I was surprised. The older I get the more disconcerted I am by the vagaries of human nature.'

'I've caused you pain. I'm so sorry, Nell.'

Nell got up from the bed. 'Don't let's go there, lovie. Now let's get the charity sacks down to my car. I'll take them into Penzance tomorrow.' She paused. 'Gabby, have you thought this through? You're going to be so much on your own in London. There's plenty of work in Cornwall, you know. Here, at least you have access to us all, we are a phone call away.'

Gabby turned away and looked out of the window. This view had sustained her through so much. She said, with her back to Nell, so quietly Nell had to strain to hear her, 'It is where I can grieve, Nell. There is such a hole here . . .' She thumped her chest. 'Sometimes I can barely breathe for the loss of him.'

Sometimes I can barely breathe for the loss of him.

In this bedroom she had once shared with Ted, Nell once stood exactly where Gabby stood now, staring out past the daffodil fields to a sea that changed colour as fast as the clouds flew, and she grieved and ached in stunned shock that she was there in a life with someone else.

Grief settled over the years, like any loss must in the business of living. It faded, but never left. A sentence, a smell, a place, the angle of a head in a crowd, a laugh, a beautiful piece of music shared, all, all pulled you back years later to the moment in a room with another woman and another grief.

Before Gabby left she walked down to the cove for the last time with Shadow. The light in October changed subtly as the sun got lower in the sky. Everything was golden. The sea seemed to take on the tinge of autumn, the colours of the fields and trees. The beaches were empty, the roads clear. Silence and a feeling of space returned to the countryside. Familiar noises of everyday living settled in the stillness with a sigh.

As Gabby walked down the familiar stony track, she felt overwhelmed. How many hundreds of times had she walked this way? She closed her mind to the memory of a tiny fat hand in hers, singing and waving his small yellow bucket and spade or fishing net, because the memory would destroy her.

She was leaving for a house with no one in it, and she knew as she did so it was not a house or a place that mattered, but the person within it. Without Mark, with no Josh and with no place in Cornwall, Gabby knew she would feel lonely and isolated at times. She could no longer remember a time or a life without Josh. It compounded Mark's death, unbalanced her in these acres of blue sea and sky which had sustained and steadied her each and every day of her life here.

She perched on the rocks, stroking Shadow's head and looking out at a sea like a mirror. A sea mist hovered over the horizon and fishing boats catching the late morning tide chugged out to sea, bright orange buoys cheerfully gathered on their sides like balloons. *Everything the same as it always is, always has been and will be.*

Gabby turned to take it all in, like snapshots she could take out in the dark. There was no danger of her forgetting a world that was engraved inside her, but she wanted also to remember exactly what she felt now; pin down the moment of love and regret; hold all that this place had given her so that it might sustain her, and even in this moment of intense pain at leaving she could know something else would grow from it, if she let it.

From way above her, Charlie, checking the fences that separated his fields from the coastal path, saw a small figure sitting on the rocks below. He stared down. She did not seem to move at all. Her stillness was like the sea, unusually glassy and unnerving. He thought of all the years he had caught sight of her flitting through field or path, farmyard or cove, her dark head bobbing, a coloured sweater between the trees. Happily alone, a given, a fixture, a part of his life.

Gone. The thought of her gone from here. No longer in the kitchen, no longer scattering corn for the bantams. No longer a dark head submerged under the covers as he got up in the half-light of an early morning.

His chest tightened. A pain seized him, so fierce he doubled up, held on to the fence and cried out at the thought of her gone. When he looked down again the rocks were empty. Charlie turned and leapt over the fence and began to run down the coast path, afraid of the sound he was making as the small stones flew under his pounding feet.

Isabella could not resist the pull of early morning, and leaving Thomas to Lisette's care she ran out and across the road and took the coast path. There was no one about and she lifted her face to the early sun, felt the soft new grass and clover under her feet.

She stood and looked down at the cove where she and Tom used to meet. She could see small fishing boats pulling up their nets from the silvery calm sea. She walked onward towards the boatyard intending to take the village road back to the house.

As she rounded the corner she saw him. He was leaning against the wall of the boatshed with his eyes closed and his head thrown back to the early sun. His fair hair was a little long, his white shirt was open at the throat, and he wore tan-coloured canvas trousers. His body was lean and young and brown. One leg was bent, foot flat against the wall in effortless grace. He was so beautiful Isabella's heart leapt. She would like to watch him forever.

Tom turned lazily in her direction, thinking it might be his father or brother ready for work. His eyes widened in surprise and then wonder at Isabella standing there. Her hair was loose and she wore a casual dress the colour of honey.

They stood staring at each other, rapt, as if no time had passed, overwhelmed by this moment they had imagined so long. They both moved together. Isabella ran and Tom caught her and whirled her round, laughing, his teeth white against his sun-baked face.

'Isabella! Are you real or a mirage? Have I been too long at sea?'

'I am real, Tom! I am real!'

'So you are!' Tom said, holding her to him. 'So you are, Isabella.'

'How is it that you are here suddenly in the boatyard, Tom?' Isabella wrapped her arms around him as if he might disappear.

He laughed. 'I came at dawn in a fishing boat. It was too early to wake you or my father, so I watched the sun rise, wondering if you were still here, worrying how soon I would see you again.'

Isabella stared at him. 'I am still here.'

Tom bent and took her face in his hands and kissed her mouth. The kiss was sweet and the blood rushed to Isabella's face as she balanced holding on to his arms so that this kiss might last and last. With their eyes closed they trembled, for everything was exactly as it always was, all doubts were stripped away in a single moment.

When they pulled away Isabella felt dizzy, for she had had no breakfast, and Tom went to pour her water from the pump.

'You are not ill?' he asked anxiously.

She smiled. 'I am well now. I grow stronger every day.'

Tom was unsure what this meant. He stared at Isabella, afraid to ask the question. She said, smiling, 'You have a son. He is small but very beautiful. His name is Thomas Benjamin.'

Tom let his breath out, rested his head on the top of hers. *I have a son. I have a son.*

'And you, Isabella? Are you well? My father wrote how frail you were.'

Isabella closed her eyes and whispered happily, 'I am better now, Tom.'

Tom said gently, 'Shall we climb into my old musty bedroom and you can tell me your news while we rest? I am weary for I have not slept for two days.'

Once there Tom shook the mattress and took the bedcover from a drawer, and they lay together holding each other, talking and talking until they slept.

Tom woke first and gently woke Isabella. 'Will Lisette be out looking for you?'

'She will be worried. I must go, Tom, for the baby will need me, but I am afraid to leave you, so afraid of losing you again.'

Tom laughed. 'There is no chance of that. I have travelled the world to get home to you, Isabella.' He bent to kiss her neck. 'How soft your skin feels.'

Her breasts were larger and Tom said, 'Do you feed your baby, Isabella?'

She nodded, faintly embarrassed for she remembered Richard's eyes upon her.

'I must get back, he will be hungry.'

Tom turned her small hand in his. 'Isabella, I cannot believe I have you and a son.'

'I love you,' Isabella said. 'I love you as much as ever I did.'

Tom closed his eyes, sighed. 'I want you as my wife . . .'

'Tom, Richard knows I will never return to Botallick House. I have obtained the deeds of the Summer House from him. I believe he is resigned to my freedom.'

'Do you think your husband will ever divorce you, Isabella?'

'I do not know, Tom. I do not know. I have your child and I feel as wedded to you as I will ever be, no matter what people think.'

Tom smiled. 'So you still have my grass ring?'

'Of course I do!'

'Come, you must go to my baby. I will come after dark, Isabella, to see you and my son.'

'You will?' Her eyes lit up.

'Oh, I will,' Tom said, helping her down the ladder. 'But this time

I will be very careful, for all that I love is lodged under the roof of your Summer House.'

Nell could see the two of them walking along the edge of the field, heads bent close together. Charlie seemed to be doing all the talking but they did not appear to be arguing. Gabby seemed to be listening. Had they come across each other by mistake? Were they discussing Josh?

She heard Elan's Jeep coming slowly up the lane and he parked beside her, followed her eyes. The two figures had stopped and were facing each other. Shadow had stopped too and was sitting looking up at them.

'What a mess it all is, Elan. Josh, Gabby, Charlie; all utterly miserable.'

'Not to mention you and me, darling, skulking in the wings.'

'She's so fragile. Elan, do you think she realizes what she's doing, cutting herself off from us?'

'She's in good old-fashioned mourning, Nell. How can she stay here with you and cry her heart out for a man who isn't her husband, who isn't your son?'

'Oh, you're right, as usual. I hope they are down there reaching some sort of understanding. Charlie said some dreadful things . . . Come on, come inside and have a drink, lovie.'

Gabby, walking back to the house, was startled by the sound of running and loose stones on the path. It was Charlie and she was afraid he was going to start haranguing her all over again. He was out of breath and could not immediately speak. She stopped and faced him, fervently wishing she was safely gone.

But when she looked at him she saw he was deeply upset.

'Gabby, this is nonsense. Don't go.'

'What do you mean . . . ? I . . .'

'I don't want you to go. I don't want you to leave the farm.

I didn't mean any of the things I said. It was wicked of me . . . I was way out of line.'

'Charlie, that's not why I'm leaving. I'm leaving because . . .'

'Because you were in love with another man and you were going to leave me for him and you were probably right. But he's dead, Gabby, nothing is going to bring him back. I know things will never be as they were, they can't be, but I want you to stay here. I don't want you to go. Whatever's happened I don't want you to leave. I'm miserable, Nell's miserable, Josh is way beyond misery . . . I can't say it all in one go. I can't . . . I'm no good at this, you know I'm not, it's probably why we're in this mess . . .'

'Charlie, Charlie . . .' Gabby, astonished, reached out to touch his arm, was horrified to find he was shaking like a leaf. 'Oh, Charlie, you're doing a pretty good job of saying a lot.'

She was going to cry. 'I can't switch my emotions round . . . I am so sad . . . I can't be around you and Nell feeling like this . . . I feel like a traitor. I don't understand. Why do you want me to stay, Charlie?'

'When you don't love me, you mean? When you are still grieving for someone else?'

'Yes.'

'Because,' Charlie said, 'one day you will stop grieving and being unhappy. I know his death will never go away or leave you, but one day you will wake up and it will be spring and you will suddenly realize the birds are singing and you do want to get out of bed. And then this life, me and Nell and Josh, Shadow, the bantams, we'll all still be here, you won't be alone.'

Charlie smiled, ran his hand through his hair anxiously. Gabby brought her hands up to her face and crumpled to the ground, sobbing. Charlie stood for a moment awkwardly, undecided, and then he went and knelt by Gabby and waited.

Eventually she lifted her face up and said, 'Charlie . . . I have to leave.'

'Why?'

'I'm pregnant.'

The blood drained from Charlie's face. He stared at her. 'But I thought you couldn't have any more ... All these years ...' He thought quickly back. 'It's not mine?'

She shook her head.

'How do you know? Gabby, what about that day on the beach?'

'I got my period that night.'

'But it could have been?'

'Yes.'

He got up, turned away, and Gabby saw he was crying. She went and stood by him, dared not touch him. 'All those years ...' he repeated, '... when we hoped and tried, and nothing ...' His tone was bitter.

'I'm sorry. I'm truly sorry, Charlie. What you said just now was more than I deserve. How sad ...' her voice broke again, '... that we only start to talk on the point of leaving.'

Gabby moved away and walked slowly up the field towards the house. She needed to leave quickly and was relieved to see Elan's Jeep parked in the yard. Charlie called out and Gabby turned and waited till he caught her up.

'Gabby ... No one will know it's not mine. We can bring it up here on the farm like we did Josh. You know we've always wanted another child. It can have a wonderful childhood. Please. Stay. Let us look after you, please.'

Gabby took his hands. 'Charlie, you say I don't love you ... I have lived with you for twenty-odd years, you are the father of my child ... I care deeply, but I cannot stay as if nothing has happened. Believe me, it wouldn't work, really it wouldn't.'

Charlie held on to her hands for a minute. 'Then will you think about it? Will you not rule it out of your life completely?'

'I will think about it, Charlie. Thank you.'

She reached up to kiss his cheek. 'Take care.'

Then she moved quickly towards Elan and Nell in the yard.

Chapter 79

'He has your eyes,' I say in wonder, hardly daring to touch my tiny son.

'But he has your hair.'

'And both his parents' foolhardiness, I shouldn't wonder,' Lisette says, pretending crossness, but her eyes tell me she is feeling no such thing. 'I am going to my bed. Do not keep Isabella from her sleep, Tom.'

She pauses. 'Take care when you leave.'

I look up. 'Is there something I should know, Lisette?'

Lisette sighs. 'I am uneasy but cannot say why. It may be only that I am old-fashioned and nervous about the impropriety of you being here, Tom.'

'I will leave like a shadow, Lisette.'

We lie on the bed with the baby between us. I am silent and Isabella asks, 'What is it, Tom?'

'I, too, am uneasy. I do not like creeping round like a guilty lover. Isabella, we cannot stay here and I am afraid you have grown fond of the place and of the people.'

'I have. But Tom, I am not a child, we cannot remain here under Richard's nose, it would be cruel and impossible. This house and this village will always be here. It is a house we can return to with our children. I will arrange for it to be rented out so that it will not remain empty and fall into disrepair.'

I smile, surprised. 'I can see that you have thought about this carefully.'

'I have. I wanted to know there was always a place to return to and that my children might also know this. Not my father's house or my husband's, but my own. A piece of my heart will always remain here.'

I sit up and take her hand. 'Isabella, do you feel the same sense of urgency to be gone as I do?'

'I do, Tom. That is why I have tried to put my affairs in order and have spoken to my father and to my solicitor with instructions. Tom, it means so much to me to be reunited with my father. He seems suddenly old and gentler and somehow it has made me feel safer. Oh, I have so much to tell you ...'

I laugh. 'We are going to have a whole lifetime of talking, my beautiful and clever Isabella ...'

How she has changed in only a few months. The girl is gone. This is a woman who can think for herself, for our child and for me. It is instinct, I think, like a mother in the wild with her cubs, who thinks ahead in order to survive. I worry less now about taking her to an unknown and strange destination.

'I have obtained work in Prince Edward Island and a place for us to live. But I have also accepted work in Newfoundland for a few months. Even in summer it is a very bleak place. It comes with lodgings, but it may be better for you to wait for me in Prince Edward Island ... I am worried that this new life will be strange for you and lonely.'

I feel suddenly anxious, unsure that I am doing the right thing. Maybe we should stay in England ...

Isabella lifts the baby to her shoulder for he is grizzling and she pats him gently.

'Tom. You know I have always wanted to travel and see foreign places. Why, I have hardly been out of Cornwall ... But I do not want to be parted from you ever again. I want to come with you to New-found-land. I will be content anywhere as long as you are with me.'

I lie back on the bed in relief. Isabella gets up and goes to the small nursing chair by the window and starts to feed our baby. I place my arms behind my head and watch her as she croons to him. I am consumed with love and pride and desire.

All I want is here in this room and I long to carry them off to safety across the sea to begin our lives together.

I say, 'I made inquiries for passages to New England from Calais. It is a larger port and therefore easier to mix with the crowds. We will just be one more family seeking their fortune.'

'And how shall we travel there, Tom?'

'As yet I am unsure. We cannot take passage here in St Piran or from Falmouth, but I have friends in Penzance and Newlyn. I am afraid it will be another uncomfortable journey for you ...'

Isabella smiles and changes the baby to her other breast.

'Do not think to dissuade me from an uncomfortable life with you, Tom, for I am afraid Thomas and I are going to accompany you everywhere.'

We hear an owl out in the dark and smile at each other. We are warm inside and we are together. Isabella puts Thomas back in his crib and lies beside me on the bed. We lie entwined sleepily for a while, silent in the dark, but I cannot relax. I gently disentangle myself and kiss her forehead.

'I must leave you to sleep, Isabella. I want to be up early to arrange things. If you do not see me tomorrow, do not worry, it is only that I am about my business ...' I go back to kiss her once more, then shut the door quietly.

I am just about to open the door at the back of the house and slide out when I feel a hand on my arm. I jump and stifle a shout.

'Ssh!' Lisette says and draws me down the passage and into the kitchen. My father sits at the table where a single candle burns, looking grim.

I can feel my chest tighten with anxiety. 'What is it, Pa?'

'Thy sister's husband, John, is being paid by Sir Richard to spy on this house. He will know thou art back.'

'How do you know this?'

'Mr Vyvyan called me to his house earlier. He had overheard a conversation which worried him and then thy stupid brother-in-law was flashing money about in the public house. I followed him; he watches the house till dusk and returns at daybreak, but he is out there now, across the road, under the trees at the front. He is watching Isabella's room.'

'I have seen him too once or twice on the road but thought

nothing of it, only that he was keeping out of Ada's way on the route to the public house,' Lisette says.

I sit down heavily on a kitchen chair. 'What does this mean?'

'Mr Vyvyan thinks Sir Richard might be going to drag Isabella through the London Courts, ruin her reputation to get custody of the child.'

'But the child is not his!' I cry. 'Why would he want another man's child?'

'Because he has no heir,' my father says. 'Mr Vyvyan can think of no other reason for him having the house watched.'

'I do not think anyone saw me come here,' I say. 'I did not come by the road and I came in the back door. It was dark when Lisette let me in.'

'Good,' my father replies. 'Mr Vyvyan is arranging a boat to France. Thou must be ready at dusk tomorrow, Tom. Lisette will get Isabella up to the house.'

'How?'

'John will know Isabella's routine. I dare not wake her now in case he is still out there. But the baby is due his next feed just before sunrise,' Lisette says. 'A light is always on in her room at this time and I can prepare her to move quickly.'

'John always returns to Ada's bed some time in the night and he likes his breakfast. Isabella must leave the house then.'

'One of the maids is the same size as Isabella. She will take her place for the rest of the day in and around the garden.'

I stand up, shaken.

'There is no fool like an old fool, Tom. Let me check John has gone, then get thysen back home and I will follow.'

A few hours later Lisette touched Isabella in the half-light, trying not to startle her. She put a hand to her lips and Isabella sat up, instantly awake. The baby still slept and Isabella, trembling, started to take things out of drawers and place them on the bed. She knew she could take little.

She took her private letters and the deeds to the house and placed them in her bag to give to her father, then she pulled a drawer out of the little carved chest of drawers and placed Tom's

554

letters and the grass ring between the back of the drawer and the base. She paused and abruptly went to her desk, wrote one more letter and placed that behind the drawer with the others.

Hanna, the little maid, came in and put on one of Isabella's dresses. Lisette had made a bundle of a doll for her to rock and croon to. The house was full of a sense of urgency which must remain within the walls.

Isabella threw Hanna's cloak around her with shaking hands and announced she was ready. Then come the worst moment: leaving Lisette.

'Miss Isabella, do not say goodbye to me. I will come to your father's house late this afternoon, but I must keep to my routine. I will visit Anna as usual with my bundle, and then I will make my way to you. We have always known this day would come . . . now you must go.'

Isabella and Bridget, the other maid, slipped out of the back door. The day was still misty and they were glad of it. They linked arms with small Thomas hidden beneath Isabella's cloak and made their way round the house and gained the path to the road. This was the one place any watcher from the front would see them, and they turned along the coastal path which would join the bottom of Daniel Vyvyan's garden.

It was a good three miles and Isabella could not believe how heavy a small baby felt after a short distance. When they were well on their way along the lonely path Bridget took the baby from Isabella, keeping him hidden. The girl was stronger than Isabella, and Isabella realized she had not yet got her strength back.

Charlotte was waiting for them by the small hidden gate the family used to get to the cliffs. She was in gardening clothes, though certainly not gardening but watching for them, and was very relieved to see Isabella. She took the child and they hurried up to the house.

Her father greeted her at the door. 'Come in, come in, Isabella. Come, you must breakfast, then we must talk. You are very pale.'

Isabella turned to Charlotte. 'Will you take care of Bridget, Charlotte? Do you not think it better that she return with Lisette later?'

'I do. Come, Bridget, I will take you to the kitchen.'

Her father poured Isabella her tea and she saw that his hand was not quite steady. She looked around the breakfast room. She had not been here since she was fourteen years old and yet it was much as she remembered it.

'Papa, what is it that you heard that so concerns you?'

Daniel sighed and drank his tea. 'I have thought for a while that Richard has not been himself. Allowing for his distress over your . . . all this business, Isabella, he has been behaving most oddly of late. He consults with me less often, that too is understandable in the circumstances, but some of his decisions have been uncharacteristically rash.

'At the board meetings, when shareholders start to question his judgement, which has always been sound, he grows most obstinate and rude. Men are beginning to withdraw their money, after all it is not just Richard's money that may be lost over an inadvisable investment.'

Charlotte came back into the room, followed by a maid with thin slices of bread and a pot of honey for Isabella.

'Thank you, Charlotte. Is my baby . . . ?'

'He is safe on Cook's knee. I will return him to you as soon as you have breakfasted.'

Daniel went on. 'I really do believe your husband to be quite irrational at present, Isabella. Whether this is due to drink or grief, I do not know. I am not the only one of his friends who has come to this conclusion. It was Trathan who gave me warning, Isabella.'

'Mr Trathan! Why, he has been with Richard since his naval days. He is a loyal servant and devoted to Richard.'

'That is why I took note of what he had to say. He told me the Summer House was being watched and that Sir Richard had been behaving out of character, and that he did not know how or for what reason, but he believed you to be in danger. He told me it was with profound sadness he came to me but he genuinely believes Sir Richard is about to do something he will deeply regret while he is not of a sound mind. That is why he came. And I consider that a loyal servant.'

'I, too, Papa. So I have driven Richard to act . . .'

'No, Isabella. I have seen lately what I could not have known before. Richard's family have a long history running a small empire. He is used to control and totally unused to not having his way. I also see him as something of an obsessive. He cannot come to terms with what has happened.'

'Papa, he used to be one of the kindest men I knew.'

'But a jealous one?'

'Very, Papa.'

'And there you have it, Isabella. Will you rest for half an hour while I see to the day's business? I want to check … I will talk to you later. I will leave you with Charlotte.'

He squeezed his wife's shoulder and was gone.

'Charlotte, I know it is silly, but I need Thomas within sight of me.'

'I am not surprised. Come, we will go upstairs and then I will bring him to you.'

She took Isabella's arm. 'I thought you might like to rest in your mama's old room.'

Helena's rooms had been redecorated beautifully, the colour of primroses. And the piano was in the same place. When Charlotte had gone, Isabella lifted the lid and ran her fingers along the keys, and the ghost of her childhood and Helena's voice filled the room. Isabella wept and realized she was weeping for the thing she had done to Richard. The terrible, irreparable hurt that would lie side by side with her happiness with Tom.

Thomas was brought to her and she lay with him on Helena's bed with her eyes closed, not sleeping but listening to the movements of a once familiar house which had not changed much and which comforted her. She tried to still her heart, which would not be still until Tom was there, until they were both gone from St Piran to their new life.

The rest of the day was spent signing things for her father, giving him powers to send her money on to her. To oversee the Summer House as part of his estate. Sensibly he asked her to sign a will in order that Thomas might be financially safe, for his estate would eventually go to his grandson.

'I am unsure of the law, Isabella. If you remain legally married to

557

Richard, if he will never grant you a divorce, your money must be safeguarded for you and your children. As you know, Charlotte has no children so all I have will come to you.'

'Papa, we will not leave England forever, my heart is in the Summer House and my children will come there and their children. It is a place of happiness . . .'

Her father smiled. 'And illicit love, it seems.'

Isabella blushed. 'Papa, I love Tom so much. He is my whole life. I could love no other, no other at all.'

Her face was alive with her happiness and Daniel Vyvyan said gently, 'I have the greatest respect for Ben and I do not doubt Tom is like his father. I have no fear for you.'

'Thank you, Papa.'

'Tonight I have arranged a vessel into the cove. The tide is right and although it is not ideal I cannot risk any harbour or port this side of the coast. But you will have to be rowed out, no schooner can come beyond the rocks and there are the neap tides. She will sail to a small port in France . . . where I have bought three passenger tickets on a schooner to Newfoundland.'

He smiled at his daughter. 'The schooner is the safest one I know for you to travel on. I have just bought her for a great sum of money. You will be three or more weeks at sea, Isabella, and it will not be an easy voyage, but you will be free to lead a life you have chosen and I denied you . . .'

His voice broke and Isabella went to him. 'Oh, Papa . . .'

He held her for a moment and then kissed her forehead. 'Go and rest, feed your baby and then prepare for your journey.'

At the door, Isabella said suddenly, 'Three passenger tickets, Papa?'

'Did you think Lisette would let you and young Thomas leave without her? You are a Mr and Mrs Foye travelling with your baby and nursemaid.'

At midnight a little procession slipped out of the small gate and crossed to the coastal path, dangerous in the dark, until they reached the cove. Charlotte and Daniel held Isabella's arms as they stumbled down the steep stony path to the cove. Two servants held lights to guide them as they descended. Isabella was afraid of falling with the baby but would not let anyone else carry him.

There was a rowing boat swinging gently on the black slate sea and a moon so rapidly come from the clouds they did not need their lights and extinguished them. Standing by the rowing boat were Anna, Lisette and two seamen.

Isabella embraced Ben and Anna, Charlotte and her father, and then the baby was handed to Lisette in the boat. Tom lifted Isabella in and climbed in himself.

'God go with thee,' Ben whispered.

'God be with you this day and always,' Daniel echoed.

The sailors pushed the boat away and jumped in. Isabella watched the four people on the shore who seemed to move closer together for comfort. The night was silent except for the slap of the oars in the water. She stared and stared back at them, in sudden anguish for the loss of a father she had only just found again, and for Ben and Anna who were losing Tom and their grandson.

She felt suddenly afraid and cut off from all she knew. Her father, her home, her place of safety. But she made no sound. This was just the beginning. Her life was with Tom. She was with Tom, and all would be well.

Chapter 80

Josh visited Marika before he left for his posting in Germany.

'Did you have a good holiday?'

'I would have preferred to go with you. Two blokes do different things. But I loved Turkey.'

They were silent, looking at each other.

'What did you do?' Josh asked.

'I worked in Marks and Spencer's and was very miserable.'

Another silence.

'Marika, I don't want it to be like this. I don't want something my mother did to come between us.'

'But it is not your mother coming between us, Josh. It is a thing in you I do not understand, and which makes me afraid because you are so totally inflexible in your first judgement. And even when you have had time to think you remain immovable.'

'Don't you see that you too are obstinate, Marika? If I'm judging my mother, you are judging me. I thought when you loved someone you supported them whatever your own feelings were?'

'Exactly!' Then Marika thought about this. 'Maybe I am judging you. But Josh, I cannot understand how you can seem to stop caring and worrying about someone overnight.'

'Did I say I had stopped caring?'

'Of course I know in my heart that it is not possible that you do not still love Gabby, she is your mother. But to let her go on thinking you might not care . . . when you are so much part of her life. To go on with this for so long, that is what I am having difficulty with. I do not want that ever to be me.'

Josh said quietly, 'I could write or speak to Gabby and say something trite I do not mean. I could do it to please you, to sleep better at night. But I would not mean anything I say now, and until I can speak words I truly feel I will not speak to her at all, Marika.'

Marika nodded. 'I see that. You are honest.' She held out her hand. 'Good luck with your posting.'

Josh felt sick, could not take her hand. 'What are you going to do?'

'I am going back to Sarajevo to teach for a while.'

Josh stared at her, laughed, threw back his head in pain.

'I can't believe this is happening. I'm going to wake up. This is a bloody nightmare. Marika, I love you. That's it. I have no doubts. It's always going to be you. I want to marry you and live in army quarters in Germany with you . . . I can't get my head round . . . this . . .'

Marika was crying without sound. 'I love you, too. Do you think I can believe this either? Can you not feel something? Say something you mean to Gabby before you leave? Can you not find anything in your heart for her before you get on that plane?'

Josh turned and made for the door. He did not look back once. He got in the car and drove and drove with no idea where he was going. It was only a few hours later he realized he was heading home to Cornwall. As he bumped down the lane he saw Nell's familiar figure feeding the bantams and Charlie way up by the new houses, ploughing, with the seagulls flocking behind him, diving in the new-turned earth. He thought for a second Nell was Gabby, that she was home. He suddenly remembered an odd dream he had once, where Gabby disappeared in mist, and how disturbed he had felt.

He turned the engine off and sat, his shoulders shaking with grief.

Gabby, Gabby. She had always been here, at the farm, *always*. Not a part of his childhood, *the whole of it*. There at the school gates, hair as dark and shiny as a raven's wing, smiling at his anxious little face.

There in the dark if he was ill. Long days down at the cove where she read to him until her voice gave out . . . Endless days running wild with friends, but she was always there in the kitchen at the end of them . . . and *he knew, knew* she loved him above all others. There was Charlie, Nell and Elan, but they all had other lives and interests.

The sea and the sky and the fields and the farm were theirs, his and Gabby's. The canvas of his life and the security. A thing he could return to again and again with his own children. His parents, a perfect painting he could walk into any time, because the dynamics would never change.

But they had, and the shock of it . . . the terror of memories of happiness crumbling into something less perfect than the ones that lived inside his head, the terror of getting too close and hearing words that would shatter all that he believed he had shared here with the people he loved, was a thing Josh could not risk.

He drove the car into the side of the lane and jumped over the hedge, made his way across the fields and down into the cove. He sat on the jagged rocks throwing stones into the dark November sea. A little dinghy with a tan gaff-rigged sail was tacking bravely across the mouth of the cove, flying with the wind back and forth. It took a brave man to sail on this coast and Josh thought about his mother's figurehead, when small boats without engines would set forth valiantly for foreign shores through seas that would make most men quail nowadays.

The fishermen, the lifeboat men, and the air-sea rescue were the heroes now. He had watched them all his life chugging back and forth across the cove from the harbour, disappearing into huge vicious seas. He had looked up at the helicopters clattering across the sky, buzzing along the coastline during long hot summers. It was partly why he had wanted to fly.

He looked up at the cliffs where the noise of the tractor and Charlie were lost in the pounding of the waves, and he felt what he suddenly realized Charlie felt every single day; the continuation of something, Charlie's pride in the land that had been ploughed by his father and his father's father. It would skip a generation, but Josh had a sense of his own son here and the shadows of his ancestors.

Whatever, life went on and you adapted, if you were wise. He jumped from the rocks, took a last look at the rough sea and made his way up the path, home.

He had been furious with his mother, but he knew he could never stop loving her. The memories of those long golden days were indelible, he saw that now. They could not be taken away by either words or deeds. They were a part of what he was; Gabby had made sure of that. He could and always would look back on his childhood with utter happiness.

Chapter 81

The small boat arrived on the Brittany coast at dawn. It had been an uncomfortable crossing and Isabella and Lisette disembarked with relief. The only person who had slept was small Thomas, who lay in his father's arms throughout the voyage.

A gentleman was leaning on the quay wall waiting for them. He introduced himself as a Captain Abrahams. He saw Isabella shivering and suggested they all boarded his vessel without delay so that she might drink tea to revive her and then she could rest in her cabin. He called them Mr and Mrs Foye and guided them quickly in the dark to the vessel which was moored to the quay. Isabella saw with a shock that it was the *Lady Isabella*.

I have booked you on the safest vessel I know. She turned to Tom and saw that he knew and the irony was not lost on him. She looked upon the wooden features of herself and her fear rose again. Was it wise to escape to a new life on her husband's ship? She kept her hood tight around her head as she was helped aboard. She did not know how much the captain knew of their circumstances.

They were shown to their cabins. Tom and Isabella in one, with Lisette and the baby next door. The captain smiled before he left them.

'I am very happy to have you onboard my ship. Mr Vyvyan and my father grew up together and we have long owed him a favour ... I hope you will be comfortable. We set sail within the hour.'

Isabella sank down onto the small bunk.

'Tom,' she said, 'to sail on the *Lady Isabella* ... is it not perverse? Is it not bad luck?'

Tom looked down on her. 'The *Lady Isabella* is bound for

Newfoundland, Isabella, and Sir Richard is no longer the owner. He sold the schooner on to your father. There were passages to be had on her and your father knows the captain, and most of all, as far as he was concerned, this is the safest and most comfortable ship there is.'

Isabella sighed. 'You are right. I am tired and anxious and it seems odd to be on this ship, that is all.'

She looked around and tried to cheer herself. 'I had forgotten how comfortable you and Ben made the cabins.' She smiled. 'Perhaps you are right, Tom, this is going to be a more comfortable voyage than we have had so far.'

Lisette changed Thomas and then handed him to Isabella.

'Feed Thomas, Miss Isabella, and then I will come and take him while you sleep.'

'I do not think I will sleep until we are underway.'

Lisette went to her own cabin and Tom undid his case and took out a thick fisherman's jersey and hat.

'I am too restless to stay still, Isabella. I will go up on deck while you feed young Thomas. I am not far away. I think it best that you and Lisette keep to your cabins until after we have sailed.'

Isabella lay on her bunk with the baby at her breast.

She crooned softly to Thomas. He was happy and as he lay in her arms he suddenly smiled at Isabella and she laughed with delight.

'Thomas smiled, Lisette,' Isabella said as Lisette came into the cabin.

Lisette laughed. 'I think my little bird has the wind. The sun is about to rise, Miss Isabella, on a new day.'

They stared at each other. Neither could really believe they were leaving England.

'You are brave to accompany me, Lisette. I am so glad to have you with me. We have been through much, you and I, have we not?'

'We have indeed, Miss Isabella. I surprise myself at journeying at my age, but I looked after you and I will look after my little Thomas until he no longer needs me.'

'He is very lucky. Will you leave him with me? He is so cosy here and fast asleep.'

'No, Miss Isabella, you must rest. You are exhausted and feeding Thomas. I will return him to you in an hour or so.'

Isabella kissed the top of Thomas's head and handed him to Lisette. Then she slept almost immediately. She stirred when the gangplank was withdrawn. She faintly heard the sound of the ropes and chains and footsteps about the deck but slept again, the deep, exhausted sleep of someone who had not slept for days.

There was a sudden draught as the cabin door opened, then it was quickly shut again, but Isabella did not stir.

Tom watched the sun edge over the land and turn the new day a brilliant gold that sparkled across the water. This was a new beginning. He was responsible for two lives, not just his own. He thought of the voyage ahead and prayed for good weather and a safe passage.

Behind him the ship was all activity as they made ready to sail. Relatives and friends were making hasty goodbyes. He heard the gangplank pulled up and turned suddenly with a need to make sure all was well below.

He caught a snatch of colour on the quay, three people walking quickly away from the ship. The gap between land and sea was widening. He clattered down the steps to the cabins. Lisette's cabin door was ajar and he leant inside but it was empty. He pushed his own cabin door open and Isabella was sitting upright trying to wake up. She stared at him, trying to remember where she was, and Tom went to her, gently pushed her hair from her eyes, said, 'Did Lisette take the baby on deck?'

Isabella looked at him. 'I fell asleep. I think they are in her cabin, next door.'

'I will go and look for her. Lie back and wake up slowly.'

Tom went into Lisette's cabin and looked around. Her luggage was there and her cloak. He went back on deck and walked right around a ship he knew every inch of. For a moment he leant on the rail and fought his fear.

He went to find the captain. He listened to Tom and then sent two sailors to search again round the ship and in each cabin. The *Lady Isabella* was not a large vessel and there were few places for a woman and baby to disappear into.

It was then the second mate knocked on the door.

'Captain, it was just as the last guests were leaving. A woman between two men was being pushed towards the gangplank. I saw her anxiety and that she was carrying a child, but as I went towards the gangway to help her the two men caught her up and with a flourish lifted her off her feet and off the ship and away, one taking the baby for her. I thought no more about it . . . but now . . . I'm sorry I did not say anything . . .'

Tom turned pale and hurried back to Isabella. She was standing in Lisette's cabin holding a letter.

'Where is Lisette, Tom? Where is the baby?'

'What have you got there?'

'I have just picked it up from the floor.'

Tom tore it open.

We have the authority of the English courts and the French police to make the arrest of Lady Isabella Magor for the abduction of Sir Richard Magor's son, Richard Daniel Charles Magor, aged two months. A court order was gained on . . . forbidding his removal from English soil pending the custody hearing in June . . . Lady Isabella Magor's arrest may be avoided if the child is returned forthwith to his legal father . . .

Isabella stared at Tom, clutched him, knew by his face. 'Where are Lisette and the baby, Tom?'

'They are gone from the ship, Isabella,' Tom whispered. 'Taken.'

He saw again that flash of colour, the two men bundling someone between them. 'Come, we must go to the captain.'

Isabella gave a long, low, agonizing moan of despair and Tom was reminded of the cows in the fields when their calves were taken, heads raised to the sky in an endless lament.

'Come,' he said gently.

The captain looked down at the piece of paper.

'I doubt this is a genuine legal document. The words seem couched to frighten . . .'

He hesitated. 'Unfortunately Sir Richard is a very influential and powerful man. A lot of our jobs ride on his recommendation. Did you know he sold the *Lady Isabella* to your father only three weeks ago? It was difficult to understand why when the tonnage is good, but ...' he stared at Isabella, '... I understand now. Your likeness to the figurehead is profound ...'

He stopped, seeing her distress. 'I am sorry; this is nothing to you at this moment. We stop briefly at Cadiz for two more passengers; I will go to the British Consul as soon as we arrive. I am sorry, I can do no more than this at present.'

He stood up and went round his desk to stand with them.

'I was asked to take care of you and it seems I did not take the request seriously enough, knowing none of the circumstances. The only comfort, Lady Isabella, is that your baby will not come to harm. He will, in these circumstances, be given the greatest care.'

'He is only two months old,' Isabella whispered, then vehemently, 'I have not been Lady Isabella for some time. I do not use that title.'

'I am so very sorry,' the captain said again.

'Thank you,' Tom said, 'I do not think there is anything you could have done to prevent this. It would have been executed in one way or another. In one place or another.'

Back in their cabin Tom ordered tea and made Isabella drink, helped her undress and placed her under the covers. She whimpered like a small animal and it broke Tom's heart.

'Hold me,' she whispered. 'Hold me, Tom.'

He climbed into the tiny bunk and lay awkwardly holding her until he thought she slept, and then he fell into a restless sleep himself. He woke and her skin was burning, her petticoats sodden and she could not speak to him coherently.

Tom went to the jug and bathed her face, and then frightened he went out to find help. There was a middle-aged woman taking a turn round the deck and Tom asked her if she would come to look at his wife who was unwell. The woman went with him willingly and bent immediately to Isabella.

'Where is your child?' she asked Isabella. 'You need to feed the child.'

Tom could not answer and just shook his head.

The woman, thinking Isabella's child must have died, said, 'Oh the poor dear. Will you please call the steward and would you mind going to my cabin, number twenty-four, and calling my daughter to come and assist me with your wife?'

Tom left the women and went up on deck. There was a sudden and terrible heaviness in him. He moved to the front of the ship, watching the water racing past the gown of his figurehead. Her head was raised proudly in front of the ship. Lady Isabella.

He had brought this about. Isabella might now be standing in her garden at Mylor, bored perhaps, but safe. Not enduring a fever on a ship going hundreds of miles to a place she could not even imagine, without her child.

He had seen how tight and painful her breasts were. How she flinched when touched. How would those women fix her heart? A woman whose baby had been snatched so cruelly from her.

When Tom returned to the cabin Isabella looked cooler. The two women had bound her breasts tightly to try and stop the milk coming and Tom felt awkward and useless and to blame.

He kept thinking of his tiny son taken from under his nose and guilt and tiredness made him want to curl into a ball. He had done nothing but travel for months to reach Isabella and his child, and when he reached them he was incapable of protecting either.

Isabella, seeing his face, held out her hand. 'Tom, it is not your fault. I know that is what you are thinking.'

'It is. Isabella, are you feeling better?'

'I will for a little while, but the pain will return. Tom, poor Lisette, she must have been so frightened.'

'She will not let anything happen to her Thomas.'

'That is true.'

'I think Sir Richard may not have the law on his side.'

'Tom, how will Lisette feed Thomas? He will be so hungry. He is still so small.'

'I think your husband will have thought of that. He has thought carefully about many things concerning you and the baby. He will not hurt Thomas; he merely wants to own him.'

'But he cannot, he is our baby.'

'We will reach Cadiz in two or three days and the captain will wait for the mail boat while oranges are loaded. I hope we have word from your father while we are there.'

*   *   *

There was no word waiting when they arrived in Cadiz. The captain went to the British Consul and found them unhelpful. There really was nothing they could do. No crime had been committed on Spanish soil. It was an internal matter for the French and English authorities.

He returned to the ship. He was sorry, he told Tom, but he could not delay the sailing of his ship for more than a day. There were other passengers and too much money involved in the timing of their destination.

Isabella and Tom dared not alight from the ship. Tom was afraid now of Sir Richard's extended powers and terrified Isabella too would be taken from him. They were standing at the rail, four hours from sailing, when they saw the *Peninsular Steam Navigation Company* appear over the horizon carrying the mail from Falmouth.

Isabella stood clutching Tom, praying there was word from her father.

There was. It was short and to the point and obvious he had written in a hurry to catch the mail boat.

> *My Dear Daughter,*
>
> *I am afraid all is as I feared. My grandson and Lisette are returned to England in custody of the court. They are both safe and well. Lisette is still in charge of Thomas in Falmouth and she has employed a wet nurse.*
>
> *Isabella, were you aware that your husband had registered himself as the father of your child? This is a legal document and it will be most difficult to disprove him as the father who has a right to his son and heir. I understand he is prepared to make Lisette swear that he had knowledge of you during your time at the Summer House or he will separate her from Thomas.*
>
> *Isabella, do not disembark but proceed on your journey. I will not have you dragged through the courts by a man deranged. I will start to put my own case as well as yours to the lawyers but this will take many, many months.*
>
> *My child, I can only imagine what you must be feeling.*

I regret that, against my better judgement, I waited too long to help you.

Take comfort that Charlotte and I will never lose sight of our grandson and that Lisette is with him and that no harm will come to him, save that he has lost his mama, and I my beloved daughter.

I will get word to you in Prince Edward Island and with the advent of steam and faster ships the distance between us all will grow less …

I remain, your loving father.

Isabella was very still. There was such relief that she had had word of Thomas; that he was safe and that he was still with Lisette. But her heart was like stone. She knew deep, deep inside her that she would never see her small son again. He would be called another name and would have no memory of her.

They left Cadiz. Left it in a golden and beautiful haze that could not touch their misery and guilt. Isabella turned to Tom.

'Tom, we did wrong. I humiliated a proud man and this is my punishment.'

Tom could not answer, turned away from the wretchedness of Isabella's pale, drawn face.

Isabella moved forward to the prow, her back to the land. Her profile matched that of the figurehead, carried the same expression of haunting sadness. A seaman raising a for'ard sail looked down at the mirror image of their figurehead and shivered. Stared at the woman, this rumoured Lady Isabella, and thought it was not a good omen.

The captain too looked down and was uneasy. He wished he was not carrying this beautiful woman. The start of this voyage had been inauspicious, bedevilled with setback. The crew were apprehensive. It was a long, perilous voyage and they needed fair winds, luck, and God to go with them.

The crew were proud of their ship and of their figurehead but they were superstitious. The figurehead on the prow, resolute and immobile, was to guard them from all ills. They were afraid to cast their eyes upon the flesh and blood woman with her terrible air of loss.

Chapter 82

It was March and Gabby had reached her eighth month. She had lived in the empty London house all winter, working consistently, filling the hours. Pain would still catch her unawares under her ribs and she could not remove Mark's dressing gown from the door.

Nell rang her every week with news of the farm, of Charlie, Elan, Peter; small everyday things, as if to root her somewhere, one foot still on the farm. Gabby had been like a hermit, closed into the house, keeping to a routine as if her life depended on it. She waited for Nell's phone calls in the same way she waited for the coloured postcards to fall through the letter-box from Germany. One day there would be a letter, Gabby knew this.

John Bradbury rang Gabby and asked if she could go down to look at the figurehead, he had found some flaking on the face. He met Gabby off the train at Truro. The fire in the cottage was alight and Gabby felt a little surge of pleasure to be back.

'Gabby, it is so good to see you again. I've asked Nell and Peter to supper, is that all right?'

'Of course it is. Nell rings me each week, John, and it will be great to see Peter again. Can I go across and look at Isabella now?'

'Gabby, will you be all right going over on your own while I organize supper?'

Gabby smiled. 'I am pregnant, not ill! Of course I will.'

As she stood before the figurehead once more, she felt

her stomach lurch with memory of Mark. She peered up at the supposed peeling which was really not too bad and she suspected that Isabella was a combined ploy to draw her back to Cornwall.

Gabby smiled, touched. It was good to be back. Primroses coated the banks in rashes of yellowy-green and she was glad her child would be born in spring. At the farm the fields would lie sloping to the sea, acres of moss green buds ready to open. The pickers would descend as they always did. She turned to look through the arched window. *Season follows season in exactly the same way, yet we are always somehow surprised that all goes on so casually without us, no matter what we do or where we are.*

Today Gabby could not tell what Lady Isabella was thinking. Her eyes looked down, impregnable, giving nothing away.

'When I've had my baby,' Gabby told her, 'I will come and give you your last beauty treatment. I am too awkward at the moment.'

She switched the light off and locked the door again and went out in the late afternoon to look at Lisette's grave. The old part of the graveyard had been cleared of brambles and generally tidied up.

'Yes,' John said when she got back to the vicarage, 'we have a group of wonderful volunteers from an adult college nearby for pupils with learning difficulties.'

When Gabby heard Nell's car she went out and they hugged in the little cobbled yard.

'I've brought you bantam eggs and homemade bread, Gabby . . .'

She stood back and looked at her. 'You look very beautiful.'

'Huge, you mean,' Gabby said, taking Nell into the little cottage.

'What a very atmospheric room,' Nell said, a little unsure she liked the stillness of it. 'I suppose it is because it is the oldest part of the house.'

She pulled a letter from her pocket. 'Gabby, this came for you.'

Gabby's heart raced. 'From Josh?'

'No,' Nell said. 'I'm afraid not, lovie.'

Disappointed, Gabby opened it and sat abruptly on the bed.

'What is it?' Nell asked anxiously.

'It's from the Salvation Army. They trace people, don't they? Clara, my mother, has died. Her sister, Aunt Bella, asked them to trace me.'

Nell sat beside Gabby and waited.

Gabby said, after a while, 'It's strange, I feel angry, not sad. With Bella mostly because she just walked away and left me to it.'

Nell rubbed Gabby's back gently. 'It might be good to know if she had a reason?'

'Maybe.' Gabby got up. 'I hope Clara didn't have a horrid death, Nell, but it is no good pretending I feel very much.'

Nell thought, as they went out of the little cottage, Gabby may not feel anything immediately but she will feel sadness later for a life lost.

She said abruptly, 'Will you come over to the farm, Gabby? Charlie was so wistful when he knew I was seeing you. He won't put you under pressure. I think he just wants to see you. Come to lunch. I'll ask Elan, too.'

Gabby nodded. 'Of course I'll come, Nell.' She turned away. She could not tell Nell her caution was not because she did not want to visit the farm but because she missed it so much.

'Before we go into the house . . . Have you heard from Josh, Nell? How is he? Is he enjoying Germany?'

'He's enjoying his job. I am not sure he has enjoyed Dortmund particularly, except that it is a good base for his seemingly constant holidays that the army allows. He always asks after you. He still sends postcards?'

Gabby smiled. 'Yes. It's wonderful to have them, but you can't get much news on a postcard.'

It was so long since Gabby had socialized with anyone at all that she suddenly felt dread. John said gently, seeing her face go pale at the sight of the dining-room table laid, 'Dear Gabby. It is only that my kitchen is always such a pigsty that I have laid the table in here. You leave us whenever you feel like it.'

Peter had brought some clippings. 'Gabby, I meant to post these on to you, very dilatory of me. Our young reporter found this. Do you remember? He came to cover the figurehead when it first arrived.'

He handed Gabby an old *Cornishman* newspaper dated 1865. A small paragraph covered the launch of the *Lady Isabella* in St Piran.

> *Despite the inclement weather the schooner* Lady Isabella *was launched with much solemnity from St Piran's quay. The village band played and food and drink were available free of charge, in celebration of the event. However, thunder and lightning and a heavy squall forced band and villagers alike to scatter for shelter from the elements. Mr Trevannow the undertaker was heard to comment this bode ill luck for the small schooner to which Ben Welland the shipwright retorted, 'Aye, I am sure that is what thou would like, for much of thy business depends on the elements.' This to much laughter from the villagers . . .*

Gabby smiled at the quaintness of the report. 'But Mr Trevannow the undertaker was right, wasn't he, Peter?'

'I'm afraid he was. Here is the second thing of interest, Gabby. When Mark looked down the Lloyds List of wrecks he found the *Lady Isabella* there, date and position registered, but there were no Wellands, Magors or Vyvyans on the passenger list. However, one of Mark's young researchers completing his dissertation contacted me. He had travelled back in Mark's footsteps to Newfoundland and had found the graves of the passengers retrieved from the sea at the time of the wreck.

'They had been found by local *Inuit*. The bodies were a Captain Abrahams, the skipper, one old man, and a young woman and young man, both of the approximate ages of Isabella and Tom, who were bound together. They were thought to be a Mr and Mrs Foye who were on the list of passengers. These two names were also on the Lloyds List. I checked.'

Gabby stared at him, took an excited breath. 'Peter, could it be Tom and Isabella?'

'I think so. If they were travelling under a pseudonym they were escaping from something.'

'Without their baby.'

'Without their baby.'

'How sad,' Nell said.

'There is one thing more,' Peter said, excitedly.

Gabby, Nell and John stared at him, waiting.

'Please,' John said, 'put us out of our misery.'

'In 1888 a Thomas Richard Welland sailed out to Newfoundland and brought the bodies of Mr and Mrs Foye home to Cornwall.'

Gabby shivered suddenly. 'Here?' she whispered. 'To St Piran?'

'That is the mystery. It seems not. Where are the graves of Isabella and Tom? Not in St Piran, it seems.'

Charlie was thinner, Gabby saw and he looked a little older because of it. They were awkward with each other, her size didn't help, and Charlie's eyes seemed to be drawn again and again to her stomach.

Elan and the wine at lunch made it easier. Whenever he had been in London they had spent time together.

'I'm trying to inveigle Nell up to my next exhibition, darling. She's got a bad dose of Cornwallitis.'

Nell laughed. 'Well I just might get myself on a train, Elan, especially as you keep threatening us with retiring.'

'It will never happen, Nell. Elan couldn't stop painting even if he wanted to.'

'Don't you be so sure. I am growing old and may retire to a warmer climate.'

After lunch Charlie took Gabby round the farm and showed her the changes in the last few months, and they talked about Josh. 'I've even started to write letters,' he said.

'It's the busy time coming up,' Gabby said. 'How are you doing for pickers?'

'I have to be so careful, there are checks for illegal immigrants all the time and they have got clever at false papers.'

'The fields look beautiful,' Gabby said. 'The weather's just right at the moment.'

'Yes. We start to pick tomorrow. I've got a new lad ready for when Matt retires. He's just finished college, he looks promising. Are you OK to walk along the path for a bit?'

Gabby smiled. 'Of course, but I won't make it down to the cove.'

Charlie said after a while, 'How have you been?'

Gabby did not answer immediately. She knew if she said, 'lonely', Charlie would say, 'come home', and it wasn't fair for she didn't know her own feelings.

'I've worked pretty much to stop myself thinking,' she said eventually.

'How long are you staying at John Bradbury's?'

'A week or so. I'm not sure.'

They turned back to the house. 'I know you may not want to stay at the house, but Nell would love to have you in her cottage, Gabby. She misses you. Could you spend a few days with her?'

Gabby looked at him. 'Of course I could.' She smiled. 'I'm not going anywhere. It's just . . . I don't want to hold your life up, Charlie. I want you to be getting on with it, moving on if you need to.'

'You're not holding me up.'

Elan was coming out of Nell's cottage. Gabby waved. 'I'd better go, Charlie. Elan is giving me a lift back to John's and I feel guilty, he likes to nap in the afternoons.'

'Stay on. Spend the afternoon with Nell. I'll take you back after milking.'

'Are you sure?'

'Yes. Go and tell him.'

Gabby fell asleep by the fire and then Nell cooked scrambled eggs and they sat with Charlie and watched a film, and somehow it was all, for a while, just as it used to be. Then Charlie drove her home. You don't realize how lonely you are until you are with people again, Gabby thought.

Isabella could hardly remember what the sight of land felt like. It seemed to her as if the ship had been ploughing bravely through huge seas for half her lifetime. But for Tom, she would have been very afraid, but he assured her the *Lady Isabella* had been built to withstand waves as large as the ones which broke over her.

Isabella had tried not to grieve so openly when Tom was with her, for she could see it broke his heart. He felt he had not protected her or their child and Isabella knew there was nothing either of them could have done. She should have understood more clearly the nature of her husband.

They had no doubt Thomas would be loved and given all material things, but he would not have a mother ... and there Isabella had to stop dwelling on it for she wept and became ill. She was glad of one thing. She had told Lisette where she had hidden her diary, her grass wedding ring and a letter to her son. She trusted her and knew that when Thomas was grown, if for any reason they did not return, Lisette would tell him the truth of his parents and of his birth.

Meanwhile they clung together, and looked to the future they must make for themselves and for happier times when they would both be reunited with their son. They talked long into the night in their small cabin of their many plans, and Tom described the wonderful places they might one day visit. He had a notion to visit Italy again in order to examine at leisure their statues. He believed Florence to be the most beautiful city in the world.

Now Isabella had recovered from the birth of their son they could lie with each other again, but it was not the same as before for the act now had a sweet and poignant sadness, a knowledge that the world could be cruel and happiness snatched in a second, and they could never forget this or be as they were.

As they drew near New England Isabella overheard Captain Abrahams tell Tom that bad weather was ahead and it would be a rough night and best all passengers kept to their cabins until it had blown itself out.

Tom went round the cabin stowing everything that might fall or harm them away. In the night Isabella heard him leave the cabin and go out for a minute. He was soon back and held her tight and she heard the wild hammering of his heart and then she slept again.

She was awakened and hurled out of the bunk onto the floor. Tom reached for her and held her tight and they stayed on the floor. The noise was fearsome, everything was crashing around them. There was frantic shouting and then the shouts were drowned in the roar of wind and sea. They were tossed around the cabin and the small ship listed on one side, then the other.

Isabella began to pray, 'Hail Mary, Mother of grace, the Lord is with thee … Blessed art thou among women and blessed is the …' when there was a terrible tearing and a crash and splintering, then quiet.

'What is it, Tom?' she whispered, terrified.

'One of the masts is split.'

The pounding started again and in the chaos of the cabin they were twisted nearly upside down. When the ship righted itself Tom staggered up and pulled the lifejackets towards him. He helped her into one and put his own on.

She stared at him. 'Tom?'

'Isabella, I do not think even the Lady Isabella can withstand the force of this storm, but we are not far off land. The small lifeboats will be launched and you must get into one when the order is given …'

'I will not go anywhere without you, Tom.'

Isabella could hear the crew calling and the cabin door was pushed open. Tom pulled her after him and she held on so tight her frozen fingers burnt. The passengers came out of their cabins and staggered forward, all clinging to each other.

The sight that greeted them made some of the women cry out

in panic. The *Lady Isabella* was breaking up. Pieces of her floated on the huge waves breaking over her. Men were trying to launch small boats and they watched in horror as two were washed away into the sea like matchsticks.

Tom turned to Isabella and she cried, 'Bind me to you, Tom. I want to die joined to you as we were in life. Bind me to you.'

Tom did so quickly. 'Isabella, I love you more than life itself.'

'And I you, Tom. I would rather have loved you for a short while than never to have known you at all.'

They looked upon one another and thought how glad they were that their child was not here now. It was true that God did work in mysterious ways. Thomas would have a life. Their lives would go on in him.

Together they saw the wave that would swallow them. They braced themselves, held tight to one another in desperate courage; experienced a moment of terror as the wave towered over them and swept them from the ship, and all was darkness, like a light going out.

Gabby woke screaming, clamped a hand over her mouth. Terrified she switched the lamp on by her bed. It was two o'clock in the morning. Her heart was racing. She sat up trying to calm herself. She was drowning. How Freudian, she thought, and got heavily out of bed.

She made tea and thought about the wisdom of staying with Nell, going back to the farm, and yet she was reluctant to return to London.

She could not sleep again and lay listening to the radio until the birds started singing, then she pulled a jacket over her nightdress and went out to watch the sunrise. She walked carefully on the cobbles, in case she disturbed John, and round into the garden. She sat shivering slightly on an old wooden bench watching the sun come up over the trees. There were shadows across the lawn and she thought she could hear a baby cry but when she listened there was nothing.

She moved down the garden to the trees, for behind them

the sun would rise up above the sea. She walked through the little gate at the bottom and onto the disputed land. It was the most glorious golden sunrise and Gabby shivered for the wonder of it in a garden alone. She placed her hands over her stomach and thought of Mark. How close he seemed.

She went back inside and brought her toast back out. A little gaggle of cheerful volunteers had arrived and were strimming the overgrown land beyond the garden. John came out with his coffee.

'Sorry, Gabby, did they wake you?'

Gabby smiled. 'I've been up for hours. I watched the sun rise.'

'Good heavens . . . It is a glorious morning, though.'

There was a cry from the field and all strimming stopped.

'Oh, Lord,' John said, 'I hope no one has cut their toes off. I'd better go and look.'

He disappeared behind the shrubs and Gabby lifted her face to the early sun.

'Gabby! Come and look! Just come and look at this!' John called, excitement making his voice quiver.

Gabby got up and moved as quickly as she could over the grass. John was poking about, clearing something with the help of some of the boys.

'Gabby, look, look what this youngster found.'

Gabby bent awkwardly down. She saw an edge of granite and then under the pulled-back grass, so thick it was like a carpet, she saw two small gravestones.

She knelt next to John who was still pulling the vegetation away and felt herself start to shake with excitement. Two small graves, side by side.

Tom Welland
Died at Sea
 AFL 1867
Home to Rest
1889

My Mother
Isabella Vyvyan
Died At Sea
AFL 1867
Buried here
Summer House
1889

John beamed at her. 'Who is to say this is not consecrated ground now?'

Gabby grinned back and got to her feet, dizzy with excitement, and stepped back onto a fallen branch grown slippery with lichen. She lost her balance, put out her hand to save herself, but landed heavily. John was beside her in a second.

'Gabby! Oh, my dear! Are you all right?'

Gabby lay for a moment in the wet grass, her hands on her stomach, frightened for her baby, then slowly she sat up and John and the volunteer leader helped her to her feet.

'Oh, Gabby, Gabby, I shouldn't have called you like that . . .'

'John, rubbish! You didn't put the log there!' She smiled at his worried face. 'John, I'm fine. I'll go and lie down for a bit.'

'Now, you are sure? Should I call a doctor?'

'No, John. I'm quite sure. Go and finish your breakfast.'

'I'll check on you in an hour. Buzz if you need me.'

Gabby lay carefully on the bed and breathed slowly.

Mark. We found her, your Isabella. We found her, and you were part of her story, and of mine, too.

After a few minutes, Gabby felt suddenly compelled to go over to the museum. She stood in front of Isabella. The newly risen sun flowed in through the windows at an angle and cast a shaft of light across Isabella's face.

'Thank you, Isabella,' Gabby whispered, 'for showing us the end of your story.'

She stood for a long time looking up at her face and

suddenly out of nowhere came the picture of a tall dark man standing in front of a garden containing washed-up treasures and debris from the sea. What had drawn Mark subconsciously to visit the house of his childhood, a place he could hardly remember? What shadows and echoes had drawn him back there?

Isabella looked steadily down, giving nothing away. Yet her expression seemed to change with the light, seemed suddenly at peace.

Gabby looked down at her right arm, so badly copied it did not meet the lily.

I will come and fix that, Isabella, I will make you perfect.

The air moved suddenly; changed. The arc of sun slid lower across Isabella's face and away. Her face was in shadow again and Gabby knew at once that Isabella did not want to become perfect again. She needed to stay as she was, flawed and imperfect.

Gabby went closer and smiled. Isabella had the face of an angel, but she had been a woman with all the vanity and selfishness and needs of a human being.

Her work here was finished and Gabby reached up to touch the face one last time. As she did so a sharp pain started up in her back, making her gasp.

Nell sat on the edge of the hospital bed. 'Honestly, Gab, what were you doing trotting about in your nightdress, uncovering buried graves, in the half-light?'

'I'm fine, Nell. They are only keeping me in as a precaution, but I did give poor John a fright.'

'Well, there is no way I am letting you out of my sight when they let you out. You are coming to me until the baby is born. You are too precious, Gabby.'

'Nell, I won't put up a fight, thank you. But, I don't want to hurt Charlie. It is not that it would be difficult to come back to the farm, it is just I don't know that I would be doing it for the right reasons. I'm scared that I would

583

be returning to Charlie just to feel safe and because you are there. Do you see?'

'Yes, I do. Leave it for now. Just let things unfold or resolve in their own way. Concentrate on that baby of yours. I'll come back later. I'll go and get your room ready, air your bed.'

'Nell, don't come back, it's too far. I'll ring you tonight. I'll be out by tomorrow.' But she wasn't.

It was a long and painful birth. Josh had been so easy, but then she had been so much younger then . . .

Gabby was so, so, tired.

'Come on, dearie, you are nearly there . . .'

And then it was over. There was silence for a second, then the baby gave a croaky little cry. Gabby relaxed, closed her eyes.

'What is it?' she whispered.

'A little girl. A beautiful little girl.'

'Is she all right?' Gabby asked, hearing a little flurry of activity in the corner and lowered voices.

There was silence, the atmosphere in the room changed.

'What's happening?' she called out, turning to look. 'What's wrong?'

'Your baby is fine, Gabrielle. Absolutely fine. We'll need to pop her into an incubator for a few hours, because she's premature, but nothing to worry about . . .'

The nurse was swaddling her and then brought her to Gabby, smiling, but watching Gabby's face. 'Here she is, isn't she a little beauty?'

Gabby looked down. Her daughter was tiny with tufts of dark hair. She understood the sudden silence in the room for the baby had skin the colour of dark coffee. Gabby unfolded the minute fingers like spider crabs and was suffused with love and a sense of wonder. *This is the missing part of Mark. The piece he was looking for. The part I hold.*

Chapter 83

Mark watched the clouds floating past the small square of window. Utterly beautiful. Great white cumuli, peaked and pure as icing sugar. Naimah next.

Oh Gabriella, how far away you seem, how far away, and yet I feel you everywhere I move.

He closed his eyes. They ached and pricked with tiredness and guilt. The plane gave a small lurch and the seat-belt light came on and a cheerful voice warned of a bumpy ride ahead. He saw again the startled look in Nereh's eyes. Disbelief.

'So, Dad, when are you thinking of telling Maman?'

A father who has feet of clay after all.

The plane lurched, bumped again and then dropped. Mark opened his eyes and looked out. The pilot had dropped to try and avoid the weather but this sudden dark storm did not look good. There were murmurings from the other passengers and the stewardess, smiling, brought round plates of sweets.

Mark closed his eyes again. He wanted to get back to snow. It calmed him, made a division and a diversion between these difficult weeks before he could get on a plane to the house by the river, to the woman he loved.

He smiled; he had found an old copy of Peter Nero's version of *The First Time Ever I Saw Your Face* and he had posted it to Gabby.

The plane seemed to give a shudder and the pilot came on, less cheerful this time.

'Ladies and Gentlemen, we are experiencing some bad

weather. Please keep your seat-belts on. We have a bumpy ride for the next few minutes. This is nothing to worry about . . .'

The small plane was tossed sideways. A girl screamed and a child cried and was hushed. Out on the wing Mark saw ice glitter and heard an engine cough. The woman beside him started to pray, her rosary moving fast and practised through her fingers.

The sky was darkening. Lightning flashed ahead and inside the plane all was suddenly quiet. Something stirred on the edge of Mark's memory and he eagerly moved towards it. This . . . thing that had eluded him all his life. He was dimly aware of the pilot asking everyone to pull their seats up and get into the emergency position and not to panic. The cabin staff rapidly checked the babies and small children.

He did not want to lose this, this answer, this clue to what he is.

The plane was tossed like a kite. It strained and creaked like a damaged animal and out of nowhere Mark heard this incredible sound. Deep, breathy sounds that made a rhythm so familiar the hairs stood out on his arms and on the back of his neck.

He saw two women facing each other, muffled up in coats and fur. One hand touched the upper arm of the other as if for balance. Their faces and mouths were very close and they were making this amazing sound deep in the back of their throats. One led, the other responded. They swayed gently, their lips almost touching, one using the other's mouth cavity as a resonator.

The words appeared meaningless to Mark and yet he understood them as he understood the snow and the space and what fills each. It was all a part of him and he leant closer to glimpse the face of the woman he knew was his mother. He wanted to laugh. She was throat-singing, controlling her breath in a vocal game with her friend. On the sounds went; a story, a cry of a bird, a name.

She turned, this forgotten woman, and Mark saw how

young she was. How young. Remembered how he was taken from her as harshly as she was taken from her own kind. Plucked from her frozen body in a lonely house she hated.

Her eyes held his. She smiled and he remembered with sadness the warmth of her body as they slept wrapped together on cold nights, when she would make this sound to herself, this throaty, comforting echo in the lonely dark of night.

The pilot lost control and the nose of the plane dived. The screams were loud in his ears. Mark thought, how strange to remember who you are, the small piece that has always been missing, in the moment of death.

I am Inuk, which means person. I am Inuk.

Chapter 84

Wildflowers clustered in purple clumps on the cliffs. Away, down in the cove, oyster catchers swooped and called on the wet sand.

Gabby had parked her car by the gate to the cottage where Elan once lived, and walked along the coastal path wanting to approach the farm from the sea.

It was odd; in her mind, the top field was still a great expanse of verdant green, and scarlet poppies grew among the weeds and clustered under the hedge. Rabbits still scurried away from the openness of a huge space where a bird of prey could swoop at any time, clean and straight and deadly, spoiling the rural bliss she hung on to, but which no longer existed. For houses had spread like a rash, inland.

She walked on until she stood at the head of the valley looking down on the farmhouse. The day was still and trapped and Gabby stood and leant against the gate. A butterfly came and landed on her hand, one antenna seeking the sweat above her veins.

Gabby was seized, enveloped by memories so intimate, so violently visceral that she gasped and closed her eyes. She could so easily believe she was young again, content with her lot, filling the space she was in because she knew no other. Each day filled with the farm. With Charlie, Josh, Nell. With Shadow, now dead, the bantams that followed her round the farmyard . . . Milly, Virginia, Agatha . . . speeding towards her, their heads poked forward, running like greedy old ladies, making Josh howl with laughter.

Had she known she was content? Did she realize, then, what she had?

Nell's words came back. Filled her throat with the sweet ache of remembrance.

'My dear Gabby, you were sleepwalking. Contentment means no highs or lows. Just that equitable middle way, conscious of how lucky we are, how much we have, yet acutely aware at the approach of a stranger, when the heart gives that terrifying leap of recognition, of how much we have missed. That exciting chance to explore the height and depths of a life we might have led.'

Nell, her face transformed and alight with the memory of someone other than her husband. Gabby remembered the shock of realizing that Nell too had been a sleepwalker in her own life, wedded to the farm, the seasons, her family, while her face turned in her dreams to the open window and the breeze from the sea and the stars glittering over the fields into infinity. There, a quite different life unfolded in Nell's mind. A sweet interior life no one could spoil, unravelling like an endless story no one guessed at. Nell, making a success of the life she had, and smiling and giving and being.

The call had come when Gabby was wheeling a trolley through Gatwick with her daughter sitting on top of the luggage. They had just disembarked off a flight from Canada.

Lucinda, walking just behind Gabby, had heard her cry out, 'Oh, God, no, Charlie!'

'It just seems to be taking hold so fast . . . Gabby, she watches the door for you . . .' Charlie's voice had faltered.

'I'm on my way, Charlie. I'm at Gatwick. If I can get a flight to Newquay, can you meet me?'

'Of course. I've rung Josh.'

'I'll ring you back. Charlie, will you tell her I'm on my way? Where is she?'

'She's still at home at the moment. She's had Macmillan nurses for the last week . . .'

Oh, Nell, Nell. 'Charlie, I'll be there as quick as I can.'

'I'll go and tell her.'

'Lucinda, I've got to get down to Cornwall . . . I've got to catch a local flight . . .'

'OK, let's find a desk or someone who can help us. I'll take Issy.'

There had been a cancellation and Gabby had taken the last seat on the flight just leaving.

'Thank you, God,' she had whispered. 'Thank you, Lucinda.'

She had run leaving her daughter and luggage in a pool behind her.

By the time Gabby had got to Newquay, Nell had been transferred to the hospice and Charlie had driven her straight there.

'She knows you're coming. They are trying to control the pain. She's been hanging on for you.'

Charlie had looked pale and drawn and Gabby dared not touch him.

He had said, after a while, 'Nell told me it was your money that saved the herd. She said you didn't want me to know. It tipped the balance. I would have lost them otherwise. It was generous. I'll pay you back when I can.'

'Charlie, there's no need. It came out of the blue from an aunt. I know you and Nell had an awful time and it was something I really wanted to do.'

The package with the American stamps on it had been posted to her in London. Aunt Bella had died, too, and her solicitor had forwarded it on. It had lain addressed to Gabby for months.

'We got off lightly compared to farmers who did have foot and mouth or whose herds were slaughtered,' Charlie had said. 'But of course I couldn't move or sell and it's taken us a long time to recover.'

Nell had been watching the door when Gabby arrived.

'Gabby!' she cried.

How small Nell was. How small and impossibly old. Gabby had rushed over and there was so little for her to hold.

'Nell, darling, I'm very cross with you. You should have told me. That's why you had an appointment in London in the summer, wasn't it? Why didn't you tell me?'

'For the same reason I didn't tell Charlie. You would have both fussed and wanted me to take treatment. I wanted to enjoy these last months with you all . . . Now, sit down, I'm longing to hear all your news.'

A nun had brought her a cup of coffee, but when she turned to Nell again she was asleep.

'Morphine.' The nun had smiled at Gabby. 'She's comfortable, we've managed her pain. She will slip in and out of sleep . . . If you need us, ring the bell.'

There were two other women in the room and two empty beds, just vacated or just waiting to be occupied. The room was bright with light curtains. Outside there was a garden and beyond a huge chestnut tree, the leaves turning a glorious red.

Gabby laid her cheek on the old leather armchair and watched Nell sleep. Her breathing was so shallow she seemed not to breathe at all. Nell. Something momentous and heavy had pressed down on Gabby's chest.

There was no preparation for losing the most important person in your life. She had closed her eyes and in the peace of the buttery yellow room, she slept.

When she woke, Nell had been propped up on the pillows like a small bird and was watching her.

'Oh, God! How long have I slept? Was I snoring?'

The nurse laughed. 'No. I hear you are jetlagged.'

'I remembered,' Nell smiled. 'Poor lovie. You've been to Montreal and back. Was it a good conference? Those Fine Art thingies are usually good fun and interesting, too.'

'I'll leave you girls to gossip.' The nurse had touched Nell's arm gently. 'Ring if you need anything, Nell.'

'It was wonderfully organized. It was fun, lots of interesting people. Lucinda came of course, and Issy.'

'How is that little Issy?'

'She's fine, travels like a little pro.'

Nell reached for Gabby's hand. 'And did you meet any of Mark's family, Gabby?'

Gabby folded Nell's papery hand between her own. 'Nell, I'm frightened of tiring you by talking too much.'

'If I fall asleep suddenly, you'll have to forgive me, it will not be disinterest, just the morphine, but Gabby I so want to hear all your news.'

'I met Nereh again, she was the one who turned up at my door in London. And I met Inez and her two children. Nell, Issy is so like Nereh. She's small, dark and vivacious with masses of wild curly hair . . . Inez is much fairer. Then . . .'

'What?' Nell asked opening her eyes.

'Well, it was rather odd. Veronique suddenly came to the hotel we were staying in. I was completely thrown. I knew Mark's daughters were curious . . . but, there was a knock at the bedroom door and there she was. I knew immediately who she was, she was so French and elegant. I think it was Issy she really wanted to see.'

'What did she say?'

'She told me she had known in her heart that Mark was having an affair but chose to ignore it. She did not think there was any danger of him leaving her. She said she wanted to see what sort of woman could take him from his family.'

'She was hostile?'

'Just very cold, at first, as if I deserved to have her presence imposed in my own hotel room. Issy helped. She went to her as if she was a bosom friend and Veronique melted. I thought she was going to cry.

' "It's like Nereh all over again," she said. "The child most like Mark, the one he adored most; he couldn't help it." '

Nell had closed her eyes, leant back against the pillows. 'Don't stop talking. Please go on. I want to hear everything, lovie.'

'Well, she stared at me a lot and I imagined her thinking if it hadn't been for the figurehead, Mark would still be with her, might still be alive.'

'Like that film with Paltrow? *Sliding Doors* or something?'

Gabby smiled. 'Something like that, Nell! She said suddenly and fiercely, looking at Issy, "This child is part of Mark, part of us. We are her roots, her extended family. It is important she grows up knowing about us for we were the greater part of her father's life. There is so much that only his family can tell her."'

Nell opened her eyes. 'Ouch!'

'Yes. I said lamely that I was so sorry that I had hurt her. She softened slightly. Said, "I hurt myself. I was grossly overweight when he was alive and I immersed myself in my children's lives. I still do. But I wish Mark could see me now; thin and running my own little school." Then she hugged Issy and left. At the door she said, '"I'm glad Nereh sought you out. I'm glad you've become friends, it's a link for Mark's daughter." And she was gone.'

Nell's lips were dry and Gabby held the glass to her mouth. Two feverish circles coloured her cheeks. Nell was making a supreme effort for Gabby.

'Sleep now, darling, or I'll tire you out. Charlie is coming later.'

Nell had said, her eyes as piercing as ever they were, 'Roots. They are important to you, too. Are you glad Issy will have this family to refer to or do you feel threatened?'

'I'm glad, Nell. I want her to know exactly where she comes from and who her family are, at least on her father's side.'

'You are all right, lovie? You are in the right life? I so want you to be happy.'

In the right life? Some nights when the wind sounded like the sea, she longed for the farm, for the cove, for Nell and a life she had once had, but memory was selective and threw up only the happy things, buried the rest.

She said slowly, 'A package came some months ago from an aunt in America. She never got to post it. Her solicitor sent it on when she died. She had to come back to England when her sister – my mother – died, to see to her affairs, and she found all these letters, Nell, from herself, written

593

to me when I was a child. Clara had hidden every one. I could only bear to read a few. Bella had offered me a life in America with her and I never knew . . . Sliding doors again! All the hundreds of lives we might have led . . .'

Nell had reached for her hand and Gabby smiled and said, 'I'm fine, darling. I'm living a different, city life, but I have good friends and I love my work. I've just always missed you so very much.'

'You're here now. How good it is. Bliss.' And Nell slept.

Gabby had gone out into the lifeless garden. In a field a bonfire was being stacked with wood and old orange boxes. A limp Guy Fawkes sat on the top.

When she had returned to the room, someone had put a little table by her chair with a knife and fork and something to eat. As if they knew that now she was here she was not going to leave Nell, not for a moment.

'Look, Nell,' Charlie had said. 'Look who's here.'

Josh put his head round the door. 'Hello, Trouble!' he said to Nell.

Nell beamed and held her hand out to him. 'Josh! What are you doing here?'

He hugged her carefully. 'I've got some leave and who would I come and see but you?'

Gabby saw Josh's shock at Nell's appearance but he hid it well. He produced freesias. 'I hope you still like these, Nell. I couldn't find anemones.'

'They smell wonderful, thank you, Josh.'

Josh sat on the bed.

'Tell me your news,' Nell said.

'Well, I've just bought a very expensive sports car to explore the island in . . . I bought it just to frighten you along the lanes when I get home, so you'd better get out of here fast.'

'What colour?' Nell asked, playing along.

'Silver. And the hood slides down like a dream, at the press of a button. I will even let you drive it . . .'

'Big of you,' Nell said in her old voice, and Josh laughed.

Gabby and Charlie went out into the garden to leave them alone. They walked along the fence between the garden and the field in silence.

Josh sat in the chair, fighting not to let his feelings show on his face.

Nell said gently, 'Don't be sad, lovie. Please don't be sad.'

Josh couldn't speak. He took a deep shaky breath and put his hand over his mouth.

Nell took his hand. 'Josh, listen. If it makes it easier, think of that poem, you know . . . something about being in the next room . . .'

'Nell, you hate tracts like that.' Josh grinned, despite himself.

'I know I do. But death seems so final to the young and the thought of being in the next room is somehow comforting. For me, too. I like to think of myself near you through your life. A room you can walk into sometimes when you miss me.'

'Nell, I can't imagine a world without you in it.'

'I know, lovie, but I can't last forever, even for you. Now tell me, how are you really?'

'I'm pretty busy. I love Cyprus. I still love flying, but . . . I wish Marika would marry me.'

'Tell me about that lovely girl?'

'She comes out to see me. We can't seem to stay apart. In fact we are sharing a house in Kyrenia at the moment. But she won't marry me.'

Nell had closed her eyes. 'I want you to make it all right with Gabby, Josh. I love you both so much.'

'I do write, well, postcards and things. We do sometimes talk on the phone . . .'

'You have a little half-sister. Two parents who love you and a girlfriend, I think, who waits for you to do the right thing.'

Josh said slowly, 'I will make it all right, Nell. I promise.'

'I'm glad. I'm going to have a little snooze, lovie. Will I see you tomorrow?'

'You can't get rid of me that easily,' Josh said, getting up.

Charlie put his head round the door. 'Is there anything you need, Nell?'

'No, Charlie, bless you. You get back to the milking. Love to the family . . .'

'Are you all right?' Charlie had asked Gabby at the door of the Land Rover. 'I mean you can come back and stay at the farm. You look all in.'

'Charlie, do you mind if I stay with Nell? I want to. I'm not stepping on toes, am I?'

'Of course not. Gabby, I can't bear to see her like this. I can't cope with it.'

Josh said, 'Gabby, I could stay with you. I don't mind at all.'

'No, Josh. Go with Charlie and keep him company. Come back in the morning. If there's any change I'll ring you both.'

Josh had looked down on her, hesitated and then opened his arms to his mother, and they had held each other for a long, long time in the cold November afternoon with the faint smell of bonfires.

That night Gabby had lain on the bed next to Nell. Nell had been sleeping for a long time and every now and then a nurse came in and checked her. She woke once and whispered in the dark, 'Are you there, Gabby?'

'I'm here.' Gabby moved off the bed to her side.

'Peter came to see me.'

'That was nice, Nell.'

'He was so upset, Gabby. Could you tell him when you see him that it's quite all right?'

'What is, darling?'

Nell was silent, gone again into her own little world. Then she said, 'I was terribly in love with him. He left me for a man.' Nell smiled bleakly. 'I guess I married Ted on the rebound. All a long time ago.'

Gabby was astonished. Peter! She had never even thought of him as gay, just aesthetic, an academic. Nell and Peter, lovers!

'We were so close. We did everything together. In those days he had a wonderful sardonic sense of humour ... great fun. He could never be doing with the camp gays. He thought it wasn't dignified. I don't think, in a way, he really enjoyed or quite accepted being gay ... Why am I talking too much ... it must be the drugs.'

'He broke your heart, Nell?'

'He broke my silly heart. Never tell Charlie.'

'Of course not. I wish he hadn't hurt you.'

'I don't. It would be a terrible thing never to know love or passion for another human being, wouldn't it?'

She opened her eyes and looked at Gabby.

'Yes,' Gabby said. 'Like being half-alive.'

Nell smiled. 'Exactly! My wonderful Gabby. Let's both sleep for a while.'

Gabby lay back on the bed. Outside, she could hear the wind through the trees and every now and then the moon appeared from clouds in the gap in the curtains. Inside, all was hushed. Soft voices somewhere. Rubber soles in the corridors. Every now and then a nurse appeared to monitor the other two women in the room as well as Nell.

With Nell gone there would be no excuse to come back. A door would shut. A light would go out. A huge chunk of her life would end. Nell. She could not even remember a time before Nell. Gabby longed to wail like the lost child she had been, *Don't die, Nell. Don't die and leave me.*

She had been woken by a noise and was off the bed and beside Nell in an instant. In the light from the corridor she saw Nell was trying to say something.

'What is it, darling? Are you in pain?'

Nell couldn't answer. Gabby looked into her eyes and saw fear. She pressed the bell. 'Nell, it's all right. It's all right ...'

Nell's mouth was working and Gabby bent closer. 'Always . . . loved . . . you,' Nell breathed.

'Oh, Nell. Oh, Nell.'

The young nun bent to Nell. 'Hello, Nell . . . let's take your pulse. All right sweetheart, let's give you a little injection to ease the pain.'

They watched Nell's body relax as the morphine took hold. The nun drew Gabby to the door. 'I'll ring her son. It's a matter of hours now.'

'But she's been so chatty all today . . . it can't be . . .'

'Gabrielle, I don't know how she has gone on this long. She has made a supreme effort for you. Let her go gently now . . . She has been so brave.'

Gabby pressed her hand to her mouth and went back to the bed. The nun hurried out to ring Charlie. When she returned she whispered to Gabby, 'I am just across the room.'

Gabby took Nell's hand. It was hot and dry and each breath seemed to take forever. Nell's eyes suddenly opened. She leant forward and tried to say something again and Gabby was desperate to understand. The nun came and held Nell, bent to her again . . .

'Well,' was the only word Gabby could make out, then Nell's eyes closed and she leant back on the pillow and the awful laboured breathing started up again.

'Can she hear me?' Gabby asked.

'I don't know, dear. Talk to her all the same.'

Gabby talked about Charlie and the farm, about Josh and all the funny and good moments they had all shared. And then she prayed for the awful rattling breathing to stop. She didn't want Charlie to see this. She stroked Nell's hand and rocked, whispered over and over like a mantra, 'I love you, Nell. I love you. I love you, Nell . . . I love you so, so much . . .'

And suddenly the breathing stopped and the room was silent. Gabby looked at the hand between her own and could not let it go.

The nun said gently, 'It's over, Gabrielle. It's over, my dear.'

And still Gabby could not relinquish Nell's hand. She laid her cheek on the hand and the tears poured out of her. Her body shook with grief. *Nell. Nell. Nell.*

She watched Nell's face change and the light go out of it. Nell gone.

Infinitely gently, the nun had eased her hand away and had held her, had led her into another room. She had let her weep until she was exhausted, then she had said gently, 'Gabrielle, did you hear what Nell was trying to say?'

Gabby had shaken her head.

'It's from St Julian of Norwich. "All will be well. All will be well and all manner of things will be well."'

All will be well. All will be well and all manner of things will be well.

Gabby looked down again at the farm. The walled garden was neglected again. Small garments hung on the line. Tricycles and bicycles and carts lay around the yard among bantams that no longer had names. It was hard to believe that Nell was no longer there.

She walked on down the lane. A small girl ran out of the back door to her tricycle. Soon the dark car would arrive and fill the yard. A page turned some time ago. Other lives were being lived on the farm now.

Charlie was married again, to Sarah, and had two little daughters and another life. She saw Josh come out to look for her. He took her arm, hugged her.

'It's goodbye to Nell, Gab.'

'Yes, darling, it's so hard to believe.'

Charlie came out and bent to kiss Gabby, held on to her hand.

'Nell. So much a part of our lives, wasn't she?'

'She was. Charlie . . .' Gabby hesitated, '. . . I don't regret a minute of that life.'

His sad face lit up. 'Don't you, really?'

'No, I don't. It was a life we all led together.'

Josh moved nearer and put his arm round his father.

'Dad, Nell would hate us to greet her like a trio of wet ducks.'

They turned and watched the black coffin coming slowly up the rutted lane. It turned, and they prepared to follow it on foot to the little village church that overlooked the cove from the headland.

Gabby and Josh walked together behind Charlie, Sarah and the twins, and they suddenly saw, as they walked, the people from the village coming from all directions for miles and miles to say goodbye to Nell. Charlie, choked, turned automatically for Gabby, to hold on to the last vestige of a life he had lost, for the careless chance of a love he had wasted.

Gabby walked with her arm firmly round him and Josh. She knew once she was gone Charlie would return to the life he now had; to the plump, uncomplicated wife and the children he had now and loved. He would once more be content. Nell had gone and all their lives had moved on. Life did move on . . . whether we liked it or not. Yet Gabby, too, with the warmth of Charlie's arm against hers, had a sense of a life just missed.

When Josh and Gabby arrived back in the London house it was late, but they saw the lights from the downstairs rooms shining out over the river.

Two faces were looking out for them. One fair-haired, one dark. The front door was thrown open and Isabella Hannah came running down the steps in her pyjamas to Gabby.

'Mummy, Mummy, I've made a drawing to make you not sad, look, look.'

They went inside and Josh kissed the pregnant Marika.

'Hello, how are you both?'

'We are both hugely well.' She went to hug Gabby. 'Was it very sad?'

'It was sad and wonderful . . . Nell's send off.'

'Nell would have been highly amused,' Josh told her.

'I'm afraid I could not keep your daughter in bed,' Marika said.

'Come on, darling, it's very late.'

'But . . . there's no school tomorrow, it's Sunday.'

'Then you'll be too tired to go to the Eye with us. Ha! I thought that might make little madam nip up the stairs smartish . . .'

Josh grinned at Gabby. 'I'm whacked, let's all go to bed.'

'Shall I bring you up some tea?' Marika asked Gabby.

'Bless you!' said Gabby and thought suddenly, I sound like Nell!

She tucked Issy in and the child said sleepily, 'Stay with me till I sleep, Mummy . . . Do you know what?'

'Tell me.'

'I am going to be Mikka's bridesmaid.'

'How wonderful, darling!'

Gabby lay down beside her in the glow of her small night-light, and the child turned as she always did, thumb in her mouth, with the other hand running her small fingers over the birds and small animals carved on the little chest she insisted on having by her bed. It had been in Josh's room and now it was here, in London.

When Isabella was asleep, Gabby opened the small drawer in the top of the chest and took out an unopened envelope with Bella's handwriting on. She bent to the small lamp. It was time she had the courage to open this.

She drew out a letter, and a folded document. She stared at it and then started to read Bella's letter. '*You will see,*' Bella wrote, '*that although there is a space on your birth certificate, this document proves you had a father who provided for you until the day he died, certainly long after you left home. I send you proof of this in Clara's bank statements and in the letters he wrote to her concerning your welfare.*

'*It seems, my dear Gabby, that I was not the only one who was kept away from you by Clara. I have to think of my* sister as mentally ill rather than wicked. I think that you will see this from the copious letters she kept from your father in reply to her obviously unbalanced ones . . .'

Gabby reached for the document and opened it slowly. Too late, really, for what did it matter who her father was now. Beside her, Issy made little snuffling noises in her sleep.

In the half-light she read that her father was a merchant captain . . . *David Thomas Welland* . . . of Prince Edward Island. In the dark, Gabby shivered, turned and looked at the small chest she had carried everywhere with her all her life. Again she had a fleeting, unformed recollection of a man holding her gently, smoothing with his hand the small animals on the drawers before he placed her on the floor and she heard the sound of heavy footsteps going down the stairs. She understood now why Clara had so surprisingly let Olive's brother collect it for her, all those years ago.

She went slowly down the stairs and stood in front of the photograph of Isabella. Her eyes looked steadily back. Mark seemed very near her at that moment and Gabby realized suddenly that all their lives were necessarily unfinished. His. Hers. Nell's. Elan's, who had died of a heart attack in Goa.

Sometimes there were no neat and tidy endings.

She went back upstairs and placed the envelope back in the little drawer of the chest, kissed her daughter and went back to the room she had shared with her love.

She would never know that once that small drawer had held a dried grass wedding ring. More binding than a ring of gold.